The *Amish* Cooking Class

TRILOGY

The *Amish* Cooking Class

TRILOGY

3 Romances
from
New York Times
Bestselling
Author

Wanda E. Brunstetter

SHILOH RUN  PRESS

An Imprint of Barbour Publishing, Inc.

THE SEEKERS

Dedication

To my friend Mae Miller, who has treated us
many times to some of her delicious Amish meals.

*But seek ye first the kingdom of God, and his righteousness;
and all these things shall be added unto you.*
Matthew 6:33

Prologue

Walnut Creek, Ohio

A deep moan escaped Heidi Troyer's lips as she glanced at the clock on the far wall. Lyle was late for supper again, and she'd fixed his favorite meal—sweet-and-sour spareribs, pickled beets, Amish broccoli salad, and German-style green beans. For dessert she'd made an oatmeal pecan pie. But in all fairness, her husband had no way of knowing supper had been waiting for the last hour. This morning Lyle said he could possibly be late and had suggested a sandwich or bowl of soup for supper once he got home. Since the auction was only ten miles away in Mt. Hope, Heidi expected her husband would be home by now.

"That's what I get for assuming. Shouldn't have gotten carried away cooking a big meal." She sighed. What else was there for her to do this afternoon but cook? She'd washed clothes, hung them out to dry, cleaned the house, and pulled weeds in the garden. Boredom had set in until she'd decided to cook something—her favorite pastime. Heidi enjoyed spending time in the kitchen and often shared her baked goods with others in their community who had less time for cooking.

Woof! Heidi's Brittany spaniel rubbed against her leg, wagging his stubby little tail and interrupting her musings.

"I know. I know. You're desperate for attention." Heidi filled her plate with food and took a seat at the kitchen table. "Looks like it's just you and me again this evening, Rusty."

The dog whined then grunted as he turned around in a circle before lying down under the table. He gave a long doggy sigh and rested his silky head on Heidi's bare foot.

"Your life is pretty tough, isn't it, boy?" Reaching down to rub his soft, feathery ears, Heidi felt grateful to have Rusty with her. He was a good companion—someone to talk to when her husband was away.

Heidi wiggled her toes and giggled when Rusty started snoring. She rarely wore shoes in the house unless she had company or was fighting the bitter cold of winter. With spring less than a week away and warmer weather making its appearance in Holmes County, Heidi saw no reason to confine her feet in a pair of shoes unless she went out.

Bowing her head, she closed her eyes and offered a silent prayer before eating. *Heavenly Father, please keep my husband safe as he travels home this evening. Help me be more patient while I wait for him. Bless our family and friends with good health. Thank You for the food set before me. And thank You for getting us safely through the winter months. Amen.*

As Heidi bit into a succulent sparerib, she thought about the letter she'd received this morning from her mother's sister, who lived in Shipshewana, Indiana. Aunt Emma had been teaching quilting classes in her home for the past several years, and every class brought a variety of interesting students. A few years ago, when she and her husband, Lamar, spent the winter in Sarasota, Florida, Aunt Emma opened her vacation home to six local people wanting to learn how to quilt.

One line in her aunt's letter caught Heidi's attention. It read: *"I enjoy quilting, and because I like meeting new people, I'm thankful for the opportunity to share my ability with others."*

Heidi took a sip of water, letting a new thought take root in her brain. Having been married eight years, with no children to care for, she spent a good deal of her time rambling around the house, looking for things to do once all the basic chores were done each day. She was finally about caught up on things—even the decluttering in closets she'd put off doing until yesterday. She felt good about donating several items to the local Share and Care Thrift Store in nearby Berlin.

Heidi would soon plant a garden. She'd started growing tomatoes inside by the kitchen window from seed packets purchased at the local hardware store. She enjoyed keeping watch on their progress and tending the plants each day. Unfortunately, supervising the tomatoes' growth didn't take up much of her time.

She had been good at cooking since she learned as a child under her mother's tutelage. Whenever the days became boring or lonely, she brought out her kitchen utensils and whipped up a favorite old recipe or tried something new. Lyle sometimes teased her about trying to make him fat, even though he had nothing to worry about. His six-foot frame was lean and trim. It amazed Heidi how much he could eat and never gain weight.

She drummed her fingers along the edge of the table. *I wonder if I should consider teaching a cooking class. It would give me something meaningful to do and provide a little extra money.*

Heidi looked at the calendar hanging on the kitchen wall. If she made up several flyers and placed a few ads, perhaps enough people would sign up so she could begin her first class the second Saturday of April.

Heidi smiled as she forked a piece of broccoli into her mouth. *I can teach a total of six classes every other week from April through June and still keep up with the chores needing to be done around here.*

Grabbing a paper and pencil, she began sketching the layout of the flyer advertising her cooking class. Now Heidi could hardly wait until Lyle got home to get his approval on this new venture.

Chapter 1

Sugarcreek, Ohio

Loretta Donnelly's vision clouded as she sat on the front porch, watching her children play in the yard. Conner, with dark curly hair like his daddy's, was three. His sister, Abby, whose hair was medium brown like Loretta's, had recently turned five and would go to kindergarten in the fall.

"They are growing too fast and missing out on so much," Loretta murmured, pulling her long hair into a ponytail. She squeezed her eyes shut, struggling not to cry as she often did when she thought of Rick. He'd been gone nearly a year, but it felt like yesterday when she'd received the news of his death. Rick had been on a business trip. Loretta wished she had urged him to spend the night somewhere before heading home for the weekend. But having been gone for six days, Rick was anxious to get home. Loretta was excited for him to return, and so were the children. It was a shock when she'd received the horrifying news that an accident had occurred on the freeway. Rick had apparently fallen asleep at the wheel, causing his car to hit a guardrail and flip onto its side. Fortunately, no other vehicles were involved.

Loretta's eyes snapped open when her daughter touched her arm. "Mommy, can I have a ponytail like yours?"

"Sure, sweetie, turn around." Loretta reached into her skirt pocket and found an extra hair band. Pulling Abby's shoulder-length hair back, she secured the ponytail with the band.

"Thanks, Mommy. We look alike now."

"You're welcome." Loretta bent down and gave Abby a hug.

After Abby joined her brother again, Loretta's thoughts turned to her financial situation. They'd been living on the money from Rick's life insurance policy, but it wouldn't last forever. Eventually, Loretta would need to look for a job, which meant finding a full-time babysitter.

Loretta's parents lived in Pittsburgh, Pennsylvania. Soon after Rick died, Mom and Dad suggested Loretta sell her house and move in with them. She appreciated their offer but didn't want to uproot the children. Loretta wanted to give Abby and Conner a simpler life, like they had here in Amish country, rather than exposing them to big-city living. Besides, it wouldn't be fair to move the children closer to one set of grandparents but farther from the other. Rick's parents lived in Colorado, and Loretta had no desire to move there. Residing in this simple home in this quiet town helped her feel closer to Rick. This was where she wanted to raise her children. Unless God told her otherwise, she planned to remain right here.

Loretta's attention turned to her children when she heard Conner's cry. She rose from her chair and hurried into the yard. "What's going on with you two?"

"He threw dirt at me." Abby wrinkled her nose. "Then he pulled my ponytail."

"Did you throw dirt back?"

Sniffling, Abby nodded.

Oh, great. Now they're both crying. "No more dirt throwing or hair pulling." She shook her finger at the children before taking hold of their hands. "Let's go inside now and get you cleaned up. After that, we'll have lunch."

Once Loretta made sure Conner and Abby were clean, she made peanut butter and jelly sandwiches. The two sat giggling about something on the cereal box still sitting on the table from breakfast. It was good to see how quickly they recovered from the argument they'd had outside. It was one of the benefits of kids their age—they could be mad one minute and happy the next.

While Abby and Conner ate their lunch, Loretta sat at the table, sipping a cup of tea, reading the latest edition of *The Budget* newspaper. After seeing what some of the local Amish scribes had written, she noticed an ad for cooking classes. The first class would begin next Saturday. Anything related to the Amish interested her, and it would be fun to learn how to make some traditional Amish dishes.

She took a sip of tea, letting the idea float around in her head. *I probably shouldn't spend the money right now, but if I can find someone to watch the children, I may sign up for those classes.*

Dover, Ohio

"How are things coming along with your wedding plans?" Charlene Higgins's friend Kathy Newman asked as they took seats inside Sammy Sue's Barbeque restaurant.

Placing both hands beneath her chin, Charlene groaned. "What wedding plans? Len and I haven't even set a date for the wedding, much less made any plans."

"I thought after he proposed last week you two would be working out the details for your future together." Kathy's pale eyebrows squeezed together.

Charlene drank some water before giving her response. "Len wants to wait until he's told his parents about our engagement before we set a wedding date."

Her friend leaned slightly forward. "When does he plan to tell them?"

"I—I don't know." Charlene fingered the fork lying on her napkin. "I'm worried his folks—especially Annette, won't approve of Len's choice for a wife."

"For goodness' sakes, why not?" Kathy lifted her gaze toward the ceiling. "They should be happy their son's fallen in love with someone who is not only beautiful but smart."

Slowly, Charlene pulled her fingers through the ends of her long hair. Ever since she was a girl she'd been complimented on her creamy complexion and shiny brown hair with golden highlights. When she'd reached her teenage years, her friends suggested she become a model. Charlene wasn't interested in pursuing that profession. After high school graduation, she'd gone to college and graduated with a Bachelor of Science in early education. For the last year she'd been teaching kindergarten at one of the elementary schools in Dover.

"Are you ladies ready to order?" their waitress asked, stepping up to the table.

"Most definitely. I'll have the pulled-pork flatbread." Kathy smacked her lips. "I love the caramelized onions and cheddar cheese on it."

Charlene looked over the menu a few more seconds then ordered the same thing. With so many choices, it was easier to go with a familiar sandwich rather than try something new.

"Now, getting back to Len needing to tell his folks about your engagement. . ." Kathy paused to pick up a slice of lemon and squeeze it into her water. "Why do you think he needs their approval? Is Len one of those guys who must check with his parents on everything?"

"I don't think so, but. . ." Charlene pointed at the window. "Look at that! Wish I'd brought my camera with me today."

"What are you pointing at? I don't see anything out of the ordinary."

"A flock of geese heading for the Tuscarawas River, but you missed them." Charlene continued to watch out the window. "Their wings were stretched out for a landing. Bet they made quite a splash." She slouched in her seat. "Wish I was over there on the bridge right now. I could at least get a picture of the geese on my cell phone."

"Too bad I missed it, but at least you got to see them come in for a landing." Kathy stretched her arms out like a bird. "I'm surprised you don't have your digital camera with you. You take it nearly everywhere."

"I was running late and didn't think to grab it before I went out the door. Wouldn't you know the one day I didn't have it was when I could have gotten a great shot?" Heaving a sigh, Charlene shrugged. "Oh, well. I'm sure there will be other times I can photograph geese."

"Okay now, before the geese captured your train of thought, what were you going to say? Was it something about Len's parents?" her friend prompted.

"Yeah. Len's mother is quite domesticated. Her house is spotless, and she's an excellent cook." Charlene pursed her lips. "I, on the other hand, can barely boil water, which is why Len and I always go out to eat, rather than me cooking him a meal."

Kathy's forehead wrinkled as her mouth opened slightly. "You'll never learn to cook if you don't practice."

"I am not going to use my fiancé as a guinea pig. He could end up with food poisoning."

"Don't you think you're being a bit overly dramatic?"

"Maybe, but the one time I had Len's parents to my condo for supper, I burned the roast, and the vegetables were overcooked." Charlene picked up her water glass and took another drink.

"Maybe you need a new timer for your stove."

"Or maybe I ought to take some cooking lessons."

Kathy smiled. "Hey, not a bad idea. In fact, I saw an ad in the paper the other day advertising cooking classes. If you're interested, I'll give you a call with the information as soon as I get home."

Charlene lifted her shoulders in a brief shrug. "I'll give it some thought, but unless the person teaching the classes is a miracle worker, I may be a lost cause."

"Don't be silly. You know what you need, my friend?"

"What?"

"A good dose of self-confidence."

Charlene didn't argue. Although she had little or no confidence when it came to cooking, she was plenty confident when it came to teaching her students. Of course, she couldn't feed her future husband properly by being a good teacher. *Maybe I will consider taking those cooking classes.*

Walnut Creek

Eli Miller had just started cleaning his barn when his neighbor Lyle Troyer showed up. They'd been friends a good many years.

"Hey, what's new with you?" Eli set his shovel aside.

"Not much. I have a box for you in my buggy, though." Lyle grinned. "A gift from my *fraa*."

"You don't say. What kind of gift did Heidi send for me? It's not my birthday or any special occasion."

"Doesn't have to be. She made you one of her famous peanut butter *kichlin*."

Eli chuckled. "Your wife's cookies are good, but I didn't realize they were famous."

"Bet they will be after she starts teaching her cooking classes." Lyle thumped Eli's shoulder. "Heidi also asked me to find out if you'd like to come over for supper tonight."

"I'd be pleased to, but what's this about Heidi teaching cooking classes?"

Lyle leaned against the barn wall, folding his arms. "As I'm sure you know, she's a pretty fair cook."

"*Jah*, and so was my fraa, but she never taught anyone." Eli rubbed the side of his bearded face. As always, thinking about Mavis caused him to miss her. He could hardly believe she'd been gone a year already. If only she hadn't ridden her bike to visit a friend and stayed until the sun began to set, when there'd been less visibility. If Mavis had been using her horse and buggy that evening, she might still be alive.

Lyle bumped Eli's shoulder again. "Say, I have an idea. Why don't you sign up for Heidi's cooking classes?"

Eli's eyes widened as he touched his chest. "Me? You're kidding, right?"

"Nope. You've mention many times about how bad your cooking is. If you learn how to cook, you'd be eatin' a lot better meals than tuna sandwiches and hard-boiled eggs."

"Not sure I'd be comfortable taking classes. It'll probably be a bunch of women, and I'd feel as out of place as a child tryin' to guide a horse and buggy down the road." Eli walked over to the barn's entrance and gazed out across his property. Looking at everything, one would never know his wife was gone. The daffodils she'd planted a few years ago were bursting with yellow blossoms. The colorful hyacinths, in an array of pink, white, and purple, bloomed near the porch. Eli could almost visualize Mavis reaching down to take a whiff of their fragrance. She loved the smell of hyacinths, and in the spring she'd put a few in a vase on the kitchen table.

Several bird feeders swayed as soft breezes wafted through branches where they hung. Cardinals, goldfinches, and bluebirds ate in friendly comradery. An image of Mavis standing in front of the kitchen window came to mind, and Eli recalled her contented expression.

A few times she'd caught him watching her, and then they'd stood together and gazed at the birds gathering around the feeders. It seemed everywhere he looked these days a vision of Mavis materialized before his eyes. Eli hoped he could hold those precious moments in his mind forever. He never wanted to forget her sweet face.

Little things, such as feeding the birds, gave pleasant memories, but walking into the house was a different story. Gone were the days when he'd enter the kitchen and mouthwatering smells reached his nostrils. Eli remembered how his wife's pumpkin cinnamon rolls filled the whole house with their spicy aroma. Since Mavis knew they were his favorites, she made them quite often. Sometimes, even the fragrance of Mavis's hair would capture traces of what she had baked. When Eli greeted his wife after a long day's work, he wanted to hold her until the sun went down, filling his senses with the warmth of her body and scent of her hair.

Cherished flashbacks like these were bittersweet, popping into his mind at unexpected moments. While agonizing to think about, they were also more precious than ever.

At least I have those treasured memories tucked away safely right here. Eli touched his chest, aware of his heart thumping beneath his hand.

"Hey, are you feeling okay?" Lyle nudged Eli's arm. "Did you hear what I said a few seconds ago?"

"What? Oh, uh. . .*jah.* I. . .I was thinkin' about something, is all." Eli's face warmed as he focused on his friend. "What were you saying?"

"Said you may be surprised who all shows up at Heidi's cooking classes." Lyle bent down to pluck a piece of straw off his trousers. "Heidi's aunt Emma hosts quilting classes in her home, and she's taught several men to quilt. Fact is, it's my understanding that they enjoyed it almost as much as the women did. According to Emma, some of the men became quite good at quilting."

"Is that a fact?" As he tugged his earlobe, Eli sucked in his lower lip. "*Danki* for the mention. I'll give it some thought."

Chapter 2

Mt. Hope, Ohio

Kendra Perkins turned toward the window, hoping the sunny sky would brighten her mood. She'd been staying with her friend Dorie Hampton for the past week—ever since Kendra's parents kicked her out of their house. She had only been allowed to take her clothes and personal items—nothing else. A year ago, Kendra would have never believed something like this would happen to her. It wasn't fair. What kind of parents could do such a thing? She shouldn't be punished for one little mistake.

Guess it's not a little mistake. Fingers clenched, Kendra swallowed hard. *What I did was wrong, but are Mom and Dad so self-righteous they can't admit to ever having made a mistake? Is there no forgiveness in their hearts toward their wayward daughter?*

Determined not to succumb to self-pity, Kendra turned her attention to the newspaper want ads on the kitchen table. She couldn't live in Dorie's tiny mobile home forever. She needed to find a job so she could support herself. She had to make a decision about the future of her unborn child before her October due date.

"Find anything yet?" Dorie asked, walking into the kitchen.

Kendra shook her head. "But then, I only began looking a few minutes ago."

Dorie handed Kendra a glass of cranberry juice and took a seat at the table. "Maybe you should have stayed in college and continued working toward a career in nursing."

Kendra gave an undignified snort. "If Mom and Dad kicked me

out of their house, they sure weren't going to keep paying my tuition." Her face contorted as she brought her fingers to her lips. "They think I'm a sinner, and they're ashamed of me for giving in to my desire and becoming intimate with Max. Since I'm the oldest daughter, I'm supposed to set a good example for my two younger sisters."

"Maybe they need more time to come to grips with this. After all, it's their grandchild you're carrying."

"Doesn't mean a thing. My dad's on the church board, and he made it clear that I've humiliated him." She sniffed deeply, shifting in her chair. "Guess he thinks the church wouldn't forgive me if they knew. So mum's the word, if you get my meaning. And Mom. . . Well, she can't think for herself these days. Even if she did want to help me, she'd go along with whatever Dad says."

Kendra wished she could forget what had happened, but how could she erase her pregnancy or her parents' rejection? She had considered not telling them about the baby, hoping her boyfriend, Max, would marry her. But things blew up in her face when she told him about the child and he'd asked her to get an abortion. Max was out of her life now. He'd found another girlfriend and joined the navy. With any luck, she'd never see him again.

Kendra wished she could have hidden her condition from her folks as long as possible, but with her small, 110-pound frame and five-foot-two height, it would be fruitless to try and cover up her pregnancy once she started to show. Consequently, she'd decided to tell her folks right away. She had hoped that, for once, Mom would stick up for her. *Guess I should have known better, 'cause she never has before—at least not on things where she'd have to go against Dad.*

Kendra wondered what excuse her parents had given to her younger sisters, Chris and Shelly, when she moved out. Had they told them the truth or made up some story, making it look like Kendra left of her own accord? No doubt, they'd kept it a secret, too embarrassed to tell her sisters the facts.

Swallowing against the bitter-tasting bile in her throat, Kendra left her seat and got a drink of water. She would never forget the look on Dad's face when she told him and Mom about her pregnancy. His eyes narrowed into tiny slits as his face turned bright red. Kendra feared he might explode. Instead, he turned his back on her, staring into the fireplace. Dad stood quietly several minutes, shoulders rising up and down as he breathed slowly in and out. Then, when she thought she could stand it no longer, he turned to face her. Speaking calmly, as though he was talking about the weather, Dad told Kendra he wanted her out of the house by the next day, and said she was not to say anything to her sisters about any of this. Without another word, he left the room and never looked back. Like a whipped pup with its tail between its legs, Mom followed meekly behind him. Kendra's own mother said nothing to her. Not a single word.

Scattering Kendra's thoughts, Dorie pulled the newspaper over and circled several ads. "I see a few openings for hotel housekeepers and waitresses."

"Okay, I'll check them out." Kendra gave an impatient snort. "Can't remember when I've ever felt so depressed. It feels like nothing in my life will ever be right again."

"Sure it will. It's gonna take time, but you'll see—eventually things will get better and work out." Dorie tapped the newspaper with her pen. "Hey, check this ad out. An Amish woman will be teaching cooking classes at her home in Walnut Creek."

Kendra squinted. "What's that got to do with me?"

"The classes are every other Saturday, beginning next week and going through June. You should go, Kendra. It'll give you something fun to do."

Kendra sat down with a huff. "I don't even have a job yet. How can I afford to take cooking classes? And what if I get a job and have to work on Saturdays?"

"You can worry about your work schedule once you find a job." Dorie gave Kendra's arm a gentle tap. "There's no problem with the classes; I'll pay for them. Even though your birthday isn't till December, let's call it an early present."

❧❧❧

Berlin, Ohio

The muscles in Ron Hensley's neck twitched as he drove around town, looking for a parking space big enough for his motor home. He settled on the German Village parking lot, but his vehicle took up two parking spots. Ron noticed a few other free spaces and hoped no one would complain. His pounding headache and jitteriness indicated a need for coffee and something to eat.

Ron's funds were getting low, and he had to find a place to park his RV for a few days. It wasn't cheap to put fuel in the tank, so for now, road travel must be curtailed.

Sometimes Ron wondered why he'd chosen this way to live, but his rationale took over. This was the way it had to be. How many times had he told himself the outdated motor home was less expensive than owning a real home or finding an apartment to rent? It also gave Ron a chance to travel and meet new people, even if he did take advantage of their hospitality. His predicament could be frustrating, though—especially when funds ran low and he couldn't afford to buy food, cigarettes, or beer. Ron figured at this point in his life things were as good as they were going to get. His motor home didn't have all the bells and whistles, like newer models, but it served his purpose, and that's what mattered.

Stepping inside the German Village market, Ron spotted a small café. He went in and ordered a cup of black coffee and a ham sandwich, then took a seat at one of the tables. As Ron watched the people in the market, many of them Amish, he thought about how trusting most Amish folks were. Not like most English people he'd met.

Last week Ron had parked his RV on an Amish man's property in

Baltic. He'd eaten several good meals the man's wife had prepared, and they'd even given him money when he told them he was broke. The week before, Ron had camped in Sugarcreek a few days then moved on to Charm. This was his second time in the area. He'd been to Holmes County a year ago, but he didn't hang around too long.

Might stay longer this time if I find a good place to park my rig. Ron scratched his receding hairline. If he remembered correctly, Amish communities were abundant here, so it shouldn't be too difficult to find the right house.

Ron lingered awhile after he finished eating and drank a second cup of coffee. He slid his fingers over his short, slightly gray beard and smoothed his mustache. The sandwich and coffee sure hit the spot, and the trembling had stopped.

Ron belched then quickly looked around. Activity continued in the marketplace. No one seemed to have heard the rude sound. At least nobody looked his way.

Sure could go for a piece of pie. Ron noticed a young Amish man's plate on the table close by. Creamy chocolate spilled out between the crust of his pie, and a mountain of whipped cream swirled over the top. Ron's mouth watered, and he turned his head away so his stomach wouldn't win out. *Nope. I don't need any pie. Can't afford to spend the extra money on it, either.*

Feeling more alert after two cups of coffee and ready to hit the road, Ron cleared his dishes from the table and headed out of the market. He was almost to the door when he spotted some flyers pinned to a bulletin board. One advertised an auction in Mt. Hope. Another told about a tour of an Amish home, which included a meal. A third flyer advertised some cooking classes in Walnut Creek. He pulled it off the board, because there were directions to the Amish home. Ron wasn't interested in cooking classes, not to mention he had no spare money to pay for them. But this might be a good place to park his motor home for a while. If the lady of the house cooked well enough to offer classes, she might offer him some free meals. In return, he could help around the place. Walnut Creek was less than ten miles away. *Think I'll head over there right now and check things out.*

✦ ～✦～ ✦

Walnut Creek

On her way back from the mailbox, Heidi stopped at the phone shack to check for messages. She found one from her mother. Heidi listened as Mom told her how things were going at their home in Geauga County. The message ended with Mom saying she'd talked to her sister, Emma, the other day and had passed on the news about Heidi's plans to teach cooking classes.

Heidi smiled, sitting up straight on the stool. *Mom's obviously happy about this or she wouldn't be spreading the news. I'm happy too, but a bit* naerfich, *wondering how things will go.*

Heidi was about to step out of the phone shack when the telephone rang. She turned and picked up the receiver. "Hello."

"Heidi, is that you?"

"Jah. Is this Aunt Emma?"

A chuckle erupted on the other end of the line. "It certainly is. I heard from your *mamm* the other day. She said you were making plans to teach cooking classes."

"I am. The first class will begin next Saturday. To be honest, I'm a bit apprehensive, wondering how it will go."

"I understand. When I taught my first quilting class, I was so naerfich I could hardly eat breakfast the morning it started."

Heidi's stomach tightened. If Aunt Emma, an experienced quilter, had felt nervous, she could only imagine how she would feel next Saturday morning.

"Not to worry, though," Aunt Emma quickly added. "Once all your students show up and you begin cooking, your nerves will settle, and your skills will kick in. Believe me, you'll simply relax and have a good time."

"I...I hope so." Heidi shifted the receiver to her other ear. "Cooking for Lyle, or even when we have company, is one thing, but teaching strangers to cook could prove to be a challenge."

"You'll do fine. I have every confidence in your ability to teach your students. Speaking of which, how many are signed up for your class?"

"Only one woman and our neighbor, Eli, so far, but I'm hoping I'll get more before next week."

"I'm sure God will send the people He wants you to teach." Aunt Emma's tone sounded so confident. "Ask for His guidance, and remember, I'll be praying for you."

"Danki. I feel better after talking to you."

"Do keep me posted, and should any of your students share a personal problem with you, don't hesitate to seek God's wisdom on their behalf."

Heidi gulped. She remembered hearing how Aunt Emma had mentored several of her quilting students. *Maybe those who come to my class won't have any problems they need to share. I hope that's the case, because I'm not sure I'm up to the task.*

"I sense by your silence you still have some doubts."

"I do have a few," Heidi admitted, "but it helps knowing you'll be praying for me."

"I'm sure others will pray as well."

Heidi opened the door and peered out when she heard the rumble of a vehicle outside. It surprised her to see an older model RV coming up the driveway. "Someone's here, Aunt Emma, so I'd better hang up. Danki for calling, and I'll keep you informed on how things go with my classes."

"All right, dear. I'll be anxious to hear. Now have a good day."

Heidi told her aunt goodbye, hung up the phone, and stepped outside in time to see a vehicle stop near the house. *I wonder who it is and what they want.*

Chapter 3

"May I help you?" Heidi asked, walking up to the man who had gotten out of his motor home. She figured he might be lost and in need of directions.

He took a step toward her and extended his hand. "My name's Ron Hensley, and I'm havin' a problem with my rig. It hasn't been runnin' right today. I'm afraid if I keep pushing, the engine might blow."

"I'm sorry to hear it. Maybe you need a mechanic to look at your vehicle."

"Well, the thing is. . ." He paused, rubbing the back of his neck. "I don't have the money for repairs right now. What I need is a place to park my RV till I figure out the problem and fix it myself." He looked down at his worn-looking boots then back at Heidi. "I'm kind of in a bind. Would ya mind if I stayed here a few days?"

Taken aback by his unexpected question, Heidi glanced toward the road. *I wish Lyle was here so he could handle this situation.*

"I understand your hesitation." Ron shifted his weight. "I don't want to put you out, and I normally wouldn't ask, but I'm kinda desperate right now."

Heidi swallowed hard. *Please, Lord, help me do the right thing.*

No sooner had she silently prayed than Lyle's driver, Eric Barnes, pulled in. *Thank You, Lord.* She hurried down the driveway to speak with Lyle.

"You look upset. *Was is letz do?*" Lyle asked in Pennsylvania Dutch after he waved goodbye to Eric.

"I'm hoping nothing is wrong here, but I am a little concerned."

Heidi gestured to Ron and told Lyle the man had asked if he could park his motor home on their property a few days while he worked on it.

Lyle's forehead creased as he rubbed the side of his bearded face and glanced toward the man standing beside his RV with hands in his pockets. "What'd you tell him?"

"Nothing. I was hoping you would get here and could handle things." Heidi clasped her husband's arm. "He introduced himself as Ron Hensley. I'm thankful you came home when you did, because I wasn't sure how to respond."

Lyle patted her hand tenderly. "Don't worry; I'll take care of this. You can either go with me to talk to him or head into the house."

"I'll go inside." Glancing briefly at Mr. Hensley and his dented motor home, Heidi hurried inside. Pausing in front of the living-room window, she watched her husband approach the man. *I wonder if Lyle will let Mr. Hensley stay here. Or will he ask him to find someplace else to work on his vehicle?*

Heidi felt sorry for Ron. He looked unkempt and dejected, like his paint-chipped motor home. The man's eyes didn't sparkle, and he seemed to have trouble making eye contact. He was obviously down on his luck and needed a place to stay, but she hoped it wouldn't be here. With her cooking classes starting soon, she didn't need the distraction. Besides, Lyle was in and out because of his auctioneering duties, and Heidi would feel uncomfortable having a stranger on the premises.

Moving to the kitchen, she took some leftover lentil soup from the refrigerator to heat for supper. After pouring it into a kettle, Heidi placed the soup on the propane-gas stove and turned on the burner. While it heated, she'd make a tossed green salad and set out the bread she had baked yesterday, along with fresh, creamy butter and a jar of local honey. It'd be more than enough for the two of them.

By the time the soup was thoroughly heated, Heidi had finished making the salad, so she set the table. *I wonder what's keeping Lyle.*

Seems like he's been talking to Ron a long time.

She headed for the living room to look out the window, but saw no sign of Lyle, Ron, or his RV. *How strange. I wonder where they could be.*

Goose bumps erupted on her arms. *Could Ron have kidnapped my husband?* Heidi had read about the kidnapping of two teenage girls up in Canton a few months ago. Their parents were wealthy, and the girls had been held for ransom. Fortunately, the police found and rescued them, and they'd been returned to their parents, unharmed, while the kidnapper went to jail. Things didn't always turn out so well, however.

But why would anyone kidnap Lyle? she reasoned. *We're not rich.*

Heidi began pacing. *I need to calm down and stop allowing my imagination to run wild. If Mr. Hensley took Lyle, surely I would have heard the rumble of his vehicle, like I did when he drove into our yard. Of course, I was outside at the time.* She moved across the room. *I should quit fretting and go check for myself.*

Heidi was almost to the door when Lyle stepped in. Relief washed over her, and she rushed into his arms. "What's going on? Is everything okay? When I looked out the window and didn't see you or Mr. Hensley, I became concerned."

"We were on the back side of the barn, where he parked his RV so he'd be closer to the outhouse we no longer use."

Her eyes widened. "He's staying?"

"Jah. We talked awhile, and he seems like a decent enough person."

Heidi pursed her lips and, placing her hands on her hips, she stared up at him. "Ron's going to use the outhouse?"

"He probably won't use it himself, because there's a bathroom in his motor home. But the holding tank is getting pretty full, so I suggested he empty it in the outhouse." Lyle took off his straw hat and hung it on a wall peg. "I agreed to let Ron stay a few days, and told him he could get water from our garden hose."

Heidi fingered her apron band, wondering if she should express her opinion or remain quiet. She wouldn't usurp her husband's authority.

Still, she had the right to express her opinion, since there were times she'd be here by herself. Sometimes, her husband could be too trusting.

Lyle lifted Heidi's chin with his thumb. "You're not pleased with my decision to let him stay, are you?"

"We don't know anything about Mr. Hensley."

"You're right, he's a stranger, but I don't believe he means us any harm." Lyle slipped his arm around Heidi's waist. "He's down on his luck. Maybe the Lord sent Ron to us for a reason. We need to show him God's love."

Heidi remained quiet. She would pray Ron got his vehicle fixed soon and could be on his way to wherever he was going.

Ron's stomach growled as he leaned against the pillow on his bunk and drew a deep breath. The sandwich from lunch had worn off, and all he could think about was the pie he wished he'd gotten for dessert. Once he had taken care of the RV and gotten himself settled, all he'd eaten for supper were a few crackers and cheese slices, which weren't nearly enough to fill his growling belly. The compact refrigerator in his tight kitchen area was practically empty.

Shoulda used what little money I had left to buy some food when I was at the market in Berlin today. Jaw clenching, he groaned. *Sure can't drive over there now, or anywhere else, for that matter. The Troyers would figure out I lied about my rig not running right. If there's another market close to their place, I'll walk over there tomorrow. I need to find a way to make some money, too.*

Ron crumpled the cracker wrapping. *This old vehicle not only eats up gas, but I'll need to get more propane for the stove and water heater soon.*

Since he'd shot off his mouth and asked if he could stay here until he got his rig fixed, Ron would have to walk everywhere until he moved on. He'd have to pretend he was working on the rig, or it might look suspicious. *If I can find a ride into town, maybe I'll buy a new set of spark plugs when I get my retirement check at the end of April. Then, when I'm ready to move on, I can replace the old plugs and say my rig's running good again.*

Ron had to admit the Troyers seemed like nice people. Their farm wasn't elaborate, but at first glance he noticed it was well kept. It was especially nice to be parked at a place where he could stretch his legs and breathe in the country air. Open space was what he needed. It helped him feel less claustrophobic.

"Sure can't say the same about this tin can on wheels," Ron grumbled, looking around his tightly confined home. Even though his bunk wasn't as comfortable as a real bed, at least it was someplace to lay his head. From his position at the back of the rig, Ron saw all the way through to the driver's seat. The small kitchen area was directly behind the driver's seat, with a table and a bench that folded down from the wall. These could be made into an extra bed, but Ron never bothered, since he had the bunk area in the back. If he chose to, the passenger and driver seats could be swiveled around and used with the table when eating. Since Ron was always by himself, he didn't bother to do that, either.

He grimaced. *Even if I wanted to, it would be impossible to entertain in this sardine can. I can barely move around in here myself.*

One nice feature in the motor home was a decent-sized closet. Ron kept a lot of his things there and in the storage box attached to the outside of the vehicle.

The small bathroom sufficed, with a shower, sink, and toilet. And here, in the area where he slept, a dresser had been built into the wall, with several drawers where he stored clothing.

Ron wadded the cracker wrapping and threw it toward the garbage bag by the side door. It missed by inches. *Great! Story of my life. No wonder the Amish couple agreed to let me stay here a few days. All they had to do was look at me and this junk heap I'm driving to figure out I'm hard up.*

Determined to put his problems out of his mind for the night, he closed his eyes and tried to sleep. Things might look better in the morning. After a good night's rest, maybe he'd have a clearer head and could decide what his next move should be.

Tap! Tap! Tap!

Ron's head jerked as his eyes snapped open. Unexpected noises always put him on alert. Once he figured out someone was knocking on the outside of his rig, he leaped up, nearly tripping over the garbage sack. He combed his fingers through his hair. *Get ahold of yourself.* Ron forced a smile and opened the side door. "Hey, what's up?"

Lyle blinked and took a step back. "If you haven't already eaten, I thought you might like some of Heidi's lentil soup. She made a big batch and we had plenty left over." He held out a lidded container. "It's still warm, if you'd like to eat it now. She also wrapped two slices of homemade bread for you."

The mention of soup caused Ron's stomach to rumble. "Yeah, I'd appreciate it." He took the soup gratefully, noticing a nice-looking dog sitting by Lyle's feet with its ears perked and head tilted to one side. It looked almost like the critter was trying to figure Ron out.

"By the way. . ." Lyle pointed to the animal. "This is Rusty. He's pretty friendly once he gets to know you."

"Okay. Umm. . .tell your wife thank you. Oh, and I'll bring the container back to your house in the morning. Will that be soon enough?"

Lyle nodded, and Rusty's tail wagged. "Have a good night, Ron."

"Same to you." Ron closed the door, grabbed a spoon, and took a seat at the table. Opening the lid, he dug into the soup, not bothering to get a bowl. From where he sat, the fridge was easy to reach. Fortunately, he still had a little butter left. Spreading some over the soft slices of bread, Ron couldn't wait to take a bite. "Lyle's wife is some cook. If I play my cards right, I might get to sample a lot more of her cooking."

Chapter 4

"Today's the big day, jah?"

Lyle's question startled Heidi. She hadn't realized he'd come in from doing his morning chores.

"Yes, it is a big day for me, and I'm a little naerfich," she admitted.

He walked over to the table where she'd been going over the list of things she wanted to cover during the first class. "There's no reason to be nervous. I'm confident you'll do fine." Lyle placed his hands on Heidi's shoulders, massaging them a few minutes before leaning down to kiss her cheek. "More than fine, in fact."

She smiled. Her husband had a positive attitude and always offered encouragement when she felt discouraged or had doubts about something. Was it any wonder she'd answered with a confident yes when he'd asked her to marry him? In addition to his pleasant personality, Lyle was a fine-looking man. He'd caught her eye the moment she'd first seen him at a young people's singing in Geauga County. Noticing his thick brown hair and dark brown eyes, Heidi had found it difficult to look away.

Lyle had been working at his uncle's farm in Middlefield the summer they'd met, and by the end of August, when he returned to his home in Holmes County, Heidi was head over heels in love. Afterward, they'd kept in touch through letters and phone messages, and Lyle came back to her house several times to visit and get better acquainted. Heidi felt as though they were meant to be together and had no doubts about leaving Geauga County and moving to Holmes County to spend the rest of her life with Lyle.

Glancing at the clock, Heidi rose from her chair. "I'd better get breakfast started. Soon it'll be time for my students to arrive."

"Why don't you keep it simple this morning? You won't have as much kitchen cleanup to do." He opened a cupboard door and took out a clean mug. "In fact, coffee and toast would be enough for me."

"But I usually fix ham and eggs most Saturday mornings. Since you have an auction today, a big breakfast is a good way to start your day."

"I don't need it, Heidi." Lyle poured himself a cup of coffee. "But if you insist on fixing more, I'll settle for a bowl of cold cereal to go with the toast. If I get hungry later on, there'll be plenty to eat at the auction. In fact, if you'd like, I can bring something home for supper."

"Okay. We both have a busy day ahead of us, and it would be a treat if you brought something home. Danki for offering, Lyle."

"You're welcome. Life has many small pleasures, and getting a take-out meal now and then is one of them." The look Lyle gave her was no less than adoring. She watched her husband open the pantry door and take out a box of cereal. "Think I'll fix a bowl and take it out to Ron."

With her lighthearted mood twisting in a different direction, Heidi released an exasperated sigh. "I can't believe he's still parked behind our barn. Isn't he ever going to get his vehicle running well enough to leave?" Tugging on the narrow strings of her head covering, she frowned. "Ron originally asked if he could spend a few days, but he's been here a week already."

"He doesn't have money for the parts he needs." Lyle set the cereal on the table and took three bowls down from the cupboard. "Ron's done a few chores to help me outside this past week. The least we can do is offer him a few meals and a place to stay until—"

"Until what, Lyle?" Heidi crossed her arms. "If he has no money to fix his motor home, how is he going to earn any staying here? I'm beginning to wonder if Ron plans to stay on our property indefinitely. Doesn't he have a job or a family to call for the help he needs?"

"Ron's made no mention of family, but he did say the RV is his only home. He also said he has no job, only a small monthly retirement check."

"If he has no home, then how's he getting his mail?"

"A post office box, but he didn't say where."

Heidi touched the base of her neck, feeling warmth beneath her fingers. "How can we be sure he's telling the truth? Maybe he's a drifter who uses people to give him money and food."

"I haven't given him any money."

Heidi felt relief hearing that much at least. Still, she had to wonder how much longer it would be before Ron moved on.

"Are you okay with me giving him a bowl of cereal?" Lyle nudged her arm.

"Jah. While you're out there, though, would you please find out how much longer he's planning to stay?"

Lyle nodded. He went out the door a few minutes later, and Heidi got out the bread to make toast. As much as it bothered her to have Ron parked in their yard, she needed to be kind and put her Christianity into practice.

Sugarcreek

Loretta scurried around the kitchen, hurrying to get breakfast made for the children before her pastor's eighteen-year-old daughter, Sandy, came over to watch them while she attended the cooking class. She'd been worried about finding someone to watch Conner and Abby and felt grateful when Sandy offered.

Loretta poured Conner's favorite cereal into a bowl then took out the kind Abby liked best. After placing a hard-boiled egg and a piece of toast on a plate for herself, she joined the children at the table. "It's time to pray." She clasped both of their hands. "Dear Jesus, thank You for this food we are about to eat. And thank You for Sandy, who will be coming here soon to spend time with Abby and Conner. Help them be good and have a fun time while I'm at the cooking class today. Amen."

"Amen," Abby echoed.

Grinning, Conner bobbed his head. "Amen."

Loretta smiled. How thankful she felt for her two little ones. They'd become even more precious to her since Rick died. Closing her eyes, she added a brief silent prayer: *Help me be the kind of mother my children need, and show me how to guide them down a path of humility and simplicity.*

Mt. Hope

"Are you okay in there?"

Kendra groaned as she stared at her pale face in the mirror. "I'll be okay, Dorie. Give me a few more minutes and I'll be out." Bile rising in her throat, she turned toward the toilet and vomited a second time. When her stomach emptied, she rinsed her mouth and wet a washcloth to wipe her cheeks. She'd hoped the morning sickness would have passed by now, but this past week it seemed even worse. In addition to her stomach doing flip-flops, some mornings she'd experienced dizzy spells or awakened with a pounding headache. Fortunately, nausea was the only symptom plaguing Kendra so far today.

"Wish I could eat something in the mornings without feeling sick to my stomach," she muttered, pushing her short auburn hair behind her ears. Since she'd become pregnant, most breakfast foods and some of her other favorite meals, like pizza, upset her stomach.

Many times when Kendra was growing up, her mother would make dippy eggs and toast for breakfast. For now, until the morning sickness passed, she'd switched from eating eggs or even pancakes, to having saltines and mint tea. Usually by lunchtime, Kendra was able to eat without getting sick.

Taking a deep breath, she left the bathroom and joined her friend in the kitchen. "Sure hope I can get myself together. I should be leaving for the cooking class soon, and if I keep feeling this way, I won't be able to go."

Dorie opened a cupboard door and took out a box of saltine crackers. "I'll fix you some tea while you nibble some of these."

"Thanks." Kendra massaged the bridge of her nose, hoping a headache wasn't forthcoming.

"It's good you don't have to drive far to get to the Amish lady's house." Dorie gave Kendra a cup of tea then finished eating her scrambled egg and bacon sandwich.

"Yeah, it's only about nine miles from here. If traffic is light, I should be there in ten minutes or so." Kendra had to take a few more deep breaths as she chewed; then she swallowed the cracker. She loved bacon, but this morning even the smell of it on Dorie's sandwich made her queasy. "Sure hope I don't get sick while I'm at the class. Think how embarrassing it would be. And what if the Amish lady's only bathroom facility is an outhouse?"

"Don't worry; I'm sure their house will have an inside bathroom." Dorie poured herself a glass of tomato juice. The site of the thick reddish-colored juice made Kendra's stomach turn, and she had to look away.

After Dorie drank her juice, she got up and took her dishes to the sink. "I don't think you have anything to worry about."

"I'm gonna take a few crackers with me, too." Kendra opened a drawer and took out a sandwich bag. "What if the odor of whatever she teaches us to cook makes me feel nauseous?"

"You worry too much." Dorie stepped behind Kendra and massaged her shoulders. "I'll put some mint tea in a thermos, and you can take it along."

"Okay, thanks." Tea would be better than coffee. Kendra found even the smell of the dark brew to be objectionable. "Oh, I'm supposed to bring an apron with me to the class. Do you have one I can borrow?"

"Sure thing." Dorie opened a drawer and pulled out a lime-green apron. "Here you go."

"Thanks." It wasn't Kendra's favorite color, but at least the apron would cover her baggy shirt and jeans and hopefully keep them clean.

"Do you have any plans while I'm gone today?" Kendra asked.

"Thought I'd tidy up around here and maybe repot my African violet." Dorie pointed to the flower sitting by the kitchen window.

While Dorie got out the thermos and brewed more tea, Kendra returned to the table. She reflected on how she and Dorie had been friends since high school. *If I'd only listened to her when she voiced concerns about Max, I wouldn't be in this predicament right now.*

Walnut Creek

Ron was about to pour himself a second cup of coffee when a knock sounded on his side door. He'd been somewhat prepared for it, since Lyle usually came out to talk to him each morning and often brought something to eat.

Lyle smiled when Ron opened the door. "If you haven't eaten already, I brought a bowl of cereal for your breakfast."

"That's mighty nice of you." Ron took the bowl gratefully. The other day he'd walked to the market nearby and spent his last few dollars. Now, only a little food remained in his dinky refrigerator, so any food offered by the Troyers was appreciated.

"I'll be leaving for an auction soon," Lyle announced. "You're welcome to come along if you like."

Hesitating a moment, Ron shook his head. "I have no reason to go to an auction, but I'll chop some wood while you're gone if ya like."

"It would be helpful. Heidi and I are having friends over for a bonfire next week, so the wood will be put to good use." Lyle started to walk away but turned back to face Ron. "I was wondering how much longer till you're able to work on your rig."

Ron glanced up at the house then back at Lyle. "You want me to leave? Is that what you're sayin'?"

"No, it's not. I only asked because when you first came here you told us it would only be a few days." Squinting, Lyle shuffled his feet. "How much money do you need to buy the parts to fix your motor home?"

Ron shrugged. "Can't say for sure. My retirement check should arrive by the end of the month. Maybe then I can hire one of your drivers to take me to get the check as well as the parts I need."

"So you want to stay till then?"

"Yeah. If it's okay with you. Don't want to put you out or be an inconvenience to anyone, though."

"No, it's fine." Lyle gave a quick nod.

"Thanks for your understanding." Ron quickly shut the door before Lyle had a chance to change his mind. He'd made the right decision choosing this Amish house to stop at. From what Ron could tell so far, the Troyers were easy marks.

Chapter 5

Dover

Charlene glanced in the hall mirror one last time, to be sure her hair looked okay. She had debated about wearing it down, but since she'd be taking cooking classes, it might be best to wear her hair in a ponytail so it didn't get in the way. Her stomach tightened, thinking about the classes she'd agreed to take. *What if the recipes she gives us are too difficult for me? What if I'm not teachable? I could end up making a fool of myself. Well, at least Len's mother won't be there to see me mess up.*

Charlene cringed, reflecting on the time she'd been invited by Len's parents to join them for Thanksgiving. When his mother, Annette, asked Charlene to bring a pumpkin pie, she'd considered buying a store-bought one. However, wanting to impress her future mother-in-law, Charlene made the pie from scratch. Big mistake. She'd ended up using too much evaporated milk and, to make matters worse, hadn't cooked the pie long enough, for the inside was runny. Fortunately, Len's mother had made an apple pie to serve. But things really fell apart when Annette asked Charlene to whip the whipping cream. Charlene was horrified when she started up the mixer and liquid splattered out of the bowl, some ending up on Annette's lovely blue dress. Was it any wonder the woman had never warmed up to her? No doubt she hoped her son would choose someone who was capable in the kitchen. Charlene wanted Len to be proud of her cooking abilities and hoped by taking the classes there might be a chance to prove herself to Len, as well as his mother.

"What do you think, Olive?" Charlene looked at her cat sitting on the couch, head bobbing as he silently watched her. She'd given the name to the feline because of the cat's pretty, olive-green eyes that were a sharp contrast to his fluffy gray fur. "Am I crazy for going to these cooking classes?"

Olive meowed and curled into a ball, oblivious to her owner's nervousness.

"Guess not." Charlene shrugged her shoulders then picked up her purse. She was about to head out the door when she remembered she'd left her cell phone on the kitchen table. Besides having the phone for emergency purposes, she planned to GPS her way to Heidi Troyer's home. She'd been to Walnut Creek a few times and knew the back roads could be tricky. Charlene had never been good with directions, so without the GPS she'd probably end up driving around for hours and be late for the class or miss it altogether.

Charlene got in her car, set the GPS, and headed down the road toward Holmes County. After passing through Sugarcreek, it suddenly dawned on her that the apron she was supposed to bring remained on the back of a chair in her kitchen. *How did I miss seeing the apron when I went back to get my cell phone?*

Glancing at the clock on her car dash, Charlene figured she would have enough time to stop at Walnut Creek Cheese and pick up an apron from the kitchen supplies section.

A short time later, Charlene entered the store and found a pretty lavender apron—her favorite color. She paid for it and hurried back to her car. As long as she didn't get lost, arriving on time shouldn't be a problem.

Walnut Creek

Eli left his house and headed for the barn to get his bike. Since the Troyers lived nearby, it was kind of pointless to hitch his horse to the buggy. Riding the bike would be quicker, and the fresh air and exercise would do him some good, even though it wasn't his favorite mode of transportation.

"What was I thinking, agreeing to do this?" Eli muttered. "Lyle must have caught me in a weak moment when I agreed to take his wife's cooking classes. I'll probably bumble my way through every lesson and end up looking like a fool."

He thought about the stale toast he'd had for breakfast and was reminded, once again, how badly he needed to learn how to cook. Hopefully a few other men would be in the class, or maybe Lyle would be there to offer moral support. The thought of taking a cooking class with a bunch of females made Eli's stomach tighten. Most women he knew were good cooks, so he wasn't sure why any Amish women in their community would need to take Heidi's class. One thing was for sure—he was not wearing an apron, even if it had been requested, although if he had a mind to, he could have taken one Mavis used to wear.

"Whelp, I may as well get this over with." Eli slapped his straw hat on his head, pushed his bike out of the barn, and climbed on. *Sure hope Heidi lets us eat whatever we cook today. I could use a decent meal for a change.*

Loretta squinted at the address on the mailbox in front of a white, two-story home to be sure she had arrived at the right address. She felt relief seeing the house numbers were the same as the one on the form she'd filled out to sign up for the classes.

She pulled her car into the driveway in time to see an Amish man with brown hair and a matching beard get off his bike. Since he had a beard, it meant he was married, so she assumed he was Heidi's husband.

When Loretta got out of the vehicle, the man glanced her way and gave a quick nod; then he stepped onto the front porch and knocked on the door.

That's odd. Loretta stood beside her car, watching. If he was Heidi's husband, surely he wouldn't knock on his own door—unless it was locked, and he'd forgotten the key.

A few seconds later, the door opened, and the man went inside.

She glanced around the property. Although modest, the house, barn, and other outbuildings were neatly kept, and the yard looked well maintained. Noticing the fenced-in fields behind the place, she assumed the land also belonged to the Troyers. But an RV was parked near a freshly tilled garden. *I wonder why an Amish person would have a vehicle like that.*

Loretta looked quickly away when she saw a man peek out the motor home's side window. *Guess it's none of my business.* She turned and hurried toward the house. Remembering her apron and notebook were still in the car, she spun around to get them.

Except for the motor home, Loretta didn't see any other vehicles in the yard. She figured the others were either late, or perhaps she was the only one who'd signed up for the class. If that was the case, she'd receive more individualized attention and could learn to cook Amish-style meals quicker than if other students were there, asking questions.

Loretta grabbed her apron, and as she closed the car door, another vehicle pulled in. A few seconds later, a young woman, wearing her long hair up in a ponytail, got out of her car, holding her purse in one hand and a lavender apron in the other. She offered Loretta a pink-cheeked grin. "Are you here for Heidi Troyer's cooking class?"

"Yes, I am." Loretta smiled in return.

"Same here."

They stepped onto the porch together, and Loretta knocked on the door. When it opened, an Amish woman, who appeared to be in her late twenties, greeted them with a welcoming smile. "I'm Heidi Troyer; welcome to my class."

Loretta could hardly take her eyes off this beautiful young woman. Her shiny dark hair peeking out the front of her white, cone-shaped covering and her sparkling blue eyes set against a creamy complexion made her appear almost angelic. If not for her plain Amish clothes, she could have been a runway model. With her own medium brown hair and average-looking brown eyes, Loretta felt plain by comparison.

"Come in and take a seat." Heidi motioned to the living room, where the Amish man who had entered the house before them sat in the rocking chair. He gave a nod then looked down at his black boots. Loretta expected Heidi to introduce him, but instead, she moved over to the window and peered out. "Our last student hasn't arrived yet, but when she gets here, I'll ask everyone to introduce themselves, and then we'll move into the kitchen to begin our first lesson."

Loretta took a seat on the couch, and the young woman with the ponytail sat on the opposite end. It felt awkward sitting here without proper introductions.

Glancing at Heidi, who continued to look out the front window, Loretta guessed their teacher felt as anxious as she did right now.

Picking a piece of lint off her dark blue maxi-dress, Loretta discreetly dropped it into her purse. She wasn't about to let it fall on the floor of this spotless room. While the living room had no decorative items or pictures on the walls, a few candles sat on the end tables. Two sets of mounted deer antlers hung on either side of the fireplace. A man's straw hat hung on one, so Loretta figured since the antlers were being put to good use, they would be allowed in the Amish home. A beautiful antique oil lamp sat on the mantel, and an oval braided throw rug lay on the floor under the coffee table in front of the couch.

The coziness of this room was so inviting, Loretta wished she could duplicate it in her own home. She'd never been one to display a lot of fancy doodads and didn't even own a TV. To some her decor might seem meager and plain, but it met her and the children's needs.

I'm too practical to spend money on things if they don't serve a specific purpose other than for decoration, she mused. *Sometimes I wish my parents had joined the Amish church, because I'd probably have fit right in.*

"She's here!"

Heidi's excited tone startled Loretta, and she nearly jumped off the couch. Apparently, only three women had signed up for the class, which meant, with so few here, they'd be able to move through the lesson quickly and hopefully learn a lot. Loretta could hardly wait to begin.

————————⚬⚬⚬————————

Curious as to what was going on outside, Ron peered out the side window of his motor home. According to the flyer he'd seen on the bulletin board in Berlin, this was the day Heidi's cooking class was supposed to begin. No more cars had arrived at the Troyers', so everyone who signed up was probably here.

Ron needed to get the garden hose in order to refill the motor home's fresh-water tank but had waited until he was sure no one else was in the yard. The last thing he wanted was to be pulled into a conversation with anyone right now—especially a bunch of strangers.

Ron stepped outside and headed for the outdoor spigot on the side of the house. It was a bit chilly for April, but he felt the sun's warmth on his face when he looked up.

As he walked by the vehicles parked in the driveway, Ron noticed two of them were smaller cars, and the other was a minivan. They all appeared to be older models. Near the vehicles, a bicycle leaned against a big tree. Ron remembered seeing an Amish man ride in on it.

He turned on the spigot and pulled the hose toward his RV. While the tank filled, a red-tailed hawk caught his attention. Gripping the nozzle, Ron watched the majestic bird sailing round and round in the expanse of the open blue skies. For a fleeting moment, he wished he were as free as the hawk as it caught a draft and went farther out of sight.

Ron's thoughts returned to the people who'd arrived, wondering why they'd chosen to take a cooking class. "Must be nice to have a purpose in life," he muttered under his breath.

He turned and watched the road. For a Saturday, hardly any traffic went by. Of course, on a back country road such as this, there weren't many cars—mostly horse and buggies.

It was nice having his motor home parked closer to the Troyers' house. Lyle had suggested it the other day, saying it would be easier for Ron to get fresh water from the garden hose. The view of the fields by the back of the barn was okay, but since his holding tank was now empty, there was no point staying parked near the outhouse. Here, closer to the house, was better. It gave Ron the advantage of seeing what was going on around the place, as well as the comings and goings at the house. It would also give him a chance to see if the Troyers followed a routine, so he'd know when they were gone.

"Oh, great!" Ron jumped back. He hadn't been paying attention, and water gushed out of the full tank, soaking his pant leg. Quickly, he turned off the hose and screwed the lid back on the water tank. Dragging the hose, he walked toward the house. Once there, he turned off the spigot and reopened the hose's spout. This way all the water would drain out as he rolled the garden hose back on the reel.

"Guess I need to change my trousers." Ron swept his hand over the wet spot. *Wonder if Heidi would mind if I hung my pants on her clothesline to dry? Then again, maybe I'd better not. I'll drape 'em over the passenger seat and they can air-dry that way.* Tapping his foot, he grunted. "What I really need is a cup of hot coffee."

Ron stepped into his motor home, grabbed the teakettle, and went to the sink to fill it. In his haste, he turned on the faucet full force. It sputtered loudly, and before he could react, water squirted out, spraying his face and the front of his shirt. "Super! I forgot the air needs to be forced out of the line before the water flows smoothly." Ron set the teakettle on the counter and turned the water pressure down until he heard the pump switch off.

"Now I need to change my shirt." Ron's knuckles whitened as he clenched his fingers. "I can tell this is gonna be a great day." What he wouldn't give for a real cup of fresh-brewed coffee right now. But all he had was some of the instant kind. *Maybe after I change my shirt and trousers I'll see if Heidi has some java to spare.*

Chapter 6

Loretta felt sorry for the Amish man sitting in the room with her and the other young lady. As he fiddled with his suspenders and stared at the floor, it became obvious the poor fellow felt out of place.

So as not to stare at the man or make him feel worse, she glanced quickly out the window. *What looks even more out of place is the beat-up motor home in the yard. I wonder who owns it and why it's parked here.*

From where she sat, Loretta had a good view of the yard. She'd watched intently as an older man came out of the motor home and stood near her minivan. She'd been curious when he came closer to the house. In fact, it appeared as if he had walked underneath the window near where she sat. A few minutes later, he pulled a hose toward the RV. While filling the tank, he looked first at the sky then toward the road. The man moved his mouth, too, like he was talking to himself.

Loretta had to stifle a giggle when she saw water spurt out of the tank. The man didn't look too happy when he came toward the window again. She looked away so he wouldn't see her watching him then glanced toward the RV again as he went inside and shut the door.

Turning her attention back to those in the room, Loretta tried to think of something to say. She wanted to ask their names and why they'd signed up for the class but didn't want to appear nosy. Leaning back in her chair, she remained quiet.

———•∽∽◦∽———

Eli felt as out of place as a donkey showing up for church. It reminded him of the day he'd found Mavis hosting a quilting bee at their home.

Fifteen women sat around a quilting frame in her sewing room, chattering like a bunch of noisy magpies. He'd tried to be polite and even managed a quick "hello" but then hurried from the room before anyone engaged him in conversation.

Eli had no trouble talking with a group of men, but when he had to talk to more than one woman at a time, he became tongue-tied. It was worse with women he'd never met before, like today. If not for his need to learn how to cook, Eli would have rushed out the door and pedaled home as fast as his legs could go.

He glanced around the room and noticed one of the women wearing a long blue dress with matching apron in her lap. She seemed to be staring at him. *Sure hope she doesn't say anything to me.* Eli wished a trapdoor would appear in the floor so he could crawl inside and disappear. Averting his gaze, he studied a worn spot in the knee of his trousers. *Probably should've worn a different pair. Didn't want to get too dressed up for a cooking class, though. I'm likely to spill something and end up with food on my clothes.*

Eli reflected on the time he'd helped Mavis shuck corn and ended up with a mess all over his clean shirt. In a gentle tone she'd scolded him for wearing one of his nicer shirts to take part in a messy job. So this morning he'd put on clothes he thought were the most appropriate.

Heidi returned to the room a few minutes later, accompanied by a young woman with short auburn hair and dark brown eyes. She then asked everyone to introduce themselves and tell what they hoped to learn during the cooking classes.

When nobody responded, Heidi motioned to the young woman with a ponytail. "Why don't you go first?"

"Oh, okay. My name is Charlene Higgins, and I signed up for these classes because. . ." She paused, blinking rapidly. "Well, to tell you the truth, my cooking is terrible. I've heard most Amish women are excellent cooks, so I signed up, hoping by the time I get married I'll be more comfortable around the kitchen and won't starve my poor husband."

Heidi smiled. "Thank you, Charlene. Now who would like to go next?"

Eli sat quietly, wishing he wouldn't have to say anything, but his turn would eventually come. He was on the verge of introducing himself when the woman with long brown hair spoke up.

"I'm Loretta Donnelly, and I'm interested in the Amish way of life, so I'm hoping to learn how to make some traditional Amish dishes."

Heidi nodded and motioned to the auburn-haired woman standing beside her, holding a lime-green apron and beige-colored tote in front of her stomach.

"My name's Kendra Perkins. I can make a few things fairly well, but my friend, Dorie, thought taking the cooking classes would be something fun for me to do."

"Thank you, ladies. That leaves you." Heidi motioned to Eli.

"Well, umm. . . My name is Eli Miller." His face heated as he gripped the arms of the rocking chair. "To be honest, I can't do much more than boil water, so I'm here to learn how to cook." He looked over at Heidi and grimaced. "That is, if you think I'm teachable."

"I believe anyone who has a desire to cook can learn, and if you can read, you should be able to follow a recipe. Why don't we all go into the kitchen now and begin our first lesson?" Heidi's sincere smile caused Eli to relax a bit.

After everyone washed their hands and put on their aprons, they took seats around Heidi's long kitchen table. Eli insisted he didn't need an apron, so Heidi didn't force the issue.

She handed each of them several pieces of paper and then stood at the head of the table. "For those of you unfamiliar with the basics of cooking, I've written down some necessary information, including how to measure the liquids, dry ingredients, grated cheese, dried fruit, eggs, butter, shortening, molasses, and syrup." Heidi paused to be sure everyone paid attention. She tried to make her voice clear enough and did her best to keep her composure. It wouldn't be good to let on to her students that she was a bundle of nerves. *I hope my decision to teach these classes wasn't a mistake.*

Heidi drew a quick breath as she collected her thoughts. "Let's see.... Oh, yes, I've also included a list of the different types of flour, sugar, creams, cooking oils, and yeasts. In addition, I've written down how to reduce or increase a recipe, included a list of substitutions when you don't have an exact ingredient, as well as given directions for selecting the proper kitchen utensils, kettles, skillets, and baking pans." She looked at each of her students. "Before we proceed, does anyone have a question?"

Charlene's hand shot up.

"Yes?"

"Will we be expected to use all the ingredients you have listed during our every-other-week cooking classes?"

Heidi shook her head. "There's no way we can make enough dishes in our six weeks of being together to use everything listed on your papers. You will, however, need this list when you are cooking in your own kitchens." Since Charlene and Eli had already admitted they had limited cooking skills, it had been a good idea to put together the handout sheets.

Heidi was about to give everyone the ingredients and utensils they would need to make her favorite breakfast casserole when a knock sounded on the back door. She excused herself to answer it, hoping whoever it was wouldn't stay long, because they only had until one o'clock to finish the first lesson.

"Should I, or shouldn't I?" Ron contemplated out loud as he looked down to make sure the clean shirt he'd put on was buttoned.

A reasonable amount of time had passed since the young

auburn-haired woman had went into the Troyers' house, so now seemed as good a time as any to knock on Heidi's door.

Ron toyed with his mustache as he shook the few grains of instant coffee left in the jar. "Maybe she'd let me hang my clothes on her line to dry."

Stepping outside, he had walked briskly toward the house. *Come on now. What's the worst she could say?* He'd ask for a cup of coffee first, then bring up his need to wash clothes.

Holding his coffee mug while toying with his mustache, he had second thoughts about interrupting Heidi's class. But it was too late to worry about it now; she'd already opened the door.

Heidi tipped her head. "Did you need something, Mr. Hensley?"

"Uh. . .yeah, and please call me Ron. Would you happen to have any fresh coffee made?"

"As a matter of fact, I do."

"Would ya mind filling my cup? I'm almost out of the instant kind, and it doesn't taste the same." He made a choking noise while shaking his head. "Nope. Nothin' beats a good cup of the real thing."

"No problem. If you'll follow me to the kitchen, I'll pour you a cup."

Ron hesitated, shuffling his feet a few times. "Well, uh, I saw you have company and don't want to interrupt. I can wait here on the porch."

"Not a problem. The people in my kitchen have come for a cooking class, but it'll only take me a minute to fill up that mug. Come on in, Mr. Hensley. My students won't mind."

Ron was well aware of Heidi's cooking classes, but he didn't let on. He wasn't about to tell Heidi he'd seen her ad on the board at the market in Berlin, and it had prompted him to show up here. He followed her into the kitchen and stopped short when he saw three women and an Amish man sitting at the table, looking at him with curious expressions.

Heidi's kitchen was spacious. A far cry from the tiny one in his motor home. It almost made him dizzy seeing all this space in one room. Ron had been cramped up in his RV so long, he'd forgotten what living in a house was like.

"Class, this is Ron Hensley." Heidi motioned to him. "He's here to—"

"Whew! This is good news." The Amish man pushed his chair away from the table and hurried across the room. "It's nice to know I'm not the only man attending Heidi's cooking class today. I was worried for a while there." The man shook Ron's hand vigorously. "My name's Eli Miller. It's nice to meet you."

"Oh, well, I. . ." Ron stopped talking, as an idea formed. *If I were to attend Heidi's class, it would give me an opportunity to be in her house and scope things out. Who knows what kind of treasures are scattered about that could bring a good price at the pawnshop in one of the bigger towns outside of Holmes County?*

Putting on his best smile, Ron looked over at Heidi. "Would you have room for another student? I can't pay you now for the classes, but I should have enough money in a few weeks, when I get my retirement check."

Heidi stared at him quizzically. "I didn't realize you were interested in learning how to cook Amish-style meals."

He bobbed his head enthusiastically. "It's always good to learn new things. Especially if it's a simple meal I can make easily in my RV."

The Amish man thumped Ron's back and pointed to an empty chair at the table. "I'm sure glad you're here. Why don't you sit down?"

Ron handed Heidi his empty mug and took a seat. *Sure hope this isn't a mistake.* He bit the inside of his cheek. *I'd better wait and ask about doing laundry some other time. I'll have to be careful what I do and say while I'm in this house so neither Heidi nor her husband catches on to my plan.*

Chapter 7

Thank goodness this class is only twice a month. Ron fidgeted while everyone else sat quietly, waiting for Heidi to get started. He felt like a rabbit wanting nothing more than to bolt. Fact was, he'd rather be doing anything other than sitting here with a bunch of strangers. Ron had no desire to get acquainted with any of them, either. The fewer people who knew him, the better.

Maybe I should have offered to do something for Lyle out in the barn today. As soon as possible, Ron planned to have a talk with him about doing a few more things around the place to help out. He didn't want to appear as if he were taking advantage of their good nature. It could arouse suspicion.

As Ron sat in his chair, he looked around the kitchen, trying to take everything in. He'd already noticed how spacious it was, but the room was also clean and neat. Everything seemed to have a place. Raising his eyebrows, Ron glanced at the floor. It was so clean and shiny a person could probably put their plate down there and eat off the floor. There was nothing unnecessary in this kitchen. Most things he saw had a purpose.

Something in particular caught Ron's attention—a collection of oil lamps on top of the kitchen cabinets. They looked old. He figured they might be worth some money. Since Lyle was an auctioneer, he may have picked them up at one of the events he'd attended. Of course they could also be something one of their relatives had handed down.

An idea formed as Ron counted the lamps—ten altogether—a sizable collection. *I'll bet if two or three suddenly vanished, it would be a while before they'd be missed. How often do Heidi or Lyle look up there to admire the lamps? I wonder what other treasures are in this old house.* Ron rubbed his chin, shifting in his seat. *Getting inside the barn to look around for treasures shouldn't be a problem, but if I can figure out a way to come into the house when nobody's at home, bet I could walk away with a lot of good stuff.*

───── ❧❦❧ ─────

Doubts clouded Heidi's mind about having Ron take part in her cooking classes. Did he plan to stay parked on their property from now until the end of June, when the classes would end? If he moved on, would he return every other week to finish the classes? She suspected he might be up to something but couldn't put her finger on it.

Lyle had no objections to Ron being here. Perhaps she shouldn't, either. Besides, Eli seemed pleased to have another man in the class. Maybe for some reason Ron was meant to be here.

Pulling her thoughts back to the matter at hand, she took a baking dish from the refrigerator. "Today we'll be making what I call, 'Amish country breakfast,' and this is what it looks like after it's been put together. Since we won't have time for everyone to make their own dish today, we will take turns mixing the ingredients. Once everything is in the nine-by-thirteen pan, it will go into the refrigerator and stay there overnight." Heidi placed the baking dish she'd taken from the refrigerator on the table and removed the foil covering. "In the meantime, I will bake this dish, because I put it together last night and it's sufficiently chilled. When it's done, everyone will get a sample to eat, along with a bowl of cut-up fruit, which we'll be making next." She paused and gave each of them a recipe card. "I've written the directions for Amish country breakfast on each of your cards so you can make it in your own home whenever you like." Heidi didn't mention it, but she'd also included some scripture on the back of everyone's card. After praying about this, she felt led to do it. Today's quotation was from Psalm 46:10: "Be still, and know that I am God." Hopefully, one or more of her students would find it meaningful, as it had been to her since she'd become a Christian. Many days when she'd been bustling around the house or yard, Heidi paused to reflect on those words. Then she'd take a break and sit quietly to pray and thank God for all He'd done in her life.

"Who gets the breakfast casserole you'll be baking tomorrow?" Ron leaned forward, staring at the dish with hungry eyes.

"Two of my friends will be coming over Monday morning to help plant a few early vegetables in my garden, so I'll serve it to them."

Ron heaved a sigh and sat back in his chair.

Heidi's heart softened toward him a bit. "You and the others will get to eat the one I'll be baking today."

He grinned. "Okay."

"Now, before I put the casserole in the oven, we'll need to add the topping." Heidi gestured to the three cups of cornflakes she'd set out. "One-half cup of melted butter needs to be added to these." She took out the butter she'd measured before her students arrived, placed it in a small kettle, and set it on the stove. "When melting butter, it's important to keep the burner on low so it won't burn."

Everyone gathered around the stove as Heidi demonstrated. Once the butter was melted, she brought it to the table and poured the liquid in with the cornflakes. Then she handed Loretta a wooden spoon and asked her to stir it until the cornflakes were thoroughly coated. Afterward, Heidi asked Kendra to pour the mixture over the top of the casserole.

"Now it's time to bake this delicious country casserole." Heidi put the foil over the dish again and pointed to the recipe cards she'd given each student. "You'll see the oven needs to be set at 375 degrees."

After Heidi put the casserole in the oven and set a timer for forty-five minutes, she got out another nine-by-thirteen pan. Then she gestured to the three-by-five index cards. "The first thing we'll need to do is grease the pan. I usually use coconut oil for this purpose, since it's one of the healthiest oils and works equally well as shortening for greasing."

She placed a jar of coconut oil on the table. "Who would like to do the honors?"

"Maybe I should," Charlene spoke up. "Since greasing a pan is easy, I shouldn't goof up." She went on to tell about the mistake she'd made at Thanksgiving with the pumpkin pie, and then the whipping cream fiasco at her future in-laws' house.

Poor Charlene. Heidi couldn't comprehend how the young woman could have so much trouble with what she, herself, saw as a simple task. Heidi had learned to mash potatoes at a young age and caught on quickly. She set the baking pan and coconut oil in front of Charlene then handed her a paper towel.

Charlene tilted her head, causing her ponytail to swish over her shoulder and rest against her chest. "How much oil should I use?"

"Take only enough to grease the bottom and sides of the pan," Heidi prompted.

All eyes were on Charlene as she dipped a piece of the paper towel into the creamy, solidified coconut oil. It wasn't enough to grease the whole pan, but before making any comments, Heidi waited to see how well Charlene did with the small amount she'd taken.

With lips held tightly together, Charlene squinted as she spread the oil on one side of the pan. "Looks like I may need more." She reached back into the jar and spread some more around, until the other three sides and bottom of the pan were greased.

"Good job." Heidi handed each student two slices of bread, keeping four of them for herself, to show them what to do. "We'll start by layering half of the bread, ham, and cheese, and then each of the layers will be repeated."

Heidi opened the refrigerator and took out the ham she'd cut into small enough pieces to cube, along with a one-pound brick of cheddar cheese. After giving everyone a knife and small cutting board, she asked them to cut their pieces of ham into small cubes. She watched as everyone did as she asked, and hid a grin when Ron popped a piece of ham into his mouth. *The poor man must be hungry.*

Next, Heidi demonstrated how to grate the cheese. Then she passed the brick of cheese around, along with the grater, and each person took a turn. With the exception of Eli scraping his knuckles, things went fairly well.

"Are you okay? If you need a bandage I have some with me." Loretta reached for her purse. "Between my two little ones, someone always has a boo-boo, so I make sure to keep bandages on hand."

"I'm fine." Eli held up his hand. "My knuckles aren't bleeding. It'll take me a while to get the hang of using this thing, though." He handed the grater to Ron. "Your turn."

Ron made quick work out of grating a pile of cheese, causing Heidi to wonder if he'd done it before.

"Now that we have the cheese shredded and the ham cut, you'll put them in the baking pan on top of the bread slices," she instructed.

"Which goes first. . .the meat or cheese?" Charlene questioned.

"Start with bread, then meat, followed by cheese. This way, the cheese melts down over the meat. Once the first set of ingredients is down, you'll place a second layer of bread, meat, and cheese."

Heidi watched her students take turns creating the layers. Little conversation transpired between them as they all seemed to be concentrating on the task at hand.

Next, she took six eggs from the refrigerator and gave one to each student, keeping one for herself. She also placed six bowls on the table, along with wire whisks for everyone. Then Heidi demonstrated how to beat the egg with the whisk and asked the others to follow her example.

It took Eli a few tries to get his egg beaten, but the others managed okay with theirs.

Heidi set a container of milk on the table and poured enough to make three cups, which she divided equally into six small bowls. "The next step is to pour the milk into your beaten egg mixture and stir until well blended."

Charlene groaned when some of the liquid in her bowl spilled out and onto the table. Her shoulders hunched as she looked up at Heidi with furrowed brows. "Oops. Sorry about that."

"It's okay. You didn't spill much." Heidi handed Charlene a clean sponge to wipe up the mess.

When Charlene rubbed the area, her sponge caught the bowl of egg-and-milk mixture, sending it spattering onto Heidi's clean floor. "Oh, no!" Gasping, Charlene slapped her forehead. "Now look what I've done."

"Don't panic. It could have happened to any of us." Heidi went to the utility room to get the mop.

When she returned, Charlene jumped up and took it from her. "Since I'm the one who made the mess, I'll clean it up." A blotch of red erupted on both of her cheeks.

"If ya give me a sponge I'll wipe off the table where some of the egg mixture landed," Eli offered.

Loretta took the bowl and whisk and then put them in the sink to wash, while Kendra dried the pieces.

This is not going as planned, Heidi thought with regret. But everyone seemed to be taking it in stride and helping to clean up the mess. Everyone but Ron. He stood with arms folded, gazing around the kitchen.

Heidi got another egg, along with more milk, and handed them to Charlene.

"Let me see if I can attempt this again." Charlene cracked the egg and gently whipped it with the whisk. Slowly, she poured in the milk. This time she did it perfectly, and blushed when everyone clapped. "Thank you. Thank you very much." Giggling, she stood and took a bow.

Maybe this incident wasn't such a bad thing. Heidi licked her lips with cautious hope. Everyone seemed to be more relaxed, and it was nice to see them working together and encouraging Charlene. Even Ron's attention seemed to have returned to the matter at hand.

Next, Heidi asked her students to pour the milk-and-egg mixture over the layered items in the baking dish. When finished, she covered the dish with a piece of foil and placed it in the refrigerator to set overnight.

"Does anyone have any questions?"

Kendra, whose face had grown pale all of a sudden, raised her hand. "Where's your bathroom? Think I'm gonna be sick."

Heidi pointed. "Down the hall, last door on the left."

Covering her mouth, Kendra dashed out of the room.

Chapter 8

S ure hope that little gal doesn't have the flu." Ron's face tightened as he plucked at his shirt collar. "The last thing any of us needs is to get sick because of her. If she wasn't feelin' good, she should've stayed home today."

"There's a virus going around at the school where I teach, but so far I've managed to escape it." Charlene crossed her fingers. "I hate taking sick leave. It confuses my young students when they have a substitute teacher. "

"What grade do you teach?" Loretta asked. She felt it was time for a little conversation.

"Kindergarten at an elementary school in Dover. To some of the children I'm like a surrogate mother; they become dependent on me."

Loretta smiled. "My daughter will start kindergarten in the fall. She's excited about going to school."

"How many children do you have?" This question came from Heidi.

"I've been blessed with two—Conner, who's three, and Abby, who recently turned five. Do you have children, Heidi?"

Heidi's shoulders drooped a bit as she slowly shook her head. "The Lord has not seen fit to bless my husband and me with children, but we find plenty to do here to fill our days." She glanced toward the hall door. "I'd better check on Kendra. Loretta, if the timer goes off, will you please take the baking dish out of the oven?"

"Certainly."

After Heidi left the room, Loretta's attention turned to Eli. Even though he smiled occasionally, she detected a sense of gloom in his brown eyes—the same look of sadness she felt whenever she thought about her deceased husband. It was hard to hide one's pain when it felt so raw. Loretta did her best to keep a cheerful attitude—especially around her children. When she was alone in her room at night, however, she let her guard down. During those times, Loretta gave into her grief and allowed the tears to flow. Weeping was part of the healing process, just as her acceptance of what could not be changed. When some people lost a loved one, they became bitter and angry at God, but Loretta's faith remained strong through it all. Instead of turning against God during her time of grief, she leaned heavily upon Him for strength and guidance.

The timer dinged. Since Heidi wasn't back yet, Loretta opened the oven door, took out the baking dish, and placed a pot holder under it on the counter. She inhaled deeply as the delicious aroma flooded her senses. Apparently, it had affected the others, too, for they all lifted their heads and sniffed the air.

"The casserole smells like somethin' my wife used to make." Eli looked longingly at the dish.

"Used to make? Doesn't she make it for you anymore?" Ron asked.

Eli lowered his gaze. "Mavis died a year ago. She was hit by a vehicle while riding her bicycle."

"I'm sorry for your loss." Charlene's quiet tone was sincere.

"Life ain't fair," Ron muttered. "In fact, if you ask me, most of the time it stinks."

"I lost my husband a year ago, too. It's been hard for me and the children, but I won't allow bitterness or despair to set in." Loretta returned to the table, and as she spoke, she looked at Ron. "Life isn't always fair, but we all have much to be thankful for, even if it's something little. So it's best to focus on the positive."

———⌖———

Kendra's legs trembled as she stood at the sink and rinsed her mouth with a paper cup she'd found on the vanity. She hated making a spectacle of herself and dreaded going back to the kitchen where she'd have to face those people. Did they suspect she was pregnant? How much longer could she keep it hidden? The tops Kendra liked to wear when she wasn't pregnant would soon be unable to hide the baby bump, revealing her condition.

Kendra thought about her parents and how they'd asked her not to tell anyone about her predicament. Of course, it wasn't for her sake they didn't want the word to get out. Dad's only concern seemed to be about how he would look to the people at church if they found out one of their board members had a daughter who'd really messed up. He was so self-righteous.

It doesn't matter what anyone thinks, she told herself. *Since I'm not attending church anymore, I don't have to face those people.* Kendra pulled her shoulders back. *I don't know the people who are here taking Heidi's class, and until today, they weren't acquainted with me. So it shouldn't matter whether I tell them or not. Some might look down their noses at me, but maybe a few won't think I'm a bad person. After all, everyone's made a few mistakes at some time in their life.*

Tap. Tap. Tap. "Are you all right, Kendra? Is there anything I can do for you?"

"No, I'm okay. I'll be out in a few minutes." Kendra appreciated the Amish woman's concern, but she wasn't about to let Heidi come into the bathroom and see her looking like this.

After splashing cold water on her face and pushing damp hair behind her ears, Kendra drew a deep breath and opened the door. It surprised her to see Heidi standing in the hallway. She figured the teacher would have returned to the kitchen.

"Your face is awfully pale, and you appear to be shaken." Heidi gently touched Kendra's arm. "I'm concerned about you."

"No need to worry. I feel better since I emptied my stomach."

"Maybe it would be best if you went home and rested. I can send some of the breakfast casserole with you to eat when you're feeling better."

Kendra shook her head. "No, I'm okay. I'm sure I can make it through the rest of the class without getting sick again. In fact, my stomach is growling from smelling your casserole. Oh, and I also brought some mint tea and saltine crackers. They usually help settle my stomach."

Without a word of argument, Heidi slipped her arm around Kendra's waist and walked with her back to the kitchen. The comforting gesture brought tears to Kendra's eyes, and she blinked to keep them from falling onto her cheeks. Now was not the time to give in to her up-and-down emotions.

Still shaken and drained, Kendra took a seat at the table. "Sorry for the interruption. My stomach started doing flip-flops all of a sudden."

"Maybe you've come down with the flu," Ron suggested. "It might be better if you went home so none of us gets exposed to it any more than we've already been."

"I've had the bug many times over the course of my twenty-two years, and it's not what's troubling me." Kendra's jaw clenched. "Believe me. What I have is not the flu."

"What do you have?" Charlene asked.

Kendra placed both hands on her stomach. "I'm expecting a baby, and for the last several weeks, I've been dealing with morning sickness."

———————— ⁘ ————————

Eli looked at Kendra, remembering his wife's pregnancies a few years back. Those started out as happy days, when all seemed perfect and right. The first time Mavis got pregnant, she had no morning sickness. The second time was quite the opposite. Almost from the start, when she suspected she was in a family way, nausea hit the poor thing every morning and sometimes lasted throughout the day. Mavis never complained about feeling sick. She'd put on a brave face and say, "This is the best kind of sickness. It means my pregnancy is normal."

She loved every minute of being pregnant—until the first miscarriage. What a disappointment for both of them. They'd thought the second pregnancy was going well, until the unexpected happened.

Eli flinched, remembering the day as if it had just occurred. Mavis had been doing laundry. She'd made several trips up and down the basement stairs and then trudging outside to the clothesline. Eli had been cultivating an area in the backyard for a new flower bed his wife wanted. Leaning on his shovel, he'd stopped to watch Mavis come out with another load of clothes to hang. Her smile seemed like a permanent part of her face as she hummed a pleasant tune. It made Eli smile, too.

Since it was close to noon, Mavis suggested they have lunch on the porch. "You keep working on the flower bed, and I'll bring some sandwiches out." Whenever the weather cooperated, Eli and Mavis often took the opportunity to eat lunch on the porch. Sometimes they'd have a picnic under one of their lofty maple trees.

Eli had worked diligently, his appetite increasing, while he looked forward to taking a break with his wife. Time passed as he got the ground ready, and soon he began to wonder what was taking Mavis so long to make those sandwiches. Even now, chills ran up his spine as he thought about the soft whimpers he'd heard that day when he'd set the shovel down and gone into the house.

His heart thumped when he entered the kitchen and found his wife lying on the floor. He ran to Mavis, cradling her body, while she kept repeating, "It happened again, Eli. We've lost another *boppli*."

Eli forced his thoughts back to the present. *I hope Kendra's pregnancy goes well for her.*

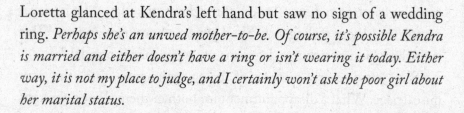

Loretta glanced at Kendra's left hand but saw no sign of a wedding ring. *Perhaps she's an unwed mother-to-be. Of course, it's possible Kendra is married and either doesn't have a ring or isn't wearing it today. Either way, it is not my place to judge, and I certainly won't ask the poor girl about her marital status.*

"I can't speak from experience, but it's my understanding that morning sickness goes away after the first few months," Charlene interjected.

Loretta nodded. "She's right, but then everyone is different. I felt queasy all the way to my sixth month when I was expecting Abby. But with Conner I hardly had any morning sickness at all."

Kendra gave a brief shrug before placing her elbows on the table.

Loretta motioned to the baking dish on the counter. "The timer went off while you were out of the room, Heidi, so I removed the casserole from the oven."

Heidi smiled. "I appreciate it. By the time we get our fruit cut up, the breakfast casserole should be cool enough to eat."

"Then let's get to it!" Ron clapped his hands so loud Loretta nearly jumped out of her chair. "I'm starvin', and the smell of that country breakfast is about to drive me crazy."

───────── ❧ ─────────

By the time the casserole cooled sufficiently, Heidi's students had finished cutting the fruit. Loretta and Charlene had peeled a few apples and cut them into bite-size pieces. Kendra sliced bananas while Ron and Eli peeled some tangerines and separated them into sections. Heidi expected Ron to eat a piece, but to her surprise, he put them all in the bowl she'd provided.

Once vanilla yogurt had been mixed in, Heidi took the bowl to the dining room and set it on the table. Since they'd used the kitchen table for putting the meal together, it would be nice if they ate in the other room, where she'd previously set the table.

When Heidi returned to the kitchen for the casserole, she invited everyone to take seats at the dining-room table.

"Is there anything I can do to help?" Loretta stepped up to Heidi.

"There's a pitcher of water in the refrigerator. You can take it to the dining room and pour some in everyone's glass."

Loretta did as Heidi asked then joined the others at the table.

"This is a simple yet tasty breakfast meal." Heidi gestured to the baking dish. "The best thing about it is it can be made the night before and then popped in the oven the following morning."

Ron smacked his lips noisily. "I can hardly wait to dig in."

"We Amish always offer a silent prayer before our meals," Heidi mentioned. "I hope each of you will thank God with me for the food we are about to eat."

Ron's brows drew inward. "I'm not much of a prayin' man, but out of respect for you, I'll bow my head."

Heidi understood some of her students might not be Christians, but she saw no reason not to pray like always. And since no one had offered an objection, she bowed her head and closed her eyes. *Heavenly Father, thank You for the opportunity to share with these people some of my Amish recipes. After the short time of being with Ron, Eli, Loretta, Charlene, and Kendra today, I have come to realize You may have led them all to my home for more than cooking lessons. As You did for my aunt Emma, please give me the wisdom I need to conduct the next five classes.*

Chapter 9

Sugarcreek

Loretta smiled as she watched her children playing in the yard. Soon after she'd returned from the cooking class, she'd come outside to till the soil in her garden and do some planting. Seeing Heidi's garden plot had given Loretta the incentive to get a few of her vegetables seeds started. Being in the house all winter made her long to be outside in the warm sunshine. Spring brought forth a healing strength, rejuvenating deep within her soul. God had a way of helping a person mourn their loss, and Loretta found nature and the welcoming of the new season part of that process.

While she planted a row of peas, Abby and Conner played happily nearby. They enjoyed being outside and were full of energy. Her children got along well, although at times Abby could be a bit bossy. For now, at least, her little brother went along with whatever she wanted to do. No doubt there would come a time when Conner would want to be in charge and become his own person.

Humming as she went down the first row, dropping peas into the freshly cultivated soil, Loretta thought about how things had gone during the class today. Heidi had been so kind. Even when things got a little out of hand, she'd been patient. Heidi explained things well, too, always demonstrating before asking the students to do what she asked. *What a shame she has no children. I'll bet she'd make a good mother.*

Loretta glanced at her kids again. *I can't imagine my life without them.* She'd thought it so many times before, but it was the truth.

She could hardly wait to go back to Walnut Creek for another class in two weeks. The breakfast casserole they'd eaten before heading home turned out delicious and had been quite easy to prepare. Loretta planned to fix it for breakfast soon, and hoped the children would enjoy it, too. She figured whatever they made at the next cooking class would also be a treat. Loretta also wondered if Heidi would give them another recipe card with scripture on the back, as she had today. It was a good idea, as everyone needed God's Word to guide and direct them through life. Loretta especially appreciated the reminder to be still and focus on God. As busy as she kept these days, she didn't feel complete until she opened her Bible and spent time alone with God.

Loretta's thoughts went to the people she'd met today. Despite coming from different walks of life, Heidi's students had one thing in common—they all wanted to learn how to make some traditional Amish dishes. Of course, for some it went beyond that. Charlene, Eli, and maybe even Ron needed to learn the basics of cooking. Loretta hoped that, as they took five more classes together, she would get to know the others more personally. After only one lesson, they felt like strangers to her. *Of course,* she mused, *they might not want to talk about their personal lives.*

Loretta wasn't sure how much of her life she'd be willing to share, either. It was much easier to open up to people she knew well than discuss personal matters with strangers.

Spending time at Heidi's house had made Loretta feel a bit connected with the Amish way of life. This was another reason she looked forward to going again. She hoped to learn more simple ways to incorporate in her life, as well as the children's.

"Mommy, come quick! There's a snake over here!" Abby's shrill voice drove Loretta's thoughts aside.

Jamming the seed packet into her pocket, she hurried over to where her daughter stood pointing. While Loretta had no fondness for snakes, for the sake of her children, she was determined to put on a brave front. *Sure hope it's not a big one, though.*

"Look, Mommy. . .it's right over there." Abby moved close to Loretta and stood clutching her hand as she continued to point a shaky finger.

Conner, who'd been playing with his truck in a pile of dirt several feet away, joined them. "I wanna see the snake!" Hopping on one foot and then the other, he spoke with the excitement of a three-year-old.

When Loretta spotted the creature, she sighed with relief. "That's not a snake, sweetie. It's a salamander. Come, take a look." Leaning down, she put her arms around both of the children and urged them forward. "See, it has little legs, and there's a red stripe down the middle of its back."

Eyes wide, the children bobbed their heads. Abby got brave and moved a little closer.

"Salamanders live in damp areas, such as under leaves and rocks," Loretta explained.

"Can I pet it, Mommy?" Conner's eyes widened.

"Oh, I don't think it would hold still for that. If we get too close the salamander will most likely scurry under a rock."

"Can we put the critter in something and bring it in the house?" Abby squatted down and reached out to touch the tiny amphibian. "It's cute. We could name him Oscar. He could be our pet."

Although Loretta felt no connection to the salamander, she understood the way her daughter felt. When she was Abby's age and discovered the wonders of nature, she often brought things home. Now she'd have to tell her children the same thing her father told her when she was a girl. In fact, Loretta could still hear his words echoing in her ears. "As nice as it would be to take care of this salamander, he belongs here in his natural environment," she told the children.

Abby's lower lip protruded. A few minutes ago she'd been afraid of the creature, and now she wanted to make it a pet.

"Our yard is his home, and I'm sure you will see him again. When you do, be sure to sit quietly so you don't scare him."

Abby seemed satisfied with Loretta's explanation. Conner was content, appearing almost spellbound as he studied the salamander. Loretta stayed with the children, observing the creature until it finally crawled off.

Conner clapped his hands. "That was fun!" He turned and scampered back to the dirt pile and his toy truck.

Abby reached up and took Loretta's hand. "Can I help ya put seeds in the ground?"

"Of course you may." Loretta squeezed her daughter's fingers tenderly, then handed her the packet of seeds. It pleased her to see how the children found pleasure in simple things. She hoped, with her guidance and love of nature, Abby and Conner would grow up to appreciate everything God created.

Mt. Hope

"How'd things go at the cooking class?" Dorie asked when Kendra entered her friend's cramped living room. "Did you have a good time?"

"The Amish teacher's nice, and we made a tasty breakfast casserole, but I really messed up." Kendra flopped onto the couch with a groan.

"How so?" Dorie took a seat in the chair across from her.

"I got sick to my stomach and barely made it to the bathroom before I threw up." Kendra frowned deeply. "It was embarrassing, but that's not the worst of it."

"What do you mean?"

"I blurted out in front of everyone that I'm pregnant."

Dorie's eyes opened wide. "What made you tell them?"

Kendra shrugged. "Figured I may as well admit it so they didn't think I exposed them to the flu. Plus, after my parents' negative reaction to the pregnancy, guess I was hoping for a positive response from at least one of Heidi's students."

"What did they say?"

"Not much. The one lady—Loretta—mentioned how she'd felt during her pregnancy. No one even asked if I was married, or when the baby's due. If they had learned I'm not married, they might have been condemning like Mom and Dad were." Kendra massaged the back of her neck, hoping to release some of her tensions. "Sure hope when I go back in two weeks, I don't get sick again."

Dorie left her seat and stood behind the couch to take over massaging Kendra's neck. "If you do throw up again, at least no one will be concerned about getting the flu. Hope your teacher didn't have a smelly outhouse." She coughed several times, as though gagging.

"I didn't see one, and they did have indoor plumbing. In fact, except for the lack of electric lights, Heidi's bathroom didn't look much different from yours or any other bathroom I've been in."

"Really? I figured the bathroom in an Amish home would look pretty plain."

"Well, I didn't see pictures on the wall there or in any other part of the house I was in. But some pretty towels hung in the bathroom, in addition to scented hand soap and hand lotion on the vanity."

"Interesting. So getting back to the people you met. . . Maybe they didn't know how to react when you told them you were expecting a baby. You don't have a ring on your finger, and my guess is they weren't going to pry with a bunch of nosy questions."

"Yeah, I guess." Kendra closed her eyes, letting Dorie's magic fingers relax her muscles. "Once I get better acquainted with everyone, I'm hoping I'll feel more comfortable. I'd especially like to know Heidi. She seems nice. Sure wish my mom was more like her." Kendra sighed and quickly changed the subject. "Thanks again for letting me use your car today."

"No problem. I wasn't going anywhere."

Kendra's cell phone rang. She pulled it out of her pocket and swept a hand across her forehead. "It's Shelly. I wonder what she wants."

"Why don't you answer and find out?"

"Most likely, Mom told her the reason they kicked me out. She's probably calling to say how disappointed she is in her big sister and wishes I'd been a better example for her and Chris. As Dad likes to point out, 'they're still impressionable teenagers.'" Kendra shook her head. "I can't deal with it right now. Shelly can leave a message if she wants to."

Dorie took a seat on the couch beside Kendra. "This isn't the first time your sister has called. You should be honest with her." She clasped Kendra's chin, turning her head so she was looking directly at her. "Shelly's reaction might surprise you. How long will you keep avoiding her?"

"I'll return her call eventually, but not today." Kendra stood, arching her back. "I'm tired. Think I'll go take a nap." She grabbed her cell phone and hurried from the room. She appreciated her friend's concern but didn't like being told what to do.

Walnut Creek

"How'd things go with your first cooking class?" Lyle asked, entering the kitchen where Heidi sat at the table making a list of things she wanted to cover at the next class.

She looked up at him and sighed. "The cooking part went well enough with the students, but I think I may have underestimated my job as their teacher."

Lyle pulled out a chair and sat down. "What do you mean?"

"Two of the students, Eli and Charlene, can't cook at all, so I had to go over some of the basics before we started making the breakfast casserole."

"It's understandable. For some folks, cooking doesn't come easy like it does for you."

"I didn't have a problem with sharing some of the fundamentals, but I wasn't expecting a few of the people who came here to share their troubles." Heidi went on to tell Lyle about Kendra's pregnancy. "Then there's Eli, who obviously still misses Mavis, and right before she left today, Loretta mentioned being a widow."

"Do you want my opinion, Heidi?"

She nodded slowly.

Lyle placed his hand on her arm. "In addition to showing your students how to make some special Amish dishes, I believe you could end up helping them deal with whatever problems they have."

"I've been thinking the same thing, since that's how things turned out with Aunt Emma and some of her quilting students." She pulled in a breath and released it slowly. "I only hope I'm up to the task."

"If you ask God to help, He will give you the wisdom to say the right things and know when to say them."

Heidi patted Lyle's knee. "You're right, of course." She appreciated her husband's insight and would try to take his advice.

"Something else interesting happened this morning, shortly after my students and I came to the kitchen."

"What was it?"

"Ron showed up and is now officially taking my class."

Lyle's mouth opened slightly. "I'm surprised he'd be interested in a cooking class, and even more surprised you agreed to teach him."

"Why wouldn't I?"

"Since you expressed concern about Ron parking his motor home in our yard, I wouldn't think you'd be open to him coming into our home and joining your other students."

"I couldn't very well say no—especially since Eli seemed to want Ron in the class."

Lyle leaned slightly forward. "How exactly did this all come about?"

Heidi explained how Ron had come to the door asking for coffee, and then Eli had assumed Ron was part of the class. "One thing led to another, and the next thing I knew, Ron was a new class member. It all happened so fast."

"But your classes will go through the end of June. Does Ron plan to stick around our place that long?"

Heidi lifted her hands, turning them upward. "I never got the chance to ask."

Lyle rose from his chair. "I'd better get this straightened out right now and see what he has to say about it. By the way, I brought sub sandwiches home for our supper. Got one for Ron, too."

"Oh, good. It will be nice not to have to cook tonight. We'll have the leftover coleslaw from the other day along with the sandwiches."

"Great." Lyle grinned.

Heidi watched as her husband went out the door. *I hope Ron doesn't take it wrong when Lyle questions him. I felt like I got to know Ron a little better during class, but I still feel uncomfortable around him. Sure hope he can be trusted and that I won't regret letting him take the class.*

Chapter 10

Ron opened his closet door and peered in. With the exception of his few items of clothes, nothing else occupied the space. Of course, he'd recently emptied it after visiting a pawnshop the week before he'd shown up at Heidi and Lyle's place. The closet was useful and could hold a good deal of things. He hoped within the next few weeks he'd have it filled again. First things first, though. He needed to figure out a way to get inside the Troyers' when no one was home.

Ron considered flaking out on his bunk for a short nap, but before he could head in that direction, someone rapped on his side door. Yawning, he opened it and was surprised to see Lyle, holding a plastic sack. "Didn't know you were back from the auction." Ron stepped out and shut the door behind him. "Never heard a vehicle pull in."

"I asked my driver to drop me off out front by the mailbox so I could check for mail." Lyle shuffled his feet, kicking a small stone with the toe of his boot. "Is it all right if I come inside? There's something I want to talk to you about."

"No problem. I've been wantin' to talk to you, too." It was a good time to let Lyle inside the RV. Aside from being a little messy, nothing looked out of the ordinary.

Lyle stepped inside, and Ron swung the driver and passenger seats around so they could sit comfortably. "Should I start, or do you want to go first?" he asked after they'd both taken seats.

"Guess I'll say what's on my mind." Lyle cleared his throat. "Heidi mentioned you took part in her cooking class today."

Ron gave a nod. "I enjoyed it, too, and hope I'll get the chance to be part of the next five classes."

Lyle gave his earlobe a tug. "I see. Well. . ."

"So I was wonderin' if you would mind if I kept my rig parked on your property a few more weeks."

Lyle worked his fingers through his thick, full beard, while looking steadily at Ron, as though sizing him up. Letting his hand fall in his lap, he spoke. "Did you come here, thinking you would stay indefinitely?"

"Course not. I needed a place to park my motor home until I could get it running smoothly again." Ron shook his head. "Never expected to get involved in a cooking class, but now that I have, if it's okay with you, I'd like to see it through."

"If I'm hearing you right, you want to stay here through the end of June?"

"Yeah, but I'm willing to do some chores in exchange for letting me stay. Could we work something out?"

Lyle sat several seconds then slowly nodded. "I'll make a list of several things needing to be done and give it to you in the morning."

"Thanks for the opportunity." Ron held out his hand, as if to seal the deal. After shaking Lyle's hand, Ron thought of something else. "Say, I was wondering. . . . Do you think your wife would mind if I use her clothesline to dry some of my things?"

"That shouldn't be a problem. Do you have a way to wash your clothes?"

Ron scrubbed his hand down the side of his face. "Unless I'm close to a laundromat and have money to spare, I usually wash 'em there." He pointed to his small kitchen sink. "Wouldn't expect Heidi to wash my clothes. Nope, that'd be asking too much."

"Umm. . .we'll see how it goes." Lyle lifted the plastic bag he'd brought in with him. "Before I forget, I picked up some submarine sandwiches on my way home and got one for you. Hope you like turkey with cheddar cheese."

"Much obliged. Truth is, I can eat most anything, but I've always had a fondness for hoagies." Ron took the plastic bag. "At least that's what I've always called 'em."

Lyle remained in the chair a few more seconds then stood and moved toward the side door. "See you tomorrow, Ron. Have a good night."

"Yeah, same to you."

As soon as Lyle left, Ron took a seat at his table and dug into the sandwich. It would be too risky for him to get close to these people, even though they were kind and hospitable. He couldn't afford to let any sentimental emotions take over, or he might leave here with nothing but a few pleasant memories. While pleasant memories were nice, what Ron really needed was money.

<hr />

Saturday evening, as Eli ate a bologna and cheese sandwich for supper, he reflected on his day. The cooking class had been interesting, and he'd felt relief when another man showed up. Being the only Amish person in the class, though, he didn't fit in with the rest of them. Of course, Heidi was there, and even though she was Amish, she was also the teacher, not to mention an expert cook.

"Maybe I'll never be able to cook a halfway decent meal," Eli muttered. "Might be eatin' sandwiches and hard-boiled eggs the rest of my life."

He thought about the three English women in Heidi's class. Two of them, Kendra and Charlene, wore makeup and dressed in what he saw as clothes made for a man. Loretta, however, wore a long skirt with a cotton blouse. From what he could tell, she had no makeup on her face, either. If her hair had been pulled back in a bun, and she'd worn a Plain dress, she would have almost looked Amish.

Eli's musings scattered when he heard scratching on the door. "Okay, Lady, I hear ya." He rose from his chair, opened the back door, and let the black lab out.

Returning to the table to finish the rest of his sandwich, Eli's thoughts were redirected to Heidi's cooking class. *I wonder what her other students would've thought if I'd told 'em I make caskets for a living.*

Eli's profession, which he'd learned from his grandfather, wasn't something he normally talked about with English people. Everyone in his Amish community knew what he did for a living, but he had a hunch the women in class, and maybe even Ron, would think making caskets was a creepy kind of job. Well, it might be disturbing, but when someone died, their family needed to purchase a coffin, and his were made according to Amish custom. Nothing fancy, just a simple pine box. What Eli never expected was the one he'd worked on only a few weeks before his wife's death would end up having Mavis buried in it.

Eli drank the last bit of milk in his glass and took the dishes to the sink to wash. *Mavis never minded doing dishes.* He filled the sink with detergent and warm water then reached for a sponge. He didn't hate doing dishes, but it wasn't his favorite chore, either. Of course he didn't enjoy doing any of the inside chores his wife used to do. *Mavis isn't coming back,* Eli reminded himself. *And unless God directs me otherwise, I'll never get married again. So I may as well do the inside chores without complaining.*

Canton, Ohio

Bridget Perkins had no more than entered the kitchen to begin making supper than her middle daughter, Shelly, stepped into the room. "I called Kendra again today, but I only got her voice mail." Tilting her head to one side, Shelly pursed her lips. "I don't understand why Kendra doesn't return my calls. Doesn't she realize I'm worried about her?"

Bridget moaned. "I don't believe your sister cares about anyone but herself."

Shelly pushed her shoulder-length auburn hair behind her ears. Her resemblance to Kendra was uncanny. If Shelly's hair were shorter, they could have almost passed as twins.

Leaning against the counter, Shelly folded her arms. "Something's going on, Mom, and I have a right to know what it is. Don't you agree?

After all, I'm part of this family, too, and I'm not a kid. I'm eighteen years old."

"There's nothing going on you need to know about." Bridget reached for a potato to peel.

"It doesn't make sense for Kendra to move out and not tell us where she's living." Shelly moved closer to the sink. "Did you and she have a disagreement about her boyfriend? Is that the reason she moved out?"

"Your sister left this house because we asked her to. End of story."

Bridget turned at the sound of her husband's deep voice. "Gary, I didn't realize you'd come home. You mentioned this morning you'd be working late this evening."

"I changed my mind." He looked at Shelly and narrowed his eyes. "You are not to have anything to do with your sister! No more phone calls or text messages. Do you understand?"

Shelly blinked. "How come? Has Kendra done something wrong?"

"She's pregnant." His voice lowered to a more reasonable pitch. "And you're not to tell anyone about this situation. Understand?"

Shelly's mouth formed an O. "What are we supposed to say when people at church ask where Kendra is?"

"We'll tell them the truth. She moved out, and we don't know where she is." His nostrils flared like a bull ready to charge. "I will not bring shame on our family because your sister couldn't keep her emotions in check. She messed up and needs to pay for her mistake."

Bridget pressed her lips tightly together. She didn't agree with the way Gary chose to shut Kendra out of their lives, but she wouldn't usurp his authority.

Dover

It was five o'clock, and Charlene and her fiancé, Len, were on their way to dinner. When Len said he wanted to take Charlene someplace special, she'd suggested a four-star restaurant in Millersburg. Chinese food was one of Charlene's favorites, and she'd been to this place last year with her friend Kathy. It was about an hour's drive through some pretty country, plus it would give them more time to talk privately.

"You're beautiful." Len reached across the seat of his Suburban and clasped her hand, bringing it to his lips. "You look great in that lavender dress."

"Thanks." Charlene squeezed his warm fingers. She'd taken extra care getting ready for her date with Len. *Could this be the time we'll set our wedding date?*

Charlene had been blessed with thick, shiny hair. Since it was long and hung past her shoulders, she could wear it in several styles. Tonight, she'd worn it down and had used a special brush to add body and soft, bouncy curls. She'd pulled one side up and secured it with a sparkly barrette. Charlene wore dangly, bronze-colored earrings with tiny jewels, blending well with her simple but stylish dress. She'd brought along a cute little shrug to ward off the chilly night air. The April days were getting warmer, but evenings could still be cold, reminding her it was only the beginning of spring.

"Len, your car still smells new inside." Charlene ran her hand over the smooth leather seat. "You keep it so nice, and it looks brand new."

"Yeah, it's hard to believe I've had it almost a year already." Len patted the steering wheel. "I hope to have this baby a long time."

"How'd your day go?" Charlene asked.

"It went well. The clients I saw were impressed with the solar panels and ended up placing an order for their new home."

Len was a sales representative and worked for his father, who owned an energy company. Solar panels were becoming more popular, especially with the farming communities.

"I'm glad to hear it. You don't normally work on Saturdays." Charlene looked at her handsome fiancé, thinking, *How did I get so lucky to land a guy like him?* Len was incredibly good looking, with dark, wavy hair and dreamy chocolate-brown eyes. There was a certain ruggedness about him. At times she couldn't help thinking what a handsome cowboy he'd make.

"The people I met with today own a huge dairy farm and want to go totally solar," Len explained. "They have quite an operation going at their place, and today was the best time they could see me. So tonight we are celebrating my closing of a pretty big deal."

Charlene felt a bit disappointed but managed to keep her composure and remain in a happy frame of mind. This was something important for Len, and she was glad for him, but she had hoped he might be ready to set a wedding date. *Now that would be something to celebrate.*

"Sure hope you like the restaurant I chose." She reached across the seat and gave his arm an affectionate pat. "I've been there once with a friend, and what we had to eat was exceptionally good."

"I'm so hungry I don't know what I'll end up getting, but with Chinese food, we could order several dishes to share, and probably have leftover to take home."

As they drove east on Route 39 toward Millersburg, Charlene stared out the window. The farmland and countryside were beautiful, as it had been in Walnut Creek when she'd gone to the cooking class earlier today. She had planned to tell Len all about it but changed her mind, wanting in the weeks ahead to surprise him instead.

"How was your day?" Len glanced Charlene's way.

"It went well. I've been thinking of a project I want to do for my kindergarten class before the school term lets out."

"What kind of project?"

"I'd like to take a group photo of our class and then take individual photos of each of my students." Charlene's excitement mounted, thinking about it. "The pictures will be gifts for the children, as well as their parents. It will give them something to remember me by."

"Sounds like a nice idea." Len gestured to Charlene's camera bag. "I see you brought your camera along this evening."

"You know me—I try not to go too many places without it. I missed taking some photos of geese when Kathy and I went to lunch in Dover recently."

"Well, maybe you can take a picture of our food at the restaurant." Len chuckled.

"You're such a tease." Charlene giggled, then her eyes widened as they passed a field where a few horses grazed. "Len, quick, turn around. I saw a horse lying down, and I'm sure it's giving birth. If it is, I'd love to get a few pictures. Can we go back, please?"

"Okay, but we can't be too long, 'cause we don't want to eat a late meal. I'll pull in to this road up ahead, and then we'll turn around and go back to where you saw the horse." Traffic was light, and Len had no problem turning around. No one was behind them, and he drove slowly.

"There! It's right there!" Charlene pointed as she got out her camera and made sure the setting was correct.

Len maneuvered over to the lane they'd previously been in then pulled his vehicle onto the shoulder of the road and turned off the engine. They both got out and stood by the fence rails. Fortunately, the horse she'd seen lying down wasn't far from the fence, or Charlene might never have seen it.

What an amazing sight to watch this event occur. She and Len had gotten there in the nick of time. The owners of the horse, a middle-aged man and woman, must have known their mare was about to foal, for they arrived in a utility vehicle shortly afterward.

Out of respect, Charlene asked, "Is it okay if I take a few pictures?"

"Sure, go ahead." The lady smiled then turned around to help the man, who Charlene assumed was her husband.

The mare was a beautiful chestnut brown with a black mane and tail. Charlene was in awe.

"Can you believe we're seeing this?" Len poked Charlene's arm. He seemed as thrilled as she was.

She held her camera steady, snapping a sequence of pictures. Some feet appeared; then a nose; and soon after, the colt's head emerged. The man helped by pulling the shoulders and hips out, followed by the back legs. As Charlene took more photos then paused to watch the process, she was amazed at how efficient these people were in helping with the foal's delivery. While the woman wiped the small horse off and cleaned out its nostrils, the man commented that they needed to wait and make sure the foal was able to stand okay. All seemed normal when the mare turned around and started licking her baby.

Tears sprang to Charlene's eyes as she watched the foal try to stand on wobbly legs then stumble and fall. The colt was precious, and a replica of its mother, with a dark mane and tail and chestnut-colored body.

Shortly after, the woman walked over to the fence to join them. "My name's Kitty Albright, and that's my husband, Ward, over there. Is this the first time you've seen a foal being born?"

"Yes," Charlene murmured, almost reverently. "I couldn't believe it when we drove by, and I'm so glad I had my camera with me. Thanks for allowing me to take the pictures. I'll make sure you get some copies, if you like."

"Thanks anyway, but this is sort of 'old hat' to us." Kitty grinned. "I'm glad you got to witness what I like to call a miracle. Here on our farm we see plenty of miracles."

"I can imagine." Charlene took more photos when the colt managed to stand and started to nurse shortly thereafter.

"Guess we'd better get going," Len suggested, leaning close to Charlene.

"Oh, okay." She looked back one last time and noticed that behind this amazing scene, a beautiful sunset had formed. *I have to get this shot.* As she snapped one last picture of the adorable colt, a loud crash occurred.

"Oh, no!" Holding his hands against his cheeks, Len groaned. "Someone just hit my car!"

Chapter 11

Walnut Creek

"My, my. . .where does the time go?" Heidi shook her head, staring at the calendar. It was Monday already, and not much time to spare before her friends arrived to help plant the garden. "I am so *narrisch*."

"Foolish about what?" Lyle stepped behind Heidi, resting his chin on her shoulder.

"During my cooking class on Saturday, I mentioned two of my friends would be coming over today to help with my garden." Heidi massaged her forehead. "Goodness, I've had so much on my mind lately, I almost forgot. I'd better take out the breakfast casserole and get it heated before Sharon and Ada arrive." She glanced at the clock. "Oh, dear, I don't have much time."

He kissed the side of her neck. "Slow down and try to relax. Seems like you're always rushing about."

Heidi couldn't argue the point, but keeping busy helped keep her mind occupied, especially during times of self-doubt.

As she took the casserole dish from the refrigerator and placed it in the oven, Heidi reflected on how her inability to give Lyle a child had created self-doubts. The doctor had explained that some women with an ovulation problem like hers eventually became pregnant. Heidi apparently wasn't one of those fortunate people. She'd suggested they adopt, but Lyle felt differently, and his answer never changed: *"If God wants us to have kinner, it will happen in His time."*

Heidi kept quiet and accepted her husband's decision. But it was hard seeing others enjoying their children. Ever since she was a young girl, Heidi had looked forward to becoming a mother someday.

Refusing to dwell on this, lest she fall prey to depression, Heidi took the coffeepot from the stove, filled Lyle's thermos, and handed it to him. "How long will you be gone today?"

"Besides running a few errands this morning, I need to be in Farmerstown at noon. The auction is supposed to be over by four, so I'll be home by suppertime." He gave her a hug. "Enjoy your visit with Sharon and Ada, but don't work too hard in the garden, okay? Looks like it'll be a warm day."

"I'll be fine." Heidi smiled. "Enjoying time with my two best friends is almost a guarantee, but I won't promise not to work hard. You know how I get when I'm busy with something."

Lyle tweaked the end of Heidi's nose, gave her a kiss, and headed out the door. "Don't fix a big meal tonight," he called over his shoulder. "How about sandwiches?"

"All right." Once more, she appreciated her husband's thoughtfulness.

Heidi leaned her forehead against the kitchen window and watched as Lyle patted Rusty's head before getting into his driver's van. The dog barked in protest and sat in the middle of the driveway, watching as the van drove toward the road.

Lord, please be with my husband today, she silently prayed. *Keep Lyle safe, and help things go well at the auction.*

———————⁓·◦⌐◦·⁓———————

Careful not to let them see, Ron stood back from the window as he watched Heidi and two other Amish women working in the garden. Squinting, he pinched the bridge of his nose. *Since she's busy right now, I'll go out to the barn and do one of the chores on Lyle's list. It'll give me a chance to see what's in there that might be of value.*

Slapping his baseball cap on his head, Ron opened the door and stepped out of the RV.

Heidi looked up from her kneeling position and waved. He waved back and hurried toward the barn. The last thing he wanted was to engage in a conversation with three women chattering in a language he didn't understand as they planted seeds.

Wonder what they're saying. For all I know, they're talking about me.

When Ron entered the barn, he grabbed a shovel to muck out two empty stalls. Lyle had explained the other day that one of the horses pulled his buggy and the other belonged to Heidi. Both animals grazed in the pasture now, where Lyle had put them this morning before his driver arrived. Ron assumed that Lyle might be at an auction someplace in the area. Auctions fascinated him—especially how fast auctioneers could talk. If he didn't forget, he planned to ask Lyle how he'd gotten into such an interesting line of work. In any case, if it was like before, Lyle wouldn't arrive home for a good many hours.

After Ron finished cleaning the first stall, he took a break to look around the barn. Several old milk cans stood against one wall, but those were too big to fit in the closet where he kept his stash. He'd look for some smaller items he could hide in his RV, and hopefully Heidi or Lyle wouldn't notice some things were missing—at least not till he was long gone.

Moving toward the back of the building, Ron spotted several old canning jars on a shelf. Looking at them closely, he discovered their blueish-green color and several bubbles in the glass. *These should easily fit in my closet, but I'd better wait till the Troyers are in bed some night before I sneak in here and get them. Sure hope I won't get caught in the act.*

Ron reflected on a time, a few years back, when a feisty old farmer in Kentucky threatened to shoot him if he didn't put back the old milk cans he'd taken. With his rifle pointed right at Ron, the man ordered him off his land, saying if he saw him again, he'd shoot first and ask questions later.

"Coulda used a guy like him at my side when I was fightin' the war in Vietnam," Ron muttered.

"I appreciate you both coming to help me today," Heidi told her friends as they sat on the back porch, taking a break. "Now that I'm teaching cooking classes, I'll be spending more time in the kitchen planning menus and making a list of things I'll need to cover during the next five classes."

Sharon leaned forward, one hand on her knee. "We're happy to help with your garden."

Ada nodded. "Once things start growing, if you need help weeding, please let us know."

"What about your own gardens? I'm sure you'll be plenty busy with those."

"Our kinner will help." Sharon drank some of the iced tea Heidi had made earlier. "My two oldest will soon be out of school for the summer, so they'll keep busy helping me in the garden, among other things needing to be done."

The mention of children caused Heidi's body to tense. Thankfully, Ada changed the subject and asked how the first cooking class went.

"Quite well. Five students attended, and they all seemed interested in learning to make some traditional Amish dishes." Heidi chose not to mention anything about her students' personal lives. She'd only just met them and, from the little she'd learned, felt it best to keep quiet about any personal problems her students had rather than turn it into something akin to gossip.

"Who's watching your youngest kinner today?" Heidi asked Sharon.

"My mamm." Sharon's dimples deepened when she smiled. "She's always pleased whenever she's able to spend time with Timothy and Eva."

"My two little ones are with their *grossmudder* today," Ada put in.

Heidi's own parents came to mind, and she remembered Mom saying when she and Lyle got married, how she looked forward to having more grandchildren. Struggling not to give in to self-pity again, Heidi thought about her brothers, and how they'd been blessed with children. Lester and his wife, Vera, had two boys and two girls. Richard, the oldest, was married to Edith, and they were parents of three girls and four boys.

Heidi pulled her shoulders back. She would not give in to despair. "Whew!" She fanned her face. "It's like summer today, instead of early spring."

"You're right," Ada agreed. "I hope things don't start coming up in our gardens and then get zapped by an early-morning frost that often happens during the first month of spring."

"I don't usually put things like tomato plants in the ground until all danger of frost is gone." Heidi gestured to her garden plot. "But it's fine to plant peas, radishes, and beets this early in the year."

They continued to visit until Sharon suggested they get back to work, since she only had a few hours left to help.

While her friends headed back to the garden, Heidi took their empty glasses inside and placed them in the sink. Glancing out the kitchen window, she spotted Ron tinkering with something under the hood of his motor home. It still concerned her that Lyle gave permission for Ron to remain on their property until the end of June. He'd even said it was okay for Ron to hang his clothes on Heidi's clothesline. It almost seemed as if he planned to remain there permanently.

Will Ron leave after the last cooking class or come up with an excuse to stay longer? Heidi hoped he didn't have that in mind, because she wasn't used to having a big old motor home sitting on their property. It looked so out of place on an Amish farm—more so than English clothes hanging on the line.

Dover

Charlene stood in the corner of the playground, keeping an eye on her kindergarten class as they enjoyed recess. *Oh, to be young and carefree again.* She flexed her tense shoulder muscles, thinking about all that happened Saturday night. Her date with Len had started so well. Up until they'd stopped to watch the foal come into the world, things had been nearly perfect. What excitement to see the mare give birth and capture it all on camera. The photos turned out amazing, including the one of the mare and nursing colt, with a beautiful sunset in the background. Too bad their evening ended on a negative note. Once Len's vehicle was hit, everything fell apart.

Charlene squirmed, remembering the horrible ordeal when the car crashed into Len's Suburban. Poor Len. The vehicle wasn't even a year old. The accident ruined their whole date. Because the car's bumper had gotten pushed into one of the back wheels, the Suburban had to be towed back to Dover, and their dinner plans were canceled.

Charlene apologized—it seemed like a hundred times—but her fiancé assured her, "It wasn't your fault."

The people who'd hit Len's car also apologized, saying they felt terrible about the unfortunate accident. The driver explained they were gawking at the colt and hadn't noticed Len's Suburban at first. By the time they did, it was too late.

After exchanging insurance information, Len called for help, and he and Charlene rode back to Dover with the tow-truck driver. Len and the driver talked the whole time, but Charlene tuned them out, fretting over what happened. Len squeezed her hand and said, "It's gonna be okay." But even with his assurance, she felt terrible. If they hadn't stopped to see the mare give birth, everything would have been fine.

Charlene breathed in and out slowly. *If Len found it his heart to forgive me, then I need to get past this guilt, because the accident really wasn't my fault.*

Sugarcreek

Loretta felt as if the chores would never end. By the time the children went down for their naps, she was exhausted and tempted to lie down, too. But if she stopped now, the rest of her tasks would never get done, at least not today.

Hoping to increase her energy, she drank another cup of coffee then headed for the clothesline, making sure the back door was left open. With the storm door closed, no bugs could get in, but enough screen was exposed so Loretta could hear the children if they called out.

A sense of peace settled over her as she took the towels off the line, breathing deeply of their fresh-air aroma. Loretta owned a dryer, of course, but whenever she washed clothes and the weather was nice, she hung them outdoors. It wasn't merely to save money on electricity. She enjoyed the lingering scent—especially on the sheets and towels.

When the clothes were all off, Loretta picked up the basket and started for the house. The storm door held fast when Loretta tried to open it. *That's strange. I'm sure I didn't lock it from inside before I stepped out.*

Perplexed, she set the basket on the porch and yanked on the door handle once more. A piece of heavy furniture would have been easier to move. Despite not wanting to wake the children, she pounded on the door. If the only way she could get in was to rouse Abby and Conner, then they'd have to do with less sleep now and go to bed earlier tonight.

After knocking on the glass door several times with no response, and wiggling and jiggling the handle again, a sense of panic came over Loretta. She paused to pray. *Heavenly Father, please help me get this door open. My children are inside, and they need me.* The words from Psalm 46:10 Heidi had written on the back of the recipe card for the breakfast casserole came to mind: *"Be still, and know that I am God."*

Chapter 12

Loretta's heart pulsated as she pounded on the storm door, thunder sounding in the distance. *Lord, please get me inside. If only one of the children would hear her.*

"Abby! Conner!" She called their names repeatedly, continuing to beat her fists on the door. *Lord, I need Your help. Why aren't You answering my prayer?*

"Be still, and know that I am God."

She drew a deep breath, forcing herself to calm down.

After what seemed like hours, Conner showed up, rubbing his eyes.

"Honey, please open the door for Mommy." Loretta spoke softly, so as not to upset her son.

He tipped his head, looking at her curiously through the glass. "The door is open. Come in, Mommy."

She shook her head. "Only the big wooden door is open. The door with glass and screen in it won't open for me. Sweetie, pull down on the handle, please."

Conner jiggled it, but the door didn't budge.

More frustrated than ever, Loretta asked her son to go get his sister.

"Abby's sleepin'."

"I realize she's taking a nap, but you need to wake her up."

"What if she yells at me?"

"Tell your sister I asked you to wake her up and she needs to come open the door for me right away."

"Okay." Conner trotted off and returned a short time later with Abby at his side.

Loretta felt relief. "Abby, I can't get the door open. See if it will open from inside."

Abby pushed the handle down, but nothing happened.

"Try pulling the button above it straight up," Loretta instructed. "If it's locked, that should let us open the door."

Standing on tiptoes, Abby kept trying but to no avail.

Loretta saw no other choice but to remove the storm door from its hinges. First, she'd need to find the right tool in order to do the job.

"I'm going out to the garage to look for a tool," Loretta called to her daughter. "I want you and Conner to go to the living room and wait for me there."

"Okay."

Loretta hurried across the yard. Before she made it to the garage, her elderly neighbor, Sam Jones, showed up.

"Is everything all right, Mrs. Donnelly? With a storm approaching, I wanted to check." The wrinkles on his forehead deepened. "Heard you shouting and pounding. Wondered if you'd gotten locked out of the house or something."

"I did, in fact. I can't open the storm door from the outside, and the kids can't get it open from inside." Loretta gestured to the garage. "I came here to find the right tool to remove the door from its hinges."

He held up one hand. "Not to worry. I've been locked out of my house a time or two. I'll get the door off for you." Sam stepped inside the garage.

Loretta walked back to the porch. No need to tell her neighbor where the tools were. Sam used to come over to visit with Rick while he did things in the garage. The two became good friends. Sam was devastated when Rick died. He told Loretta once that he felt like he'd lost a son.

"Mommy! Mommy!" Abby yelled from the living room.

"What is it, sweetheart?" Loretta peered in through the glass door but couldn't see the children.

"I hear thunder," Abby whimpered, finally stepping up to the door. "Conner's scared, too. He's on the couch, holdin' two pillows against his ears."

"Don't worry. I'll be with you both shortly. Sam is getting a tool from the garage to help me get inside."

Telling Abby about Sam seemed to calm her fears, for she went back to the living room. Loretta stayed by the door, relieved when she heard the children giggling. It sounded like Abby was reading her brother a story.

A few minutes later, Sam showed up, and in no time, he had the storm door off.

"Thank You, Lord," Loretta murmured. *What a blessing to have a good neighbor like Sam.*

Mt. Hope

Tired from a day of fruitless job hunting, Kendra went to bed early. Dorie was on a date with her boyfriend, Gene, so the house was quiet.

Kendra plumped up her pillow and crawled into bed, thankful her friend's mobile home included this small guest room. Sleeping on the couch held no appeal, but Kendra would have crashed there if Dorie had nothing else to offer.

Distant thunder rumbled, and a gentle rain fell from the storm that had passed through earlier. For her, the rain hitting the metal roof of the mobile home worked like a lullaby on a baby.

As Kendra closed her eyes, lulled by the soothing sound, the scripture verse Heidi had written on the back of the recipe card for the breakfast casserole came to mind. *"Be still, and know that I am God."* She thought about praying, the way she'd done since she was a young girl. But what was the use? God hadn't responded to the one thing she'd recently prayed about.

Kendra felt discouraged and wondered sometimes if God was real, or just a supernatural being someone had made up so they'd feel better when praying. Well, Kendra didn't need some Bible verse to make herself feel better. What she needed was a job and someone to tell her what to do about the baby. Should she keep the child and try to raise it alone? Would it be better to put the infant up for adoption? *Mom and Dad sure won't help me raise my baby, even if this innocent child will be their first grandchild.*

She rolled onto her side, trying to find a more comfortable position. *If I keep the baby, what kind of a life do I have to offer? What if I never find a suitable job? Even if I do secure employment somewhere, who'll watch the baby when I'm at work?*

The sensible thing would be to adopt it out, but Kendra couldn't do it unless she knew for certain the little one growing inside her would be raised in a good home with loving parents. Since God hadn't answered her prayers about this, maybe, if He did exist, He was mad at her, too.

She clenched her fingers until her palms ached. *That creep, Max. If he'd asked me to marry him instead of getting involved with someone else and then running off to join the navy, this wouldn't be a problem right now. While Mom and Dad might have been angry about my promiscuousness, they may have eventually accepted things if I'd gotten married.*

Though the rain slowly stopped, faint flashes of lightning reflected on the wall, and occasional claps of thunder continued to rumble.

Kendra rolled onto her back again, staring at the ceiling. *What a pickle I've gotten myself into.* Her eyes and nose burned with unshed tears. *I need some answers, and soon.*

Walnut Creek

Heidi entered the bedroom to the sound of her husband's gentle snores. Thankfully, the storm had abated, or she'd be hearing that, too. The battery-operated light on the nightstand glowed, and Lyle's Bible lay across his chest. He'd had a long day and gone to bed soon after they finished supper.

Gently, she lifted the Bible and carried it to her side of the bed. She'd meant to do her devotions this morning, but Ada and Sharon arrived earlier than expected, so she'd put her Bible reading on hold.

Taking a seat on the edge of the bed, Heidi opened the Bible to Psalm 127. Reading silently, her eyes came to rest on verse three. *"Children are an heritage of the Lord: and the fruit of the womb is his reward."* She'd read this passage many times, and it always put an ache in her heart.

Tears welled and her shoulders slumped as the longing for a child took over yet again. *Help me, Lord, to be content and stop dwelling on what I cannot change.*

Heidi finished the psalm, set the Bible aside, and picked up the notepad on her nightstand. *I should concentrate on my next cooking class and decide what dish to teach my students how to make. Haystack might be a good choice. It's a healthy, traditional Amish meal to serve for lunch or supper. It's not difficult to make, either.*

Heidi turned off the light. With one less thing on her mind, hopefully sleep would come easy. She was pleased her garden had gotten planted today before the rain fell. *Thank You, dear Lord, for all my blessings, and the rain we needed.*

———— ❧◦❧ ————

It was close to midnight when Ron looked outside. The rain had stopped an hour ago, and now he'd have to dodge puddles. Regardless, a little water or mud wouldn't stop him from carrying out his plans. *No light coming from the Troyers' windows—that's good.* He grabbed a flashlight, stepped out of the motor home, and headed for the barn.

When Ron entered the building, the horses neighed and moved around restlessly in their stalls. "Hush, you two. There's nothin' to get excited about." Ron went to each horse and patted them on the nose, hoping to get them comfortable with his voice.

He'd need to work fast and hoped neither Lyle nor Heidi woke up because of sounds from the horses. If they caught him in the barn at this time of night, he'd have to come up with a legitimate excuse for being here.

Ron made his way to the back of the building, thankful the horses settled down. Shining his light up ahead, he spotted the canning jars he'd seen earlier today. Four of them sat side by side on a shelf, but Ron only took two. *Would they miss a third?* With no more thought, he reached for another jar. As Ron wrapped his fingers around the cool glass, something wiggled in his palm. In the nick of time, before dropping the jar, he caught it in his other hand, seeing a spider crawl out between his fingers. The eight-legged creature must have been on the back of the jar when he took it down from the shelf.

Seeing all the cobwebs, he should have known better. Ron put the third jar back, shook the spider to the floor, and stomped on it. No point pushing his luck. Since he'd be sticking around the Troyers' several more weeks, there'd be plenty of time to get more loot. A little here…a little there… Soon there'd be enough items to make a trip to the pawnshop in Dover or New Philadelphia. Of course, he'd go when Heidi and Lyle weren't home. They'd become suspicious if they saw him driving his rig when it hadn't been fixed.

"Bide your time," Ron whispered as he opened the door to his rig. Stepping inside, he kicked off his shoes and left them lying by the door. Tomorrow he'd knock the mud from the soles. His RV looked messy enough without getting dirt all over the floor. *Heidi and Lyle are so trusting, by the time they realize some of their treasures are missing, I'll be long gone.*

Chapter 13

"Are you ready to teach your second class this morning?" Lyle asked as he sat beside Heidi at the kitchen table.

She nodded. "We'll be making haystacks."

"Yum." He smacked his lips. "Might be good for supper tonight. Unless you have something else planned."

Heidi smiled, lightly brushing her hand against his. "I'd figured on serving it for supper since all the ingredients are here."

"Will there be enough?"

"Jah. I bought plenty of everything."

"I look forward to it. Oh, before I forget, I spoke with Ron after the auction." Lyle reached for his cup of coffee and took a drink. "He's eager to take part in your class today."

"I'm glad, and I hope the rest of my students feel the same way."

"How could they not?" Lyle set his cup down and clasped her hand. "They're learning from the best cook in all of Holmes County."

Heidi rolled her eyes at him. "I doubt I'm the best, and you might be a wee bit prejudiced."

"Maybe so, but you're an excellent cook. Why else did I choose you among all the other young women who wanted to marry me?" Chuckling, he winked at her.

She swatted his arm playfully. "You're such a big tease."

"True, and isn't it one of the reasons you love me so much? You enjoy a little teasing."

She gave his beard a gentle tug. "A little humor is good for everyone. Which is why I chose Proverbs 17:22 to write on the back of everyone's recipe card today. 'A merry heart doeth good like a medicine.' It's one of my favorite verses."

"God's Word is full of good advice." Lyle leaned closer to Heidi and kissed her cheek before pushing back his chair. "I'd better get going or I'll never get to Abe Miller's place to find out how much he'd charge for a new open buggy."

"Can we afford it right now?" Heidi questioned.

"I'm not sure. That's why I need to ask about the price. Afterward, I'll be heading to Charm to pick up a few things. Should be home by the time your class is over or possibly a bit later, depending on if I run into anyone I know and end up chatting a spell." Lyle grabbed his straw hat from the wall peg, lifted his hand in a quick wave, and headed out the door. "Hope you have a good class," he called over his shoulder.

"Danki. See you later, husband."

When the door clicked shut, Heidi left the table and put their empty cups in the sink. As she washed them along with the breakfast dishes, she watched out the window until Lyle's horse and buggy was out of sight. Already she felt lonely without him.

Mt. Hope

"How are you feeling this morning?" Dorie asked when Kendra entered the kitchen.

"Not bad. I felt a little queasiness when I first woke up, but it's better now. With any luck, I'll make it through the day without throwing up." Kendra moved across the room to fix a cup of mint tea. "How was your date with Gene last night?"

"Good. Better than our last date when it rained, although we had fun bowling once we dried off after running from Gene's car through the parking lot. This time, we drove up to Canton, had dinner, and went to see a movie. Since I don't have to work Saturdays, it was nice going out on a Friday night rather than a Monday evening." Dorie took a box of cold cereal from the cupboard. "What'd you do all evening?"

"Not much. Went to bed early again. Had a hard time falling asleep, though. Like almost every night here of late, too many thoughts swirled in my head."

"Were you rehashing the situation with your parents?"

"Yeah, but I can't stop fretting about what to do when the baby comes." Kendra gave a slight shake of her head. "Any way I look at my options, it's a no-win situation."

"What do you mean?"

"If I put the baby up for adoption, I'll always wonder where the child is and if he or she is well cared for." Rocking back and forth, Kendra placed both hands across her stomach. "How could I forget about a baby I carried for nine whole months? The child is already a part of me. It's not something easily forgotten."

"Like I've said before, no one's forcing you to put your baby up for adoption." Dorie put two bowls on the table and took a carton of milk from the refrigerator. "You could keep the child and raise it yourself. A lot of single mothers are doing that these days."

Kendra pulled the silverware drawer open and removed two spoons, placing them on the table. "When you say it like that, it sounds so right, but raising a child by myself would be a challenge—especially since I won't be getting any help from Mom and Dad." Frowning, she lifted one hand. "And how will I take care of the baby financially? I have no job yet, and what if I'm not able to find one?"

"I'm sure the right one's out there, Kendra. You have to keep looking. Don't give up."

"Easy for you to say. You have a good job. Besides, even if I worked at a fabulous place, I'd need to find someone to watch the baby after it's born." She sank into a chair as a heavy sigh escaped her lips. "Paying a babysitter could be expensive, not to mention all the things I'd need to buy for the baby. Sure wish I had lots of money in the bank."

"I'd offer to babysit, but my work hours might not be the same as yours." Dorie took the seat beside her. "Too bad your folks won't let you move back home. Maybe your mom would babysit, and you could go back to college and get your degree."

Kendra's jaw clenched as she lifted both hands in defeat. "Fat chance! It will never happen—not with Dad feeling the way he does and Mom with no apparent mind of her own. She goes along with whatever he says."

"Never say never. Sometimes people change their minds on issues they once held firm to."

"Not Dad. When he decides something, he doesn't budge. And as far as my education goes. . .well, let's just say, my dream of becoming a nurse is just that. . .a dream. It's never gonna happen." Kendra grabbed the cereal box and poured some into her bowl. For the moment, her stomach had settled. "Can't solve this problem right now, so for today at least, it'll be fun to learn how to make another Amish recipe."

"Do you know what she'll be teaching you today?"

"Not sure, but I'm anxious to find out."

Walnut Creek

"No, Lady, you cannot go with me today." Eli shook his finger at the shiny black lab. The persistent dog followed him to the end of the driveway, wagging her tail as she barked at him.

Since the weather was nice, Eli chose to walk to the Troyers' house. He and his dog often went for walks, so Lady probably figured she'd be welcome to come along.

"Guess I'd better put you in your pen, or you'll end up following me all the way there." Eli grabbed Lady's collar and led her to the chain-link pen. "Now be good, and no barkin' while I'm gone." He made sure the dog had plenty of water, gave her a quick pat, and closed the gate.

Woof! Woof! Woof!

Eli whirled around. "Quiet now! I'll be back in a few hours. Then you can run all over the yard and carry on all ya want."

Whimpering, the dog quieted and lay down, nose between her paws.

As Eli headed down the road in the direction of the Troyers', he puckered his lips and whistled a pleasant tune. Although he hadn't expected to like the class, he'd enjoyed helping make the breakfast casserole during the first cooking lesson. Heidi's patience and ability to explain things well made it easier for him to come back. He'd known the Troyers a good many years, and that made being there more comfortable, too. The best part, though, was when Ron showed up. Eli felt less conspicuous no longer being the only man in the class.

Heidi had included some scripture on the back of the recipe card she'd sent home with him. Eli appreciated the reminder to be still and focus on God. Sometimes he got busy in his shop or around the yard and didn't take time to be one-on-one with his Lord.

Following the directions on the front of Heidi's recipe card, Eli had tried to duplicate the breakfast casserole in his own kitchen. It hadn't tasted too bad, but the texture wasn't quite the same, and most of it stuck to the baking dish. He'd managed to dig it out, though, and enjoyed eating the casserole for breakfast three days in a row. *Sure was better than cold cereal or a boiled egg,* he mused. *Next time, though, I'd better use more cooking oil to grease the baking dish. Think Mavis would be pleased I'm learning how to cook.*

Eli stopped walking for a moment, and glanced around. From the way things looked, today's weather was off to a good start. Spring was getting into full swing now, with flowering shrubs blooming and tree seeds whirling through the air. Despite the few cooler days they'd had this month, warmer temperatures were slowly winning out. Eli was glad the days were getting longer, too. It was no longer dark when he quit work for the day and came inside to start supper. He looked forward to the longer days of summer, when he could get more done in the yard.

Overhead, Eli watched a pair of Canadian geese fly past, honking in their own conversational way. Some birds in the area had already nested, while others were in the stages of building a nest. The other day, Eli had noticed a pair of tree swallows taking up residence in a bluebird box he'd mounted on the fence. No wonder this time of year made him feel ambitious. As Mavis used to say, "Spring is a glorious season—especially after a long, cold winter."

Eli started walking again, and had only gone a short distance when a minivan pulled up beside him. He recognized the driver right away.

Loretta leaned toward the window on the passenger side and rolled it down. "Are you heading to Heidi's?"

He gave a nod.

"Would you like a ride?"

Eli felt tongue-tied and could barely make eye contact with her. *Sure hope I don't stutter.* "Umm. . .thanks." He opened the door and got in, keeping his gaze on the seat belt as he fumbled to get it hooked. The silly thing wouldn't connect, so with a huff, he gave up trying.

Loretta reached across the seat. "Here, let me help you. That seat belt buckle can be kind of stubborn at times." She clicked it together. "There you go."

His ears burned. *She must think I'm a dunce for failing to do something as simple as hooking a seat belt.* "Thanks," he mumbled, barely able to look at her.

When Loretta pulled onto the road, the silence grew unbearable, until Eli sneezed—not once, but eight times. He blew his nose and shyly muttered, "Sorry. Spring allergy season."

It seemed to break the ice a little when Loretta glanced at him and smiled. "How have you been these last two weeks?"

"Nothing to complain about. How are things with you?"

"Not too bad except for when I got locked out of my house a few days ago and my kids were still inside."

"What'd you do?"

"Sam came over and took the door off its hinges. In the nick of time, too, before a storm came through."

"Yeah, it hit here, too." Eli wondered who Sam was. *Maybe he's Loretta's boyfriend. Well, it's none of my business, and I'm sure not gonna ask.*

"I'm anxious to find out what we'll be making today. Did you enjoy the first class?" She seemed determined to carry on a conversation.

"Yep."

"Same here. I made the breakfast casserole last week, and my kinner loved it."

Eli jerked his head. "You know Pennsylvania Dutch?"

She laughed. "I don't speak it fluently, but I can say a few words."

"How'd you learn 'em?"

"Well, I. . ."

Seeing a cow had wandered into the middle of the road up ahead, Eli only had time to point and shout, "Look out!"

Chapter 14

"Oh my, that was too close!" Loretta's heart palpitated after swerving to avoid hitting the cow. Thankfully, no cars were coming in the other lane, where the animal now stood, looking like it couldn't care less about what had almost happened.

"Bet that critter belongs to the Troyers." Eli scanned the area. "Don't see any other cows at least. I'll hop out and see if my coaxing is any good. Go ahead up the driveway so you're not sitting in the middle of the road. I'll follow behind with the cow and guide her into their yard." He opened the door and stepped out of the van.

Loretta wiped her sweaty palms against her long skirt as she turned up the Troyers' driveway. She hoped Eli could get the cow to do what he wanted. The thought of him in the road sent chills up her spine. What if a car came and didn't see him in time?

After looking in the rearview mirror, Loretta felt relief seeing Eli and the cow meandering up the driveway behind her van. With little urging from Eli, the cow seemed as if it knew where it belonged. She remained in the van until he pushed the gate fully open and got the animal inside, giving its rump a pat.

When Loretta got out of her vehicle, Eli stepped up to her. "Sure hope this cow belongs to the Troyers. Even if it doesn't, it'll remain here till our cooking class is over. Then I'll go looking till I find the owner."

"Based on how it acted, my guess is the cow belongs here." She looked directly at him, slowly shaking her head. "I'm glad you called out to me in time. I hate the thought of killing, or even injuring the cow. Not to mention damaging my van. Since it's my only vehicle, I can't be without it."

"All's well that ends well." Eli offered her a shy-looking grin. "Should we go on up to the house now?"

"Yes." Loretta glanced around the yard. So far hers was the only vehicle in the yard, other than Ron's motor home. "Looks like we're the first ones here."

Walking side by side, she and Eli stepped onto the porch. After a brief knock, the door opened, and Heidi greeted them. "It's good to see you. Please, come inside."

When they entered the house, Eli told Heidi about the cow on the road, and how he'd put it in the pasture. "I assumed it was your cow."

Heidi's lips compressed. "I bet it is. Soon after Lyle left this morning, I went outside to hang a few towels and noticed the gate to the pasture was open. I shut it, of course, but the cow probably made her escape before I came out."

"Could be." Eli bobbed his head. "I made sure the gate latched after I put her in."

"Danki for taking care of it. I have no idea how the gate got open, but I appreciate your help." Heidi motioned to the living room. "You're welcome to sit in there until the others arrive. I'll join you as soon as I finish what I'm doing in the kitchen."

Eli removed his straw hat and shuffled into the living room. Loretta followed. He took a seat in the rocking chair and got it moving, while she seated herself on the couch. Uncomfortable with the silence and needing to say something, she asked how long Eli had lived in Walnut Creek.

"I was born in Mt. Eaton, but when I turned six, my folks moved to Sugarcreek, which is where they still reside."

"What a coincidence. Sugarcreek is where my children and I live."

He stopped rocking. "You're lucky to have them. My wife and I wanted kinner, but she miscarried twice. To make matters worse, she got cancer and had to have her uterus surgically removed." Eyes closed, Eli massaged his forehead. "Our hope of having children ended, of course."

"I'm sorry for your loss. It seems you and your wife went through a lot."

"We did, but our love proved strong, and we enjoyed every minute we had together." Opening his eyes, Eli lifted his hands and let them fall in his lap. "Life is hard, but God's been with me through it all. Wouldn't be where I am today without His help."

She nodded. "He's been with me, as well. I couldn't have coped with my husband's death if not for the strength I continue to draw from the Lord, as well as Christian family and friends."

Heidi entered the room and was about to take a seat when a knock sounded on the front door. "Sounds like someone else has arrived." She went to answer it and returned with Ron at her side.

Eli let his head fall against the back of the chair and drew a deep breath through his nose. Loretta assumed he was glad Ron had come back for another class. Even for a sociable English man, which Eli was not, being among a bunch of women—in a cooking class, no less— would probably be difficult. From what Loretta could tell so far, Eli was a kind, gentle person, although a bit on the shy side.

He must miss his wife as much I do Rick. Loretta swallowed against the sudden lump forming in her throat. All this pitying got her nowhere. Determined, she directed her focus on something else.

───────────── ❧ ─────────────

Ron sauntered into the room and took a seat in the recliner.

"Nice to see you again." Smiling, Eli tipped his head.

"Same here." Ron pulled the lever back on the chair to put his feet up. It felt good to sit in a chair like this. He hadn't enjoyed such a comfort since he and Fran split up. After the divorce, it wasn't easy letting her keep the house and everything in it, but he'd seen no point in fighting for it. Since Matt and Gail were still in grade school at the time, Fran needed a home to raise them in.

Ron hadn't seen his ex-wife in a good many years and didn't even remember how old the kids were anymore. *Probably in their forties by now,* he figured. One of the reasons he'd split years ago and headed out on the road was so he wouldn't be stuck paying child support.

Things went well with him and Fran when they'd first gotten married, but a tour of duty ending after Vietnam soured their relationship. Ron had struggled with the trauma of the war ever since. Many nights he'd wake up screaming, with his body drenched in sweat. The heinous war had affected his personality. Ron's mood swings and harsh temper drove a wedge between him and Fran and caused their children to fear him. While he'd never abused them physically, his impatience and sharp tongue often left Matt and Gail in tears.

Ron's thoughts came to a halt when the grandfather clock bonged on the hour, just as Kendra and Charlene showed up.

Heidi gestured to the two young women. "Looks like everyone is here, so why don't we all go to the kitchen and get started?"

Begrudgingly, Ron put the recliner in the upright position and followed the others. The only bright spot in being part of this class was that it gave him another chance to look around the place, plus an opportunity to eat one more decent meal.

———————⟨ ⟩———————

When Charlene entered Heidi's kitchen, it surprised her to see so many items sitting on the table—lettuce, cheese, olives, tomatoes, onions, green pepper, celery, corn chips, and two cans of beans. "What are we making today?" she asked.

"It's called 'haystack,' and we Amish like to fix it for lunch or supper." Heidi went on to clarify how each of the items needed to be chopped or grated. "We'll also brown some ground beef and add mild-flavored salsa to it. The soup that will be poured over the top must be combined with milk and heated."

"What are we supposed to do with it all?" Kendra's eyes widened as she motioned to the table. "And why is the recipe for this meal called 'haystack'?"

"Once I explain the rest of the procedure, you'll understand. Now, after the vegetables are chopped, they'll be placed in separate bowls, along with rice, beans, ground beef, and cheese sauce. Afterward you can put whatever items you want on your plate, making a tall haystack." Heidi smiled. "Are there any questions?"

Charlene's hand went up. "Do the eggs need to be sliced or chopped?"

"Usually they're chopped, like the vegetables." Heidi moved toward the table. "So if everyone will put your aprons on, we'll get started. Excusing the men, if they'd rather not borrow an apron from me," she added.

Ron shook his head. "Don't need an apron."

"Me neither," Eli agreed. "Getting food on my clothes is nothing new for me."

Charlene winked when she looked over at Loretta and saw her smile. *Cutting up veggies and piling them on a plate should be easy. This is one meal I'm sure I can fix without messing up.*

While Kendra and Ron waited for their instructions from Heidi, he glanced around the kitchen.

"So, which car do you drive?" Kendra, normally quiet, struck up a conversation.

"Don't have a car. I'm staying here right now." Ron shoved his hands into his pockets. "You probably noticed the motor home parked over by the Troyers' garden."

She nodded.

"It's not only my mode of transportation, but I live in it, too."

"It's nice of Heidi and her husband to let you park on their property. How long have you been friends with them?"

"Only a little while. Since my RV isn't running right, they gave me permission to park the rig here till I'm able to fix it." Ron preferred not to say much more. He hardly knew this girl, and after these classes were over, he'd never see her or any of the others again. Besides, there was something about Kendra that got on his nerves. He couldn't put his finger on it, though.

"I've never seen the inside of a motor home, but I always thought how neat it would be to travel around in one." Kendra pushed a strand of hair behind her ears. "From what I've seen in magazines, some of the newer models are like living in a house. Some have large rooms, flat-screen TVs, and a few models are even equipped with electric or propane fireplaces."

"Mine's not that glamorous." Ron puffed out his cheeks. "I'm lucky I could afford to buy this old clunker."

"Regardless, I'd love to see what the inside looks like," Kendra persisted. "Would ya mind showing it to me?"

This girl was too bold. No wonder she irritated him. What business did she have, asking to see where he lived? Ron didn't want anyone inside his traveling home, especially now, with the items he'd hidden in the closet. If Kendra was anything like his ex-wife, she'd want to snoop in all the cupboards and the closet, as well. *I'll have to come up with some excuse not to let her into my rig.*

"The inside of my RV is no big deal." Ron kept his voice on an even keel. "In my opinion, there's nothing worth seeing in there. Besides, after class I'll be busy doing some things for Lyle."

"I'm glad to hear you're helping them around the farm." Kendra looked at him squarely. "It's the least you can do for these nice people letting you stay however long you're planning to be here."

Where does this sassy little gal get off making a comment like that to me? Ron was about to tell Kendra what he thought, when Heidi stepped between them and began explaining what they needed to do.

He gripped his wooden spoon so tightly he feared it might break. *Good thing Heidi spoke first, or I may have said something I'd later regret. Wish some people would mind their own business. I'll be glad when I have enough loot to move on down the road.*

Chapter 15

Heidi noticed how everyone sat forward, as though eager to learn something new today—even Ron, who rarely smiled. Kendra, normally quiet, had begun a conversation with him. Heidi wasn't sure if her students truly enjoyed the class or were simply enthusiastic to make haystack so they could eat the tasty meal. She, too, looked forward to eating haystack. It was one of her favorite meals.

While Heidi's students chopped their vegetables, she took two packages of ground beef from the refrigerator. "Any volunteers to brown the beef?"

"Not me. I'd most likely burn the meat. It happened the last time I tried to fry bacon." Eli stroked his throat and grimaced.

"You probably turned the burner too high." Heidi took out two frying pans and poured a little cooking oil in each. "Even if I use a nonstick pan I always put oil in the bottom for added flavor and to add a touch of moisture to the meat." She handed one package of beef to Kendra and the other to Ron. Since they'd been conversing, Heidi hoped pairing them would go well. "Why don't you start browning the meat? When it's partway cooked, Loretta and Charlene can take over. Eli, you may want to watch the procedure to see how it's done."

———————

Kendra unwrapped the ground beef and placed it in one of the frying pans while Ron followed suit. She'd felt fine when she first got here, but as the beef began cooking, the odor wafted up to her nostrils, which caused her stomach to churn. She handed Heidi the wooden spoon. "Somebody else better do this, 'cause the sight and smell of this meat has made me feel nauseous."

Loretta stepped forward and took the spoon. "Maybe you ought to step outside for a breath of fresh air. The good country air always helped when morning sickness hit me."

"A cup of mint tea might settle things down. How about I fix it for you?" Heidi offered.

Moving toward the back door, Kendra nodded. "Thanks, Heidi. I'll drink it when I come back inside. I forgot to bring some with me today."

When Kendra stepped onto the porch, she stood at the railing and drew several deep breaths. Getting out of the kitchen and away from the strong meaty odor brought some relief. She'd come mighty close to getting sick and didn't want a repeat of the last class when she'd barely made it to the bathroom in time.

She gazed at the landscape, while recollections circled inside her head. *Before I got pregnant, the odor of meat cooking never bothered me at all. My belly wasn't sensitive to much of anything back then.* Kendra placed her hands firmly on her stomach, which had begun to pooch in the last two weeks. *Are you a boy or a girl? Well, what does it matter? I probably won't get the chance to be your mama.* Tears of frustration pricked the back of Kendra's eyes. *Sure hope I find a job soon.*

She'd scoured the newspaper want ads and made numerous calls to hotels, bed-and-breakfasts, and restaurants in the area, but all the jobs she'd seen listed had already been filled. Kendra wasn't sure how she'd cope with her morning sickness even if someone offered her a job. Somehow, she would manage and make it work. Relying on Dorie indefinitely was not an option. It wasn't fair to expect it, either. Dorie had her own expenses to worry about.

Kendra tipped her head back. Not a cloud to be seen. The birds in Heidi's yard twittered and tweeted as though they hadn't a care in the world.

"Wish I could say the same," Kendra muttered. It wasn't in her nature to feel so negative, but after finding out she was pregnant and then the breakup with Max, she'd become bitter and hopeless—even more so when Mom and Dad kicked her out. Obviously, she'd disappointed them, but did it mean they no longer loved her?

Kendra's sisters came to mind. She still hadn't responded to Shelly's messages. *What's the point? I wonder what Shelly and Chris would say if I told them I was forced to leave home and the reason for it.*

Kendra moved away from the railing and took a seat on the porch swing. The gentle swaying as she pushed her feet against the wooden porch floor helped her relax.

Sighing, she closed her eyes and tried to visualize who her baby might look like when he or she came into the world. Would it have auburn hair and brown eyes like hers, or end up with curly black hair and blue eyes like Max?

Kendra nearly jumped off the swing when the back door swung open and Heidi stepped out. "We're ready to layer the ingredients on our plates. Are you feeling up to joining us now?" She handed Kendra a cup of tea.

"Umm. . .yeah, I do feel better." She lifted the cup and took a sip. "Thanks. This is good, and breathing the country air for a while helped my stomach settle."

Heidi smiled. "I'm glad. Hopefully the tea will help, too."

Kendra stood and followed Heidi into the house. She felt hungry now and couldn't wait to try the haystack.

———————⌐∞⌐———————

"Charlene, are you crying?" Loretta felt concern when she noticed tears rolling down the young woman's cheeks.

Charlene shook her head. "It's those onions I chopped. They made my eyes water."

"Their strong odor has a tendency to do that sometimes." Heidi handed Charlene a tissue. "Now that everyone has finished chopping their vegetables, let's begin the layering process." She demonstrated on her own plate how to put the items down in the order given, to create their individual haystacks.

Once everyone piled the ingredients on, Heidi demonstrated how to pour the cheese sauce over the top. "Some of you may want to add your favorite salad dressing, too." She pointed to the bottles of ranch, thousand island, and Italian dressings she'd set out.

Following behind Charlene and Kendra, Loretta filled her plate with all the goodies. The sight of everything piled up on her plate made Loretta's mouth water. It looked and smelled delicious.

After the men filled their plates, everyone followed Heidi to the dining room. When she bowed her head for silent prayer, Loretta and the others did the same. Once the prayer ended, they all dug in.

"How have you all been doing since our last class?" Heidi questioned.

"I've been looking for a job, but haven't had much luck." Kendra clicked her fingernails against the tabletop. "I'm willing to take almost anything, but I keep hearing there are no openings right now."

"Don't give up." Loretta wished she could do something for this girl. "Keep watching the newspaper or use a computer. The Internet is a great search tool."

"I've done that already. Since my folks kicked me out of their house when they learned I was pregnant, I don't have a computer anymore. My friend, Dorie, whom I'm living with now, has a laptop." Groaning, Kendra leaned her elbows on the table. "She's done so much for me already. I hate to ask if I can keep borrowing hers."

"So you're not married?" The question came from Ron.

Kendra shook her head. "If I was, I wouldn't be in such a mess and might not need a job at all."

"I'll keep my ears open, and if I hear about something, I'll let you know," Charlene spoke up.

"Jobs often become available here in our Amish community," Heidi added.

Loretta couldn't imagine what it must be like to be in Kendra's situation. It would be difficult enough to try and raise a child on her own, but to have been thrown out of her parents' house was beyond belief. What kind of a person would force their own child to leave? Kendra needed help, not condemnation.

Kendra lowered her gaze. "Okay, let's not talk about me anymore."

As if sensing Kendra's discomfort, Heidi turned to Loretta next. "How did your week go?"

"There were a few tense moments when I got locked out of the house." Forehead wrinkling, Loretta dropped her hands to her sides. "My children were inside, and I panicked because they couldn't get the door open, either."

"What did you do?" Charlene leaned forward.

"Fortunately, one of my neighbors heard me pounding on the door and came right over. Sam took the door off its hinges so I could get in before the storm hit."

"For the most part, things went well for me since the last time we were all together." Charlene's brows puckered. "Except for the date with my fiancé, which started out perfect, but ended horribly wrong."

"What do you mean?" Loretta asked.

"Len and I were on our way to Millersburg for dinner. Halfway there, we passed a field where a mare was giving birth to a foal. I asked Len to pull over, since I'd never seen the birth of a colt before. I'm glad I had my camera with me, but when we were ready to head back to Len's vehicle, everything fell apart." Charlene paused and took a breath.

"What happened?" This question came from Kendra.

"Someone hit his Suburban. He had to have it towed back to Dover, and we never made it out to dinner." Charlene wrinkled her nose. "I ended up fixing sandwiches after we took a taxi to my place, where Len called his dad to come get him."

"At least neither of you was in the car when it got hit. You could have been hurt." Heidi commented.

"Yes, we were thankful."

Heidi gestured to Eli. "How have you been?"

He shrugged his shoulders. "Same old, same old. Always busy in my shop."

"You have an interesting profession. Would you mind telling everyone what you do?"

Eli pulled at his shirt collar then rubbed the back of his neck. "Well, I. . .uh. . .make caskets, and also some wooden furniture." He cleared his throat a couple of times. "Most of us don't like to be reminded of death, but the truth is, out of five thousand people, five thousand will die, and most will need a coffin."

No one said a word, until Charlene started asking several questions about his profession. Eli seemed to relax and was willing to respond.

"Ron, do you have anything to share?" Heidi looked in his direction.

"Nope. I'll just listen to the rest of you yammer."

Loretta cringed. Did he have to be so rude? In an effort to put a positive note on things, she gestured to her plate. "This haystack is delicious, Heidi. My children might enjoy helping me make it, so I'm going to try this recipe at home sometime next week."

"It's good, but all that chopping of so many ingredients seems like a waste of time," Ron garbled around a mouthful of food. "Don't think I'll ever make it, though." His chin jutted out. "It ain't worth all the effort."

Tension showed on Heidi's face as her lips compressed. She was obviously hurt by Ron's comment.

It was difficult, but Loretta refrained from saying anything about the man's negative attitude. If it wasn't worth the time to fix a nice meal, why was he taking the class?

She glanced at Eli, who'd been gobbling the food down like it was his last meal. "What about you, Eli? Will you try making haystack on your own?"

He lifted his broad shoulders in a brief shrug. "Maybe. Except for browning the beef, it wasn't too hard. Can't go wrong cuttin' up vegetables and opening a can of beans."

"Don't forget the rice we cooked on the stove after we browned the beef," Charlene interjected.

"True, but if I were to use the kind of rice that cooks in a minute, I could probably manage." Eli took another bite and blotted his lips with a napkin.

Loretta smiled at Heidi. "Thanks for showing us how to make this healthy meal."

"You're welcome." Looking a little more subdued, Heidi handed them each a recipe card with the directions for making haystack. "Now you'll be able to try it at home. Oh, and please don't forget to look at the Bible verse I included on the back."

"I may make this for my future in-laws sometime." Charlene blotted her lips with a napkin. "My fiancé doesn't know I'm taking these classes. I want it to be a surprise."

"It's always fun to surprise someone," Kendra spoke up.

"Yeah, unless it's an unpleasant surprise. Some surprises, like my ex-wife kickin' me out of our house years ago—now that was anything but pleasant." Ron looked over at Kendra. "See, you're not the only one who was given the boot."

The room became quiet as all heads turned to look at Ron.

Loretta couldn't form a response. Since she knew none of the details, she thought it best to keep quiet.

Heidi, on the other hand, spoke quickly. "You're right, Ron. A surprise such as that would certainly be difficult to take."

"Are you and your wife back together?" Eli questioned.

"Nope. Been divorced a good many years." Ron forked more food into his mouth. It was obviously a topic he'd rather not talk about.

***

Ron listened as the others discussed various topics, but he remained quiet. Discussing his messed-up life was something he wouldn't even consider. No one could fix his problems anyway, so no use talking about it. He'd already said too much. *Wish I had never mentioned my ex-wife. If I'd continued the discussion, someone would have probably asked if I have any children. Blabbing the whole story would have been a mistake. These people would most likely look down on me. Either that or feel sorry for the poor Vietnam vet.* He drew his fingers into his palms. *I don't need anyone's pity.*

"Did you have a good two weeks since we last saw you last?" Eli nudged Ron's arm.

"Didn't do much. Tinkered around the RV's engine a bit and helped Lyle with a few chores," Ron mumbled. *I'm sure this fellow means well, but I don't feel like answering a bunch of questions. Guess this is what I get for taking Heidi's cooking class. Don't think Eli realizes I'm not the sociable type.*

"My fiancé likes to work on vehicles when he isn't busy at his job," Charlene interjected. "I could ask him to take a look at your motor home. Maybe he'd find the problem."

"I ordered a part, and thanks, but no thanks. I'll fix my rig once the part comes in."

Ron finished eating and set his fork down. He felt relief when Charlene pulled a photo out of her purse to show everyone. It took the focus off him. Ron had to admit, the picture of the colt and its mother looked interesting—especially with the beautiful sunset in the background.

"I saw a local photo contest advertised in the paper the other day," Kendra commented. "You oughta enter your picture. The ad mentioned it's being sponsored by a photography magazine."

"Maybe I will." Charlene's straight white teeth showed when she gave a wide smile. "Someone has to win, right?"

All heads nodded.

A few minutes later, Heidi's husband entered the room. "Sorry to interrupt." He paused near the table and grinned at Heidi. "I got home earlier than expected, but I didn't think I'd find you here in the dining room. I assumed your class would take place in the kitchen."

"It did, but we came out here to eat the meal." She gestured in the direction of the kitchen. "There's plenty left if you'd like to fix a plate and join us."

"Okay, I'll get some food in a minute." Lyle opened the china hutch door and removed a tall vase. Then he put something inside it and closed the door. From where Ron sat, it looked like money Lyle stuffed inside the dark blue vase.

What's that guy thinking, hidin' money in such an obvious place? And with all of us sitting here, watching, no less. Some folks are too trusting.

Chapter 16

Dover

Three days passed since Charlene attended Heidi's second cooking class, but she'd been too busy to try making haystack. With school winding down in a few weeks, there were so many extra things to do. She planned to have a special program for her kindergarten class the last day of school. The children would entertain their parents with songs they'd learned during the year, as well as acting out a story Charlene chose from one of the books she'd read to the children. She'd taken individual photos of her students the other day, and those would be given out during the program, as well.

As soon as school is out at the end of May I'll get serious about practicing my cooking skills, Charlene told herself as she heated a few pieces of leftover pizza in the microwave for supper.

Olive, who lay on the throw rug near the sink, lifted her gray head as though sniffing the air. *Meow!*

Charlene clicked her tongue while shaking her head. "No pizza for you, my little feline." She pointed across the room to the cat's dish. "Your dinner's over there."

The timer went off, and after Charlene took the pizza out of the microwave, she poured herself a glass of iced tea and took a seat at the kitchen table. Savoring the tangy pepperoni, sausage, and mozzarella cheese, she took time to scan the local newspaper. Her eyebrows rose when her gaze came to rest on the newspaper article Kendra had mentioned during the last cooking class. AMISH COUNTRY PHOTO CONTEST.

Kendra was right. The contest was sponsored by a well-known photography magazine, one Charlene had paged through many times at the grocery store. As she read the details and learned what was required, the thought of entering the contest sparked an interest. The photos would be judged on different categories, such as nature, scenic, seasons, or animals—all taken in an Amish community. Unlike many photo contests, and to be respectful of the Amish, this one did not include a people category, since most Amish objected to having their picture taken.

The photo Charlene took of the foal and its mother depicted Amish country and qualified for three of the categories—scenic, nature, and animals.

Charlene stopped reading and pulled the envelope out of her purse, where she'd put the picture on Saturday. In her opinion, this photo was the best she'd ever taken. In fact, she might even enlarge and frame it.

It still surprised her that she'd managed to capture the sunset's glow illuminating both horses' coats. *I wonder if the judges will notice.*

As she read the rules further, Charlene became more determined to enter her picture. The photo's orientation was required to be in a portrait layout and not the landscape option. An address was listed where it should be mailed, or it could be submitted via a JPEG attachment to the website they listed. She'd already printed the picture from her printer to show everyone in Heidi's class, but it would be easier to submit online. As stated, she had to make sure her name was included, as well as where the picture was taken. The photo needed a title, not longer than six words. *Think I'll call it "Ending to a Perfect Day."*

The article also indicated the judges would pick a winner from each of the categories mentioned. The winners would receive a year's subscription to the sponsoring magazine. What made Charlene sit up and take notice was the last part of the rules. *"A Grand Prize will also be selected from all the photos received. The winning photo will appear on* the cover of the magazine, and the photographer shall receive a two-year subscription to the publication."

Charlene saw no reason this picture would not qualify. *I'm going to submit it and see what happens. How nice it would be to have a photo I took on the cover of a magazine.* Leaning back in her chair, she heaved a sigh. *Maybe it's wishful thinking.*

Mt. Hope

Kendra stared out the kitchen window as she sat at the table, eating supper alone. Dorie went out with her boyfriend again, leaving Kendra to fend for herself. "This is becoming a habit," Kendra muttered, picking at her salad. "But then, I can't expect my friend to stay home all the time just to keep me company."

Dorie had a life of her own before Kendra showed up, and she'd already been more than hospitable. She was Kendra's only friend who had responded to her frantic call the day Dad kicked her out of the house.

Kendra wondered if Dorie and Gene's relationship was getting serious. They'd been seeing a lot of each other lately. Dorie was lucky to have a boyfriend who, from what Kendra could tell, practically idolized her. Gene always seemed willing to do whatever Dorie wanted, and he was good about bringing her little gifts, not to mention complimenting Dorie on her looks.

The skin under Kendra's eyes tightened as her lips parted slightly. It wasn't right to envy her friend, but she couldn't help it. Dorie had a job, a boyfriend, and a place to call home. Her parents were still speaking to her, too. Kendra had nothing but an unborn baby she had no idea what to do with, plus a lot of unpleasant memories from her relationship with Max. It hadn't always been that way. Things were good with them in the beginning, but everything went sour when

Kendra got pregnant. Max turned on her like a badger going after its prey. He'd accused her of having been with someone else. Heaping coals on the fire, he'd eventually admitted having a relationship with another woman the whole time he'd been seeing Kendra.

I wonder if his new girlfriend is pregnant, too. Bitterness welled in Kendra's soul, and she covered her face with her hands, trying to get the image out of her mind of Max pointing his finger and accusing her of having cheated on him.

Kendra pounded the table and gritted her teeth. "Yeah, right. How dare he accuse me, when he was the one cheating? I must have been blind not to have seen it."

Max had rejected Kendra and wanted nothing to do with their baby. He'd even suggested she get an abortion. Although Kendra had drifted from her Christian beliefs, she could never end her child's life. The baby deserved a chance to live and grow up in a healthy, stable environment.

Tears stung her eyes as she pressed her hand against her baby bump. *Short of a miracle, I can never offer you a good home or stable environment, little one. It would be you and me against the world, always needing a handout from a friend like Dorie.* She swallowed hard, nearly choking on the sob rising in her throat. *If things got really bad, we might end up on the street, begging for money.*

Kendra's head jerked when her cell phone rang. She'd barely managed to pay the phone bill for April, and if she didn't find a job soon, she'd have to cancel the service, which would mean no more calls or text messages.

She picked up the phone and looked at the caller ID. *Oh, great, it's Shelly again. I may as well answer or she'll keep calling.*

Kendra swiped her thumb across the screen. "Hi, Shelly. What's up?"

"That's what I'm hoping you'll tell me. I've tried calling several times but you never answer or respond to my messages. Are you avoiding me, Kendra?"

"Not avoiding exactly." Kendra switched the phone to her other ear. "Just don't have anything to say."

"How about telling me why you left home without letting me know where you were going?" Kendra heard the irritation in her sister's voice.

"Did you ask Mom or Dad?"

"Yes, and they said they didn't know where you were."

"What else did they tell you?"

"Dad said you're pregnant. It is true, Kendra? He kicked you out?"

"Yeah, I'm expecting a baby, and Dad sent me packing when I told him."

Kendra half expected her sister to hang up, or at least make some negative comment.

A few seconds ticked by before Shelly spoke. "So where are you staying?" No caustic comments or accusations. Only a simple question.

"I'm in Mt. Hope, at my friend Dorie's."

"Well, you need to come home so we can help you. You can't take care of a baby alone."

Neck bent slightly forward, Kendra folded her arms over her stomach. "Didn't you hear what I said? I'm an embarrassment to our parents—especially Dad. He doesn't want me there anymore, and he made it clear that I should keep my mouth shut about the pregnancy. I'm sure he's worried someone at church will find out." She sucked in a breath. "And of course, that would be terrible. Someone might frown on a board member who couldn't keep his daughter from messing up."

"That's ridiculous. We're family, and family needs to stick together during good times and bad. I don't care about Dad's threats or what he's worried about, either."

"What do you mean? What else did he say?"

"Dad told me not to contact you. No text messages or phone calls." Shelly laughed. "But you see where that got him. Even though he's our father, I don't agree with what he said, because it's just not right."

"You'd better do as he said, Shelly. Same goes for Chris. Don't make things worse for yourself."

"I don't care. He can't keep me from talking to my sister."

"It's a tough time for me, and it hurts to know Mom and Dad don't care about anyone but themselves." Kendra flexed her fingers. "Don't worry about me, sis. I'll manage somehow. Just keep your grades up in school and stay away from untrustworthy guys like Max. Oh, and make sure you don't do anything wrong, or you're likely to get kicked out of the house."

"Kendra, I. . ."

"Can't talk any longer. Dorie's car pulled in." Kendra muttered a quick goodbye and clicked off the phone. In some ways she felt better for having talked with Shelly. In another way she felt like pond scum because, by succumbing to Max's charms, she'd let her whole family down.

Kendra cleared her dishes and had begun putting them in the sink when Dorie came in. Thankfully, Gene wasn't with her. The last thing Kendra needed right now was to watch those two hanging all over each other.

"Guess what?" Dorie's face broke into a wide smile. "Gene and I ate at Mrs. Yoder's Kitchen tonight, and I found out they are looking for a part-time dishwasher."

Kendra bit the inside of her cheek. "I need more than a part-time job. Besides, washing dishes isn't the kind of work I want to do."

"Beggars can't be choosy." Dorie draped her sweater over the back of a chair. "It could work into a full-time job, or maybe a waitressing position will open up." She moved closer to Kendra. "I'd apply for the job if I were you."

"Okay, I'll go to the restaurant tomorrow and put in my application. Since it's within walking distance, I won't need to borrow your car." Kendra gave a halfhearted shrug. "But then since you'll be working tomorrow, I wouldn't be able to borrow it anyway."

Dorie slipped her around Kendra's waist. "Try not to worry. Things will get better soon; you'll see."

"Yeah, right." Kendra turned away from the sink, pressing her hands to her temples. "Nothing ever works out for me."

Walnut Creek

Ron watched out the side window of his motor home as Heidi and Lyle got into their buggy and rode out of the yard. Earlier, Lyle had mentioned joining some of their friends for supper this evening and said they wouldn't be home for a few hours.

This is the perfect opportunity to sneak into their house. Ron rubbed his hands briskly together. *Providing the doors aren't locked, that is.*

He waited until the horse and buggy were out of sight then stepped out of his rig and glanced around. *Good thing they don't have close neighbors.*

When he got to the front porch and tried the door, he discovered it was locked. *Drat!*

Hoping the back door might be unlocked, Ron hurried around the side of the house. There, he spotted the Troyers' dog, lying on the porch with his nose between his paws.

Ron stepped cautiously onto the porch, but the dog didn't budge. *Stupid mutt. Some watchdog you are.* But then Rusty was used to him by now. Ron shook his head when the dog lifted his head, tail thumping against the wooden floor. "Go back to sleep, Rusty."

He turned the doorknob and felt relief when it opened. Upon entering the kitchen, Ron grabbed a few cookies from the plastic container he spotted on the counter. He ate one and stuffed two more in his shirt pocket. Then he made his way to the dining room, opened the hutch, and lifted out the vase he'd seen Lyle put money in on Saturday. Ron whistled when he saw the bills were still there. Placing the money on the table, he counted ten twenty-dollar bills.

Ron chewed on his lower lip. *How many should I take?* He knew better than to take all the money. A few missing bills may not raise any suspicion. Lyle might think he'd miscounted when he'd put the money in the vase. Ron put seven twenties back and kept three. Given the opportunity, he'd check the vase again in a few days and see if any additional money had been added. If so, he'd take a few more.

"Easy-peasy." Ron made his way back to the kitchen. He'd stayed at many places during his time on the road, but none quite as easy as this. By the time he left here at the end of June, he'd have quite a haul. People who left their doors open when they weren't home were just asking to be ripped off.

Ron looked up at the oil lamps above one of the cupboards. Since he was here, he might as well take a few of those, too.

Chapter 17

Sugarcreek

Loretta stoked the logs in the fireplace and took a seat on the couch. While the afternoon had been warm, the evening grew chilly. She tried to relax, watching the flames rekindle as the wood popped and sparks disappeared up the chimney. Today seemed long, and it had been difficult getting the children settled in their beds. "It's my fault," she murmured. "I shouldn't have let them eat candy so close to bedtime."

Recently, Loretta had tried to practice better eating habits—for herself, as well as the children. But when they whined, she sometimes gave in to their requests for sugary treats, which made them hyper.

Since Rick's death, it had been difficult to keep from giving in to their whims. They needed their father, especially as they were growing up. A parent's "tough love" approach was never easy, but even more of a challenge for a single parent. Loretta reminded herself it was how a child learned—even if it meant refusing them something they enjoyed.

From where she sat in the living room, looking out the side window, Loretta enjoyed watching a few birds flitting around to find a roosting spot for the night. She glanced toward Sam's place and thought about his raspberry patch, which was slowly coming to life. He'd mentioned how he'd planted the bushes a number of years ago when his wife was still living, and each year the mass seemed to get thicker. The long stems leafed out, and tiny white flowers became visible. Loretta could almost taste the sweetness of the juicy red berry and how they melted in her mouth. Sam was good about sharing his bounty with her and other neighbors. This year it might be fun to make raspberry jam. *I wonder if Heidi makes jelly. Bet she does.*

When Loretta closed her eyes, a memory, which seemed like yesterday, popped into her head. It had been a quiet, warm summer evening. After she and Rick took turns reading a bedtime story and had watched their daughter fall asleep, they'd tiptoed out to the front porch for some alone time. They'd visited awhile, and when Loretta surprised Rick with the news he'd be a daddy again, he'd pulled her into his arms. "I'm so glad. Do I dare hope it's a boy this time?"

Loretta had smiled and gently pinched his cheek. "Whatever God chooses to give us will be a blessing."

Shortly after, Sam ventured over and joined them on the porch. He'd brought a bucket of raspberries he'd picked that afternoon.

"If you've got some ice cream, I've got the topping," Sam announced.

After Rick shared their good news with Sam, he suggested they make it a celebration. The three of them enjoyed vanilla bean ice cream, topped with Sam's luscious ripe berries. Sam had seemed as excited for them as they were with the blessing and promise of another child.

Loretta opened her eyes and picked up the cup of hot chocolate she'd fixed herself after tucking the children in bed. How many nights had she and Rick sat here, enjoying each other's company and the warmth of the fire? How lonely she felt without him.

Sighing, Loretta reached for comfort by lifting her Bible from the coffee table and opening it to her favorite passage—Psalm 23:1–3: "The LORD is my shepherd; I shall not want. He maketh me to lie down in green pastures: he leadeth me beside the still waters. He restoreth my soul: he leadeth me in the paths of righteousness for his name's sake." She closed her eyes. *Thank You, Lord, for leading and guiding me. Help me become a blessing to all those I meet. Give me wisdom in raising my children, and keep us safe throughout this night. Thank You for every blessing in my life. Amen.*

Sparks flared upward from the burning log in the fireplace, fizzling out as they rose higher. Her husband's life had vanished like the fire's sparks—here one second, gone the next. *Will my life ever feel complete again?* Loretta hoped so, for her sake as well as the children's. Difficult as it was to remember those days, Loretta wanted—no, needed—to keep the memories alive. When the children grew older, they'd no doubt have many questions about their father. There were so many good memories she could share with Abby and Conner.

Loretta lifted her cup and was about to take a drink when the telephone rang. She set the cup down and hurried to the kitchen to answer it. *Sure hope I remembered to turn the ringer off the extension upstairs so it doesn't wake Conner and Abby.*

As soon as Loretta entered the kitchen, she grabbed the receiver. "Hello."

"Hi Loretta, it's Becky from church."

"It's nice hearing from you. How have you been?"

"Super busy right now. I'm on the planning committee, and I wondered if you'd be able to help with our church yard sale, which is a week from this Saturday."

Loretta's face tightened, feeling a twinge of irritation. Becky hadn't even bothered to ask how she and the children were doing. Didn't she care?

"I'm sorry, Becky, but I won't be able to help with the yard sale. I have another commitment that day." Loretta looked at the calendar, where she'd circled the date of the next cooking class. *No point telling Becky what I'll be doing that Saturday. She'd probably think it wasn't as important as the church function.* She stared at the floor. *When did I become so cynical? Who am I to say what her response would have been?*

"It's fine. I understand," Becky replied sweetly. "I hope you have a nice evening, and I'll see you at church this Sunday."

"Okay. Bye, Becky." Loretta hung up and returned to the living room to finish her drink, which was now lukewarm. Looking upward, she prayed, *Lord, help me avoid being judgmental.*

Walnut Creek

"You're awfully quiet," Lyle commented as he and Heidi headed for home. "Didn't you have a good time at the Rabers' tonight?"

"Jah, I did. It was a pleasant evening, and I enjoyed holding their new boppli." She pulled her shawl tighter around her neck to ward off the chill permeating the buggy. It was hard to believe the weather had been so nice earlier today.

Lyle nodded. "He's a cute little guy."

"Holding him made me long for a child of our own even more." Heidi released a lingering sigh. She could almost smell the baby lotion reaching her nostrils when she'd held the precious bundle an hour ago. "We're missing out on so much not having children of our own. If only God would give us a miracle."

Lyle let go of the reins with one hand and took hold of Heidi's hand. "We agreed to accept our situation as God's will."

"No, it's what you decided. This is easier for you than me." She inhaled sharply, hoping to hold back forthcoming tears. Every time the topic of her inability to conceive came up, an unseen barrier wedged between them. If only Lyle would change his mind about adoption. Tonight had been such a pleasant evening, and Heidi didn't want it to end on a sour note. Whenever she was around children, her longings sprang to the surface, even though she tried hard to keep them buried.

"Let's talk about something else." She squeezed his fingers. "You never did say what you found out about getting another open buggy."

His teeth clicked together. "Don't think it's gonna happen this year, Heidi. The price I was quoted is more than I care to spend right now."

"It's okay. Our old buggy is fine."

"Jah, it's probably good for another year or so."

"Say, when we get home, would you like a few of the molasses kichlin I made earlier today?"

"Normally I'd go right for 'em, but I ate too much supper tonight, so I'm still pretty full." He let go of her hand and thumped his stomach.

"You gobbled down your fair share of fried chicken, all right." Heidi chuckled. "I'll make sure to put several cookies in your lunch bucket tomorrow."

"Sounds good."

They rode in silence the rest of the way. While being lulled by the buggy's gentle sway, Heidi almost fell asleep listening to the steady *clip-clop, clip-clop* of the horse's hooves against the pavement.

When Lyle pulled the horse up to the hitching rail, he handed the reins to her while he got out and secured the animal. Bobbins usually cooperated and remained at the rail, but Lyle never took chances. A few years ago, two small children in their community waited in their father's buggy. Before he got his horse secured, it backed up, turned, and bolted. The children were lucky their dad caught up with the buggy and was able to subdue the horse before it ran into the road. What turned out to be a frightening adventure for the little ones ended well. Unfortunately, that wasn't always the case. There had been many accidents due to horses bolting when they became spooked by something, or sometimes for no apparent reason at all.

Once certain Bobbins had been secured, Heidi got out of the buggy. While Lyle put the horse in the barn, she headed for the house, using a flashlight to guide the way.

Upon entering the kitchen, she turned on the gaslight over the table, which illuminated the room with a warm glow. Since her nerves were a bit frazzled, and she felt more awake now, Heidi turned on the stove to heat water in the teakettle. While getting a cup from the cupboard, she noticed several cookie crumbs on the counter. "Well, that *schtinker*," she murmured. "Looks like my husband sampled some of the molasses kichlin before we left home."

Grabbing a sponge from the kitchen sink, Heidi cleaned up the mess and put the crumbs in the garbage can. After the water heated, she fixed herself a cup of chamomile tea and took a seat at the table.

Several minutes later, Lyle came in. "How about a cup of tea?" she asked.

"Sure, and I've changed my mind about the kichlin. Think I'll try a couple to go with the tea." With a playful grin, he winked at her.

Heidi lifted her gaze toward the ceiling. "From the looks of the *grimmel* I found on the counter a few minutes ago, I'd say you already had a taste of my cookies."

His forehead wrinkled. "No I didn't, Heidi. Never went near the cookie container."

Setting her cup down, she pursed her lips. "I suppose I could have dropped a few crumbs when I put the cookies away and just didn't notice."

"You know how it is. We all do things without realizing it." Lyle's eyes widened, and his voice lowered to a whisper. "Or maybe we have a *maus* in the house."

"Oh, dear. Don't even suggest such a thing, especially since I'm conducting cooking classes here in the kitchen. I can only imagine my students' response if a mouse made an appearance during one of our classes."

Lyle tickled Heidi under her chin. "I was only teasing." He opened the plastic container and took out three cookies. After placing two on a napkin, he ate the third one. "Yum. Yum. I'm a *glicklich* man to be married to such a good cook."

"Danki." She smiled. "And I'm lucky to have a man who appreciates my efforts." Heidi truly was thankful for her husband. Once more, she vowed to quit feeling sorry for herself because they had no children and remember to count her blessings.

After tossing and turning several hours, Eli got out bed. *Think I'll head to the kitchen and get a drink of water.*

He'd only taken a few steps toward the door when he tripped over a boot and bumped into his dresser. "Ouch!" Eli leaned over to rub his knee, and when his head came up, he clipped it on the top of the dresser. "Not fun."

Fumbling for his flashlight, he clicked it on and looked in the mirror above the dresser. The bump on the head didn't look too bad, but boy, his knee sure hurt.

Limping his way to the kitchen, Eli gritted his teeth. *If Mavis were here now she'd get me a glass of water, and put Arnica ointment on my knee. My wife always did pamper me.*

After turning on the gas lamp over the table, Eli stood at the sink, looking out the window while he filled his glass with cold water. The moon, reflecting on the pond at the edge of his property, caught his attention. Little ripples formed when a slight breeze occurred, turning the moon's image into diamond-like shapes, sparkling on the water's surface.

His stomach rumbled as he turned back around. There were no snacks in the refrigerator, and not a single cookie filled the cookie jar. What he wouldn't give for something sweet to munch on right now.

Sure hope Mom gives me more kichlin soon. He tilted the glass, gulping down the water. *Store-bought doesn't taste the same as homemade.*

Eli limped across the room and lowered himself into his favorite chair at the table. Staring into space, he reflected once again on the wonderful years he and Mavis shared, and some of the silly things they used to do. He laughed out loud, recalling the night neither of them could sleep. They had no dessert or snacks that evening, and both craved something sweet. After tossing and turning to no avail, Mavis came up with a crazy idea. "Let's make a batch of kichlin." Of course, Eli didn't disagree. Later, as they sat at the kitchen table sharing milk and peanut butter cookies, he announced, "These are the best tasting cookies I've ever eaten. Think they taste better when they're right out of the oven."

Mavis smiled and poked his belly. "Now, don't get used to the idea. I'm not planning to get out of bed in the wee hours and bake cookies often."

Eli looked at his empty cookie jar as his mind snapped back to the present. *Think I'll drop by my folks' place later this week and see if Mom's made any cookies recently. If not, I'll stop at one of the bakeries on my way home. It's not good to have an empty cookie jar in the house.*

Chapter 18

Thursday afternoon, while Heidi was taking a pie from the oven, Lyle came into the kitchen. "What smells so good?" He breathed deeply. "Yum."

"I made a pie using some of the peaches I canned last year." Heidi noticed Lyle held the vase from the dining-room hutch.

"Did you take any money from this?" His forehead creased as he lifted it up.

She shook her head. "Since the money we put in there is for things we're saving up for, I'd never take anything without checking with you first."

He tipped his head. "Hmm. . . Could have sworn I put $200 in here the other day, but now there's only $140. Maybe I had less than I thought." He scratched the side of his head. "Am I getting forgetful all of a sudden? I'm only thirty. Could old age be creeping in already?"

Heidi touched his arm. "Don't be silly. We all forget things."

"True, but I'm almost sure. . ." His voice trailed off as he leaned against the counter. "You don't suppose one of your students took it?"

She shook her head briskly. "I don't see how. We were all here in the dining room at the same time, so there was no chance anyone could have taken it without the others seeing."

"Guess you're right. Even so, I'd better put this in a less conspicuous place." Lyle opened the cupboard door where their dishes were kept and placed the vase on the top shelf next to some empty canning jars. Then he turned to face Heidi again. "If you haven't started supper yet, why don't we go out for a bite to eat?"

"Well. . ." She tapped her chin. "I'd planned to fix a meat loaf, but if I don't have to cook this evening, it'll keep the kitchen cooler. And when we get home, I can work on my lesson plan for the upcoming cooking class."

"Then it's settled." He pulled her into his arms for a sweet kiss. "Besides, you work hard around here and deserve a break from cooking once in a while."

"I got a break the other night, when we went to the Rabers' for supper, remember?"

The skin around Lyle's eyes crinkled when he smiled. "You're right, but we spent the whole evening visiting, which didn't give you any time to prepare for your next class, as you'd hoped to do then. Speaking of which, what dish will you be teaching them how to make this time?"

"I thought of sweet-and-sour meatballs at first but changed my mind. Think I'll teach them how to make German pizza instead."

His eyes gleamed as he wiggled his brows. "It's one of my favorites."

Giggling, Heidi gave his stomach a gentle poke. "You have a good many favorites, dear husband."

Sugarcreek

"It's good to see you, son." Mom gave Eli such a tight squeeze it nearly took his breath away. For a woman of small stature, she had great power in her hugs.

"It's good to see you, too." Eli sniffed the air. "Whatcha been bakin', Mom?"

She took a plastic container from the cupboard and opened it.

Eli's mouth watered. "Banana whoopie pies. You're a good mamm. You always remember those are one of my favorite cookies."

She chuckled and squeezed his arm tenderly. "Don't worry. I'll send plenty of them home with you."

"How about now? Do I get to eat one before I go?"

"Certainly, and you're welcome to stay for supper."

Eli shook his head. "As hard as it is to turn down the offer, I have a few errands to run in Berlin. Then I'm heading right home. There's work waiting for me in the shop."

Mom's forehead wrinkled. "Okay, but you have to promise to come over for a meal soon. I always fix more than your *daed* and I can eat." She put a whoopie pie on a plate and handed it to Eli. "Would you like some milk to go with it?"

"Sure, but I can get it."

"That's okay. Please take a seat at the table and let your old mamm wait on you. I don't get the chance to do it often."

Eli pulled out a chair and sat down. "One of these days I'm gonna invite you and Dad to my house for a meal."

She peered at him over the top of her glasses. "Oh? Have you found a woman friend? Are you courting again?"

His body stiffened. "Course not. No one could ever replace Mavis."

"Starting over with a new fraa would not mean you are replacing your first wife." She poured him a glass of milk and placed it on the table.

His mother meant well, but insinuating he find a new wife did not sit well with Eli. She ought to realize how much he'd loved Mavis and still did. Did Mom think he could forget what they'd once had and move on with his life as though Mavis never existed?

Eli took a breath and blew it out. The best thing to do was change the subject. "So where's Dad this afternoon? Figured he'd be off work by now."

"He went to the dentist's. They'll be seating his new crown, so it could be a while before he gets home."

Eli glanced at the clock above the refrigerator. "Guess I won't get to see him then, 'cause as soon as I finish this treat I need to go."

Mom's lower lip protruded. "But Eli, you only got here a few minutes ago. We don't get to see you as often as we'd like. For that matter, we even hoped you might sell your place and move closer to us."

"I'm not sellin' my place." Eli's shoulders tensed. "It's been my home since Mavis and I got married, and it'll be my home till the day I die. I won't change my mind, neither."

Mom winced. "Calm down, son. You don't need to be so testy. I meant no harm."

A sense of guilt came over Eli, and he quickly apologized. "Sorry, I'm a bit sensitive when it comes to the idea of leaving my home. Mavis was everything to me, and I miss her something awful. I could never leave the place that holds so many special memories."

Mom rested her hand on his shoulder. "I don't understand exactly how you feel because I haven't lost my mate, but a mother's heart hurts to see her child, grown or otherwise, brokenhearted." She paused, clearing her throat. "I won't bring up the topic again, but if you ever want to talk, I'm here for you, Eli."

"Danki." He bit into the whoopie pie. "This is *appeditlich*."

She took a seat beside him. "I'm not one to brag on my baking abilities, but I must agree—these cookies turned out delicious."

———◦◦◦———

A short time later, as Eli headed down the road with his horse and buggy, he glanced at the container on the seat beside him. As much he liked Mom's banana whoopie pies, even over a period of a few days, he could not eat all twelve of them. *Mom means well, though. She only wants the best for me, even with her insinuating I should get married again.*

He clicked his tongue and snapped the reins to get Blossom moving a little quicker. He'd brought Mavis's horse out today, thinking she needed a workout. Trouble was, the lazy animal wanted to poke along. Time was dwindling, and if he didn't get to Berlin soon, he'd have to take care of his errands quickly in order to get home at a reasonable time to finish some work.

To save precious minutes, Eli took a shortcut. As his rig crested a hill, he caught sight of a woman by her mailbox, near the edge of the road. "*Ach*, it's Loretta." Eli pulled back on the reins. Then he waved and called out to her.

With her mouth open slightly, she waved in response.

On impulse, he directed Blossom up Loretta's driveway, even though he was pressed for time. For the moment, it didn't seem to matter. "So, is this where you live?"

Smiling, she nodded. "What brings you out my way?"

"I was at my folks' place. I believe I mentioned they live here in Sugarcreek. Funny thing is, I've been past this place many times but didn't know until today that you lived here."

"Most likely it's because our first meeting was at Heidi's cooking class. So even if you'd seen me, it would have meant nothing. You'd have probably thought I was just another English woman working out in her yard."

"Maybe so." Eli couldn't put a finger on it, but he felt relaxed talking to Loretta right now. Something about her mannerisms reminded him of Mavis. Her looks were different, of course, but Loretta's soft-spoken voice and quiet demeanor were similar to his wife's.

Remembering the container of cookies, he picked it up. "Do you or your children like whoopie pies?"

"What child doesn't like whoopie pies?" Loretta giggled. "Call me a kid, but I love 'em, too."

"Well, good, 'cause my mother gave me several banana-flavored whoopies, and I'd like to share 'em with you."

"How nice." Deep dimples showed in Loretta's cheeks when she smiled. "I'll run up to the house and get another container so you can keep yours." Before heading up the driveway, she added, "I'd invite you in, but Abby and Conner are napping. They'd most likely wake up if they heard us talking. Then I'd never get them back to sleep."

"It's okay, I understand." Eli handed her the container. "I'm actually heading to Berlin to get a few things, and afterward I need to go right home. There's plenty of work waiting for me there."

"Okay, I won't be long. How many should I take?"

"Leave me two and you can have the rest."

"Are you sure? I don't want to cut you short."

"Not a problem." He thumped his stomach. "I don't need the extra pounds, and I'm most happy to share."

While Eli waited for Loretta to return, he glanced around her place. It looked like the house and garage sat on half an acre or so. The lawn appeared to have been recently mowed, and he noticed a weed-free garden on one side of the yard. Did Loretta take care of it herself, or might a friend or relative help out? Another home sat next door. Eli saw a man walking around a berry patch.

Mavis's horse grew restless and stomped her front hooves. "Settle down, Blossom. We'll be on our way soon."

Loretta returned a short time later and handed him the container. "The children will be happy when they wake up to such a nice snack. Please tell your mother thank you."

"I will."

"Oh, and feel free to stop by anytime you're in the area. I'd like you to meet my kinner."

Eli grinned. *There she goes again, using a Pennsylvania Dutch word.* "I'll take you up on the offer, 'cause I'd enjoy meeting them, too." He gave a small wave. "See you at the cooking class a week from Saturday."

"Yes. I'm looking forward to it."

Eli paused long enough to watch Loretta wave at her neighbor then walk over to his yard. *I wonder if the man she's chatting with is the "Sam" she's mentioned a few times during class. He looks old enough to be Loretta's dad.*

Eli shrugged his shoulders and whistled a tune as he backed the horse and buggy onto the road. For some reason, after seeing Loretta, he felt carefree and was glad he'd given her some of Mom's whoopie pies. It felt good to do something nice for someone. *Paying it forward—*

that's what it's called. Eli thought of the scripture on the back of the haystack recipe card he'd received from Heidi. This was what it meant to have a merry heart.

⸙

Mt. Hope

When Kendra left Mrs. Yoder's Kitchen and headed back to Dorie's, her spirits lifted a bit. She'd been hired to wash dishes. Even though it wasn't her first choice, at least some money would be coming in soon, which meant she could help her friend with expenses. Kendra felt grateful she'd be working afternoons and some evenings, because mornings were still the worst for her when it came to dealing with the nausea. The best part of all was that she wouldn't have to work Saturdays and miss any of the cooking classes. Tomorrow would be her first day on the job, and then she wouldn't work again until Monday. She'd have a day to get oriented to her duties, and then two days off.

Sure wish there was something fun to do this weekend. It's boring to sit around while Dorie goes out with Gene. When he comes to her house, it's even worse, 'cause I have to hide out in my bedroom to give them private time together.

Kendra stopped walking and bent to pick up an aluminum can someone had carelessly thrown on the sidewalk. *Some people have no respect. Littering to them is no big deal.* She tossed the can in the nearest trash container and continued on.

Kendra looked at her shadow, which, like her profile, revealed a small baby bump. Instinctively, she rubbed her hand over the swell on her stomach. Then she glanced up as she rounded the corner. Approaching Dorie's house, she came to a halt. "It can't be." Seeing a familiar car parked in the driveway, Kendra groaned. Her body tensed as her hand went from her stomach to her forehead. *Oh no, it's Dad. What does he want?*

Chapter 19

Kendra's legs trembled as she approached her father getting out of his car. Did she dare hope he had come to apologize and ask her to return home, or could there be something else on his mind?

"Hi, Dad. I. . .I'm surprised to see you here."

His eyes narrowed as he glared at her. "Don't know why. You should have expected me."

"Wh—what do you mean?" Her hands moved jerkily.

He took a step closer, nostrils flaring. "Don't play games. You know precisely what I mean. You disrespected me and turned a blind eye to what I asked you not to do."

"What was that?"

"You talked to Shelly about your pregnancy and blamed your mom and me for throwing you out."

"It's the truth, isn't it?"

"Don't get smart." A vein on the side of his head twitched. "To make things worse, Shelly blabbed the whole thing to Chris. Now they're both upset."

And I'm not? "Are they upset with me for getting pregnant or upset with you for kicking me out?" Kendra kept her chin high and her voice even, refusing to let her defenselessness show. She'd always knuckled under when dealing with her dad. But no matter how much energy it took, today Kendra would not let him intimidate her.

His voice rose a notch. "Watch your attitude, Kendra."

She shifted her weight. *He's avoiding my question.*

"I came here to warn you."

"Warn me about what?" Kendra's anger increased. It took every ounce of resistance to keep from shouting at him.

"Your sisters are impressionable, and they've always looked up to you." He loosened his collar. "I've forbidden them to contact you again, and I warned them that if they do, they'll also be kicked out of the house."

Her mouth dropped open. "You're kidding! It's not right to punish Shelly and Chris because you're angry at me." She'd never dreamed her dad could be so cruel or unreasonable. What had come over him to be treating his family like this?

"I'm not punishing them. I am protecting my youngest daughters. If you care anything about your sisters, then do as I say, and stay away from them." His thick brows squished together. "Do you hear me? No more interaction, including phone calls, text messages, e-mail, or social media communication."

Before Kendra's response spewed from her lips, he got back in his car and drove away. She'd wanted to tell him to leave. This was her home, although temporary. Dad had no right to come here and berate her. *How could my own father, who I used to look up to, treat me like this?*

Shoulders sagging and eyes watering, she shuffled toward the mobile home. *So much for the verse from Proverbs 17:22 Heidi gave us. If Dad has anything to say about it, my heart will never be merry. Thank goodness Dorie isn't home yet, because I need to be alone right now so I can cave in and have a good cry.*

Kendra had never deemed herself a weak person emotionally, but since she'd become pregnant, her emotions were all over the place.

She entered the mobile home and sank to the couch, letting her head fall forward into her hands. It was bad enough the future of her unborn baby grew more uncertain each day, but having no communication with or support from her family made it ten times worse.

"What I allowed to happen with Max was wrong, but must I pay for my sins the rest of my life?" Trembling, Kendra looked upward.

No response. Not that she expected any. Her throat constricted. *God's abandoned me, just like Mom and Dad.*

The front door opened, and Dorie stepped in. She stood next to the couch, looking down at Kendra through squinted eyes. "From the looks of your gloomy expression, I'm guessing you didn't get the dishwashing job."

"No, I got it, all right. I start work tomorrow."

"Then why the sad face?"

"My dad paid me a visit. He was waiting outside when I got home from the job interview."

"Uh–oh. What'd he say?"

"Chewed me out for talking to Shelly and confirming that Dad kicked me out. I guess the truth hurt." Kendra wiped the moisture from beneath her eyes. "He told me under no uncertain terms that I am to have nothing to do with my sisters."

Dorie sat on the couch beside Kendra. "You're not a child. He can't tell you what to do. Besides, you're not living under his roof anymore."

"No, but he can make life difficult for Shelly and Chris. If I try to contact my sisters, he vowed to kick them out, too."

"How terrible." Dorie gave Kendra a hug. "I'm sorry you have to go through all this turmoil, and your sisters, too. Your dad's being so unreasonable. Someday he'll regret how he's treated his family."

"I hope he does, but Dad's so stubborn I doubt he cares about anyone but himself. And he calls himself a Christian?" She sniffed. "If I do get to keep my baby, none of my family will get the privilege of knowing him."

"Or her." Dorie bumped Kendra's arm. "It could be a girl, you know."

Kendra forced a smile. "Thanks for letting me vent. I needed to get some stuff off my chest."

"No problem. That's what friends are for."

Berlin

"Thanks for the ride," Ron told Lyle's driver as they left the post office in Berlin, where he'd picked up his government check. "If you'll swing by the bank in Walnut Creek before we head back to the Troyers', I'll cash my check and get you paid."

Eric nodded. "I'm curious. How long have you known the Troyers?"

"Met 'em early April."

"And you've been staying with them ever since?"

Ron rubbed the back of his neck. *What's with this guy and his inquisitions?* "I'm not stayin' with them. They've allowed me to park my rig on their property till I could get it running good again."

"And have you?"

"Not yet. Had to order a part, and it hasn't come in." He held up his check. "Until I got this, I had no money to pay for the part." Quickly changing the subject, Ron pointed to a line of cars up ahead. "Looks like traffic's stopped for some reason. Hope we won't be late getting to the bank."

Eric craned his head. "From what I can see, there's road work up ahead. Don't think it'll take long to get through it, though. I see a flagman letting one lane go."

They waited alongside a huge field. Ron noticed the acreage had already been cultivated and how healthy looking the turned soil seemed to be. An Amish man with three plow horses skillfully maneuvered his team down the next row, along with what looked to be some sort of seeder attached. One big tree, almost completely leafed out, stood stoically in the open field.

"It's amazing what the Amish accomplish in our modern-day world, isn't it?" Eric looked in the same direction as Ron.

"I guess so." Ron shrugged. To him, plowing with horses seemed like too much labor. He also wondered why a tree as big as this one would be left in the middle of the field to work around. *It'd be easier to cut the thing down, wouldn't it?* He'd no sooner thought it than he noticed the Amish man stop and wave at someone coming from the back of the field, where the barn and farmhouse stood. It was a woman, and as she approached the big sprawling tree, he saw that she carried a picnic basket.

Ron didn't want to watch anymore, but he couldn't turn away. While this lady, who he assumed was the man's wife, smoothed a dark-colored tablecloth over the ground and took things out of the basket, the farmer steered his team of well-behaved horses around the back of the tree.

For a split second, Ron experienced a tinge of regret, observing a simple act between the Amish couple. *If only Fran and I. . .*

He leaned back and tried to relax, but sitting in this traffic got on his nerves. *When will we ever get going?*

Walnut Creek

It hadn't taken Eli long to get home after he'd run errands in Berlin. Work awaited him in the shop, but he no longer felt ambitious.

"Think I'll take a minute to relax before I delve into work." Eli talked as if someone was there with him. He'd done it often since Mavis passed away.

After making himself a cup of coffee and taking a whoopie pie from the container, he went outside to do a little porch sitting. Blowing on the cup of steaming brew, he stared out toward his pond. Mavis had wanted a pond so badly, and they'd been fortunate to come across this farm to buy. Eli felt his body relax as he bit into the sweet treat. Except for the rippling from a mallard duck swimming peacefully over the surface, the rest of the pond held a coating of film from pollen settling on the top.

Eli rubbed his hand over the armrest of his chair, observing the pollen there, too. *Guess I should have wiped this off before I sat down.* An image of Mavis bustling around to wipe off the porch furniture came to mind. Another pleasant memory to reflect upon.

After taking off his boots and wearing only his socks, Eli tucked his feet under Lady, slumbering in front of him. As a frog croaked and several others joined in, a grunt escaped the dog's lips. Then Lady stretched her legs out to the side and made lapping noises as she settled in.

"You like the peace and quiet, too, don't ya, girl?" Eli rubbed his foot over her fur. This was the kind of quietness he immersed himself in every chance he got. Almost every occasion brought memories of things he and Mavis had enjoyed. When spring arrived, once the chores were done, the porch always drew their attention. Many evenings they'd watched deer grazing on tender sprouts coming up in the meadow adjoining their back property.

Among the daisies, which recently started blooming, spotty clusters of mustard weed glowed yellow near the pond. Colorful butterflies, and even a few dragonflies, made their way through the warm spring air. One dragonfly was not so lucky when it ventured out over the pond. A fish jumped out at the exact moment, grabbing the tasty meal. As the fish splashed down under the water, the duck spread its wings and took flight. Quick as a flash, Lady jumped up, barking on the porch's edge while watching the duck fly away in protest.

As the mallard flew over the house, still quacking, Eli smiled and took the last swig of coffee. Reluctantly, he pushed himself out of the chair. "Guess I better get something done instead of sittin' here watching time go by." Looking back toward the woodshed, Eli noticed a black-and-white critter heading to a stack of wood he'd piled near the shed the other day. "Oh, great. Hope that skunk doesn't decide to take up residence here. Sure don't need that."

———————————— ❦ ————————————

Sugarcreek

"Anyone want a banana whoopie pie?" Loretta asked when Conner and Abby woke up from their naps.

They both nodded with eager expressions. "Did ya bake 'em while we were sleepin'?" Abby questioned.

"No, a man I met at the cooking class brought them by a while ago. His mother made the whoopie pies, and he wanted to share some with us."

"Is he a nice man?" Abby clambered into a chair.

Scrambling into his booster seat, Conner echoed, "Nice man?"

"Yes, he is." Loretta appreciated Eli's quiet, pleasant demeanor from the first time she'd met him. He'd seemed shy at first, but after visiting with him a few times, he'd become more relaxed and talkative. With the exception of Ron, everyone attending Heidi's classes seemed nice. Something about Ron bothered Loretta, though.

Heidi and her husband are kinder than me. Loretta took a seat between her children. *Since Rick died, maybe I've become too paranoid, but I'd never let a stranger stay on my property a full day, much less the three months it will take to complete Heidi's cooking classes.*

"Mama, are ya gonna give us the cookies?"

Loretta blinked. "Of course, Conner. I'll also pour you a glass of milk."

A few minutes later, Loretta sat at the table with her children, eating the delicious whoopie pies. She looked forward to seeing Eli again. Someday soon, maybe the children would get to meet him.

Chapter 20

Walnut Creek

Eli leaned against the porch post, breathing in the morning's damp air. Fog was lifting, while shafts of sunlight patterned streaks through the misty break of day. Spiderwebs in various parts of his yard hung heavy with the morning dew. The temperature climbed as the sky's milky haze parted and a beautiful blue spread out in its place. "Looks as if a nice day is rolling in." Eli leaned down to pat his dog's head then stretched and leaned back, getting the kinks out of his sore muscles. His knee felt better this morning, but his back hurt some, due to bending over to work on a coffin he'd started making yesterday.

Glancing toward the woodpile stacked close to the house, he put his work gloves on and yawned. It would have been a good morning to stay in bed a bit longer, but Eli never cared much for sleeping in. For as long as he remembered, even as a young boy, he liked morning. *"A body misses a lot if they stay in bed too long,"* his dad always said. Mavis had been an early riser, too. One more of the things she and Eli had in common.

Eli looked toward the sky again. *Better get this woodpile relocated before I head to the Troyers'*.

Turning his attention downward as he walked toward the firewood, Eli spotted more ruts in the grass. "I'm getting sick and tired of that irritating *bisskatz* makin' holes all over my yard. Probably diggin' for grubs." Eli stomped the divots back down, making them level with the lawn. Lady followed him, head down, sniffing the ground.

Eli had waited up last night, and the night before, too, but never saw any sign of the skunk. He'd also set out a cage to trap the critter but ended up catching the neighbor's cat instead. "Guess the animal's only doing what skunks know how to do." Eli tried to make light of the situation, even though his yard had begun to look like swiss cheese.

I'll worry about finding the little schtinker later on. Eli filled the wheelbarrow and hauled the wood over to the shed, while Lady returned to the porch and flopped down. Despite the clumps in his yard, Eli's mood was cheery. Every day since the last cooking class he'd read Proverbs 17:22, reminding him of the importance of having a merry heart. Not even the skunk put a damper on his mood this morning. He looked forward to going to Heidi's again and wondered what plans she had for their class today. Eli was also eager to talk with Loretta and hear how she and her children enjoyed the whoopie pies he'd given her. *Think I'll walk to the Troyers' house again. Maybe Loretta will drive by and, like the last time, offer me a ride.* He smiled. Whistling through his lips, a merry tune followed.

Walking back for another stack of wood, Eli glanced toward his pond. The mallard duck was there again, only this time a female swam with him. Slowly they zigzagged through the water then went to the far end where a cluster of cattails grew. It wouldn't be the first time a pair of wild ducks nested on the pond's bank. Eli looked forward to seeing little ducklings that could hatch most any day.

After several more trips to get the firewood stacked, Eli figured one more load would finish the job. When he'd moved the last heap, Eli had noticed a hint of skunk odor on the bark of the wood. Now as he put each piece into the wheelbarrow, the sickening smell became stronger. "Bet this is where the skunk's been hiding."

He picked up the next log, and an all-too-familiar black-and-white critter sat looking at him. Jumping backward, Eli jerked his arms around. The skunk turned and lifted its tail. It all happened so fast. Waving his hand in front of his nose, he watched in defeat as the rascal darted out of the yard toward the fields behind his place. "Go ahead and run! That's where you belong, you smelly ole critter!"

Eli's dog slept on, as though nothing out of the ordinary had happened. Eli shook his head. *Good thing, too. Lady would have gotten sprayed if she'd gone after the skunk.*

Luckily, the full brunt of the spray missed Eli. Only a little spritzed on his arm. Remembering how his mother used tomato juice on the family dog when it got sprayed by a skunk, Eli headed back to the house.

He'd bought a few tomatoes at the store in Berlin the other day, so he cut one in half and rubbed it on his arm. Too bad he'd rolled up his sleeves earlier while he was stacking the wood. Otherwise, his shirt might have gotten sprayed instead of his skin. Next, he gave his arm a good scrubbing with soap and water. Then, leaning close to his arm, he took a whiff. His sinuses were clogged due to spring allergies, but as far as he could tell, no smell lingered.

Eli glanced at the kitchen clock and grimaced. "Don't know where the morning went." Hurrying to his room for a clean shirt, he heard Lady barking outside. "Sure hope that ole skunk didn't return, but if I don't leave now, I'll be late for the cooking class."

Sugarcreek

The phone rang as Loretta gathered up her things and waited for the babysitter to arrive. She was tempted not to answer, since the last call she'd received was a person trying to sell her something she absolutely didn't need. However, when Loretta glanced at the caller ID and saw it was Sandy, she answered right away.

"Sorry to be calling at the last minute, but I woke up with a sore throat and don't want to expose your kids. I'd hoped I might feel better after sucking on some throat lozenges and gargling with salt water, but it seems to be getting worse. In fact, as soon as I hang up the phone, I'm heading back to bed."

"Oh, okay. I'm sorry to hear you're not feeling well, but thanks for letting me know."

When Loretta hung up, she glanced at her watch, debating what to do. It was too late to find someone else, which meant she'd either have to miss the cooking class or take the children with her.

Loretta drummed her fingers on the edge of the counter. *I wonder if Heidi would mind.* She could call and ask, but it wasn't likely Heidi would check messages in the phone shack before Loretta left home.

Guess I'll chance it and take the kids with me. Loretta cupped her hands around her mouth. "Conner! Abby! Grab a book to read. You're coming to the cooking class with me."

Walnut Creek

Heidi moved about in the kitchen, checking her list and making sure all the ingredients were out for the main dish her students would make today. Lyle had made himself scarce, saying there were some things to do outside and in the barn this morning.

A knock sounded on the door, and Heidi went to answer it. She found Kendra and Charlene on the porch. Charlene, her usual cheerful self, grinned as she entered the house. Kendra, on the other hand, shuffled in with shoulders slumped and lips pressed tightly together. Heidi noticed dark circles beneath the young woman's eyes. Kendra looked like she'd lost her best friend. *Should I say something? Do I ask her what's wrong? No, she might think I'm being pushy and ought to mind my own business. If Kendra wants to talk about what's bothering her, I'm sure she'll speak up.*

"You're the first ones here, so feel free to take a seat until the others arrive." Heidi gestured to the living room.

"What are we making today?" Charlene seated herself on the couch.

"German pizza." Heidi smiled. "It's not a traditional pizza made with a flour crust, but I hope you'll enjoy making it."

"If it's as easy as haystack to make, I'll be pleased." Charlene clasped her hands to her chest. "Oh my, it tasted so good. I'm anxious to fix it for Len and his parents when they come to my place for supper next week." She crossed her legs, bouncing her foot up and down. "Or maybe, if I like what we make today, I'll fix it instead."

"Either would be a simple yet satisfying meal." Heidi glanced at Kendra. She sat in the rocking chair with her head down and hands resting against her stomach. "Have you had a chance to make haystack since our last lesson, Kendra?"

The sullen young woman's only reply was a brief shake of her head.

Heidi was about to ask if Kendra felt all right when the front door opened and Ron poked his head in. "Hope I'm not late. Had trouble sleeping last night, and by the time I did fall asleep, the light of day was streaming through the RV's windows and woke me." He ambled into the room and took a seat on the recliner, where he'd sat the last time.

"How come you didn't sleep well?" Charlene asked.

Curling his fingers, Ron scrapped them through the ends of his short beard. "Just didn't, that's all."

Heidi figured she'd better say something to release the tension in the room. She looked over at Ron and smiled. "I was telling the ladies we'll be making German pizza today."

Ron's eyes brightened a bit. "Good to hear. I like most kinds of pizza—especially pepperoni with black olives."

"This isn't a traditional pizza with a regular crust." Heidi went on to share what she'd told Kendra and Charlene before he showed up.

"What? To me, a pizza with no crust doesn't sound like pizza at all." Ron's forehead wrinkles deepened. "How's a person supposed to eat it, anyway?"

"I'll explain how it's made and the best way to eat it once Eli and Loretta get here," Heidi replied.

Ron seemed satisfied with her response, for he flipped the recliner back and closed his eyes. Would he snooze right there on Lyle's chair? Heidi glanced at the grandfather clock across the room. *What's keeping my other students?*

Chapter 21

Ron opened his eyes and glanced around the room. *Still no Eli. What's wrong with that guy?* As far as Ron was concerned, time was wasting, sitting here waiting for Eli to arrive. Ron took a frustrated breath. *If the guy had to make the rest of us wait, he oughta quit the class. Course, Loretta's not here yet, either. Wonder what's holding them up?*

"Did you have a good week, Ron?" Charlene asked.

"Okay, I guess. Got the part for my RV, but I've been too busy helping out around here to do anything with it yet." Ron yawned and readjusted the chair's footrest. Sitting here doing nothing, he felt sleepier by the minute.

"If you need to get your vehicle running, don't worry about us. Take care of your motor home first," Heidi interjected. "If the chores don't get done right away, it's okay, they can wait."

"I'll see," he mumbled. "I promised Lyle I'd get certain things done, though. Since I don't need to go anywhere right now, what's a few more days going to matter fixing my rig?" Ron grasped the handle on the side of the chair and put it back to its normal position. "How much longer are we gonna wait on Eli? Shouldn't we get started now?"

"We're not waiting just for him," Kendra spoke up. "Loretta's not here yet, either."

Ron folded his arms. "Humph! Maybe they both need to learn how to tell time."

Kendra stopped rocking and rose from her chair. "Ya know what, Mr. Hensley? You're rude and crude!" She walked over to the fireplace, staring up at the mantel.

Ron's face heated. "I'm only being honest, and you oughta mind your own business, young lady." The last thing he needed was some smarty-pants girl giving him a piece of her mind. *What is it with young people today, thinking they can talk to adults any way they choose? Where's the respect?* He shifted on the chair, ready to recline again. If he really thought about it, who was he to complain about disrespect when he'd stolen from the Troyers, right under their noses? It surprised him, but he actually felt a twinge of guilt.

Heidi left her seat, too, and moved over to the window. "I see Loretta getting out of her minivan now, so as soon as she comes in, we'll go to the kitchen and get started. When Eli arrives he can join us."

———————

Tension knotted Kendra's neck and shoulders as she stood by the fireplace. *The audacity of that man, Ron. He is so ill mannered.* She focused on the beautiful oil lamp sitting on the mantel. This was certainly more charming than her parents' mantel, always cluttered with candles, fake flowers, statues, and the like. Framed pictures of Kendra and her sisters would have been better than all the junk Mom thought was important to display.

Kendra's clenched fingers dug into her palms. *First Max, then Dad. Why do men treat me so awful?* Of course Kendra knew not all men were bad. The affectionate gestures she'd seen Lyle give Heidi on the few occasions he'd been here had almost brought her to tears. Good men were certainly hard to find, though. Now she had to deal with someone like Ron, when the whole purpose of learning to cook from an Amish woman was supposed to be putting some fun in her life.

She scrubbed a hand over her face. *I can't win.*

———————

Eli pedaled as fast as his legs would allow. He didn't want the class to start without him. He'd planned to walk to Heidi's, but cleaning up after the skunk meant he was running late. Riding his bike was quicker than harnessing the horse to the buggy, and besides, a little exercise would probably be good for him.

Coasting down the hill, Eli felt the warm breezes gently brushing his face. Today's weather was beautiful, and everything seemed right with the world. Maybe the fresh air would help mask whatever might be left of his skunky smell. While the birds sang, nature's blooms burst at the seams. Eli breathed deeply, hoping to capture the wind's sweet scent.

Even though he was in a hurry, the ride was peaceful and soothing, until a car came up behind him. The noisy muffler filled the otherwise serene morning with an annoying reverberation.

Eli watched as the car sped up the road. For no reason that he could see, the driver slammed on his brakes. Then the vehicle spun around and came back, whizzing past Eli way too close. In an effort to keep from losing his balance, he gripped the handlebars tightly.

Eli kept pedaling and never looked back, but he sensed what was about to happen. The blaring muffler drew closer, until the older model Mustang pulled up beside him, keeping pace with his bike. Four teenage boys—two in the front seat and two in the back—pointed and jeered at him. Several dents on the front fender of the car, amid scratches and dings throughout the paint, gave evidence of neglect.

"Hey there!" The freckle-faced driver snickered. "Where's your horse and buggy, Mr. Amish man?"

Eli ignored them, looking straight ahead. *Who needs this type of aggravation, especially this morning? I'm gonna be late for sure.*

"Come on, man." One of the boys in the backseat snickered. "Can't ya pedal any faster than that?"

The teens whooped and hollered. *Do they get a thrill out of harassing me?* This wasn't the first time something like this had occurred. Others in his community had been teased and taunted by boisterous kids out for a good time. *If I ignore them, maybe they'll go away.*

Luckily, no other vehicles passed on either side, as the driver pulled away from Eli, weaving in and out of both lanes. *They must be drunk or high on something.*

When the vehicle slowed up and moved closer to him again, one of the teens leaned out the window and knocked Eli's straw hat off his head. Eli wouldn't give them the satisfaction of watching him peddle away without his hat. He stopped and went back to retrieve it. Eli hoped the boys would drive onward, but to his disappointment, the car stopped. The young driver got out and, like a menacing cat on the prowl, meandered slowly toward him, while the other guys, arms folded, stood by the car and watched.

Eli held his arms stiffly at his sides. *Keep calm. Don't do anything foolish that could rile them further.*

"Hey man, ya know what? You smell like a skunk." Pointing a bony finger at Eli, the lanky adolescent plugged his nose.

Eli's brain told him to stand his ground—*Be polite, don't cause a scene.* But his body tensed, hands drawing into fists. Giving this boy a piece of his mind would bring much satisfaction. The words formed in his head, but Eli kept quiet. Though it would get him nowhere, a good tongue-lashing would have made him feel better.

The snickering kid came almost face-to-face with Eli. He stood several seconds then, eyes growing wide, whirled around and rushed back to the car. Eli raised his arms to shield his face when stones kicked up from the spinning wheels. He coughed as the dust settled down and the car's motor grew fainter, until it was out of sight.

"You okay?" Lester Hendricks, one of the patrol officers in the county, pulled up alongside Eli.

"Yeah, I'm fine." Eli dusted off his hat. "Just a bunch of kids having fun, I guess. They sure took off when you came along."

"I saw the Mustang and know the teen driving it." Lester frowned. "I've had a little trouble with him before—nothing big that would put him behind bars, but several warnings. If you want to file a report, I wouldn't blame ya."

"Naw, I wanna forget it. Kids will be kids. I'm glad the incident's over."

"Okay, but if you experience any more trouble with that bunch, you'd better contact the sheriff's office."

"Will do." Eli nodded and got back on his bike. "Thanks for stopping."

When Heidi opened the front door, she was taken aback, seeing a young boy and girl standing beside Loretta.

"My babysitter canceled at the last minute, and I didn't want to miss the class, so I brought Abby and Conner along." Loretta glanced down at the children. "I hope you don't mind."

Heidi shook her head, holding the door open for them. "It's fine. I'll find something to occupy them with while we're having our class." She showed Abby and Conner a basket of toys. "I keep these on hand to entertain my nieces and nephews." Heidi turned to Loretta. "The children can either play in the living room or come to the kitchen with us and play on the floor while we cook the meal I have planned for today."

"If you don't think they'll get in the way, I'd feel better if they came with me so I can keep an eye on them," Loretta replied.

"Whatever you prefer is fine with me."

Loretta glanced around the room. "Isn't Eli coming today?"

"I believe so. When my husband checked for messages this morning there were none from Eli. I'm sure he would have called if he couldn't make it."

"Here, let me carry that to the kitchen." Ron took the toy basket from Heidi.

After the adults were seated around the table and the children got settled on the throw rug in front of the basket, Heidi went to the refrigerator and took out the ingredients they would need.

"Today we're making German pizza," Heidi explained to Loretta. "Instead of a regular crust, baked in an oven, we'll use shredded potatoes for the base and cook the meal in a skillet on top of the stove." She handed everyone a three-by-five card with the recipe printed out. The verse she'd included on the back this time was Psalm 71:1. "In thee, O LORD, do I put my trust: let me never be put to confusion." Heidi hoped this scripture would be helpful to one or more of her students during the next few weeks.

"It certainly seems different than a regular pizza." Loretta stared at her recipe card.

"It is, but I hope you'll enjoy it." Heidi gestured to the ingredients after placing them on the table. She also gave everyone a small skillet. "The first thing you will do is brown the ground beef with chopped onion, diced green pepper, salt, and pepper. We'll do this two at a time, since it'll be easier to double up at the stove. Charlene and Kendra, after you get your onion and pepper chopped then you can go first."

While everyone got busy, Heidi watched Loretta's children at play. Abby seemed fully engrossed in a book as she sat cross-legged on the braided throw rug, thumbing through the pages. Conner found a wooden horse and buggy belonging to Lyle when he was a child. A smile formed on Heidi's face as she watched the young boy push the horse along, making *clip-clop* noises with his tongue. He was obviously familiar with the sound.

Loretta has children but no husband. A knot formed in Heidi's stomach. *I have a husband but no kinner. Since I haven't suffered the loss of my mate, I should feel thankful. Poor Loretta's heart must be broken, becoming a widow at such a young age. She needs her husband, and these precious children need their father. It's hard to understand why certain things happen. At times, life can be so unfair.*

Hearing a knock on the back door, Heidi jumped. Before she could get to the door, it opened and Eli let himself in. "Sorry I'm late. Ran into a little problem at home this morning, and also on the way here."

"Are you all right?" Loretta's fingers touched her parted lips.

"Yeah, I'm fine. Hope I didn't make you all wait too long." Eli slipped his straw hat over a wall peg near the door.

"It's okay, we've barely gotten started." Heidi pointed to an empty chair at the table. "You can begin by chopping the onion and green pepper set out for you."

As Eli walked past Heidi, her nose twitched. *Is that a skunky odor?*

When Eli took a seat at the table, Ron's nose wrinkled, sliding his chair to the left, which put more distance between the men. When it appeared Ron might say something more, Conner hopped up and darted over to his mother. "What's that yucky smell?" He closed his eyes and plugged his nose.

Loretta put a finger to her lips. "Shh. Conner, don't be impolite."

Then Abby walked over to Eli and sniffed. "Phew! You stink, mister."

"Abby Donnelly!" Loretta shook her finger. "Apologize to Mr. Miller this instant."

Kendra and Charlene sucked in their breath, while Ron sneered at the child. Heidi's sympathy went to Abby when her little chin quivered.

"There's no need to apologize, little lady." Eli's face flamed. "I'm afraid the yucky smell is me. Got my arm sprayed by a skunk hiding in my woodpile this morning."

"What did the skunk do after he sprayed you?" Abby took a step back before asking her question. Conner walked over and stood next to his sister.

Eli rubbed his beard. "Well, the last I saw of Mr. Skunk, he was making a run for it toward the field behind my place."

Abby giggled. "You're funny. You called him 'Mr. Skunk.'"

"Do you think he'll come back?" Conner tilted his head.

"I hope not." Eli lifted his arm. "Skunks are kinda cute, but they don't smell good when they lift their tail and let loose with a spray."

"Did you use anything to get the smell out?" If he hadn't, there were a few things Heidi could suggest.

"I rubbed half a tomato on my skin, plus lots of soap and water." Eli's mouth stretched downward. "Figured the smell was gone."

"Hardly." Ron rolled his eyes. "It's far from gone, Eli. Can't ya smell it?"

"Not really. But then, I've been havin' a little trouble with my allergies lately, so my sniffer isn't working as well as it should." Eli pushed back his chair. "I'd better head back home so I don't ruin your cooking class. Don't want your house to get all skunked up."

Heidi shook her head. "Nonsense. I want you to stay. The odor isn't so bad, and if I open the kitchen window it'll ventilate the room. After we're finished with our German pizzas we'll take them outside and eat our meal at the picnic table. How's that sound?"

"Oh, boy. A picnic!" Abby jumped up and down. Conner joined in.

"Settle down now, you two," Loretta scolded.

Still a bit red in the face, Eli returned to his seat. Heidi hoped no one else would comment about the aroma of skunk. *Eli has been embarrassed enough.*

Chapter 22

While Loretta shredded potatoes, she glanced at Eli. Perspiration covered the poor man's forehead, and he sat as far away from the others as possible. The smell wasn't so horrible—at least from where she sat. Her eyes watered, but the odor from the onions she'd cut up could be the reason.

Since Eli had been the last to arrive, Loretta wanted to be polite and introduce her children to him. She could have made introductions sooner, when the kids made comments about the skunky odor, but it didn't feel appropriate right then. Besides, Loretta had been so embarrassed by what they'd said, she wasn't thinking clearly. Now Abby and Conner were happily playing again, and Eli left the table to brown his ground beef. It might be best to wait until they'd finished making the pizza and were relaxing at the picnic table outdoors to make formal introductions.

⸻

Between the pungent odor of ground beef cooking and the telltale stench of skunk coming from Eli, Kendra struggled with nausea. She tried chewing gum and some peppermint candy, but neither helped much. She had forgotten to bring mint tea and saltine crackers again and would be glad when they finished making their pizzas and could go outside to eat it. At least the air would be fresher out there. She even thought of asking Heidi if she had any menthol rub. Smearing the ointment on the end of her nose would surely mask the odors making her stomach queasy. Eli seemed like a nice person, so Kendra wouldn't embarrass him further by asking

Heidi for menthol rub. Aside from Heidi's husband, Lyle, Eli was probably one of the nicest men she'd met. Certainly more polite and respectful than Ron.

Kendra glanced at Loretta's children and noticed Heidi staring at them. In fact, she seemed more interested in the kids than teaching her class this morning. Kendra almost pitied their teacher, with that faraway look in her eyes. Even her smile appeared forlorn.

Too bad Heidi doesn't have children of her own. I'll bet she'd make a good mother. Kendra tapped her chin. *I wonder if she and Lyle have considered adoption.*

"Here are some cut-up veggie sticks to go with your pizza." Heidi placed the platter on the picnic table and took a seat on the bench where Loretta sat with her children. She'd already given Conner and Abby cheese sandwiches and potato chips. Lyle joined them for lunch and suggested they all bow their heads for silent prayer. When the prayer ended, everyone began to eat.

"This is yummy," Charlene spoke up. "I never imagined pizza could taste so good without a crust."

"The shredded *grummbier* makes up the crust," Eli interjected.

Abby nudged her mother's arm. "Mommy, what'd that man say? He said a strange word."

"I'm not sure, but first things first. Let's get proper introductions made." Loretta gestured to Eli. "This is the nice man who gave us the whoopie pie cookies the other day. His name is Eli Miller." Loretta placed her hands atop her children's heads. "Eli, I'd like you to meet my daughter, Abby, and my son, Conner."

"Nice to meet you both." Eli shook their hands. "Oh, and the word I said—*grummbier*—is the Pennsylvania Dutch word for potatoes."

"Grummbier," Abby repeated. Then Conner said it, too.

"Thank you for the cookies." Abby grinned while rubbing her

stomach. "They were yummy."

"I agree with you." Eli bobbed his head. "Would ya like to learn the Pennsylvania Dutch name for cookies?"

Both children, as well as Heidi's other students, nodded.

"The word for cookies is *kichlin*."

"Kichlin." Abby giggled. "That's a funny word."

Loretta tapped her daughter's shoulder. "Now, don't be impolite."

"Sorry." The little girl lowered her head.

"It's okay." Eli's brows jiggled up and down playfully. "To most English people, many of our Amish words sound funny."

Lyle chuckled. "I remember once, as a young lad, our English neighbor girl, Yvonne, told us everything my brother and I said in our native language sounded funny to her. She used to laugh and try to figure out what the words meant. Sometimes we'd tell her, and sometimes we didn't. Whenever she was with us, we had fun speaking words only the two of us understood."

"Is anyone hungry for dessert?" Heidi asked. "I made a peach cobbler last night."

"Sounds good to me." Ron thumped his stomach. "I'm always in the mood for dessert."

"Me, too," Charlene added.

Everyone else agreed.

Heidi got up. "I'll clear some of these dishes and get the cobbler when I'm inside."

"Let me help." Kendra grabbed the plates and silverware, piling them on the serving tray.

"I'd be glad to help, too," Charlene offered.

"Same here." Loretta rose from the bench.

"No, that's okay." Kendra motioned for them to stay put. "I used to work part-time as a waitress when I was taking some college classes, so I'm pretty good at managing dishes by myself."

After Heidi and Kendra entered the kitchen, Kendra placed

everything in the sink then turned to face Heidi. "Mind if I ask you a personal question?"

"Not at all. What would you like to know?"

"I watched how you interacted with Loretta's kids earlier. Made me wonder why you don't have any children of your own."

"Oh, that's right. You were in the bathroom during our first cooking class, when I told the others about my situation." Heidi released a lingering sigh. "My husband and I would like to be parents, but in the eight years we've been married, I've not been able to get pregnant."

"That's too bad. Have you considered adoption?"

"I'd love to adopt, but Lyle..." Heidi stopped talking. Why discuss this with Kendra? She probably wouldn't understand Lyle's refusal to adopt. Heidi didn't understand it, either.

"If you'd like to take small plates from the cupboard, as well as enough forks for everyone, I'll get the peach cobbler." Heidi moved across the room to the refrigerator.

"One more question." Kendra set the dishes and silverware on a tray.

Heidi placed the cobbler on another tray. "What is it?"

"Would it be all right if I come by here sometime between our classes, to visit and get to know you better? My dishwashing job isn't full-time, and I have Saturdays off."

Kendra's question surprised Heidi, but it pleased her, too. She was almost certain Kendra needed someone to talk to. Maybe she would open up and share her struggles.

Heidi gave Kendra's arm a gentle pat. "Feel free to drop by anytime. I'd enjoy getting better acquainted." She picked up the tray and followed Kendra outside.

"Eli, I noticed you rode your bicycle today." Heidi pointed to the tree it leaned against.

He nodded. "I wanted to walk, but since I was running late, I chose the bike instead." It still bothered Eli to ride a bike because it stirred emotional feelings concerning Mavis's accident. He had to admit, in light of what happened on the way here with those teens, walking wouldn't have been much better. In hindsight, Eli wished he'd brought the horse and buggy.

"This peach cobbler is excellent," Charlene commented as everyone ate the dessert.

"Yes indeed. . . My wife can cobble with the best of them." Lyle's eyes twinkled as he winked at Heidi.

Eli's shoulders hunched, unable to deal with his envy. His wife used to make good cobblers, too. But the dessert wasn't the cause of his jealousy. Lyle's look of adoration, and the sweet smile Heidi gave him in return, tugged at Eli's gut. He longed for such a relationship and continued to miss the special moments he and Mavis had shared. *Well, I can't bring her back, so I need to quit feeling sorry for myself and get on with life.* How many times had he given himself this lecture? How often had he fallen prey to self-pity and longing for something he couldn't have?

"The others are right," Eli told Heidi after taking a bite. "It is good cobbler." Then looking at Lyle, he added, "I'm surprised you're not auctioneering someplace today."

Lyle swatted a bug when it landed on the picnic table. "This is the first Saturday in a long while I haven't been called to an auction."

"I've always been fascinated with auctioneers and their ability to speak so fast." Loretta wiped her fingers on the napkin beside her plate. "How did you get into that line of business, Lyle?"

"I've been wonderin' about that, too," Ron put in. "Just kept forgetting to ask."

"Well,"— Lyle scratched behind his left ear—"in my teenage years I became fascinated with auctions and the fast-talking people who conducted the events." He paused and drank some water. "Had to be at least eighteen in order to learn the trade, though. So when I was old enough I took classes to learn how to legally run an auction."

Kendra leaned her elbows on the table. "I thought the Amish didn't go to school past the eighth grade."

"It wasn't like high school or college," Lyle explained. "Following the classes, I had to take a test. Afterward, I served a yearlong apprenticeship and then took another test. Once I passed, I got my auctioneer's license."

"Don't it make you nervous to stand in front of a bunch of people and talk so fast?" Ron questioned.

Lyle shook his head. "At first it did, but not anymore."

"I can talk to my kindergarten students easily, but if I was faced with what you do, I'd be a nervous wreck." Charlene gave her ponytail a tug.

"I like my job. Standing in front of a large crowd gives me a rush of adrenaline."

"Hey look! There's a big balloon in the sky."

Eli looked where Abby pointed. Everyone else did the same.

"See how colorful it is." Charlene's eyes widened as she continued to watch the enormous balloon.

"I'd love to be up there right now," Kendra said wistfully.

"Same here." Even Ron seemed intrigued by the colorful sight.

"Could be one of the balloons coming from Charm, or it might be one from Millersburg." Lyle tipped his head back, holding one hand above his brows. "Every now and then we see 'em drifting over our farm."

"From what I've heard, they have several locations around Ohio where you can take a balloon ride," Eli stated.

The children ran farther into the yard, while the rest of them stood and watched the brilliant balloon against the deep blue sky.

Eli chuckled when the kids waved at the people in the balloon. It was almost overhead now, and low enough that he could make out a few people in the basket suspended underneath the giant orb. The children squealed with delight when the riders responded by waving back.

"They're waving at us!" Abby shouted, while Conner jumped up and down.

Everyone watched as the balloon drifted onward, until it could barely be seen.

"Now that was an unexpected surprise," Heidi said when everyone returned to the picnic table to finish eating their cobbler.

Eli couldn't quit watching the children as they giggled and chattered to each other. Obviously seeing the balloon was a magical moment for them, and to be honest, it seemed to put the others into a friendlier, more relaxed state of mind. He grinned as Loretta tried to calm her children when they asked to go for a ride in a balloon.

"Maybe someday, when you're older, we'll see about taking a ride, but for now, I don't believe you'd be tall enough to see over the basket you'd be standing in." Loretta looked at Eli and smiled.

Seconds later, Abby changed the subject. "We have a salamander in our garden."

"His name is Oscar." Wide-eyed, Conner clapped his hands. "He lives under a rock."

While Charlene and Kendra questioned the children about Oscar, Eli glanced at Heidi, gazing at the children with what could only be considered adoration. He could almost read her mind and felt the same sadness he saw in her eyes. Loretta was fortunate to have two great kids. The joy on their faces as they explained about the salamander and their excitement when the balloon floated over were priceless. Ron even commented on the children's pet salamander. *I wonder if he has any children?*

Arf! Arf! The Troyers' Brittany spaniel bounded up to the picnic table, wagging his tail.

Eagerly, Abby and Conner left their seats and began petting the dog. "Can we get a doggy like this?" Abby looked up at her mother.

"Not right now." Loretta tapped her daughter's arm. "Maybe after you and your brother are a little older and can take care of a pet."

Conner's lower lip protruded. "I'm a big boy, Mommy. I wanna dog."

She squatted beside them and stroked Rusty's silky hair. "I know, son, but it will have to wait until I get a job. Feeding a dog and taking care of its needs is an added expense we don't need right now."

Eli imagined how difficult it must be to turn down a request as innocent as Conner's. He finished his cobbler and set his fork down. *It may not be as long as you think, Loretta.*

Chapter 23

The following Saturday, Eli hitched his horse to the closed-in buggy. His first stop would be his folks' place, and then on to Loretta's.

He climbed into the buggy and took up the reins. *Sure hope she's home today. I'm eager to see her children's faces when they find out what I brought 'em.*

Heading out onto the road, Eli whistled his favorite tune. Since Mavis's death, mornings were usually the worst for him. Grasping for something to look forward to each day, he felt thankful for a job that kept him busy. Even so, making coffins was work, not fun. But he was good at his craft, and the money Eli earned paid his bills.

Since beginning to take Heidi's cooking classes, Eli's spirits had lifted some, and he no longer dreaded getting out of bed on those days. Of course, it might have more to do with meeting Loretta and her kinner than learning how to cook. Since the time he'd become a widower, Eli hadn't felt as comfortable with any woman until now. It made no sense. Loretta wasn't Amish, and he'd only met her a little over a month ago. He shouldn't even be thinking about her.

"Maybe I'm desperate for female companionship."

Eli's horse twitched its ears.

"Just keep movin' girl; I wasn't talkin' to you." He leaned back in his seat, enjoying the ride. In his book, traveling by horse and buggy beat any other mode of transportation. Walking was fine if the destination was close. Riding a bike was okay, too, and provided a good workout. But because Mavis had died while riding her bike, every time Eli got on one, he felt apprehensive. He'd felt even more hesitant to ride his bicycle after last week when he'd been taunted by those teenage boys. Thanks to the deputy showing up, they'd moved on. Hopefully, Eli had seen the last of them.

———⟶❧⟵———

"Just look at how quickly these weeds have grown." Heidi knelt on a foam pad next to her vegetable garden.

"You talkin' to me?"

Heidi jerked her head, surprised to see Ron standing a few feet from her. "Uh, no. I didn't see you there. I talk to myself now and then."

He chuckled. "I do it sometimes, too. I'll only become worried when I start answering my own questions."

Heidi smiled. *So Ron does have a humorous side.* He often seemed so serious and sometimes a bit grumpy. Of course, living all alone, with no home of his own, would be quite depressing.

"Need help pullin' weeds?" he asked.

"No, thanks. Since there's only a few, I can manage. Besides, shouldn't you be working on your RV now that you have the part you need?"

He tugged on his ear. "You're right, I need to get started with it, but I can't seem to get in the mood." He pointed to the blue sky above. "It's nice out today, and I feel like takin' a walk."

"Maybe you should. Fresh air and exercise is always a good thing."

"Yeah." Ron hesitated, as if he might want to say more, but then he mumbled, "See you later, Heidi," and sauntered off.

She watched as he headed down the driveway and out toward the road. Heidi still felt a bit uneasy around Ron, but the longer he stayed here, the more compassion she felt for him.

As Heidi returned to weeding, her thoughts went in another direction. She reflected on her brief conversation with Kendra during last week's cooking class. She'd been surprised when Kendra had asked about coming by sometime to visit and get better acquainted. The poor girl obviously needed a friend. Heidi hoped if Kendra did drop by, she would have an opportunity to talk with her about the best friend anyone could have—Jesus Christ.

Concentrating on the job at hand, Heidi plunged her trowel into the ground to attack a few more weeds. The sun beating down on her scarf-covered head made it feel like summer instead of spring. "Even my dress is sticking to me." She pulled the material away from her skin. The garden gloves she wore felt confining as well, but she'd put up with them until she finished weeding. The warm weather persisted today, as it had all week. *If summer is going to be like this, our grill will get a real workout, because it'll be too hot to heat up the kitchen by using the stove.*

Heidi's hand went to her growling stomach. It was way past lunchtime. Setting her trowel aside, she rose to her feet and headed inside.

"Whew! That feels better." Heidi peeled off her garden gloves, turned on the cold water, and lathered soap over her sweaty hands. Grabbing a towel, she glanced out the kitchen window just as a car pulled into the yard. "Oh, good, Kendra did come for a visit." Heidi dried her hands and opened the door to let her young student in.

"I hope you don't mind me dropping by unannounced." Kendra offered Heidi a sheepish-looking grin. "I borrowed my friend's car today to run a few errands, so I decided to stop here on the way back to see if you were home and had time to talk."

"Certainly." Heidi led the way to the kitchen. "I was about to fix myself some lunch. If you haven't eaten, you're welcome to join me."

"I ate a late breakfast, but even so, I am a bit hungry." Kendra smiled. "If it's no trouble, I'd enjoy having lunch with you."

"No trouble at all." Heidi gestured to the table. "Take a seat and I'll fix us a sandwich. Is ham and cheese okay?"

"I love ham and cheese, but let me help you."

Heidi took out the loaf of bread she'd baked yesterday and asked Kendra to get the ham and cheese slices from the refrigerator. "There's a jar of mayonnaise in there, too, and also some lettuce."

"Do you have any dill pickles?" Kendra snickered. "For some reason I've been craving pickles lately. It's the weirdest thing. The other night when I couldn't sleep, I got up and raided my friend's refrigerator."

"I'm not speaking from experience, but from what other women tell me, craving certain foods is common during pregnancy."

"Yeah, I've heard the same thing."

Heidi cut their sandwiches in half and took out a pitcher of lemonade. "Here we go."

After they took seats at the table, it pleased Heidi to see Kendra bow her head.

Following their silent prayers, Heidi poured lemonade into their glasses. "How's your new job, Kendra?"

"It's okay, but I'm hoping it turns into full-time. I won't keep sponging off my friend forever." Kendra touched her stomach. "Then there's the expense of having a baby."

"Won't your parents help with the costs?"

Kendra's eyes narrowed as she shook her head. "Since my folks tossed me out when they found out about the pregnancy, I don't expect any help from them at all." Her forehead creased. "My dad paid me a visit the day I got my new job."

"How did it go?"

"Horrible. He chewed me out for talking to my sister, Shelly. Worse than that, he warned me not to make any contact with her or my other sister, Chris. Said if I did, he'd show them the door."

Heidi's brows furrowed. "You mean he'd make your sisters move out?"

"You got it." Kendra bit into her sandwich. "He's a mean man, and I hate him. He's not my dad anymore; he's my enemy now."

"Hate's a pretty strong word." Heidi placed her hand on Kendra's shoulder. "The Bible tells us in Luke 6:27 and 28: 'Love your enemies, do good to them which hate you, bless them that curse you, and pray for them which despitefully use you.'"

Kendra's lips curled. "I'm all too familiar with Bible verses and prayer. Grew up attending church with my family. But as far as I can tell, the church is full of hypocrites—the biggest one being my dad."

"If you pray for him, perhaps in time he'll come around."

Kendra picked up her glass and took a drink. "Can we please change the subject? I don't want to talk about Dad anymore."

Heidi said nothing more on the topic. She would remember, however, to pray for Kendra, as well as for her father, asking God to remove the anger and bitterness from both of their hearts.

Sugarcreek

Taking a whiff of the air-freshened towels while putting them in the basket, Loretta heard the whinny of a horse. When the buggy pulled closer, she recognized the driver even before he got out. *Eli. I wonder if he came for a visit, or perhaps he brought us more cookies.*

After securing the horse, Eli walked toward her and tipped his hat. "Wasn't sure if I'd find you at home, but I'm glad you're here 'cause I brought your kids a special gift." Looking directly at her, he quickly added, "I hope you'll let 'em keep it. It's in my buggy if you wanna take a look."

Loretta's eyebrows rose, but she followed him to the buggy. When he reached inside and lifted out a small brown-and-white puppy, she gasped. "Oh, Eli, I don't think—"

"Please don't say no. I saw the way Conner and Abby loved on Heidi's dog last week. I bet they'd enjoy having a puppy of their own."

"You're right, but puppies are a lot of work, not to mention an additional expense I don't need right now."

"Since I don't live close by, I can't do much to help ya take care of the pup, but I'd be happy to help with the expense."

She shook her head. "Oh, no, I couldn't ask you to do that."

"You don't have to ask; I'm volunteering. In fact, I brought a bag of dog food along so you won't have to worry about feeding the puppy for a while." Eli scratched the pup behind its ears. "When the food runs low, let me know, and I'll buy some more."

"You're a nice man, Eli."

His face colored, and he lowered his head. "Tryin' to help out a friend, is all."

Loretta smiled. She'd begun to think of Eli as her friend, too.

Walnut Creek

When Kendra left the Troyers' house that afternoon, she reflected on the things she and Heidi had discussed. *She doesn't understand my situation. Heidi's never been in a predicament like mine.*

Country scenery went practically unnoticed as Kendra headed back to Mt. Hope. She hit the switch to put the window down farther and rested her elbow there. Even with the warm breezes blowing through her hair, Kendra's thoughts would not elude her. *What did I do to deserve all this? How can some be so lucky in life, and others, like me, seem to attract trouble?*

Kendra noticed something brown by the high weeds along the side of the road. Glancing in the rearview mirror to be sure no vehicles were close behind, she slammed on the brakes. Kendra raised her eyebrows when she noticed a lone female duck standing like a statue, as if waiting for something. Then, one by one, ten little ducklings surrounded their mama.

Hesitating on her next move, the female quacked and looked in Kendra's direction. Water glistened in the sunlight as Kendra caught a glimpse of a pond on the other side of the road. Watching in the mirror, she gripped the gearshift and put it in REVERSE and then PARK.

After getting out of her car, Kendra slowly approached the mother duck. "Okay girl, it's safe to cross." She bent low, making a shooing motion with her hands. "But then you probably already knew that, didn't you?" She continued to guide them until the mother and babies waddled safely across and under a fence. Kendra giggled as the tiny ducklings followed like soldiers trailing a drillmaster during boot camp.

Getting back into the car and buckling her seat belt, Kendra gripped the steering wheel with such force her knuckles turned white. "To think what could have happened if I hadn't stopped in time." She put her hand protectively over her stomach. *I have a little one to protect as well.*

Kendra watched the ducks enter the water. At least now they were in a safe place. *If only my parents had half the concern toward me as that duck has for her babies.*

While her father hadn't done anything to despitefully use her, like the verse of scripture Heidi had mentioned, he'd despitefully kicked her out of his house and, worse, now threatened her sisters with the same punishment. *He's not deserving of my prayers. It would serve him right if the church found out about my pregnancy and kicked him off the board. I oughta let someone there know.*

Chapter 24

Sugarcreek

"Come see what Mr. Miller brought," Loretta called through the screen door.

When Loretta glanced back and smiled at him, Eli stood taller. The puppy squirmed and wiggled and licked his nose, as if it knew this was going to be home. The dog was so cute it almost made him regret not keeping one of the litter. If not for Lady, the decision would have been easy. As the pup grew languid and nestled comfortably in his arms, its milky breath reached Eli's nostrils.

A few seconds later, Loretta's children came out. Abby's eyes lit up when she saw the dog. "It's so cute! Whose puppy is it?"

"It's yours and Conner's, if you want it." Eli set the pup on the porch. Instinctively, it went to the children and let out a *yip* while wagging its tail. It ran in circles around them, and woofed several raspy barks, as if it was learning to talk. The puppy seemed to enjoy being the center of attention.

"Yippee! Yippee!" Conner jumped and down, while Abby's eyes seemed to grow larger by the minute.

Abby knelt beside the dog and stroked its head. "Can we keep it?" She looked up at her mother with pleading eyes.

Loretta nodded. "The question is, what shall we name the little guy?"

Conner, sitting cross-legged on the other side of the dog, shouted, "Donnelly! Cause he belongs to us." The puppy seemed happy getting so much attention from two excited children. It went from Conner to Abby, and back to Conner again, while the kids giggled and took turns petting the dog.

"Donnelly's a pretty big name for such a small dog, but if that's what you want, it sounds good to me." Eli grinned. The boy choosing his last name for the dog was kind of cute.

As if accepting the name, the pup crawled into Conner's lap and licked his chin with a slurpy tongue. Everyone laughed, Eli most of all. What a happy morning it turned out to be. Eli's heart seemed to beat faster to keep pace with all the joy pumping out of it.

"This pup is a Miniature American Shepherd, so he won't get too big. It's from a litter my mother's dog gave birth to eight weeks ago," Eli explained. "Homes were found for all the other puppies except this little fellow."

"We'll take good care of Donnelly, I promise." Enthusiasm shone in Abby's dark eyes.

Eli bent down and patted the top of her head. "I knew I could count on you and your *bruder*."

"What's a 'bruder'?" Abby tilted her head, looking up at him with the curiosity of a child.

"It means 'brother.'"

Abby snickered and pointed at Conner. "You're my little bruder."

"What do you both say to Mr. Miller for giving you such a nice gift?" Loretta prompted.

"Thank you," the children answered in unison.

Conner clambered to his feet and hugged Eli's leg. "I love our puppy."

"You're most welcome." Eli's throat clogged.

"Is that horse yours?" Conner pointed to the fence post where Blossom stood, swishing her tail.

"She certainly is. Her name is Blossom. She used to belong to my wife before she. . ." Eli's words trailed off.

"Can I pet her?"

"I have no problem with it, if your mother says it's okay." Eli looked at Loretta.

"As long as you're there with him, it's fine with me."

"Absolutely." Eli reached down and scooped the boy into his arms. His heart swelled with pleasure when Conner hugged him tight. *I'd give nearly anything to have a son like this boy.* He glanced at Abby. *A daughter would be nice, too.*

"Reach out your hand now and pet her gently," Eli instructed when he stood beside his horse.

The boy complied and laughed when Blossom let out a whinny. "I think she likes me." The horse nickered in response.

"I believe you're right." Eli ruffled Conner's hair. "Say, how'd you like to go for a ride in my buggy? Then you can see how well the horse pulls."

"If Mommy says it's okay."

"Of course. Maybe she and your sister would like to ride with us."

———————— ⟨∽∞∽⟩ ————————

Riding in the buggy brought back a time when Loretta was a little girl, visiting her grandparents. Oh, how she wished Grandma and Grandpa Zook were still alive. Memories of them were faint, and sitting beside Eli as the buggy jostled along felt like a new experience. She considered telling him about her heritage, but would he understand if he found out Loretta's parents never joined the Amish church and left their families soon after they were married? Loretta had always been hesitant to discuss it with anyone—especially when she didn't know the details herself. She'd always been curious about the reason her folks had chosen to be part of the English world rather than join the Amish church, but never asked. Loretta often wished her parents had joined the Amish church, because she'd be Amish now, too.

Pushing her musings aside, she glanced over her shoulder and smiled. Wearing huge grins, Conner and Abby sat in the seat behind them, with their hands on Donnelly's head. The pup closed his eyes and let out a whiny yawn.

"It seems they tuckered little Donnelly out." Loretta turned back around.

"Or maybe it's the other way around." Eli grinned. "Don't know who's more tired, the kids or the puppy."

"I see now my kids needed a dog." Loretta paused, briefly touching his arm. "Thank you, Eli, for your kindness."

His smile increased. "My pleasure."

As they rode around Sugarcreek, the kids chattered and giggled. Occasionally, their new puppy let out a small *woof*.

"Sounds like they're having a good time back there," Eli commented.

"They are, and so am I sitting up here. It's nice to ride at a much slower pace."

"Jah." Eli clucked to the horse then began to whistle.

Every muscle in Loretta's body seemed to relax. Was it the buggy ride or spending time with Eli? *Wish I felt this content all the time.*

Abby leaned forward and tapped Eli's shoulder. "Could ya teach me how to whistle, Mr. Eli?"

"I'd be happy to." He reached back and patted Abby's hand. "Next time I come to Sugarcreek, I'll stop by your house and give you a lesson. How's that sound, little lady?"

"Sounds good."

Yip! Yip! The puppy barked, wiggling around. Riding past a farm, Eli pulled on the reins so they could watch the activity going on by the edge of the field. Several children and a few adults held on to strings as their kites danced far overhead.

"Look there!" Conner pointed. "See the big smiley face?"

"Yes, and some kites have pretty colors, too," Loretta added.

"Remember, Mommy, how Daddy used to fly kites with me?" Abby spoke in a bubbly tone. "It was fun."

"I remember." Loretta had not heard Abby recount many memories about her father since his death. It was good to hear her talking about him now. Conner had only been two when Rick died.

No doubt, he remembered very little about his father. Loretta had shared things about Rick with the children and answered questions when they asked.

Eli flicked the reins, and they continued on down the road. "Let's go, Blossom. No reason to dally."

"Can we ride in your buggy again, Mr. Eli?" Abby tapped his shoulder again.

"Most definitely. Next time, I'll take you by to meet my folks."

"That would be nice," Loretta responded. "It'll give me a chance to thank your mother in person for the delicious banana whoopie pies."

"How about next Saturday when our cooking class is over?" Eli suggested. "I'll follow you back to your house after we're done, and we can pick up the children. It'll also give me a chance to see how Donnelly's doing."

"Can we bring our puppy along so he can see his mama?" Abby questioned.

"Great idea. Should've thought of it myself." Eli glanced at Loretta and smiled. "That's a smart daughter you have."

Walnut Creek

Ron watched out his side window as Lyle hitched his horse to the buggy and climbed in beside Heidi. They hadn't mentioned going anywhere, but this might be a good opportunity to sneak into their house again and take more money or some other item of value.

Ron waited until the buggy was out of sight then stepped out of his motor home and glanced around. The Troyers' dog lay sleeping in its pen. That was good. He wouldn't have to deal with the mutt barking or pestering him for a treat.

Tromping up the porch steps, Ron tried the front door but found it locked, like it had been the last time they'd gone away and he'd come in uninvited. He hurried around back and discovered that door was also locked.

Drat! Wonder if they discovered the missing money or the oil lamps I took. Do they suspect me? Is that why the doors are both locked?

Ron took a seat in one of the chairs on the porch, resting his chin in the palm of his hand. He couldn't help but notice the clean white wicker. Years ago, he and his wife purchased a wicker rocker for their front porch. It didn't take long for the dirt to show, despite countless cleanings. Eventually they'd gotten rid of the chair and replaced it with something easier to maintain. It was easy to see the Troyers took good care of all their belongings—something Ron didn't choose to do anymore. What was the point?

Ron rose from the chair. *Whelp, I can't sit here all day reminiscing. I need to check the windows and see if any of them are unlocked—or maybe the basement door.*

Since going through the basement to get into the house would be easier than squeezing through a window, he checked there first. Not only was the basement door unlocked, but it was partially open.

"A lot of good it does to lock the front and back door but leave the basement door open," he muttered, stepping into the dark room. "Guess the Troyers slipped up on that one, but it's to my advantage."

He took a few steps and bumped into something. "Should've brought a flashlight." He was about to give up when a thought popped into his head. *There might be something valuable down here. Think I'd better go back to my rig and get a light so I can scope out this basement before I head up to the main part of the house.*

Ron went out the door and was almost to his RV when a van pulled in. A few minutes later, an elderly Amish couple got out with two small suitcases.

"Who are you?" the woman asked, looking strangely at Ron.

"My name's Ron Hensley. And who might you folks be?"

"I'm Emma Miller, and this is my husband, Lamar. Heidi's my

niece. Is she at home?"

Ron shook his head. "Heidi and Lyle went somewhere."

"Oh, I see. Do you know when they'll be back?"

"Nope."

She looked at her husband then back at Ron. "I'm surprised they're not here. I wonder if they forgot we were coming."

Ron shrugged. "Beats me. Neither of 'em mentioned anything to me about expecting company."

"Are you a friend of theirs?" Lamar pulled his fingers through the ends of his long gray beard.

"Guess you could say that." Ron scrubbed a hand down the side of his face. "They let me park my rig here when it needed repairs. I'll be stayin' awhile since I'm taking Heidi's cooking classes."

Eyes widening, Emma's mouth formed an O.

"Don't look so surprised." Lamar elbowed her arm. "Think of all the men who've taken your quilting classes."

"True." She looked at their driver and gave him a wave. "We'll go on in the house and wait till Heidi and Lyle are home."

Ron was on the verge of telling them both doors were locked but changed his mind. They might wonder how he knew and become suspicious if he told them he'd already tried both doors.

"Nice meeting you folks," he mumbled before heading off to his motor home. It seemed odd that Heidi and Lyle would take off if they were expecting company—especially family members. *Oh well, it's none of my business. Just wish Heidi's aunt and uncle hadn't shown up when they did. Now I'll have to wait for a better time to check out the basement, not to mention gain entrance to the house. Just hope when there is a next time that at least one of the doors will be unlocked.*

Parting the curtain an inch, Ron watched the relatives try the front door. When they found it locked, they went to the back of the house. *If they're smart enough to try the basement door they'll be able to get in. If not, they'll just have to wait on the porch. Either way, it ain't my problem.*

Chapter 25

"The meal at Der Dutchman tasted good as always," Heidi commented as she and Lyle headed toward home Saturday evening. "I'd considered cutting into the banana loaf I made earlier today when we get home, but I ate so much, I don't believe I have enough room." Patting her stomach, she took a deep breath and sighed.

"I hear ya. I'm so full, I think I might pop." Lyle stuck his finger inside his mouth and made a popping noise. "Whenever we eat from their buffet, I take too much. Guess the ole saying holds true, because my eyes are certainly bigger than my stomach."

Heidi smiled. Lyle could sure poke fun at himself. It was one of the many traits she loved about him. "Now don't get me laughing, or I might end up with the hiccups."

"Laughter's good medicine. The Bible says so, right?"

"True, which is why I included that scripture on the back of one of the recipe cards I gave my students."

He reached across the seat and clasped her hand. "Good thinking."

"Oh, Lyle, before I forget. . . While you were at the auction today, Kendra stopped by for a visit." She squeezed her husband's fingers.

"Isn't she the young, auburn-haired woman who attends your cooking class?"

"Jah, and during our visit she opened up to me about a few things."

"Such as?"

"Kendra is bitter toward her father."

"How come?" Lyle let go of Heidi's hand and snapped the reins, signaling to the horse to pick up speed.

"After Kendra informed her parents she was expecting a baby, her dad told her to leave his house and have nothing to do with her sisters."

"I take it she's not married?"

"No, and the father of her child has moved on with his life and wants nothing to do with helping Kendra raise the child." Heidi had gotten this bit of information during her last visit with Kendra.

Lyle's brows furrowed. "Family is family, regardless of what she did. It's too bad her daed doesn't see it that way."

"Hoping to offer Kendra some support, I shared scripture with her."

"Did it help?"

"From what I could tell, she didn't want to hear it."

"If the Lord laid it on your heart to share a passage from the Bible, then you did the right thing."

"I hope so. I don't want Kendra to feel that I'm forcing my religious beliefs on her."

Lyle shook his head. "To my knowledge, you've never done that with anyone. But we do need to be in tune with the hurts of others. Sometimes the best way to help them is through God's Word."

"True." Heidi sighed. "I only wish I could do more to help her. From what I understand, Kendra's only real friend is the young woman she's staying with in Mt. Hope."

"Don't forget prayer. There's power in our prayers."

"Jah." Heidi felt thankful for her husband's wisdom and godly counsel. Another trait he was blessed to have. She appreciated being able to talk to him about Kendra.

As Lyle guided the horse and buggy into their yard, Heidi pointed out the front window. "Someone's sitting on our front porch, and it looks like. . ." She stifled a gasp. "For goodness' sake, it's Aunt Emma and her husband, Lamar."

Lyle's forehead wrinkled. "Did you know they were coming?"

She shook her head. "I had no idea whatsoever."

As soon as Lyle brought his horse to the rail, Heidi stepped down to secure the animal then hurried up to the house.

"Aunt Emma, what a surprise!"

"Surprise? Didn't you get my letter about us coming for a visit?" Aunt Emma rose from her chair and gave Heidi a hug. Lamar did the same.

Heidi's face radiated with heat as she shook her head in disbelief. "I haven't received any letters from you, at least not recently."

Peering at Heidi over the top of her metal-framed glasses, Aunt Emma tilted her head. "How strange. I wrote to tell you we'd be arriving today for a short visit before heading to Geauga County to see your folks."

Heidi's eyebrows squished together. "I bet your letter got lost in the mail. If I'd known you were coming, we would have stayed home this evening. Did you try to call?"

"I meant to yesterday, but things got busy and I plumb forgot." Aunt Emma thumped her forehead. "Must be old age setting in. Things come to mind—then they flit right out again."

"You don't have to be old for it to happen, either," Lamar interjected with a chuckle. "Just busy."

Heidi laughed. "I can certainly relate to that." She gestured to the porch chairs. "How long have you been sitting out here waiting for us?"

Lamar pulled out his pocket watch. "Oh, a couple of hours."

"I apologize. You should have gone in and made yourselves at home."

"We tried the front and back doors, but they were both locked." Aunt Emma yawned. "So we sat out here and took a little nap."

"Sometimes we leave the basement door unlocked."

"Guess we should have checked there, but it's okay." Lamar stretched his arms over his head. "It's such a warm evening, and it felt relaxing to sit on your porch, listening to the evening sounds. Guess that's the reason we snoozed a little."

"Ach, listen. Isn't that the sound of a whip-poor-will calling?" Aunt

Emma pointed to the closest maple tree.

"Jah, I believe so. They arrive every year about this time. Some nights they come in close and 'whip and will' for minutes on end. It almost sounds like those silly birds are singing their name." Heidi giggled. "One evening a whip-poor-will became so annoying Lyle threatened to open our bedroom window and throw his pillow at the winged creature. But I told him, 'You'll do no such thing. How many people get to hear a whip-poor-will serenading them by their window?'"

"So true," Aunt Emma and Lamar said in unison.

It amazed Heidi how alike these two were. Lamar was her aunt's second husband, and the two of them seemed to be soul mates. After Uncle Ivan passed away, Aunt Emma had been lonely. But then ever-cheerful Lamar came into her life and changed all that. It helped, too, that the couple had quilting in common. Lamar designed beautiful quilt patterns, and Aunt Emma made equally lovely quilts. They worked well together, and Lamar often helped teach his wife's quilting students.

"Well, enough talk about the birds." Heidi moved toward the front door. "I'll bet you two haven't had supper yet."

Heidi's aunt shook her head. "We thought you'd be here, and I figured on helping you make supper."

"I'm so sorry. Lyle and I ate supper at Der Dutchman, but there's leftover chicken from last night's meal in the refrigerator. I'll heat some up for you."

"Don't go to any trouble on our account." Aunt Emma gave a quick shake of her head. "A sandwich would suit us just fine."

"We'll see about that." Heidi clasped her aunt's hand. "How long can you stay?"

"Until tomorrow. We'll go to church with you in the morning, and then our driver will be back in the afternoon to take us up to your folks' place." A wide smile stretched across Aunt Emma's face. "It'll be good to see my sister again. It's been too long since our last visit."

After taking care of the horse and buggy, Lyle stepped onto the porch. "This is certainly a pleasant surprise." He shook Lamar's hand then gave Aunt Emma a hug. "We didn't realize you were coming."

"Aunt Emma sent me a letter, but it must have gotten lost in the mail." Heidi pointed to their suitcases. "We really ought to go inside. After I've fed these dear people some supper, we can spend the rest of the evening catching up with each other's lives."

"I'm anxious to hear about your cooking classes." Aunt Emma slipped her arm around Heidi's waist.

"And I'm eager to hear if you've taught any more quilting classes."

"Heidi, I heard the whip-poor-will when I came out of the barn. Sounded like it was back by the fields along the tree line somewhere," Lyle mentioned.

"We heard one, too, only it was out front in the maple tree." Heidi pointed.

"Guess they've returned for the spring and summer months—in time to entertain us in the wee hours of the night."

"Oh, Lyle, just admit it." Heidi poked his arm. "You enjoy hearing them as much as I do."

"You got me there." Lyle poked her back before winking at Aunt Emma.

The men picked up the luggage, Heidi linked arms with her aunt, and they all went into the house.

Mt. Hope

Kendra sat at Dorie's kitchen table, staring at the phone book. *Do I call Deacon Tom, and if so, what do I say? Should I blurt out the truth about my pregnancy and then tell him Dad kicked me out? Or would it be better if I make small talk first and lead slowly into the reason I called? Ha! Dad would probably get kicked off the board if this news got out. Well, he deserves whatever's coming to him.*

Kendra reached for her cell phone but hesitated. *If I tell Deacon Tom, he's bound to confront Dad, and then it could explode in my face. Dad might be so mad he'd kick Shelly and Chris out of the house to get even with me.*

Overwhelming anger had gripped Kendra's senses when she'd left Heidi's house this afternoon. Talking about her situation hadn't helped at all. Kendra's heart fluttered and her ears rang just thinking about everything. Maybe it would be best not to contact anyone from church about this mess and wait to see how it all played out. One thing for certain: she would not pray about her situation, like Heidi had suggested. Nope. She'd done enough praying in the past, and where had it gotten her?

Kendra thought about the verse on the back of the recipe card for German pizza. *"In thee, O Lord, do I put my trust: let me never be put to confusion."* She frowned. *The only person I'm trusting is myself.*

"I may as well face it," Kendra muttered. "I've lost my family, and if I decide to give up my baby, I'll lose him or her, too." Truthfully, Kendra saw no hope for her future. Even if she got hired full-time at the restaurant, she wouldn't make enough money to rent her own place and also provide for a child. The only sensible thing to do was relinquish her rights as the baby's mother and put him or her up for adoption.

Kendra wrapped her arms tightly around her middle. *Now I know how that mama duck must have felt, wanting to protect her little ones.* No matter how Kendra looked at it, whatever she chose to do would be difficult. If adoption was the best answer, should her baby go to strangers or someone she knew?

Dover

"Stop fidgeting and try not to appear so nervous." Len rubbed Charlene's back as they stepped onto his parents' porch. "Be nice to my mom, and she'll be nice to you." He lowered his arm and slipped it around Charlene's waist then leaned over and kissed her cheek. "Remember, sweetie, I love you."

"I love you, too." She drew in a few deep breaths. *Let's get this over with.*

Without knocking, Len opened the door and entered the house. "Mom! Dad! We're here."

Len's mother, Annette, stepped out of the kitchen, wearing a white apron of all things. If Charlene wore a white apron, it'd be dirty within minutes of putting it on.

"You're early. Supper's not quite ready." Annette's pale blue eyes held no sparkle. Not even a hint of a smile on her face, either.

"It's okay, Mom." Len gave her a peck on the cheek. "I'd rather we be early than late."

In order to break the ice, Charlene thought to offer Len's mother a friendly hug, but with Annette's cold reception, she changed her mind. Squaring her shoulders and putting on her best smile, she tried something else. "Is there anything you'd like me to help you with?"

"I suppose you could cut more vegetables to put in the tossed salad. I'm not done making it yet."

"I'd be happy to finish the salad." After learning to make Amish haystack, with so many ingredients, Charlene felt sure she could manage a simple tossed salad.

"I'll visit with Dad while you ladies get supper on. Is he in the living room?" Len asked.

"Your father probably didn't hear you arrive." Nodding toward the other room, his mother frowned. "He's watching some documentary on birds of prey, and he'd better turn off the TV and come to the table when I announce supper's ready." She turned and tromped off to the kitchen.

Charlene cringed. Obviously Len's mother wasn't in a good mood this evening. *Sure hope I don't make things worse.*

Chapter 26

P leased she had done well finishing the tossed salad, Charlene asked Len's mother if she needed help with anything else.

Annette brought a kettle over to the counter and placed it on a pot holder. "You can mash the potatoes while I make some gravy."

"Okay. Do you use a potato masher or portable mixer?"

Annette blinked rapidly, neck bending forward. "A mixer, of course. No one uses a potato masher anymore. It went out with the Dark Ages." She opened a drawer and handed Charlene an electric hand mixer.

"The Amish don't use electric mixers," Charlene commented.

Annette quirked an eyebrow. "The Amish? What do you know about them?"

"Well, I . . ." Charlene caught herself in time. She'd been about to say she was taking cooking classes from an Amish woman. Since Charlene hadn't even told Len, she wasn't about to reveal it to his mother. "I've read some things about the Plain People. It's common knowledge they don't have electricity in their homes."

Annette lifted her shoulders and gave an undignified huff. "Sounds ludicrous to me. I can't imagine anyone living in our modern-day age and not making use of electricity." She placed a stick of butter and a carton of milk on the counter, along with salt and pepper. "Make sure the potatoes aren't lumpy. Oh, and Todd likes them nice and creamy, so you'll need to put in enough milk."

Charlene offered no response to Annette's comment about the Amish. She obviously thought they were old fashioned and perhaps even foolish. Charlene thought quite the opposite. Since meeting

Heidi and spending time in her home, she viewed the Amish people as hardworking, responsible, and caring. They were dedicated to living a simpler life, without all the fancy things so many English people thought they needed. Charlene felt the Amish people's desire to live life as their ancestors had done was no less than amazing, especially in this day and age. Their focus was on serving God and family, not worldly things.

"I'll do my best with the potatoes," she murmured, hoping they would meet with Annette and her husband's approval. The last thing she needed was to look bad in anyone's eyes tonight. When she and Len went out to dinner last night, they'd set a wedding date. Len planned to tell his folks the news this evening. Charlene hoped they'd be happy about it, but she wasn't holding her breath. She'd figured out almost from the beginning of her and Len's relationship that his mother wasn't fond of her. Perhaps with Len being an only child, Annette wouldn't be happy with any woman he chose. In order to make her marriage to Len peaceful around his family, Charlene would need to win his mother's approval. But how?

"Why are the potatoes so soupy tonight?" Todd's question was directed at Annette. "You ought to know by now the way I like them—creamy, with lots of butter." His nose wrinkled. "I don't enjoy spuds runny enough to eat with a spoon."

Charlene swallowed hard as she watched Len's father hold up his fork, while the potatoes poured through the tongs. "Sorry about that. I'm the one who whipped the potatoes. I may have added too much milk."

Annette's eyes narrowed when she took a small bite. "My husband's right; these potatoes are horrible."

"I didn't say they were horrible," Todd corrected. "They're just too runny, is all." Charlene glanced at Len, wondering if he might say something negative about the potatoes or, better yet, come to her defense. Instead he sat silently, eating his salad. *Guess the tossed salad passed the test, at least. So far, no one's complained about that.*

Charlene's thoughts were overridden when Len's mother poked her fork into the salad and pulled out a cucumber chunk. "My goodness, Charlene, didn't anyone ever teach you how to cut vegetables for a salad? They need to be finely cut. This cucumber is so large it won't even fit in my mouth."

Len picked up his knife and waved it in the air. "Come on, Mom, give it a rest. If the cucumber's too big, just cut it to the size you want. Charlene did the best she could."

"Thanks," Charlene murmured. She took pleasure in hearing Len finally stick up for her.

Annette glared at him, giving no response as she pushed the cucumber aside.

Charlene couldn't believe the woman's stubbornness. She behaved like a child. *Is this kind of behavior what I'll have to put up with every time I'm around her?*

Len cleared his throat, while tapping his water glass with a spoon. "Charlene and I have an announcement to make." He reached over and clasped her hand. "We're planning to get married the last Saturday of September."

"What?" Annette's mouth dropped open. "Why, that's not nearly enough time to prepare. It only gives us four months to plan things out for the wedding."

"I'll do most of the planning." On this matter Charlene would not relent. "In fact, I already have my wedding dress picked out."

"Well, haven't you been the busy bee? You know, there's a lot more to prepare for a big wedding than choosing a dress." Annette picked up her napkin and dabbed her lips daintily. "We need to make out a guest list, choose a caterer for the reception, and—"

Len held up his hand. "Whoa, Mom, you're getting carried away. Charlene and I will discuss all those things, and if we need your help, we'll ask."

Once again, Charlene felt pleased by her fiancé's response. Len stood his ground, not letting his mother take over the wedding. Besides, Charlene's parents needed to be included in their plans.

"We can talk about this later." Annette gestured to the platter of chicken. "We need to eat before our food gets cold."

After everyone finished their meal, Charlene got up to clear the table. On her way to the kitchen the silverware slipped off one of the plates she held and bounced on the floor. Wincing, she bent down, picked them up, and made a hasty exit, but not before overhearing Len's mother say, "Your girlfriend is not only a bad cook, but she's clumsy."

Hearing Annette's cutting remark, Charlene struggled with the desire to flee. *Wish I hadn't come here tonight. Seems I can't say or do anything right.* Curious to know if anything more would be said, she paused at the kitchen door and listened.

"Mother, that's enough. Charlene is my fiancée and your future daughter-in-law. Things are awkward enough and will only get worse if you can't find a way to get along with her."

Charlene felt a little better hearing Len speak on her behalf. But it did nothing to alleviate her concerns. What would her relationship with Annette be like once she and Len were married? Would he always take her side, or could there be times when Len stuck up for his mother?

———— ❧ ————

Walnut Creek

"Mind if I ask you a question?" Heidi moved closer to her aunt on the couch and clasped her hand. They'd been visiting since Aunt Emma and Lamar finished supper. The men were in the barn, feeding the horses, so it was nice to have some time alone with her aunt.

"Of course, dear. I'd be happy to answer any question. What would you like to know?"

"Do all the people who come to your house to learn how to quilt have some sort of problem they share with you?"

"Jah, quite often many of them do. Some have come with more serious issues, but many were minor." Aunt Emma held her hands together, as though praying. "With some people, I offered advice and often shared scripture, while others I simply prayed for."

"This is my first group of students, and I've already discovered most of them are facing some sort of problem." Heidi's lips parted slightly. "Some, like the young unwed woman who's expecting a baby, have sought my advice, while others, like Ron, only shared a bit with me and the class."

"Who is Ron?" Aunt Emma asked.

Heidi pointed to the living-room window. "He lives in the motor home parked in our yard."

"Oh, so he's the man we met when our driver dropped us off." Aunt Emma's forehead wrinkles deepened. "I asked if he was a friend of yours, and he said you'd allowed him to park his vehicle here. Is that true?"

"Yes. Until a little over a month ago, we'd never met Ron. He showed up one day, saying his motor home wasn't running right and asking if he could stay here a few days until he got it fixed. Then he ended up taking my cooking classes, so we agreed he could stay until the final class, near the end of June."

"It's kind of you to allow him to stay so long. Is he a pleasant person to be around?" Aunt Emma fluffed the throw pillow on the couch and positioned it behind her head.

"Truth is, Ron's hard to figure out. Sometimes he seems nice and polite. Other times, he says rude things and acts kind of jittery, especially around the others during our class." Heidi reached for her cup of tea and took a sip. "He hasn't told us much about his past, but I believe he's dealing with some serious issues."

"He needs prayer, then, and perhaps in time you'll have a chance to tell him about God's love."

"I hope so. Even more so, I hope he is willing to listen."

"A deer in the road—look out!" Sweat poured down Ron's face as he slammed on the brakes. He'd passed the place now, but in his side mirror, he could see the deer lying motionless by the side of the road. It was getting dark. Nobody cared about a deer. Ron drove onward. Maybe it wasn't a deer. It could have been a Vietnamese soldier.

Moaning, he rolled to the other side of his bunk as the scene changed in his head.

Machine-gun fire—grenades going off all around him. The swamp made sucking sounds as he lifted one boot, and then the other. The humidity was hard to bear. His clothes stuck to his skin. Off the bank, he saw an enemy soldier coming toward him with a bayonet. Ron hoisted his gun, as he'd been trained to do, and fired. The soldier collapsed in a heap, sinking slowly below the bog's surface. Ron cupped his mouth with his hand. He's dead. I'm a murderer. The poor fellow never stood a chance.

An owl hooted, and Ron's eyes snapped open. Drenched in sweat, he rose from his bed, relieved to see familiar surroundings. It had only been a dream—a reoccurring nightmare.

Shuffling to the kitchen area, Ron grabbed a glass to fill with water. In need of fresh air, he opened the side door and stepped out, taking a seat on the entrance step. Although well after midnight, the bright moon illuminated the Troyers' yard. Looking at their house, he saw that all was dark.

Ron shivered, running his hands over his arms as he sucked in a gulp of air, hoping to calm himself. *Why can't I get the war out of my head? Will the terrible nightmares ever cease?*

Ron's thoughts turned to his only brother. *Oh, Mike, I miss you so much. If not for the war, you'd still be alive, and I never would have enlisted.*

Ron's chin quivered as he held his churning stomach. *It should have been me who died, not you.*

Chapter 27

Sugarcreek

The next Wednesday, Charlene met her friend Kathy for dinner at a restaurant in Sugarcreek. A few minutes after the hostess seated them, a waitress came to take their orders. Kathy ordered fried chicken and mashed potatoes, with a side order of corn. Charlene asked for spaghetti and meatballs, accompanied by a small dinner salad.

"How'd your school week go?" Kathy leaned her elbows on the table.

Charlene shrugged. "Okay, but I dread Friday, since it's the last day of school until fall."

"Aren't you glad to have the summer off? I certainly am."

"The first few weeks are nice, but I soon become bored. Besides, I always miss my students."

"Guess you would." Kathy drank some water. "Try teaching fifth graders, and then see how grateful you are to have the summer off. As much as I enjoy teaching, the kids in my class can sure try my patience sometimes."

"Have you considered teaching a lower grade?"

"Yeah, but with the younger ones comes another set of problems. I'll probably stick with the grade I teach. That way, I'll always have something to complain about." Kathy snickered, tucking her shoulder-length blond hair behind her ears. "So how'd your dinner at Len's parents' go on Saturday?"

Moaning, Charlene slumped in her chair. "What a fiasco it turned out to be."

"Oh no. What happened?" Kathy leaned forward, as though straining to hear above the voices around them.

"For one thing, I made a complete fool of myself."

"How so?"

Charlene explained how she had turned the mashed potatoes into soup. "Oh, and according to Len's mother, I didn't cut the vegetables for the salad small enough, either. I also dropped some silverware while clearing dishes from the table." Charlene poked her tongue lightly into the side of her cheek, inhaling a long breath. "Then, while heading to the kitchen, I overheard Annette say to Len and his dad that I'm clumsy."

"Oh boy. Unless you're able to gain his mother's favor, you may be faced with trouble once you and Len are married."

"I know, but the way things are going, I doubt I'll ever find favor with her." Charlene's neck muscles tightened as she shook her head. "Annette goes out of her way to be rude. I'm afraid she'll eventually turn Len against me."

"Perhaps you should reconsider marrying him. Now's the time to bail, not after the wedding."

"I'm not bailing, Kathy. I love Len. If I could talk him into moving away from his parents it might help the situation. At least then, we wouldn't have to see them so often."

Kathy raised her eyebrows. "Good luck with that. Len's job is here, and so are his folks. I'd be willing to bet money he won't leave."

"Well, I won't know till I ask."

"And if he says no?"

Charlene bit the inside of her cheek. "I'm not sure. Guess I'd better wait and see what Len's response is before I make any decision that could affect my future with him."

Walnut Creek

Eli grinned as he stepped out of the phone shack. After checking messages, he'd called Loretta to confirm their plans for Saturday. When class was over, they'd meet at Loretta's house, and Eli would take her and the children to get acquainted with his folks. He looked forward to spending time with Loretta, Abby, and Conner and was eager to find out how things were going with Donnelly. A warm sensation spread throughout Eli's body. *I'm glad I gave them the dog.* He visualized the look of joy on Abby's and Conner's faces. Those kids were so cute and smart. Once again, Eli wished he'd had the good fortune to become a parent. But it must not have been meant to be, or Mavis would have lived and been able to bear children.

Eli's mood shifted, his peppy step gone as he shuffled up the driveway. *I shouldn't let negative thoughts take over like this. Nothin' good comes of it.*

As Eli approached the house, his nose twitched. A foul odor told him something was burning. Remembering the eggs he'd put on the stove to boil, he jerked the door open and rushed inside. Luckily, the kettle hadn't caught on fire, but all the water had boiled out, and the pan was completely dry. Worse yet, all the eggs exploded, and now the mess was stuck to his ceiling. The horrible stench of burnt eggs made his stomach roil. In addition to cleaning up the mess, the whole house needed a good airing.

Eli sputtered and coughed as he made his way through the house, opening windows and doors for ventilation. "Sure hope this putrid odor doesn't linger or seep into the furniture."

He got out the step stool and scraped off the eggs on the ceiling above the stove. Next, Eli filled the sink with soapy water and cleaned the whole area. Following that, he placed an open box of baking soda on the kitchen counter, hoping to absorb some of the remaining unpleasant aroma. *If I wanted to give the folks in my cooking class a good laugh, all I'd have to do is tell 'em about this.* He smacked the palm of his hand against his forehead and groaned. *What a horrible way to end the day. Guess now I'd better hitch my horse to the buggy and go out to eat supper.*

It had been a busy day for Heidi, with baking, cleaning house, paying bills, and making sure everything was lined up for her class on Saturday. Now for a much-needed break.

Settling into the rocker on the front porch, she closed her eyes, listening to the melodic tinkle of wind chimes. Lyle found the chimes at an auction last week and hung them on the porch eaves close to the kitchen window so Heidi could hear the music when she stood at the sink. As the breeze lessened, the tinkling sound diminished, but a dove's soft cooing took its place.

Smiling, Heidi opened her eyes. Even during tense moments, the sound of a dove's gentle coo offered solace. At a time such as this, when Heidi felt content, her relaxation went deeper. She couldn't sit out here much longer, though. Lyle would be home soon, and she'd have to start supper. They'd invited Ron to join them for burgers cooked on the grill. Since it turned out to be such a nice day, they planned to eat outside.

She glanced at Ron's motor home, wondering why he'd kept to himself today. By now he'd usually be out walking around the property or in the barn doing chores for Lyle.

I may have missed him, she thought. *I wasn't watching out the window all day. I hope Ron will be on time for our six o'clock supper.*

Ron leaned forward, rubbing his forehead. He'd sat in his RV most of the day, brooding. Today would have been his brother's sixty-ninth birthday. Ever since Ron was a boy, he'd looked up to Mike. He'd hung on his every word. With only two years between them, they'd always been close and understood one another.

When Mike joined the marines, Ron felt such pride in his brother. He'd worried, though, when Mike was sent to Vietnam.

Ron sucked in a deep breath, remembering the peaceful and quiet afternoon when Ron and his parents had relaxed in the living room after their usual big Sunday meal. Ron heard the crunch of tires as a car pulled in and would never forget what happened when his father opened the door.

Standing somber at the entrance was a casualty notification officer and a chaplain. Ron covered his ears, but not even that could drown out his mother's screams. Dad tried to console her, while struggling not to break down himself.

Nothing was ever the same. It was difficult, but Ron and his parents moved forward, taking one day at a time. Ron felt like a robot, though. Several months later, the sadness in Mom's and Dad's eyes remained. Why wouldn't it? No parents expected to outlive their children.

Ron was lost without his brother and angry at God for allowing it to happen. Even though his parents begged him not to, six months after Mike's funeral, Ron enlisted in the marines. Not long after, he, too, ended up in the ravages of the Vietnam War. It was exactly where he needed to be. Ron wanted—no, needed—to seek revenge for his brother's death.

Bringing his thoughts back to the present, Ron looked out the RV window and muttered, "Life stinks, but it keeps going on." Reaching for his wallet, he pulled out a folded piece of worn-looking paper. His vision blurred as he stared at Mike's named etched in pencil. Years after finishing his tour of duty, Ron took his parents to Washington, DC, to visit the Wall at the Vietnam Veterans Memorial. While there, he had the chance to etch his brother's name. It was mind boggling to see all those other names and realize, like Ron and his parents, thousands of families mourned the loss of their loved one, while trying to get some semblance of normalcy back into their lives.

But in the years after Mike's death and Ron's time in the marines, as hard as he tried to get back to living a normal life, the nightmares still came. Even getting married and having children didn't make them go away. Ron came to the conclusion this was how it was going to be.

His life would never be the same.

Rubbing his finger over his brother's name, Ron whispered, "Happy birthday, Mike. I love you, brother."

Ron's thoughts halted when a knock sounded on his side door. "Just a minute," he called, folding the paper and returning it to his wallet. He went to the sink and splashed cold water on his face then opened the door.

"Supper's ready," Lyle announced. "Heidi made plenty, so I hope you're hungry."

Ron managed a fake smile and nodded. Truthfully, he felt like he couldn't eat a thing. He'd only had one cup of coffee all day, which likely caused some of the jitteriness he felt at the moment. Thinking about Mike had diminished his appetite.

"You okay?" Lyle asked. "I have a hunch you're not feeling so well."

Ron crossed his arms as he gave a slow nod. "Been thinkin' about my older brother, who died in the Vietnam War. Today would have been his birthday." Ron blinked fast. Saying the words out loud made it all too real.

"Loss is hard." Lyle gave Ron's arm a squeeze. "I understand if you'd rather not join us, but maybe a juicy burger and some friendly conversation will offer some cheer."

"Yeah, okay." Ron stepped out of the RV and shut the door. At moments like this, when Lyle was so nice, Ron felt guilty for taking advantage of them. *If Lyle and Heidi knew I'd stolen things from them, they'd probably throw me off their land. And most likely would call the sheriff. Then I'd be sitting in some jail cell, instead of here, where I have it so good. If I still had the stuff I took from their house and barn, I'd put it back. But those items I pawned, and the money I stole from the blue vase is gone.*

Another thought popped into Ron's head. *Maybe I ought to leave now, before I'm tempted to steal anything more.*

Chapter 28

Heidi glanced at the kitchen clock. In thirty minutes class would begin, but everything hadn't been set out. The morning started out a bit hectic. She'd slept longer than planned, and it put her behind.

"I suppose it won't matter if we begin a few minutes late," Heidi murmured, taking a sack of flour from the cupboard and placing it on the table.

"Were you talking to me?" Lyle wrapped his arms around Heidi's waist and nuzzled the back of her neck with his nose.

She snickered. "Talking to myself, silly, and you shouldn't sneak up on me like that. I should have remembered to set the alarm last night so I'd have plenty of time to get ready for my class this morning."

He turned Heidi to face him, rubbing both her arms. "You'll do fine. Some of your students will probably show up late, like they did the last time. So don't fret about starting right on the button."

She smiled and gave his cheek a gentle pinch. "You're right, as usual."

Lyle gave a quick shake of his head. "I don't claim to know everything. Just don't want you to stress out. Remember, these classes are supposed to be fun."

"Oh, they are—at least for me. So far my students seem to have enjoyed themselves." Heidi placed a bowl of red-skinned apples on the table. "Although Ron sometimes acts a bit standoffish. It's hard to read him most of the time."

Lyle's face sobered. "Speaking of Ron, did he say anything to you about leaving?"

"No he didn't. I thought he planned to stay until the end of June, when the cooking classes are over."

"So did I, but when I spoke to him earlier this morning, he said he'd gotten his RV running and figured on heading out today right after class."

Heidi's forehead creased. "It seems strange he'd want to leave now, with only two classes left to take. Did he say why?"

"Nothing clear-cut. Just mumbled something about not wanting to take advantage of our hospitality anymore."

Heidi pursed her lips. "That's silly. He's been here this long. He should stay and finish the classes."

"I told him the same thing. Not sure he'll listen, but at least I tried." Lyle went to the kitchen sink and filled a glass with water. "Ron shared a few things with me the other evening when I went out to his motor home, just before our cookout."

"Oh?"

"The poor fellow was grieving because if his brother hadn't been killed in the Vietnam War, it would have been his birthday." Lyle slowly shook his head. "I feel sorry for Ron. He seems almost lost, and I think he needs a friend."

"You've said before you thought God brought Ron here for a reason. Maybe it's so we can be his friends," Heidi suggested.

"Jah, I believe you're right."

Heidi glanced out the window and spotted Ron sitting on a camp stool outside his motor home with his hands pressed against his head. "I hope by the time my cooking classes are done, that my students, Ron included, will feel as if they've made some new friends. I also hope, due to the scriptures I've shared, that some will have found help for whatever problems they might be going through."

Lyle kissed Heidi's forehead. "Jah, God can minister to them through His Word, as well as things you might say during class, just as He's done to many of your aunt Emma's quilting students."

Sugarcreek

"There ya go." Loretta gave Abby a hug. "Why don't you take Donnelly outside? Then you can sit on the porch and wait for Sandy to arrive."

"Okay, Mommy." Her daughter skipped out of the room, with the dog frolicking at her side.

Loretta smiled. Abby looked cute in her bright red top. It was a summery shirt her mother-in-law had given Abby at Christmas. Thank goodness, she'd purchased a large enough size. Abby was growing fast, and the cotton shirt, which was too big in December, fit her perfectly now.

"All right, big boy." Loretta scooped Conner up to get him ready as she heard the screen door slam. Glancing out the window, Loretta saw Abby walking the puppy toward the backyard.

Loretta hummed while she changed Conner from his pj's to a pair of jeans and a striped T-shirt. She'd dressed both kids in something comfortable since they'd all be going with Eli later today.

She closed her eyes, breathing deeply. After having the windows closed all winter, it was nice having them open, as the comfortable breeze wafted through the screens. Loretta appreciated the opportunity to allow her children to grow up in this environment. There was plenty of space for them to run, play, and use their imagination. Abby and Conner enjoyed pretending while they played with their simple toys. She'd decided early on not to own a TV so it wouldn't be a distraction for her or the children.

Loretta also felt grateful for the elderly neighbor next door who'd do about anything for them. It was a comfort being able to call on him if needed. Sam took good care of himself, too. Instead of wasting away in front of TV, he kept moving and doing, many times offering to take care of outside chores for Loretta.

Through the open window, Loretta heard Abby coaxing Donnelly.

"Come on, puppy. Do your business now."

Eli had given her children such a wonderful surprise. Even with all the pup's little accidents, once again, Loretta wished she had gotten a dog for them sooner. Although the puppy wasn't consistent yet, the new member of their family was learning quickly. The other night, for the first time, Donnelly scratched on the door to be let out. Afterward, they all praised the dog and gave him a treat for being good.

"Donnelly! Donnelly!" Conner giggled, pointing to the window.

"Yes, I hear him barking." Loretta combed her son's hair. "Okay, let's join your sister now, and we'll wait for Sandy to arrive." Loretta was grateful Sandy was available to watch the kids again while she went to class. When she got home, Eli would swing by with his horse and buggy, and off to his parents' house they'd go—Donnelly included.

When Loretta went outside to the porch with Conner, she didn't see her daughter in the yard. She'd assumed Abby was with Donnelly, but the barking pup, straining against its leash, sat on the porch by himself. Abby had apparently wrapped the end of the dog's leash around one of the lawn chairs, and Donnelly, even though little, had dragged the chair over and was about to go down the porch steps with it trailing behind him.

"Conner, do Mommy a favor and stay right here with Donnelly, while I go look for your sister." It wasn't like Abby to leave the puppy alone. She'd been watching over Donnelly like a mother hen ever since Eli gave them the dog.

Loretta's heart filled with gratitude when Sandy pulled in. She sprinted to the babysitter's car before the motor was even turned off.

Sandy rolled her window down. "Is everything all right?"

"Oh, Sandy, I'm so glad you're here. I have an emergency, but I need you to stay with Conner." Loretta pointed to the porch. "He's waiting there, and I'll explain later."

"Of course." Sandy turned off the ignition and ran toward the porch.

"Abby, where are you?" Loretta hurried toward the garage. She turned the knob, but the door was still locked, so her daughter couldn't be there. *Don't panic. Stay calm.* Her brain sent messages, but her mother's instinct kicked in, ignoring all reason. As she headed toward the back of the property, something red caught her eye.

The property that adjoined the back of her and Sam's lots belonged to a farm over the ridge. Normally the cows didn't graze this far. From Loretta's home, the farm buildings weren't visible, but on rare occasions, the herd would venture farther and wind up at this end. Abby and Conner always wanted to see the pretty black-and-white Holsteins, so Loretta would take them to the fence to watch. Sometimes they'd feed them grass. But what Loretta saw now made her eyes grow wide as her hand went to her mouth. Abby stood in the field, a few feet from a monstrous black bull. Holding a clump of grass, her daughter walked slowly toward the massive animal. Loretta faintly heard Abby coaxing, "Here's somethin' for you to eat."

Loretta took no thought of the beautiful wildflowers blooming along the fence row or the birds tweeting merrily from the trees. Her focus was on the giant beast flicking its ears while staring back at her precious child.

As Loretta ran toward the fence, her breath burst in and out. Abby probably thought this was one of the gentle cows. The bull looked Loretta's way then back at Abby. *Oh, why did I put a red shirt on my little girl this morning?* Maybe it was a myth, but Loretta had heard bulls didn't like the color red.

"Abby." Loretta spoke calmly as she climbed over the fence and walked slowly toward her daughter. "Don't go any closer, honey."

Loretta approached Abby and scooped the child into her arms then stood trembling as she kept an eye on the bull. His neck and shoulders were huge and muscular. Loretta's impulse was to run, but it might set him off. Without breaking contact with the bull's steady gaze, she backed slowly away. Despite her best efforts, the beast began pawing the ground with both his front feet, sending dirt flying in all directions. *What to do now?* Loretta trembled when Abby asked, "Mommy, is the cow mad at us?"

"I'll explain later. Just hold on to me." Loretta turned. The fence was at least sixty yards away, but it might as well have been five miles. If the bull wanted to, he could run the distance in seconds, before she reached the fence.

Loretta's lungs burned as she sprinted toward safety, the whole time praying for help. She looked back once and shuddered when the bull lowered his head, shaking it from side to side. Big puffs of air escaped the animal's nostrils. All Loretta wanted to do was get her precious child to safety. *Please Lord, help us.*

As though God heard her plea at that very moment, there was Sam, running past her, waving his arms and shouting, "Boo-Boo. It's all right now, settle down."

The bull lifted his head and, for the moment, seemed subdued. Was it the name Sam had called him?

"Walk to the fence, Loretta. Don't run," Sam instructed. "I called the Blakes. It's their bull, and as you heard, his name is Boo-Boo."

Abby laughed as she clung to Loretta's neck. "I like his name, Mommy. Don't you?"

All Loretta could think about was how in the world an animal that massive could be called Boo-Boo and how grateful she was that Sam had shown up when he did. God most certainly had answered her prayer.

Walnut Creek

Charlene glanced at the clock on her dashboard and grimaced. She'd never seen so much traffic on this stretch of road.

Ah, so there's the reason. Everyone seems to be heading for the Walnut

Creek Cheese store today. The parking lot was full of cars. Even the hitching rail for Amish horse and buggies looked full to capacity. *The store must be having a sale. Either that or everyone picked this particular Saturday to do their shopping.*

After pausing to let a car turn in front of her, Charlene moved on. Even though she looked forward to attending the fourth cooking class, her nerves were a bit on edge this morning. This time, however, it wasn't for fear of making a fool of herself in front of the class. Today she struggled with her plans to speak with Len about his mother during their dinner date this evening. Charlene had spoken to him only once this week, to make plans for tonight. While she could have told Len what was on her mind then, Charlene preferred not to do it over the phone. It might go over better if she discussed it with him in person.

She held tightly to the steering wheel. *What will I do if Len says no to my request? If he's not willing to move, maybe I should end our relationship before his mother ends it for us.*

Tears pricked Charlene's eyes, and she blinked rapidly to keep them from spilling over. She loved Len and couldn't imagine spending the rest of her life without him. *Is it right to make him choose between me and his mother?*

Charlene sniffed deeply and kept her focus straight ahead. *If I get the chance to speak to Heidi alone today, maybe I'll ask her opinion.*

───── ⌒◦◦⌒ ─────

Eli couldn't stop smiling as he guided his horse and buggy in the direction of the Troyers' house. Normally, he wouldn't have bothered to take the buggy such a short distance, but since he'd be heading to Loretta's as soon as the cooking class was over today, it made sense. No point walking or riding his bike then going home and hitching the horse. This way would save time.

He looked forward to seeing Loretta again and taking her and the children to meet his folks. *Bet Mom will enjoy seeing the puppy again, too. Wonder what she'll think of the name Abby and Conner gave the hund. Personally, I like it. It's a catchy name. Course Loretta's kids are cute, so everything they say and do is liable to impress me.*

Eli shook his head. *They're not angels, though. I'm sure Conner and Abby are naughty sometimes. But I'll bet their mother handles it well. Loretta seems kind and patient. Even so, I doubt she'd let her kinner get away with anything.*

With little coaxing, Eli's horse turned up the Troyers' driveway. Of course, since they were in the same church district and Eli was Lyle's friend, he'd been here a good many times. The trusty animal could have probably found the way, even without Eli's guidance.

As he pulled up to the hitching rail, Eli spotted Ron walking toward the house with his head down and shoulders slouched. *Wonder what his problem is. Maybe he's not happy to be here today.*

When Loretta pulled her van into the Troyers' yard, she spotted Eli's horse and buggy. Her pulse raced a bit as she thought about his invitation to take her and the children to visit his parents this afternoon. Abby and Conner looked forward to it, and if Loretta was being honest, so did she.

Her hands still shook from the morning's experience, but thankfully, her daughter had been unscathed. In fact, when they'd walked back to the porch, Abby couldn't wait to relay the story to her brother and Sandy.

Loretta was eager to tell Eli but would wait and let Abby share her adventure. In her childlike eyes, it had been an adventure, and Loretta wanted to keep it that way. She did not wish to instill fear into her children's minds but had calmly explained how most bulls were uncomfortable around people.

Thank goodness Sam heard me calling for Abby and saw the bull when he looked out his kitchen window.

Loretta thought's returned to Eli. *Did I do the right thing agreeing to go with him this afternoon? I hope his parents won't get the wrong idea and think Eli and I are courting.*

Loretta thumped her head. *What am I thinking? We're only friends. I'm sure Eli's informed his parents of that. I do have to admit, though, I enjoy his company, and if he were English. . .*

Loretta turned off her engine and stepped down from the van. She was almost to the house when her shoe caught on an odd-shaped rock. All the contents of Loretta's purse spilled out as she lost her balance and landed flat on her back.

Chapter 29

Straining his ears, Eli hoped it was Loretta's minivan he heard pulling in. She was the only one left to arrive. When he went to the living-room window to look out, he was stunned. Loretta lay flat on the ground. Without a second thought, he rushed out the door and dropped to his knees beside her. "Loretta, what happened? Are you hurt?" His heart beat so fast he found it hard to breathe.

"I tripped on a rock, and. . ." Moaning, she turned onto her side and sat up. "My ankle hurts. I. . .I hope I can stand."

Heart still pounding, Eli stood and swept Loretta into his arms as if she weighed no more than a feather.

Heidi was at the door waiting for them when he stepped inside. "What happened? Is she hurt?"

"She tripped on a rock and fell." Eli spoke between ragged breaths. "She injured her ankle. I hope it's not broken."

"Better take her to the couch."

As Eli placed Loretta gently down, everyone gathered around.

"I'm okay. Don't look so worried." Loretta winced when Heidi touched her ankle. "Guess I should have been paying closer attention."

"You might want to go to the hospital and get an X-ray taken," Kendra suggested.

Loretta shook her head. "I'm sure there's no need for that." She stood and took a few steps then lost her balance and fell back onto the couch.

"Here, let me take a look." Charlene stepped forward, and Eli moved aside. "I'm trained in first aid."

Eli held his breath as Charlene examined Loretta's ankle. "The good news is, I'm almost sure it's not broken—maybe just a sprain. Heidi, do you have an ice pack we can put on Loretta's ankle?"

"Yes. I'll get it right now." Heidi hurried from the room.

Eli felt relief hearing Loretta wasn't seriously hurt. His main concern now was that she might not feel up to visiting his folks this afternoon. *What's wrong with me? I'm being selfish. Above all else, Loretta's comfort is the important thing.*

"How do you feel now?" Heidi asked after Loretta sat for fifteen minutes with her leg propped up and an ice pack on her ankle.

"It feels a little better. Look, it's not even swollen." Loretta twirled her ankle in a circular motion. "Sorry for holding up your lesson, Heidi. We should head to the kitchen now so you can get started."

"Are you sure? If no one's in a hurry, we can wait awhile longer."

"Oh, please don't." Loretta waved her hand and pushed herself to a sitting position. "I'm fine, really."

Heidi led the way to the kitchen, and everyone followed. Glancing over her shoulder, she saw Eli offer his arm to Loretta as she gingerly walked beside him. After observing the look of concern on his face when he carried Loretta into the house, Heidi wondered if Eli had more than a casual interest in Loretta. Although she was a sweet woman, Loretta wasn't Amish. It would be difficult for them to develop a serious relationship without one of them giving up their current way of life.

Pushing her concerns aside, Heidi pointed to the table. "Today we're making apple cream pie, so we'll take turns mixing and then rolling out the crust." She gestured to the finished pie she'd made this morning. "This is what it looks like when it's taken from the oven. Once we're finished, you'll each have your own pie to take home today, along with the recipe for it." The scripture Heidi had written on the back of their cards was Ephesians 4:32: "And be ye kind one to another, tenderhearted, forgiving one another, even as God for Christ's sake hath forgiven you." She hoped it might speak to someone this week.

"Is your oven big enough for all the pies to bake at once?" Kendra asked.

"No, but two pies can bake at the same time. If no one's in a hurry to go, there should be plenty of time to get them all done."

"The young woman I hired to watch my children today has somewhere she needs to go later this afternoon, so I'll have to leave by one o'clock," Loretta spoke up.

"Not a problem. We'll make sure yours is one of the first pies to go in the oven." Heidi looked at the others. "What about the rest of you?"

"I can stay awhile longer," Charlene responded. "I have plans with my boyfriend, but not till this evening."

"I'll leave when Loretta does, because…" Eli paused and moistened his lips. "Well, I have some plans for this afternoon." He glanced quickly at Loretta then back at Heidi.

"It's fine. Your pie can go in with Loretta's." Heidi looked at Kendra. "How about you?"

"I'll stay longer."

Heidi smiled. "And Ron, since you're staying here on our property, I would assume you won't mind if your pie goes in last?"

Ron hesitated then nodded. He seemed quiet today. Could it have something to do with him telling Lyle he planned to leave? As soon as class finished, she'd speak to him about it.

———— ⁓ ⁓ ⁓ ————

Just what I need, Ron grumbled to himself. *Sure didn't want any delays today.* He'd planned to cut out right after class. He was afraid that with any more holdups, he'd end up changing his mind. The last couple of days, Ron went back and forth with the idea of leaving. But he'd already told Lyle he would go. Otherwise, it wouldn't take much for

Ron to relent and stay, at least until the final cooking class was over.

The other evening, while listening to the radio in his RV, Ron had heard an advertisement about the mobile display of the Vietnam Wall coming to the Columbus area. He'd considered heading in that direction today. The Moving Wall was being set up for the upcoming Memorial Day holiday next week, to honor and recognize those who'd served and sacrificed their lives in the Vietnam War. The half-size replica of the original wall had been touring the country for more than thirty years, which made it easier for people who didn't have the opportunity to travel to Washington, DC, to get some idea of what the Wall was all about. Since Columbus was a little over one hundred miles away, the drive would take about two hours. Once there, Ron hoped to find a place on the outskirts of the city, reasonable in cost, where he could set up camp for a few days. It had been years since he'd taken his parents to the original Wall, and now he felt the need to see his brother's name again, especially with the holiday to honor veterans approaching. Ron wanted to retrace Mike's name, too, since the one in his wallet had become tattered and worn.

Ron almost felt guilty leaving the Troyers like this, especially since they were kind of growing on him. Had Lyle told Heidi about his plans to leave, or should Ron spring the news on her after class?

A knot formed in his belly. This farm felt more like home than any other place he'd stayed. Even Lyle's horse seemed like a friend. Ron had found himself unloading on the animal when he just needed someone to listen to him. The horse's soft nickers offered solace for Ron, even if Bobbins didn't understand.

What's more, Heidi and Lyle's Brittany spaniel had gotten used to seeing Ron around the place. Some mornings, Rusty came to the entrance of Ron's RV and barked until he responded. The dog sat patiently waiting for Ron to open the door and pat him on the head or give him a scrap of food before returning to the porch to lie down.

While Ron listened to Heidi explain more about the pies, he

figured anytime he bugged out would work, as long as he didn't lose his nerve. If he could find a place for his RV by nightfall, it was half the battle—at least that's what he kept telling himself. But Ron wasn't sure what would come next after the Memorial Day holiday.

Don't worry till the time comes, he told himself. Ron felt like a lost soul moving from one place to another, without any real goals or purpose. Truth was, his life had no meaning anymore. He had no family, no friends, and no real reason to get up each morning.

———————⌇∽⌇———————

When Charlene's turn came around to roll out her piecrust, she picked up the rolling pin with trembling fingers. Mixing the ingredients for the crust had been easy enough, but she wasn't sure how to roll it correctly. The last thing she wanted was a too-thick piecrust. Or worse yet, one she could see through. *You would think by now my nerves would settle down, especially with Heidi as a teacher. Too bad Len's mother doesn't have Heidi's patience. Otherwise, I wouldn't be faced with the discussion I'll be having with Len this evening.*

"Press firmly and roll from the inside out," Heidi instructed, leaning close to Charlene. "That's it. You're doing fine."

Charlene smiled. It wasn't as difficult as she'd expected. In fact, the whole process ended up being fun. Carefully, as Heidi guided her, she picked up the dough and placed it in the pie pan.

"Here's a tip I'd like to share with all of you about fluting the edges of a piecrust before it's baked. Once the pie shell has been put into the pan, place it on a cake stand. This will make it easier to turn the pie plate, and you won't have to stoop over. Of course you may use your fingers to flute the edges, but it's also fun to try some kitchen utensils to make more decorative edges." Heidi picked up a spoon and made a few scalloped edges. "You can also use a fork for different patterns."

"The spoon looks easy enough. I'll try that." Between the lessons she'd already taken, and the time spent practicing at home, Charlene felt confident she'd be able to cook a decent meal for Len soon. And maybe even surprise his parents.

———————•❧•———————

"How are you doing, Loretta?" Eli asked as she walked slowly to the stove to check on her pie.

"My ankle still hurts, but not as bad as it did earlier." She smiled, appreciating his concern.

"Glad to hear it." Eli moved closer and lowered his voice. "If you're not up to going over to my folks' today, we make can it another time."

She shook her head and whispered, "I'll be fine. Abby and Conner would be disappointed if we didn't go, and I'd never hear the end of it." Loretta glanced back and felt relief that no one seemed to be watching them. "Besides, I'm eager to meet your parents."

"Okay, then." He peered into the oven and grinned. "Our pies are lookin' pretty good. Maybe I'll take mine along to Mom and Dad's, and we can eat it while we're there."

"I'll take my pie, too. That way, if we're all hungry we can have a second piece." How long had it been since Loretta felt this lighthearted? Nothing, not even her sore ankle, could keep her from going with Eli as planned. After what happened earlier today with the neighbor's bull, an afternoon with Eli and her children was just what she needed.

"Yum. I can almost taste the pie already." Eli's smile widened. "I'm looking forward to this afternoon."

Feeling warm and fuzzy inside, Loretta gave a nod. "So am I, Eli." *More than you know.*

Chapter 30

As soon as Ron took his pie from the oven, he set it on the countertop and headed for the door. Kendra's pie cooled next to his, and since she and Heidi were engrossed in conversation, he figured it was a good time to make his escape.

Ron's hand touched the doorknob when Heidi called out to him. "Where are you going, Ron? Don't you want your pie?"

He halted and turned back around. "Uh, it's too hot to carry right now."

"You're right, but here's a box to put it in, like I did for the others before they left."

Ron hesitated. "Sure, okay then. Guess I can take it with me."

Heidi put on a pair of oven mitts and placed the pie inside a cardboard box. Then she handed it to Ron and followed him out the door. "May I ask you something?"

"Yeah, sure." With his back to the porch railing, he turned to face her.

"Lyle mentioned you were planning to leave without finishing the cooking classes."

Ron shifted the box as heat crept up the back of his neck. "Well, yeah, I was. Figured I ought to be moving on before I overstayed my welcome."

She shook her head. "You haven't, Ron. We'd be pleased if you'd stay until the classes are done."

"Okay, I'll stay." What else could he say with her looking at him so kindly? To be honest, Ron didn't really want to leave—at least not until he'd finished the class. He shuffled his feet. "See, the thing is, there's someplace I want to go for a few days."

"To visit your family?"

"No way! My ex-wife and kids don't want anything to do with me, but I can't really blame 'em." He scratched behind his right ear. "I'll be driving down to Columbus to see the Vietnam Veterans Memorial Wall. Saw the original many years ago in Washington, DC, and figured since it'll be this close for a few days, even though the replica is only half the size, I'd like to take the opportunity to see it again."

"How long will you be gone?"

"A few days. I'll be back before your next cooking class."

"Good to hear. If you know when you plan to leave, I'll make sure you have some snacks to take along."

"It's nice of you, but don't go to any trouble on my account."

Heidi smiled. "It's no bother. I'm always baking and trying out new recipes, which means I usually end up with more food than Lyle and I can eat."

"Okay, I'll let you know before I head out." Ron stepped off the porch and made a beeline for his motor home. *Sure wish the Troyers weren't such nice people. They've been nothing but kind to me. I told Heidi I'd be coming back, but maybe after I leave Columbus, I should head in some other direction. Guess I'll have to wait and see how it goes. Don't know why I can't make up my mind.*

Heidi returned to the kitchen, and Kendra hoped this would be a good time to finish their talk. She'd barely opened her mouth when Lyle came in, saying their horse and buggy waited and they could head to town to do some shopping now.

Kendra picked up the box with her pie in it and started for the door. "I'll see you in two weeks," she called over her shoulder.

"If you're free next Saturday, please drop by," Heidi responded.

"I'll see how it goes. Since next weekend's a holiday, I might do something with Dorie." Without waiting for Heidi's response,

Kendra hurried out the door. Before getting into Dorie's car, she glanced at the horse and buggy waiting at the hitching rail. *I wonder what it's like being raised Amish. "The simple life." Isn't that what some call it? Sure hope I get a chance to talk to Heidi before our next cooking class. If she and Lyle would agree to adopt my baby, the child would be a lot better off than living in the English world with me.*

Sugarcreek

When Eli directed his horse and buggy onto Loretta's driveway, he saw Abby and Conner sitting on the porch with their dog between them. As Eli approached, Donnelly's ears perked up and his tail started wagging.

Loretta came out of the house. "I'll get my pie and be right with you," she called.

"Sounds good. I brought my pie along, too." Eli got out of the buggy and secured his horse to the fence post. Then he helped the children into the backseat of his buggy.

"Don't forget Donnelly," Conner reminded him.

"No worries." Eli bent down, scooped the pup into his arms, and put him in the buggy between the children. "There's a box on the floor by your feet, Abby. Please don't step on it, and don't allow Donnelly to get near it, either."

"I won't, Mr. Eli." Abby shook her head. "We'll hang on to the puppy the whole ride."

Eli smiled. "Good to hear."

When Loretta came out carrying a box, he took it from her and placed it on the floor of the passenger seat. "Here, let me help you." He held his hand out to her. "How's that ankle?"

"About the same, but no worse, either." She barely made eye contact with him.

After Loretta got situated, Eli asked her to hold the reins while he untied his horse. A few minutes later, he hopped into the buggy and she handed back the reins.

"I'm glad your horse didn't bolt, because I'm not sure about handling a horse and buggy. I've never driven one before."

"If you're interested, I'd be glad to teach you sometime."

Loretta nodded slowly. "I'll let you know if I can work up the nerve."

I'd enjoy being your teacher. It would give me more opportunity to spend time with you. Eli didn't voice his thoughts. The feelings creeping in toward Loretta were unexpected. *Must be because I miss Mavis and desire female companionship.* He mentally shook his head. *But that's not really true. When I'm with other women, I don't feel like I do when I'm with Loretta. Is it possible that she feels the same way about being with me? Sure wish I had the nerve to ask.*

Loretta felt lighthearted as she glanced over at Eli. He was such a kind, soft-spoken man. The more time they spent together, the more she enjoyed his company. Abby and Conner liked Eli, too. They'd mentioned him several times since he'd given them the puppy. *If only he weren't Amish.*

Twisting her watchband around her wrist, Loretta shifted on the buggy seat. As much as she looked forward to meeting Eli's parents, she couldn't help feeling apprehensive. *What if they don't approve of him seeing me? Of course, Eli and I are not courting. We're friends—nothing more—so it shouldn't matter.* The trouble was, Loretta had been thinking about Eli a lot lately. *Too much, maybe.* She'd even fantasized about them becoming romantically involved, which wasn't even possible, since she was not Amish. It was difficult to admit, even to herself, but Loretta hadn't felt this way about anyone since Rick died, and she'd known Eli shy of two months.

Perhaps I'm merely in need of male companionship. Yes, that's all it is. Of course, Loretta visited with her neighbor Sam quite often, so maybe it wasn't a simple need to spend time with a man.

"Mr. Eli, did Mommy tell you about the big cow I tried to feed this morning?" Abby leaned over the seat and touched Eli's shoulder.

"Why no, she didn't."

"The cow was bigger than the other ones we feed. His name is Boo-Boo, and he had a ring in his nose."

"Is that so?"

"Uh-huh. But I don't think he liked me too much, 'cause he looked kinda mad. Then Mommy climbed over the fence. She carried me out of the field while Sam helped Boo-Boo's owner take him back where he belonged."

"Sounds like you had quite an adventure. I'm glad it turned out okay." Eli reached back and patted the child's hand. "Better sit back in your seat now, Abby. Don't want you to get jostled around."

Without question, Abby did as he asked.

Loretta leaned closer to Eli and whispered, "I didn't want to scare her about Boo-Boo, but he's a mean bull. I feared for Abby's life and needed to get her out of there right away."

"It's important for you to stay in your yard, Abby," Eli called over his shoulder. "A cow like Boo-Boo is a lot bigger than you, and you should never leave your yard without your mother's permission."

"Okay, Mr. Eli."

Loretta smiled and mouthed the message, *Thank you, Eli.*

He grinned back at her. "Guess what, kids? My parents have a few cows, and one big bull, too. I'll take you out to the barn to see him if he's in there today."

While Abby and Conner clapped their hands, Loretta grew nervous. Eli must have sensed her fear, because he added, "Don't worry. My parents' bull is a big ole baby. His name is Biscuit."

"Biscuit." Conner giggled.

"How'd he get that name?" Loretta questioned.

"Well, when he was about a year old, my mom took some home-made biscuits out of the oven and wrapped them in a cloth to keep warm. She put the biscuits, along with some butter and jelly, in a picnic basket and took them out to the barn where Dad was working."

"Mommy makes good biscuits," Abby said. "She gets 'em at the store and they're in a tube."

Loretta's face heated. *Oh my, Abby. Did you have to bring that up?*

"They are good, aren't they? I make that kind sometimes, too." Eli winked at Loretta. "Anyway, my folks' little bull was in a stall next to where Mom and Dad sat on a bale of straw. They weren't paying attention to the sneaky animal as they talked and enjoyed Mom's home-baked treat. Then, unexpectedly, the young bull stuck his head through the railing and pulled the plate of biscuits into his stall."

Loretta and the children laughed. "What'd they do then?" Loretta asked.

Eli chuckled. "By the time my dad got in the stall and took the plate away, the overzealous critter had eaten every last one of those homemade rolls."

"That's funny." Abby giggled again.

"Yep. My poor dad only got one biscuit that morning. My siblings and I didn't get any till Mom made another batch. This time she told us the biscuits were not to leave the kitchen. So that's how Biscuit got his name."

Loretta held her hands loosely in her lap, enjoying the interesting conversation. "I can almost picture it, Eli. What a cute memory, and a good name for the bull, too."

"My folks have told that story many times when people ask why they gave our bull such an unusual name."

"Is Biscuit friendly?" Loretta still felt a bit concerned—especially after what had happened with Boo-Boo.

"He's quite massive, and definitely not little anymore, but Biscuit still thinks he's a baby." Eli glanced back at the children. "Not all bulls are friendly, but as long as I'm there, you don't have to worry about Biscuit at all."

As they traveled farther, Loretta tried to concentrate on the passing scenery instead of thinking about Eli. Seeing how good he was with her kids, she felt sure he would have been a wonderful father.

Soon, they pulled onto a gravel driveway. "We're here," Eli announced. "This is where I grew up and where my folks still live." He glanced over his shoulder at the children. "This is where the mother of your puppy lives, too."

"Bet Donnelly will be excited to see her," Abby said.

"Bet Donnelly will be excited to see her," Conner repeated.

Eli chuckled. "I'm sure she'll be glad to see her pup again, too."

Loretta watched as an Amish couple came out of the house. The man, who appeared to be in his early sixties, walked up to the horse and secured him to the hitching rail, while the woman waited on the porch.

When Eli got out of the buggy, Loretta did the same. After she reached in and took out her pie, Eli came around and helped the children and their puppy down. Loretta assumed they'd feel shy and stick close to her, but with Abby holding Donnelly, they both darted up the porch steps and stood directly in front of the Amish woman.

"My name is Abby, and this is my brother, Conner. We brought our puppy to visit his mama."

Conner bobbed his head. "His name is Donnelly. He used to live here."

The woman leaned down and shook both of their hands. "It's nice to meet you. I'm Eli's mother, Wilma Miller."

Loretta glanced at Mrs. Miller then looked back at Eli, still talking with his father. *Should I go up and introduce myself or wait for Eli?* Repositioning the box that held the pie, Loretta gave herself a pep talk. *Quit being such a scaredy-cat and get on up to that porch.* She drew a deep breath, straightened her shoulders, and headed for the house.

Chapter 31

Mom and Dad, I'd like you to meet Loretta Donnelly and her children, Abby and Conner." Eli motioned to Loretta after he and his dad stepped onto the porch.

His mother smiled. "I've already met Loretta and the children." She leaned over to pet Donnelly's head. "Looks like Sadie's pup has found a good home."

"The children love him," Loretta interjected. "He seems to have adjusted well to his new surroundings."

When his folks' dog started whining from inside the house, Mom opened the screen door. "Come out Sadie and see your pup."

Eli chuckled as Sadie, tail wagging, greeted Donnelly with slurps and yips. "It's almost like a family reunion watching those two get reacquainted."

"I hope your dog won't be upset when we leave with her pup." Loretta looked at Eli's mother.

Mom shook her head. "Sadie might miss her at first, but she'll be fine."

"So, Mom, I promised Abby and Conner I'd take 'em out to see Biscuit." Eli pointed to the barn. "Is he there?"

"Nope. He's in the pasture," Dad responded. "Let's walk out to the fence. Maybe he'll come over to greet us." He gestured to Donnelly. "Better not take the pup along, though. Biscuit gets a bit spooky around dogs."

"I'll keep him with me," Mom volunteered. "And our dog, too." She held out her arms and the pup went willingly to her, while Sadie stood watchfully by. "I doubt Sadie will let Donnelly out of her sight."

"Before I forget, Loretta and I brought pies." Eli handed a box to his mom. "How 'bout a little later on we all have some?"

"Okay, let me take them inside."

"I'll help." Loretta walked in behind Mrs. Miller with her pie but glanced back at Eli. "Will you please wait till I come back out?"

"Of course." Eli remained on the porch with the children until Loretta joined them again. "Okay kids, are you ready to meet Biscuit?"

Together, Abby and Conner hollered, "Yes!"

"I'd better go along to keep an eye on the children." Loretta eyed the field with a cautious expression.

"Don't worry. I'll be with them the whole time." Eli took each child's hand. "Loretta, why don't you wait with Mom on the porch so you two can get better acquainted?"

Loretta seemed hesitant at first but finally smiled and said, "Okay." She held a paper sack under one arm and handed it to Eli. "Your mother said to give you this."

Eli tilted his head. "What's inside?"

"Biscuits, and I don't think they came from a tube."

Loretta's cute little grin charmed Eli. He was tempted to stay on the porch and visit with her and Mom but didn't want to disappoint the children. He took hold of Abby's and Conner's hands. "Now don't worry, Loretta. I won't let these two out of my sight."

———— ⟨⟨∘∘⟩⟩ ————

Abby stood on the fence rail, while Eli's father held Conner. "Watch this." Eli opened the paper sack and held it in front of him. It wasn't long before Biscuit the bull trotted over to the fence, tongue swiping over his big lips.

"Would you like to feed him?" Eli asked the children.

Abby eagerly nodded, while Conner answered, "I'm gonna watch."

"Come down here with me." Eli motioned for Abby as he took a biscuit from the bag and hunkered down on one knee. "Here ya go.

Hold this treat in your hand and through the two rails."

Abby squealed when Biscuit's long tongue scooped up the pastry. "He's a nice bull and a pretty color, too." Her eyes sparkled with enthusiasm as she watched the tan-colored animal. "The cow I saw this morning was all black."

"Sounds like it could have been an Angus. Ole Biscuit here, he's a Jersey," Eli's dad explained. "Most times he's quite docile."

"What's that word mean?" Abby looked up at him inquisitively.

Eli's dad glanced at him and grinned. "Docile means the same thing as tame. But I never turn my back on Biscuit, because you can't completely trust a bull. Believe me, I learned the hard way."

"Was Biscuit bad?" Conner asked innocently, while his sister fed the bull another bun.

"Well, let's just say I gave him an opportunity to be bad." Dad scrubbed a hand down the side of his face. "I bent over the water trough one morning to fill it with fresh water. Ole Biscuit must have thought he was a goat, 'cause the next thing I knew, he butted me into the water." He chuckled. "I ended up with two baths that morning."

Abby and Conner laughed, and Eli joined in. Even though he'd heard the story a good many times, it still made him chuckle.

"Maybe the next time you and Conner come for a visit, you can help me brush Biscuit." Eli snickered. "He likes to have his ears scratched, too."

"Can I scratch his ears now?" Conner asked.

"Don't see why not." Dad picked Conner up and held him in a safe position to reach Biscuit's ears. Biscuit leaned closer, and more giggles escaped Conner's lips.

* * * * *

Loretta took a seat in the chair beside Eli's mother. "I want to thank you for the banana whoopie pies Eli shared with my children and me a few weeks ago."

Wilma's eyebrows lifted. "He gave you some?"

Loretta nodded. "They were delicious."

"Well, I shouldn't be surprised. My son's always had a giving nature." She laughed. "Once, when Eli was a boy in school, he gave away his lunch to a girl who'd forgotten hers. What made it even more sacrificial was I'd put several of Eli's favorite cookies in his lunch pail that morning."

Loretta smiled. Although she'd only known Eli a short time, she could picture him doing something so kind. His personality was a lot like her husband's. Rick always did good deeds and helped others.

"Eli seems to enjoy Heidi Troyer's cooking classes," Wilma commented. "Maybe now he can fend for himself without worrying about burning the house down or starving to death from lack of eating proper meals." She looked pointedly at Loretta. "How come you signed up for the classes? Are you lacking in cooking skills, too?"

Heat flooded Loretta's face as she shook her head. "I took the class for two reasons. One, to do something fun, and two, because I'm interested in the Amish way of life and their home-style cooking."

"I see." Wilma rocked slowly in her chair. "Eli's wife, Mavis, was an excellent cook. He still misses her a lot."

"I'm sure he does. I miss my husband, Rick, as well."

"Eli took her death hard. I doubt he'll ever recover from it."

Unsure of what to say, Loretta merely nodded. It felt as if Mrs. Miller might be throwing hints about her son not looking for another wife. Did she suspect Loretta was beginning to have feelings for her son?

A short time later, Eli, his father, and the children returned. "Biscuit's big, but he's nice." Abby announced. "Do ya wanna see him, Mommy?"

"Maybe some other time, Abby. I'm visiting with Eli's mother right now."

"Eli said next time we come we can brush Biscuit." Abby's eyes gleamed.

"And scratch his ears," Conner added.

Loretta glanced at Eli and noticed *his* ears had turned red. It pleased her to know he wanted to bring them here again.

"Why don't we have some of the apple cream pie Loretta and I brought along?" Eli looked at his mother and wiggled his brows. "The children and I are *hungerich*."

"That means 'hungry.'" Abby grinned. "Mr. Eli taught us that word while we were talkin' to Biscuit. He said the bull was hungerich."

"Well then, if someone will take the sleeping pup from me, I'll go inside and slice those pies." Mom stood and handed Donnelly to Eli, as Sadie moaned from her comfortable position and got up with a doggy grunt. "Since it is so nice out today, why don't we eat our pie on the porch?" she suggested.

"Good idea. I'll help you, Wilma." Loretta rose from her chair but paused to look at Eli. "Would you please keep an eye on the children?"

"Sure thing. It's a privilege to watch your kinner."

When Loretta held the door open for Wilma, she heard Abby say, "Mr. Eli, are you gonna teach me how to whistle today?"

"You bet. How about a lesson right now?"

Abby bobbed her head.

Once more, Loretta couldn't get over how well Eli responded to her children.

Berlin

"Oh, look, there's your sister, Regina," Heidi mentioned when she and Lyle entered the market.

He looked in the direction she'd pointed. "You're right. Guess we'd better say hello before we start shopping, in case she's getting ready to leave the store."

Heidi followed him to the other side of the store, where Regina stood beside her three-year-old daughter, Mary.

"Hey, big sister, it's nice to see you today." Lyle gave Regina a hug, and Heidi did the same.

"Nice to see both of you, too. It's been a while." Regina smiled at Heidi. "How are things going with your cooking classes?"

"Quite well," Heidi replied. "It's fun teaching, and I've enjoyed getting acquainted with my students."

"All but one of Heidi's students are English," Lyle added.

Regina tipped her head. "Interesting. Who's the Amish person learning to cook?"

"Our friend Eli Miller." Lyle bent down and gave little Mary a hug. "How's my favorite niece?"

The child's blue eyes sparkled as she looked up at him with a dimpled smile.

Regina poked Lyle's arm. "She may not be your favorite niece much longer. I'm expecting another boppli, and it could be a *maedel*."

Heidi forced a smile and gave her sister-in-law another hug, even though the news cut deeply into her heart. "Congratulations, Regina." *If only it were me announcing a pregnancy.*

"Danki. Irvin's hoping for a boy, but a little sister would be nice for Mary."

"I'm sure." Heidi nodded.

As though he sensed her discomfort, Lyle gently squeezed Heidi's arm. She was certain her husband also wanted children. If only he wasn't so against adoption.

In an effort to take her mind off the situation, Heidi changed the subject. "Did you plant a garden this year, Regina?"

"Oh, jah." Regina gestured to her daughter. "Mary even planted some lettuce, carrots, and bean seeds in her own little garden plot."

"She'll enjoy watching the seeds sprout into plants," Lyle commented. "Maybe growing her own vegetables will make her want to eat them when they mature."

"I'm hoping." Regina took her daughter's hand. "We should be moving on now. I have a few more things to get, and then I need to go home and start supper."

"Okay. Hope to see you soon. Tell Irvin I said hello." Lyle bent down and tweaked Mary's nose. "You'll always be my number one niece, little one."

As Heidi and Lyle moved on through the store, she glanced over her shoulder. *Does Regina realize how fortunate she is to have Mary and now another child on the way?*

Dover

"You're kind of quiet this evening," Len commented as Charlene sat across from him at Sammy Sue's Barbeque, fidgeting with her napkin. Coming into their dinner date, she'd been set to ask if he'd be willing to move to some other town. Now she was beginning to lose her nerve. Charlene had hoped to discuss her situation with Heidi last Saturday but never got the chance. Now she wondered if she should bring up the topic at all.

Len reached across the table and took her hand. "Charlene, did you hear my question?"

"Umm. . .yes." She took a drink of water.

"Is something wrong?"

"Not exactly, but I do have a question."

"What is it?"

"Well, I've been wondering about something." Why was this so hard?

"And?" Len flapped his hand, as though encouraging Charlene to speak.

"I was wondering if you would consider moving after we get married."

Deep wrinkles formed across his forehead. "Move? Move where?"

She shrugged. "I. . .I'm not sure. Some other town, where we can start over."

"Why would we want to start over? You have your teaching job here in Dover, and I'm working for my dad. His business is doing quite well." Len looked at her earnestly. "The solar business is growing, and I can't leave now. I'm in a good position—one we'll both benefit from someday."

"Yes, but I'm sure we could find other jobs, and—"

He held up his hand. "Wait. What brought this on all of a sudden? You've never mentioned wanting to move before. I thought you loved teaching the kids here. You're getting to know their families, too."

"You're right, Len, and that would be the hard part." Charlene drank more water and set the glass down. "It's your mother. She does not like me, Len. If we stay here in Dover, we'll see your folks more often, and she'll always find fault with everything I say or do, like she already does."

Len shook his head briskly. "First of all, my mother doesn't find fault with everything you say or do."

"Yes, she does. You heard her curt remarks the last time we were at your parents' place for supper."

"I'll admit, sometimes Mom tends to speak when she should be silent, but I'll have a serious talk with her if you want."

Charlene's spine stiffened. "If I want? If you truly love me, Len, then you should have already put your mother in her place and stood up for me."

Len's face flamed. "I have stood up for you, and you're making too much of this. Once we're married, I'm sure Mom's attitude will change and you two will learn to get along."

"Learn to get along?" Charlene's voice rose. "I've tried to get along with her, Len. She doesn't want to get along with me, and I can't believe you're defending her."

Glancing around at the other tables, when the room grew quiet, Len leaned forward, putting his fingers to his lips. "Keep it down, Charlene. Everyone's looking at us."

Charlene drew a frustrated breath. Seconds later, when the restaurant's chatter began again, she took a quick look around. All seemed normal.

"Now listen, Charlene," Len spoke in a low voice. "I'm not defending my mother. I only meant. . ."

"Are you willing to move once we're married or not?" Now that she'd found the courage to bring up this topic, Charlene was determined to make him understand.

"No. My job is here, and if you ask me, you're overreacting to my mom. Anyway, how are you going to get close to her if we move away?"

"First of all, I am not overreacting. As I said before, your mother doesn't like me. If she has her way, she'll turn you against me." Charlene spoke through gritted teeth. Why didn't Len seem to get it? Was he blind where his mother was concerned?

"No, she won't turn me against you." Len looked around again. "And please, can we drop this? People are staring."

"You know what?" Charlene dropped her napkin over her half-eaten plate of food. "I've lost my appetite. Would you please take me home?"

"You're kidding, right?"

"I'm not."

"Come on, Charlene, you're blowing this whole thing out of proportion."

"You think so? Well, I'm beginning to wonder whether you love me or not."

"Of course I love you. I wouldn't have asked you to marry me if I didn't."

"But you don't love me enough to move out of Dover, right?"

Len lowered his gaze. "I don't see any reason to move, and it's unfair of you to expect me to. Especially now, when the business is booming."

Charlene folded her arms. "This discussion is getting us nowhere, and if you won't take me home, I'll call a cab."

"Okay, okay. I'll get the waitress to bring our bill, and then we can leave without finishing our meal. Will that make you happy?"

Charlene gave no reply. Her hands trembled and tears stung her eyes as she reached for her glass of water once more. It was hard to believe Len didn't love her enough to move. Well, if that's how he felt, there would be no marriage. If Len cared more about his job than honoring her request, he wasn't the man for Charlene.

Chapter 32

The next Wednesday afternoon, Charlene sat at the kitchen table, staring at her cell phone. She was off work for the summer, and school would not resume until early September.

"What to do? What to do? What to do?" Charlene drummed her fingers on the table. She'd already vacuumed her condo and washed the breakfast dishes. She had plenty of time now to pursue her photography hobby. Trouble was, she didn't feel like doing anything.

Charlene hadn't heard from Len since their dinner date last Saturday evening. Their conversation went round and round in her mind. He'd been upset when she asked him to move, but she'd hoped by now he would have thought it over and called to discuss things with her.

Should I call him? She shook her head and stubbornly pounded her fist on the table. *No. If Len wants to talk, he ought to call me.*

Charlene got up and poured herself a cup of coffee. She blew on it and took a tentative sip, trying to calm down as she reevaluated things. *Len's right, I enjoy my teaching job here. If we moved, I'd have to find another position at a new school. I wouldn't get to see my former students, either.*

Len had also been right in what he'd said about her students' families. Charlene had gotten to know the parents quite well. Whenever she saw one of them at the store, she always made it a point to say hello. Charlene felt a part of the community. She got along well with the other teachers at the school.

Maybe moving to another town isn't the best choice. I might not be happy living someplace else, and Len wouldn't be, either. It wasn't fair to ask him to leave his family's business, especially since it's growing and doing so well. What would I do, though, if we stayed in Dover? I'm not sure his mother will ever accept me as part of their family.

Tears welled in Charlene's eyes and dribbled down her cheeks. She either had to make a clean break with Len or improve her relationship with Annette. She reflected on the verse printed on the back of the apple cream pie recipe card Heidi gave her and the other students. Ephesians 4:32: *"And be ye kind one to another, tenderhearted, forgiving one another, even as God for Christ's sake hath forgiven you."*

I need to be kind to Len's mother, and forgive her for the put-downs she's aimed at me. Lord, thank You for Your forgiveness. Please help me show love to Annette.

Walnut Creek

Eli had no more than finished filling the bird feeders than a horse and buggy pulled into his yard. Surprised to see his mother, he stepped up to the hitching rail and secured her horse.

"Wie geht's?" Mom asked when she climbed down from the buggy.

"I'm doin' fine." Eli gave her a hug. "Wasn't expecting you to come by today. Are you here for any particular reason?"

She gave his arm a playful pinch. "Can't a *mamm* drop by to see her *sohn* for no particular reason other than to say hello?"

He grinned. "Course you can, and this son of yours is happy you dropped by. Feel free to do so anytime you like."

"Actually, I do have a reason for coming here." She reached into her buggy and took out a plastic container. "I baked peanut butter *kichlin* this morning. Thought you might like some."

"Might?" Eli thumped his stomach. "Of course I would. But if you keep bringing me desserts all the time, I'm gonna get fat." He took the offered cookies.

She shook her head. "As hard as you work in your shop and around the place here, I doubt you'll ever struggle with your weight."

"You're probably right. I never gained weight when Mavis was alive. She was an excellent cook."

Mom hugged him. "You still miss her, don't you?"

"Jah, but it's gotten easier since I met Loretta and her kinner. They're a lot of fun to be with."

Her brows furrowed. "Have you taken a personal interest in Loretta?"

"Well, I . . ."

"If you have, you need to nip it in the bud."

"What are you talking about, Mom? We're only friends."

"She's not one of us, Eli."

Eli clenched his teeth. He wasn't prepared to deal with this right now. Moving toward the picnic table, he took a seat on the bench and motioned for his mother to do the same. "You have nothing to worry about. Loretta's a nice person and, like me, she's lonely. I've enjoyed getting acquainted with her and also the children. Spending time with them has given me something to look forward to. In fact, I haven't felt this lighthearted since Mavis died."

Mom touched his arm. "I'm glad you've found someone you can relate to, and it sounds like you've made a good friend, but you need to be cautious. While you may not have serious feelings for Loretta, what if she has them for you?" Her brows lowered. "She could try to talk you into leaving our way of life and turning to the English world."

Eli shook his head vigorously. "I would never choose the English way of life, and I'm sure Loretta wouldn't expect me to, either."

Mom's face relaxed a bit as she squeezed his arm tenderly. "I'm thankful your daed and I raised a *schmaert* sohn."

Eli wasn't sure he was all that smart. Truthfully, he hadn't admitted to himself until now, but if Loretta were Amish, he could easily be interested in her beyond friendship.

———————⁓~⌾⁓~⌾⁓———————

Carefully, Heidi climbed the ladder to the hayloft. One of the barn cats had given birth to a batch of kittens yesterday, and Heidi wanted to check on them.

Following the sound of pathetic *mews*, she located the black-and-white kittens and their mother, whom Heidi had named Mittens.

Heidi made herself comfortable on a bale of hay and sat quietly, observing the kittens as they nursed. As adorable as they were to watch, a deep sadness came over her. She cupped her mouth, hoping to stifle the urge to cry. *Mittens can have* bopplin. *Why can't I? It isn't fair that I'll never experience motherhood firsthand.*

Giving in to self-pity, Heidi's guard was broken, and the tears flowed. *If only Lyle would agree to adopt. Why is he being so stubborn?* She had asked herself the same question so many times. When she'd convinced herself she could be happy without a baby and feel comfortable living a childless life, something always happened, causing Heidi to focus on her need to be a mother. The other day, hearing Regina was expecting another baby had reopened Heidi's emotional wounds. Avoiding the painful subject seemed to be the best way to deal with it, although the desire to raise a child was never far from her thoughts.

Heidi's contemplations halted when she heard the barn door creak open and click shut. Wiping her nose with the tissue she clutched, and drying the tears on her cheeks, Heidi crawled to the edge to go back down the ladder. Thinking Lyle was home from his errands, she was about to call out to him when she heard a muffled voice. Heidi remained quiet and still, and when she looked down, she was surprised to see it was Ron who'd entered the barn. Was he talking to Bobbins?

Heidi had no trouble recognizing the soft nickers of her husband's buggy horse. In all the times she'd had conversations with the animal, Bobbins always nickered at the right time, as though she understood everything being said. By now the horse was no doubt used to Ron, since he'd often mucked out her stall.

Heidi continued to listen but only caught bits and pieces of what Ron was saying. Being careful not to make any noise, she scooched on her stomach to the far side of the hayloft. When Heidi looked down, she saw Ron stroking Bobbins's neck.

He'd left their place over Memorial Day weekend and returned late last night, but this was the first time she'd seen Ron since he'd come back. Seeing his motor home parked in the usual spot this morning, Heidi had known he was there. Quite often Ron came up to the house in the mornings to have coffee with Lyle and ask what chores he wanted done. This morning, however, Ron remained in his motor home. Heidi assumed he was tired after the drive back from Columbus and had slept in. But why was he here in the barn now, talking to Bobbins?

What Heidi heard next made the tears flow again, only this time, it wasn't for herself. The heart-wrenching sight below caused Heidi to cover her mouth.

Standing beside the stall, Ron continued to rub the horse's neck, and as if she understood, Bobbins lowered her head. With his forehead pressed against the mare's head, Ron spoke again. "Oh, Bobbins, right now you're my only true friend."

The horse nickered in response, and Ron started to cry. His shoulders shook as the sobs grew louder and more intense.

Barely breathing, lest she be heard, Heidi kept listening as Ron poured out his grief.

"Dear God, please help me deal with this agony. I miss my brother so much. Seeing that wall again made me realize how much I've messed up in every area of my life." Ron's voice cracked. "Wish it had been me You took, instead of Mike. My brother was a good person and deserved to live. I don't deserve anything except trouble, because I've done nothing but hurt everyone in my life."

Heidi's heart went out to this poor soul. She wished she could offer Ron comfort, if only a listening ear. But he hadn't opened up and shared his pain with her—only a bit to Lyle. She certainly would not let him know she was eavesdropping on his conversation with Lyle's horse.

Sniffing, Ron shuffled over to a bale of hay and sat down, hands cradling his head.

Heidi remained motionless until, several minutes later, he left the barn. Ron truly was a troubled man. Did he for some reason blame himself for his brother's death? Or maybe it was God he was angry with. If only Ron would talk freely about his situation, perhaps she or Lyle could help. She wondered if Ron had read any of the scriptures she'd put on the back of the recipe cards. If he had, she hoped he might find comfort or direction through God's Word.

Closing her eyes, Heidi lifted a prayer on Ron's behalf. Then, brushing pieces of hay from her dress, she slowly descended the ladder.

———⚬❧⚬———

Canton

Kendra's hands grew moist as she drove up the driveway to her parents' home. She'd worked the early-afternoon shift at the restaurant and borrowed Dorie's car this evening. Coming here wasn't easy, but Kendra felt compelled to speak to her mother. She had chosen this particular evening because she was almost certain Dad would be at church for the monthly board meeting. When Kendra saw Heidi again, she was prepared to ask if she and Lyle would consider adopting her baby. But if there was the slightest chance. . .

She turned off the engine and leaned her forehead against the steering wheel. *If Mom agrees to let me move back home, maybe Dad could be persuaded.*

Kendra stepped out of the car and hurried up the porch steps, glancing around to see if the neighbors were watching. *I wonder if they've heard I was kicked out of my parents' house. Is the word out around the neighborhood that Bridget and Gary Perkins' oldest daughter got pregnant?*

She drew a deep breath and rang the doorbell. Several seconds later, the door opened and her sister Shelly appeared. She blinked rapidly. "I'm surprised to see you here, Kendra. Did you tell Mom and Dad you were coming?"

Kendra shook her head. "Dad's not here, I hope."

"No, he's at church for the board meeting."

"That's good, 'cause I need to talk to Mom." Kendra stepped quickly into the house. "It's important."

Shelly clutched the book in her hand as though holding it as a shield. "I hope you realize what you're doing. I'd be in trouble if Dad knew I'd talked to you, much less let you into the house."

"He won't know who let me in unless you tell him." Kendra glanced around. "Where's Mom?"

"She's in the kitchen with Chris, putting the clean supper dishes away."

"Okay, thanks." Kendra moved speedily in that direction, glancing over her shoulder as Shelly retreated to the living room.

When she entered the kitchen, she cleared her throat a couple of times. Mom turned around, and seeing Kendra, let out a gasp. The dish she held slipped out of her hand and fell on the floor. Luckily, it didn't break. "Kendra! What are you doing here?"

"Came to see you. There's something I need to say. Can I speak to you privately for a few minutes?"

Mom pursed her lips. "Your dad would not approve of you being here, Kendra."

"I'm well aware, but what I have to say is important."

Mom gave a huff then bent down to pick up the plate. She turned to Chris. "Would you please leave us alone?"

Glancing briefly at Kendra with a placid expression, Chris left the room.

Mom placed the plate in the sink then pulled out a chair at the table and sat down, gesturing for Kendra to do the same. "What do you need to talk to me about?"

"The baby." Kendra sat down and placed both hands on her stomach. "*My* baby."

Mom stared at her blankly, making little circles on the tablecloth with her finger.

Kendra rubbed her damp hands down the side of her jeans. There was no way to say this, except to blurt it right out. "I'm putting my baby up for adoption, unless..."

"That's a wise decision. Under the circumstances, I'm sure you're not able to properly care for a child on your own."

"No, I can't, but I hoped maybe..."

"What are you hoping for, Kendra? Did you think we would offer to help raise the child?" Mom spoke in a monotone voice.

Does she have no feelings at all? Kendra curled her fingers into the palms of her hands until her nails bit into the skin. *Dad sure did a number on her. Mom and I used to be close. It's as though she can't think for herself. Doesn't she care how much I'm hurting?*

Kendra decided to try a new approach. "Don't you want to be a part of your grandchild's life?"

"I would if it were under different circumstances." Mom blew out a quick breath. "I'm sorry you got yourself into such a predicament, but I will not go against your father's wishes, so there's really nothing I can do." Mom's hands flailed in front of her. "Your child will be better off with adoptive parents."

Kendra's mouth twisted as the muscles in her shoulders and neck tightened. At that moment, it hit her how truly alone she was in this. She had no other choice. Kendra could not be the mother of the baby she so desperately wanted to keep.

Leaping out of her chair, she turned and fled from the house without bothering to say goodbye to Mom or her sisters. Unless they came crawling to her, begging for forgiveness, she would never return to this place or make contact with anyone in her family again.

Chapter 33

Dover

Charlene had gotten up later than planned this morning and rushed around to get ready to leave for Heidi's fifth cooking class. She looked forward to going, because it would give her something meaningful and hopefully fun to do. Other teachers might be enjoying their time off from school, but Charlene had quickly become bored.

I wonder if Heidi will have another class after ours is finished in two weeks. If she does, maybe I should take it. At least learning to cook new things might help take my mind off the situation with Len. He still hadn't called her, and as the week had dragged on, Charlene had debated calling him.

She didn't know why it was so hard to make the first move, but since Len hadn't, Charlene had convinced herself that he no longer loved her.

If I don't hear from him by this evening, I'll make the call. She grabbed her purse, apron, and keys then headed for the door. Charlene's footsteps halted when her cell phone rang. She paused to check the caller ID, hoping it might be Len, but the number on the screen was not familiar. Normally, she would have ignored such a call, but her curiosity was piqued, so she answered. "Hello."

"Is this Charlene Higgins?"

Charlene didn't recognize the woman's voice. "Umm, yes, it is."

"I'm calling about the picture you submitted several weeks ago for a contest in the magazine I represent. I want to congratulate you. The photo you took of the mare and her foal won first place."

Stunned, Charlene could barely form a response. "Oh my. I never expected... I'm so surprised." She moved back to the kitchen and sank into a chair.

"Yes, and unless you already have one, we'll be sending you a copy of this month's issue, showing the picture you submitted on the cover."

"No, I don't have the magazine." Charlene hesitated but explained anyway. "I normally look at your magazine when I'm at the store, but I haven't purchased a copy in a while."

"I'm glad I had the opportunity to surprise you with this news. You'll also receive a two-year subscription to our magazine."

"Thank you." Charlene could hardly believe her good fortune. "It means so much that you thought the photograph I entered was good enough for the cover."

"It certainly is, and we thank you for entering. Now, don't forget, we have a contest every year, so keep your camera clicking."

After Charlene exchanged a bit more information with the woman, the phone call ended. She sat in stunned silence. This exciting news added a bright spot to her day. She couldn't wait to share it with someone.

Walnut Creek

When Kendra pulled into the Troyers' yard, she spotted Ron sitting on a camp stool outside his motor home. She'd come early, hoping to talk to Heidi before the others arrived. Since no other cars were here, unless Ron decided to come inside right away, it looked like she'd get the chance.

Kendra got out of the car, hurried up the steps, and knocked on the door. A few seconds later, Heidi greeted her.

"Hope it's okay I came early." Kendra smiled while Heidi held the door open for her.

"No one else is here yet, and I'm still setting things out in the kitchen, but you're welcome to visit while I finish up."

"Okay, thanks." Kendra entered the house and followed Heidi to the kitchen. "Is there anything I can do to help?"

"You can get out the sour cream, bacon, and onions." Heidi gestured to the refrigerator.

"Sure, no problem. What are we making this time?"

"German potato salad." Heidi pointed to the potatoes on the counter. "It's served warm instead of the traditional cold potato salad."

"Sounds good." Kendra went to the refrigerator and took out the ingredients; then she placed them on the table. "I've made a decision about my baby." She moved closer to where Heidi stood at the sink, washing the potatoes.

Heidi turned to look at her. "Oh?"

"My folks want nothing to do with me or the baby, and I'm not in a position to take care of a child by myself." Kendra paused to rub her forehead before she continued. "I've thought about it long and hard and will be putting the child up for adoption." She made direct eye contact with Heidi. "So I was wondering—well, hoping might be a better word. Would you and your husband be interested in adopting my baby?"

Heidi gasped and dropped the potato in the sink before bringing both hands up to her chest. "You. . .you want us to raise your baby?"

"Yeah, that's right. After getting to know you these last several weeks, I believe you would be a good mother, and—"

Heidi lifted her hand. "Wait a minute, Kendra. I don't think you fully understand what that would mean. If Lyle and I agreed to such an arrangement, your child would be raised Amish. When he or she got older, they might join the Amish church, as so many of our young people do."

"I've considered that and have no objections. In fact, the child will most likely be better off raised in a simpler fashion."

Heidi took a deep breath and released it slowly. "I can't give you an answer right now. I'll need to talk it over with Lyle."

"Of course." Kendra placed her hand on Heidi's arm. "I've given this a lot of thought. You and your husband are the parents I want for my baby."

After the other students arrived, it was difficult for Heidi to concentrate on the lesson. How could she think about teaching someone to make potato salad when a short time ago she'd been offered the chance to become a mother? She could hardly wait for Lyle to get home this evening so they could talk about Kendra's offer. Heidi closed her eyes briefly. *Dear Lord, please let my husband say yes.*

"Is something wrong with the way I cut my potatoes?" Charlene's question cut into Heidi's thoughts.

"Uh, no. Why do you ask?"

"You looked at them with a curious expression."

Heidi blinked. "I'm sorry. My thoughts were someplace else." She motioned to the ingredients set out. "Now that your boiled potatoes have been cut and placed in a bowl, you'll need to combine the dry ingredients, vinegar, sour cream, onions, and bacon pieces, making sure to stir them well." She waited for everyone to do as she instructed then said they should toss lightly, until the potatoes were coated well with the dressing.

"Do we eat the potato salad while it's still warm?" Loretta questioned.

Heidi nodded. "It's a bit different from traditional potato salad, but I personally believe it's every bit as good, and hope you'll enjoy it, too."

"It's not hard to make, either." Eli looked at Loretta and grinned. "Don't you agree?"

Smiling in response, she nodded.

Heidi noticed how Eli had taken a seat beside Loretta this morning. They'd conversed quite a bit, smiling and laughing whenever the other said something. It didn't take a genius to see the attraction between them. *Might there be a future for Eli and Loretta as a couple? If so, one of them would leave behind their way of life.* Heidi hoped Eli would not abandon the faith he'd belonged to for so many years. But if he should choose to leave, she felt sure Eli would adhere to his strong religious beliefs and not stray from his faith in God. It would be difficult for Loretta to become Amish, but not impossible.

It's none of my business. I have my own things to worry about. Redirecting her thoughts, Heidi glanced at Ron, to see if he might comment on the potato salad. However, he sat silently, toying with his wooden spoon. Was he still thinking about his brother who'd been killed in the Vietnam War?

Heidi had told Lyle what she'd overheard Ron saying to Bobbins in the barn, and Lyle had a talk with Ron the following day, but he wouldn't respond.

It wasn't good for a person to hold their feelings inside, but if Ron didn't want to talk about it, at least they'd tried. Their prayers would continue for him, in hopes that he would someday find peace.

Turning her attention to the task at hand, Heidi posed a question to her students. "I have some German sausages, as well as a package of hot dogs we can barbecue on the grill. How would you all like to join me for lunch outside?"

All heads nodded, even Ron's.

Eli chuckled. "And this time we won't be eating outdoors because I smell like a skunk."

"Did you ever solve the problem with the skunks in your yard?" Charlene asked.

"I believe so. At least I haven't seen or smelled any around my place lately." Eli gestured to his bowl of potato salad. "Think mine's as done as it's gonna get."

"It looks fine, Eli." Heidi smiled. "If everyone else is finished, we can move outside and start the grill."

"How are Conner and Abby?" Eli asked as he sat on a picnic bench beside Loretta.

"Doing well. Of course, those two are always full of energy, which keeps me on my toes."

"How about Donnelly? Is he settling in okay?"

She nodded. "The pup can be a handful at times, but the children enjoy him so much. I'm happy about that."

Eli leaned closer to Loretta and was about to whisper something when Charlene stood up and tapped a fork against her glass, making a tinkling sound.

"I have something I'd like to share with all of you." Charlene's dimples deepened when she smiled. "I took your advice, Kendra, and entered a photograph in the contest you told me about."

"To tell you the truth, I'd forgotten all about it. Did you enter the picture you showed us a few weeks ago?" Kendra asked.

"Yes. It was the one of the foal and mare," Charlene continued. "After I entered, I'd forgotten about it, too—until a lady from the magazine called me this morning."

"And?" Heidi waited, as did the rest of the group.

"Well. . ." Charlene held back.

"Oh, please," Loretta coaxed. "Don't keep us in suspense."

Even Ron seemed eager to hear, as he leaned slightly forward.

Charlene took a deep breath before announcing her news. "Well, I found out this morning that I won first place."

"Wow, that's great!" Kendra left her seat and gave Charlene a hug.

There were many congratulations, and a few more hugs.

"What did you win for coming in first place?" Ron questioned.

"The photo I submitted is on the front cover of this month's photography magazine." Charlene shook her head, as if still trying to comprehend it. "It's so weird. I usually stop by the stand and browse through the magazine when I'm at the store, but I haven't done it in a while. If I had seen the recent addition, I'd have discovered the picture of the mare and foal I'd taken."

"Is that all you get—just the satisfaction of having your picture on the cover?" Ron's brows furrowed. "Seems like a lame prize."

"It's an honor for me to have one of my photographs on the cover of a prestigious magazine, not to mention I'll get a free two-year subscription to the magazine."

"Now you won't have to stand in the store and read the magazine." Everyone laughed at Kendra's remark.

"You got that right," Charlene agreed.

"With your interest in photography, maybe this will open the door to other opportunities for you," Heidi commented.

"It might, but if it doesn't, I'm okay with that." Charlene sighed. "Having a photograph I took be good enough for the cover of this magazine is a dream I never expected to see fulfilled. It speaks volumes for me—more than money."

When things settled down, Heidi scurried about, making sure everyone had what they wanted. While everyone else engaged in conversation, Eli took the opportunity once again to ask Loretta a question. "Do you have plans for supper this evening?"

She shook her head.

"Would you and the children like to join me at Der Dutchman here in Walnut Creek? I could come by your place later this afternoon with my horse and open buggy. Then after we visit awhile, we'll head out to eat."

Loretta glanced around, as though worried someone might be listening. "Since Sugarcreek is a ways for you to go, how about I drive my car and meet you at Der Dutchman?"

Eli dropped his gaze to the table. He'd hoped for some extra visiting time with Loretta and the children before they went out for supper. "How would it be if we ate at one of the restaurants in Sugarcreek? It would be closer to your house, and I believe you and the children might enjoy riding in my open buggy."

"It sounds like fun. Once Abby and Conner find out you're coming, they'll be excited. Don't be surprised if they're waiting on the porch, like the last time you came by."

Eli smiled. Despite his mother's warning, his yearning to get better acquainted with Loretta and her children increased. If he had his way, he'd drop by to see them every day this coming week. But with work piling up in his shop, he wouldn't have time for that.

Chapter 34

Sugarcreek

Noticing how quiet her children had become, Loretta glanced over her shoulder. The motion of Eli's buggy must have put them to sleep, for Conner's head leaned against his sister's arm, and both children's eyes were closed. Since neither Abby nor Conner had taken a nap today, it was nice to see them resting. Hopefully, they would both be in good moods when they got to the restaurant.

"Traveling in an open buggy is fun." Loretta looked over at Eli and smiled. "It reminds me of riding in my dad's convertible many years ago."

"My friend Dennis had a convertible when we were going through our *rumschpringe*. We enjoyed running around in it. Of course," Eli added with a snicker, "for me, it wasn't nearly as much fun as taking my horse out with the open buggy."

"It is kind of nice to travel at a more leisurely pace." Loretta motioned to the trees alongside the road. "While driving my minivan, all these lovely trees wouldn't be much more than a blur."

Eli grinned. "Don't believe I've ever met an English woman who sees things the way you do. I find it refreshing."

"Must be my Amish heritage."

"What?" Eli's mouth opened slightly.

"My grandparents were Amish but have since passed away. Unfortunately, I didn't get to be with them much because my parents never joined the Amish church. Mom and Dad moved from Lancaster,

Pennsylvania, to Cleveland, Ohio, soon after they were married. They live in Pittsburgh now."

When Eli shook the reins and made a clucking noise, the horse began trotting a little faster. "Well, no wonder you're different. The Amish way is in your blood." He cocked his head to one side, looking at her through narrowed eyes. "How come you never mentioned this before?"

She pursed her lips. "I wasn't sure how you'd respond."

"What do you mean?"

"I was worried you might frown on my dad and mom moving away from their Amish families and choosing the English way of life."

Eli shook his head. "It's not my place to cast judgment on others. Your folks must have had their reasons. Besides, not everyone raised Amish decides to join the church and remain part of the Amish culture. We're all given the opportunity to choose. Course," he quickly added, "most Amish parents are disappointed when one of the children doesn't join."

"It's understandable. In all honesty, a part of me has always wondered what my life would have been like if my parents had joined the Amish church. I wish I knew their reasons, but it's never been talked about, and I wasn't sure if my folks would be upset if I asked."

"Did they teach you some of the Pennsylvania Dutch language? Is that how come you know a few words?"

"No, I learned those words from my grandparents when we went to visit them one summer. Wish I could have known them better, though." Loretta fiddled with the straps on her purse, wondering if she should say more. "Umm... I've been wondering about something, Eli."

"What's that?"

"How hard would it be for someone like me to join the Amish church?"

His brows shot up. "Are you serious?"

She gave a decisive nod.

"A few English people have made the transition, but it's difficult, due to the language barrier, plus giving up modern conveniences and following the church rules."

"I believe I could give up modern things, and I am interested in raising Abby and Conner in the kind of life where the emphasis is on God and family, rather than gaining material things."

Eli smiled. "If you're serious about this, I'd be happy to help you take the necessary steps to make the transition."

"Yes, yes. I'd appreciate it." Loretta didn't admit it to Eli, of course, but in addition to seeking a simpler way of life, if she joined the Amish church, it would open the door for a possible relationship with him. That is, if he was interested. So far, Eli hadn't given any indication that he cared for her as more than a friend.

———— ◦ ————

Dover

The muscles in Charlene's shoulders felt strained as she stood on the deck at the back of her condo. For the last fifteen minutes, she had been holding her camera in the same position, hoping for a close-up picture of a hummingbird. She'd hung a feeder out the other day after seeing a couple of hummers flitting around an azalea bush behind her place, but so far she hadn't seen any at the feeder. *Oh well, maybe another time. I can't stand here all day.*

Charlene took a seat in one of the deck chairs and leaned against the cushion behind her head. She hadn't called Len yet, and the longer she put it off, the more difficult it became. What if he didn't want to talk to her? Maybe in his mind, their relationship was already over.

But if I don't call, how will I know? Charlene rose from her chair and headed to the kitchen, where she'd left her cell phone. Punching in the first three numbers, she paused when the doorbell rang. Placing her phone on the table, Charlene went to the door and leaned toward the peephole to look out. She gasped, seeing Len standing there. With no hesitation, she opened the door.

"Mind if I come in?" Rubbing the back of his neck, he shuffled his feet and gave her a sheepish grin.

"Of course not. I was punching in your phone number when you rang the doorbell." She opened the door wider, and he stepped inside.

Len handed Charlene her ecru-colored shrug. "You left your sweater in my car the last time we were together, and there's something wrapped inside."

Charlene looked down. "Our date did end abruptly."

Len pointed to her sweater. "Go ahead; open it."

Charlene unfolded the shrug and was surprised to discover a floating frame—the kind used for protecting and displaying magazines. Framed inside was the photography magazine, exhibiting the winning cover. "How did you get this?"

"Saw it on the magazine rack at the drugstore." Len smiled. "Congratulations!"

"Thank you." It touched Charlene that he would go to the trouble of framing this special edition.

"It was worth getting my car banged up so you could get this great shot and win the competition. I'm proud of you, honey."

Her throat constricted, and she swallowed hard. He'd called her *honey*, and it nearly melted her heart.

Len took a step toward her. "The magazine isn't the only reason I came by, though."

"Oh?" Her hand trembled as she placed the frame and sweater on the entry table. Did she dare hope they could work things out? Charlene held her breath as Len clasped her hands.

"I'm sorry for not calling you since our disagreement. Believe me, it was a struggle not to, but I needed time to think things over." Pausing, Len cleared his throat. "I love you, Charlene, and I don't want anything, or anyone, to come between us. Seeing you standing here now, I don't know how I stayed away this long." He squeezed her hands more snugly. "I guess what they say about 'absence makes the heart grow fonder' is fact, not fiction."

"You've always had my heart, Len." Unconsciously, she parted her lips.

"Ditto. I want to tell you something else, too. I've come to a decision."

"Oh? What's that?"

"If you really feel relocating is the best thing for you, then I'm willing to move. In fact, I'll start looking for another job right away. You just need to tell me where you'd like to go."

Love swelled in Charlene's heart, and with no hesitancy, she rushed into his arms. "I've been thinking things over, too, and it wouldn't be fair to ask you to give up your job in the family business. I don't want to give up my teaching position here, either."

"But what about my mother?"

"I need to quit worrying and make the best of the situation with her."

Len pressed his forehead against hers. "I don't want you to make the best of the situation, honey. I'll talk with Mom again and try to make her understand how hurtful she's been toward the woman I love and plan to marry." His lips brushed hers with a tender kiss. "Now, how about going out to dinner with me so we can make up for our last dinner date that ended on a sour note?"

She took several deep breaths, savoring the moment. "I have a better idea. Let's eat here, where we can talk without the distraction of other people and restaurant noise."

"Good idea. Should I make a call to get some pizza delivered?"

Charlene shook her head. "Tonight, I'd like to fix something special for you. It's a simple yet tasty meal the Amish enjoy."

Len's eyebrows squished together. "I'm confused."

"I have been waiting to tell you this, but every other Saturday since the first part of April, I've been attending cooking classes at an Amish home in Walnut Creek. Heidi Troyer, the woman who teaches the classes, is an excellent cook. She's helped me feel more confident in the kitchen." Charlene squeezed Len's arm playfully. "You can be my first guinea pig."

He lifted his gaze toward the ceiling. "So I've gone from being your future husband to a guinea pig now, huh?"

She giggled. "It was only a figure of speech. I am anxious to see what you think of haystack, though."

His brows lifted a bit. "Haystack? Will we be eating a meal or harvesting a field?"

Charlene felt lighthearted since the worry had been lifted off her shoulders. "You're silly." She gave his stomach a gentle poke. "The way to a man's heart is through his belly, you know."

Len placed Charlene's hand against his chest. "You'll always have my heart, too, sweetheart."

Charlene didn't resist when he pulled her close for another kiss. When the kiss ended, she linked arms with Len. "Okay now, future husband, come to my kitchen, and I'll show you my newfound culinary skills."

<hr />

Walnut Creek

Heidi paced the kitchen floor, waiting for Lyle to come home. He'd gone to another all-day auction, and she had been counting the hours until his return.

Ever since Kendra's offer to let them adopt her baby, Heidi had thought of little else. She had no idea how she'd even made it through the cooking class today. Heidi hoped and prayed Lyle would be willing to adopt the baby, because she felt sure this was the answer to her prayers. All they would need to do was find an adoption lawyer to draw up the papers to make it legal. Hopefully, his fee wouldn't be too high, but at this point, she would gladly borrow the money if she had to, so she and Lyle could raise a child together.

"I'll teach more cooking classes to help with the expense," she murmured as she took out a loaf of bread for bacon and tomato sandwiches.

"There you go—talking to yourself again." Lyle stepped up behind Heidi, turned her to face him, and gave her a warm, gentle kiss.

"You startled me. I didn't hear you come in." She spoke breathlessly.

"Had my driver drop me off by the phone shack so I could check for messages. That's probably why you didn't hear his car." Lyle stroked Heidi's arms, sending chills up her spine. "So, what's this about teaching more cooking classes?"

"If we need extra money I'm willing to teach additional classes. Maybe every Saturday, instead of every other week."

"Heidi, there's no reason for that. I'm making a decent living, and there's nothing we need extra money for right now."

She sucked in her lower lip. "There would be, if we had a boppli."

"What are you saying, Heidi?" His eyebrows lifted. "Has God given us a miracle? Are you expecting a boppli?"

"No, but we've been offered the chance to adopt."

"How can it be? We haven't contacted an adoption agency."

Heidi pulled out a chair at the table. "Let's take a seat, and I'll explain the situation."

Lyle hesitated at first but did as she suggested. Heidi took the seat beside him.

"Kendra, the young expectant mother who attends my class, arrived early today so we could talk before the others got here." Heidi reached for Lyle's hand. "She wants us to adopt her baby."

He sat quietly for several seconds then slowly shook his head. "It's out of the question, Heidi."

"How come?"

"We don't know much about this girl, and besides. . ."

"I know she wants us to raise her child."

"We've discussed adoption before, and I've made myself clear on the topic. I don't feel it's right for us." His voice was steady and lower pitched than normal.

"But why? You've never really explained your reasons." Heidi could barely speak around the burning thickness in her throat.

"Jah, I have explained, Heidi—many times. Maybe you just weren't listening. If it were God's will for us to have children, you would have gotten pregnant by now."

"Perhaps God sent Kendra to my cooking class for a reason. Maybe this is His will."

Lyle's shoulders pushed back as he shook his head. "No, Heidi. I don't believe this is the way."

"Why not? Kendra must believe we would make good parents to have asked if we'd raise her baby."

"That's just it—*her baby*. Would we ever feel like the child was completely ours?"

"I believe so."

He shook his head once again, more firmly this time. "It's not meant for us to raise someone else's child." Lyle's hands touched his chest. "It hurts to think I'm not enough for you."

"Oh, no, Lyle, it's not that at all." Heidi clasped his arm. "You mean the world to me, Lyle. I only want us to have a family." Heidi's throat constricted as tears sprang to her eyes.

"I've always thought we were a family." Lyle placed his hand on hers. "You're all I need."

When he put it that way, it was hard to know how to respond. Heidi wanted to say Lyle was all she needed, but the words seemed to be stuck in her throat. She loved him with all her heart, but so many times—especially during the long hours he was gone—loneliness set in, and her arms ached to hold a baby. Why couldn't he understand her feelings and share in the desire to have a child?

"All right, I understand," she murmured, struggling not to break down. "I won't bring it up again." Heidi pushed her chair back and stood. "I'd best get the sandwiches made so we can eat."

Lyle got up from his chair. "While you're doing that, I'll take a quick shower." He gave her a peck on the cheek. "I love you, Heidi."

"Love you, too."

When Lyle left the room, Heidi turned toward the refrigerator to get the bacon and tomatoes. She dreaded seeing Kendra again and having to tell her she'd need to find someone else to adopt her child. Her shoulders drooped as she lowered her head. The disappointment Heidi felt penetrated her soul.

Chapter 35

Sugarcreek

Perspiration beaded on Loretta's forehead as she crouched beside her garden to pull weeds. It had been four days since she'd told Eli she might be interested in joining the Amish church, but she hadn't heard from him since. *Maybe he's changed his mind about helping me. Or perhaps he's been too busy with work.*

Sitting up from her bended position to wipe her forehead, she noticed Sam next door, walking up and down the rows in his raspberry patch. About the same moment, he glanced her way and gave her a neighborly wave.

"How are the berries doing?" Loretta hollered.

"Should be ready to pick in another week or so. I'll see you get some."

"Thanks, Sam. I'm looking forward to it."

Sam was such a good neighbor. Loretta smiled when she saw him come to the edge of the yard as Abby and Conner took their dog over to greet him. Then she noticed Sam take something from his pocket and hand it to each of the kids. Abby and Conner ran over to Loretta, with Donnelly nipping at their heels. Sam gave another wave then headed toward his house.

"Look what Mr. Sam gave us." Abby held out a five-dollar bill, and Conner did the same. "He said we can use the money to buy Donnelly something."

Conner's wide-eyed expression revealed his excitement as he repeated what his sister said.

"Better let me hang on to that for you. Did you both remember to thank him?" Loretta was pleased when they both bobbed their heads before handing her the money and running off to play with the dog again. She slipped the bills in her skirt pocket then went back to weeding her garden, humming a merry tune.

"Only one more row to do, and then I'm done." Loretta spoke out loud. As she looked toward the sky, she added, "Oh Rick, I hope I'm making you proud, raising our children the best way I know." As if on cue, a bluebird landed on a nearby branch, singing in soft, warbling tones. This might have meant nothing to most people, but to Loretta it was special, since bluebirds had been Rick's favorite birds. She felt as though God sent the bird to give her a sense of assurance that she was doing right by her children.

With renewed energy, Loretta set back to weeding and thought about what to have for lunch. Today would be a good day to pack the children's lunch so they could eat under the big tree. Conner and Abby always enjoyed having a picnic, even here in the yard. The fresh air did them good, too.

Loretta sat up on her knees to watch Abby and Conner trying to teach Donnelly how to fetch a stick. *Could my children adjust to the Amish way of life? How would they feel about wearing Amish-style clothes?* They were still young, so learning a new language would probably be easier for them than it would Loretta. But with help, she felt sure she could learn. Giving up modern conveniences shouldn't be too difficult for the children or Loretta, although turning in her van for a horse and buggy might prove to be quite a challenge. Perhaps she could ease into the simple life—giving up a few things at a time to see how it went. Taking it slow might be a better adjustment for the children, too.

"Mommy, come look at Donnelly!" Abby's excited tone drew Loretta's thoughts aside once more. "See how he goes after the stick?"

Loretta turned her head in the direction Abby pointed. Sure enough, the pup bounded across the yard to fetch the stick. Donnelly's tail wagged, and he let out a *woof* after dropping the stick at Conner's feet. Conner cheered and Abby clapped. Loretta did the same.

"Kids, don't forget to praise Donnelly, so he will know he did well."

"Good boy!" Abby patted the dog's head, while Conner gave Donnelly a hug.

"Now you should teach him how to sit or speak," Loretta coached. "I'll go inside and get the doggy treats. When he does what you ask, you can reward him with one."

Abby and Conner were all smiles. What a joy to see her children so happy. They would be even happier when she surprised them with a picnic lunch.

While the kids continued to work with their pup, Loretta went inside and packed their lunch. She hoped as Conner and Abby grew into adults, they would always find something to be joyous about, especially the little things in life.

———— ⚬⌁⚬ ————

Walnut Creek

Heidi clipped a pair of Lyle's trousers to the clothesline and paused to rub her throbbing forehead. She'd woken up with a headache this morning—no doubt from lack of sleep and clenching her teeth. Ever since Lyle had refused Kendra's request to adopt her baby, Heidi felt depressed. She dreaded telling Kendra Lyle's decision. Surely, the young mother-to-be would look for another adoptive couple as soon as she found out, or contact an adoption agency.

It wasn't right to feel this way, but Heidi could barely look at Lyle without feeling bitter. In her mind, he was being unreasonable and selfish. Didn't he comprehend how much love they had to offer a child? Truth was, Heidi had enough love in her heart for both of them.

Keeping busy helped some this week. In fact, she tore into housework like never before. One day, she'd cleaned out the closets.

Another time, Heidi did the kitchen cabinets. The floors were so spotless and shiny she could almost see her reflection. But even with all the work, her thoughts returned to the situation with Kendra.

Several birds chirped in the trees nearby as Heidi forced herself to concentrate on hanging the rest of the laundry. When she finished the chore, she picked up the empty basket and hauled it into the house.

Thirsty after being outside in the heat, Heidi went to the sink and filled a glass with cold water. Popping an aspirin in her mouth, she swallowed it down. *I hope this takes hold quickly.*

Glancing out the kitchen window, she noticed Lyle talking to Eli near the barn. Eli's bike rested against the fence. *When did he arrive?* With her thoughts so internally focused, Eli could have been talking with Lyle for over an hour, and she wouldn't have noticed.

Normally, Heidi would have gone out to say hello and offer the men some refreshments. Not today, though. She wasn't in the mood to converse with anyone, much less act as a joyful, gracious hostess.

Sighing, she turned away from the window and wet a paper towel, holding it against her forehead. *Think I'll go to my room and take a nap.*

⎯⎯⎯⎯⎯⎯ ༄ ⎯⎯⎯⎯⎯⎯

"Got a question for you. Would ya happen to know anyone who has an easygoing buggy horse they might want to sell or loan?" Eli asked, moving closer to Lyle.

Lyle quirked an eyebrow. "What's wrong with your buggy horse? Is he havin' a problem?"

"Nope. Timmy's good, and so is Mavis's horse, Blossom. The horse is for a friend of mine, and I think she'll eventually need one."

"Anyone I know?"

Eli's ears warmed. "It's, uh, for Loretta Donnelly."

"Isn't she one of Heidi's students?"

"Jah."

Lyle leaned against the barn, near the slightly open door. "Why would she need a buggy horse?"

"Loretta's thinking about joining the Amish church, and I'm gonna teach her how to drive a horse and buggy. If she catches on, she'll probably want her own horse and carriage."

"Wow! Does Heidi know about this?"

Eli shrugged. "Loretta may have told her. I'm not sure, but I've said nothing to anyone else. I found out about her desire to seek a simpler life when we were together last Saturday evening." He removed his straw hat, flapping it at a persistent fly buzzing around his head. "I took Loretta and her kinner out to supper."

"Ah, well, did you tell her how difficult the transition would be?"

"Jah, but it's not impossible. See, Loretta's grandparents were Amish, so she already has a connection."

"What about her parents? Weren't they Amish, too?"

Eli shook his head. "They never joined the church. Guess they preferred to go English."

Lyle eyed Eli with a curious expression. "Is there something going on between you and Loretta? Something more than casual friendship?"

"Sure is gettin' warm out." Eli felt sweat trickling down the back of his neck and reached up to swipe it away.

"Umm...we weren't discussing the weather." Lyle's shoulders lifted almost up to his ears. "But if you don't want to talk about Loretta, it's fine by me."

"I. . .well. . .maybe I should." Eli licked his parched lips and swallowed hard. He hoped he could express his feelings without stumbling over every word. "Well, actually, there could be more if she became Amish, although I haven't expressed my feelings to Loretta yet. I don't want to rush things and need to be sure she has feelings for me before I blurt anything out."

A slow smile spread across Lyle's face. "Heidi's had an inkling about you two, and I guess she was right." He gave Eli's shoulder a hefty squeeze. "Good for you. I hope things work out."

Eli lowered his head a bit. "This doesn't mean I've forgotten about Mavis. She'll always hold a place in my heart."

"I understand. You two had a special relationship."

Eli nodded. "Same as you and your fraa do."

Lyle looked away then back at Eli. "There is only one thing coming between me and Heidi right now."

"Can't imagine anything getting between the two of you. I hope everything's okay. Or am I bein' too nosy?"

"She wants to adopt a baby, and I do not." Lyle closed his eyes briefly, drawing a deep breath. "I believe if God wanted us to have kinner, Heidi would be able to conceive."

"Hmm. . ." Eli folded his arms, clasping both wrists. "Children are a blessing, and fatherhood is something I've always longed for. If Mavis had lived, we may have considered adoption."

"Really?"

"Jah, only, thanks to that hit-and-run driver, her life was snuffed out before we had a chance to talk about it." Eli's toes curled inside his boots, reliving the instant he'd been notified of his wife's untimely death. No moment could have been worse. His whole world seemed to fall apart. Until he'd met Loretta, Eli had never thought he could even consider falling in love again, much less with an English woman. Now if he just knew how Loretta felt about him.

———————⸎———————

Grabbing a broom, Ron began knocking down cobwebs in the barn when he heard voices outside. Setting the broom aside, he moved toward the door to see who it was. When he spotted Lyle and Eli outside, Ron stepped back, hoping they hadn't seen him and wouldn't pull him into their conversation. He'd had another nightmare last night about the deer, an old silo, and a soldier holding a bayonet. No way would he be good company today. In fact, Ron wasn't sure he could speak a pleasant word to anyone right now.

After all these years, why was he still tormented by memories of the war that took his brother's life and so many others? He was reminded once again that thousands of families had been affected in the same manner. Ron wondered how they coped and moved forward.

No air stirred in the barn, and a cold drink of water would surely taste good right now. Swatting at an annoying bee, Ron's ears perked up when he heard Eli talking to Lyle about his wife's death.

"Every time I drive past that old silo on County Road 172, I think of how Mavis was killed that evening, a year ago on April 24." Eli paused and cleared his throat. "I can't understand how the person who hit her bike could have left the scene of the accident and never called for help or reported it to the sheriff."

"It's hard to believe anyone could do such a thing." Lyle's voice rose a bit. "It's even harder to understand why the law never found out who was responsible."

Ron froze in place, his heart beating so hard he thought his chest might explode. He'd been driving that road last year, on the evening of April twenty-fourth, and remembered seeing the silo seconds before he'd hit a deer. At least he'd thought it was a deer. The silo had been in his nightmares as well, but until now, he'd never thought much about this detail.

A sudden coldness hit the core of his being. He'd suffered a flashback from the war moments before the impact, but kept going, since he saw no point in stopping to report a dead deer.

Oh no! Ron's hands seemed to rush toward his mouth of their own accord, as he stifled a gasp. *I hit a woman, not a deer. It was me. I killed Eli's wife.*

Sickened by this revelation, Ron dashed to the back of the barn, grabbed a bucket, and threw up. As he leaned against the wall for support, Ron tried to catch his breath. With nothing left in his stomach, dry heaves took over, making him lurch to the point where his throat felt raw. The knowledge of what he had done to poor Eli's wife was far worse than any nightmare he could imagine. The right thing to do would be to turn himself in, but the thought of spending years in jail with hardened criminals was too much to bear. If only the earth would open up and swallow him. It would be a far better punishment than a lifetime in jail. Wishful thinking wouldn't make it happen, though. Ron needed to get far away from here and, if it were possible, forget what happened.

Chapter 36

A s Heidi cleared the table after eating lunch by herself, she thought about the rest of her afternoon and what she would do to keep busy. Soon after Eli left on his bicycle, Lyle went to a dental appointment. He'd told Heidi he planned to grab a bite for lunch when he got to Mt. Hope, where he had some business to take care of concerning an upcoming auction.

One could probably hear a hairpin drop with the quietness of the house. Heidi found herself at a loss for something to do. At least the nap did her some good, and the headache was gone.

"Wish I could get away for a few days," she murmured. "Maybe go over to Geauga County and visit with Mom and Dad." Since Heidi's next cooking class wasn't for another week and a half, she couldn't come up with a reason not to go, unless Lyle preferred she stay home. When he returned this evening, she would ask if he'd mind if she hired a driver so she could visit her folks.

Some time away might be good for me. She glanced at the calendar on the kitchen wall. *If I share my situation with Mom, she might help me deal with what I'm going through right now.*

Heidi put the dishes in the sink and glanced out the window. It surprised her to see Ron's RV pulling out of the driveway and onto the main road.

I wonder where he's going. Maybe Ron is low on food or supplies and is heading to the store. Since Ron's motor home was running well again, he went in and out of their place, although he usually mentioned to either Lyle or Heidi where he planned to go.

Heidi filled the sink with warm water and added detergent. *I'll bet he told Lyle he'd be going out.*

A short time later, Heidi was surprised when she spotted Kendra getting out of her car. Because of her job, she usually didn't stop by on a weekday—especially at this time of the day.

Heidi dried her hands and went to answer the door. "I'm surprised to see you, Kendra. Did you get off work early today?"

Kendra shook her head, tears gathering in the corners of her eyes. "I lost my job at the restaurant. The person I've been filling in for came back, so now I'm once again out of a job."

"I'm so sorry." Heidi gave her a hug.

Kendra sniffed. "Guess I should have expected it. Nothing ever works out well for me."

Heidi cringed. *When Kendra finds out Lyle and I won't be adopting her baby, she'll be even more disappointed.*

"Would you like to come in and have a glass of iced tea?" Heidi offered. "I made some fresh this morning."

"Sounds good." Kendra followed Heidi to the kitchen and took a seat at the table.

Heidi took the jug of cold tea from the refrigerator, put ice in two glasses, and poured some for both of them. *Should I tell Kendra right out about not adopting her baby, or wait till she asks?*

Heidi didn't have to wait long for Kendra to bring up the subject. "Have you talked to your husband about adopting my baby?"

Heidi sat in the chair across from her, wishing she could vanish in thin air when she saw the hopeful look in Kendra's eyes. "Yes, I have spoken to Lyle, but he feels it's not the right thing for us to do."

"How come?"

Heidi swallowed hard, hoping her swirling emotions wouldn't spiral out of control. "Lyle believes if it were meant for us to be parents, I would be able to get pregnant."

Kendra's brows furrowed as she pinched the bridge of her nose.

"If every person who couldn't bear children felt the same way, no baby would ever get adopted."

Heidi couldn't argue with that, but at the same time, she wouldn't say anything negative about her husband. Lyle was the head of their home, and whether Heidi agreed with him or not, she must accept his decision.

Kendra's chin quivered as her eyes filled with fresh tears. "I'm sorry to hear it. I truly thought, and still do, that you would be the best choice for my baby." She placed one hand on her stomach, rubbing in circles. "Guess now I'll have to look for someone else who might want my baby, or contact a lawyer who specializes in adoptions."

"You could also get in touch with an adoption agency. I'm sure there are some listed in the phone book or on the Internet." It hurt to make the suggestion, but Heidi wanted to give Kendra some positive feedback.

"Yeah, I'll check on those options." Kendra gulped down her tea then pushed the chair aside and stood. "I'd better get going. My friend let me borrow her car today because I told her I'd be stopping by to see you. But she'll be getting off work soon, and I need to pick her up."

Heidi left her seat and walked Kendra to the door. "This may not be much consolation, but I wish things had worked out differently." She slipped her arm around Kendra's trembling shoulders, wishing there was more she could say.

"Yeah, me too." Sniffing, Kendra turned and hurried out the door.

Struggling to squelch the sob rising in her throat, Heidi shuffled into the living room and lowered herself to the couch. She sat several seconds, staring at the floor, before grabbing the throw pillow and giving in to her tears. One thing was certain: her future was clear. She would never become a mother.

────── ·❦· ──────

Sugarcreek

Eli grinned when he pulled his horse and buggy into Loretta's yard and spotted Abby and Conner frolicking on the front lawn with their puppy. He'd no sooner secured his horse to a post than the children ran up to his buggy. Eli was thankful they'd held back until he had the horse safely tied. Of course, with Loretta sitting on the porch, he felt sure she would have warned them.

"Mr. Eli, come see what our puppy can do," Abby shouted.

Conner clung to Eli's hand. "Donnelly sits. Donnelly speaks. Donnelly—"

"Plays fetch," his sister interrupted.

Eli chuckled. "It sounds like you two have been quite busy teaching your dog some tricks. I'm anxious to see for myself what little Donnelly can do."

Conner ran over and grabbed a stick. He threw it across the yard, and the pup chased after it. Tail wagging, Donnelly dropped the stick at Eli's feet.

"Oh, so you want me to play now, do ya?" Eli bent down and picked it up. Then he gave the thin piece of wood a hefty toss. Eli laughed, and the children jumped up and down when the dog leaped into the air and caught the stick in his mouth.

"All right you two, settle down now." Loretta called the children to the porch. "Here you go. I packed a surprise lunch, so why don't you go over to the big tree and have a picnic?"

"Oh boy, a picnic just for me and Conner," Abby squealed. "Thank you, Mommy."

"I'm hungry." Conner thumped his stomach.

"While Mr. Eli and I talk, you and your sister can eat what's in the picnic basket." Loretta handed the wicker basket to Abby. It was one they had used many times when Rick was alive. "Conner, you can carry this tablecloth and help Abby spread it over the grass to sit on."

"Okay, Mommy." After Loretta gave him the checkered tablecloth, Abby took her little brother by the hand, and they ran toward the mighty oak, with Donnelly at their heels.

"Have fun!" Eli called.

"We will, Mr. Eli." Conner turned and waved.

Eli joined Loretta on the porch. "Those two are sure well behaved. You've done a good job with them, Loretta."

"Believe me, I try." She smiled. "My husband was a good father. In fact, he set a fine example for all of us."

Eli quickly changed the subject, so he wouldn't end up feeling sorry for himself because he had no children. "I came by to tell you what I found out about the things you'll need to do in order to become Amish."

Her eyes brightened. "Wonderful! I'm anxious to hear, but before you explain, would you like something cold to drink? Oh, and have you had lunch? I made two extra sandwiches."

Not one to pass on an invitation that included food, he gave an eager nod. "That'd be nice."

Loretta excused herself. When the door closed behind her, Eli sat quietly, listening to the squeals of laughter as Abby and Conner sat on the tablecloth, enjoying their picnic lunch. *If I married Loretta, I could help raise her children.* He removed his straw hat and placed it on his knees. *Now, don't hitch the buggy before the horse. Loretta would have to be Amish before I could consider asking her to marry me. And if she does decide to join the church, I'll need to make sure we truly are compatible.* Eli couldn't deny the definite attraction he felt, but he didn't know Loretta well enough yet to be sure it was love.

Loretta came out of the house and handed him a glass of lemonade and a sandwich. She also had one for herself. "Here you go. Hope you like ham and cheese."

"Danki. I like most any kind of sandwich." Eli bowed his head for silent prayer. It pleased him when she did the same.

When he finished praying and opened his eyes, Loretta smiled and took a sip of lemonade. "I'm eager to hear what you have to tell me."

"One of the things you'll need to do to become Amish is learn the Pennsylvania Dutch language." He shifted in his chair. "That might be the most difficult part."

"I believe you're right. What else, Eli? I want to know everything that will be expected of me." She leaned slightly forward with an eager expression.

"Well, first off, one of the ministers in our church said you should live in an Amish community for at least a year." He winked at her. "Think you've already covered that one, since you live here in Sugarcreek where there are many Amish folks."

Loretta moved her head slowly up and down. "Rick and I came here because the community is slow paced and peaceful. I've always felt comfortable around my Amish neighbors." She paused to take a bite of her sandwich. "What are some other things I'll need to do?"

Eli held up three fingers. "Attend Amish church services every other Sunday. If you'd like to attend church in my district, I'll act as your go-between to introduce you to the church and its members."

"I would like that. At least then I'd know someone and wouldn't feel like a stranger."

"Also, if you decide to seek employment, it would be best if you found a job working among Amish people. It'll help you understand our work principles and get more familiar with Amish customs."

"If my husband's insurance money holds out, I plan to get a job once Abby starts school. I'll either hire a babysitter for Conner, or put him in preschool or daycare. Of course, any of those choices will cost money."

"I'm sure one of the Amish women in this area would be willing to watch the kids for a reasonable price while you're at work." *But if you married me, you wouldn't have to work outside the home.* Eli kept his thoughts to himself. It was too soon to speak of marriage.

Loretta looked out in the yard. "Just listen to those two." Smiling, she shook her head. "Ever since you gave Abby a whistling lesson, she's been trying to teach Conner."

"Your daughter is smart and learns quick." Eli finished his sandwich and brushed the crumbs off his pant legs. "The day I showed her what to do, she began whistling in no time."

"Don't I know it?" Loretta laughed. "I hear Abby nearly every night after I put the little munchkin to bed. I believe she whistles herself to sleep."

Eli clapped his hands. "Now that's cute."

"Is there anything else I'll need to do in order to become Amish?" Loretta questioned.

"Jah. After a year's gone by, which could be sooner where you're concerned, you'll receive instruction in the ways of the church and its ordinances. Then the church members will take a vote on whether to allow you to join. If they vote yes, you'll become a full member of the Amish church."

"There's a lot more involved than I realized."

"Also, I've been trying to find a well-trained horse you can borrow for a time, as well as a used buggy. As I stated before, I'd be glad to teach you how to handle the horse and get used to using a carriage."

"It would be most helpful." Loretta released a lingering sigh. "It won't be an easy road, but I'm willing to try. In fact, I'll give it my best."

Walnut Creek

"Whelp, guess it's about time we head for bed." Lyle looked at the clock on the fireplace mantel. He yawned and stretched his arms over his head. "It's been a long day, and I'm bushed."

"I'm tired, too, but before we go to our room I want to tell you something."

He turned to look at her. "I'm all ears."

"Kendra dropped by early this afternoon. I told her we wouldn't be adopting her baby."

"How she'd take it?"

"Upset, of course, but I suggested she contact an adoption agency, so I'm sure things will work out for her and the baby." Heidi looked away, hoping to hide her disappointment. The decision had been made, so no point in trying to get Lyle to change his mind. Besides, she'd promised not to ask again.

"Before I forget. . ." She moved toward the living-room window. "Did you notice that Ron's motor home is gone?"

Lyle's forehead wrinkled. "It is?" He walked over to the window and stood beside Heidi, looking out.

"Jah. I saw him pulling out earlier today, but figured he'd be back by now."

"I hope his RV didn't break down."

"Does he have our phone number? Do you think he would call if he had a problem?"

"I believe so. If he isn't back by morning, I'll check the phone shack for messages."

"Good idea." Heidi walked beside Lyle toward the bedroom. "Say, I have another question. Would you mind if I went up to Geauga County to see my folks for a few days?"

"I don't have a problem with it." Lyle clasped Heidi's hand. "You've been working hard lately. A little getaway might do you some good."

"Okay. I'll call my driver in the morning. If she's available to take me, I'll let Mom and Dad know to expect me sometime tomorrow afternoon."

Geauga County, Ohio

When Ron had first pulled out of the Troyers' yard, he had no destination in mind. He'd driven around Holmes County a few hours and then headed toward Geauga County. He'd heard some Amish communities were in the area and hoped he could park his rig at one of their farms.

All afternoon and into the evening hours, the conversation he'd heard earlier today, between Eli and Lyle, came back to haunt him. Even now, the man's words echoed in his head: *"Every time I drive past that old silo on County Road 172, I think of how Mavis was killed that evening, a year ago on April 24. I can't understand how the person who hit her bike could have left the scene of the accident and never called for help or reported it to the sheriff."*

Before, when Ron dreamed about hitting a deer, he'd felt like he was a murderer. Now the proof was there—it was true, only it wasn't a deer. He'd thought the flashbacks were bad. How could he deal with what he now knew was reality?

Chapter 37

Middlefield, Ohio

As Heidi sat in the front seat of her driver's van, she felt herself relax. They were almost to her parents' house, and she was eager to see them. The Geauga County Amish were fewer in number than those in Holmes County, but growing up here had been slower paced. In some ways, Heidi missed it. Fewer tourists came here. Where she and Lyle lived, people often gawking at the Amish and snapping pictures became annoying at times.

But the main reason Heidi wished she still lived in Middlefield was to be closer to her folks. It would be nice to drop in at the spur of the moment and have tea with her mother, or invite Mom and Dad for dinner at her place. As it was, they only saw each other a few times during the year. Heidi missed going shopping, canning, and baking with her mother, as they'd done before she married Lyle.

Guess I should be glad we're only a few hours away. Some of their Amish friends had family living in a different state, which meant costly trips to hire a driver or travel by train or bus for visits.

Heidi reflected on Philippians 4:11: *"I have learned, in whatsoever state I am, therewith to be content."* It was the scripture she'd included on the last recipe card she'd given her students. The message was meant for Heidi as much as for those who attended her class.

Closing her eyes, she sent up a silent prayer. *Thank You, God, for all I have. Help me remember to count my blessings.*

As Heidi's driver, Sally Parker, turned onto the next road, Heidi spotted a motor home. If she wasn't mistaken, it looked identical to

Ron's. The RV was pulled into a deserted-looking lane. *But if it is Ron's, what's he doing here? Surely Ron is back in our yard by now. I'll ask Lyle about it when I call to let him know I got here safely.*

"When do you want me to come back for you?" Sally asked when she pulled into the yard of Heidi's parents'.

"How about Monday of next week? It'll give me a chance to go to church with my folks on Sunday, and I'll be home in plenty of time to prepare for my last cooking class next Saturday."

Sally smiled, pushing her short brown hair behind her ears. "Monday works for me. If I leave Walnut Creek around ten in the morning, I should be here shortly after noon. Or would you rather I pick you up a little later in the day?"

"Why don't you try to be here around noon? Then you can join me and Mom for lunch. I'll say goodbye to Dad in the morning, since he'll be at work when I leave. We can head home after we eat. It'll be better to travel on a full stomach, and we won't have to look for a place to stop along the way."

"Good point," Sally agreed. "I'll make sure I'm here as close to noon as possible."

When Heidi got out of the vehicle, she spotted both of her parents heading toward her with happy smiles.

"It's mighty good to see you, daughter." Mom gave Heidi a welcoming hug, and Dad did the same. "We're so glad you came to spend a few days."

Dad bobbed his head. "Your mamm's right. It's been too long since we had a good visit. I'm only sorry Lyle couldn't join us. I'm always interested in hearing about things that go on when he's conducting auctions."

"He has a few of them to preside over this week," Heidi explained, "but we'll both come up some other time when he isn't so busy."

"Sounds good." Dad said a few words to Sally before taking Heidi's small suitcase out of the van. "Have a safe trip back." He waved before turning to Heidi again. "Now let's go up to the house so we can catch up on each other's lives."

Heidi said goodbye to Sally and was getting ready to follow her folks up the sidewalk when she remembered the phone call she needed to make. "I'll meet you two in the house shortly. First, I want to call and leave a message for Lyle so he knows I made it safely."

⌘

Later in the day, Heidi returned to the phone shack to see if Lyle had left her a message. Sure enough, there was one. She listened to it twice to be sure she heard everything.

"Heidi, thanks for letting me know you made it to Middlefield. I miss you already, but I hope you have a great time with your folks. In response to your question about Ron: No, he has not come back. It would seem as if he's gone for good. Sure seems strange he'd leave so suddenly, without telling either of us where he was going or if he'd be back."

After Lyle's message ended, Heidi remained on the wooden stool, rubbing her chin. *Could the motor home I saw earlier have actually been Ron's? But why would he be parked in such an odd place? Sure wish I'd had the chance to talk to him and find out why he left Walnut Creek so suddenly.* Ron had always kept somewhat to himself, but after returning from Columbus, where he'd spent Memorial Day weekend, he'd become even more aloof.

Heidi reflected on the day she'd heard Ron talking to their horse in the barn, and how the poor man's gut-wrenching sobs pulled at her heartstrings. *If only we had been able to help him. Now all we can do is continue to pray for Ron and hope he finds the help he needs.*

⌘

Dover

In an effort to make peace with Len's mother, Charlene had invited his folks to her place for dinner this evening. She'd made German pizza and a tossed green salad—a simple yet tasty meal. She felt pleased it had turned out well. Of course, it remained to be seen what Annette would say about it.

"Well, everything's ready." Charlene smiled at Len, who sat on the living-room couch. "We can eat as soon as your folks arrive."

He glanced at his cell phone and frowned. "They should have been here by now. Sure hope they didn't forget."

"Maybe you ought to give them a call."

"If they don't show up in the next five minutes, I will. Can you hold supper a little longer?"

"Yes. I turned the stove down. It'll be fine." She took a seat beside him and smiled when he clasped her hand. Charlene was glad she and Len hadn't parted ways because of his mother. She doubted she could find another man she loved so much.

They sat quietly together until the doorbell rang. Charlene jumped up. "It must be your folks."

Len went to the door with her, holding his arm around her waist, as if to offer support. Charlene relaxed a bit. *He must sense how nervous I am.* She opened the door and, putting on her best smile, greeted Mr. and Mrs. Campbell.

"Sorry we're a little late." Annette looked at Len's dad. "Todd had a phone call to make before we left, and it took a while."

Todd shrugged his shoulders. "What can I say? Business is business, and it couldn't wait."

"Well, everything's ready, so if you'll take a seat in the dining room, I'll bring dinner out." Charlene headed for the kitchen, and she was surprised when Annette followed.

"Is there anything I can help you with?" she asked sweetly.

"You can get the tossed salad from the refrigerator if you like."

"Certainly." Annette took out the salad and started toward the dining room with it but then turned back around. "Len showed us the photography magazine with the picture you took on the cover. You did a great job, Charlene. Congratulations."

"Thanks. Photography's only a hobby for me, but I truly enjoy it."

"Have you considered doing it professionally?"

"No, not really."

"Perhaps you should. You have an eye for capturing a good photo." Annette glanced at the stove and sniffed. "And if the delicious aroma in here is any indication of the meal we're about to eat, I'd say we're in for a treat."

Charlene clamped her teeth together to keep her mouth from dropping open. Could this be a sign of things going better between her and Len's mother? It certainly appeared so this evening.

———— ❧ ————

Mt. Hope

Kendra had been lying around Dorie's place most of the afternoon, bored and depressed over her situation. After spending the morning searching the Internet, she still had no job prospects. But one problem would soon be solved. She'd decided to call a lawyer to discuss finding adoptive parents for her baby. Between the loss of her job, plus the uncertainty of her baby's future, worrying had become part of her life.

Sighing, she repositioned herself on the couch. *I can't rely on Dorie indefinitely. Sure wish I could get a place of my own. But without a steady income, there's no way that's gonna happen. Why can't anything be easy? Things seem to go well for other people. I must be jinxed.*

Hearing a vehicle pull into the yard, Kendra got up and looked out the window. When she saw Dorie get out of her car, she sat back down.

A few minutes later, Dorie entered the house. "I'm home," she called from the hallway. "Did you have a nice supper?"

Kendra waited until her friend joined her in the living room before responding. "No, I haven't eaten. Thought I'd wait for you."

Dorie blinked rapidly. "You're kidding, right?"

"What do you mean?"

"I told you before I left this morning I'd be having dinner with Gene after I got off work." Dorie took a seat in the rocker across from Kendra.

Kendra folded her arms across her stomach. "Guess I forgot."

"You seem to be forgetting a lot of things lately," Dorie muttered. "I asked you to take the garbage out yesterday, but there it still sat, under the kitchen sink this morning."

"Sorry." Kendra leaned her head against the back of the couch and groaned. "My brain isn't functioning well these days."

"Kendra, I understand you're dealing with a lot of stress, with a baby coming and no job." Dorie rubbed her fingers across her forehead. "I hate to dump one more thing on you right now, but Gene and I plan to get married next month. So you'll need to find another place to stay as soon as possible." Dorie offered Kendra a too-quick smile. "I'm sure you realize how awkward it would be with you, me, and Gene living here in the same house."

Kendra stiffened. "Yeah, I agree, but this is all kinda sudden, don't ya think?"

"Not really. I told you last month Gene and I were talking marriage. Guess you weren't listening then, either."

Kendra had no recollection of Dorie mentioning plans to be married. She wondered how much worse her life could get. If only she could convince her folks to take her back. But it seemed highly doubtful. She may as well try to move a mountain with her pinkie finger. Kendra had no idea where else she could go. Maybe some women's shelter in one of the larger towns in the area would take her in.

"Will you have a big wedding, Dorie?" she asked. "If so, you don't have much time to plan."

"No, Gene and I are going to save the money we'd spend on a wedding and put it in the bank to someday buy a house. We don't want to live in this rental too long. Our folks are all for it and agree with our plans."

"Sounds nice." *So much for learning to be content, like that Bible verse Heidi wrote on the back of the recipe card for German potato salad.*

Kendra swallowed hard, struggling not to break down. "I'll be moved out before the month is over." She clenched her teeth. *Oh man, where do I go from here?*

Chapter 38

Middlefield

"What a beautiful Saturday it's turned out to be." Heidi's mother pointed to the cloudless sky. "This is certainly good gardening weather."

Heidi pulled another handful of weeds then paused to wipe the perspiration from her forehead. "It certainly is. I only wish it were a little cooler. This heat is getting to me, and my clothes are sticking to my skin."

"Let's finish weeding this row of peas, and then we can stop for a glass of iced tea and some of those delicious ginger kichlin you made yesterday." Mom's voice sounded light and bubbly. "I appreciate you chipping in the way you have, but these last few days have not been restful. You should relax while you're here visiting."

"It's okay, Mom. I didn't come here to rest. I came to spend quality time with you and Dad. I'm still not one to sit around, and I am more than happy to help out. Besides, how could I do nothing while you and Dad are doing chores?"

"You've always been a hard worker. Even as a little girl, barely able to walk and talk, you were eager to help." Mom chuckled. "I remember one time when I cleared the breakfast table, and you pointed to the silverware and declared, *'Wesch's gschaar.'*

Heidi laughed. "Wash dishes, huh? Guess I didn't see it as a chore, but something fun to do."

"More than likely you simply wanted to help." Mom shook her head. "Never had much luck getting your brothers to do the dishes."

"But Lester and Richard have always helped Dad a lot."

"True, and those young men still do whenever they come over from their homes in Burton."

"How are they both doing?" Heidi grabbed another clump of weeds. "I'd hoped to see them and their families while I'm here."

"They're good, and so is their masonry business. Richard and Lester, as well as their wives and kinner, will join us for church tomorrow, since it's an off Sunday for them in their church district." Mom stood and arched her back. "Whew! I've had enough weeding for now. Let's rest awhile and enjoy some refreshments."

"Sounds good." Heidi stood, too, and followed her mother into the house.

After they were seated at the table with cookies and iced tea, Heidi felt it the perfect time to bring up the topic of adoption. "There's something I've been meaning to talk to you about."

Mom tipped her head to one side. "I'm all ears."

"There's a young woman who's been attending my cooking classes, and she's expecting a boppli."

"Oh?" Mom reached for a cookie.

"Kendra Perkins is her name, and she's not married."

"I see."

Heidi took a drink of iced tea before she continued. "Kendra's been coming over to visit me between classes. Recently, she asked if Lyle and I would be willing to adopt her baby when it's born."

Mom's eyebrows lifted. "Is this something you and Lyle are agreeable with?"

"I would be, but Lyle won't agree to it. He believes if God wanted us to have kinner, I'd be able to conceive. Since my husband is the head of our house, I need to abide by his decision." Heidi sighed deeply, touching her chest. "It hurts right here, and my arms ache more than you can imagine to hold a child of my own."

Mom leaned closer and put her arm around Heidi's shoulders. "Can't say as I fully understand, since I've given birth to three kinner of my own, but as your *mudder*, I feel your pain, dear one."

Heidi was sure her mother probably would have liked to have had even more children, but getting married later in life and having her first baby when she was forty-two didn't give her too many childbearing years.

Tears sprang to Heidi's eyes, blurring her vision. "I'm trying to accept Lyle's decision, but still praying he will change his mind. Is it wrong for me to hold out hope?"

Gently, Mom stroked Heidi's cheek. "It's not wrong, but if he doesn't change his mind, then you should accept it and look for the good things in your marriage."

Heidi sniffed. "I'm trying to remain positive and content. With God's help, I hope to become stronger and able to accept things as they are."

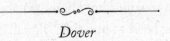

Dover

Charlene pulled into the Campbells' driveway and turned off the ignition. She'd baked an apple cream pie and felt somewhat proud of herself. The pie turned out like the one Heidi taught them to bake last month at one of the classes. "If this tastes as good as it looks, I have half the battle won."

Last Wednesday, when Len's parents came over for dinner, the evening had gone better than Charlene hoped. But the urge to make sure things continued in the right direction with Len's mother had prompted Charlene to pay this unexpected visit.

With one last look in the visor mirror, Charlene was glad she'd taken extra time to fix her hair. She wore it pulled back away from her ears and secured with a pretty ribbon. "Here we go." She glanced at the pie container sitting next to her on the seat.

When Charlene got out of the car, she gripped the dessert carefully and walked slowly toward the house. The last thing she needed was to drop the pie.

"Hello, Charlene." Annette greeted her, coming from the other side of the house, holding a box of flowers. "What brings you by today?"

Charlene smiled. "This morning I was in a baking mood, so I made a pie. Since I can't eat the whole thing by myself, I wanted to share it with you and your husband."

"That's so nice of you. After I'm done, we'll go inside, and I'll put the coffee on. I have one more batch of flowers to transplant and water." Annette walked to the flower bed near the house. "Why don't you put the pie on the kitchen table? Then come back out and join me."

"Okay, I'll return in a jiffy." Charlene stepped inside. The house felt cool and comfortable, since the air conditioner was running, so she saw no point in putting the dessert in the fridge. They'd be cutting into it soon.

When Charlene returned to the yard, Annette finished putting extra dirt around the flowers she had just planted.

"I've been anxious to transplant this clump of mums so they can spread in this area of the flower bed. It'll look nice this fall when they bloom." Annette adjusted the triangle-shaped scarf covering her hair. "Now all I have to do is water them." She pointed toward the hose. "I already unraveled the hose, but could you please turn the water on at the spigot? It's over there on the other side of the porch."

"Sure, I'd be glad to." Charlene walked past the porch and clasped her hands together near her chest. *Thank You, Lord, for things going better between Len's mom and me.* Annette was acting like a totally different person toward Charlene.

When Charlene turned the spigot handle to open the water line, Annette let out an ear-piercing scream. Charlene didn't know what had happened. *Did Len's mother get stung by a bee?*

Charlene ran back around and couldn't believe what she saw. The water came out full force, aimed right at Annette. The poor woman held out her hands as if to shield her face, but it was no use.

"Oh, no!" Charlene bolted to get to the end of the hose, which spewed water like a dancing snake. In the process of turning the nozzle off, she also got wet. Afterward, she looked at Annette, now soaked to the bone, and watched as Len's mother flailed her arms in an attempt to get some of the water off. Charlene couldn't speak. What would she say? Why now, when things seemed to be going so well between them? Would this incident ruin it all?

Annette looked at Charlene, while Charlene looked back in disbelief, wishing she could disappear. It did not look good. Just when things couldn't get any worse, Len's mother started laughing hysterically. In fact so hard, she doubled over, holding her stomach. "Look at me! I must look like a drowned cat." She twisted the bottom of her blouse and wrung water out. "Guess I forgot to turn the nozzle off last time I used the hose."

"Oh goodness, should I go get you a towel?"

Nodding, Annette pointed at Charlene. "From the looks of your wet clothes, I think you'll need one, too. Come on. Let's go in the house so I can find us both something dry to wear."

When she approached, Len's mother draped her cold, wet arm around Charlene's shoulders. "Too bad you didn't have your camera with you. What a great picture I would make."

As they giggled and stepped onto the porch, Charlene said, "I think it's time for some of that pie." *Who knew a mistake with the hose could end on a positive note?*

———————⌒⚬⚬⌒———————

Walnut Creek

As Kendra headed down the road in Dorie's car to visit Heidi, she struggled to keep from breaking down. She'd promised her friend she would move out by the end of the month but had no idea where to start looking.

"I thought our friendship meant more to Dorie," she mumbled. "How could she do this to me? Doesn't she care that I have no place to go? I won't even have a car to drive once I move out."

Kendra closed the car windows and switched on the AC. All that blew out was hot air, worse than what was outside. After a few minutes, hoping it would eventually cool the car inside, she opened the windows again. "Oh, come on! What else is gonna go wrong? Dorie didn't tell me the air-conditioning broke in her car. Or did she?" Kendra hit the steering wheel and accidently blew the horn. The driver in front of her flung his arm out the window and made a fist. She could see him yelling something in the rearview mirror.

"Sorry mister," Kendra mumbled. "It was a slipup, for goodness' sake." *Seems like my whole life lately is one big mistake.*

Kendra hoped Heidi might be able to help or at least offer some advice. She might know of someone in the area who needed a live-in housekeeper or babysitter. Kendra felt desperate.

When she arrived at the Troyers' a short time later, Kendra spotted Heidi's husband in the yard, filling one of the bird feeders. She parked the car near the barn, got out, and headed across the yard. "Is Heidi here, Mr. Troyer?" Since Lyle hadn't agreed to her adoption request, she could barely make eye contact with him.

He shook his head.

"When will she be back?"

"Not till Monday. She's up in Geauga County right now, visiting her folks."

"Oh, I see." Kendra turned to go but stopped in her tracks when Lyle called out to her.

"Wait, Kendra! If you have a few minutes, I'd like to talk to you."

She walked back to him, a bit uncertain. "Sure. What'd you wanna say?" Kendra picked nervously at her chipping nail polish.

"I wanted to explain my reasons for not wanting to adopt."

She shrugged her shoulders. "I'm aware. Heidi told me."

"Okay, but there's something you don't know. After praying about it since Heidi's been gone, and talking to a good friend who's had adoptive parents since he was an infant, I've changed my mind. If you're still willing to let us adopt your baby, I'll contact a lawyer to get the paperwork started."

Barely able to believe her ears, Kendra teared up. "I'm willing." *Maybe things will work out after all. Now if I could only find a job and a place to live.*

<hr/>

Middlefield

Not wishing to ask favors of anyone, Ron had parked his RV in a secluded spot off the main road. He'd barely been able to eat or sleep since he left the Troyers' place. When he managed to fall asleep, recurring dreams tormented him about hitting the deer.

"Only it wasn't a deer." Ron pounded the table where he sat drinking a bottle of beer to help numb the pain and shame of what he'd done. "It was Eli's wife I hit. If he found out what I did, he'd probably hate me for the rest of his life."

As the day wore on, it turned warmer and more humid. Ron felt like everything had closed in around him. At the Troyers', where his RV had been parked, shady trees kept it cooler, not to mention their neat little farm was more scenic to look at than this dreary place.

Here it was secluded but hardly picturesque. From what Ron could tell, this was an old tractor path he'd pulled onto, no longer used by anyone. Somewhere farther down the path, Ron imagined there'd be a wide-open field once used for farming, although he didn't care to find out.

Overgrown shrubs and out-of-control weeds made up the landscape Ron saw out his motor home windows. Even the worn-out gate off to the side of the path was held in place by invading weeds.

Not only did Ron's nightmares keep him from getting a good night's sleep, but the sounds and smells outside kept him tossing and turning, as well.

One night, two animals were out there fighting. Shortly thereafter, the disgusting odor of a skunk permeated his RV. Now he knew how

Eli must have felt when he'd shown up at class with skunk smell on his arm. Another time, Ron heard something snorting. Later, headlights from a vehicle pulling in behind him lit up the inside of his living quarters. Ron heard someone yell about finding another place to go, and then a second person giggled. He figured this old path might be a parking spot young people frequented for partying. Ron remembered those days well, when he and his brother hung out with friends.

Not only did these new surroundings make him feel suffocated, but the knowledge of what'd he done to Eli's poor wife seemed to choke the life out of him.

Ron shook his head, wondering where things had gone wrong. He hadn't been aware of it then, but for a little while, he'd gotten used to a routine at the Troyers', making him feel like he belonged somewhere. In an unplanned sort of way, Ron felt he had somewhat of a family. How long had it been since he'd believed someone actually cared?

He finished drinking the remainder of the beer and tossed the bottle in the garbage can under his sink. At first Ron thought he could run away from all this, but the guilt weighed so heavily, he felt as if he were drowning in his sins.

A plaque he'd seen on the wall in Heidi and Lyle's kitchen came to mind. Burned into the wood were the word of Proverbs 10:9: *"He that walketh uprightly walketh surely."* It had been a long time since Ron had done anything uprightly.

I need to go back and admit what I did. No matter what punishment awaits, it'll be better than living with the agony of this. Eli deserves the truth, and I deserve to be punished.

Ron rubbed his pounding temples. He didn't know where Eli lived, but Eli would be at Heidi's last cooking class a week from today. *Should I wait and go there to tell him, or would it be better if I bite the bullet and turn myself into the sheriff, and then let the law do the telling?*

Chapter 39

Walnut Creek

Heidi stepped out of her driver's van and smiled when her dog ran up to her. "Hey, Rusty. Did you miss me, boy?"

The dog wagged his tail and licked Heidi's hand when she leaned down to pet him. Rusty had the softest wavy coat, and an almost fawn-like color mixed in with mostly white fur.

She glanced around the yard, wondering where Lyle could be and why he hadn't come out to greet her. Figuring he might be busy in the barn, Heidi paid her driver and hauled her suitcase up to the house, with Rusty following close behind.

Once on the porch, she turned, waving to Sally as she drove out toward the road. She'd had a nice visit with her folks, but like always, it felt good to get home.

Heidi paused to look at the bird feeders, active with many types of birds. A quick glance around the farm told her all but one thing looked normal. Ron had not returned. It looked odd to see the empty spot where his motor home had been parked. She'd become used to seeing it there. A dry patch of grass where the RV once sat was the only evidence Ron had ever been there. *Guess I'd better water that spot and hope it turns green again.*

When Heidi entered the kitchen, she found a note from Lyle on the table, saying he'd gone out to run an errand and would be home in time for supper. In the center of the table, a vase filled with stems of honeysuckle sent a sweet fragrance throughout the room. Honeysuckle bloomed along the fence row on the far side of their farm, and depending on which way the wind blew, sometimes the pleasing scent drifted all the way to the house.

Heidi remembered when she was little her mother had taught her to get the droplet of nectar from the honeysuckle by pulling the stamen out of the flower. No wonder the hummingbirds enjoyed it, too.

A few daisies intermixed with the sweet-smelling blossoms made a pretty bouquet. Heidi loved when her husband made these simple, yet thoughtful, gestures. It was a pleasant reminder of what they had together.

Rusty seemed content to have Heidi home, as he made himself comfortable by the door. Round and round he went, until he plopped down with a grunt. Heidi giggled when the dog groaned and stretched his legs out to the side. "If only my life could be as easygoing as yours."

The dog raised his head as his stubby tail wiggled back and forth.

Clicking her tongue against the roof of her mouth, Heidi shook her head. *What a life.*

After inhaling more of the flowers' sweet fragrance, she put away the banana bread Mom had given her before she left and then picked up her suitcase. By now, Rusty slept deeply, so he didn't budge when Heidi left the room.

After she unpacked, she would find something to do until Lyle got home. No doubt there'd be plenty, because the house hadn't been cleaned since she left for Geauga County.

Sugarcreek

Loretta paused in front of the full-length mirror in her bedroom to get a better look at the Amish-style dress she'd put on. She had bought it, as well as a few other plain dresses, at a local thrift store the other day. Loretta hoped wearing the simple dresses might help prepare her for becoming Amish.

Eli would be coming over later today to give her a driving lesson with his horse and buggy, and she felt satisfied with her choice of clothing. Hopefully he'd approve and understand her reason for wearing it. Loretta wasn't rushing things or trying to make a statement, and she certainly didn't want Eli to get the wrong impression.

Since she didn't own an Amish bonnet yet, Loretta had found a black scarf to wear over her bun and secured it to the back of her head. She'd seen several Amish women in her neighborhood wearing scarves when they worked in their yards and felt it would be appropriate.

Loretta's stomach tightened as she tried to imagine how it would feel to drive a horse and buggy. Controlling a full-sized horse with a mind of its own would be a lot different than driving a car. She wouldn't let her fears get the best of her, though. "I'll have to learn many new things if I want to be part of the Amish community." She spoke out loud. More and more, the reality of this change grew stronger, but Loretta felt ready for the work and new challenge.

Sam had offered to keep an eye on Abby and Conner while she was having her first lesson from Eli. Anxious to help Sam pick raspberries, the children had asked to go to his place as soon as they finished eating lunch. Loretta walked them over and, after returning to the house, went to her room to check her attire, in readiness of Eli's arrival. She tried not to feel too eager, but her emotions won out. Each time she and Eli were together Loretta found herself eagerly looking forward to the next time she would see him.

The affection Loretta had developed so quickly for Eli frightened her. She'd heard of people falling in love soon after meeting someone, but it had never happened to her. Even with Rick, it took several months of them dating before she acknowledged he was the one for her.

"Maybe my feelings for Eli stem from loneliness and missing Rick," Loretta murmured. "Sure wish I knew how he feels about me."

In an effort to keep her mind on other things, Loretta rose from her seat and went to the kitchen to make a jug of iced tea. Eli would likely be thirsty when he got here, so she'd offer the cold drink before they headed out for her driving lesson.

———————— ❦ ————————

Walnut Creek

Eli stepped into the phone shack to check for messages and jumped with surprise when the telephone rang. Quickly, he picked up the receiver. "Hello."

"Am I speaking to Mr. Eli Miller?" a man's voice asked.

"Yes, I'm Eli."

"This is the sheriff calling. Can you come to our office as soon as possible?"

Eli's heart hammered. "What is it about?" He hoped no harm had come to his folks or anyone he knew in the area.

"Are you sitting down?"

"Umm. . .yes." Eli lowered himself to the wooden stool.

"The person responsible for your wife's death came forward and confessed. I'd like to give you all the details and would prefer to do it in person."

A rush of adrenaline coursed through Eli's body as he gripped the edge of the wooden shelf where the phone sat. "What did you say?"

The sheriff repeated himself. "I hate to spring it on you like this but figured you'd want to hear. We need to know if you want to press charges."

Eli tilted his head from side to side, weighing his choices. "Umm. . . no, it's not the Amish way. But I do wonder what type of person could have done this, and why they didn't stop or report the accident when it happened."

"I'll explain it all when you get here. Oh, and since you're not willing to take this person to court, the state will no doubt press charges."

"I'll be there as soon as I can. I'm glad you called, Sheriff." Eli's hands shook as he hung up the phone. After more than a year of wondering who was responsible for Mavis's death, the guessing would finally be over.

He stepped out of the phone shack and was about to shut the door when he remembered something. *The driving lesson. I'd better call Loretta.* He lifted a shaky hand to rub the perspiration from his forehead. He couldn't teach her today. In addition to making a trip to see the sheriff, he felt so shook up he wouldn't be able to think clear enough to teach anyone anything. And why risk putting Loretta in danger? After receiving such startling news, it could be some time before he felt up to doing much of anything. Already, his body felt drained from the anticipation of what would take place at the sheriff's office.

Eli stepped back inside to call his driver for a ride and notify Loretta their plans would need to be canceled. Surely, she'd understand.

Sugarcreek

When Loretta hung up the phone, she sat at the kitchen table, pondering the things Eli had told her. She couldn't imagine how he must feel right now. Most likely, there were mixed emotions. While it would be good to finally learn who was responsible for his wife's death, he'd no doubt feel like someone opened an old wound and poured hot water on it. Now the agony of what happened to his wife would cause him to grieve all over again. Loretta could almost feel his pain.

She shifted in her chair. *If I were in Eli's place I could barely function right now. I wonder how he will handle all this.* Closing her eyes, she sent up a prayer on his behalf. *Please, Lord, be with Eli and send healing balm for his emotional wounds. He needs You now more than ever.*

Sighing, Loretta opened her eyes. *Guess I'd better go check for the mail. Better yet, think I'll give my mother a call.* She'd been meaning to talk to her folks about her idea of becoming Amish but had put it off, unsure of their reaction. *With the children over at Sam's place, guess now's as good a time as any.*

She reached for the phone and punched in her parents' number. Her mother answered on the second ring. "Hi, Mom, it's me."

"What a coincidence, Loretta, I was just going to call you. How are you and the children?"

"We're all fine. Uh, there's something I wanted to tell you, though." Loretta drew a deep breath.

"I have something to tell you, as well."

"Oh. Should I go first, or do you want to?"

"You go ahead."

Loretta sucked in another breath then blurted, "I'm thinking of becoming Amish."

Silence on the other end.

"Did you hear what I said, Mom?"

"Yes, I heard. You took me by surprise, is all. When did all this come about?"

Loretta twisted a strand of hair around her finger, wondering how much she should share or where to begin. "Well, as you know, when Rick and I moved here to Sugarcreek, we wanted Abby and Conner to grow up in a quiet, simple community."

"Yes, I'm aware."

"For some time now I've yearned for a simpler way of life, without the distraction of modern things."

"You don't have to be Amish to simplify your life." Mom's tone seemed more like a caution, rather than one of disapproval, but Loretta figured she should explain a little more. "Before I go any farther, I need to ask you a question."

"Sure, go ahead."

"What was the reason behind you and Dad not joining the Amish church and choosing to become part of the English world?"

Mom cleared her throat. "I was wondering when you'd get around to asking me that. I'm actually surprised you didn't ask sooner."

"Is it a deep, dark secret?"

"No, not at all. We just saw no reason to talk about it."

"So what was the reason?"

"During your dad's running-around years, he bought a car, as many young people do when they want to try out the English way." Mom paused a few seconds. "The truth is, when we decided to get married and were trying to decide if joining the Amish church was right for us, your dad's desire to own and drive a car won out."

"I see." Loretta toyed with the saltshaker in the middle of the table. "So instead of appreciating the simple life, he wanted modern, worldly things?"

"I wouldn't say that exactly. Your dad and I have never gone overboard when it comes to buying, or even wanting, worldly things."

Loretta couldn't argue with that. She remembered, growing up, her parents never had to have the best of everything. They didn't, however, shun modern things like electric appliances, Dad's truck, Mom's car, and a home where decorative items were displayed. If not for the few visits they'd made to visit her grandparents, Loretta would never have known her parents had once lived the Plain life with their parents and siblings.

I wished I'd had this talk with Mom sooner. Loretta set the saltshaker aside. "Would you have any objections if I did join the Amish church?"

"None at all. The choice is yours, Loretta. Have you made friends with any Amish? You'll need someone to mentor you."

Loretta pursed her lips. *Do I tell her about Eli? Would it make a difference?* "Actually, I do have an Amish friend who is willing to help me with the necessary steps." Loretta wasn't ready to share her feelings about Eli yet, especially when she wasn't sure how he felt about her. If things got serious at some point, she would then inform her parents.

"That's good. How do the children feel about all this?" Mom asked.

"They don't know yet. I'm waiting to explain it to Abby and Conner until I'm certain it's the right thing for all of us."

"Makes sense. Please keep me informed, Loretta."

"I will." A slight breeze had picked up and filtered through the open window, giving Loretta some much-needed fresh air. In preparation for becoming Amish, she'd only been using electricity for necessary things like cooking, hot water for baths, and lights turned on as needed. The air conditioner had been staying off, with windows opened for ventilation. "So, what was the reason you were going to call me?"

"From years of going up and down ladders in his painting business, your dad's knees have gotten pretty bad."

"I'm sorry to hear it."

"The doctor has finally talked him into getting knee replacements, and he's agreed to have the left knee done next month. I was hoping you and the children could come here to visit for a few weeks during his recovery. It'll help cheer him up, and you can assist me in keeping him from doing things he's not supposed to do."

"Of course, Mom, I'll be happy to come, and I know the children will be eager to see you and Dad, too. I'd like to be there the day he has surgery."

"Thank you, Loretta. I'd better go now, but I'll talk to you again soon. Oh, and I'll be praying that God shows you what to do in regard to becoming Amish."

When Loretta hung up the phone, she sat several minutes, mulling things over. All this time she'd wondered why her parents left their Amish families to start over and had never asked why. She felt as if a weight had been lifted from her shoulders. From now on, if anyone asked, she wouldn't be afraid or ashamed to tell them her parents had grown up Amish, or why they'd chosen not to stay. She appreciated Mom's understanding about her desire to live the Plain life.

Loretta rose from her chair. It was time to head outside and get the mail. She'd just stepped out the door when she heard Abby scream. Looking out across the yard, she saw the child running toward her, frantically waving her hands.

"Honey, what's wrong?" Loretta broke out in a cold sweat. "Where's Conner?"

Abby pointed to her little brother, trailing along behind her. "He's bleedin' real bad!"

Loretta raced toward them, but as the children drew closer, and she saw blotches of red on her son's face, hands, and clothes, her apprehension faded. Smiling with relief, she bent down, enveloping both children in her arms. "Conner's not bleeding, Abby. He's splattered with berry juice."

Conner smacked his lips and held out his hands. Opening his closed fingers, he grinned at Loretta. "Want some, Mommy?"

She stared at the smashed berries and laughed. *Oh, the sweet innocence of a child.* Loretta thanked God for giving her these two beautiful children and for blessing her with wonderful parents. Whether she joined the Amish church or not—and even if nothing serious developed between her and Eli—she would enjoy every moment with her precious son and daughter and always try to be honest with them.

Chapter 40

Today was Heidi's final cooking class—at least for this group of students. She'd gotten up early this morning, to make sure everything was ready. She planned to teach her students how to make a special meat loaf her mother had taught her many years ago. Heidi also made a delicious broccoli salad. After the lesson, they would share a final meal together before everyone went home.

Today will be bittersweet. Heidi's mouth twisted grimly. She'd miss seeing her students and felt bad Ron wouldn't be here to join them and take the final class. They still hadn't heard a word from him, and she couldn't help wondering where he'd gotten to, and whether it had actually been his motor home she'd seen in Geauga County. Perhaps she'd never find out, but whenever she thought of Ron, she would say a prayer on his behalf.

"You're up awful early this morning."

Heidi turned at the sound of her husband's voice. "Today's my final cooking class. I wanted to make sure everything is ready before everyone arrives."

Lyle stepped up to Heidi and placed his hands on her shoulders. "Speaking of your students...there's something I've wanted to tell you, but things have been so busy this week, we haven't had much chance to talk."

"What is it?" Heidi reached up and curled her fingers through his full beard. After eight years of marriage, it had gotten quite long. She'd almost forgotten what Lyle looked like without it.

"Kendra stopped by here last Saturday to see you."

"Oh? Did you tell her where I was?"

"Jah." Lyle motioned to the table. "Let's sit down, and I'll tell you what else Kendra and I talked about."

Curious, Heidi pulled out a chair and sat. Her husband looked so serious, she worried. She hoped he hadn't said anything hurtful to Kendra about the request she'd made for them to adopt her child. The poor girl had gone through enough without receiving a lecture from Lyle.

He took the seat beside Heidi and clasped her hand. "I told Kendra we would adopt her baby."

Heidi's eyes widened. "What?"

"It's not easy to admit, but I've been selfish and was wrong not to consider your feelings about wanting to adopt."

"Oh, Lyle." Heidi touched her chest, acutely aware of her heart's rhythmic beating beneath her fingers. "Are you positive about this? Please don't do it just for me."

"I'm certain." Lyle looked at her tenderly then pulled her into his arms.

Tears coursed down Heidi's cheeks as she leaned her head on his shoulder. "Danki, Lyle. Thank you so much." Heidi feared her heart might burst with the joy overflowing. Sometime in October, she would finally become a mother.

When Kendra arrived at Heidi's, her heartbeat quickened. Had anything changed since last Saturday, when Lyle agreed to adopt her child? She hoped he felt the same and was still willing. Despite the worry, Kendra had a good feeling. The day's weather couldn't be better, with clear skies so blue it almost hurt her eyes. A slight breeze blew in the fresh, comfortable air. Kendra breathed deeply, and with outstretched arms, she shouted, "It's good to be alive!"

No sooner had Kendra stepped onto the porch than Heidi came out and greeted her with a hug. "Lyle told me he spoke to you last week and agreed we should raise your baby."

"I'm so relieved." Kendra smiled through her tears as they walked inside together. "I still haven't found another job, and since my friend Dorie will be getting married soon, I'll have to move out of her place by the end of June." She sniffed. "But at least I don't have to worry about what will happen to my baby."

Lyle, who had been sitting on the sofa in the living room, got up and came over to them. "Maybe you can stay here with us until you're able to make it on your own." He looked at Heidi. "Would this arrangement be all right with you?"

With no hesitation, Heidi nodded, tears glistening in her eyes. "We have an extra guest room, so it shouldn't be a problem at all."

"Would you really do that for me?" Kendra could barely speak around the lump in her throat.

"Yes, we would," Lyle responded. "Having you here will give us a chance to get better acquainted and make plans for the baby's future."

For the first time in a long while, Kendra sent up a silent prayer. *Thank You, Lord, for these special people. I'm even more sure now that they'll make the best parents for my little girl or boy.*

———————⚬~⚬⚬~⚬———————

A short time later, as Heidi gave instructions to her four students on how to make sweet-and-sour meat loaf, she noticed the smile that never left Charlene's face. It was in sharp contrast to her sullen expression during the previous cooking class.

"How are things with you, Charlene?" Heidi handed her a small baking dish.

"Absolutely wonderful." Charlene's smile widened. "Len and I had a disagreement, but things are better now, and it's been working out between me and his mother." She clasped her hand to her chest.

"Guess what else? Remember the colt I took a picture of?"

Heidi nodded.

"Well, I got a call from the owner, and they decided to name the colt after me—Charlie."

"Aw, that's so cute." Kendra grinned. "Bet you feel flattered."

"I do. And get this," Charlene added. "They want me to have little Charlie."

Heidi sucked in her breath. "Are you going to take the little fella?"

"Well, I don't have a place to keep him right now, since I live in a condo, but Len's parents volunteered to keep him at their place until Len and I are married and are able to buy a home of our own—which, of course, would need to have enough property for a horse." Charlene stopped talking long enough to take a breath. "Kitty and her husband also said they'd keep the colt until we're ready, so I'm not sure what we'll end up doing."

"Goodness, a lot has happened since our last class." Loretta patted Charlene's arm. "I'm happy for you."

"I'm sure we all are." Heidi nodded at Charlene then looked over at Loretta, noticing for the first time that she wore a plain, Amish-style dress and a dark-colored scarf on her head. "How have you been, Loretta?"

"Really good." Loretta glanced at Eli then back at Heidi. "I'm taking steps to become Amish, and Eli's helping me make the transition."

"Now that's a surprise. I had no idea you were considering becoming part of the Amish community." Heidi set the ingredients for the meat loaf topping on the table.

"The Amish way feels right to me, and it's actually part of my heritage, which I'd like to share with you sometime." Loretta's eyes sparkled. "I believe it will be good for my children, as well."

"You may face some challenges," Heidi commented, "but if it's what you truly desire, then I wish you the best."

Eli opened his mouth, as if he might want to say something, when a knock sounded on the back door.

Heidi excused herself to see who it was. She felt surprise when she opened the door and found Ron on the porch. "Can I come in?" he asked, looking down at his shoes.

"Of course. It's good to see you, Ron." She stepped aside. "The others are in the kitchen, preparing to make a special meat loaf, and then we'll share a meal together one last time before everyone goes their separate ways." Heidi wanted so badly to ask where Ron had been all this time, but if he wanted to tell her, it should be of his own choosing. Silently, she led the way to the kitchen.

Ron stood inside the kitchen door a few seconds then walked over to the table. "I wasn't planning to be here today, and I won't be stayin' for a meal," he murmured to no one in particular. "But I had to come back because I've done something terrible and couldn't face the consequences. My conscience got the best of me, though, so I'm here to confess."

He drew a deep breath and turned to face Eli, heart thumping hard in his chest. Telling this nice man the truth would be the hardest thing he'd ever done, but he had to do it. "I owe you a heartfelt apology, but I don't expect forgiveness, because what I did is. . ." He paused and tried to swallow, wishing he had something to drink because his mouth felt dry as the desert. "Well, it's inexcusable."

Eli tipped his head. "What are you referring to?"

"I'm talkin' about your wife. I heard a conversation you and Lyle had a while back, and you mentioned the date and place where your wife had been hit." Ron paused and wiped the sweat tricking down his face. "This is hard for me to admit, but I was driving on that same road the very same evening last year. Something triggered a flashback from the war in my mind during the drive, and about that time I thought I hit a deer." One more quick pause, and another deep breath. "But I realized after what you said that it must have been your wife, on her bicycle, I hit, not a deer."

Eli sat several seconds, looking at Ron through squinted eyes. Then, slowly, he shook his head. "You may have hit a deer, Ron, but it was someone else who killed my wife."

The women gasped, and a shiver ran up Ron's spine. "Wh–what?"

"The sheriff got in touch with me a few days ago, and when he gave me the details, I learned that the young man who did it turned himself in and confessed to the hit-and-run." Eli's voice quavered. "When he gave me a description of the teenager, I realized it was the same kid who tried to run my bike off the road last month." Eli paused to wipe a tear that had fallen onto his cheek. "The evening I was first informed of the accident, the sheriff mentioned they'd found a dead deer at the scene. Said he thought the person responsible for the tragedy may have hit Mavis in an effort to avoid hitting the deer. I didn't give it much thought until now." Eli leaped to his feet and clasped Ron's shoulder. "I'm glad you weren't the one responsible for my wife's death. You're a good person for coming here to speak with me about it."

The room got deathly quiet as everyone seemed to digest this information.

———————⸱❦⸱———————

Heidi stood quietly beside Ron, until he expelled a deep breath and sank into an empty chair. "It's a relief to know I'm not the one responsible, but I am not a good person. I've done many things I'm not proud of, including. . ." He looked at her and winced. "I'm ashamed to admit this, but I took money from a vase in your house, as well as some old oil lamps and a few other things of value. I can't get any of the items back because I pawned them, but here's the money I took, plus some extra." He reached into his pocket and handed her a wad of bills. "I'm so sorry. What I did was wrong—especially after the kindness you and Lyle showed me."

Heidi stared at him, and then with no hesitation she placed her hand on his arm. "I'm glad you came back to tell the truth, and I forgive you, Ron. I'm certain when Lyle joins us for lunch and hears your confession, he will also forgive."

Ron dropped his gaze to the floor. "Thanks, but I don't deserve your forgiveness."

"God commands us to forgive others, just as He forgives us," Eli spoke up. "I've been reminded of that myself recently. Plus, the verse on the back of a recipe card Heidi gave us during one of our classes mentions forgiveness."

Ron nodded. "I've made a decision to see a counselor for help with my postwar issues, and I plan to return to my hometown and try to make amends with my grown children, as well as my ex-wife." He smiled at Heidi, pointing to the plaque on the kitchen wall. "When I thought about that verse of scripture, I realized it was time for a change."

"Good for you, Ron." Smiling, Kendra looked at him. "I'm right there with you and am all about change."

"None of us is perfect, and we all need to be forgiven," Charlene put in. "Coming here to this class has opened my eyes to a few things." She stepped up to Heidi and gave her a hug. "Thank you for all you've taught us."

"You're welcome, and I thank all of you for being such good students." Heidi went to her desk and took out five notebooks then handed one to each person. "This is a small recipe book I put together so you can make some other traditional Amish dishes on your own. There's also a list of helpful kitchen tips at the back." She pointed to the recipe card she'd given everyone today. "I also want to leave you with one final verse to reflect upon. It's Matthew 6:33, and this is how it reads: "But seek ye first the kingdom of God, and his righteousness; and all these things shall be added unto you."

"Thank you, Heidi." Charlene grinned, her face fairly glowing.

"The recipes will be helpful when I get married, and all the scriptures you have shared with us will guide me along the way."

The others were unanimous in thanking Heidi, too.

As she stood watching her students finish making their meat loaves, Heidi felt rewarded in so many ways. She was glad she'd acted on her idea to teach cooking classes, and appreciated the opportunity to become acquainted with each of her students, as well becoming instrumental in their lives. Perhaps sometime in the future she'd have the opportunity to teach more seekers—not only how to cook but how to strengthen their faith in God, as well.

Heidi's Cooking Class Recipes

Amish Country Breakfast

Ingredients:

14 slices whole wheat bread
2½ cups ham, cubed
1 pound mozzarella cheese,
   shredded

1 pound cheddar cheese,
   shredded
6 eggs
3 cups milk

Topping:

½ cup butter, melted

3 cups cornflakes
   (do not crush)

Grease 9x13 baking pan and layer half the bread, ham, and cheeses. Repeat layers. Beat eggs in a mixing bowl, add milk, and pour over layers in pan. Refrigerate overnight. Next morning, preheat oven to 375 degrees. Mix butter and cornflakes. Spread mixture over other ingredients in pan. Cover loosely with foil and bake for 45 minutes.

Amish Haystack

Ingredients:

½ pound saltine crackers or one bag corn chips, crushed

2 cups cooked white or brown rice

2 heads lettuce, chopped

6 to 8 tomatoes, chopped

1 (6 ounce) can black olives, sliced

2 cups tomatoes, diced

2 cups onions, diced

2 cups green pepper, diced

2 cups celery, diced (optional)

1 quart cooked navy or pinto beans

2 eggs, boiled and chopped (optional)

2 cups nuts, chopped (optional)

1 (14 ounce) can condensed milk

2 cans cream of cheddar soup

1 (16 ounce) jar Ragu spaghetti sauce or salsa

3 pounds ground beef, browned

Put each of first 12 ingredients into separate containers. Mix soup and milk together in a saucepan and heat. Add the Ragu sauce or salsa to browned ground beef and heat.

Each person creates their own haystack by layering items in order given on their plate. Pour cheese sauce and favorite salad dressing on top and enjoy! Serves 12 to 14 people.

German Pizza

Ingredients:

1 pound ground beef, browned

½ medium onion, chopped

½ green pepper, diced

1½ teaspoons salt, divided

½ teaspoon pepper

2 tablespoons butter

6 raw potatoes, shredded

3 eggs, beaten

⅓ cup milk

2 cups cheddar or mozzarella cheese, shredded

In 12-inch skillet, brown beef with onion, green pepper, ½ teaspoon salt, and pepper. Remove beef mixture from skillet. Drain skillet; then melt butter in it. Spread potatoes over butter and sprinkle with remaining 1 teaspoon salt. Top with beef mixture. Combine eggs and milk and pour over all. Cook, covered, on medium heat until potatoes are tender, about 30 minutes. Top with cheese; cover and heat until cheese melts, about 5 minutes. Cut into wedges or squares to serve.

Apple Cream Pie

Ingredients:

3 cups apples, finely chopped	1 rounded tablespoon flour
1 cup brown sugar	1 cup cream
¼ teaspoon salt	1 (9 inch) unbaked pastry shell

Preheat oven to 450 degrees. Mix apples, brown sugar, salt, flour, and cream. Put in unbaked pastry shell. Bake 15 minutes. Reduce heat to 325 degrees for an additional 30 to 40 minutes. When pie is about halfway done, take a knife and push top apples down to soften. After pie cools, store in refrigerator.

German Potato Salad

Ingredients:

- 4 boiled potatoes, cut into chunks
- 1 teaspoon sugar
- ½ teaspoon salt
- ¼ teaspoon dry mustard
- Dash pepper
- 2 tablespoons apple cider vinegar
- 1 cup sour cream
- ½ cup onions, thinly sliced
- 2 to 3 slices bacon, fried and cut into small pieces
- Paprika

Place potato chunks in large bowl. Combine sugar, salt, dry mustard, pepper, vinegar, sour cream, onion, and bacon pieces. Pour over warm potatoes and toss lightly until coated with dressing. Serve warm with a dash of paprika.

Heidi's Sweet-and-Sour Meat Loaf

Ingredients:

- 1½ pounds ground beef
- 1 medium onion, chopped
- 1 cup saltine cracker crumbs
- 1 teaspoon pepper
- 1½ teaspoons salt
- 1 egg, beaten

Preheat oven to 350 degrees. In mixing bowl, combine ground beef and onion. Add cracker crumbs, pepper, salt, and egg. Mix well. Shape into loaf and place in a 9x5 pan.

Topping:

- ½ cup tomato sauce
- 1 cup water
- 2 tablespoons apple cider vinegar
- 2 tablespoons mustard
- 2 tablespoons brown sugar

In a mixing bowl, combine tomato sauce, water, vinegar, mustard, and brown sugar. Spread over meat. Bake for 1½ hours.

Discussion Questions

1. Heidi wanted desperately to have a baby, but her husband wasn't willing to adopt. Was it right for her to keep asking, or should she have accepted his decision from the beginning?

2. Heidi's husband, Lyle, thought it must not be God's will for them to have children, so he closed his mind to adoption. Do you feel everything that happens to us is for a reason? If you were unable to have a child, would you see it as God's will, or would you seek to adopt?

3. Was it right for Lyle to think only of himself when it came to adopting a child, or should he have considered his wife's need to become a mother?

4. When Kendra's parents, who professed to be Christians, forced her out of their house after she told them she was expecting a baby, she became bitter against them and their religion. Is there ever a time when a parent should turn their back on a grown child?

5. Because of Kendra's father, her mother didn't stick by her, either. Would you be able to choose sides between your husband or child, knowing one of them would be hurt? Was Kendra right in trying to get her mother to take her side against her father's orders?

6. Loretta wanted a simpler life for her children. Could she have found it without joining the Amish church? What are some ways you can simplify your life and still remain English?

7. After the death of his wife, Eli convinced himself he would never fall in love again. Is it possible for one who's lost one's mate to feel the same kind of love the second time around? Why would some widows or widowers feel disloyal to their deceased spouse if they were offered the opportunity for love again?

8. Charlene struggled with feelings of inferiority because she wasn't a good cook. How did attending Heidi's cooking classes help Charlene rise above her insecurities and self-doubt?

9. Should Charlene have made the first move to call her boyfriend after their disagreement, since it was because of her request to move out of the area that she didn't hear from him? Should she have even made such a request, knowing his job, which he enjoyed, was in Dover?

10. Ron had flashbacks and nightmares from the things he'd encountered during the Vietnam War. The things Ron said and did seemed to be related to the emotional scars left from the war. Do you know someone who is suffering from physical or mental postwar trauma? How can you help that person deal with the pain?

11. Ron's children were now adults. Even though his life was messed up due to traumatic things that happened to him during the war, should he have tried to locate his children and attempt to be part of their lives? Have you or someone you know been abandoned by a parent? If so, how did you cope?

12. Eli waited over a year until the law caught the hit-and-run driver who killed his wife. Could you find the strength to move forward and have the patience Eli did in waiting to find out who and why? Would you be able to forgive the person responsible, as Eli did? What does the Bible say about forgiving others?

13. Kendra was devastated when she lost her job and the same day found out the Troyers would not adopt her baby. If something similar happened to you, would you find it difficult to keep a positive attitude and not give up?

14. What are some things you learned about the Amish from reading this book?

15. Could you relate to any of the characters in the story? Were there any scriptures Heidi shared with her students that you found helpful? What is your favorite Bible verse, and how has it helped you during a difficult time?

THE BLESSING

Chapter 1

Walnut Creek, Ohio

Heidi Troyer's skin prickled as a gust of wind blew into her kitchen. After peeling and cutting an onion to go in the savory meat loaf she was making for supper, she'd opened the window a few minutes ago to air out the room.

Glancing into the yard, Heidi watched as newly fallen leaves swirled over the grass. Across the way, freshly washed laundry she'd hung on the line a few hours ago fluttered in the unseasonably cool breeze. Even the sheets made a snapping noise when the wind played catch and release.

They'd soon be saying goodbye to the month of August, and Heidi was glad. A long dry spell had caused some of the trees to drop their leaves early, and the rustling of those still clinging to the branches sounded like water rushing down a well-fed stream after a heavy rain.

"I wish it would rain. Even a drizzle would be nice." Heidi looked toward the sky, but not a single puffy cloud was in sight. September was a month of transition, teetering between warm, summer-like days and cool, comfortable nights, so maybe the rain would come soon. She looked forward to its fresh, clean scent, not to mention it removing the necessity of watering her flowerbeds and garden.

Heidi glanced at the plot where she'd planted a variety of vegetables in the spring. The potatoes and other root vegetables still needed to be dug and put in the cellar, and she wanted to get the chore done before Kendra's baby was born and the adoption became official. Once the infant came, Heidi would put her full attention on raising the child. She'd already made the decision not to teach any more cooking classes—

at least not until her son or daughter was older and didn't require round-the-clock attention. Heidi certainly couldn't teach and take care of the precious baby, and she didn't want to juggle between the two—especially after waiting so long to become a mother.

Heidi's senses were heightened, and she giggled out loud as she visualized herself holding the infant while stirring a batch of cookie dough. After being married to Lyle for eight years and finding herself still unable to conceive, the idea of soon becoming a mother was almost more than she could comprehend. In a matter of weeks, her dream would finally come true. How thankful she was that Kendra had moved into their home and agreed to let them adopt her child. Once the baby was born and Kendra got her strength back, she would find a better-paying job and move out on her own. It wouldn't be right to ask her to leave until she was physically and financially ready.

Heidi sighed. *What a shame Kendra's parents turned their back on her and she felt forced to give up her baby. But then if they hadn't, Lyle and I would not have been given the opportunity to raise Kendra's child.*

Satisfied the onion smell was gone, Heidi took one more breath of the late summer-scented air, then closed the window and took a seat at the table. She owed her aunt Emma a letter and would start writing it while the meat loaf cooked. Maybe by the time supper was ready, Kendra would be back from her doctor's appointment, and Lyle from Mt. Hope, where he'd put his auctioneering skills to good use most of the day.

I can hardly wait for us to be sharing a warm meal at the kitchen table, so I can hear about the events of their days. Heidi was most anxious to get updates on Kendra's doctor's appointment. She'd offered to go with her this afternoon, as she had several other times since Kendra moved in with them. Today, however, Kendra had said she had a few stops to make after seeing the doctor and didn't want to take up Heidi's day.

I wouldn't have minded. I enjoy being with Kendra. Heidi's nose tickled, and she rubbed it, trying to stifle a sneeze. Smelling onion on her fingers, she wet her hands under the faucet, then rubbed them along the sides of their stainless steel sink. After a few seconds, she smelled her fingers again and was amazed the onion scent was gone.

Heidi didn't know how it worked, but she was glad her friend Loretta had recently given her this unusual tip.

"I'll have to keep this in mind to share with my students once I decide to start up the cooking classes again." Heidi wrote a note to remind her, since it would be a good while before she taught more classes.

After she stuck the note in her recipe box, Heidi turned her attention to a daily devotional book lying near her writing tablet. She read Psalm 9:1, the verse for the day, out loud: "'I will praise thee, O Lord, with my whole heart; I will shew forth all thy marvellous works.'"

Closing her eyes and bowing her head, Heidi prayed: "Thank You, Lord, for Your many blessings. I praise You with my whole heart for all Your wonderful works. Thank You for this day, and for my family and friends. Protect us, and shower Your people with many blessings. Amen."

Heidi had no more than finished her prayer when she heard a car pull into the yard. She went to the window and looked out, smiling as she watched Kendra get out of her driver's car. Since Kendra didn't have a vehicle of her own, she'd hired one of Heidi and Lyle's drivers to take her into town. If Heidi had gone with her, they might have traveled by horse and buggy; although it would have taken them longer.

Keeping an eye on Kendra, as she made her way toward the house, Heidi couldn't help noticing her slow steps, and how she pursed her lips, while holding her stomach, as though in pain.

Heidi's shoulders tightened as she rushed to open the door. She hoped the doctor hadn't given Kendra unsettling news today.

"Sorry I'm late." Kendra entered the house, avoiding eye contact with Heidi, and took a seat at the kitchen table. "We need to talk." She pushed a lock of auburn hair behind her ears.

Heidi pulled out a chair and sat. "What is it, Kendra? Is everything okay with the baby?"

"No, not in a physical sense at least." Kendra's brown eyes looked ever so serious as she took the seat next to Heidi.

"What do you mean?"

The young woman's shoulders curled as she bent her neck forward.

"The whole way here, I thought about how I should tell you this." Kendra took a shuddering breath. "And still, I don't know where to begin."

Heidi held her hands in her lap, gripping her fingers into her palms. "Please, tell me what it is you need to say."

"Well, the thing is. . ." Kendra shifted in her chair. "Miracle of miracles—my dad called my cell phone this morning. He asked if I'd be free to come by his office this afternoon." She paused and drew a quick breath. "I went there after I left the doctor's office, and. . ." Her voice faltered, and she paused to swallow before continuing. "He said it had been a mistake to kick me out of the house after I told him and Mom I was pregnant."

Heidi smiled. "That's good news, Kendra. I've been praying for it to happen. I hope things will be better between you and your parents from now on."

"Yeah, well, Dad wants me to move back home so he and Mom can help raise the baby."

"Raise the baby?" Heidi blinked rapidly, her breath bursting in and out. "Does this mean you've changed your mind about Lyle and me adopting your child?"

Kendra gave a slow nod. "Since my parents are willing to help, there's no reason for me to give up the baby now. And since the contract the lawyer drew up says. . ."

Heidi held up her hand. "I know what it says; although I never expected you would go back on your word."

"I. . .I wasn't planning to, but things have changed." A few tears trickled down Kendra's cheeks. "I never wanted to give up my baby; you have to know that. I only agreed to it because I had no support and knew I couldn't take care of a child by myself." She touched Heidi's hands: both of them had turned cold. "I can see you're disappointed, and I'm sorry, but I hope you understand."

Understand? Heidi's stomach clenched, and she pressed the wad of her apron against it. She sat in stunned silence, unable to form a response. The tension felt so strong, she could almost touch it. It didn't seem possible, after all these months of Kendra living with them, that she had changed her mind. Heidi wanted to be happy for the young, pregnant woman sitting at her table. It was good Kendra had reconciled with her parents and been invited to move back home. But Kendra's decision to keep the baby put a hole in Heidi's heart—one she felt sure would never close. Her dream of holding a tiny baby she could call her own was just that—only a dream. The walls in this house would not echo with the laughter of children. Tiny feet would never patter across the floor. No chubby arms would reach out for a hug. Heidi fought for control. The ringing in her ears was almost deafening.

She glanced toward the hall, knowing the nursery that had already been set up would have to be dismantled. All the baby blankets and clothes would have to be packed away. The crib would be disassembled. She'd have Lyle haul it out to the barn, for having the crib in the house would be a painful reminder of their loss. Heidi didn't even want to look at it now.

She thought about the scripture she'd quoted several moments ago and wondered if she would ever praise the Lord again.

Less than an hour later, Heidi checked on the meat loaf, decided it was done, and turned the oven temperature to low. It was all she could do to get supper ready for when Lyle got home. Kendra's shocking announcement numbed her mind. She wondered what Lyle's reaction would be when he heard the news.

Kendra came into the kitchen and stood watching as Heidi took a sack of potatoes from the pantry. "Would you like help getting supper ready?" she asked.

"We need a kettle for boiling the potatoes." Heidi could barely make eye contact with the young woman. Truth was, she wished she could be alone to deal with her grief.

Kendra went to the lower cupboard and took out a medium-size pot. "I'll add water to the kettle and set it on the propane burner to heat."

Without a word, Heidi slid over the jars of home-canned beans she'd taken out earlier. After removing the lids, she dumped the contents into a kettle and sprinkled some leftover onion bits on top. She stirred them around a bit, set the lid in place, and put the pan on the stove. She felt like a robot, merely going through the motions of preparing their meal.

"Is there anything else I can do?" Kendra waited by the stove.

"We'll have iced tea to drink. Could you make that while I cut up a few carrot and celery sticks?" Heidi glanced at Kendra. *This meal will be so awkward. I'd give anything if Kendra's decision wasn't absolute.*

Her hands trembled as she took out the carrots and began slicing them. She wished it was still morning and things were as they had been before Kendra's shocking announcement. *Is there even a chance she might think things over and change her mind? Is it right to cling to that hope?*

"When I'm done making the tea, I'll set the dining-room table." Kendra put the tea bags in the pitcher of hot water.

"Okay." Heidi washed celery stalks and cut those as well, pausing briefly to glance at the clock. Lyle would be home soon, and he'd be hungry. Her insides twisted; she had no appetite at all.

Silently, Kendra got out the plates, silverware, napkins, and three glasses. She placed them on a large tray and headed for the dining room, elbows tucked into her sides. This had to be difficult for her, too. Heidi and Kendra had become close during the months she'd been living here. Heidi felt sure the young woman did not want to hurt her. But she had, and Heidi needed to come to grips with it, despite her disappointment.

A few minutes later, as Heidi watched the water bubbling over the potatoes, she heard the familiar sound of Lyle's horse and buggy pull in. She glanced at the timer on the counter. The potatoes had ten more minutes to go. It felt like it was a countdown to the moment she would give Lyle the news. *Should I tell him before supper or wait until we've finished eating?* Either way, there simply wasn't a good time nor an easy way to say it.

The back door squeaked open and clicked shut. A few seconds later, Lyle entered the kitchen, carrying his lunch box. He placed it on the counter, then pulled off his straw hat and smoothed back his thick auburn hair. "How was your day, Heidi? Did everything go well here?"

She moved away from the stove and gave him a much-needed hug. At the moment, Heidi felt so overwhelmed she could barely speak.

"You're trembling, Heidi. Is something wrong?" He patted her back gently. "Wasn't Kendra supposed to see the doctor today?"

"*Jah.*" Heidi's voice sounded muffled as she held her face close to his chest, hoping to draw strength from his embrace.

"There's nothing wrong with the *boppli*, I hope."

"No, Kendra's baby's fine."

Kendra came into the room just then. "Are we about ready to eat?"

"Almost." The timer for the potatoes went off, and Heidi stepped back to the stove to shut off the burner. The beans were also well heated, so she turned them off, too. "I'll set everything on the dining-room table, and we can take our seats." She'd already decided not to tell Lyle about Kendra changing her mind regarding the adoption until they were alone this evening. It would be too difficult to say it in front of Kendra.

"Okay, just let me get washed up." Lyle gave Heidi's arm a tender squeeze before he left the room.

Kendra picked up the amber-brewed tea sitting near the refrigerator. She also got out a tray full of ice before turning to face Heidi. "Lyle doesn't know about me moving back with my folks, does he?"

"No, I haven't said anything yet." Heidi's voice caught in her throat. She picked up a pair of pot holders, opened the oven door, and brought out the meat loaf. After placing it on a platter, she sliced up their main course.

Kendra paused a minute, blinking rapidly, then without a word, she made a hasty exit with the tea and ice cubes.

Soon Lyle returned from washing up and offered to carry the meat loaf to the table. Heidi gave a brief nod and followed him with the beans and potatoes. Then, remembering the carrots and celery that had been sliced, she returned to the kitchen to get the container. When Heidi returned to the dining room, she took a seat across from Kendra, and they all bowed for silent prayer. Lyle sat at the head of the table, and he cleared his throat when he'd finished praying. Heidi took this as a cue, and she lifted her head. It had been difficult to even formulate a prayer. Although she was thankful for the food on their table, she felt no gratitude for the fact that her hopes and dreams of being a parent had been crushed. She couldn't let it defeat her, though; she had to be strong.

After the food was passed around, Lyle looked over at Kendra and smiled. "I was asking Heidi about your appointment earlier. How did it go?"

Kendra picked up her iced tea and took a drink. "Umm. . . It went fine. The doctor said the baby and I are doing okay."

"Good to hear." As if sensing Heidi's gloomy mood, Lyle reached over and lightly touched her arm. "You're not eating much."

Her lips quivered. "I–I'm not really hungry tonight."

"How come?" He reached for the bowl of potatoes and helped himself to several pieces. "Did you have too much to eat for lunch?"

Before Heidi could respond, Kendra blurted, "I believe it's my fault Heidi's not hungry. She's upset." She paused and looked at Heidi before continuing. "I can't blame her, and I'm sure you'll be upset, too, with what I have to tell you."

Lyle's brows drew together. "What is it, Kendra?"

"I've changed my mind about giving up my baby."

His eyebrows shot straight up. "What?"

Kendra explained the situation and said her parents wanted her to move back home. "I'll be packing up my things and leaving in the morning."

Heidi wished Kendra hadn't said anything—especially during their meal. Her shoulders slumped as she dropped her gaze and stared at her uneaten food. Heidi felt her husband's eyes upon her, and she couldn't help wondering what Lyle must be thinking right now. Her heart felt like it couldn't sink any lower. *It's so unfair. How could this be happening to Lyle and me?*

Chapter 2

Lyle placed his hands on Heidi's shoulders, where she stood at their bedroom window watching the remaining colorful leaves swaying gently in the trees. "Are you all right? You've been staring out the window for the last ten minutes. If we don't get ready for church soon we're going to be late."

"It's our off-Sunday," she reminded. "We can stay home today and do our own private devotions."

"I realize that, but I thought we were going to visit a neighboring community today, like we often do between our own church district's biweekly Sunday services."

Groaning, she flopped onto the bed. "I don't feel like going. It would be hard for me to sit and watch other women holding their *bopplin*."

"There are babies in our own district, too. Are you going to stay home from church every Sunday because of that?"

Heidi blinked several times, willing herself not to cry. She'd had enough tearful spells since Kendra had moved out two weeks ago.

The bed creaked beneath his weight as Lyle took a seat beside Heidi and clasped her hand. "Don't you think it's time to let go of your grief and get back to the business of living?"

She pulled away from his grasp. "That's easy enough for you to say. You never really wanted to adopt Kendra's baby. You only agreed to it because of me."

He shook his head. "Not true, Heidi. It may have been the case at first, but I changed my mind, and was looking forward to being a *daed*." Lyle pressed a hand to his chest. "I'm hurt by Kendra's decision as well."

She tipped her head. "Really? You haven't shown it that much."

"I keep busy with my work and try not to dwell on what happened. Don't you think it was hard for me to take the crib down and haul it out to the barn? Like you, I couldn't bear looking at it." Lyle leaned his head against Heidi's. "We can't change the situation; Kendra's moved out and gone back to live with her parents." He paused and drew a deep breath. "I've reached the conclusion that the adoption must not have been God's will for us."

Heidi stiffened. "So are you saying God doesn't want us to become parents?" Her throat felt swollen from holding back tears, and she swallowed hard to push down the lump that had formed.

"I don't know if God wants us to have children or not, but if it's His will for us to become parents, then we'll be given another chance to adopt."

"Oh, so you think some other pregnant woman is going to show up at our doorstep and ask us to adopt her child?" It wasn't right to speak to her husband in such a sarcastic tone, but Heidi couldn't seem to hold her tongue this morning.

"That is not what I meant."

"What then?"

"We can put our name in with the adoption lawyer, and. . ."

"I don't want to." Folding her arms, Heidi shook her head stubbornly. "Not now, anyway. Even if the lawyer found another birth mother seeking adoptive parents to take her child, she might change her mind at the last minute, like Kendra did." Heidi's voice cracked. "I can't deal with another disappointment, Lyle."

He slipped his arm around her waist. "Let's wait a few months, then we can talk about this again. Okay?"

She lifted her shoulders in a brief shrug. What choice did she have?

"Have you thought about teaching another cooking class? You enjoyed the last one you taught, and your students learned a lot more than cooking from you. It would give you something meaningful to do, and teaching six more classes might prove to be fun."

Heidi couldn't deny having enjoyed teaching her first set of students.

During the six classes she'd taught, some wonderful things had happened. She would never forget how Ron Hensley turned his life over to Christ and went back to his hometown to make amends with his grown children and ex-wife. Then there was Loretta Donnelly, who'd formed a relationship with their friend and neighbor, Eli Miller, and was preparing to join the Amish church this fall. Heidi had been pleased when Charlene Higgins, engaged to be married, learned how to cook under her tutorage. The young school teacher had gained more confidence in the kitchen, which in turn, gave Charlene a better relationship with her future mother-in-law. Even Kendra Perkins had changed during the time she'd been in the class, focusing on the positive, rather than letting negative thoughts fill her mind.

Despite Heidi's disappointment over not being able to adopt Kendra's baby, she wished the young woman well. "Maybe it is time to teach another class," she murmured. "At least it would keep me busy."

Lyle patted her arm. "Good for you."

Drawing strength from deep within, Heidi turned toward the closet. "I'll change into my church clothes and be ready to leave for church by the time you have the horse and buggy ready."

He smiled and leaned down to give her a kiss. "You'll be glad you went once we're sitting in church and singing familiar hymns from the *Ausbund*."

"Jah, you're probably right. The songs of old, as well as our ministers' sermons are enough to lift anyone's spirits."

------ ◦◦◦◦ ------

Coshocton, Ohio

"Hey, buddy, what's for breakfast? You're not gonna give us any leftover stew, I hope."

"No, Andy, I'm certainly not. We're gonna have cold cereal this morning." Bill Mason ground his teeth together. He and a couple of his buddies had gone camping at his cabin for the weekend, and as usual, he'd gotten stuck with all the cooking.

Andy, Russ, and Tom wrinkled their noses. "Come on, Bill,"

Russ said. "Can't you do better than that? If I wanted cold cereal for breakfast, I could have stayed home."

"Maybe you should have then." Bill poked Russ's arm. "Whenever we go camping you guys always want me to cook, but then all you do is complain."

Tom shifted on his canvas camping stool and leaned toward the fire he'd recently built in the pit outside Bill's cabin. "Know what I think?"

Bill shook his head. He had a mind to throw his gear in his rig and head for home. *Let 'em fend for themselves and see how they like it.*

"I think you oughta take some cooking classes. If you started on 'em right away, by the time deer season starts, you might be ready to cook us some decent meals."

"Humph!" Bill folded his arms. "Maybe you should be the one to take cooking classes." It was hard not to let his so-called friends get under his skin this morning. Bill hadn't slept well last night, even though his was the only bed inside the cabin. The other men had bedded down near the fireplace with their sleeping bags on fold-away cots.

Tom shook his head. "Nope. Out of the four of us, you're the only one who likes to cook."

"Tom's right." Andy gave a nod. "Even if I took classes, it would do me no good."

Bill grunted. "Well, you'd better get used to my cooking then, 'cause I ain't takin' no cooking lessons—end of story." He grabbed a box of cereal and set it on the metal folding table he'd set up near the fire pit. "And by the way, I don't actually like to cook; we just wouldn't eat if I didn't do it, 'cause none of you guys can do much more than boil water."

Tom threw another log on the fire. "You're right about that, but even if we could cook a decent meal, you'd probably still do it." He pointed his finger at Bill. "'Cause you like to be in control of things, since this is your hunting cabin."

Bill massaged his temples. *I wonder if it would have been better for* me to go to church today instead of camping with this bunch of ingrates. The truth was he hadn't been to church in a good many years. More than likely, he'd never step into a church building again.

———————— ⌯⌯⌯ ————————

Millersburg, Ohio

Clutching a plastic container, Nicole Smith ambled across the room and placed it on the table. "Here you go, Tony. Are you happy now?"

Nicole's freckle-faced, nine-year-old brother looked up at her and frowned. "Is that all I get for breakfast—just some boiled eggs?"

She pointed to the plate in the middle of the table. "You can have some of the bread I toasted, too."

Tony squinted his blue eyes, and wrinkled his nose. "You don't have to be so bossy, Nicki."

She shook her finger at him. "Don't call me that. My name is Nicole. Do you hear me, Tony? N–i–c–o–l–e. Nicole."

He puffed out his cheeks and grabbed a piece of toast, then slathered it with strawberry jam. "Mama calls you Nicki."

"That's right, and she knows I don't like that nickname." Nicole looked at her twelve-year-old sister. "Are eggs and toast okay for you, Heather, or do you want a bowl of cold cereal?"

"I don't want either." Heather shook her blond head. "I want pancakes this morning."

Tony bobbed his head. "Yeah, that'd be a nice change."

Nicole felt like telling her siblings if they wanted pancakes, they should get out the ingredients and fix them, but that would be a mistake—even worse than if she made them herself. "Listen, you both know I'm not good at making pancakes. The last ones I made turned out all rubbery." Nicole plopped both hands against her slender hips. "I'm tired of you both wanting something different every day. Can't you eat what I fix for breakfast without complaining?"

"I don't like cold cereal." Tony wrinkled his nose again.

Heather clutched her throat, making a low-pitched gagging noise. "The taste of boiled eggs makes me feel sick to my stomach. You oughta learn how to make somethin' else for a change."

"All right you two; don't give your big sister a hard time. Nicole does the best she can." Dad came into the kitchen and took a seat at the head of the table. He paused long enough to add some cream to his coffee, then helped himself to a piece of toast.

"She needs to learn how to cook somethin' besides cold cereal, boiled eggs, and toast." Heather looked at Nicole. "Maybe you should take some cooking lessons. Then you can make us some yummy-looking stuff like that lady on TV who has the cooking show."

"Dad doesn't have enough money to pay for cooking lessons." Gritting her teeth, Nicole grabbed a hard-boiled egg and cracked it open. *Cooking meals for my sister and brother, as well as Dad, shouldn't be my job anyway. It was Tonya's responsibility, and she oughta be here taking care of us right now.*

Nicole tried not to dwell on it, but there were times, like now, when her anger bubbled to the surface. She was a sophomore in high school and should be having fun during her teen years, not babysitting, cooking, cleaning, and doing all the other things her mother used to do before she started drinking and ran off with another man. The high hopes Nicole once had for her high-school years had died. Everything she did now was an unappreciated chore.

Nicole couldn't fault Dad for agreeing to the divorce Tonya asked for—especially when she said she didn't love him anymore and had started seeing another man. But that didn't make it any easier to deal with the disappointment Nicole, Dad, and her siblings all felt. The responsibilities on Nicole's shoulders had increased this past year, and it was hard not to feel bitter and let anger take control.

Nicole had given up on her dreams of going to the upcoming homecoming dance that would be held the night before the big football game against her school's biggest rival. Win or lose, after the game there'd be a big bonfire. Guess she'd be missing all that, too. Well, what did it matter? She had no one to go with anyhow. She couldn't really blame the few friends she used to hang out with for not wanting to include her when she always turned down their invitations to go places and do things with them. Even after-school clubs like being on the yearbook staff, which she wouldn't have minded joining, were out of the question now. Nicole always had to get home right away, do several chores, and of course, get dinner going before Dad got there.

Nicole rubbed her forehead and heaved a sigh. Becoming a cheerleader was an even bigger pipe dream—a far-fetched hope that would never come true.

She jumped when Dad placed his hand on her shoulder. "You know, your brother and sister could be right. Taking some cooking classes might be a good idea, Nicole."

Her eyes narrowed. "You're kidding, right?"

He shook his head. "It might be fun and even good for you. I think I'll start looking around to see if there are any classes being offered in our area."

Lips pressed together, Nicole slunk down in her chair. She hoped if Dad did start looking, he'd come up empty-handed, because the last thing she wanted to do was take cooking classes, with some stranger telling her what to do. Besides, when would she have time for that? Nicole was already on overload.

⸻ ⟡ ⸻

Canton, Ohio

Kendra gripped the grocery cart, as she pushed it down the baby aisle. Since moving in with her parents, she'd tried to make good use of her time and help wherever, and whenever, she could. Her mother needed a few groceries, so Kendra had volunteered to go—if for no other reason, than to get out of the house for a while. Now, she wondered if it had been such a good idea.

Since early this morning, she'd been having what she thought might be the early stages of labor. A dull, persistent pain throbbed through her lower back, but not bad enough to stop her from doing anything. Kendra wanted to keep mobile and stay busy, to help keep her mind off things, and grocery shopping would do just that.

As the time drew closer to her due date, Kendra grew increasingly apprehensive. What was labor like, and how long would it last? Could she withstand the pain? Would she have any complications? Would her baby be born heathy? Kendra had all the normal questions of a first-time mother, but she had even more important things to ponder. *Did I make the right decision to move back home? Would it have been better for my child to be raised by the Troyers and not under my parents' influence? Mom can be so spineless, and Dad. . . Well, he's impossible to please most of the time. He may have invited me back, but I don't think he's ever forgiven me for bringing shame on my family.*

Already, Kendra's folks had been suggesting things they thought would be best for their first grandchild. But Kendra did not commit to anything. She placed her hand on her stomach. "This is still my baby, and I have the final say, no matter what Mom and Dad might suggest," she huffed under her breath. Kendra kept walking when a shopper looked quizzically at her.

"Didn't you ever talk to yourself?" Kendra mumbled low enough so the man wouldn't hear her. Then she stopped at the diaper section, which took up a large part of the shelves. Kendra didn't realize how many selections there would be, and how many different brands of disposable diapers were available for purchase. It was a bit mind-boggling.

Pulling an envelope from her purse, Kendra flipped through the coupons inside to see if any were still active and hadn't expired yet. "Oh good." She took out a dollar-off coupon. "Here's one I can use." Thankfully, this store carried the brand, and she could save a dollar, at least. After realizing she'd need to buy two packs of diapers to qualify for the coupon, Kendra made room in the cart to put them. When she grabbed the second pack off the shelf, a sharp pain stabbed from her lower back all the way to the front of her swollen middle.

Grasping her stomach, the pack of diapers fell, and she shuffled over to her cart to hang on. At the same time, a young woman, who was also pregnant, but not as big as Kendra, stopped to see if she needed any help.

"Are you okay?" the kindly lady asked. She picked up the diapers and placed them in Kendra's cart.

"I—I think so." Kendra remained still until the pain subsided. "It's not my due date yet, and I'm hoping these aren't labor pains I've been having."

"By the way, my name's Delana." The woman rubbed her stomach. "I'm not due until the beginning of December, but in the last maternity class I attended, we learned about false labor. Do you think that's what you might be having?"

"I'm not sure. I've had a backache all morning." Kendra reached around and rubbed the small of her back. "But then, since I've grown larger, my back always hurts, so who knows?"

"Okay, well, maybe you'd better finish your shopping and get back home, just to be on the safe side," Delana suggested. "Would you like me to call your husband or someone else?"

"No, that's okay. I only live about fifteen minutes from here." No way would Kendra admit to a stranger that she had no husband. Her situation was no one's business but her own. Kendra hadn't even bothered to introduce herself—not even after the woman had said her name.

"Well, if you're sure." Delana hesitated a minute. "It was nice talking to you, and good luck."

"Same to you." Kendra pointed to the diapers in her cart. "Thanks for assisting me."

"Sure, no problem." Delana moved on.

Looking at her mother's list, Kendra headed for the frozen food aisle. *Let's see. . . Mom wants four packages of mixed vegetables.* This morning, her mother had mentioned wanting to make soup for supper. Luckily the store was having a sale on a well-known brand this week. *Ten packages for ten dollars. Sounds like a good deal.*

As Kendra held the freezer door open to get the frozen vegetables, another pain, worse than the last one, made her scream. This time, the cart's support did no good, and she doubled over and crouched on the floor, barely able to deal with the pain. By this time, several patrons gathered around, including the young pregnant woman she'd spoke to minutes ago.

Delana didn't ask any questions. She got out her cell phone and called 911. An older woman took her sweater and bunched it up to make a pillow for Kendra's head. "There, there dear, lie down on the floor and try to relax. Help will be here soon."

By then, Delana had made the call and hunkered down next to Kendra, taking her hand and patting it gently. "Looks like you might be having your baby a little sooner than you expected. Just breathe deeply and think positive thoughts. The paramedics will be here soon."

Delana looked up at the other people gawking at Kendra, and said, "She'll be okay. The ambulance is on the way. No need to hover all around. Please, just give her some space."

A few people hesitated, but then they finally dispersed and went about their shopping.

When only Delana and the older woman were kneeling beside Kendra, she didn't feel quite so intimidated.

Delana leaned closer. "I never got your name."

"It–it's Kendra." She tried to get up, but the older lady told her to stay put.

"But the pain is gone now, and I feel okay. My water hasn't even broken yet, so I don't think the baby's coming right away."

"Still, you should get checked out." Delana placed her hand on Kendra's shoulder. "What if you were driving home and had another bad contraction? You don't want to have an accident and get hurt or injure the baby."

"I guess you are right," Kendra relented, even though the floor was hard and uncomfortable.

As she remained there, trying not to think about her situation and willing herself to relax, Kendra looked toward the end of the aisle. For a fleeting moment she saw a man who'd been looking her way, turn quickly and scurry around the corner.

Was that Dad? If it was, then why didn't he come see if I was okay?

Millersburg

Later that evening, Nicole reclined on her bed, working on a math assignment. She laughed out loud, thinking about her dad's silly idea of her taking a cooking class. "I can't believe he'd even suggest such a thing."

Soon, her bedroom door opened, and Heather walked in. "I heard you laughing. What's so funny in here?" She flopped on the end of Nicole's bed.

Nicole rolled over and sat up, swinging her legs over the side of the bed. "You heard me laugh?"

Her sister gave a nod. "Were you talkin' to yourself, too?"

"Yeah. I was thinking about Dad saying I should take a cooking class. Can you imagine me doing something like that?"

Heather shrugged. "It's not a bad idea, you know. We get tired of eating the same old things all the time."

"You can take over for me anytime you want." Nicole stretched her arms over her head. "It's not easy being in my shoes, you know."

"It's been hard for all of us since Mom left." Heather's chin quivered. "I wish she'd come back, Nicki."

Nicole gave a quick shake of her head, choosing not to make an issue of her sister calling her Nicki. "Not with her drinking problem, Heather. That's what got her messed up in the first place." Her gaze flicked up. "Besides, she's married to someone else now." *And he's a big creep,* she mentally added.

Heather sniffed. "Don't know why she'd want to leave Dad. He's a great guy, don't you think?"

"Absolutely. He works hard and does the best he can for us. We're lucky to have a dad like him." Nicole gave her sister's arm a pat. "You'd better get ready for bed, and I need to finish my homework."

"Okay." Heather scooched off the bed. "See you in the morning."

Nicole smiled. "Yep. I'll have your cold cereal ready and waiting."

Her sister paused at the door and wrinkled her nose. "If Dad can afford it, I think you'd better take a cooking class." Heather hurried out of the room before Nicole could form a response.

Nicole picked up her math book and stuffed it in her backpack next to the bed. She was too tired to do any more problems. If she got up early tomorrow maybe, she could finish then.

Yawning, she stretched out on the bed again and closed her eyes. A vision of her mother popped into her head—scraggly blond hair she sometimes wore pulled back in a ponytail, and blue eyes often rimmed with red. *Why'd you have to ruin things between you and Dad? How come you chose your new husband over us? He's not even a nice man.*

Chapter 3

Walnut Creek

The sun's announcement of morning cast an orange tint to the dimly lit kitchen, where only a small, battery-operated lamp had been turned on. "You look *mied*, Heidi." Lyle poured himself a second cup of coffee and took a seat at the kitchen table. "Are you sure you're feeling up to teaching a cooking class this morning? We can still go out to supper this evening, but maybe you should take it easy the rest of the day."

Heidi yawned. "I didn't sleep well last night, but I'll be fine."

"Did you have a bad dream?" He added a spoonful of sugar to his cup and stirred it around.

Heidi poured hot water over her tea bag and sat in the chair across from him. "Jah. It wasn't really bad though—just unsettling."

"What was it about?"

"Kendra's boppli. Only in the dream, the baby was ours. At least it seemed that way. She was beautiful, Lyle, with golden hair, so soft and downy." Heidi lowered her head and massaged the back of her sore neck. "We were in the nursery with her. I watched, while you held the precious infant tenderly in your arms. You wore your Sunday clothes, and I needed to finish getting ready for church. It was our first service with the baby. I was thrilled to show her to everyone."

Heidi lifted her head and looked at Lyle. Sympathy showed on his face as he lightly stroked her forearm. "All at once, we were at church," she continued. "I sat on a wooden bench, holding the baby and singing a hymn from the Ausbund. Then I noticed a woman I'd never met before, sitting next to me. She leaned over, and whispering, asked what I had named the baby." Heidi paused and took a sip of the herbal tea, then set her cup down. "I stammered and hesitated with what to say, not knowing what the infant's name even was. I looked across the room, where you sat beside your friend Eli, hoping to get your attention, but that didn't work."

Her brows furrowed. "I excused myself to the woman and rushed out of the barn where the service was being held. Holding the boppli close, I gulped in some air." Perspiration beaded on Heidi's cheeks, remembering the stress she'd felt in the dream. "The next thing I knew, there was no baby. I was standing in our kitchen with my first cooking class. Kendra was there, wearing an apron, like my other students. Smiling, she stepped up to me and asked what we'd named the baby. My jaw dropped. We still hadn't named her yet." Heidi began rubbing her neck again. "Then I woke up."

"Sounds like quite a strange *draame* you had." Lyle took over massaging her neck. "No wonder my *fraa* seems deprived of her rest. After having such a night of strange dreaming, who wouldn't be?" His tone was gentle and soothing. "Once more I have to ask—are you sure you're up to teaching the class today?"

"I'm tired, but I'll be able to teach my students." Heidi released a lingering sigh. "I have to follow through with this, Lyle. Five people have signed up for my class, and I won't let them down." Squinting her eyes, she turned to face him. "Besides, as I recall, it was your suggestion that I teach another group of students."

"True." He took a sip of coffee and set his mug down. "But I could have been wrong. You might not feel up to it yet."

"I'm fine physically, and keeping busy will help to ward off my depression." She glanced toward the door leading to the hall and grimaced. "It's still hard for me to look at the empty room that would have been our baby's nursery without thinking about Kendra and how she went back on her word. It seems so unfair."

He touched her hand. "But can you really blame her? Kendra's back with her folks again, and you were praying for that."

"Jah." Heidi pushed away from the table. "I wonder if she's had her baby yet."

"Didn't she promise to let us know?"

She gave a slow nod. "Maybe she changed her mind about notifying us, the way she did about giving us the boppli. Guess I'm overreacting. The baby's not due until next month."

"Well, October is only about two weeks away." Lyle left his chair and pulled Heidi into his arms, gently patting her back. "I'm sure Kendra or someone from her family will give us a call after the baby is born."

"Maybe so. I hope you're right." Heidi tried to remain positive. It wasn't in her nature to carry a grudge or think negative thoughts, but she hadn't fully come to grips with them losing out on the opportunity to become parents. Somehow, she would need to work through it, though, and the only way she could think to do it was to stay busy and keep her focus on something else.

Heidi glanced at the clock on the wall near the stove. In one hour her new students would arrive, and then she'd have something else to concentrate on.

———————⌖———————

Canton

Grabbing his notebook and pen, Todd Collins rushed out the front door of his condo. Today he was going to test the limits of his palate— or at the very least, attempt something he hadn't tried before. As a food critic, Todd had learned to try almost any food he came across, no matter how strange or foreign it might seem. He'd been in many different restaurants—Italian, Chinese, Mexican, and several others, critiquing countless entrées and various meals. Some small, ordinary places served delicious dishes, while some high-end locations were not so good. Todd had even traveled to food festivals and become obsessive in his search for new food trends and ideas. He'd also researched other food critics and chefs, and taken a few cooking classes as well. Today, however, Todd was about to embark on something unique.

Normally, when he was critiquing a restaurant, Todd had to go incognito—never meeting the owners or getting to know them personally. A few times, however, he'd introduced himself and even made a few acquaintances. This morning, though, he could just be himself, as he was sure no one would recognize him. Besides, even with other people there taking the class, he didn't plan to broadcast his profession. It would be better that way, since the Amish teacher might be offended if she thought someone was critiquing her. And she probably wouldn't like it if she knew Todd eventually planned to write an article for his column about his experience of taking a cooking class in an Amish home.

I'm not really being dishonest, acting like a dumb schmuck who can hardly boil water. That part is actually true. I can say, however, that I'm one of the best at discerning good food from bad. Tasting all kinds of fare that I hope to write about is my goal with the job I currently have.

Todd kicked a stone with the toe of his shoe as he approached his flashy red car. He stood close to the side mirror, gazing at his reflection. *I'm not such a bad guy, really. Just misunderstood, that's all. It's an Amish lady teaching the cooking classes, and those attending with me are probably a bunch of little old ladies who are bored and need something to do. There's no way Heidi Troyer will know who I am or figure out the reason I signed up for her class.*

———— ⌖ ————

New Philadelphia, Ohio

Allie Garrett had never been a morning person, and rushing around to get the kids ready to drop off at the babysitter's only added to her frustration today. Nola, age five, and Derek, who was nine, had been pokey eating breakfast, and now sat in the backseat of Allie's minivan squabbling over some nonsensical thing. Allie was tempted to pull over and have Derek move to the third seat, all the way in the back of the van, but she was running late and didn't want to stop and take the time to separate the two. Her kids would just have to work things out themselves.

She blew out an exasperated breath. *Such things kids find to quarrel about.* The latest, being the pull-down arm rest between her daughter and son, which somehow had become a boundary line. When one had even a finger on the other's side, the bickering instantly flared up, and a shoving of hands and arms followed. Then, every time Derek said something, his sister mimicked him, which only made things worse.

Resisting the temptation to scold them, Allie clasped the wheel even tighter, and concentrated on the road ahead. She hoped by ignoring their childish attempts to win out, they would eventually quit.

She looked forward to attending Heidi Troyer's cooking class today, if for no other reason than to get away from the children for a few hours. She was a devoted mother and loved Nola and Derek very much, but sometimes they got on her nerves. One of the reasons could be because Allie worked as a receptionist for a pediatric dentist and had to deal with whiny children four days a week. But the biggest reason Allie felt overwhelmed when her kids acted up was because she shouldered most of the responsibility for their care. Her husband, Steve, was a policeman and worked odd hours, so he often wasn't around when Nola and Derek were home. To make matters worse, Steve frequently filled in for others on the force when they needed time off.

Allie felt like a widow sometimes, and knowing how dangerous his job was, she worried she might become one. Any time the phone rang at odd hours, her fears heightened, and she always thought the worst.

Pulling up to the babysitter's house, Allie turned off the engine and went around to the side of the van to let the children out, thankful they had finally settled down. It was fortunate for Mrs. Andrews, their babysitter, who never hesitated to report how well her children got along. *Why is it that kids are usually on their best behavior for someone else?* Allie wondered.

Switching mental gears, Allie thought about the cooking classes her husband had paid for on her behalf. If nothing else came from taking the classes, at least she would learn how to cook some traditional Amish meals, and it might even prove to be fun. Maybe she would come away with some new ideas for what to fix for supper. Steve might be impressed with her cooking—at least on the evenings he was home and could join her and the children at the table. It had been some time since he'd complimented Allie on anything she'd made. Maybe the gift of the classes was his way of letting her know she needed to improve her cooking skills. Either that, or Steve wanted her to do something fun and creative so she'd stop complaining about him being gone so often. Well, no matter the reasons, she was committed to giving these classes a try.

Dover, Ohio

Lisa Brooks stood in front of the bathroom mirror, staring at her dark circles and red-rimmed eyes, accentuated by her fair skin. In addition to meeting with a client about the five-tiered cake, as well as the meal she would be catering for the couple's wedding reception next week, she'd stayed up late last night, reading a book she'd recently bought about the Amish culture. Since Lisa would be attending a cooking class this morning, taught by an Amish woman, it was a good idea to learn what she could about their lifestyle. The last thing she wanted to do was embarrass herself by saying or doing something foolish or that went against the teacher's customs and religious beliefs.

One thing Lisa had been surprised to learn was that some Amish who lived in Holmes County, Ohio, had installed solar panels in their homes. She wondered if Heidi Troyer's house had the advantage of solar power. It would certainly make it easier to cook meals and run appliances. She couldn't imagine trying to operate her catering business without the advantage of electricity.

The more she'd read, the more intrigued Lisa became with the way this group of Plain people lived. She couldn't believe they had no electrical appliances in their homes or that they used gas lanterns or battery-operated devices in the evenings for lighting. *How amazing!* Lisa scratched her head. *They seem almost like pioneers in our modern day. And yet, this Amish lady can still give cooking classes.*

Lisa hoped to learn some things about Amish cooking during the six classes and incorporate them in some of the meals she offered to her clients. She couldn't say her business was booming, but over time and through word of mouth, Lisa trusted her income from the catering business would increase. She did advertise in the local paper but intended to branch out to papers in neighboring towns. Or perhaps she would create a website, if she could find someone to help her design it.

Lisa picked up the comb and ran it through her short blond hair. Regardless of how tired she looked, it was time to go.

Chapter 4

Walnut Creek

Lisa gripped the steering wheel and studied the mailboxes as she watched for Heidi Troyer's address. Approaching the right one, she jumped when a horn honked from behind. "What in the world?" She glanced in the rearview mirror and saw a flashy-looking red sports car following much too close.

Signaling her intent to go left, Lisa turned up the driveway. The other vehicle did the same. She was about to pull in next to a pickup truck, when the sports car zipped past her and took the spot.

Lisa gritted her teeth. *What's wrong with that driver, cutting me off like that? And in someone's driveway, no less! Whoever it is, they don't seem to care about anybody but themselves.*

She found another place to park, and when she got out of the van, Lisa had to force her mouth to keep from saying something she might later regret. The sports-car driver had also exited his vehicle and was walking toward the house. He paused and turned to look at her. "Guess I was a little quicker than you. Sorry about that." He motioned to his fancy car. "That baby gets me where I want to go."

Lisa nearly had to bite her tongue to keep from saying anything sharp to the belligerent man. She trailed behind him as he hurried toward the house, like a little kid needing to be first. She had to admit the guy was quite handsome. He was tall, dark-haired, and wore a pair of navy blue dress slacks, a crisp pale blue shirt, and black well-polished shoes. He walked with a purpose and an air of confidence. Lisa envied him for that, because at the moment, her stomach felt as though it were tied in knots.

As she reached up to touch her short strands, Lisa couldn't help staring at his thick, slightly curly hair. *What some girls wouldn't give for a head of hair like that.* This man was well-groomed from head to toe, and not a hair on his head looked out of place.

As he approached the porch, he turned again, this time glancing over his shoulder, and gave a stiff nod in her direction. She forced a smile she didn't really feel, and followed him onto the porch. *I hope this fellow, wearing heavy cologne, isn't here for the reason I am. What would a guy like him be doing at a cooking class anyway? Or maybe he's not here for that. He could be selling something, I suppose.*

<hr />

Heidi had let Bill Mason into the house a few minutes ago, and now someone else was knocking on her door. She told Bill to take a seat in the kitchen, then stepped into the entryway and opened the door. Heidi shook hands with a young, dark-haired man and a pretty woman with blond hair after they entered the house.

She looked a little closer at the woman, and noticed faint dark circles under her appealing blue eyes. Heidi wondered if the young woman may have had trouble sleeping. She tapped a finger against her chin. *One thing for sure, if I can put others ahead of myself, maybe I'll be too occupied to focus on my own discomfort. I wonder what I'll learn from this group of students.* Teaching her previous set of students had felt like finding hidden treasures, the way some of them shared from their past, present, or what they hoped for in the future. Each session Heidi had taught so far seemed interesting in its own way; especially when her pupils caught on to whatever she was teaching them to make and gained confidence in their abilities. Deep down, Heidi was glad her husband had suggested she teach cooking classes in their home. It had been as meaningful to her as it was to her students.

"I'm Heidi Troyer. As soon as the other students get here I'll ask everyone to introduce themselves." She gestured to the door leading to the kitchen. "Please go in and make yourselves comfortable." Heidi picked up the clipboard from her desk and put a check mark next to the name of each person who had arrived.

"Okay, thank you." The young woman stepped quickly in front of the man and hurried into the other room, fanning her crimson cheeks with one hand.

The man mumbled something under his breath and followed.

I wonder if these two know each other. Heidi's lips compressed. *Could there be some kind of problem between them? I hope things don't start off on the wrong foot for this class. I'm not up to dealing with any issues today.*

After hearing another vehicle pull in, Heidi opened the door again. A teenage girl with short brown hair got out of a dark blue car. The man driving the vehicle waved and headed out of the yard. With shoulders hunched, the girl walked hesitantly up the path and onto the porch.

Heidi smiled and extended her hand. "You must be Nicole, my youngest student."

"Yeah, that's me. Hope I'm not late."

Heidi shook her head. "Three others are already inside, but I'm still waiting for another woman to arrive." She opened the door for Nicole, and they both went into the house. Heidi led the way to the kitchen and asked Nicole to take a seat at the table. She was pleased the young lady had signed up. Most of Heidi's students were a bit older, like the ones who had already arrived.

Glancing at the clock across the room, she realized it was five minutes after ten. Heidi was about to suggest everyone go ahead and introduce themselves, when a knock sounded at the door. She excused herself and went to answer it.

A lovely, dark-haired woman waited on the porch. "Are you here for the cooking class?"

"Yes. I'm Allie Garrett, and I am sorry for being late. I had to drop my kids off at the sitters, and then. . ." She paused and drew a quick breath. "My GPS wasn't picking up signals for a time, so until I saw the address on your mailbox, I thought I might be lost."

"It's okay." Heidi placed her hand on Allie's arm. "You're only a few minutes late, and we haven't yet begun."

"Oh good. That's a relief."

She led the way to the kitchen, and after Allie took a seat, Heidi stood at the head of the table. Her stomach quivered with nervous apprehension, which made no sense. This wasn't the first class she'd ever taught. Maybe it was the students' somber expressions that caused her nerves to flare up. The teenaged girl avoided eye contact; the dark haired woman picked at her cuticles; the young man dressed in clothes nice enough for church glanced around the room as though checking things out; the blond-haired woman fingered her gold-chained necklace; and the older man with partially gray hair kept looking at his watch. She hoped they weren't already bored. Or maybe everyone felt as nervous as she did right now.

Heidi cleared her throat and moistened her parched lips with her tongue. "Hello, everyone. I'm Heidi Troyer. Welcome to my cooking class. Before we begin, did everyone remember to bring an apron?"

Lisa, Allie, and Todd held up their aprons, but Nicole shook her head. "Didn't know I was supposed to bring one."

"Me neither," Bill mumbled.

"It was on your registration form," Heidi explained.

"I didn't see it. Dad filled out the paper for me, since coming here was his idea," Nicole said.

Bill's forehead wrinkled. "Guess I missed the part about the apron, too."

"Well, don't worry about it. I have extra ones you can both use today." Heidi opened a drawer and took out two aprons. She handed the green one to Nicole, and the blue apron she gave to Bill. Then she returned to her spot at the head of the table. "Now I'd like everyone to introduce themselves and tell us the reason you signed up for this class." She gestured to the blond-haired woman. "Would you mind going first?"

"No, of course not." The young woman sat up a little straighter, as though gaining more confidence. "My name is Lisa Brooks. I have a catering business, and I'm taking this class to broaden my cooking skills." She turned to the dark-haired man sitting beside her. "You're next."

"Yeah, okay. My name's Todd Collins, and. . ." He paused and pulled his fingers down the side of his clean-shaven face. "Umm. . .I enjoy eating different kinds of food, so the reason I'm here is to taste, and hopefully learn how to cook, some traditional Amish dishes."

Heidi smiled, motioning to the older man who'd arrived first.

He pushed his chair aside and stood. "My name's Bill Mason, and I'm here to learn how to cook something other than hunter's stew." With no further word or explanation, he returned to his chair.

Heidi gestured to the teenage girl. "Would you please tell us your name and the reason you came to my class?"

"I'm Nicole Smith, and like I said before, my dad signed me up for the class. Guess he figured I should learn how to make something other than cold sandwiches and frozen microwave dinners. He and Tonya got a divorce, so all the cooking and cleaning falls on me now." Nicole's lips curled, and her tone sounded tart. "I'm also stuck taking care of my little brother and sister."

"Was Tonya your stepmother?" Lisa asked.

"Nope. Tonya's my real mom."

"Oh, I see." Lisa lifted her gaze to the ceiling, before looking away.

Heidi's heart went out to Nicole. It had to be hard for her, living without her mother and shouldering the responsibility for taking care of her siblings. It surprised her, though, that the teenaged girl would refer to her mom by her first name.

"I guess that leaves me now." The dark-haired woman who'd been last to arrive pushed an unruly strand of hair away from her slender oval face. "My name is Allie Garrett, and as a birthday present, my husband gave me a gift certificate to take this class. He said he thought it would be something fun for me to do. I agreed to take it because I hoped I might learn how to make some different dishes for my husband and our two children." She gestured to Heidi. "Do you have any kids?"

Heidi swallowed hard. She'd hoped this touchy subject wouldn't come up today. Every time someone asked if she had children, it felt as though her heart had been pierced with an arrow. "No, my husband

and I have not been able to have any children."

"Oh, that's a shame." Allie's tone was soothing, and Heidi feared if she didn't change the subject right away, she might give in to her tears, which always seemed to be just below the surface. Crying was certainly the last thing she wanted to do in front of her new group of students.

"All right then, that's enough about me." Heidi clasped her hands together. "I hope you will all enjoy the class. And now, let's begin, as I share with you a few helpful hints about cooking."

"What are we gonna learn how to cook?" Bill leaned forward with his elbows on the table.

Allie resisted the temptation to roll her eyes. *Does the man have to be so impatient? He should at least give the teacher a chance to speak.*

"The recipe I'm going to teach you how to make this morning is baked oatmeal. But first, I'd like to give you a few handouts with some tips for the kitchen." Heidi passed out a sheet of paper to each of them. "Before you all go home today I'll give everyone a three-by-five card with the recipe you learned to make this morning."

"Good thing, 'cause with the way my brain's been workin' lately, I'd probably forget everything you told us by the time I got home." Grinning, Bill's gaze traveled from person to person sitting around the table.

Allie studied the first handout Heidi gave them. It listed everything from how to keep hot oil from splattering out of the frying pan, to the best way to store dried pasta, rice, and whole grains. There was also a tip about how to get onion odor off your hands, but with the exception of that, most of the other things she knew already, since she'd been cooking since she was a teenager.

While Heidi offered some measuring tips, Allie shifted in her chair as an unexpected image of Steve flashed before her. He'd worked all night, and by the time she left for the babysitter's, her husband still hadn't come home. *Is he okay? Has Steve been hurt in the line of duty?* Allie was accustomed to Steve not always being able to get in touch with her. Many times his duties became hectic, and he often came home late. It was difficult not to worry about him.

She squeezed her eyes shut. *Get a grip; you've had these worrisome thoughts before, and Steve's been okay. Just relax and keep your concentration on learning how to make baked oatmeal.*

Chapter 5

Baked oatmeal? Eyes narrowed, Todd tugged at his shirt collar. *I signed up for this class to learn about Amish cooking, not bake oatmeal of all things. Besides, who ever heard of baking oatmeal? It's supposed to be cooked on the stove in a kettle or even microwaved in a bowl.*

He glanced at the others as they looked expectantly at Heidi while she told how to combine the eggs, sugar, and butter in a baking dish, and then add the oatmeal, baking powder and salt, stirring until blended. Everyone but Allie seemed interested. She sat rubbing her forehead while staring at the kitchen table. *Maybe she's as bored as I am. Hopefully the recipes Heidi shares during the next five classes will be more interesting than today's.*

Todd looked across the table at Lisa. She glanced at him briefly, then looked away. Since she was in the catering business, she'd obviously come here to get some new meal ideas. It was nice to know he wasn't the only one with an agenda.

He studied Lisa a few seconds—shiny blond hair, vivid blue eyes, and deep dimples in both cheeks. Her only flaw was the dark circles encompassing her eyes. Todd tried not to stare at Lisa; he didn't want to appear nosey, but he'd like to know a little more about her. Other than an interest in food, he didn't know if they had anything in common. *I wonder if she's married.* He glanced at her left hand and saw no wedding ring. She'd made no mention of a husband or children, either.

"Mr. Collins, did you hear what I said?"

Todd's head jerked as he turned his focus back to the Amish teacher. "Uh. . .no, I guess not. Would you mind repeating it for me?"

"I asked if you're ready to start mixing the ingredients for your baked oatmeal now." Heidi gestured to the bowl and mixing spoon sitting on the table in front of him.

357

Todd noticed the others had also been given a bowl and large spoon. He figured from their impatient expressions, they were all waiting on him. "Yeah, sure. I'm ready to begin." Todd slid his bowl closer to Lisa's, hoping to engage her in conversation. He hoped she wouldn't think he was being too forward. Todd watched as the others began measuring and putting the ingredients in their bowls. Lisa did the same, appearing confident and happy with the pleasant smile she wore. Todd tried to copy what she did, but ended up bumping her arm, causing Lisa to add too much oatmeal.

"Oops, sorry about that. I'm not used to sharing a work space like this." Todd's face heated. He wasn't off to a good start this morning— at least not with Lisa.

Her eyes narrowed. "Well, if you weren't sitting so close."

He moved to one side, pulling his bowl with him. "Don't worry. It won't happen again."

"It's not a problem, Lisa," Heidi spoke up." Since you haven't added any liquid yet, you can just scoop out the excess oatmeal."

"Okay." Lisa did as Heidi suggested, giving Todd a sidelong glance. He wanted to say something more to her but figured it'd be best to keep silent for now.

⸻ ❧❧ ⸻

Before Allie began mixing the ingredients Heidi had given her, she pulled her cell phone out of her purse. No voice mails or text messages, so everything must be okay with Steve. No doubt she'd conjured up the earlier vision of him unnecessarily, believing he might be in some sort of trouble. Worry was a difficult habit to break.

Determined to keep her focus on the job at hand, Allie returned the phone to her purse, picked up the first egg, and cracked it into the bowl. If the baked oatmeal turned out good, she would make it for her family someday.

As she mixed the ingredients, Allie's thoughts went to Nola and Derek. *I hope they're behaving for Mrs. Andrews today.*

Allie was about to pour the runny oatmeal mixture into the small baking dish Heidi had provided, when Bill bumped her arm.

Everything in her bowl spilled onto the table. She gasped, then glared at him. "I see Todd's not the only one sitting too close to someone at this table. I hope you're planning to clean up this mess."

Red-faced, Bill gave a quick nod. "Sorry about that. You're right; I shouldn't have been sitting so close."

"I guess not." Allie glanced down at her white blouse and peach-colored maxi-skirt. "It's a good thing none of it got on my clothes." A trickle of perspiration rolled down her cheek.

"Not to worry." Heidi hurried to the sink and grabbed a sponge, as well as a dish towel. "Bill, while you are cleaning the table, I'll get out some more ingredients for Allie to mix."

Allie almost said, "Don't bother, I'm going home," but she wouldn't waste the money Steve had spent for her to take the Amish woman's cooking classes. So she forced herself to smile and said, "Thanks, I'll try to hurry mixing the ingredients so I don't hold up the class."

Heidi glanced at the clock before handing Bill the towel and sponge. "We have plenty of time left before our class ends, so don't worry about holding us up, Allie." She hoped nothing else went awry today. Her nerves were already jangled, but for the sake of her students, she had to remain calm and keep a positive attitude. When the class was over, and everyone went home, she planned to check their phone shack for messages, then lie on the couch and take a nap. Lyle wouldn't be home until suppertime, so she had all afternoon to relax and do whatever she pleased.

Once the table was cleaned, and Allie's ingredients were mixed and poured into her baking dish, Heidi explained the baking process. "Since the oatmeal mixture needs to bake for thirty minutes, and I only have one oven, three of you can put yours in now. While we wait for them to bake, I'll answer questions any of you may have."

"Sounds good to me." Bill lifted his hand. "I have a lot of questions."

After several attempts to ask Heidi questions, and Todd putting his 'two cents' worth' in, Bill gave up. *If this Todd guy knows so much, why is he taking this class? Maybe he should be the one teaching the class, instead of Heidi.*

Bill turned his attention to Nicole, who had been rather quiet during the class so far. A few times, he had caught her staring at him, but when he made eye contact with Nicole, she quickly averted her gaze. She was obviously the youngest in this group, perhaps even high-school age. There was something familiar about the girl, but Bill couldn't put his finger on it. Could it be that she attended the high school where he worked? Maybe she was a student there. But after working as a maintenance man all these years, the students became a sea of faces walking down the halls.

For almost thirty years Bill had been working at the school in Millersburg. He'd started out as a janitor, but along with that, he was taught other duties as well. This enabled him to be promoted to the position of managing maintenance. Of course, the men under him weren't the ones doing all the work at the school. Bill worked right alongside of them, and sometimes alone, when the need arose.

Manager. . .humph. . .a lot of good that title has done for me. His wife, Mona, now his ex, left him for someone else—a man she considered better.

Bill remembered how, during all the years they were married, his wife had been embarrassed about his job. When someone asked what her husband did for a living, she would answer, "He works at the school." This evasion succeeded for a while, especially when their son, Brent, was young. Most of his wife's friends assumed he was a teacher, until their own kids grew up and attended high school. Then they caught on. Some of Mona's acquaintances teased her about it and drifted away from the friendship, while others remained loyal and didn't seem to care what Bill did for a living. Still, when anyone turned their nose up, Mona had been affected deeply.

Bill's pay was decent, and they'd always had money to meet their bills, but it wasn't good enough for Mona. She left and married this so-called better man named Floyd. He was the owner of a huge equipment company, and they lived high-off-the-hog, so Bill hoped

Mona was finally happy.

One day, Bill had made the mistake of driving by Floyd and Mona's house. It was huge, in a prominent neighborhood on the other side of town. *I hope they stay on their side of town.* Bill ground his teeth together, reflecting on how he'd felt at that moment. So far, even though he'd seen Mona on a few occasions involving their son, he'd been lucky not to cross paths when she'd been with her new husband. Bill wondered if he'd ever find love again, or if he could reach the point where he could trust another woman. It would be nice to have someone waiting for him when he got home from work. On the other hand, since the divorce, he'd become set in his ways and had come to think he could do things, including cooking, on his own. He really didn't need another wife, or even a lady friend.

Nicole tapped her fingers on the edge of the table. The aroma of food baking whet her appetite. It had been a while since she'd eaten breakfast, and the bowl of cereal she'd had didn't stick to her ribs. Her baking pan was one of the first three to go into the oven, and now the last batch had been put in. Nicole would be glad when they were done and she could go home. The cooking class wasn't as much fun as she'd hoped it would be. But then, maybe that was because she was the only teenager present. Truthfully, she felt out of place here among these strangers. *Too bad I'm not the only student in the class. It would be a lot easier if Heidi could teach just me. I have some questions, but would be embarrassed to ask them in front of the others. They might think I'm stupid.*

She glanced around Heidi's modest, but well-equipped kitchen. Everything appeared neat and in order. Nothing like the kitchen at home after Nicole finished cooking something. It was a lot easier to make a mess in the kitchen then it was to clean it all up. Of course, Nicole's mother had never kept a tidy kitchen. In fact, whenever she'd been drinking, the whole house was neglected.

As though she could sense her frustration, Heidi, who sat beside her now, reached over and touched Nicole's arm. "You've been awfully quiet today. Is there anything in particular you'd like to know?"

"No, not really." Nicole dropped her gaze to the table.

"Okay. If you think of anything, please let me know."

"I'd like to ask you something," Lisa spoke up.

"Certainly." Heidi looked in her direction and smiled. "What would you like to know?"

"Can you tell us a little about the Amish way of life, and why you do without so many modern conveniences?"

"Yeah, I'd like to know that, too." Todd winked at Lisa. "In fact, I was about to ask the same question. How come there's no electricity connected to your home?"

Lisa squinted her eyes at him, then looked away. Nicole had enough smarts to know when someone was flirting, and she had this guy pegged. It wasn't right. For all Todd knew, Lisa was married. She glanced at Lisa's left hand. *Although she's not wearing a wedding ring. I hope she doesn't fall for Todd. I know his kind. He reminds me of the jerk Mom ran off with when she divorced Dad.*

Nicole turned her attention to Heidi as she began to tell the history of the Anabaptists, and how the Amish faith was a breakaway from the Mennonites. She found it interesting when Heidi explained the reason they didn't allow TVs, computers, and many other modern things to run off electricity in their homes. Those items represented a negative distraction that could take their focus off God and family.

Nicole's thoughts went to her mother again and how she used to sit around most of the day drinking while watching soap operas and game shows on TV. When she wasn't doing that, she often hung out at one of the local bars. It was difficult to count all the times Dad had gone after Mom and brought her home in a drunken stupor. Why he hadn't been the one to file for divorce was a question Nicole had asked herself many times. Did Dad love Mom so much that he was willing to overlook the mess she'd created for herself by not seeking help for her drinking problem?

Nicole couldn't remember when her mother had quit taking care of her family or if she ever had been attentive to them. Maybe when she was a baby, and too little to remember. Mom hadn't been there for Tony and Heather, either. Nicole had been responsible for taking care of them several years before her mother left. She clenched her fingers, making a fist. *I hate that woman. She's my mother in name only, and I hope I never have to look at her again.* These days it was easier to refer to her as Tonya, instead of Mom, like her siblings still did. Dad had stressed to Nicole many times that it was wrong to hate anyone and it wasn't good to dwell on the past, but she couldn't let go of her anger. She was glad Tonya had agreed to let Dad have full custody of the children. The thought of spending time with that woman and the creep she'd recently married was enough to turn Nicole's stomach.

"So how long have you been teaching cooking classes, Heidi?" Allie's question drove Nicole's thoughts aside.

"I taught my first set of classes this past summer, so this is only my second group of students."

"How many were in the first classes?" Bill asked.

"Five—same as this time."

"Guess you wouldn't want many more than that or it might get too crazy." Bill gestured to the oven when the timer across the room rang. "Oh, good. My baked oatmeal must be done, along with Todd's." He rose from his chair, but Todd beat him to the stove, jerking open the oven door.

Nicole frowned. *How rude. Who does that man think he is? Todd monopolized much of the conversation when Bill was trying to ask Heidi questions earlier; he winked at Lisa several times; and now this? If I were Bill, I'd put that guy in his place.*

Heidi stood on the front porch, watching as the last vehicle pulled out of her yard. Nicole had been the first to leave, when her father picked her up, and Bill had been the last to go. He was quite a talker, especially when he didn't have to compete with Todd.

Heidi wasn't sure how much anyone had learned today, but at least she'd sent them all home with the recipe for baked oatmeal, as well as a meaningful scripture on the back of the card. She had done the same thing with her previous students. She'd read the verse she shared today during her devotions a few days ago. It dealt with anxiety and fear: "I sought the LORD, and he heard me, and delivered me from all my fears" (Psalm 34:4). Hopefully it would speak to someone's heart this week.

She sighed. *Well, one class is finished, and there are five more to go.* Her next class would be in early October, two weeks from today. Maybe by then Kendra's baby would be born.

Remembering she was going to check for phone messages, Heidi headed down the driveway to the small wooden building. When she stepped inside, she clicked the "message" button on the answering machine.

"Hello, this is Kendra Perkins's mother, and my message is for Heidi Troyer. I'm calling at my daughter's request. She wanted you to know that she gave birth to a baby girl this morning. The infant came a little earlier than expected, but both mother and daughter are doing fine."

Heidi sank onto the metal folding chair, holding both hands against her chest. Her heart felt as if it had been broken in two. She was happy for Kendra, as well as her parents, but, oh, how she wished the baby could be hers—a daughter to raise and cherish. Even though the infant had arrived early, Heidi would have been more than ready to care for the child. Everything had already been purchased for the nursery. Of course, it had all been put away—out of sight, but never far from Heidi's thoughts.

Tears welled in her eyes, and she blinked to keep them from spilling over. No amount of crying would change the fact—Kendra was keeping her baby, and that was that.

Heidi left the phone shack without bothering to listen to the other messages. All she wanted to do was go back to the house and sleep the rest of the afternoon. Tomorrow was Sunday; maybe things would look brighter in the morning.

Chapter 6

Heidi had no more than lain down on the couch to take a nap, when someone knocked on the front door.

Groaning, she rose and went to see who it was. When she opened the door, she discovered their mailman, Lance Freemont, holding a package.

"This was too big to fit in your mailbox, so I brought it on up to the house." As he handed Heidi the package, he leaned forward a bit, sniffing the air. "Say, what smells so good?"

"Oh, it's probably the baked oatmeal my students made during the cooking class I held this morning. Kitchen odors can linger sometimes."

Lance grinned. "Is that so? Didn't realize you taught cooking classes. How long have you been teaching people how to cook?"

"I started my first set of classes in the spring, teaching on Saturdays for six weeks. Today, I began another set of six lessons with new students." She placed the package on the entry table. "The classes aren't necessarily for beginning cooks, however. Some who come to my house already know how to cook but want to learn more about traditional Amish meals."

"I see." A lock of Lance's light brown hair sprinkled with gray, fell across his forehead. "Are the classes always on Saturdays?"

She gave a nod. "Yes, every other Saturday."

"Have you got room for one more student?"

"There are five in the class—and I could include another—but don't you deliver the mail on Saturdays?"

"Sometimes, but my schedule changes, and beginning next week I'll only be working every other Saturday. As luck would have it, I'll be off on the same days you hold classes."

"Well, you're welcome to join the class then, week after next." Heidi quoted the price, taking a little off, since Lance had missed the first day. "When you come in two weeks, I'll give you the recipe for baked oatmeal my students learned to make today."

"That'd be great." There was a twinkle in his hazel-colored eyes she'd never noticed before. "What time does class start?"

"Ten o'clock."

"Can I wait to pay you until then? I'd do it now, but I need to get back on my mail route."

Heidi smiled. "Next class is fine. I'll give you the same form to fill out like my other students received. Also, if you can, you'll need to bring an apron with you." She stepped over to her desk, grabbed a white form and handed it to him. "It has the dates of each class and my phone number, in case you have any questions. Just leave a message, and I'll get back to you."

"Okay, sounds good. I'll see you then." Lance turned, and as he started down the driveway, swinging his arms, he began to whistle.

Heidi covered her mouth to stifle a giggle. Lance's personality would be a good fit with her other students—perhaps balancing out some of their negativity. His positive attitude had helped Heidi feel a little more uplifted than she had after receiving the news that Kendra's baby had been born. She felt sure Lance's jovial spirit would bless her other students, too.

I need to send Kendra a congratulations card and maybe get something for the baby. Heidi tapped her chin. It was the least she could do to offer support and let Kendra know there were no hard feelings. Before she'd moved out, the young woman had given Heidi her parents' address and phone number, in case she'd left anything behind or needed to get in touch with her.

Heidi glanced at the package Lance had delivered and wondered who it was from. She hadn't ordered anything, but maybe Lyle had and just forgot to mention it.

She picked up the box and smiled when she saw the return address. It was from her aunt, Emma Miller, who lived in Shipshewana, Indiana.

Heidi took the package to the kitchen and placed it on the table, then sliced the lid open with a paring knife, being careful to avoid damaging whatever was inside.

Pulling the cardboard flaps aside and then removing several layers of white tissue paper, Heidi gasped as she lifted out a beautiful blue-and-white quilt in the ocean waves pattern. A note was pinned to the material. "Happy Anniversary, Heidi and Lyle. Lamar and I wish you many more good years together. Be blessed! Love, Aunt Emma and Lamar."

Tears welled in Heidi's eyes as she clutched the quilt close to her chest. The different shades of blues Aunt Emma selected were perfect. *How thoughtful of my dear aunt to remember today is Lyle's and my ninth wedding anniversary.* They'd gotten cards with money inside from both of their parents yesterday, and they would celebrate the occasion this evening by going out to supper at one of their favorite restaurants. Heidi looked forward to going. Even more so than she had this morning.

Inhaling the aroma from inside the box, Heidi almost felt like she was standing in her aunt's kitchen. *She must have been baking the day she got the package ready to mail, because this quilt smells like cinnamon and other spices.*

Heidi ran her hands over the material, then draped the lovely covering over the kitchen chair. When she picked up the box it had come in, she discovered something else inside. She smiled, lifting out a plastic container, tucked neatly at the bottom. Heidi had a pretty good idea what was inside as she opened the lid and inhaled, delighting in the sweet fragrance wafting up to her nostrils. On top of the plastic wrap was another note from her aunt about the pumpkin cookies she'd made and wanted to share. Heidi pulled up the cellophane and saw over a dozen perfectly shaped cookies lined neatly in small rows.

Think I'll sample one of these right now. Heidi licked her lips, then took a bite of the plump, spicy cookie. *How sweet of Aunt Emma to remember our anniversary by making us a quilt. Such a lovely gift and labor of love. I can hardly wait till Lyle gets here so I can show the beautiful covering for our bed to him.* She looked down at the cookies. *He'll certainly enjoy eating these tasty* kichlin, *too.*

New Philadelphia

Allie had only been home a few minutes with the children when she looked out the window and saw Steve's car pull up. Relieved to see he that was okay, she ran to the door and swung it open. The minute her husband stepped inside, Allie threw her arms around his neck and gave him a tight squeeze.

"I appreciate the hug, but you're holding me so firm. Is everything okay?" He patted her back.

"I–I'm fine." She pulled slowly away. "But I've been worried about you today."

Steve's brown eyes darkened further. "How come?"

Her muscles tensed. "How come? Your job is dangerous, Steve, and I had a mental picture of you this morning. It left me feeling as though you had been hurt."

He shook his head slowly. "If anything had happened to me, you'd have been the first to know."

She sighed. "That's a small consolation, dear. I wish you had a desk job, instead of being out on the streets where anything could happen."

He placed his hand on her shoulder and gave it a squeeze. "I'm doing what I feel called to do. You knew that when I decided to get training to become a police officer soon after we were married. You said you were okay with it."

Allie couldn't argue. She wanted her husband to be happy, despite knowing full well his life could be in jeopardy. Here lately, though, with the children growing and needing their father around, Allie had become paranoid about his safety. She'd never make it if something happened to Steve. She counted on him, not just for his financial support, but to be there whenever she and the children had a need. She relied on him for moral and emotional support, too. Along with their children, Steve was the love of her life.

Allie thought about the verse of scripture Heidi had written on the back of the recipe she'd given them today. "I sought the Lord, and he heard me, and delivered me from all my fears." She squeezed her eyes shut. *Oh, how I want to believe that. If only my fears could vanish like vapor, but I don't need to seek the Lord for that. Maybe the cooking classes I'm taking will help me learn to relax.*

Steve bent and gave Allie a kiss. "Enough about me now. How'd your first cooking class go this morning?"

She opened her eyes and shrugged. "Okay, I guess. We learned how to make baked oatmeal, but I was hoping for something more exciting than that."

"There are five more classes, though, right?"

She gave a slow nod, reaching up to run her fingers through his dark, short-cropped hair.

"No doubt you'll learn to make plenty of other things."

"I hope so. I'd like to be able to fix something Derek and Nola would enjoy."

He quirked an eyebrow and grinned. "You don't think they'd like baked oatmeal?"

She swatted his arm playfully, feeling more relaxed. "What do you think, silly?"

"Speaking of the kids. . . What are they up to this afternoon?"

Allie gestured toward the living room, at the same moment as the children started bickering. "They're watching their favorite cartoons. Or at least they were." She lifted her gaze to the ceiling and groaned.

Steve gave Allie another quick kiss. "Yeah, I hear Nola and Derek now—loud and clear. Think I'll go surprise the kids and join 'em." He wiggled his brows. "I love cartoons."

Allie gave his arm a light tap. "Okay, you big kid. While you're doing that, I'm going to feed Prissy; then I'll make us all a snack."

Allie heard Nola and Derek scream with glee when Steve entered the living room. She smiled and headed for the utility room to take care of the cat. *Those kids sure love their daddy. When I'm done, maybe I'll join Steve and the children for a while. Some microwave popcorn would be a good snack. I'll check to see if there's any left in the cupboard.*

Watching cartoons wasn't exactly Allie's favorite thing to do, but it was always nice to spend time with her family.

———————•☙❧•———————

Dover

Lisa sat at the kitchen table, drinking a cup of tea while trying to relax. Two weeks until Heidi's next class seemed like a long way off, and she was eager to go again, hoping next time Heidi would share a more exciting recipe. Not that the baked oatmeal was bad; it just wasn't anything she'd be likely to use in her catering business, unless someone hired her to fix a breakfast meal for a special event.

Blaring music caused Lisa to jump. Ever since she'd gotten home from the cooking class, her nerves had been on edge. The renters in the unit attached to her duplex had the volume on their TV up so loud it could be heard through the wall separating her half of the duplex from theirs. When Lisa agreed to let the Browns rent the unit, she'd never expected them to be so noisy. But the loud music was better than listening to Bob and Gail argue—something else Lisa couldn't help overhearing whenever they went at it.

She poked her tongue into her cheek and inhaled a long breath. The young couple had only been married a year, but they had some marital problems that seemed to be getting worse as time went on. She'd been praying for Bob and Gail. Even invited them to attend church with her, but they showed no interest.

A few weeks ago, Gail had asked Lisa if they could get a dog. Nothing was in the contract they'd signed about pets, so Lisa felt she couldn't deny them one of their own. She liked dogs, too, and thought at first having one might ease the strain between the couple. Unfortunately, it was wishful thinking. So far, their puppy had done nothing but frustrate Lisa.

When her neighbors were at work, the little thing whined and howled all the time. The poor pup was lonely, and Lisa couldn't help feeling sorry for it—especially when those sorrowful yowls went on and on. It was heartbreaking to hear.

As if that wasn't bad enough, there were times when Lisa noticed her flowerbeds had been messed up. Flowers and stems got broken, and one time she'd seen the remains of a flower lying in the yard on the Brown's side of the duplex. Lisa worried if she approached them about these issues, it would create tension between them as neighbors. They'd always paid their rent on time and spoken politely to Lisa, so she was uncertain what to do.

Lisa loved working in her flowerbeds. Getting her hands into the soil was a source of solace. The colorful mums and marigolds had been blooming so beautifully, until the pup did its damage. This was the last thing she wanted to deal with, and her patience was waning. Maybe it would be better to do some hanging baskets with flowers instead of having them in the flowerbeds. At least the neighbor's new pet couldn't bother those. She would need to figure out how many baskets would work out front, and where they could be hung so no one would run into them. Perhaps she would stop by the hardware store soon to see what was available. Since her renters were obviously not going to get rid of the puppy, she would have to do whatever was necessary to protect her property from damage.

Lisa was reminded of the sermon her pastor had preached last Sunday on how believers should let their light shine so others would see Jesus. She closed her eyes and prayed: *Lord, please help me to set an example so people, like my neighbors, will come to know You personally.*

Chapter 7

Walnut Creek

Isn't this beautiful, Lyle?" Heidi looked down at her aunt's quilt, which she had spread out on their bed the night before after returning from their anniversary meal at Der Dutchman restaurant.

Smiling, Lyle nodded. "There's no doubt about it—your aunt Emma is a gifted quilter. She makes good cookies, too."

"Jah. Her thoughtful gift surely added a bright spot to our anniversary." Heidi blinked, hoping no tears would come. "It's hard to admit, but after hearing that Kendra had her baby yesterday, I began to feel sorry for myself again."

Lyle pulled Heidi into his arms, gently rubbing her back. "Would you like me to contact the adoption lawyer again and see if he can find another baby for us to adopt?"

Heidi found comfort in her husband's arms, and even more so in his willingness to adopt. For so long he hadn't even considered it an option for them. She leaned her head against his chest, feeling comfort in his strong arms. "I still want a boppli, but I'm not sure I could handle another disappointment."

"Not every mother who agrees to put her baby up for adoption changes her mind at the last minute, Heidi. We have to trust God to give us the right child."

She pulled away and looked up at him, stroking his bearded face. "You're right; I'm just not ready right now. Maybe we can talk about it again after the first of the year." She pointed at the clock on the small table beside their bed. "Right now we need to finish getting ready for church. I'm eager to hear what our ministers have to share."

Millersburg

Nicole stepped into the living room, where her dad sat reading the Sunday paper, while Heather and Tony watched TV. "If you don't need me for anything, Dad, I'm going outside for a while."

He looked up and gave a quick shake of his head. "Go right ahead. The three of us are well-entertained."

"Are you comin' back to fix our lunch?" Tony looked over his shoulder.

Nicole grunted. "Is food all you ever think about?"

Heather snickered and bumped her brother's arm. "Before Mom left, she used to say Tony had a hole in his leg 'cause he was always hungry."

Nicole balled her hands into fists. "Of course he was hungry. Tonya neglected all three of her children."

"I've told you before, Nicole—you shouldn't refer to your mother by her first name." Dad reached up and massaged the back of his neck. "It's disrespectful."

Nicole folded her arms, remembering how her mother had shown up at her sixteenth birthday party—drunk as a skunk, and flashing her new engagement ring. "Humph! She was disrespectful to all of us— you most of all, Dad. I can't believe you're defending her."

"I am not defending her. What she did was wrong, but she's still your mother, and—"

"I'm goin' outside now, but I'll be back in time to fix lunch." Nicole whirled around and dashed out of the room.

I don't get Dad. Why doesn't he understand? After all the horrible things Tonya did, he should be angrier than I am. Nicole grabbed her drawing tablet and colored pencils, before going out the back door. When she stepped out, she nearly tripped over her brother's dog, Bowser. The critter lay on the porch in front of the door. She had to admit Bowser was kind of cute. He was part beagle, half mutt, and full of nothing but trouble. Nicole hated it when he got into a barking mode, though.

Bowser didn't seem to know the meaning of the command, "Be quiet!" *I suppose I should be grateful the mutt's sleeping. Just wish he'd find some place to nap other than by the door.* She couldn't count all the times she'd tripped over the dog when he was dozing on the welcome mat.

"You lazy pooch. Go find someplace else to snooze." Nicole nudged him with the toe of her sneaker.

Bowser merely grunted, then rolled over onto his side. Nicole stepped around him and sprinted toward the back of their property, where their yard met the woods. She didn't get much time alone these days, so it would be nice to be by herself for a while.

She took a seat on a log and placed the drawing tablet in her lap. They'd had a cold snap a few mornings this past week, and some of the leaves were starting to turn. Nicole liked this time of year, when the cooler weather set in. She remembered when she was a child, crunching through the leaves on her way to school during autumn mornings. Now that Nicole was in high school, she caught the bus. The only time she got to frolic in the leaves was after school and on weekends when she had time to be outside, which was rare. It was too bad the leaves didn't stay pretty longer, for it wouldn't be many weeks before the trees would all be bare.

Opening the box of colored pencils, she began sketching a squirrel sitting on a tree branch several feet away. She hoped the little critter would sit still long enough for her to get its outline done. Squirrels could be pretty skittish, so she had to sketch quickly.

Woof! Woof! Woof!

The squirrel leaped to another branch as Bowser came running and nearly slammed into the tree.

"Oh great! So much for a little peace and quiet." Nicole set her drawing aside and clapped her hands. "Go home, Bowser! You're nothing but a pest." She'd never get the drawing of the squirrel down now.

Looking up at the tiny critter, the mutt kept yapping. The squirrel found a different branch, and finally jumped into another tree. Of course it didn't discourage the dog. Nicole covered her ears as the barking continued.

Nicole's lips pressed together, her irritation increasing by the minute. In exasperation, she reached inside the log, where she kept another notebook. This one wasn't for sketching, though. It was a tablet full of letters to her mother. Not nice letters, either, but ones Nicole kept to herself. They were condemning, scolding letters; Nicole's way of getting back at her mother for all the hurt and shame she'd caused their whole family. Nicole had no plans of giving the letters to Tonya, but it made her feel better to write them. She saw it as a way to vent, but without telling anyone her troubles.

From pen to paper, Nicole finished pouring more of her emotions out. After the squirrel escaped through the trees, Bowser came over to where Nicole sat and stood staring up at her. She stared right back at him. *Stupid mutt.*

The dog tipped his head as though he'd heard something. She watched the nutty hound, who now seemed fixated on a nearby hole. Bowser growled and started digging like there was no tomorrow. The mutt appeared frantic as dirt tossed up and onto Nicole's lap. "Hey! Stop doing that, you goofball!" Nicole gritted her teeth.

Bowser, in his doggie state of mind, continued his endeavor until a poor ground mole was withdrawn from its burrow and carted off from sight. The pathetic prey squeaked for its life.

Still holding her writing tablet, Nicole jumped up, chasing after Bowser. "You let that poor critter go!" She waved the notebook several times, and even swatted the dog's behind. Sheepishly, Bowser finally gave in and dropped the mole. It scurried away and back down its hole.

Nicole looked at her tablet, noticing that the binding had given way, and frowned. The papers fluttered to the ground. "Bowser, this is all your fault!" She knelt and picked up the fallen sheets of paper. "Guess I should have let the sleeping dog lie," Nicole muttered.

After she'd claimed everything, Nicole tucked the papers together as best she could and put them back into the log. Then she picked up her drawing tablet and colored pencils. "Come on, mutt, let's go!" Maybe sitting on the back porch to do some sketching would be her best chance for peace and quiet.

When Nicole stepped onto the porch, she discovered Heather's cat, Domino, flaked out on the wooden bench.

"Go on, scat, dumb cat!" She picked up the feline and placed him out on the grass. "Go chase a mouse or find someplace else to sleep. Sure don't need you getting hair all over me."

It might not be right to take her frustrations out on her siblings' pets, but Nicole got tired of the messes they made, not to mention being unable to do anything just for herself. She thought about the cooking classes Dad had signed her up to take. Apparently he believed it was something she would enjoy, but the first class had been boring. And the fact that the Amish woman had written a Bible verse on the back of the recipe card she'd given Nicole only fueled her frustration. She was still angry at God for ignoring her pleas concerning her mother's drinking problem and horrid behavior. All the prayers Nicole had said went unanswered. If there really was a God, He should have done something about the situation.

Nicole looked up at the sky, shielding her eyes from the glare of the sun peeking through the clouds. *At the very least, You could open my mom's eyes to the truth; she needs help and should go somewhere to get it.*

Speaking this way to God, even in her mind, did nothing to make Nicole feel better. *If You are real, God, then why don't You answer my prayers?*

Canton

Releasing a noisy yawn, Todd grabbed the Sunday morning newspaper and flopped into his favorite brown, leather easy chair. He'd stayed up late last night, writing down his thoughts about the cooking class. Todd planned to write an article about taking lessons from the Amish woman, but not until he'd finished the last class. By then he'd have a lot more information, and could even include a recipe or two. It would generate interest and maybe take the sting out if he wrote anything negative about the Amish way of life or the types of meals Amish women served.

Laying the paper across his chest, Todd closed his eyes, to better reflect on what had happened during the first class. A mixed group of people had come to Heidi Troyer's to learn how to cook some traditional Amish dishes. Todd hoped whatever they made in the next class, which wouldn't be for another two weeks, would be a bit tastier than the baked oatmeal Heidi had taught the class how to make. It was probably okay for someone who enjoyed eating oatmeal, but he'd never liked it, even as a kid when his mother doctored it up with plenty of brown sugar and raisins. Truth was, when Todd got home yesterday, he'd thrown the baked oatmeal in the trash. He could only imagine what his mother would say if she'd seen him do such a thing. *"Todd Collins, did I not teach you better than that? Tossing out perfectly good food is wasteful. Why, do you know how many people are starving around the world and would give anything to have eaten the food you saw as nothing but garbage?"*

Todd didn't care; he'd just go by his favorite coffee shop in the morning and order a tempting creation to eat with his latte. *What my mom doesn't know won't hurt her.* He chuckled, still relaxing and enjoying himself in the overstuffed chair.

Todd opened his eyes. He felt relief that his parents still lived in Portland, Oregon, where he'd been born. He only saw them a couple of times a year and was always glad when they went home. Dad was okay, but Mom got on his nerves with her constant nagging and asking twenty questions. The one thing she quizzed him about most was whether he'd found a nice girlfriend yet, and if so, was he ready to settle down? She wanted to know all the aspects of Todd's life, and even called frequently to ask him questions. Mom was like a bloodhound, sniffing for any little evidence to gather and involve herself in Todd's life.

Todd's parents had gotten married when they were in their early twenties, and here Todd was twenty-eight years old, with no serious girlfriend, much less any plans to be married. It wasn't that he didn't want a wife. He just hadn't found the right woman yet. Of course, he admittedly was a bit picky. *And with good reason,* he thought. *I chose wrong once and won't make that mistake again.*

Pushing his thoughts aside, Todd focused on the newspaper and his column, where he'd given a negative critique of a restaurant in town. It wasn't a fancy place—kind of a hole in the wall, really, but he'd hoped for some good food when he went there, since it had been advertised as "Just like Mom's tasty home cooking."

"Tasty home cooking, my eye." Todd gave a disgusted snort. "I've eaten a better burger at the fast-food restaurant down the street from my condo."

He folded the newspaper and tossed it on the end table close to his chair. *If enough people read my thoughts about the new place, maybe the owners will sell out or vacate the building. I don't know these people, so what does it matter? Then hopefully someone who knows what they're doing will take over the restaurant.*

Todd grabbed hold of the armrests and lifted himself out of his chair. *Think I'll drive over to Akron and try out some other restaurant today. Good or bad, it'll give me an opportunity to do another review.*

Chapter 8

Berlin, Ohio

On Monday, Heidi decided to do some shopping. She needed groceries, and with all the shops to choose from in Berlin, she could hopefully find something nice for Kendra's baby, too. It had been a difficult decision, but Lyle had agreed to hire a driver this coming Saturday so they could go to Akron and visit Kendra, rather than merely mailing the card and gift.

I want to do the right thing, and if there's a pocket-sized New Testament in one of the stores, I'll buy it as well. The Bible can be for the baby when she's older and is able to read, Heidi told herself as she headed down the baby aisle in one of the stores. Even though Kendra's parents had invited her to move back home so they could help raise the baby, her relationship with God was weak. Whatever Heidi did or said could help strengthen the young woman's faith, but if Kendra took it the wrong way, Heidi's words might have the opposite effect. Heidi didn't want to create an obstacle between Kendra and God.

As Heidi approached the baby clothes, she spotted Loretta Donnelly coming from the opposite direction.

"Hello, Heidi." Loretta smiled. "It's good to see you. Are you buying clothes for the new arrival?"

Swallowing against the constriction in her throat, Heidi barely managed a brief nod. "Only it won't be Lyle's and my child wearing the baby outfit, because we will not be adopting Kendra Perkins's child after all."

Loretta tipped her head. "But I thought..."

Heidi explained about Kendra changing her mind and ended by

saying Kendra had given birth to a baby girl last week.

"Oh, she had the baby already?"

"Yes. Apparently it came earlier than expected, but both mother and daughter are doing fine." Heidi took a deep breath, hoping she wouldn't break down in front of her friend.

"I'm sorry to hear you won't be raising the baby. I know how much you'd been looking forward to it. You and Lyle would make wonderful parents." Loretta's brows lowered. "How will Kendra take care of a child by herself?"

"She's moved back with her folks, so they will help with the baby."

Loretta placed her hand on Heidi's arm, giving it a gentle pat. "How are you dealing with this?"

Heidi's posture sagged. "I'm disappointed, of course, but it's a situation I cannot change, so I am trying to accept it as God's will."

Loretta nodded soberly. "When things are out of our control, acceptance is always the best. God's way is not always our way."

"True. Now how are things with you these days? Are you still making plans to join the Amish church?"

"Yes, I am, and once I become a member, I suspect Eli will ask me to marry him. He's hinted at it several times."

Heidi gave Loretta a hug. She needed to hear some good news. "That's wonderful. I'm happy things are going well for you."

Loretta's wide smile reached all the way to her coffee-colored eyes. "*Danki.*"

"Where are your children today?"

"They're staying with a neighbor. I needed to get some serious shopping done, and it's hard to do it with Abby and Conner along—especially when they start begging for things they shouldn't have or don't need."

"Do the children know about your decision to become Amish?" Heidi shifted her weight.

"Yes, and they're happy about it. Abby and Conner love Eli, and he's made it clear that the feeling is mutual. I feel blessed to have met him during your cooking classes. I truly believe God brought us together."

"I couldn't agree more." Heidi felt blessed, too, knowing she'd had a small part in bringing two of her students together in such a special way. She thought about her current group of students and wondered if anything said or done during the upcoming classes would make a difference in any of their lives.

Millersburg

"Mr. Mason, may I speak with you a minute please?"

Bill set his broom aside and turned to face Debra Shultz, one of the high school English teachers. Debra was in her sixties and had never married. It didn't take a genius to know why, either. The woman was a complainer, always looking for something to pick about. At least that's how Bill felt whenever she started in on him. Last week, during a cool morning, it was the vent in her classroom, and how the heat wasn't coming out of it correctly. The week before that, she complained about her floors—said they hadn't been cleaned properly. As far as Bill was concerned, Ms. Shultz should have retired years ago.

"What is it, Ms. Schultz?" He tapped his foot impatiently, as she stood with arms folded, looking at him over the top of her metal-framed glasses with narrowed mousy brown eyes. Bill resisted the urge to add *this time*. He tried to remain polite and calm.

"I wanted to remind you to make sure the garbage cans in my classroom get emptied today." A muscle in her right cheek quivered. "You must have been in a hurry last Friday, because when I entered my classroom this morning, the garbage can by my desk was still full of trash."

"Sorry about that. I'll take care of it now if you like." Apparently the custodian who emptied the trash had missed one of her cans. Bill would speak to him about it, but for now, it was best to simply do the job himself.

She shook her head vigorously. "I have one more class yet today, and I don't want to be disturbed. When you're finished doing your cleaning at the end of the day, you can empty the garbage."

"Sure, no problem." Bill picked up the broom and began sweeping the hallway again, where several pieces of wadded-up paper lay. She apparently didn't realize he wasn't a regular janitor anymore. No question about it—today was definitely Monday. He hoped he didn't encounter any more picky teachers.

As Bill moved on, he stepped aside for a group of students coming out of the lunchroom. He recognized one of them right away. It was Nicole Smith, whom he'd met at Heidi Troyer's cooking class a week ago Saturday. She glanced his way, but when he nodded, smiled, and said "Hello," she turned her head the other way.

He frowned. *Surely she must recognize me. Maybe Nicole doesn't want anyone to know she's acquainted with a lowly janitor and is taking cooking classes with him outside of school.*

Bill reflected on how she'd acted the day of the cooking class. Come to think of it, the girl hadn't said much, and barely made eye contact—not just with Bill, but with the other students as well.

She could be a bit snobbish. Bill moved on down the hall. He noticed she wasn't walking with anyone right now. Nicole Smith might be a loner, or maybe she had trouble making friends.

Earlier today when Bill had started sweeping the halls because the other custodians were busy with different things, he'd slowed and stopped to listen after hearing a teacher mention Nicole's name in one of the classrooms. A water fountain was right next to the door, so as not to appear obvious, he'd stepped over to it and taken a long drink. He couldn't help overhearing the teacher tell Nicole she wasn't doing well with her grades, and then he'd listened as Nicole tried to explain.

Wiping his shirtsleeve across his wet mouth, and down on his chin, where water had dripped, he'd watched as Nicole practically flew out of the room. Bill's quick sidestep had kept the girl from plowing into him, but it appeared she hadn't even noticed he was there. He'd remembered how Nicole introduced herself at Heidi's. The poor girl had a lot of responsibility to shoulder.

Watching as she went down the hall now, Bill continued sweeping. *Maybe I ought to make an effort to get to know her better during the cooking classes.* He gripped the handle of his broom as the idea set in. *Yep. I think that little gal might just need a friend.*

Nicole walked briskly down the hall toward her history class, her mouth twisting grimly. She'd had a lecture from Mrs. Wick, her English teacher, earlier today, about not getting her lessons in on time. Nicole had a feeling this would happen, with her being on overload at home. Now this was on her plate to deal with, on top of everything else. And unless she could talk her teacher out of it, her dad would soon be involved. She couldn't let that happen. It pained Nicole to have Dad know about her failing grades. He'd not only be upset, but disappointed in her, too. Her teacher didn't mince any words about the situation, and Nicole felt worse than ever with what she'd said.

"You have failing grades in this class," Mrs. Wick warned. "If you don't bring them up, you won't pass my class. Perhaps you should stay after school a few days a week, for some private tutoring."

After trying to explain her situation at home, Nicole instantly regretted telling her teacher anything. Then Mrs. Wick suggested a conference with Nicole's father, to see if something could be worked out. The teacher said if Nicole failed one more test, she would contact her dad and suggest a one-on-one conference with him at his earliest convenience. Nicole definitely didn't want to involve Dad. He had enough to worry about. She'd begged the teacher to give her another chance, saying she'd work extra hard to get her grades up. Mrs. Wick ended the conversation by saying she was concerned for Nicole, and the matter needed to be addressed.

Nicole didn't mind English so much. In fact, she liked her teacher. It could have been worse if she'd been stuck with some other English teacher, like stuffy old Ms. Shultz. She'd heard some of the students talking about how Ms. Shultz gave no one any slack. Nicole, no doubt, would have failed the class by now, and she felt thankful for Mrs. Wick's patience. But Nicole was out of options and didn't want to fail the class. Her teacher cared; Nicole heard it in the tone of Mrs. Wick's voice as she'd explained the situation to her. Despite having a nice teacher, Nicole was still in a dilemma. She didn't have time to get all her homework done. History, English, algebra, and biology—they were all hard subjects, requiring extra study for tests and homework assignments. It seemed so overwhelming.

I don't see how Mrs. Wick thinks I'm supposed to keep up with everything she assigns when I have so many things at home to do. She scrubbed a hand over her face. *I can't believe she suggested I stay after school for tutoring lessons and wanted to have a meeting with Dad. He doesn't get home until six o'clock most evenings, and I need to be there for Tony and Heather, not to mention cooking supper every night. Who knows what kind of mischief those two would get into if I came home even a few minutes late?*

To make matters worse, when Nicole left Mrs. Wick's classroom, she'd almost bumped into the head janitor. She couldn't believe he was attending Heidi Troyer's cooking classes, and she sure hadn't wanted that guy to know she attended the school where he worked. Worse yet would be if he found out how bad she was doing with her studies and blabbed it around the school. She wondered if janitors were friends with teachers. Did they talk or take lunch together? Nicole didn't need all these extra things to worry about.

Her face tightened. *Life is not fair. I hardly ever have any time to myself. If I do flunk out, it won't be my fault.* She let out a puff of air. *I could use some help right now. Why couldn't I have had a study hall period, or an elective class like art or music?*

Nicole dabbed on some lip balm from her purse, thinking once again about her mother. *Tonya shouldn't have run out on us. She should have stayed and straightened up so she could take care of her family. If I ever get married, which is doubtful, I'll never run out on my husband and children.*

Chapter 9

Canton

A re you sure you want to go through with this?" Lyle asked, as he and Heidi sat in the back of their driver's van.

Heidi gave a slow nod, fidgeting nervously with her fingers against the package she held. "Paying a call on Kendra is the right thing to do."

"It might be the right thing for her, but is it for you?"

"Jah, I believe so."

Lyle reached over and clasped Heidi's hand. "I don't mean it in a prideful way, but I'm proud of you for this decision you've made. You and Kendra became quite close during the time she was living with us, so I'm sure our visit will be meaningful to her. She will hopefully know there are no hard feelings."

"I hope so." Heidi closed her eyes and sent up a silent prayer. *Heavenly Father, please help me to get through this without breaking down, and give me the right words to say to Kendra.*

After hearing Lyle draw in a deep breath, Heidi looked over at him. "What is it, Lyle?"

"Just enjoying this time of the year." His endearing gaze reached hers. "Can you smell and feel the fresh hay?"

"Jah." Heidi looked toward a field where hay had been recently cut and baled. "It's not October yet, but you can almost smell autumn's essence. Soon its brilliant colors will be quilting the land."

He grinned. "You have such a nice way with words. I could never have put it that way. But you're absolutely right—it's God's perfect balance, don't you think?"

Heidi gave a slight nod. *The land may be in perfect balance but not our lives.* Children would balance hers and Lyle's lives completely. Even if it only turned out to be one child, the hole in Heidi's heart would finally close.

A short time later, their driver, Ida, pulled up to a large, two-story house. "According to my GPS and the numbers on this house, we're at the right place," Ida announced. "If you'll be a while, I can go somewhere for a cup of coffee. Or would you rather I just wait here in the van?"

"We shouldn't be more than an hour or so," Lyle replied. "If you want to go for coffee, that's fine. No point in you sitting here in the driveway, waiting."

"Okay, sounds good. I'll be back in an hour, but if you're not done visiting, no problem. Please, take your time." She reached across the seat and picked up a book. "I brought some entertainment."

Grinning, Lyle got out of the van. Heidi did the same, remembering to take the package she'd brought for the baby. As they stepped onto the Perkins' porch, Heidi blew out a series of short breaths.

Lyle tipped his head to one side. "You okay?"

"I'm fine." Heidi quickly rang the doorbell, before she lost her nerve.

A few seconds later, a teenage girl with long brown hair answered. "Hi, I'm Chris, and you must be the Troyers." She smiled, revealing a set of braces on her top and bottom teeth. "I heard you were coming."

Heidi smiled, too, feeling a little more relaxed. She reached out her hand. "It's nice to meet you, Chris. Kendra has told us a lot about you and your sister, Shelly."

Giggling, Chris rolled her eyes. "I can only imagine. You probably heard about all the times we pestered our big sister."

Heidi shook her head. "Kendra only shared the good things about growing up with you and Shelly." She chose not to mention that Kendra had also mentioned how, when her father first asked her to leave his house, he'd instructed her sisters to have nothing to do with Kendra. It had been a difficult time for the young woman.

"Well, that's a relief." Chris spoke in a bubbly tone as she held the door open wider. "Come on in. My folks aren't here right now, but Kendra is anxiously waiting." She led the way down the hall. "Shelly's not here, either. Our church is having a fall craft show today, and she's helping Mom with one of the tables."

Heidi was disappointed she wouldn't get to meet Kendra's parents, but maybe it was better this way. It might be easier to visit with Kendra if Mr. and Mrs. Perkins were not present. She wasn't sure how much Kendra had told her folks about her and Lyle, but they might be a bit standoffish toward them—even wondering why an Amish couple would want to adopt their grandchild.

When they entered the house, Heidi noticed a few pictures hanging on the wall in the entry. The frames were antique gold and held what appeared to be oil paintings of scenic views. It surprised her not to see any family pictures on display. Many other English homes she'd visited had photo albums sitting out and often had several family pictures on the walls.

Heidi glanced down, noticing how the hardwood floors gleamed— especially here in the hall. The scent of baby powder filled Heidi's nostrils as they walked behind Chris. Moisture gathered in the corners of her eyes when they entered the living room and she saw Kendra sitting in an upholstered rocking chair, holding her baby.

"Oh, Heidi, I'm so glad you're here. You, too Lyle." Kendra's eyes were wide and glowing as she nuzzled her tiny daughter.

That could be me, holding my child. Heidi remembered how she'd had a vision of holding a baby while stirring food in a bowl on the table. Her chin trembled slightly as she tried to regain her composure. "Hello, Kendra. It's good to see you. How are you and the baby?"

"We're both doing great. Come see for yourself." Kendra motioned for Heidi to move closer.

As Kendra's sister left the room, Heidi placed the gift on the coffee table and made her way over to the bold flower-patterned chair. Lyle held back, taking a seat on the leather sofa. Heidi figured her husband wanted her to have the opportunity to speak with Kendra first.

She couldn't help noticing how Lyle leaned forward, looking intently at the large black piano sitting in the far side of the room. Kendra's parents had a lovely home, but Heidi was more interested in seeing the precious baby than studying this house's interior.

Heidi's lips parted slightly as she gazed at the tiny bundle of sweetness in Kendra's arms. The little girl's skin was pale and dewy, and her baby-fine hair was an auburn color, just like her mother's. The infant's wee eyes were closed in slumber, and her tiny, rose-colored lips made little sucking noises. She looked so sweet in her defenseless sleep.

"She's beautiful," Heidi murmured. "I'm happy for you, Kendra."

"Thanks." Kendra looked down at her baby and sniffed. "I never dreamed it would feel so wonderful to hold my own child. Little Heidi is my whole world, and I love her more than I ever thought possible."

Heidi tipped her head. "Her name is Heidi?"

"Yeah." Kendra looked up and smiled. "I hope you're okay with that."

Heidi nearly choked on the sob rising in her throat. All she could do was nod. When she looked over at Lyle, he gave her a reassuring smile.

"Wanna hold her?" Kendra asked.

Fearful she might break down if she held her namesake, Heidi replied, "Well, I—I don't want to wake her."

"It's okay. She's been sleeping awhile. If she wakes up, she'll go right back to sleep. My sweet little Heidi is such a good baby. Did you know, she almost came three weeks early?"

"Yes, your mother mentioned that in the message she left us."

Kendra went on to explain how she'd had contractions in the grocery store, but after getting checked out at the hospital, the doctor confirmed it was only false labor, but then a few days later the real thing happened.

Struggling against tears threatening to spill over and trying to absorb all that Kendra had said, Heidi leaned down and took the baby from her. As she stood holding the precious little girl, an image of the dream she'd had popped into her head again. *Why do I keep visualizing myself holding this boppli?* It was wrong to wish Kendra might change her mind and let Lyle and Heidi adopt her daughter, after all, but Heidi couldn't seem to control her thoughts.

Walnut Creek

Lance had barely gotten home from delivering the mail, when the phone rang. He hurried to the kitchen and grabbed his cell phone from its charger. "Hello."

"Oh, good. I'm glad you're home, Dad. Uncle Dan's been trying to get a hold of you most of the day, and he called me in desperation."

Lance shifted the phone to his other ear and took a seat at the table. "Desperation? What's that brother of mine want, Sharon? Is Dan hurt or having some kind of trouble?"

"He didn't say, but I don't think it was an emergency. Uncle Dan just said he needed to talk to you right away and wished you'd answer your cell phone once in a while."

"I left it home this morning. The battery was almost dead and it needed to charge."

"Don't you have a charger to use in your car?"

"I did, but I lost it."

"Dad, you really ought to—"

"So what's new with you, honey? How's Gavin? And are the kids doing okay?" Lance got up from the table and ambled over to his fish tank in one corner of the room. The goldfish, his only pets, had been fed this morning, and swam around the tank without a care in the world.

"Everyone's fine, Dad." Sharon groaned. "And I wish you wouldn't change the subject whenever you don't want to talk about something."

"Well, there isn't much to say on the topic. I'll buy a new charger for the car when I get the chance. In the meantime, I'll give my brother a call and see what he wants."

"Sounds good, but before you hang up, I want to extend an invitation to you."

"What's up?"

"Gavin and I are having a few people over for dinner after church tomorrow, and we'd like you to come."

"No can do. This Sunday's my time to spend with your sister and her family. I was at your place last week, remember?"

"Of course I remember, Dad, and I've already talked to Terry about this. She's fine with you coming to our house again tomorrow."

Lance rapped his knuckles on his knee. Sharon was up to something, no doubt about it. "Okay, what's the reason you want me at your house so bad? You're not trying to fix me up again, I hope." A year after Lance's wife died, both of his daughters began to think it was their job to find him a suitable wife. Well, they could forget the notion. No one could ever replace Flo. Lance and Florence had been high school sweethearts, and gotten married when they both turned nineteen. They'd had a good marriage and been soul mates, until the Lord took Flo home three years ago.

"I'm not trying to set you up, Dad, but there are two nice single ladies from church we should all get acquainted with. They moved here a few weeks ago, and—"

"Sorry, honey, but count me out. I'm having dinner at Terry's tomorrow like I said." Lance put the phone back to his other ear. "I'd better go now so I can give Dan a call. Oh, and I'll also call Terry to let her know I'm still coming."

"Okay, Dad. I'll see you tomorrow at church. Have a nice evening."

When Lance hung up, his conscience pricked him a bit. He knew Sharon was disappointed, but the last thing he needed was to spend the afternoon with not one, but two spinster women who might be eagerly looking for a man. He wished he could make his caring daughters understand that he had no intention of getting married again and was perfectly happy trying to be a good father and grandfather. Eventually they might get it, but until then, he'd keep dodging all invitations that involved single ladies.

It was bad enough how, on some Sundays after church, a few of the older unmarried women approached Lance, hinting about invitations to their place for dinner. Some men might like the idea and jump at the chance for a lady's affection, but Lance always came up with a reason he couldn't oblige, with the hope these women would take the hint.

Even some of the widows on his mail route had found out he was single again. They'd be waiting for Lance by their mailbox near the road, or on the porch where their mail container hung. Some had homemade cookies for him, while others made fudge and other types of desserts. They all had one thing in common. Like a fish taking bait, they used their sweet smiles and tantalizing treats in the hope of reeling him in. But Lance was one fish that was never getting hooked. His heart had belonged to Flo—and it always would.

Remembering his daughter's message, he picked up the phone again and punched in Dan's number. His brother answered on the second ring. "Hey, Lance, I was hoping I'd get a hold of you before the day was over. I'm in a bit of a bind right now, and need a favor."

Lance grimaced. His brother always seemed to need something. "What's up?"

"You know the townhouse I bought after Rita died?"

"Yeah."

"Well, I'm remodeling the whole place, and every room is torn up." He paused. "So now I don't have anywhere to stay."

Lance thumped his forehead. *Great. I bet Dan wants to stay here with me. There goes my peace and quiet after work and on Sundays.*

"Anyhow, the place won't be move-in ready for several weeks, so would it be all right if I bunk in with you till it's done?"

"Um, yeah, sure, that'd be fine. The guestroom's always ready for unexpected company. Bring over whatever you need; I don't have anything planned and will be home all evening."

"Thanks, Lance. And don't worry, I'll treat you to a few meals out, 'cause I owe you big."

"No problem." Lance said goodbye and clicked off his phone. He didn't look forward to having his life disrupted, but since it was for only a matter of weeks, he'd make it work.

Lance stood and ambled into the kitchen to get something to eat for supper. There wasn't much in the refrigerator, and he didn't feel like cooking, so he grabbed the container filled with leftover macaroni and cheese.

As Lance heated his supper in the microwave, he thought more about Flo. *I'm sure she would approve of me helping Dan out. She was a hospitable woman.* His eyes misted. He missed her sweet smile and wished she was with him right now. *Maybe with my brother here in the house, I won't feel so lonely.*

Chapter 10

Walnut Creek

Heidi's eyelids fluttered as she struggled to stay awake, while sitting on a backless wooden bench inside Eli Miller's woodshop where church was being held today. After she and Lyle returned home from seeing Kendra and her baby yesterday afternoon, Heidi, determined not to give in to self-pity, had looked for things to keep herself busy. Holding Kendra's baby and hearing the child had been named after her caused Heidi's emotions to jump all over the place. Consequently, she'd stayed up late doing things that probably didn't need to be done and hadn't gotten enough sleep. Her conscience said she'd done the right thing by going to see Kendra, but her heart told her otherwise. It was hard not to grieve for something she wanted so desperately. If only God had said yes to her prayer.

Along with some cute pink booties and a New Testament she'd gotten at one of the stores, they'd given Kendra a small quilt for her baby, Heidi's aunt Emma had made when they'd first told her they were planning to adopt. Kendra seemed pleased with the gifts.

Heidi shifted on the unyielding bench, trying to find a comfortable position. *Who wouldn't be pleased to receive such a special item as a handmade baby quilt?*

When the final hymn began, Heidi became more fully awake, eager to go outdoors for a bit to breathe some fresh air. Due to her musings, plus a struggle to stay awake, she'd missed most of the final sermon and felt guilty about it. She hoped no one had caught her on the verge of drifting off.

Lance was almost out the door of the church he attended when his daughter Terry approached him. "Say, Dad, can I talk to you a minute?"

He halted. "Sure, what's up?"

"I know you were planning to come over to our place for dinner today, but something unexpected came up, and I need to cancel. Can we make it next week instead?"

"Next Sunday will be Sharon's turn to have me over." Lance's eyebrows squished together as he touched the base of his neck. "What's going on that you have to cancel?"

"Nick's mother isn't feeling well, so I'm taking dinner to her and Nick's dad today."

Lance pulled his glasses down and looked over the rims. "Is there something going on here, Terry?"

She shook her head. "Of course not, Dad. Why would you think there was anything going on?"

"I thought maybe you were in cahoots with your sister. She wanted to have me over for dinner today so she could set me up with one of the new ladies from church." His forehead wrinkled. "I've told you both before that I'm not interested in a relationship with another woman. Your mother was the only lady I'll ever love, so there's no point even bothering to play matchmaker."

She tipped her head back, eyeing him curiously. "Is that what you think I'm doing?"

"Well, aren't you?"

"Absolutely not. Nick's mother is genuinely sick. I would never make up a story like that. I only suggested you go over to Sharon's this afternoon so you wouldn't have to spend the day alone. Besides, you're not the world's best cook, so I would think you'd appreciate a home-cooked meal."

Lance drew a quick breath, feeling heat rush to his cheeks. He felt like a heel. "S—sorry, Terry. Guess I'm a little paranoid these days. Am I forgiven?"

"Of course." She gave him a hug. "So are you going over to Sharon's for dinner?"

He shook his head. "Not today. Think I'm gonna grab something at the fast-food place on the way home and spend the rest of the day visiting with your uncle Dan and helping him find places in my guestroom for the rest of his things."

Terry's head tilted to one side. "Why is he putting things in your guestroom?"

Lance explained about Dan's townhouse being remodeled and ended by saying it would be a temporary situation.

She smiled and patted his arm. "It'll give you a chance to spend a little time with your brother. I'm sure you'll both enjoy yourselves."

He nodded slowly. *Sure hope it works out that way.*

Dover

Lisa rolled over sleepily, but when she glanced at the clock on the bedside table, she sat straight up. "Oh, no, it can't be afternoon already!" Lisa hadn't wanted to sleep this late, or miss church, either. When she didn't make it to church, her day seemed to lack a positive outlook, and it was harder to get through the week. But the night hours had been sleepless for her. And what a night it had been, too. After she'd gotten home from catering a baby shower, she had gone straight to bed. Lisa had been so tired, she hadn't even bothered to remove her makeup, taking time only to quickly brush her teeth.

She should have slept like a baby after all the work she had put in for the occasion, but the puppy next door howled most of the night. During the brief time the pathetic little critter wasn't carrying on, its owners' voices kept Lisa awake as they hollered at each other. She'd slept with two pillows pressed against her ears. It was worse than any nightmare. How two people who'd only been married a year could scream at each other the way those two did, made her wonder why they'd gotten married in the first place. *If I ever get serious about anyone, I'm going to make sure not to rush into anything. I'll get to know them well before we make a lifelong commitment.*

The sun streamed in through a crack in the blinds, and Lisa

clambered out of bed. Yawning, she padded down the hall to the bathroom. One look in the mirror told Lisa it was a good thing she hadn't gone to church. Her hair was a tangled mess, and her eyes were so puffy she could barely keep them open. She could never make herself presentable enough to be seen by anyone today.

Sighing, she tucked a lock of hair behind her ears. *What I need is some fresh air. Think I'll get dressed and take a walk. When I get back home, I'm going to have a little talk with my renters. They have to do something about that pup or else look for somewhere else to live.*

New Philadelphia

After Allie picked her kids up from Sunday school, she headed straight for the mall. Nola needed new shoes, and Derek a pair of blue jeans. Some people might think it wasn't right to shop on Sunday, but since Allie worked at the dentist's office during the week, she needed weekends for shopping and running errands. Besides, what did it hurt to shop on Sundays? It wasn't like the day was sacred or anything.

Allie glanced at her children in the rearview mirror. They both looked nice in their Sunday clothes. *My son and daughter are so precious. I love them more than life itself.*

She flipped on her turn signal and made a right. *Someday, when Nola and Derek are older, will their lives be better from going to church and learning memory verses? Should I consider going to Sunday school with them, rather than dropping them off and finding something else to do by myself?*

Allie had attended Sunday school when she was a girl, which was why she felt the need to see that her children went, too. But she'd quit going during her teen years and didn't feel it was necessary for her anymore. She did pray sometimes, however—especially when Steve was working and didn't come home when she expected. It was either pray or spend the whole time worrying. Besides, where had any amount of worry gotten her?

As Allie pulled her minivan into the mall's parking lot, she spotted two police cars parked side-by-side. Nearing the vehicles, she realized one of the drivers was Steve. In the other police car sat a blond-haired female cop Allie had not met before. She was obviously new on the force, but it seemed strange Steve had made no mention of her. Usually, when someone new was hired, he told Allie about it right away.

A pang of jealously shot through her. The people Steve worked with saw more of him than she and the kids did these days. Today was supposed to be his day off, but once again, he'd covered for someone on the force who needed, or maybe simply wanted, time off.

Allie's heartbeat quickened when Steve got out of his vehicle and took a seat in the passenger's side of the other patrol car. *I wonder what he's doing. Should I find a spot near their vehicles and find out for myself?*

"There's Daddy!" Derek shouted from the back of the van.

"Yes, Son, it sure is your dad."

"What's he doin'?"

Allie gritted her teeth. "I don't know. Looks like he's talking to another police officer."

"Are we gonna say hi to Daddy?" The question came from Nola.

"Yes, we definitely are." Allie found a parking space in the row behind the squad cars, pulled in, and turned off the ignition. "You two sit tight. I'll be right back with your dad."

She hesitated at first, wondering what she should say. Allie didn't want to come off as being a jealous wife. Sometimes that spurred another woman on. And she didn't want to sound like a nag, either. That might push Steve right into the arms of another woman.

When Allie approached the second patrol car, she rapped on the passenger door. Steve jumped, looking at her with lips forming an O and eyes wide open. "Allie," he mouthed.

She gave no response—just stood waiting for him to exit the car.

He said something to the blond woman, then opened the car door. "What are you doing here, Allie?" Steve's cheeks looked flushed.

"I brought the kids to buy some new clothes. How come you're here? Was there some kind of disturbance at the mall today?"

"No, I, uh. . ." He rubbed the back of his head. "I heard Officer Robbins was in the area so I met up with her to talk about some things."

Allie leaned down slightly, glancing in the window. The woman inside gave her a nod. Even with her police hat on, the woman's beauty could not go unnoticed. Her hair was tied back in a long ponytail, thick with spiral curls. She had flawless skin with vivid blue eyes. No wonder she needed so little makeup.

Absentmindedly, Allie reached up to touch her own hair. At least she'd taken the time to style it this morning. "Is Officer Robbins new on the force? You've never mentioned her before."

"Yeah, Lori came on a few weeks ago."

"I see." *I wonder what kind of things you would need to talk about with her.* Allie pointed at the minivan. "The kids are waiting. They both want to say hello."

"Okay, sure, but let me introduce you to Lori first."

Allie shook her head. "No, that's okay. Maybe some other time."

"Okay, sure." Steve told the other officer he'd talk to her later, got out of the car, and sprinted over to the van.

Allie gave the blond officer a backward glance before following Steve to their car. She tried hard not to let wandering thoughts creep into her head but couldn't help wondering if Lori was the reason Steve was working on his day off. *Has he really been covering for someone else on the force all these times, or has Steve been using it as an excuse to work the same schedule as Lori Robbins?*

Allie was on the verge of asking Steve a few more questions but changed her mind. She didn't want to start anything in front of the kids. This evening, though, if the opportunity arose, she would question her husband more about Officer Robbins.

Chapter 11

Walnut Creek

When Lance pulled onto his driveway Wednesday afternoon, he spotted his brother's sports car parked in front of the garage door. *Oh, great. How's he expect me to put my rig inside now?*

Lance wasn't in a good mood anyway. He'd had a rough day. It all started this morning when he dropped a bag of mail and had to scramble to pick it up before it started to rain. Things went downhill after that, and now this. His normally cheerful mood had gone by the wayside.

He knew his brother needed somewhere to stay, which meant making some adjustments on his part, but already, he couldn't help feeling some regret. Dan had moved his things into Lance's place Saturday evening, and for the past three days, he'd blocked the way into the garage. On top of that, Lance's brother was good at making messes and didn't bother to pick up after himself. No doubt he'd been used to having his wife clean the house when she was alive and figured he didn't have to pick up his clothes, do the laundry, or gather up the things he'd left in the living room after watching TV. Apparently Dan also thought he owned the driveway here.

Lance turned his vehicle off and got out. He shoved the set of keys in his jacket pocket and looked up when he felt a few drops of rain hit his arm. Maybe it wouldn't amount to more than a sprinkle. They'd had enough rain this morning to last a week.

When he entered the house, Lance found Dan sprawled out on the couch with the television blaring. Lance positioned himself between the TV and his brother. "So what have you been doing all day?"

Dan sat up and yawned. "Did a few loads of laundry, but not much else." He pulled his fingers through the ends of his silver-gray mustache. "Oh, and I fed your goldfish."

Lance ground his teeth together. "I did that first thing this morning. Remember when we were having coffee before I left for work, and I told you I'd fed the fish?"

"Oops. Sorry about that. Must have forgot."

"There's no need for you to feed the fish at all. They're my responsibility, so I'll take care of them from now on. Okay?"

"Yeah sure. Whatever you say." Dan stood and ambled toward the kitchen. "I'm goin' after a glass of milk. Can I get you anything?"

"No, I'm fine right now. I may get something to drink after I change my clothes."

"Speaking of your clothes, there's a pile of clean laundry on your bed."

Lance's eyebrows rose. "You washed my clothes?"

Dan grinned. "Sure did. Thought it was the least I could do to say thanks for letting me stay here till my townhouse remodel is done."

"Okay, thanks. I'm going to my room now to change. See you in a bit."

When Lance entered his bedroom, the first thing he saw was the pile of clothes on his bed. None of them were folded, which meant either having to iron the items or run them through the dryer again to get the wrinkles out.

He picked up one of his favorite shirts and gave it a shake, then dropped it to the bed in disbelief. It was at least a size smaller than it had originally been. *What'd that brother of mine do—wash all my clothes in hot water?*

Gripping the shirt, Lance marched out of the room and went straight to the kitchen. With a hand on his hip, he glared at Dan. "I'm sure you meant well, but from now on, just worry about your own laundry, and I'll do mine, 'cause I can't afford to be losing any more clothes." He held up the item in question.

Dan's cheeks colored. "Oh, oh. Guess this is my day for blunders. I won't let it happen again. If you'll tell me what color and size you want, I'll buy you a new shirt."

"Don't worry about it. What's done is done." Lance flopped into a chair at the table. As far as he was concerned, Dan's townhouse couldn't get done soon enough.

"Say, how 'bout this. . . We'll go out for a bite to eat—my treat. That way you won't have to cook anything, and you can come home afterward and relax for the rest of the evening." Dan rinsed his glass and set it in the sink. "So what do you say, Brother? Do you wanna go out to supper with me?"

Lance tapped his fingers on the table, mulling things over. After a day like he'd had, it would be nice not to worry about what to fix this evening. "Yeah, sure, a meal out will be nice. Just give me a few minutes to change and get ready. Then we can head out."

"No problem. I'll get a jacket and wait for you in my car." Dan ambled out of the kitchen.

Lance pushed away from the table and carried his withered-looking shirt to his room. "This was one of my favorites," he mumbled under his breath. *Guess I may as well throw it in my bag of rags. It's not good for much else. Sure hope nothing like this happens again.*

Millersburg

Nicole entered the house, tossed her schoolbooks on the coffee table, and flopped onto the couch. It had begun to rain again, and she was relieved to be indoors. Heather and Tony's bus should be dropping them off any minute, so she was glad she'd made it home before they did. The last time they got home before she did, they'd fixed snacks and left a mess in the kitchen. Ever since Nicole's mother walked out on the family, the kitchen had become Nicole's domain, even though she didn't know how to cook that well. Maybe after a few more lessons from Heidi Troyer, Nicole would be able to make some decent meals. Dad deserved some tasty dishes—that was for sure. After what Tonya did to him, he ought to have only good things.

Nicole had been given a ton of homework today, but she was in no hurry to get it done. All she wanted to do was get out her sketch pad, sit outside on the patio, and draw something from nature. Her dream was to have her own art studio someday. But of course, it wasn't likely to happen. "Nothing good ever happens for me," she mumbled.

"Who are you talking to, honey?"

Nicole jumped, her eyes widening when her father stepped into the room. He wore a pair of sweat pants and stood rubbing his head with a towel. "Dad, what are you doing here?"

"I live here, remember?" He chuckled. "Got off early today and just finished taking a shower."

"I didn't see your car out front when I came in."

"It's in the garage."

"Oh."

He glanced around. "Are Tony and Heather home yet?"

"Nope. Only me."

"How was school?" He took a seat in his easy chair and propped his feet on the footstool.

Nicole shrugged. "Same as usual."

"How are your grades? Are you keeping up with things?"

"I'm doin' okay." Nicole looked away from him. It wasn't right to lie to her dad, but she didn't want to worry him. She would catch up eventually. At least she hoped she would.

"Well, that's not what the e-mail I got today from your English teacher said." Dad's forehead creased. "According to her, your grades are close to failing." His voice grew louder. "Don't you think you should have let me know about this?"

Nicole sat quietly, looking down at her hands. *I shoulda known I couldn't trust Mrs. Wick. I thought she would give me another chance.*

Dad tapped his foot. *Thump! Thump! Thump!* "Well, young lady, what do you have to say for yourself?"

"I probably should have said something, but I didn't want to worry you." She looked up at him, tears pricking the back of her eyes.

His eyes narrowed. "Well, it's too late for that. . . . I'm worried now! You can't afford to fall behind, Nicole. Your education is important, and I want you to graduate from high school."

"I know." Nicole blinked and swallowed hard, hoping she wouldn't break down.

"We'll have to make some adjustments so you have more time to study and do your homework."

"What kind of adjustments?"

"For one thing, Heather can take over doing the dishes while you study."

"She doesn't do them as good as I do. The last time she washed dishes I found some dirty ones in the dish drainer and had to do them over."

"If she doesn't get the dishes clean, she will have to rewash them, not you." Dad paused, swiping a hand across his forehead. "I'll be checking my e-mails more regularly. The one I found today came in a day or two ago."

Sighing, Nicole nodded. "Okay, Dad." *Boy, what was I thinking? I should have figured Mrs. Wick would contact Dad anyway.* Her fingers curled into the palms of her hands. *Why didn't I come clean with him about this the day it happened?*

"I'm sorry for not confiding in you," she said tearfully. "I promise from now on there will be no more secrets."

Dad stepped over to Nicole and pulled her into his arms. "You know how much I love you, don't you?"

She gave a slow nod.

"And even though I don't say it often enough, I appreciate everything you do around here." He patted her back. "You're a good daughter, and an equally good sister, always putting Heather and Tony's needs ahead of your own."

Nicole pressed her cheek against his chest. "Thanks, Dad. It means a lot to hear your say it."

A horn honked behind Bill as he sat in his vehicle, waiting to pull out of the school's parking lot. He glanced in the rearview mirror and frowned. It was the picky English teacher. "Oh, don't be so impatient, Ms. Schultz. I can't pull onto the street when there's a car coming."

Bill waited a few more seconds, then once he saw that all was clear, he pulled onto the road. The sky was filled with dismal-looking clouds this afternoon, and it had begun to rain. It was a bit of a drive back to New Philadelphia, and he hoped traffic wouldn't be too bad. Sometimes, when the tourists headed out of Berlin, Walnut Creek, or Sugarcreek, it took longer than normal to get home. He looked forward to getting there today, since he had plans to meet one of his buddies for supper this evening. Of course, their main topic would focus on the big fall hunting trip they'd been planning for months. Even if Bill didn't bag a deer this year, it would be fun to spend time in the woods and sleep in his cabin.

Bill let out a deep, gratifying sigh. There was nothing better than sitting in his tree stand, watching nature prepare for winter. Except for his orange hat and vest, Bill dressed all in camouflage, right down to his boots, making it difficult for any animal to tell what he was. Even his hat and vest had a design etched through the bright orange that helped break up his image to anything looking his way. But when something did, their curiosity piqued. A few times Bill had to sit real still when a little nuthatch flew and sat on his leg. The bird remained there a few seconds and then scurried down the length of his leg, pecking at the tree pattern in the camo material of his pants before flying off.

Bill's buddies often teased him about the extent to which he would go to make his presence unknown in the woods. Before he left for hunting camp, he washed his hunting clothes in soap that smelled like autumn leaves. He also showered and washed his hair, using a scent-free soap. Lastly, to make sure there was no human odor, Bill sprayed the bottom of his boots and give a squirt to his clothes with another type of de-scenting liquid. *Sure, let my friends laugh at me, but they won't be laughing if I bag a buck first.* It didn't really bother Bill if he did or didn't get the first deer, but it had become a contest between Russ and Tom, wagering on who would get theirs first.

The squirrels found Bill interesting, too. He snickered, remembering last year when a squirrel sat on a dead tree's branch that hung close to where he sat. As it ran up and down the brittle limb, the bushy-tailed critter chattered and scolded, trying to get Bill to move. Then the branch broke, and fell onto another dead branch, breaking it as well. It was like a domino effect as the squirrel fell to even lower branches, breaking them, too. Before crashing to the ground, the squirrel rolled up in a little ball, and when it hit the leaf-covered floor, it took off running, and Bill never saw him again.

Yes, there were plenty of good reasons Bill enjoyed getting out in the woods. Unlike some hunters, it wasn't about the kill, but about everything else that encompassed hunting season. Going to his cabin couldn't get here soon enough, even if he did have to do all the cooking. Bill hoped by the time they got there, he'd have learned some better recipes to try out on his friends. In just a few more days he'd be back at Heidi Troyer's place taking his second cooking class.

He flicked on the radio for some music to keep him company the rest of the way home. *I wonder what she'll teach us to make this time.*

Walnut Creek

When Heidi stepped onto the porch to shake out some throw rugs, she saw Eli Miller riding into the yard on his bike. Earlier it had rained hard, and dark clouds still hung in close.

Heidi watched as Eli set the kickstand on his bicycle. "Hello, Eli," she called to him. "I can sure tell it's fall by the way the days are growing shorter and from all this rain we keep getting."

Nodding, Eli stepped onto the porch. "Is Lyle here?"

"No, he's auctioneering again today. Was there something you needed?" Hearing Rusty barking from inside the house, she quickly opened the door, knowing the dog wouldn't quit if she didn't let him out to greet their visitor.

Eli reached down and patted the Brittany spaniel's head.

Heidi smiled. "Rusty sure likes you, Eli. He always seems to know when you're around."

"He's a good dog, for sure." Eli grinned when Rusty plopped down by his feet. "I'd hoped to see Lyle today, but it's nothing that can't wait." He shuffled his feet a few times, lowering his gaze. If Heidi didn't know better, she'd think he was hiding something.

"I don't expect Lyle will be home until suppertime. If you'd like to come back around six o'clock we'd be pleased if you joined us for the evening meal."

"Sure appreciate the offer, but I can't tonight." Eli's hand anchored casually against his hip as his lips turned up. "I'm goin' to Loretta's house for supper."

"I see. You've been seeing a lot of her lately, jah?"

His ears turned pink as he nodded. "I'm glad she's planning to join the Amish church."

Heidi smiled. "I'm happy, too. Loretta's a good friend. It will be nice to have her in our church district." She hung the rug she still held over the porch railing. "Mind if I ask you a personal question?"

"Course not. What would you like to know?"

"Are you getting serious about Loretta? I mean, would you be thinking about marrying her?" Heidi couldn't help herself. Since Loretta had already mentioned things were getting serious between her and Eli, Heidi assumed he'd be asking for Loretta's hand in marriage.

The rosy hue coloring Eli's ears spread quickly to his cheeks. "Well, we have been courting."

"I'm aware. That's why I wondered if maybe. . ." Heidi ended her sentence. "Sorry, Eli. It's none of my business, and I didn't mean to pry."

"It's okay—no problem. I'd better get going. Would you please tell Lyle I dropped by?"

"Certainly." Rusty pawed at the hem of Heidi's dress, and she knelt to pet the dog's furry head.

Eli turned, and as he headed for his bike, he began to whistle, swinging his arms easily at his side.

Heidi quit petting the dog, picked up the first rug, and gave it a good shake. *I wouldn't be a bit surprised if Eli and Loretta don't start planning their wedding the day after she joins the church. He was probably too embarrassed to tell me. Bet the next time he sees Lyle, he'll let him know. Maybe that's why Eli came over here today.*

Chapter 12

Near Strasburg, Ohio

Todd looked at the clock on his dash and groaned. It was a quarter to ten, and he was only halfway to Walnut Creek. *Looks like I'm gonna be late. And to top it off, it's raining harder than when I first pulled out of my driveway.*

Until he'd gotten up this morning and looked at the calendar, Todd had forgotten today was the second Saturday of October, and he was supposed to attend another cooking class. Between working on his column for the newspaper, trying out a couple of new restaurants in the area, and keeping up with his social life, he'd had a busy couple of weeks.

To make matters worse, Todd's mother called a few days ago, pestering him to visit them. He didn't have time for a vacation. And if he were to take one, it wouldn't be to Portland, Oregon. He'd grown up there and, after graduating from college, had been eager to move from the Pacific Northwest and be on his own without Mom looking over his shoulder, scrutinizing everything he said or did.

Todd gripped the steering wheel and tried to focus on something else. It was hard being an only child and having your parents complain because they didn't get to see you often enough. "Well, if Mom wasn't afraid to fly, they could come visit me here in Ohio more often. I shouldn't have to always be the one to put forth the effort."

Todd's most recent trip to Oregon had been last Thanksgiving, but this year he planned to stay by himself at home. Whenever he went to his folk's place, Mom always plied him with questions about his social life, and of course, kept on him about whether he'd met anyone he might consider marrying. A few times she'd even tried to set him up with the daughter of one of her friends.

Mom doesn't even know the type of woman I'd be interested in. Todd glanced at himself in the rearview mirror. "What is it about mothers thinking their sons aren't happy unless they find a wife?" he muttered. "If I do ever decide to get married, it'll be to a woman of my own choosing. Right now, my career comes first."

Walnut Creek

As Lisa turned her van onto the road leading to Heidi's house, her excitement mounted. Even with the wet weather, she looked forward to attending the second cooking class and hoped she would learn something new today that she could incorporate in her catering business. Things were going well, and she had a wedding reception to cater next Saturday. But the opportunity to secure more clients was what she continually needed. She didn't enjoy driving places that didn't involve business in the van she used for her catering services, but money was tight, and until she was making more of it, Lisa couldn't afford to buy a smaller vehicle to use strictly for pleasure.

Lisa's cousin, Jim, was a successful lawyer, making a lot more money than she'd probably ever see. It was hard not to be envious, but he'd worked hard to get where he was, so he deserved his achievement. His wife, Carlie, and their two children, Annette and Cindy, had everything they could possibly want. Lisa, on the other hand, had yet to find a man she'd consider marrying, successful or not. She often wondered if she would ever have any children. For now, at least, she'd made growing her business a priority.

I'll just bide my time, Lisa told herself. *If I keep working hard and do my best to help the business flourish, someday it'll be a success. I may never make anything close to what my cousin does, but I enjoy my job, and if I can make a decent living, that's good enough for me.*

Heidi had begun setting out the ingredients for Amish friendship bread, when she heard a vehicle pull in. Glancing out the window, she saw Nicole get out of her father's vehicle and run quickly to the house. Too bad it had to rain again today. Heidi sensed during the last class that the young girl was deeply troubled, but she wouldn't pry. If Nicole wanted to discuss her situation at home, she would open up either during class or sometime when she and Heidi had a few minutes alone. Since no one else had arrived yet, perhaps Nicole would be more talkative.

Heidi set the sack of flour she held on the kitchen table and hurried to open the door. "Good morning." She smiled when Nicole stepped in with rain dripping off her jacket. "It's good to see you again. Just hang your wet coat on one of the wall pegs." Heidi motioned toward them. "How have you been these last couple of weeks?"

With a nonchalant shrug, Nicole stepped inside. "I've been okay, I guess."

"You're the first one here, so why don't you come with me to the kitchen? We can visit while I finish getting things set out."

Silently, Nicole followed Heidi into the kitchen and plunked down in a chair at the oversized table.

"Would you like something cold to drink? There's a pitcher of lemonade in the refrigerator."

Nicole shook her head. "No thanks."

It didn't take a genius to realize the girl wasn't eager to carry on a conversation, but Heidi felt compelled to keep trying. "Have you done any cooking these past couple weeks?"

"I cook every meal at my house, but none are very tasty." Nicole's forehead wrinkled. "At least that's what my brother and sister say about the things I fix for them. They don't appreciate anything I do."

In an effort to make Nicole feel better, Heidi touched the girl's shoulder. "Sometimes people appreciate what we do but forget to say thanks."

"Yeah, maybe. My dad says thanks once in a while, but he's got a lot of other stuff on his mind." Nicole puffed out her cheeks. "Oh, and by the way, I forgot to bring an apron again."

"It's fine. You can wear one of mine." Heidi was on the verge of saying more, when another vehicle pulled into the yard. She glanced at the clock. It was five minutes to ten. Soon everyone would be here and her second cooking class would begin.

Once everyone else arrived and had removed their wet outer garments, Heidi asked them to take seats at the kitchen table. "Today we will be making Amish friendship bread." She went on to explain that in order to make the bread, a starter must first be prepared. "You will be able to keep part of the starter and give part of it to a couple of friends." Heidi picked up a bowl that had been covered with plastic wrap. "You will notice by the texture and smell that this starter is slightly fermented." She showed each student the fresh batch from the bowl in her hands.

Bill wrinkled his nose. "If I fed that putrid-looking stuff to my hunting buddies, they wouldn't be my friends very long."

Heidi bit back a chuckle. "No one's expected to eat the starter. Only a small portion of it will be added to the other ingredients to make the friendship bread." She set the starter down and handed out recipe cards, as well as the necessary ingredients, along with small bowls and utensils for everyone.

Looking at each of the students, she smiled. "When you leave here today, in addition to the bread you will make, I'll give all of you a small amount of starter."

Todd's brows furrowed as he leaned his elbows on the table and stared at the yeasty-smelling dough. "What are we supposed to do with the stuff when we take it home?"

"We're gonna use it to make more friendship bread." Bill tapped Todd's shoulder. "If you don't have any friends you can make some new ones by giving them a loaf of the tasty bread."

Todd scowled at him. "How do you know it's tasty? We haven't even made it yet."

Bill puffed out his chest. "I have every confidence that our cooking teacher would not give us any recipe that wasn't good."

"Thank you, Bill." Heidi was pleased he had such confidence in her. Hopefully everyone's bread would turn out well.

Lisa glanced around the table. Except for Todd, who looked thoroughly disgusted, everyone else seemed eager to learn how to make friendship bread—although Allie appeared preoccupied.

She'd never say anything to Heidi, but Lisa was a bit disappointed. She had hoped that today they would learn how to make a casserole or some type of supper dish she could use in her catering business. And to be truthful, Lisa never liked getting involved in chain-type letters, which this friendship bread reminded her of—passing the starter from one person to another.

Hopefully during the next four classes, they'd be given something better to make. She stared at the starter. *Maybe I could make this recipe for the holidays, to give family members or someone from church.*

Lisa held her fist to her mouth, hoping to stifle a yawn. She wondered if the rainy weather added to her feeling extra tired this morning.

Sitting up straighter and leaning forward, she tried to concentrate. She'd slept pretty well the first part of last night—until four thirty this morning, when the puppy next door started howling. If this went on any longer with her tenants, Lisa had made up her mind to say something. She'd been hoping the situation would have remedied itself by now, but it was worse than ever. The poor puppy needed more attention and exercise after being locked up all day alone. When Lisa arrived home the other evening, she saw Gail open her front door and let the dog out by itself. With no supervision of any sort, the puppy sniffed around for a while and did what it had to do. Lisa was glad it stayed away from the street. How sad it would be if the pup got hit by a car. When the poor thing wanted in, it sat on their door step barking and yipping to no avail. Finally, after what seemed like forever, the dog was let back inside.

Now who would leave a little puppy outside all by itself? Lisa would surely never do that. *Some people just shouldn't own pets.* Her neighbors were proving to be irresponsible, and she regretted having rented to them.

Lisa looked over at Heidi's dog, lying by the kitchen door. It was content in sleep and appeared to be oblivious to everyone in the room. Rusty was well-behaved and always listened to Heidi's commands. Lisa watched as the dog stretched, opened his eyes, and closed them again. *Now there is a dog that is obviously loved and well cared for.*

Everyone laughed at something Heidi had said, and Lisa snapped to attention. *I'd better listen to what is going on, so I don't miss something important and end up doing something stupid and make a fool of myself.*

Chapter 13

Allie had a hard time concentrating on the cooking lesson. She kept thinking about Steve, and how she'd seen him in the mall parking lot on Sunday with the cute little blond patrol officer. She'd planned to talk to him about it but changed her mind. He'd probably say she was overreacting or had become paranoid. *Well, if I am, there's good reason. My insecurity or vulnerability being married to an officer of the law could be rearing its ugly head right now.*

Steve had accused Allie of overreacting many times—especially where his safety was concerned. *When did he start filling in for a coworker and working later hours or volunteering to work on his days off? Was it when Lori Robbins started working on the force?* Allie wished now she'd made a mental note of it but felt bad after thinking things through a bit more. She didn't want to draw any conclusions or become suspicious about her husband. A good marriage should involve trust. She'd need to make sure she didn't sound accusing if she and Steve had a discussion about this. Allie had a tendency to say the first thing that came to her mind, which often got her in trouble with him.

Maybe it's me. Have I let myself go? Am I putting on weight that I just don't see? Allie reached up and brushed her hair back off her face. *I could probably use a fresh style, or maybe a complete makeover like I've seen on one of those TV shows, where they take a plain-looking woman and transform her into a beauty queen.*

Forcing her contemplations aside, Allie tried to focus on what Heidi was saying. Unfortunately, making friendship bread held little appeal. Allie had hoped for a new supper dish she could make for Steve and the children. She wouldn't say anything to Heidi, however. It wouldn't be right to hurt her feelings. Maybe, when they came to

413

the next class, Heidi would show them how to make something Allie could fix more often. *Guess I can share a loaf of friendship bread with some of my friends at work. I don't want that starter to go to waste.*

———————⚬⚬⚬———————

Bill put his loaf pan full of dough into the oven, placing it next to Nicole's. *I wonder what would happen if I gave a loaf of friendship bread to the irritating English teacher at the high school.* He puckered his lips. *If it was from anybody else, she might appreciate the gesture, but coming from me, I bet she'd throw it in the trash. That feisty old lady probably wouldn't accept anything I offered, even if it was served on a fancy gold platter. Don't know why she has it in for me. I've always been polite to her, even when she got under my skin.*

Bill returned to his seat at the kitchen table to wait for his bread to bake. He glanced over at Lance, who sat beside him and smiled. "Bet with you bein' a mail carrier, you'll have plenty of people you can give friendship bread or starter to."

Lance shrugged. "Yeah, maybe so. I may make some for my two daughters, though. I think they'd enjoy sharing this recipe and bread with their families, as well as passing it along to others. My brother might even enjoy it."

"How many brothers do you have?"

"Just the one. Dan's a few years older than me, and right now he's living at my house. It's only temporary—just until his townhouse is fully remodeled. I have a younger sister, too." Lance motioned to Bill. "How 'bout you? Do you have any siblings?"

"I don't have any sisters, but I do have three brothers." Bill blew out his breath. "They all live in Cleveland, and we don't see each other much."

"That's too bad."

"It's okay." Bill shrugged. "I have some good buddies who live near me. We do a lot together throughout the year. In fact, we're heading out to do some camping at my cabin in Coshocton soon."

"Sounds like fun."

"We have a good time, but it would be nice if even one of my brothers would join us sometime." Bill frowned. "None of 'em are the outdoorsy type, though. You're lucky to have a brother living close to you. I wouldn't mind if one of my brothers lived with me, even if it was only temporary. It might give me a chance to turn them on to hunting."

"Yeah," Lance gave a quick nod.

Bill figured none of his brothers would be interested in the friendship bread, but he wished he had a daughter to give a loaf. His only child, Brent, was single and also lived in Cleveland, but he probably wouldn't want any friendship bread. Since Bill was divorced, he really had no one to share the recipe with. Someday, maybe his son would get married and he could give the recipe to Brent's wife.

Bill's jaw clenched. *It'll have to be Brent's wife if he ever marries 'cause I'm sure not getting married again. I'm doin' fine by myself.*

He thought about his hunting buddies. If the friendship bread tasted good, he'd make a few more loaves and give one each to Tom, Russ, and Andy. *That oughta show those fellows I can make something other than the same old hunter's stew.* Bill brushed away some flour clinging to his apron. *I wonder what it was like for the cooks back in the Wild West during one of those trail drives. I bet those cowboys weren't as picky as my longtime friends who like to complain about minor things.*

Bill looked across the table, where Nicole sat with her head down as though studying something on the floor. The teenage girl hadn't said more than a few words since Heidi started teaching the class this morning. What was her problem anyway? Was she thinking about the troubles she had at school, or could Nicole have some serious difficulties at home she had to deal with?

Sure wish there was something I could do to help her. Trouble is, I can barely get the gal to look at me.

Nicole tried to concentrate, but all she could think about was the test Mrs. Wick sprung on them Friday in English class. Nicole shouldn't have been surprised though, since the teacher had hinted several times about reading certain chapters. She'd been staying after school for help from Mrs. Wick, then coming home and working on the assignments while it was still fresh in her mind. Nicole had a lot to do yet to get her grades up—not just in English, but in other classes as well. It was partly her fault for not seeking help before.

Nicole sighed deeply, then looked around quickly to see if anyone noticed. The last thing she wanted was for anyone in the class, or even Heidi, to ask her if anything was wrong.

She realized something had to be done about her grades, and Nicole sure didn't want to retake any of those classes. But how could she devote more time to her studies with all the responsibilities she had at home? Her dad had been trying to come home earlier so she could study more, and he'd made her siblings do a few duties around the house to lessen Nicole's load. In fact, he'd even made a list for Heather and Tony that included some housecleaning and picking up after themselves. He was trying to help her have more time to get her grades up, but she still was stuck with cooking all the meals.

Sure wish I could be like so many other kids my age who have two normal parents. They don't realize how lucky they are.

Mondays were the hardest, going back to school, when she had to listen to fellow students talk about their weekends. Nicole and her family rarely went anywhere exciting or did fun things together; it was normally the same old routine. So sometimes while sitting there listening to her classmates, she would envision herself doing what they talked about during their weekend. It didn't help much.

Maybe getting an interesting book to read would help take me away from my real life. Guess I could go see what our school library has to offer during lunch one day.

Nicole thought about all the events going on at school, such as the football games that took place most Friday nights. When there wasn't a game, a dance was held in the school's gymnasium. On Saturdays, some of the students liked to hang out at the sub shop located on the corner near the school. The homecoming football game and dance were coming up, but Nicole wouldn't be going to those events, either. She thought the world of her dad, as well as her brother and sister, but all because of her so-called mother, Nicole was missing out on the best years of her life.

For now, Nicole had to figure out a way to keep Friday's test results from her dad. She didn't have to be a rocket scientist to know she'd failed the test miserably. *I will have to study harder for the next test. Guess I'll be getting another talking to from Mrs. Wick after class on Monday. I sure hope she doesn't e-mail Dad again or ask to speak to him in person.*

When the oven door was opened, releasing a sweet cinnamon aroma, Heidi's whole kitchen smelled so good, it made Todd's mouth water. He looked at all the golden loaves, with hot steam rising off their tops, and licked his lips in anticipation of eating a piece. The bread reminded him of the type of thing he often ordered to go with his latte at the local coffee shop.

Once everyone's loaf of friendship bread had been taken from the oven and placed on the counter to cool, Heidi gave each of them a three-by-five card with the recipe for the bread, as well as a small amount of starter. Curious to see if there was another scripture verse on the back, Todd turned his over. Sure enough, there it was: "I will instruct thee and teach thee in the way which thou shalt go: I will guide thee with mine eye" (Psalm 32:8).

His brows furrowed. *I don't need the Lord to guide or teach me how I should go. I'll set my own course, thank you very much.* Todd wasn't even sure there was a God, let alone a need to call upon Him for anything.

Heidi stood at the head of the table, facing everyone. "Before you all leave today, I would like to share a few more helpful hints with you. When freezing foods, label each container with its contents and the date it was put into the freezer. Always use foods that have been cooked and then frozen within one to two months."

Allie bobbed her head. "Those are good points which I'm already aware of."

"Mind if I add something to the topic of freezing foods?" Lisa asked.

Heidi smiled. "Not at all."

"You should never freeze cooked egg whites, because they will become tough."

Todd turned to face her. "Is that something you learned the hard way in your catering business?"

She gave a slow nod. "I'll admit, I've had a few bloopers along the way, but for the most part, things have gone well with my enterprise."

"Do you cater a variety of events?" The question came from Nicole, which was a surprise, since she'd been quiet most of the class.

"Yes, and in fact, I'll be catering a wedding next Saturday night. I'll be working on the cake for it this coming week." Lisa's dimples deepened as she gave a wide smile. Todd thought she was kind of cute. He still didn't know if she was married and needed to figure out the best way to find out. He sure wasn't going to make a play for her if she had a husband, or even a boyfriend.

"That's wonderful," Heidi said. "Will you be taking pictures of the cake?"

"Yes, definitely."

The mention of a wedding caused Todd to recall that he'd been invited to attend the wedding of an acquaintance next week. It was the owner of a restaurant he'd written a good review about. The guy's name was Shawn, and after getting to know Todd from coming into his restaurant several times, they'd become fairly well acquainted. Now Shawn and his business partner, Melanie, were getting married.

Todd leaned his elbows on the table. The parents of Shawn's future wife were quite well-to-do. *I bet whomever they hire to cater their daughter's wedding will be some top-notch caterer with a lot of experience behind them. The food will probably be worthy of a five-star review.*

Chapter 14

Dover

Lisa had worked hard all week, finalizing the wedding reception she was catering this evening. All weddings were important, and she treated each as such. So far, those she had been hired to do had turned out pretty well. In fact, each one seemed to get better. Lisa continually worked to improve her catering business, and this evening's reception would be no exception.

She felt pleased after she'd set everything up. The food tables were arranged in a buffet-style setting. The bride and groom had requested a few items they both enjoyed eating: Chicken fingers, several kinds of chips, and a sandwich platter as well. Lisa had also provided macaroni and potato salads. Fresh vegetables were arranged on a huge platter surrounding a ranch dip. Pineapple, cantaloupe, and honeydew, along with orange and apple slices had been neatly arranged on a three-tiered sterling silver fruit stand that belonged to the bride's grandmother.

The cake was the last thing Lisa set up, and everything seemed to be perfect until the unexpected happened. After getting the first three tiers of the beautifully decorated cake in place, she'd just positioned the fourth tier, when one of the front table legs gave out. Thankfully, Lisa stood close to that corner of the table and was able to react quickly enough before it collapsed.

Now what am I going to do? Lisa steadied the table, praying the cake wouldn't topple off. *I must look silly standing here holding this table up.* Of course, there was no one else in the room at the moment, so she only looked silly to herself. The one saving grace, which amazed her, was the cake was still in place, even though the tablecloth had bunched up. Lisa only had one more tier to add, plus the pair of doves at the top, in order to finish this five-tiered cake. But how in the world could she do it while balancing a three-legged table?

Biting her lip, Lisa came up with an idea. She only hoped it would work. First, she used her one leg, stretching it out under the table. *Maybe I can hook the leg of the table and pull it back in place.* After she tried a couple of times, and was unable to see what she was doing underneath, Lisa started to sweat. "Whew!" She blew air up over her forehead. "This is going to be harder than I thought."

She wondered if she could get on her hands and knees and balance the table using her back. Then she could see underneath and try to figure out what the problem was. But after pondering the situation further, she realized she'd have to pull up the tablecloth to see under the table. Plus, once she was under there, how could she keep an eye on the cake to make sure it didn't fall? Lisa's last resort was to call out and hope someone was in the next room and would hear her plea for help.

"Is anyone there?" *Oh, please, Lord, bring someone to rescue me.* In less than half an hour, this reception room would be filled with lots of people, and she certainly didn't want to be standing here feeling ridiculous as she held up the table.

"Looks like you might need some help over here."

Lisa jumped when a male voice came up behind her. "Todd, w–what are you doing here?" Even though he was the last person she expected to see, much less answer her plea for help, she felt thankful someone had arrived to help her with this precarious situation. At Heidi's cooking class last week Todd had mentioned he'd be attending a wedding soon, but she'd had no idea it would turn out to be the same wedding she'd been asked to cater.

"I'm a friend of the groom. In fact, he owns a restaurant where I like to eat." Todd took over and held the table in place, then instructed Lisa on what to do. "Check the leg and see if it's still connected underneath the table."

"Okay, but be careful the cake doesn't tip." Lisa got down on her knees and pulled up the white tablecloth. "The leg's still connected, but I bet it wasn't locked in place." Lisa pulled the leg out straight and clicked it into the slot. "I think it's okay now. Thanks, Todd. I owe you a debt of gratitude." Heat crept across her cheeks as she crawled out from under the table.

Grinning, he offered her a thumbs-up before taking a step closer. "No problem. Glad I showed up when I did."

Lisa stood and smoothed out the flare of her pretty pink dress. Then she put the final tier on top of the cake, along with the little turtle-doves. Lisa ran her hand over the tablecloth to get out the wrinkles and stood back to look at the cake. "There, that should do it."

"Looks like everything's okay now. The cake looks great, by the way. I assume it's your handy work?"

"Yes."

Todd took a few steps toward the guest tables, but stopped and turned around. "You look really nice tonight, Lisa. If you're not here with anyone, would you save a dance for me?"

"No, I came alone."

"No husband or boyfriend to help you out with the cake?" He looked at her curiously.

She shook her head. "I'm single."

"Same here. See you on the dance floor." He winked before walking away.

Now what was that all about? Lisa watched as Todd found his name card at the table where he'd be seated, but she stopped wondering about him when, minutes later, the flurry of activity started. Guests began to file in and find their seats, waiting for the bride and groom to arrive from the church. The wedding party was announced first, followed by the bride and groom.

As all eyes watched the doorway, an older man announced, "And now let us welcome the newlyweds, Mr. and Mrs. Shawn Goss."

Everyone clapped, and once the wedding couple was seated, the best man and maid of honor took the microphone to offer short speeches and toasts. Members of the wedding party had food served to them at their table. Then the rest of the guests went through the buffet line, one table at a time. All the while, Lisa scurried about, making sure everything ran smoothly. She wished she could afford to hire an assistant, because by the time she went home tonight, she'd be exhausted.

After the cake was cut, and everyone had eaten, all the lights were turned low and the dancing started. The bride and groom must have loved country music, for they'd hired a live country-western band to accompany the dancing. Lisa stood off to one side and watched. It was fun to watch the fancy footwork when the line dancing started. Even Todd seemed to be a pro at cowboy dancing, as he clicked his heels and stomped his feet, doing the two-step around the floor with a pretty, auburn-haired woman. Lisa wished she could join the fun, but she still had work to do.

After taking care of the leftover food, she boxed up the top of the cake for the newly married couple to enjoy on their first wedding anniversary. Glancing up, she saw Todd, wearing a charming smile, walking toward her.

"I'm here for that dance, if you'll join me." He held out his hand. A slow dance had begun, and the lights were dimmed even lower.

"O—okay." Lisa's mouth went dry as she followed him to the dance floor. She thought he'd only been kidding when he'd mentioned dancing with her earlier.

When Todd took Lisa into his arms, her heart did a little flip-flop. It made no sense. She didn't even like Todd. At least she'd thought she didn't. Now, she wasn't so sure. He had come to her aid in time to rescue the cake, but was that any reason to let her emotions take over?

As they swayed to the music, Lisa looked into Todd's vivid blue eyes, sparkling in the low light. He truly was good looking—enough to turn any woman's head. "Thank you again for coming to my aid earlier," she whispered, finding it hard to swallow. "If you hadn't shown up when you did, I would have looked pretty silly standing there holding the table when everyone arrived."

"No problem. Glad I could help."

At first, they danced at arm's length. Then Todd pulled Lisa closer.

"Don't you just love country music?" His lips were close to her ear now, and he held Lisa's hand against his chest. "'I Cross My Heart' does seem to be the perfect song at a wedding."

"I always did like this song." Lisa found it difficult to think. Todd was a good dancer, as he smoothly swayed to the music. She had no trouble moving along with him.

"Everyone seems to be having a good time."

"Uh-huh." She caught her trembling lips between her teeth as Todd moved his head closer to hers. Was he about to kiss her? Did she want him to? Her scrambled emotions made no sense. It must be the music.

"And at least the cake was good."

Lisa stopped dancing, no longer hearing the music. "What do you mean, 'at least?'"

"Well I didn't think there was anything special about the food." Todd's nose wrinkled, like some foul odor had descended on the place. "I don't know who catered the food for this reception, but the bride and groom would have done just as well ordering everything from a fast-food restaurant."

Lisa backed up, anger flaring in her nostrils. "Is that so?" With no explanation, she spun around and stomped off.

It was good Lisa had previously packed all the leftover food in containers and put them in the kitchen's refrigerator for the family to take later. Her job was done here, and she left in a huff, anxious to get home and out of Todd's sight before she said something she might regret later.

Lisa climbed into her van and started the engine. Gripping the steering wheel, she muttered, "Who does Todd think he is, talking to me that way? Didn't he realize I catered all the food, not just the cake? Didn't he see me hustling around making sure all the serving platters were kept filled?"

It was true that the two times Todd had approached Lisa, she was taking care of the cake. First, when she'd been balancing the table while putting the tiers together. Second, when she was boxing up the top of the cake for the bride and groom. *Maybe he forgot when we were introducing ourselves at the first cooking class that I mentioned my catering business.*

"Well, what does it matter what Todd thought? He's no expert on food." Lisa backed out of her parking space. The important thing was, Shawn and Melanie where pleased with everything Lisa had prepared to make their reception perfect. Even the parents of the newly married couple made it a point to compliment her. But somehow Todd's negative remark overshadowed the rest. In fact, it put a damper on Lisa's whole night. *When I see Todd at the next cooking class, I have half a mind to tell him what I think of his rude remark about my cooking.*

She drew a deep breath and tried to calm down. She would play like a duck and let his negative comment roll right on over her. Well, maybe she would—if she could stop thinking about his curt remark and arrogant expression.

Canton

When Todd got home that evening, the first thing he did was take off his shoes and flop on the couch. His feet were killing him, and it didn't help that he'd worn a new pair of shoes to the wedding and spent too much time on his feet, dancing the night away.

He studied his left foot. "Oh great. I have a blister forming near my little toe. What else could go wrong tonight?" Todd winced, thinking about his dance with Lisa. He realized now why she'd gotten so huffy when he mentioned the less-than-desirable food someone had catered for the reception. She'd left him standing in the middle of the dance floor, staring after her until he got his wits again. Of course, by then, the music had ended and the lights were turned up, signaling that the dancing was over for the night.

Todd had attempted to find Lisa, but to no avail. After trying to make his way through the people going back to their tables, he'd scanned the room, looking for her. Where had she gone in such a hurry? He'd even run outside to look for her, but Lisa was nowhere to be seen.

When he headed back inside, Todd was in no mood for celebration. Seeking out Shawn and his new bride, Todd wished them well and said he was heading home. He closed his eyes, replaying the conversation he'd had with the wedding couple before he left.

———— ⌇∽⌇ ————

"Before you leave," Shawn said, "have you seen Lisa? We lost sight of her after she danced with you."

Todd wasn't sure how to answer, so he simply responded, "Guess she wanted to head home."

"Okay. Melanie and I will get in touch with her later."

"You haven't paid for her making the cake yet, huh?"

"No, it's not that. We paid in advance for the cake, plus all the food she supplied. Melanie and I wanted to tell Lisa thanks, and say how much we appreciated everything she did. The food was exactly what we asked for."

Todd felt more than a twinge of guilt now that he realized Lisa had also catered the food. She'd done it according to Shawn and Melanie's wishes, too. *Each to his own. Guess everyone's taste buds are different*, he thought.

He couldn't help envying the happy couple, their faces gleaming, as they'd looked into each other's eyes, then turned to face him again. "Anyway, Todd, my wife and I appreciate you coming to help celebrate our happy occasion."

"Glad I could be here. Best of luck to the both of you." Todd gave Melanie a hug and shook Shawn's hand. "Enjoy your honeymoon in the Bahamas. It'll be a great weeklong getaway for you."

"Yes, we are looking forward to it. We'll be flying out in the morning." Melanie slipped her hand into her husband's. "Our flight time got changed, but that's okay."

"Well, again, congratulations, and have a safe trip." Todd stepped away from the couple. He wasn't considering a real relationship at this time, but if there was a special woman in his life, he'd like to be as happy as Shawn and Melanie seemed to be.

"Thanks, Todd," the couple said in unison.

Todd said goodbye, sauntered out the door, and stepped up to his shiny red sports car. He paused to admire how gorgeous his vehicle looked sitting there, freshly washed and polished. "I've got good taste," he said, opening the car door. He climbed into the driver's seat and checked his appearance in the mirror. "Of course, if it had been my wedding, I would've picked out some better food for the reception. What were Melanie and Shawn thinking? Well, at least the band they hired was good."

Allowing his thoughts to return to the present, Todd rubbed his sore feet. Since Lisa had mentioned during the first cooking class that she owned a catering business, he should have realized she'd provided all the food for the couple's reception.

Todd slapped the side of his head. "I said too much. Open mouth—insert foot. I really blew it, didn't I?"

He pulled the throw pillow down from the back of the couch and gave it a punch. *It wasn't the best food I've ever eaten, but it wasn't the worst, either. It just didn't meet my expectations. When I see Lisa at next week's cooking class I'd better apologize to her.*

Chapter 15

Walnut Creek

Lance rolled over in bed and grabbed his second pillow—the one Flo used to lay her head upon. On nights like this when he had trouble sleeping, he found comfort placing her pillow on his chest. It wasn't the thunder sounding in the distance that kept him from sleeping tonight, however. It was the noise from the TV in the living room down the hall. Lance had always been a light sleeper, and his brother's constant need to watch television grated on his nerves—especially when he planned to rise early tomorrow morning to get ready for Sunday school and church. The only time Lance missed going to church was when he was sick. Even during the vacations he and Flo used to take, they always found a church to attend. Sunday was the Lord's Day, and Lance enjoyed fellowshipping with other believers. He wished he could talk Dan into going with him, but every time he brought up the subject, his brother said he wasn't interested in sitting in a stuffy building with a bunch of hypocrites who used religion as a crutch.

Lance didn't see it that way. People, even those who went to church and called themselves Christians, were human and made mistakes. Lance remembered how his dad used to say, "Church is the place for sinners, saved by grace. It's not a fancy hotel for saints."

Lance wondered if his brother thought he was a hypocrite, too, because Dan never excluded him from the select group of people he disliked so much at church. *Maybe I need to check my own spiritual walk and be sure I'm setting the proper example to win someone like Dan to the Lord.* Lance would pray for God to show him how and direct his life fully, in order to spiritually help his wayward brother or someone else who couldn't find their way. *Sure wish I could make Dan understand the importance of committing his life to Christ.*

Lance, Dan, and their younger sister, Evelyn, had been raised in a Christian home. But Dan strayed from God, and nothing Evelyn or Lance said or did seemed to get through to him. Lance tried extra hard to set a Christian example to his brother, but having Dan living here was testing the limits of his patience. Between the loud TV, dirty dishes in the sink, clothes strewn all over the floor of the guest room, and the laundry fiasco, Lance struggled to keep from losing his temper. At least Dan had started parking his car on the street until Lance came home and put his vehicle in the garage. If the other things that bothered Lance didn't improve soon, he may be forced to ask his brother to leave. But if he did, Dan might stray even further from God, believing his brother to be a hypocrite, too.

Lance hugged the pillow tighter to his chest. *If Flo was here right now, what would she say or do? I bet she'd get out of bed, go into the other room, and politely ask Dan to turn the volume down because she couldn't sleep. Guess that's what I oughta do, too.*

Rolling out of bed, Lance slipped on his bedroom slippers and padded down the hall in his pajamas. A streak of lightning lit up the hall, and an ear-piercing crack of thunder followed, causing him to jump. This time of year they didn't get many storms, but with the change of seasons and cold fronts pushing warm air out, some feisty storms developed.

"Say, Dan," Lance said when he entered the living room and saw his brother flaked out on the couch, "would you mind turning the volume down a bit?"

Dan cupped a hand over his ear and scrunched up his nose. "What'd you say?"

"I said, would you mind turning the volume down a bit?" Lance spoke a little louder this time, making a twisting motion with his fingers. "It's keeping me awake."

"It's not that loud."

"It is to me." Lance wondered if his brother's hearing was going bad.

Dan pointed to the window behind him. Now the late autumn storm was directly overhead. "The thunder and rain are a lot louder than the TV. Are you sure it's not the weather keeping you awake tonight?"

"No, it's the TV. I'm not used to having it on when I'm in bed trying to sleep. Besides, you shouldn't have the television on when there's a storm like this. Lightning could strike and blow the whole tube out."

Dan got up and turned off the TV. "Okay, okay, I get the point. If my watching television at night is such a big deal, I'll only watch it during the day when you're out delivering mail."

"Thanks, I appreciate that." Lanced turned toward his room. "Good night, Dan," he called over his shoulder. "See you in the morning."

"Sure thing." And then his brother added, "You should get rid of this dinosaur television set and get yourself a new flat screen TV with a remote. Oh, and don't bother cooking me any breakfast in the morning. I'm going out to eat with a friend."

"Okay. Night, Dan." Lance was tempted to comment about the age of his TV, but kept his mouth shut. He even thought of mentioning church, but thought better of it, too. No point in starting a discussion that could end up in an argument. The best thing to do was just go to bed. Hopefully, with the TV off he could sleep.

"It's getting late. Are you ready for bed?" Lyle lifted himself from his easy chair.

Heidi held up the notebook in her hand and remained on the couch. "You go on ahead. I'm going to stay here awhile and finish working on my list for the cooking class next week."

Lyle tipped his head. "I thought you had everything figured out."

She sighed. "I thought so, too, but after the way some of my students responded to the friendship bread I had them make during last Saturday's class, I changed my mind."

"What's wrong with friendship bread? I've always enjoyed the variations you've made with the basic recipe." Lyle smacked his lips. "I especially like when you add raisins or chocolate chips."

"I think some of the students were okay with my choice, but others, like Allie and Lisa, seemed disappointed. Allie was probably hoping for a dish she could serve her family, and I'm guessing Lisa was looking for something to use in her catering business." Heidi fiddled with the pen between her fingers. "Neither one of them said anything, but I could sense it. And Todd. . .well, annoyance was written all over his face, too."

"So what are you going to teach them next week?"

Heidi shrugged. "I'm not sure. Probably a main dish of some sort, or maybe a salad."

Lyle glanced at the grandfather clock across the room. "Well, it's getting late, and we should be heading to bed, so can you wait till Monday to decide what dish to choose for your next cooking class?"

"You're right, Lyle. My eyes are getting heavy, too." Heidi yawned and set the notebook aside. "Truthfully, I could probably sit here all night and not come up with what to teach my class. Maybe by Monday I'll have a clearer head."

Heidi remained seated a few moments, thinking about Kendra and her baby. *I wonder how they're fairing this evening with the wicked storm and all its noise. Hopefully they aren't being kept awake because of it.* The weather was proving to be a bit unnerving, with the rumbling right above the house and bolts of lightning shooting about. *I'm sure if the baby gets fussy, it will test Kendra's new motherly skills in trying to comfort her precious daughter.*

Heidi stood, and as she followed her husband across the room, a flash of lightning lit up the entire living room. She flinched, and their dog howled when the boom of thunder hit. She could almost feel the vibration beneath her feet. Heidi's dog lay shaking near the fireplace. She bent down and gave his head a gentle pat. "It's okay, Rusty. This terrible noise shouldn't go on too much longer."

Rusty looked up at her and whined.

"Oh, all right, boy, you can sleep in our room tonight." She looked at Lyle to get his approval, and when he nodded, she clapped her hands and told the dog to come along.

Heidi followed Lyle into their bedroom, and once Rusty was inside, she closed the door behind them. She hoped by morning the storm would pass. It was never fun to travel anywhere with the horse and buggy in stormy weather, and tomorrow, church would be held in a home a few miles away.

❧

New Philadelphia

Bill hung up the phone after talking with his friend Andy Eglund. They'd been discussing their upcoming camping trip and talking about who, including Russ and Tom, would bring what.

It had been a tradition for the guys to leave on Thanksgiving, after having the meal with their families. It had been one of the things Bill's ex-wife complained about, but her fussing all those years never changed a thing. Nothing kept Bill from spending time with his friends. Going camping was a big deal. His ex just didn't understand.

Now that Bill was a free man, he usually arrived at camp Thursday afternoon. Since he wouldn't be having a Thanksgiving meal with anyone, there was no reason not to leave early. Andy, Russ, and Tom usually arrived Thursday evening or early Friday morning. They would spend the next three days getting the cabin cleaned up, and going out to scout where each of them would hunt. Sometimes Russ would bring a few board games along. He liked the friendly competition and said it was something fun to do after eating their supper in the evening.

At least Russ had the good sense to leave his dog at home. When he'd brought up the idea of bringing the mutt, Bill had put the kibosh to it.

The Monday after Thanksgiving was opening day of deer season. With his excitement building, Bill never got much sleep the night before the big day. There was nothing like sitting in his tree stand and watching the morning unfold—something he never tired of. Blue Jays chattered, squirrels gathered nuts, and if luck would have it, a buck would sneak through the area Bill hunted. He'd been told there were bears in the woods near his cabin, but to date, Bill had never seen one anywhere he hunted.

Bill started a list of what he would need to purchase for their long weekend. He got tired of eating a bunch of unhealthy snacks when they all went up to the cabin. The junk he and the guys usually ate was full of artificial colors and preservatives, not to mention too much sugar. It wasn't even fit for the squirrels. Bill didn't want to keep adding to his girth, and it wasn't easy watching his buddies eat like that. Maybe he would bring some healthy things, like some kind of a salad and cut-up veggies to have on hand.

He hoped to surprise his friends this year with some newer tasty meals he'd be learning from Heidi. So far, for breakfast one of the mornings, he planned on making baked oatmeal. Then Bill would serve a loaf of friendship bread to go along with the spaghetti meal he planned on making for one of their suppers.

As he thought about what else he could make, the phone rang again.

"Bet it's either Russ or Tom calling to discuss more about our Thanksgiving trip." Bill reached over and picked up the phone from the small table next to the chair where he sat.

"Hello."

"Hi, Dad. It's Brent."

It had been a while since Bill heard from his son, so this was a nice surprise. "Hey, Son, how are you doing?"

"I'm good. And you?"

"All's well at this end."

"Say, I won't keep you, but I was wondering if you had anything going on either the last weekend of October, or the second weekend of November? I was thinking of coming down for a few days to see you. Maybe arrive on Friday night, and spend the weekend with you. Would that be okay?"

"That sounds good, Brent." Bill smiled, anxious to see his son. "I have both of those weekends free, so whatever is good for you is fine by me."

"Okay. How about the second weekend of November?"

"Yep, that's great. I'll be anxious to see you."

"Same here."

They talked about several other things. Brent told his dad Aunt Virginia and Uncle Al had invited him for Thanksgiving dinner. "I remember that you leave for deer camp on Thanksgiving, so I thought it was okay to accept Aunt Virginia's invitation."

"I'm glad you did. If my memory serves me right, she puts out a real nice spread for Thanksgiving."

"You're right about that."

"Before you called, I was talking to my friend Andy. We were making our usual deer-hunting plans." Bill cringed when a clap of thunder sounded, rattling the windows. "Well, I'd like to talk longer, but were having a pretty bad storm right now, and the lights just flickered, so I'd better hang up before the power goes out."

"Sure, Dad. We can catch up with each other when I come to visit in two weeks."

"Sounds good. See you then."

After Bill clicked off the phone, he picked up his tablet, flipping his camping list over to start a new page. He couldn't wait to visit with Brent, and he started writing things down he knew his son liked to eat. *Maybe I'll make my son a loaf of that friendship bread, after all. Brent might enjoy it, and he can take what's left of the bread when it's time for him to go home.*

Canton

Kendra felt her chest tighten as raindrops pelted the roof and thunder cracked overhead. She'd never liked storms and used to cower under the covers when she was a little girl to try and calm her fears. Tonight, she felt like a child again, needing the comfort of her mother. But she was a mother now and didn't feel up to the task. At least, not tonight.

Another clap of thunder sounded, and little Heidi started crying. *Waa! Waa! Waa!* The noisy storm had no doubt wakened the poor baby.

Kendra turned on her bedside lamp and crawled out of bed. Then she hurried across the room and took her little girl out of the crib. "It's okay, sweet baby. Mama's got you now."

Waa! Waa! The infant continued to howl. Kendra felt sure Heidi wasn't hungry; she'd fed her just an hour ago. She checked the baby's diaper, but it was dry. It must be the storm causing her child to fuss. She couldn't blame her for that.

"Like mother, like daughter," Kendra murmured against the infant's ear. "Hush, little one. The storm will be over soon."

Another clap of thunder sounded, and Kendra's muscles tensed. It was hard to calm her baby when she, herself, felt nervous. Walking back and forth, from the crib to her own bed, Kendra patted little Heidi's back, but to no avail.

A few seconds later, her bedroom door jerked open, and Dad stepped into the room. "What's going on in here? Why's the baby crying?"

Kendra stiffened at the sharp tone of her father's voice. She couldn't get over him barging into her room like that, either. "She's afraid of the thunder, and I really can't blame her."

"Well, you'd better find some way to get her calmed down. We all have to get up early for church in the morning, and none of us can afford to lose any sleep." His brows furrowed. "If things are going to work out with you living here again, you'll have to be considerate of other people's needs."

"I am trying, Dad. I'm sure she'll stop crying once the thunder and lightning stops." At moments like this, Kendra wished she still lived with the Troyers. At least there, she was spoken to kindly and felt a sense of peace. But she'd made her choice when she decided to move back in with Mom and Dad and let them help her raise little Heidi. So she would make the best of it and try to keep the peace. She hoped Dad would let up a bit and not be so demanding. After all, Heidi was his granddaughter, not some stranger Kendra had brought home to stir up trouble.

Dad gave a quick nod, mumbled, "Good night," and left the room, closing the door behind him.

I wish Mom would've come into my room to find out what was happening, instead of Dad. He sure doesn't have much nurturing in his character. Kendra patted the baby's back. At times like this, she wished she and little Heidi could move out of this house. But they really had no other place to go.

Kendra breathed a sigh of relief when the storm abated and the baby settled down. Tomorrow would be the first Sunday to take her daughter to church, and she was a bit nervous, wondering what people would say. Of course, everyone knew Kendra had given birth to a child and wasn't married. But when she showed up tomorrow with the baby in her arms, it could cause some tongues to wag.

Well, I don't care if it does. Kendra placed the baby into her crib and gently stroked her soft cheek. *If anyone says anything unkind, I'll remind them what the Bible says about judging.* "He that is without sin among you, let him first cast a stone at her."

Chapter 16

As Kendra sat on a church pew with her parents and sisters, she breathed deeply, trying to ignore those staring at her. Were they surprised to see Bridget and Guy Perkins's wayward daughter here today, or could they be admiring her sweet baby daughter? Well, what did it matter? Like a dutiful daughter, Kendra had come here today to keep the peace, since Dad had insisted she accompany them, even though she'd been up half the night trying to calm little Heidi. It wasn't that she didn't want to attend church—just not today. She felt tired from lack of sleep and utter annoyance at her father for being so grouchy last night about her baby crying.

Kendra fussed with the baby's outfit, and then she fiddled with her necklace nervously. She could almost feel people's eyes staring at her and wondered if her family felt it, too. Kendra thought back to when she was a little girl and sat on these pews, under this same ceiling. She glanced upward, appreciating the workmanship that went into creating such a beautiful sanctuary. The ceiling was crafted of wood—which type, she wasn't sure—but the patterns in each section were a masterpiece of designs. Like a snowflake, no two pieces were the same; each was unique and had a beauty of its own. Huge beams hung strategically along the ceiling's length. Kendra remembered how, even as a child, she'd found them interesting, since they were salvaged from a local barn torn down many years ago.

This church has been here such a long time. These walls have seen a lot of weddings and other happy events, and also many funerals.

Kendra fixed her eyes on the beautiful stained-glass window close to the peak of the wall in the front of the church where the congregation faced. It was a mesmerizing piece of art, with the Lord

Jesus kneeling by a rock, hands in prayer, and a heavenly beam of light shining on His serene face.

Kendra's gaze returned to her baby daughter, nestled snuggly in her arms. Living with her parents, Kendra's situation wasn't perfect, but at least she and little Heidi had not been separated like she thought they would.

Looking back up at the image etched into the window, Kendra mouthed a silent, *Thank You, Lord.*

She turned her focus on the chorus the congregation had begun to sing, but her eyes grew heavy. Kendra had almost nodded off when the baby started to fuss. She lifted Heidi over her shoulder and patted the infant's small back. It didn't help; the baby began to wail. *Oh, no. Not a repeat of last night, I hope.*

Chris cast a sidelong glance in Kendra's direction. "You'd better do something quick or you'll hear about it from Dad," she whispered.

Kendra pulled the pacifier from the diaper bag and put it in the baby's mouth. After Dad's response to Heidi's cries last night, she knew full well what he must be thinking now. While her father had agreed to her moving back home so they could help with the expense of raising the baby, Kendra felt certain he'd never completely forgiven her indiscretion with Max. As a board member in good standing with the church, Dad saw what Kendra did as an embarrassment to him, as well as the rest of the family. Kicking Kendra out of the house was the way he'd chosen to deal with things when she'd first told him and Mom she was expecting a baby.

She had a hunch the only reason Dad let her come home was to please Mom. The first night she'd returned, her sister Shelly had confided to Kendra that their mother had been miserable since Dad forced Kendra out of the house. While Mom had never said anything in front of the girls, she may have pleaded with Dad to bring Kendra back. For whatever the reason, Kendra accepted the offer in order to keep her child. Even though she was sure the Troyers would make good parents, she would have always felt like a part of her was missing if she'd gone through with the adoption. For some unwed mothers, adoption was the best way, but given the opportunity to raise her child, Kendra had jumped at the chance.

Relieved that the baby had stopped fussing, perhaps from the quieter song they were now singing, Kendra allowed herself to relax. There was a time, not long ago, when the bitterness she felt toward Max and her own father, would have kept Kendra from darkening the door of any church. Now, even though she felt a bit uncomfortable, at least she could enjoy the service.

Dover

When Lisa returned home from church, she was surprised to see her renter's dog in the yard with no supervision. Of course, this wasn't unusual these days. From what she could tell, the poor little pup was sorely neglected. The dog started barking as soon as Lisa got out of her van. She figured with all the racket, one or both of the pup's owners would come out, but their front door remained shut.

"What's the matter, boy? Are you lonely?" Lisa bent down and stroked the animal's silky ears. The dog leaned into her hand, eyes closed and tail barely wagging. "You're starved for attention, aren't you?" Lisa couldn't figure out why anyone would get a pet and not spend time with it. A dog, or even a cat, made a good companion. *If I had a dog I'd make sure it was well cared for and give it plenty of love.*

Lisa started to walk toward her own duplex unit, when the puppy looked up at her and whined. "Sorry little fella, but I can't stay here in the yard and pet you all afternoon. I'm hungry and need to eat." She leaned over, picked up a small stick, and gave it a fling. When the pup ran after it, she hurried up the steps, unlocked her door, and stepped inside.

After placing her Bible on the coffee table, Lisa went to the kitchen for a glass of cold water. Since the room faced the front of the house, she couldn't help hearing the dog's continual yapping. She hurriedly made herself a ham and cheese sandwich, then took it to the dining room where it was quieter. She could still hear the pup faintly, but the sound didn't get on her nerves like it had previously. At least she could eat in peace.

When Lisa finished her sandwich, she went back to the kitchen and put her dishes in the sink. She would stick them in the dishwasher later, because right now she was going back outside to see why that pathetic dog was still carrying on.

She found the critter in one of her flower beds, digging a nice little hole. "Oh, no you don't, mister. You're going back inside to pester your owners." Lisa picked up the pup and marched over to the other unit. She was about to knock on the door when she saw a note stuck near the door knocker with tape. Squinting, she read it aloud: "To Lisa Brooks: This is to inform you that we can't pay the rent this month, so we moved out this morning while you were at church. We are moving in with my folks, but can't take the dog with us, so I hope you'll either take him in or find the mutt a good home."

Lisa slapped her forehead and groaned. It was bad enough the young couple had moved out with no advance notice, but to leave the dog behind, expecting her to take care of it was unbelievable. *I wonder what state they left the place in. I'll need to get the key and let myself in so I can take a good look around each room.* She held the pup securely in her arms. *What were those people thinking? How could they abandon this poor little thing?*

With a sigh of resignation, she picked up the pup and headed back to her place. For now, she would keep the critter, but as soon as she could find him a good home, he'd be gone. She had no time or patience for a pet.

When Lisa entered the house, an idea formed. This coming Saturday she'd be attending her third cooking class. Perhaps one of Heidi's other students would like a dog.

————— ⌒∞⌒ —————

Canton

Todd yawned and stretched his arms over his head. He'd slept in this morning and had spent the afternoon watching TV. It felt good to do nothing and answer to no one once in a while. The past week he'd tried out a couple of restaurants and written his review of each one. The first place he'd visited served French cuisine, and the other was a bistro a friend had told him about. He'd seen a young woman there who reminded him of Lisa Brooks, only her hair was a lighter shade of blond. Ever since his friend's wedding, when Lisa walked off the dance floor, Todd had thought about her. He wondered if he ought to look up her number and give her a call to apologize for his remark about the food at the reception. According to the bride and groom, Lisa had rushed off without even saying goodbye.

Todd got up from his chair and ambled out to the kitchen for a cup of coffee. Maybe he would go out later to look for some new shirts or a pair of slacks. Todd liked the attention he always got from the female store clerks. Of course, in all likelihood, they were only trying to get him to part with his money. Todd preferred the specialty shops tucked away in the mall. Catering to himself could almost always pull Todd out of the doldrums. He'd put Lisa out of his mind for the time being and concentrate on other things. He would see her at the cooking class this coming Saturday; then he could apologize for his unkind remarks. *Maybe I'll arrive early for class and wait in my car until Lisa gets there. Sure hope she's willing to talk to me.*

Chapter 17

New Philadelphia

"Hey, how are you, and what brings you by my place this evening?" Bill's friend Andy gave him a big grin and opened the door wider.

"Came to give you this." Bill handed Andy a loaf of friendship bread, along with a jar of starter. "I learned how to make this at the last cooking class and wanted to share a loaf with you. Was planning to give it to you and our other hunting buddies on Thanksgiving weekend but decided to come on over and give it to you now."

"I appreciate the bread, but what's in here?" Andy squinted at the jar.

"It's the starter, so you can make more bread if you want."

Andy shook his head vigorously. "You know I don't cook."

"Well, maybe one of your daughters might be interested in making the bread."

"Yeah, could be." Andy motioned with his head. "Come on in and stay awhile. I'll put on a pot of coffee and we can have some of this bread."

"Sounds good." Truth was, Bill wanted to discuss a few things with his friend about their upcoming plans to go hunting. Sunday evenings were always kind of boring for him, so he was glad he'd found his friend at home.

Andy led the way to the kitchen and told Bill to take a seat at the table, while he placed the friendship bread and starter on the counter. "I'll get the coffee going before I cut the bread."

"I have a better idea. I'll cut the bread while you make the coffee." Without waiting for his friend's response, Bill grabbed a cutting board and knife and sliced several thick pieces of bread. He placed them on a plate and set it on the table.

"Do we need butter or jelly to go with it?" Andy questioned.

"Only if you want some. The bread's plenty moist, and as far as I'm concerned, there's no need to put anything on it." Bill glanced over at Andy and grinned. "I'm kinda glad Heidi taught me and the other students how to make this bread; you're in for a treat."

A short time later, they both sat at the table, drinking coffee and eating friendship bread. "You were right. It is good bread, and it's plenty moist." Andy smacked his lips. "I hope my daughter Jenny uses the starter and makes another loaf or two. Maybe I oughta share it with one of our buddies."

"You can if you want to, but I'm planning to serve some of the bread when we all go hunting Thanksgiving weekend."

Andy's forehead wrinkled. "Uh. . .about our plans. . ." He paused and took a swig of coffee. "I can't make it this year."

Bill's jaw clenched as his shoulders slumped. "How come?"

"Well, the thing is. . ." Andy paused once more and picked up another piece of bread. "I've been invited to eat with my daughter April and her family so—"

"Not a problem. You can come up to my cabin after the meal, just like you always do."

Andy shook his head. "You didn't let me finish."

"Sorry. Go ahead."

"We won't be eating at April's house this year. Her husband booked flights for all of us to go to Disney World."

Bill's neck muscles tightened as he tipped his head to one side. "You're going to Orlando for Thanksgiving?"

His friend gave a nod. "I would've said something sooner, but I just found out about it yesterday, when April dropped by to see how I'm doing."

Bill squeezed his fingers into a fist until his hand ached. He was tempted to ask Andy if he'd consider saying no to the plans his son-in-law made, but it wouldn't be fair. Andy's family had always been tight-knit—even more so since his wife, Nadine, died. Many times Bill felt envious of this; especially since he and his son rarely saw each other. *Guess I should be glad Brent is coming to visit me next month. But at least it's not on my hunting weekend.*

Andy leaned forward, his elbows resting on the table. "You okay with this, buddy? You look sorta down in the mouth right now."

"It took me by surprise, that's all." Bill lifted his shoulders in a brief shrug. "It's been a tradition for all of us to meet at my cabin on Thanksgiving weekend, but don't worry about it. Your family comes first. I'm sure the rest of our hunting buddies won't let me down."

Walnut Creek

"What are you doing?" Lyle asked when he entered the living room with two mugs full of hot apple cider. He handed one to Heidi and took a seat beside her on the couch.

She smiled and placed it on the coffee table. "I've been going through yesterday's mail. Found a letter from Ron Hensley mixed in with the bills and advertisements."

"Is that so? It's been a while since we've heard from Ron. What's he up to these days?

"He's working part-time at the Walmart store in his hometown. Best of all, he's made amends with his children and even apologized to his ex-wife for everything he did to hurt her in the past." Heidi pointed to Ron's letter lying on the small table beside her coffee cup. "He says even though there's no chance of him and his wife getting back together, at least they can be cordial to each other from now on."

"Good to hear. Is he still seeing a counselor to help with his post-war trauma?"

"Jah. He mentioned that, too." Heidi reflected on how things were when Ron first showed up at their house asking for a place to park his motor home. She'd been surprised when he'd decided to join her first group of students for lessons in Amish cooking, and even more surprised when, several weeks later, she'd learned that Ron had stolen some things from their house and barn. Thanks to a scripture Heidi had written on the back of a recipe card she'd given her students after one lesson, Ron found forgiveness for the hurtful things he'd said and done to many people after leaving the Marine Corp, following his tour of duty in Vietnam. Several others who attended Heidi's first set of classes had also been affected by the scriptures she'd shared, not to mention a bit of mentoring from her along the way.

Of course, Heidi took no credit for any of it. If lives were changed, the glory went to God, for only He could change a person's heart and give them a new lease on life. She felt thankful for the opportunity to share God's love with others, and even more appreciative when someone responded to His calling. With this second group of students, she'd not seen any progress in a spiritual sense yet. But that wasn't to say it wouldn't come, for they still had four more cooking classes to get through. During those weeks, anything could happen.

<hr/>

Millersburg

"You look tired, honey. Why don't you go on up to bed?" Nicole's dad leaned down over the couch and tapped her shoulder.

Nicole held up her history book. "I can't go yet. Gotta test to take tomorrow, so I need to study awhile longer."

His brows furrowed. "Shouldn't you have done that sooner? You've had all weekend, and it's not good to wait till the last minute to cram for a test."

Her teeth clamped together with an audible click. "I haven't had all weekend, Dad. I've been busy with other things—like cooking meals, washing clothes, and keeping my sister and brother entertained so they didn't get on your nerves while you were watching your favorite TV shows." It irritated Nicole that Dad couldn't see how hard she'd worked over the weekend, with so little time to herself. "Now that Heather and Tony have gone to bed, this is the first chance I've had to crack open my history book."

"If you'd said you had homework sooner, I'd have taken the kids out somewhere to give you a break."

Before Nicole could comment, the doorbell rang. Dad rose from his chair. "I'll get it."

A few seconds later, he marched back to the living room, eyes narrowed and ears flaming red. Nicole cringed when she saw who'd walked in with him. "Tonya. What are you doing here?"

"Came to see you and my other two kids. And don't call me Tonya." Nicole's mother's words slurred as she staggered toward the couch. "How have ya been Nicki?"

Nicole sat up, folding her arms tightly across her chest. "My name's not Nicki." She hated the nickname her mom had given her. It made her feel like she was a little girl. *Well, I'm not. I am practically a grown woman, and I'm doing your job, Tonya.* Nicole bit her tongue to keep from spewing the words out in her mother's face.

"You've obviously been drinking, Tonya." Dad moved closer to her. "You're not supposed to show up at this house unannounced. What brought you here anyway?"

"I just told ya. Came to see my kids." She plunked down on the end of the couch by Nicole's feet.

"Tony and Heather are asleep." Dad moved toward the door leading to the stairs, as if to block the way in case Tonya decided to head in that direction.

She released an undignified belch and didn't even bother to excuse herself.

Nicole wrinkled her nose when the smell coming from her mother's mouth reached her nostrils. The odor of alcohol was so disgusting. Nicole sat up and turned her head away. A desire to flee the room was intense. She'd always hated it whenever her mother drank—not just because of the putrid odor, but because of how Mom acted when she'd had too much to drink. She became obnoxious and loud, often cursing and sometimes slapping the kids for no good reason.

"I don't care if Tony and Heather are sleeping." Tonya's voice raised a notch. "I have a right to see my kids whenever I want."

Dad shook his head. "No, you don't. You gave up that right when you ran out on your family. Do I need to remind you that when you filed for divorce, you agreed to give up all rights to the children?" His nostrils flared. "I've been kind and let you visit some weekends, but only when you're sober. You should not have come here tonight."

Tonya's face flamed, and she leaped to her feet. "Is it any wonder I left you, Mike? You're a mean man." Teetering back and forth, she lost her balance and fell back onto the couch.

"Dad's not mean." Nicole felt the need to defend him. Tonya had no right coming here and pointing fingers at Dad. He was a good parent, doing the best he could to raise his children. Tonya, on the other hand, didn't deserve the title of *Mother*.

Nicole's mom sneered at her. "You stay out of this, young lady." She blinked several times. "And why aren't you in bed, missy?"

Nicole pointed to her history book. "I'm studying for a test." Holding her nose so she wouldn't gag, she added, "Your breath smells terrible."

As if she hadn't even heard, Tonya turned away from Nicole and focused on Dad again. "Are you gonna get Tony and Heather outa bed so they can give their mother a kiss, or not?"

He shook his head, looking more determined than before. "I want you to leave, Tonya, and don't come back to this house unless you're sober."

Nicole struggled to keep from shouting, "Don't come back at all!"

Tonya lifted her chin, baring her stained teeth—teeth that used to be pearly white before she started smoking and drinking. "Don't tell me what to do, Mike. You are not my boss. Y–you have no control over me anymore."

"I never did. If I had, you wouldn't be in the mess you're in right now. You would have gone for help, like I wanted you to."

Dad's last statement seemed to enrage Tonya, for she hauled off and slapped his face. When it looked like she might hit him again, he grabbed hold of her wrist. "Enough, Tonya. It's time for you to go."

"Yeah, Mom, please go." Nicole spoke softly, hoping to calm her mother down. The last thing they needed was for Heather and Tony to wake up. They shouldn't see their mother acting this way. For that matter, as far as Nicole was concerned, they shouldn't see her at all. She wished Tonya would leave and never come back. All she ever brought with her was trouble.

Dad took Tonya by the arm and led her firmly to the front door. "Do you have a driver who's sober, or should I call you a cab?"

She sneered at him. "Arnie's waitin' for me in the car."

"Okay, good. And the next time you want to pay the kids a visit, please give me a call."

Nicole felt relief when her mother went out the door. The whole episode had shaken her badly. She set her history book on the coffee table. There was no point in trying to study anymore. All she wanted to do was go to her room and hope that things would look better in the morning after a good night's sleep. Of course, it was doubtful. Short of a miracle, nothing would ever seem right in Nicole's life—not with the way her mother was. The best she could hope for was that Tonya and her new husband would move out of town and never be heard from again. She sighed deeply. *But that will probably never happen. Tonya is so mixed up and miserable. I think she wants to pull us all down so we'll be unhappy right along with her. Well, I'll show Tonya. I don't know how, but I'm gonna make something out of my life someday, and I don't need a mother to do it.*

Chapter 18

Dover

Using her key to the other half of the duplex, Lisa opened the door and stepped inside. The evening shadows had darkened the entryway, so she flipped on the light switch. With the exception of a few scratch marks near the bottom of the front door, everything looked okay.

She made her way to the kitchen, but when she entered the room and turned on the light, Lisa's mouth dropped open. In addition to the refrigerator door hanging wide open, there was food on the table and dirty dishes in the sink. Her renters had not bothered to clean out the refrigerator or clear the table before moving out, and didn't even care about leaving grimy dishes behind. Since she'd rented the place furnished, Lisa was anxious to see what condition the living room and bedroom had been left in.

Upon entering the living room, she leaned against one wall and groaned. The leather couch had several holes; the carpet was stained; and the rocking chair, which she'd bought used but in good condition, was missing an arm.

Her jaw tightened. It seemed the young couple with exceptionally loud voices didn't care any more about the furniture in this home than they did their marriage. Several old newspapers were stacked on the coffee table, and when Lisa picked them up, she noticed a large scratch gouged in the finish. It would take considerable sanding and varnishing to fix a mark that deep.

She ground her teeth together. *How could anyone be so careless and disrespectful of someone else's property? I certainly made a mistake renting to them.*

Moving on to the bedroom, Lisa found it also to be in disarray. The linens and bedspread, which had also been included with the furniture, had been stripped from the bed and lay in a tangled heap on the floor. The mirror above the dresser bore a huge crack, as though someone had intentionally thrown something at it. The bedroom carpet was also stained, and what appeared to be fingernail polish had been spilled on one of the nightstands.

Shaking her head in disbelief, Lisa clicked her tongue against the roof of her mouth. She'd have to do a lot of cleanup and perhaps pay for some work to be done before she could rent the unit out again. And then there was the yappy pup she'd left tied up in her yard. Lisa hoped once more that she could find the little fella a good home, because she certainly couldn't keep him, even if he was a cute dog.

New Philadelphia

Allie stood in front of her bedroom window, staring at the blackened sky. It seemed like the stars were hung on invisible threads. Like so many other Sundays, she and the children had spent the day without Steve. Why couldn't he get the weekends off once in a while to be with his family? Didn't he care enough about her and the kids to want to spend time with them?

Her thoughts went once again to the female officer she'd seen Steve with a couple of weeks ago. Allie couldn't help thinking the pretty blond had something to do with him working so many hours. *I wonder how he'd respond if I asked.* She gripped the windowsill until her fingers felt numb. *Even if it were true, I'm sure he would deny it. Steve would most likely make up some excuse.*

Allie glanced at the clock on the table beside their bed. It was almost ten o'clock. *Steve should be home by now. Should I be worried about his safety or concerned that he's up to no good?*

The bedroom door clicked open and shut, casing Allie to jump. She whirled around in time to see her husband stroll across the room. He slipped his arms around her waist and nuzzled her neck with his cold nose. "Sorry I'm late."

Allie breathed a sigh of relief. Steve was back home, safe and sound. But now the other doubts replaced her fears.

"How'd your day go, honey? Did you and the kids do anything fun?"

"No, not really. After I picked them up from Sunday school, we had an early lunch. Then Nola and Derek spent the rest of the day watching TV while I read a mystery novel." Allie's voice quavered. "The day would have been a lot more fun if you'd been here to share it with us."

"Sorry. You know I had to work."

No, I don't know that. I only know you said you had to work. She turned to face the window again.

Steve put his hand on her shoulder. "Is everything okay?"

How could it be okay when you're hardly ever at home? Allie merely shrugged in response to his question. There was no point going over this again. Steve knew how she felt about him working long hours—often when it wasn't necessary.

As he stood quietly beside her, she heard his heavy breathing against her ear.

Gathering her nerve, she turned to him and voiced a question that needed to be asked. "Do you still love me, Steve?"

"Of course I do, Allie. Why would you even ask me that?"

The words stuck in her throat, and she shrugged again. Truth was, as much as she wanted to know if he was having an affair, she feared the answer. If Steve had been unfaithful, would he want a divorce? How would the children be affected if their parents split up?

"I'm not scheduled to work next weekend, so maybe we can do something fun with the kids."

She looked at him hopefully. "Really? What if someone wants you to cover for them again?"

"I'll say no."

Allie hugged her husband tightly, her doubts disappearing, at least for the moment. She could only hope Steve meant what he'd said and would stay true to his word.

Walnut Creek

As Lance stood in front of the bathroom mirror, preparing to brush his teeth, he paused to look at the red heart-shaped tattoo on his right arm. His wife's name was featured in the middle of the heart, done in dark blue ink. Every time Lance looked at the tattoo, he was reminded of how much he missed Flo. He missed her all the time, but even more since Dan had moved in with him. Flo would have been a buffer.

A muscle on the side of Lance's neck quivered, thinking about his brother's latest irritation. Dan had a habit of raiding the refrigerator at night, after Lance had gone to bed. Lance would get up in the morning and find dirty dishes in the sink, and sometimes food would be left on the kitchen counter or table. Growing up, he hadn't realized his brother was such a slob. Of course, back then, either Mom or their sister, Evelyn, did the cleaning. No doubt they picked up after Dan, so Lance hadn't noticed his brother's messy habits.

He curled his fingers around his toothbrush handle. *Well, I'm noticing them now, and if it were anyone else but my flesh-and-blood brother, I'd ask him to leave—pronto!*

To make matters worse, Dan came home the other day with one of those new-fangled flat screen TVs. "I am no more interested in one of those things than I would be with a smart phone," Lance grumbled out loud, as if it would make him feel better. His old TV may be old-fashioned, but it worked fine. Now he'd have to call someone to have it removed and the new one hooked up. Maybe he would suggest Dan return the new flat screen. But then, that would probably hurt his brother's feelings.

Lance clenched his jaw. At last report, Dan's townhouse renovations weren't even half done. So unfortunately, it would be a while before he moved out of Lance's house.

Lance squeezed the rest of the toothpaste from the tube and went over his teeth again for good measure. *Unless I can think of someplace else for my brother to live, guess I'm stuck with him awhile longer. Now if I could just come up with some way to cope.*

Chapter 19

With only one more week left in October, Heidi couldn't believe it was almost time for her students to arrive for the third cooking class. Today she would be teaching them to make Chicken in a Crumb Basket—a favorite main dish that had been passed down from her husband's family and enjoyed by everyone Heidi had prepared it for since she'd married Lyle.

Heidi spread the recipe notecards on the table, taking the time to write the verse she'd chosen to share on the back of each card. "If we love one another, God dwelleth in us, and his love is perfected in us" (1 John 4:12). She wasn't sure who among her students this scripture was meant for, but God had laid it on her heart to choose this particular verse to go with today's lesson.

Pausing from her work to glance out the kitchen window, Heidi focused on the haze sliding over the landscape. The colors of the few leaves remaining on the trees in their yard appeared muted by the morning fog. It was nothing unusual for Holmes County—especially this time of the year. Mist formed at night and in the early morning hours, when the temperatures dipped and the air became filled with moisture. Heidi didn't mind the fog, except for the unpleasant feel of cold and damp, combined with visibility restrictions. Fog, or even a light mist, could play with a person's sense of direction and make landmarks unrecognizable. This is what she feared the most whenever Lyle took the horse and buggy on the road in blurry weather conditions. Fortunately, her husband's driver had picked him up this morning to oversee another auction event. With bright beams on his truck to guide the way, she wasn't nearly as worried as she would have been if Lyle was out with the buggy.

Heidi tapped her chin with the end of her pencil. *I hope none of my students are late this morning due to the fog. Depending on the severity of it in various locations, maybe some of them will decide not to come today.*

———————⁕⁕⁕———————

Sugarcreek

As Lisa passed the road leading to the Carlisle Inn, the fog became thicker. She turned on her high beams, but that didn't help much. In fact, it made seeing through the dense haze even worse. It was hard to focus on the road when she could only see a few feet in front of her.

She kept her speed down, gripping the steering wheel with such force the veins on the back of her hands became more noticeable. *Sure hope I don't run into the rear end of a car—or worse yet, an Amish buggy.* With all the hills, it was sometimes hard to spot a horse and buggy until right on top of it, even when the weather was clear.

As moisture stuck to the windshield, Lisa gave herself a pep talk and turned on the wipers. *You still have plenty of time to get there, so try to relax and concentrate. No need to hurry. Just take it slow and easy.*

The closer she got to Walnut Creek, the denser the fog became. Lisa feared she might miss the road where she was supposed to turn for Heidi's house. She'd carelessly left her cell phone at home, so she had no way of activating her GPS to help navigate the way. If she hadn't been bothered with feeding the pup this morning and then locking the little guy in her laundry room, she probably would have remembered the phone. But the puppy she'd named Trouble needed to be someplace where he couldn't do any damage while she was gone. The little rascal was kind of growing on her, but if she could find him a good home, it would be better. With her business growing, Lisa didn't have time to train or care for a dog.

Straining to see the road signs, she pulled over to get her bearings and hopefully calm her nerves a bit. She'd only been sitting on the shoulder of the road a few seconds when another car pulled in behind her. Curls of hazy air currents kept her from observing what kind of vehicle it was. She figured the driver might also be having difficulty seeing the road.

As Lisa looked out her side mirror, the skin on the back of her neck prickled. The figure of a man had gotten out of the vehicle and was approaching her van. She quickly locked all the doors. A moment later, a face she recognized stared in at her through the window. *Oh, no, it's Todd.*

* * *

Todd knocked on the driver's-side window of the van parked in front of his car. Even through the thick fog, Todd knew right away that the vehicle was Lisa's. He'd thought he wouldn't get the chance to speak with her privately today, but as fate would have it, he'd been given the opportunity to talk to her with no one else around to interrupt or overhear what he had to say.

He lifted his hand and rapped on the window again. She stared at him a few seconds, then rolled the window down. "Hey, Lisa. Is everything okay?"

"Of course. Why wouldn't it be?" Her tone was terse, and she barely made eye contact with him.

"Well, I just thought. . . Seeing your van parked here, I wondered if you were having trouble with your vehicle."

"I'm fine. Just stopped for a minute to get my bearings. This horrible fog is like driving through pea soup, and I wanted to be sure I was on the right road." Her voice didn't sound quite so snappish, but now she was talking too fast.

He shifted his weight, leaning against her door. "Mind if I come in a minute so we can talk?"

She pulled her fingers through the ends of her shiny blond hair and gave a brief shrug. At least she hadn't said no.

Todd hurried around to the passenger's side and climbed into the van. "How have you been, Lisa?"

"You needed to get in my van to ask me that?"

Todd moistened his lips with the tip of his tongue. This wasn't going as smoothly as he'd hoped. "I really wanted to talk to you about why you ran off the dance floor in such a huff the night of my friend's wedding."

Lisa pulled at her jacket collar. "I figured you'd know the answer to that."

"I do, and I–I'm sorry."

"If you didn't like the food I prepared for the wedding reception, you could have at least kept your opinion to yourself."

"But I thought you'd only made the cake."

"I run a catering business, which I mentioned during our first cooking class." Folding her arms, she looked at him through half-closed eyes. "But maybe you weren't listening."

Todd rubbed the back of his neck. "Yeah, I remember, and as I said, I was aware that you'd made the cake. I just didn't think—"

"Whether you didn't realize I'd made the food for the reception or not is immaterial. You said it was horrible." Lisa's chin trembled.

"No." Todd shook his head. "What I said was that I didn't think there was anything special about it."

"Same difference. You obviously didn't like the food, and it hurt my feelings."

"I'll admit, it wasn't my favorite cuisine, but it wasn't all that bad, either." He placed both hands on his knees, gripping them firmly as he spoke. "Look, I'm truly sorry I offended you. I sometimes speak before I think. Can we forget the whole thing and start over?"

"I—I suppose." Her face relaxed a bit.

"Good." He smiled, then glanced at his watch. "Now that we have that settled, we'd better get back on the road or we'll be late for the cooking class. I can hardly wait to see what Heidi wants us to make today." Todd wrinkled his nose. "Hopefully it'll be something better than the crazy bread she taught us to prepare two weeks ago. I threw the starter out as soon as I got home that day."

"You did? How come?" Her vocal pitch rose, as she looked away from him, then back again.

"Because it smelled funny. Besides, I had no reason to make more bread. I have no one to give it to."

"It's friendship bread. Couldn't you have given it to a friend?"

Todd rubbed his chin. Truth was, he didn't have many friends. Since Shawn and Melanie were still on their honeymoon, he couldn't give it to them. Besides, they were more acquaintances than friends.

Ignoring Lisa's question about the bread, Todd opened the van door. "We'd better get going now, or we're gonna be late. I'll pull my car in front of your van and lead the way. That is, if it's okay with you."

She slowly nodded.

"Okay then. Toot your horn if you can't see my car or feel like you're lost in the fog." Todd stepped out of Lisa's van and climbed back into his car. He still wasn't sure if she was really his type, but it would be fun to find out. *Who knows? Maybe before the end of our class today I'll have an opportunity to ask her out on a date. Bet Mom and Dad would like Lisa. They'd probably be impressed that I found someone who's not only beautiful but has a head for business, too.*

Chapter 20

Walnut Creek

Lisa relaxed a bit as she followed Todd's car. It helped being able to see his taillights leading the way to Heidi's house. Todd was going nice and slow, which made driving less tense. Over and over she thought about the conversation they'd had minutes ago.

She pursed her lips. *I wonder if Todd truly meant it when he apologized for his remark about the food I catered for his friends' wedding. Or was he only trying to save face?* The bride and groom seemed pleased with what she'd fixed at their request, so that's all that really mattered. Lisa didn't know why she even cared what Todd thought. She'd only known him a short time, and they were not well acquainted, at that. For some reason, though, she wanted to know him better. On the one hand, he irritated her; on the other hand, she found him quite attractive and charming. Of course, a solid relationship should never be built on looks. Outward appearances could be deceiving, whereas a person's character and behavior was what made them likable.

Lisa gave her head a quick shake. *Stop thinking about Todd and concentrate on your driving. I'm sure he has no interest in me, and even if he did, I don't have time for love or romance in my life right now. I've got my hands full with my business, plus getting the duplex next door ready to rent again.* She groaned. *Not to mention a puppy to take care of if I can't find it a good home.*

———————— ✦ ❧❧ ✦ ————————

Todd glanced in his rearview mirror to see if Lisa was still following. He was glad to see the headlights of her van behind him when he turned up Heidi's driveway. The fog seemed to be clearing, and it didn't take long to realize theirs were the only vehicles here. He and Lisa were either early, or the others were late.

Good. That'll give me a little more time to visit with her. Todd felt a tingling in his chest. Lisa probably wasn't his type, but he wouldn't know for sure until he spent more time with her. *I might even do a review of one of the dinners she caters sometime in the future. If it's a good review, it could help her business, which in turn might put me in her good graces. Then again, if Lisa read the review she might think I only did it to get on her good side. Probably the best thing to do is try to see her more often and let things go from there.*

Todd turned off the ignition and got out of his car. He stood by the driver's side and waited for Lisa to exit her van.

"Were you able to see my taillights okay?" he asked when she joined him a few minutes later.

"Yes, and it helped a lot." Lisa rubbed her hands down the side of her beige slacks. "The only thing I dislike more than driving in snowy weather is fog. Unfortunately, in my business I'm often stuck driving in foggy conditions during the fall, and then the winter months often bring snow."

"Ever think about relocating to a warmer climate, like Arizona, Southern Florida, or one of the Hawaiian Islands?"

She shook her head vigorously. "Oh, my, no. My family lives here in Ohio, and it's where I call home."

"I think I could live about anywhere as long as I had a job I liked." Todd started walking beside Lisa toward Heidi's house. "What about your folks? Do they live close by?"

"Nope. Mom and Dad live in Portland, Oregon, and since I have no siblings, there's no family living near here."

Lisa tipped her head, looking at him through half-closed eyes. "If your parents live on the West Coast, why would you want to live in Ohio?"

"I have a job here, and I like my independence. When I lived in Portland, Mom tried to run my life." Todd scrubbed a hand down the side of his face. "She scrutinized nearly everything I did."

Lisa made no comment as they stepped onto Heidi's front porch. Todd had a hunch she didn't have a clue about the way he felt. No doubt Lisa was in pretty tight with her family. They probably didn't try to tell her what to do or say.

She raised her hand to knock on the door, but he put his hand in front of hers. "Uh, before we go inside, there's something I'd like to ask you."

"Oh?" Her lips parted slightly.

"If you don't have plans for this evening, how about letting me take you out for supper at the restaurant of your choice? I'd like to make up for what I said about the food you catered at Shawn and Melanie's wedding reception."

"You don't have to make up for it. You've already apologized."

He cleared his throat, while shuffling his feet. "Umm. . .yeah, I know, but I'd still like to take you out. It'll give us a chance to get better acquainted."

"Okay, but—" Before Lisa could finish her sentence, the front door swung open.

⸺⸺⸺⸺⸺•᠁᠁•⸺⸺⸺⸺⸺

Smiling, Heidi greeted Lisa and Todd. "I'm glad you both made it okay. With the fog so thick today, I wasn't sure anyone would be able to find our home."

"It's lifting in a few places, so I'm sure the others will make it here, too." Todd glanced over at Lisa, gave her a quick smile, and then looked back at Heidi.

"I'm glad to hear it's improving. It was pretty thick for a while this morning." Heidi stepped aside. "Please, come in. You can take a seat in the living room while we wait for everyone else to arrive."

The sound of Heidi's shoes clacking on the polished hardwood floors echoed in the hall. Todd and Lisa followed her into the living room and both took seats on the couch, while she seated herself across from them in the rocking chair. Heidi found it interesting how Todd leaned slightly forward, with one hand on his knee, as though anticipating or eager for something. Surely he couldn't be that excited about taking another cooking class. Lisa, however, sat with her mouth in a straight line, clutching her purse tightly to her chest as though it were a shield.

Heidi started the rocking chair moving. *Neither of them acted this way the first time they were here. I wonder if anything's wrong.* It wouldn't be right to ask, of course, so she engaged them in conversation. "In case either of you are wondering what I'll be teaching you to make today, it's an old family recipe called Chicken in a Crumb Basket. It's quite tasty, and I think you'll enjoy it."

Lisa's eyes lit up. "That sounds interesting. It might even be something I could offer to some of my potential clients who are looking for something a little different in a meal they want catered." She glanced at Todd. "Does Chicken in a Crumb Basket sound like something more to your liking than what I served at the wedding reception last week?"

Todd's ears turned pink, and his stomach growled noisily. His hand went quickly to his midsection. "I can't say for sure, since I haven't tried it yet, but I'm eager to find out what it's all about. I've never heard of chicken crumble in a basket before." He thumped his stomach when it rumbled again. "As you can tell, I'm a little hungry."

"Crumb basket," Lisa corrected. "That is what you said, isn't it, Heidi?"

Heidi gave an affirmative nod. Remembering the baking dish in the oven, she excused herself and went to the kitchen. From the way Todd and Lisa kept stealing glances at each other, she had a hunch something might be going on between them—something more than two people sharing a desire to learn how to make a few of her favorite recipes.

She smiled to herself. *Wouldn't it be something if another romance developed between two of my new students like it did between Eli and Loretta during my first set of classes?*

Chapter 21

Berlin

"You seem kind of grouchy this morning. Is something wrong?" Nicole's father asked as they headed to Heidi Troyer's cooking class. "It's not the dismal weather, I hope."

Nicole clenched her fingers. *Something is always wrong, Dad. Don't think anything in my life will ever be right again.* "No, the fog doesn't bother me that much. I'm just tired."

"You've been working hard, and I appreciate all you do." He reached across the seat and squeezed her arm. "Your brother and sister may never say it to your face, but I'm sure they appreciate the things you do for them, too."

With a slight shrug, Nicole sat silently, mulling things over. While it was nice to be appreciated, it would be a whole lot nicer if she had less work to do at home so she could spend more time on her schoolwork, not to mention making new friends and going to some of the school functions. She wanted to tell Dad her grades were still slipping but was afraid to say anything, fearful he'd get upset. Since there was nothing he could really do about it but scold her, there was no point in bringing it up.

"There's something I've been meaning to talk to you about." Dad squinted and turned on the windshield wipers. It seemed like the closer they came to Walnut Creek, the worse the fog got.

"Uh, what's up?"

"We haven't really talked about the unexpected visit your mother paid us last Sunday night."

"There's not much to say." Nicole looked in his direction. "Tonya hasn't changed, and she's still nothing but trouble. I wish she and that loser she ended up with would move out of town and we'd never have to see or hear from them again."

"As nice as that would be, it's probably not going to happen." He frowned. "But the next time she comes knocking on our door unannounced, I won't let her in. Same goes for you. Under no circumstances is she to come into our house when I'm not home."

Nicole grunted. "You'd better tell Tony and Heather that, 'cause there's no way I'd ever let Tonya in, even if you were at home, Dad."

"Good to hear, but I'd still prefer you stop calling your mother by her first name."

"But, Dad, she's so disgusting. I'm ashamed of her."

"Still, she is your mother."

"Okay, whatever." They'd had this discussion before, but Dad hadn't stopped reminding Nicole to quit referring to her mother as Tonya. Nicole would try not to say it in front of him anymore, but only to others outside their family, and of course, in her own head. She vowed she would never acknowledge that woman as anything else but Tonya.

Walnut Creek

Lance looked forward to this morning's cooking class. It would be a nice break from the constant drone of the TV, always turned up too loud. He gave his truck's steering wheel a sharp rap with his knuckles. Weekdays weren't quite so bad, since he was at work most of the day, but unless he went out somewhere, the weekends were unbearable. He'd tried his best to be patient with his brother, but it became harder with each passing day. In fact, it had gotten to the point that Lance had begun looking for places he could go in order to get out of the house for a while.

The real clincher was when he got home two days ago, and walked into the living room. There sat Dan with a big ole smile on his face, pointing to the flat screen TV. It was mounted on the wall where one of Lance's favorite pictures used to hang.

Lance shook his head, wondering how he'd remained speechless when his brother showed him how to use the remote. It was a wonder Lance didn't blow his stack right then and there. Somehow, he'd managed to keep his cool, even when Dan went on to explain how he'd made arrangements for a local charity to come take the old television set away. *The nerve of some people!*

"Too bad the cooking classes don't last all day," Lance mumbled, turning up the Troyers' driveway. He'd no sooner parked his vehicle when Bill's SUV pulled in. They got out of their rigs at the same time and walked up to the house together.

"Sure is nasty weather today," Bill mentioned.

"Yeah, I fought the fog most of the way."

"Same here, but at least we made it okay." Bill gave Lance's shoulder a tap. "How'd your week go?"

Refusing to go into detail, Lance casually answered, "Okay, I guess. How about yours?"

"Not bad at all. I took a loaf of friendship bread to a friend, which felt kind of nice. But the best part of my week was hearing that my son will be visiting me in a couple of weeks." Bill gave a wide grin. "There's nothing quite like being with family."

Lance stared at his feet as he shuffled up the stairs and onto the porch. "Yeah, right."

———————⚬◦⚬———————

Allie drew her mouth into a straight line, biting her lower lip. The fog had been so dense when she left home this morning, she'd considered turning around and heading back home. But she had already dropped the kids off at the babysitters, and her eagerness to take another cooking class drove her on. About halfway there, the fog had begun to lift, but now, as she approached Walnut Creek, her minivan seemed to be swallowed up again in more of the thick haze. This increased Allie's anxiety. Since she was getting close to Heidi's house, determination kept her going.

Sure hope the fog's lifted by the time I go home. Allie gripped the steering wheel a little tighter. *It's times like this when I wish I was rich and could hire a driver to take me everywhere.*

She thought about Heidi and all the other Amish people who lived in the area. Most of them weren't rich, but they hired a driver whenever they went somewhere too far to take the horse and buggy. *I don't think Steve would be too happy if I did that. He'd say it was a waste of money, when I'm perfectly able to drive.*

Normally, Allie had no problem driving, but when the weather became nasty, she tried to plan her errands around Steve's work schedule so he could take her. Of course, with him working more hours than usual lately, he was rarely available to act as her chauffer.

Squinting into the haze, Allie saw a movement along the shoulder of the road, but was unable to make out what it was. As the fog shifted, and her eyes focused, Allie's scalp prickled. *Is that a dog?* Turning into the Troyer's driveway, before she had time to think or react, the critter darted in front of the van. She slammed on her brakes, but it was too late. The horrible thump put no question in her mind that she'd hit whatever it was. From what Allie could see through the misty air, the animal lay in the middle of Heidi's driveway, unmoving.

Chapter 22

A llie's knees quivered as she stepped down from the minivan and knelt beside the animal. At first she thought it was a small dog, but then she noticed the animal's bushy tail and realized it was a red fox. She felt bad she'd hit the critter, but at least it wasn't someone's dog. Just to be sure, Allie nudged the fox's leg. There was no doubt about it—the poor animal was dead. *I'm glad my kids aren't with me right now. They'd both be upset—even worse if it was someone's dog.*

Allie thought about the last time she'd taken Derek and Nola to the mall. They'd stood in front of the pet store with their noses pressed against the glass. Steve said the children were too young for a pet, but maybe owning one of their own would teach them responsibility. Prissy, the persnickety cat, was the only animal in the house, but she was Allie's pet and didn't care much for the children.

Allie recalled her little dog, Rascal, when she was growing up. The two of them were inseparable, and oh how it hurt when Rascal grew old and started having problems with his hips. Her dog wasn't a purebred, but he was smart and seemed to understand everything she said. If he could have talked, Allie knew he would have all kinds of interesting things to say.

In the end, after all the medication and treatments her parents did for ole Rascal, Allie's heart broke when the vet said there was nothing more they could do for him. That was the worst part about owning a pet—having to say goodbye. Did she want to put her children through the grief she felt when that happened? Besides, Prissy had a mind of her own and might not get along with a dog.

I can't worry about that right now. I need to get up to Heidi's house, because I'm already late for class. I'll see if one of the men will dispose of the dead fox.

• ○○○ •

Hearing a vehicle approach, Heidi looked out the living-room window. "Oh, good, Allie's here now, so we'll be able to start the class as soon as she comes inside."

"Well, it's about time." Lance folded his arms and grunted. "The rest of us managed to get here on time. I wonder what her excuse is."

Heidi was surprised by Lance's attitude. He was usually soft-spoken and polite. *Something might be going on his life right now to make him edgy.* She hurried to the door to let Allie in.

When the woman stepped inside, Heidi couldn't help noticing her flushed cheeks and wide-eyed expression. "Is everything all right? You look a bit flustered."

Blowing out a series of short breath, Allie twisted her gold wedding band. "I–I'm sorry I'm late. There was a lot of fog, so I drove slowly. Then, to make things worse, a fox ran out in front of my car when I was turning up your driveway. Unfortunately, I hit it." She paused and drew another breath. "Do you think one of the men could go out and take care of the fox? I hate the idea of it lying there for some scavenger or bird of prey."

Feeling the need to comfort the distraught woman, Heidi placed her hand on Allie's arm. "Let's go in the living room where the other students are waiting. I'm sure someone will take care of the fox."

When they stepped into the living room, and Heidi explained the situation, Bill got up from his seat with no hesitation. "No problem. I'll take care of the animal right now." He grabbed his jacket and hurried out the door.

"Are you kidding me?" Nicole flopped against the sofa pillows with a groan. "Couldn't that have waited till after our class? At the rate things are going, we'll never get started. And I even remembered to bring an apron today."

"I'm sure he won't be long. While we're waiting, we can sit and chat." Hoping to ease the tension, Heidi took a seat and posed a question. "Do any of you have anything you'd like to ask concerning what we learned in our last class?"

Todd's hand shot up.

Heidi nodded in his direction. "What is it you'd like to know?"

"I'm curious why you included a Bible verse on the back of the recipe card like you did the previous week." He leaned slightly forward. "I thought we came here to learn how to make some traditional Amish recipes, not attend Bible study or feel like we just came from church."

Heidi fidgeted under his scrutiny, rubbing her forearms to dispel a sudden chill. "Well, I, uh. . ." She paused to moisten her parched lips. "I began doing it during my first set of cooking classes because I wanted to share a bit of God's Word. I'm sorry if you found it offensive or preachy."

"It's neither of those," Lisa was quick to say. "I enjoyed reading the verses you put on the first two recipe cards and hope you continue doing so." She looked at each person. "Everyone needs a little help along the way—myself included. As far as I'm concerned, the Bible is like a roadmap for life. It teaches us how to deal with all the things that are thrown at us."

"Yes, indeed." Lance bobbed his head. "The Good Book is full of wisdom, and it points the way to God's Son."

Heidi smiled. She couldn't have said it better, and appreciated two of her students' input. From the dubious expression on Todd's face, not to mention Nicole's, Heidi figured they weren't believers. She wasn't sure about Allie, who said nothing, either. *What a shame. I won't stop including scriptures on the back of the recipes cards—not unless God directs me to stop. I'm 100 percent sure that everyone in this class needs the Lord's wisdom.*

Chapter 23

As everyone sat at Heidi's kitchen table, waiting for her to hand out today's recipe cards with directions, Lisa remembered she hadn't said anything about the puppy that needed a good home.

She cleared her throat. "Before we get started, I have something I'd like to share with everyone."

Heidi smiled. "Certainly, Lisa. Go right ahead."

"Well, the thing is. . ." Lisa didn't know why she felt so nervous all of a sudden. Maybe it had something to do with the way Todd kept staring at her so intently. She also felt guilty taking up time meant for cooking to talk about the pup.

"What did you want to say?" The question came from Bill.

"It's just that I have a puppy I need to give away, and wondered if any of you might be willing to take it." Lisa quickly explained about her renters moving out and leaving the dog for her to deal with.

Bill shook his head "I own a black lab, and I don't think he'd take too kindly to me bringing another dog on the scene."

"I have several goldfish to care for, and that's enough for me right now," Lance put in.

"I have a dog, too," Nicole mumbled. "At least it seems like it's my dog, since I'm the only who takes care of it."

Lisa glanced at Todd.

He lifted both hands in the air. "Don't look at me. It's doubtful I'll ever own a cat or dog. Pets are too much trouble, and I don't want to deal with their hair everywhere."

"I have a cat named Prissy, but my kids would sure like a dog." Allie touched the collar of her creamy white blouse. "I can't believe I'm saying this, but could I bring them by your place later this afternoon to take a look at the puppy?"

"Of course." Lisa leaned back in her chair, feeling a sense of relief. Within the next few hours, the little abandoned pup might have a new home.

———————— ◦⌒◦ ————————

Todd alternated between watching Lisa, wearing a dimpled smile, and Heidi, showing everyone the ingredients for Chicken in a Crumb Basket. This particular recipe intrigued him—partly because he liked chicken—but mostly because it was an unusual dish. Certainly worth writing about if it turned out halfway decent.

Todd's mind wandered as he thought about taking Lisa to dinner this evening. He hoped she'd agreed to go. If Heidi hadn't opened the door and interrupted their conversation, he'd know for sure. *Sure wish I hadn't made a comment about the food at my friend's wedding. From now on, I'll be more careful what I say about anything—especially food—to Lisa. I'd like the chance to see where our relationship might take us. She seems like a nice person—unlike some women I've met in the past.*

Todd's thoughts went to his previous girlfriend, Felicia, and how she'd spread rumors about him, saying he had been seeing other women during the time they'd been dating. Lisa didn't seem like the type to spread rumors, so he felt safe in giving their relationship a try.

"Hey, wake up! Aren't you listening to what the teacher said?"

Todd jumped when Bill poked his arm. "Huh? What was that?"

"Heidi said we're supposed to mix all the ingredients she gave us in a bowl and then line the bottom and sides of a greased casserole dish with it, forming a basket."

Todd stared at the items set before him. He hadn't even realized she'd placed them there, much less asked him to do any mixing or lining the casserole dish. *Guess that's what I get for letting my thoughts run wild.*

He poured everything into a bowl, grabbed a wooden spoon, and started mixing. Looking around, Todd saw everyone else already had their casserole dishes lined with the "basket."

"Okay now, you'll need to take turns baking the baskets." Heidi gestured to Lisa and Allie. "Why don't you ladies go first? As soon as yours is done, Bill and Nicole can go next, then Todd and Lance will do theirs. They will only need to bake for fifteen minutes, so it shouldn't take long to get them all done."

Todd plopped his elbows on the table, watching Lisa carry her casserole dish over to the oven. She seemed so confident—a natural in the kitchen. While the first two baskets baked, everyone sat around the table and listened to Heidi explain how to mix the cut-up chicken and other ingredients for the filling. After it was cooked in a white sauce, it would be added to the crumb basket and baked another thirty to forty minutes.

When the pleasant aroma of the first two baking baskets filled the room, Todd's stomach rumbled even louder than before. He'd been in a hurry this morning and hadn't taken time for more than a cup of coffee and a bagel. *Sure hope there's enough time for us to eat what we've made before we have to go home.*

"Say, Lisa," Lance spoke with a gleam in his eyes, "didn't you mention that the duplex you rented is empty now."

"Yes, it is, but I need to get some work done, and some pieces of furniture must be fixed before I can rent or lease it again."

"Hmm. . ." Lance rapped his knuckles on the table. "My brother needs a place to stay while his townhouse is being remodeled. Would you consider renting on a month-to-month basis to him?"

Lisa tilted her head from side to side, as if weighing her choices. "I suppose I could, but I'm really looking for a full-time renter. Besides, as I explained, the place isn't ready yet."

"When it is, could you please let me know?" Lance took a small notebook from his shirt pocket, wrote down his phone number, and handed it to her.

"Of course." Lisa put the piece of paper in her purse.

Once Allie and Lisa's dishes were taken from the oven, it was

Nicole and Bill's turn. When Nicole picked up her glass dish, Lance bumped her arm. Nicole's chicken in a crumb basket slipped from her hand and landed on the floor with a *splat*!

Turning away from the others, she gripped the sides of her head. "Why does everything bad always happen to me?" Gulping on a sob, she crumpled to the floor beside the mess. "That's it—I'm done!"

Chapter 24

Bill watched in sympathy as Heidi comforted Nicole, saying it was okay, that she could mix a new batch of ingredients, and it shouldn't take long to bake. Heidi pointed to the broken casserole dish. "Don't worry about that, either. It's an old one and can certainly be replaced."

Nicole, still hunkered down on the floor, continued to sob. Bill hated to see the girl have a meltdown like this, but maybe something good would come from it. Holding one's feelings in and trying to be strong all the time were not good for anyone. He wished there was something he could say or do to draw Nicole out and make her open up, although he was fairly sure she wouldn't do it with all of them sitting here staring at her.

"Come, take a seat. I'll get you a glass of water." Heidi helped Nicole, still sniffling, to her feet. "We've all dropped things at some time or another."

Nicole sat in the chair beside Lisa and lowered her head to the table. When Heidi brought her a glass of water, she looked up again. "Th–thanks."

After Nicole finished the drink, she sat a few minutes, taking in deep breaths, while Lisa patted her back.

"It–it's not just the mess on the floor and broken dish that has me upset." Nicole paused and blew her nose on the tissue Heidi handed her. "Things are horrible for me at home, and they're getting worse all the time."

"In what way?" Allie asked.

"For starters, I'm getting behind at school and almost failing in some of my classes."

"You ought to study more and do something for extra credit. That's what I did when I was in high school." Todd looked over at Nicole.

She shook her head slowly. "You don't understand. There's a reason I can't get my homework done or spend enough time studying for tests."

Everyone sat silently as Nicole poured out her heart, telling how the responsibility of cleaning, cooking, and overseeing her siblings had fallen on her ever since her parents' divorce. "My grades are failing because I don't have time to study or get all my homework done." She sniffed deeply, dabbing at her tears with the tissue Heidi had given her. "I have no life of my own anymore."

"Why doesn't your dad hire someone to come in and clean the house at least?" The question came from Lance.

"He doesn't have enough money for that. Dad moans every time another bill comes in. Even though he's a plumber, Dad's barely making enough to keep up with all our expenses."

Bill fiddled with the buttons on his shirt. He wasn't wealthy, by any stretch of the imagination, but he made a decent living. Other than his hunting expenses, Bill didn't spend much on unnecessary things. There was no reason he couldn't help out by providing the money for Nicole's dad to hire a housekeeper. He just had to figure out a way to do it without her finding out, because he was almost certain she would see it as charity.

Nicole's cheeks, already pink, turned a deep shade of red. "As if things aren't bad enough at our house, Tonya—my mom—came by last Sunday evening, and she was drunk. I'm glad my brother and sister were in bed. They'd have been really upset if they'd seen her staggering around and heard the way she was carrying on."

Bill grimaced. *Poor Nicole. She has too much on her shoulders and is being forced to grow up before her time. I can't do anything about her mother, but I'm definitely going to do something to help ease Nicole's burden and give her more time to spend on schoolwork.*

Canton

"Are you sure you don't want me to watch the baby while you go to Mt. Hope to visit your friend Dorie?" Kendra's mother asked when Kendra began filling the diaper bag.

Kendra shook her head. "The reason I'm going to Dorie's is so she can see the boppli."

Squinting, Mom tipped her head at an odd angle. "What does boppli mean?"

"It's the Pennsylvania Dutch word for baby. I learned a few Amish words while living with Heidi and her husband."

Mom's lips pressed together. "I'm certainly glad they won't be raising my grandchild. The baby would have been raised Amish and never had the privilege of experiencing all the things you grew up with." Her nose wrinkled. "Can you imagine having to live without electricity, traveling by a horse and buggy, and dressing in Plain clothes?"

Kendra clasped the handles of the diaper bag tightly. She didn't like the way this conversation was going. "For your information, Mom, I enjoyed staying with the Troyers, and I wouldn't have minded if little Heidi had been raised in the Plain lifestyle and ended up joining the Amish church when she was older."

Mom's mouth formed an O as she leaned against the baby's crib, facing Kendra. "I can't believe you would say that."

"Why not? The Amish are good people, with strong moral values. They believe in God and putting Him first. Isn't that what our church teaches?"

"Well, yes, but. . ." Mom turned and covered little Heidi's feet, where she'd kicked the covers off. "I don't want to argue with you, Kendra. I'm just glad you decided against the adoption and came home to be with your family."

"Yeah, well, let me remind you, before you got up the nerve and convinced Dad to let me come home, you knew I was pregnant and yet you were perfectly fine with wherever and whoever I was living with.

In fact, it was not even six months ago when you said, and I quote, 'Your child will be better off with adoptive parents.' So please don't tell me your version of how much better it is living here. You don't even know the Troyers and what wonderful people they are. And I'm going to make sure they are in my daughter's life, whether you and Dad like it or not."

Little Heidi started to whimper, but calmed down when Kendra scooped her up. "There, there, my little sweet baby. It's okay. Everything is all right." She looked at her mother, who stood speechless. "There's been enough said about the Troyers, so please don't say any more negative comments about them."

Before Mom could offer a response, Kendra walked out of the room. After living with Heidi and Lyle for several months, she'd begun to feel as if they were her family. She felt thankful for the help they'd given her when she had no place else to go. Deep in her heart, Kendra still wondered sometimes if her daughter would be better off with the Troyers, but she'd made her decision to keep the baby, and it would be too hard to give her up now.

Walnut Creek

That afternoon, after everyone had gone home. Heidi sat down to eat a delayed lunch. Between Allie arriving late for class and then taking time to listen to Nicole unburden her soul, the class lasted longer than usual. Even though it was good to see Nicole open up and share her burdens, Heidi felt sorry for the girl and would remember to pray for her. She hoped somewhere down the line things would get better for Nicole and her family. Heidi's own parents had always been kind and loving. She couldn't imagine what it must be like for Nicole to deal with an undependable mother who got drunk.

Heidi had finished eating her sandwich and soup and was placing the dishes in the sink, when she heard a vehicle pull into the yard. She dried her hands on a dishtowel and hurried to the front door to see who it was.

When Heidi opened the door, she was surprised to see Kendra getting out of a car. She stood on the porch and watched as Kendra reached inside the backseat and took out her baby.

Heidi's heart pounded. For a fleeting moment she thought maybe Kendra had changed her mind and was bringing little Heidi for her and Lyle to raise, after all. But then seeing only a small diaper bag slung over Kendra's shoulder, logic took over. If she had changed her mind about letting them adopt the baby, she would have called to discuss it with them and set it all up with the lawyer again. And Kendra would have brought more than just a diaper bag along.

Kendra smiled as she stepped onto the porch. "I've been to Mt. Hope to see my friend Dorie, and since I was so close, I decided to stop by here and see if you were home. Are you busy right now, or do you have time for a short visit?"

Heidi nodded. "I taught another cooking class this morning and just finished having lunch, so I'd enjoy visiting with you for however long you can stay. If you haven't eaten, I'd be happy to fix you something." While speaking to Kendra, Heidi couldn't help gazing at the sweet bundle in her arms.

"It's nice of you to offer, but I had lunch with Dorie."

"Well, come in, and I'll fix you something to drink." Heidi opened the door, and motioned for Kendra to follow her inside. "Let's have a seat in the living room. It's more comfortable there."

Kendra shifted the baby from one arm to the other, glancing around the room. "Nothing's changed. Your place still looks as cozy as ever."

Heidi smiled. "Why don't you take a seat over there? I'm sure the baby will like being rocked." She gestured to the rocking chair.

"I have a better idea; why don't you sit and rock your little namesake while I go and fix us something to drink?" Kendra grinned. "After living here a few months, I know my way around your kitchen pretty well."

"True." Heidi lifted the baby into her arms and took a seat in the rocker, while Kendra headed for the kitchen. As she sat staring at the infant's delicate features and holding her tiny hand, a lump formed in her throat. *If she could only be my boppli, I'd be the happiest woman in Holmes County.*

Little Heidi opened her eyes briefly, then closed them again. Her breathing was sweet and even. Although Heidi was pleased Kendra had stopped by, seeing and holding the little girl who'd once been promised to her was bittersweet. Raising this child would have been such a blessing.

I don't understand why some women, like Nicole's mother, don't care about their children, while others, like me, who would give anything to be a mamm, go through life with a sense of emptiness.

Heidi blinked back unbidden tears threatening to spill over. It was wrong to feel sorry for herself and dwell on what would never be. This special baby was a blessing to Kendra, and she deserved the opportunity to raise her own child.

She put the baby over her shoulder and gently patted her small back. Closing her eyes, Heidi allowed herself to fantasize. *Maybe Kendra and little Heidi could live here with us, and even though Lyle and I wouldn't be the baby's parents, we could at least help raise her.*

"Here you go. I made us some hot tea."

Heidi's eyes snapped open. "Thank you, Kendra. You can set it there on the coffee table." She gestured to the baby. "Do you want to take her now?"

"No, that's okay. You can hold her as long as you like. Unless you'd rather not."

Heidi sighed, brushing the top of the infant's head lightly with her fingers. "I could hold your baby all day, but I guess I should drink my tea before it gets cold." Truthfully, Heidi felt if she didn't let go of Kendra's daughter now, she might never be able to let her go.

Kendra stepped up to the rocking chair. "I'll put her on the couch by me while we both drink our tea."

Heidi's arms felt empty when Kendra took the baby and found a seat on one end of the couch, placing the child close to her. "How are things going for you?"

"Okay. As good as can be expected." Kendra reached for her cup of tea.

"Are your folks enjoying their new role as grandparents?"

"I guess so." Kendra took a sip of her tea. "Sometimes the baby's crying gets on my dad's nerves, and he becomes irritable or impatient." She sat quietly for several seconds, looking at her daughter. "I think the only reason he agreed to let me come home was for my mom's sake. I found out from my sister Shelly that even though Mom stood by Dad's decision when he kicked me out of the house, she was brokenhearted and wanted me to move back home. Dad probably would have turned his back on me and little Heidi indefinitely if it hadn't been for Mom."

"That's too bad. Maybe after he spends more time with his granddaughter, he'll come around."

Kendra shrugged her slim shoulders. "I hope so, but I'm not holding my breath. Even so, I'm grateful they gave me this chance to keep my child. Things aren't the way I'd like them to be, but the good Lord above kept me and my baby together."

As they both sat in silence, watching baby Heidi, Kendra spoke again. "Remember when I told you how little Heidi almost came early?"

Heidi nodded.

"Well, when the pains got worse some really nice people at the grocery store helped me out, and even called the paramedics."

"It's good you were surrounded by compassionate strangers."

"I sure was, but get this—before the ambulance arrived, while I was still lying on the floor, this man—and I only got a fleeting glimpse of him—had been watching me, before he turned and went out of sight."

"Who do you think it was?"

"I thought it looked like my dad." Kendra frowned. "And I wondered why, if it was, he didn't come see if I was okay."

"Did you ask him later?"

"After I got home from finding out it wasn't true labor, I questioned Dad about it." Kendra sighed. "Well, it was him I saw, and he just gave me some lame excuse. He justified it by saying he had stopped to pick up a snack to take to a church meeting he was already late for, and that the woman he'd seen on the floor of the store looked like me, but he didn't think it actually was." Kendra sagged in her chair. "Can you believe that? Wouldn't you think he could have at least come over and checked?"

Heidi nodded slowly. She certainly would have checked if she'd seen someone in trouble and thought she knew them. For that matter, she'd have offered help even to a stranger. It was hard to understand how Kendra's dad, a churchgoing man, could be so unfeeling.

After a pause, Kendra continued. "I don't believe for one minute that Dad didn't know it was me, but I chose not to say anymore to him about it." She lifted her hands and let them fall to her lap. "I mean, what was the point? He's still embarrassed about me, and I'm sure he didn't want to be seen with his pregnant, unwed daughter there in the store."

"I'm sorry, Kendra." Heidi simply couldn't imagine Kendra's father treating her that way. Feeling the need for a change of subject, Heidi told Kendra how Loretta had decided to join the Amish church."

Kendra chuckled. "I'm not surprised. I'll bet she and Eli are planning to be married soon after she joins."

Heidi smiled. She hadn't talked to Loretta recently. She would have to pay her a visit soon and ask how things were going.

They visited another half hour, then Kendra said it was time for her to go.

Heidi rose to her feet and walked to the door with Kendra and the baby. "Feel free to drop by anytime you're in the area." She reached out and gently stroked the infant's head. "I would like to visit with you again and see how much the baby has grown."

Kendra smiled. "Sounds good. I'd enjoy seeing you again, too."

When Kendra left, Heidi returned to the rocking chair. Her hands went limp as she lowered her head, giving in to the tears she'd been trying so hard to hold back. Spending time with the baby had only fueled her desire to be a mother. If the pain would only subside.

"I need to get busy and keep my mind occupied." She pulled herself upright, dried her eyes, and headed to the laundry room to put a load of towels in the wringer washer. If they didn't dry outdoors in the few hours left of daylight, she'd bring the towels inside and hang them in the basement.

Heidi yawned. She felt done in from the day's activities and wished she could take a nap. But Lyle would be home soon, and she needed to get supper ready. Maybe later this evening they'd fix hot apple cider and sit by the fire and talk. She would share with him all the events of the day, including the visit with Kendra.

Chapter 25

Dover

When Allie stepped onto Lisa's front porch, she began to have second thoughts. Bringing a puppy into their house might not be a good idea, after all. Prissy would see the dog as an intruder, and the pup may not care for the cat. But it was too late to change her mind now. She'd already told her kids if they liked the dog they could have it. Nola and Derek stood beside her now, giggling and bouncing on tiptoes.

When Lisa opened the door, Allie introduced her to the children.

"It's nice to meet you. The puppy's in the kitchen. Follow me. I'll lead the way."

When they entered the room, Allie spotted the pup inside a small cage. The children saw him right away, too, and dropped to their knees in front of the enclosure.

"Can we take him out?" Derek looked up at Lisa expectantly.

"Sure, but let me close the kitchen door first. I don't want the little stinker running all over the house." Lisa wrinkled her nose. "Trouble—that's what I call him—has been known to make messes when left unattended."

Allie groaned inwardly. In addition to worrying about how the cat and dog would get along, she'd have to work at getting the puppy housebroken and trained not to chew on everything in sight. Then there was the issue of what to do with the animal during the day while she and Steve were at work and the kids were in school. *I should have thought all this through before I opened my mouth—first to Lisa, saying we'd come look at the pup—and then to Derek and Lola, offering to let them have the dog.* Allie wondered if her common sense had gone out the window lately.

After Lisa closed the kitchen door, she lifted the latch on the cage. The pup bounded out and headed straight for Nola. As soon as the child reached out to pet the dog, he slurped the end of her nose. She giggled. "Look, Mommy, the puppy likes me."

In all the excitement, the puppy made a wet spot on the floor. "Oh, oh." Nola looked sheepishly up at Lisa. "Sorry he did that."

"Oh, don't worry about it." Lisa went to get a paper towel. "This little pup is still a baby and will need some training."

Allie was on the verge of changing her mind about taking the puppy home, but she remembered her childhood dog. Her parents had been so patient with the little mistakes Rascal made, but everyone was happy when Allie eventually got the puppy trained. At least she had to give her children a chance and see how they handled this new responsibility.

"Mommy," Nola said quietly, "does the puppy making a mess mean we can't take him home?"

"I'm still thinking about it."

Nola clung to Allie's hand. "Please, Mommy. I like the dog."

"You realize that you and your brother will have to take care of Trouble and help me get him housebroken as soon as possible."

"Oh, we will Mommy," Nola shouted.

"We promise." Derek got into the act, clapping his hands and calling for the pup. Wiggling and wagging his tail, Trouble nuzzled the boy's hand and then crawled into his lap.

Derek grinned, looking up at Allie. "I think he likes us, Mommy. Can we take him home now?"

Nola's head bobbed up and down as she reached over and stroked the puppy's head.

Allie pinched the bridge of her nose. It looked like she had no choice. "If it's okay with Lisa, then Trouble will have a new home at our house."

Lisa smiled. "Sounds good. I'm sure he'll be much happier there, with children to play with, then he would living here with me."

As they were getting into the van a short time later, Allie's cell phone rang. Looking at the caller ID, and seeing it was Steve, she quickly answered.

"Hi, hon. Just wanted you to know not to expect me for supper this evening."

"Oh? How come? You said this morning that you'd be home early today."

"I thought so then, but something's come up, so I will be working later than I thought. I'll grab something to eat before I head home. Oh, and if you get tired waiting for me, go on to bed. I'll see you in the morning."

In the morning? Allie positioned herself behind the steering wheel, grabbing it tightly with both hands. *I wonder if Steve's with that female officer again. Is he really working, or could they be having an affair?*

Walnut Creek

After Lance left Heidi's, he'd run a few errands in Berlin and stopped to eat lunch at the Farmstead Restaurant. He wasn't in a hurry to go home but couldn't stay away any longer because he wanted to work on the photo albums he'd been putting together to give his daughters for Christmas. He'd set a box of pictures on his desk in the kitchen before he left for the cooking class this morning and planned to go through it this afternoon before starting supper. He especially wanted to find some pictures of Flo, beginning with when she was a girl, all the way up to when she'd married him. He was sure Terry and Sharon would treasure the albums filled with memories of their loving mother.

Lance pulled into his yard and hit the remote to open the garage door. It was nice to be able to pull right into the garage again. After having that talk with Dan, he was no longer blocking the garage door with his vehicle. Now if he could just convince his brother to move into Lisa's duplex when it was ready, things would be better all the way around.

When Lance entered the house, his nose twitched. *Do I smell paint?* The odor permeated the house, but seemed to be stronger the closer he got to the kitchen. He stepped into the room and halted, mouth hanging open. The kitchen walls had been repainted a drab beige. If the stench and putrid color wasn't bad enough, the box of photos was no longer on his desk. Everything that had been hanging on the walls now lay on the table. There was no doubt who'd done it, either. The question was why?

Following the sound of the new TV, Lance marched into the living room. Holding the remote in one hand, and a can of soda pop in the other, Dan sat on the couch with his feet propped on the coffee table.

Lance's jaw clenched as he squinted at his brother. "What possessed you to paint my kitchen without my permission?"

"It needed painting, so I figured I'd surprise you."

"Oh, I'm surprised all right." Lance slapped his hands against his hips. "Flo liked the cheerful yellow color in our kitchen, and so did I."

Dan blinked rapidly. "Sorry if I overstepped my bounds. I thought it was time for a change, and those yellow walls seemed too bright."

"I like it bright. So did Flo."

"Okay, okay. . . Don't panic." Dan held up both hands, as if to surrender. "I'll paint it back. In fact, I'll start on it tomorrow while you're in church."

"I'd hoped you might go to church with me."

Dan shook his head. "You know how I feel about church. Have ever since we were teenagers and someone in the congregation got really upset because the new carpet wasn't the color they wanted. They were so mad they ended up leaving. Then someone else left, and pretty soon half the church members were gone."

Lance clenched his teeth. "That's a dumb reason to quit going to church. People are people, and not everyone attending church is perfect. In fact, none of us are. We're all humans with bad habits and differing opinions."

Dan lifted his pop can to his lips, took a drink, and placed it on the side table. "Say what you like, but I'm not goin' with you tomorrow.

Besides, there's a football game I want to watch."

"How are you gonna do that if you're repainting the kitchen?"

"I'll paint during halftime, or turn up the TV so I can hear the score from the kitchen."

Lance figured he wouldn't get anywhere with his brother, so he left the living room and headed to his bedroom to hopefully get away from the paint smell. The last thing he wanted was to say something to Dan that he might regret later on, but now Lance was more determined than ever for his brother to move out. *Think I'll give Heidi a call and leave a message, asking if she'll give me Lisa's phone number. If I have to, I'll go over to the duplex she wants to rent and help her get the place in shape so Dan can move in.*

Remembering the pictures he'd left on his desk this morning, Lance returned to the living room. "What'd you do with the box of photos that were on my desk in the kitchen?"

Dan sat staring at the television as though he hadn't heard a word Lance said.

Lance's jaw and facial muscles tightened as he positioned himself between his brother and the television.

"Hey! What'd you do that for?" Dan's eyes narrowed. "You're blocking my view of the TV."

"I'm standing here to get your attention, because you didn't answer when I asked a question." Lance crossed his arms, refusing to budge from his spot.

Dan's forehead wrinkled as he leaned his head to one side, as if hoping to see around Lance. "What was your question?"

"I asked what you did with the box of photos that were on my desk in the kitchen. I set it there this morning so I could work on the albums I'm making for my daughters."

"Let me think. . ." Dan scratched his head. "Oh, yeah, now I remember. I put the box in the utility room, on top of the dryer. Didn't want to get any paint on the pictures, so I figured I'd better get them out of the kitchen."

"Okay; good thinking." Well, at least his brother had done one thing right. If those pictures had gotten ruined, Lance would feel sick.

Then Dan added, "I hope you don't mind, but I ended up looking through the pictures and sorted them by category for you. You know, family, places you've been—that sort of thing."

"What?" Lance never felt so exasperated in his life. "Didn't you look on the back of those photos?"

"No. Why would I?"

"Well, I have the year the photo was taken written on the back of each one." Clutching his shirt collar, Lance inhaled a long breath. "Now I'll have to re-sort them again, by the year. That's how I wanted them." Lance watched for his brother's reaction, but Dan gave none. "Oh, never mind." *No use trying to get through to him.*

"Are you done now? Can I finish watching my show?"

"Sure, Dan, we'll talk later." Lance plastered a smile on his face, but inside, his anger boiled like a pot of pasta cooking on the stove. *Who does my brother think he is, anyhow? He has no respect for my things at all.*

Lance wanted to talk to his brother about moving into Lisa's duplex right away, but since he was a bit overwrought right now, he figured this wasn't a good time. Dan was already giving him an icy stare, and if he missed any more of his TV program, he'd probably blow his top.

Lance entered his room and flopped onto the bed. *Sure hope I have better luck getting Dan to move out than I have with getting him to go to church.*

Charm, Ohio

"I hope you like Bavarian-style food." Todd pulled his sports car into Chalet in the Valley restaurant's parking lot and smiled at Lisa. "I've been here once, but not since they got a new cook, so I'm anxious to try the place out again." After the cooking class today, Todd had asked her again if he could take her out. Against her better judgment, Lisa agreed and had even let him choose the restaurant.

"If you haven't been here in a while, how do you know they've hired a new cook?" she questioned.

"Oh, I don't know. Guess someone must have mentioned it to me." Todd got out of the car and hurried around to help Lisa before she could exit on her own. She wasn't used to getting in or out of such a small vehicle, so she appreciated his gesture. In fact, ever since Todd picked her up in Dover, he'd been the perfect gentleman.

Guess I ought to give him a chance, Lisa told herself as they walked to the restaurant's entrance. She wasn't sure why, but she'd taken extra care with what to wear this evening, and had even put on a little extra makeup. She'd chosen a simple, dark blue dress, which brought out the color of her eyes. Lisa also added a matching silver necklace, adorned with a heart-shaped blue sapphire that sparkled when the light hit it.

As they entered the building, Todd rested his hand gently against the small of Lisa's back. He was certainly a gentleman this evening. Perhaps he wasn't as self-centered as she'd originally thought.

Once inside, the hostess, wearing a Bavarian-style dress, showed them to a table near the window. The restaurant, as well as the town, seemed quaint and appealing. If not for the need to be closer to the bigger towns for her catering business, Lisa thought she could be happy living in a small community like this. There was something about the area here that reminded her of pictures she'd seen of Switzerland in magazines and travel brochures. Someday it would be fun to travel to Europe and see the real Switzerland for herself. Until, and unless, that day ever came, she'd be content to visit a place such as this, here in the scenic Doughty Valley.

"You look very pretty tonight."

Lisa's cheeks grew warm. Todd's compliment caught her off guard. "Thanks." *You look nice, too,* she wanted to add, but couldn't bring herself to say it.

He grinned at her from across the table. "So what appeals to you?" Todd pointed to Lisa's menu.

"I'm not sure yet." Lisa perused the list of dinner choices. She hadn't eaten lunch today, so at the moment, nearly everything appealed. Lisa noticed near the bottom of the menu it stated that the chef used local products in many of the deliciously authentic recipes.

"The wiener schnitzel sounds good to me." Todd took a drink of water. "Think I'll have that."

Lisa continued to study the menu, then decided on a ham-and-swiss sandwich, with a side order of sauerkraut.

After placing their orders, they talked about the cooking class and how things had gone that morning.

"We're certainly a group of diversified students." Lisa took a drink from her glass of water.

Todd bobbed his head. "I'll say. What'd you think of Nicole's meltdown?"

"I feel sorry for her. Sounds like she's having a hard time dealing with her family situation."

"Yeah, it's too bad 'cause she's still just a kid and shouldn't have to shoulder so much responsibility."

Lisa was pleased to hear the compassion in Todd's tone of voice. Maybe he was nicer than she'd originally thought. With his good looks and intelligence, she was surprised he wasn't married, or at least romantically involved with someone. If Todd was seeing another woman, surely he wouldn't have asked her out or danced cheek-to-cheek with her at his friend's wedding reception. Or would he? Some men liked to play the field. Todd might be one of them.

When their food came, Lisa pushed her thoughts aside. "When I'm eating out, I always pray like the Amish do—silently," she said, smiling at Todd.

His brows lowered a bit, but then he nodded. "Fine by me."

Lisa bowed her head and thanked the Lord for the food set before her. She also offered thanks for this opportunity to get to know Todd better.

As they ate their meal, she noticed how Todd seemed to critique everything he ate, and even made a few comments about their young waitress. Here they were on a date, yet he was suddenly paying more attention to the food than her. Todd had been quite talkative on the drive here, but now his only comments were about the items on his plate or how attentive the waitress was or wasn't. She thought it was odd. But then, many things about Todd seemed a bit strange. One minute he was the perfect gentleman, saying kind and courteous things, and the next minute, Todd made off-handed remarks. He was a complicated man.

Lisa took a sip of her hot tea. *Maybe I should invite him over to my place sometime and cook a nice meal. Perhaps then he'd be more attentive. Or would he end up critiquing my dinner, and maybe even me?*

Chapter 26

Walnut Creek

B y Monday, Lance still had not heard from Heidi about getting Lisa's phone number, so he decided to stop by her house. If she was there, he would speak to her during his mail delivery, rather than putting the Troyers' mail in their box near the road.

As he neared the house, he spotted Lyle standing near the buggy shed, hitching his horse. "Morning, Mr. Troyer. Is your wife at home?"

"Yes, she's getting ready to go into Berlin with me. We both have dental appointments this morning."

"Oh, well, I won't keep you. I just wanted to ask Heidi a quick question."

"You can either knock on the door or wait here. I'm sure she'll be out soon."

"Think I'd better knock." Lance headed to the house and had barely stepped onto the porch when Heidi came out the door.

"Good morning, Lance. Do you have a package for me?"

He shook his head. "Not today, but I was wondering if you have Lisa's phone number. I need to talk to her about the duplex she has for rent, and it can't wait till our next cooking class."

"Of course. I'll see if I can find it." She turned and went back inside.

Lance leaned on the porch railing, waiting for Heidi's return. Several minutes went by, and he began to pace. *Sure hope I don't cause her to be late for the dental appointment. Guess I should have said I could stop by later for Lisa's number.*

Lance reflected on yesterday's happenings. He'd gone to church by himself, of course, and when he got home Dan had half the kitchen painted yellow. It wasn't the exact color as before, but at least it wasn't beige anymore. He'd changed his clothes and helped his brother finish the job. Afterward, due to the paint odor, they'd gone out for lunch, leaving a few windows open to air the place out and help the paint dry. When they returned home, Dan watched TV while Lance worked on his daughters' photo albums in the dining room. He'd managed to get all the pictures back in date order and had enjoyed reminiscing as he looked at each one.

Redirecting his thoughts, Lance glanced at Lyle, still standing beside his horse and buggy. "Your wife went to get a phone number for me," he called. "Sorry if I'm holding you up."

Lyle started walking toward Lance, but before he reached the front steps, Heidi came out of the house. "Here you go." She handed Lance a slip of paper.

"Thanks. I'll give Lisa a call during my lunch hour. I'll see you a week from Saturday. Oh, and I hope things go well at the dentist." Lance gave a quick wave and headed back to his vehicle. With any luck, Dan would be moved out before this week was over.

New Philadelphia

Allie tapped her fingers against the steering wheel as she waited at a stoplight while on her way to work. She'd dropped the kids off at school a few minutes ago and felt glad to be free of their chatter about the new pup. The name Lisa had given him was appropriate—he was a bundle of Trouble. At least that's how Allie saw it. Nola and Derek were enamored with the little fellow and thought everything he did was cute.

Yesterday while the kids were at Sunday school, Allie had accidentally left the door of the pup's cage unlatched, and he'd gotten out while she was in the living room visiting with Steve. When she returned to the kitchen, she found Trouble chewing on the throw rug by the sink. On top of that, he'd piddled on the floor near the back door. Then Prissy came in for a drink of water and something to eat from her dish, but the puppy wanted to play and ended up spilling cat food all over the floor.

When Allie went back to the living room to ask for Steve's help, he'd mumbled, "It wasn't a good idea to get that pup for the kids." Then he went back to reading his newspaper.

The skin around Allie's eyes tightened. To make her weekend worse, when she'd asked Steve why he'd gotten home a few minutes before midnight the night before, he gave some excuse about being called out for a domestic dispute, then quickly changed the subject. Allie felt sure he'd lied to her, but she didn't make an issue, since she had no proof. She was driving herself crazy thinking Steve may have been with another woman. When she came right down to it, the whole idea sounded ludicrous, but then, when she thought about all the facts, what else could it be? If things kept up, she may come right out and ask if he was having an affair. As much as it would hurt, knowing the truth would be better than living with her suspicions. One thing was for sure—Allie would not give up without a fight in order to save her marriage.

• ❧ •

Millersburg

Struggling to keep her eyes open, Nicole tried to focus on the test her English teacher had given the class. She'd stayed up late last night studying for it, but now she could barely stay awake. This morning, she'd overslept, so that didn't help things any as she rushed around getting breakfast ready and lunches made for her siblings, as well as herself. Dad left early for work, which meant, as usual, all the responsibility fell on Nicole.

She rolled her shoulders, trying to get the kinks out, and reached up to rub the back of her neck. *Use an apostrophe and* s *to form the possessive of a noun not ending in* s. Girl's. *Use an apostrophe alone to form the possessive of a plural noun ending in* s. Girls'.

Nicole bit the end of her pencil. *Or is it the other way around?* She opted for the first one and hoped for the best.

When Nicole looked up from her paper, she realized all the other students had turned in their tests. Earlier, before the exam started, the teacher told everyone when they were finished, they could read a book or start working on the next lesson, as long as they didn't disturb other students who were still working on the test. Nicole pursed her lips. *So, great—I'm the last to finish.*

She glanced at her watch and frowned. *Fifteen minutes left to get the test done, and I still have ten more questions to answer.*

The next question involved sentence structure, and when a comma should or shouldn't be used. By the time Nicole finished taking the test, she had a full-blown headache. She could only hope she had enough answers right and wouldn't fail the exam.

———————————⟨∘⟩———————————

As Bill headed up the hall to replace a light in the auditorium, he spotted Nicole coming out of her English class. He gave her a friendly wave, but her only response was a brief nod, then she looked the other way. Seeing her downturned facial features, Bill figured she'd had a bad morning so far.

He paused, pinching the bridge of his nose. *I still haven't done anything to help the girl, and I need to take care of that right away. As soon as I get home from work today, I'll make good on the promise I made to myself last Saturday. Like all young women her age, Nicole deserves the chance to be happy and enjoy a little time to herself.*

"Mr. Mason." A voice from behind brought Bill out of his thoughts. "May I have a word with you?"

Oh brother. Now what? Bill lifted his eyebrows as he turned to face Ms. Shultz.

"There are cobwebs in the corner of my classroom, which means there could be a spider lurking about." She stood looking at him with her arms crossed. "And I'll not put up with that."

"Now what's wrong with a little ole spider?" Bill grinned, wondering what she'd do if he put the big rubber spider he had at home in one of her desk drawers. He'd pulled a prank like that when he was a boy, and his teacher nearly fainted.

Guess I won't press my luck with Ms. Shultz today. He gave a placating nod and stepped into her class.

Chapter 27

Dover

Monday evening, as Lisa was getting ready to fix supper, her cell phone rang. She didn't recognize the number, but decided to answer anyway. "Hello."

"Is this Lisa Brooks?"

"Yes, who's calling?" She thought she recognized the deep male voice but wasn't sure where she'd heard it before.

"It's Lance Freemont from the cooking classes. I got your number from Heidi Troyer."

Lisa took a seat at the kitchen table. "Oh, I see. If you're calling about the duplex, the unit I rent out isn't ready yet."

"I figured it wouldn't be but thought maybe you could use some help with it. I'd like my brother to take a look at the place as soon as possible, too."

"Are you offering his assistance to clean and fix things up?"

"No. Thought I'd help you with that myself. Of course if he's willing. . ."

She raised her eyebrows. "Really? How come?"

Lance cleared his throat. "Figured if I helped out, you'd get the job done twice as fast."

"But don't you have a mail route during the week?"

"Sure, but I only work five days a week. A sub fills in on my days off."

"Oh, okay. Well, I suppose we could work something out." Lisa paused. "But don't you think you should bring your brother by first, to make sure he's interested in moving here?"

"Right. That's a good plan. Can I come over sometime tomorrow to help out? It's my day off and I have nothing else planned. I'll bring Dan with me so he can see the place. Then if he likes it, we'll both help out. He likes to paint, so if you're needing that done, Dan's your man."

"Sounds good. Why don't you come over around ten? I have an errand to run at eight thirty, but I should be back by then."

"Great! See you then."

Lisa said goodbye and put her cell phone on the counter. Her stomach rumbled, and she gave it a pat. It was definitely time to start supper.

Canton

After supper, Kendra's sisters cleared the table and did the dishes, so Kendra took little Heidi to her bedroom to change and feed her. Once that was done and the baby lay sleeping in her crib across the room, Kendra pulled a cardboard box out of her closet. She was surprised it was still there—especially after she'd been kicked out of the house in the early part of this year. When Kendra returned home at her parents' request, she'd half expected to discover all of her old things had been thrown out.

The box was full of old papers and memorabilia from her high school days, and she wanted to make sure there was nothing left in it to remind her of Max. When he'd chosen not to acknowledge Kendra's pregnancy and had cheated on her, she'd vowed to erase him from her life. That included getting rid of any pictures of him that may still be floating around. The last thing she wanted was for her little girl to know anything about her biological father when she grew up.

Kendra took a seat on the floor and took everything out of the box. Then, one by one, she began sorting through each item. So many mementos she'd saved in those days. It was hard not to laugh at them now. First, there was a ticket stub to a school play she'd gone to. Why she'd saved that had her perplexed, because as Kendra remembered, she'd gone there alone. Then there were the pictures of some of her classmates she'd never bothered to put in her wallet. When she came to the yearbook from when she was a sophomore, she paused to look through the photos and read a couple of pages. She'd managed to get a few signatures and autographs from teachers and some of her fellow students. Kendra had to laugh when one of them had been signed, "*To a girl who will go far in life.*"

"Yeah, right." Pushing her hair off her face, Kendra criticized her situation. "Here I am coming up on my twenty-first birthday, still living with my parents, a single mother, and no job." She heaved a sigh. "If those kids I went to school with could see me now, they'd wish they had written something different in my yearbook."

Halfway through the book, Kendra's gaze came to rest on the senior class pictures. She hadn't known many of the senior students, but recognized a few who were either involved in sports or held some position on the student body council. She recognized one of the guys—a tall, good-looking fellow named Brent. He was captain of the football team and also president of the senior class. As she recalled, Brent always had a group of silly girls around him, vying for his attention.

Then she glanced in the box and saw something else. Folded, in the shape of a triangle, was an old gum wrapper. Picking it up, she had to smile, remembering the night, like it was yesterday.

Kendra had been standing on the sidelines, cheering her school's football team as they ran out on to the field. She'd been with a group of other students when she saw a piece of paper fall out of Brent's uniform. She'd kept an eye on where it fell. Then, when everyone went back to the bleachers while the team was doing the coin toss to see who would get the ball first, Kendra hurried over and picked up the small paper and stuffed it in her pocket. It was this very gum wrapper she looked at now that had been in Brent's pocket that day.

She smiled, placing the yearbook aside, then went to the waste basket to throw the wrapper away. Ironically, to this day, she still bought that brand of chewing gum, all because of a high school crush.

I bet Brent's got a wife and a couple of kids by now. A guy like him, who had it all together, would never have given someone like me a second glance.

Sure wish I could have found somebody better to date then Max. He was a loser from the get-go. I was just too dumb to see it.

———— ⌇⌇ ————

Millersburg

"How'd things go at school today, kids?" Nicole's father asked as she and her siblings sat at the kitchen table eating the pepperoni pizza he'd picked up on the way home. It was a treat for Nicole, not having to cook.

"School was okay," Tony said around a mouthful of food. "I'd rather spend the day outside riding my bike or playin' basketball, though."

"Those are things you can do when you get home from school, Son." Dad looked at Heather. "How was your day?"

"It was good. I found a new book in the library I like. It's about a. . ."

"Hey, where's the milk?" Tony bumped Nicole's arm with his bony elbow. "I thought you were gonna put it on the table."

"I asked you to take the milk out, remember?" Nicole gestured to the refrigerator. "Why don't you get off your lazy bones and get it?"

"You're not my boss." Tony glared at her. "Only Mom and Dad can tell me what to do."

Nicole swatted at the air. "Dad's your boss, but in case you've forgotten, Mom's not here. And even when she was. . ."

Dad held up his hand. "Okay, you two, that's enough. Tony, please get out the carton of milk. And don't forget four glasses."

"Okay," Tony mumbled, pushing his chair away from the table.

Dad looked at Nicole. "How was your day at school? Didn't you mention you had a math test to take?"

"No, it was English."

Nicole cringed. She was almost certain she'd gotten at least half the answers wrong. Between lack of sleep and not studying long enough, her brain couldn't absorb all the questions on the test, let alone come up with right answers. "It's too soon to know how I did on the test." She waited for Tony to set the milk on the table and hand her a glass, then she poured herself some. No way was she going to admit she'd probably flunked the test. Dad would probably come unglued.

The telephone rang from the living room, and Dad left his seat at the table to answer it. When he returned several minutes later he wore a closed-lipped smile. "Good news, kids—especially for you, Nicole. An anonymous donor has paid for us to have our house cleaned weekly for the next six months."

"What?" Nicole's eyebrows shot up. "Why would someone do that?"

Dad lifted his shoulders in a quick shrug. "The woman who called has her own cleaning business. All she said was that she'd been paid in advance to come here and clean weekly until the last day in May. She will start this Saturday."

"Yeah!" Tony clapped his hands.

"The last day of May is when we get out of school, Dad." Heather grinned. "Nicole won't have to start cleaning again till then. Of course, I'll help her, since we won't have any schoolwork to do during the summer."

Barely able to take it all in, Nicole thought about all the people they knew. She couldn't imagine who would care enough to hire a housekeeper for them or who had that kind of money. She hoped she could find out someday who the donor was so she could thank that person for it. Even though she'd still have cooking and other chores to do, not having to clean the house every week would give her more time to study and hopefully get all her homework done on time. For the moment, at least, things were looking up.

Walnut Creek

Heidi glanced at the kitchen clock. It was almost six, and Lyle wasn't home yet. After their dental appointments, which had turned out well for both of them, he'd dropped her off at home and headed out to conduct an afternoon auction. Heidi spent the next few hours catching up with some mending and making a list of all the ingredients she would need for her next cooking class. Although it wouldn't take place until a week from this Saturday, she liked to plan ahead and be prepared.

Heidi's mouth watered as she lifted the lid on a kettle of stew and inhaled its savory fragrance. She was tempted to eat without Lyle, knowing he probably wouldn't mind, but she didn't want to sit at the table alone. She'd done it on too many occasions.

She turned away from the stove and gazed out the window. After nine years of marriage, there should be children playing in the yard, eager to come in when she called them for supper. Instead, the only thing Heidi saw was her dog, Rusty, running across the lawn. The Brittany spaniel was a loyal pet, but he could never take the place of a child.

Heidi moved from the window and shook her head. *You're doing it again—feeling sorry for yourself. When am I ever going to accept things as they are?*

The words of Psalm 103:2 crossed her mind: *"Bless the LORD, O my soul, and forget not all his benefits."* It was a timely reminder of God's faithfulness and the hope she had in Him. Heidi remembered one of their ministers saying recently that every believer should spend time naming the ways God had been good to them. This act would offer encouragement during times when things appeared bleak. He also said, "As God has been faithful to us in the past, His love for us will continue in the future. Reminding ourselves of God's goodness will keep us filled with His peace."

Heidi bowed her head and closed her eyes. *Heavenly Father, thank You for the reminder of Your faithfulness and love. Help me remember all the blessings You have bestowed on me in the past and will continue to provide in the future. Amen.*

She was on the verge of having a small bowl of the stew, when a noisy ruckus broke out on the lawn. *Groink. . .Groink. . .Arf! Arf! Arf!*

She hurried to the window and gasped. Rusty and six hefty hogs ran in circles through the freshly mowed grass. "*Ach*, the neighbor's pigs must have gotten out of their pen!"

Heidi turned off the stove, grabbed two apples from the fruit bowl on the table, and rushed out the back door. She'd seen her father lure pigs into their pen a good many times when she was a girl. Hopefully, using fruit like he did would entice them to follow her back to their owner's home.

Chapter 28

Heidi was halfway to the neighbors' house with the pigs when she saw Lyle's horse and buggy coming down the road. He must have spotted her then, too, for he pulled over to the side of the road, hopped out, and tied the horse to a fence post. "What's going on?" he called, cupping his hands around his mouth.

"The neighbors' pigs got out. Rusty was chasing them all around our yard." Moving toward Lyle, Heidi showed him the apples she held. "I'm luring them home with these."

He chuckled, slapping his knee as he got behind the pigs and cheered them on. Soon, they were back where they belonged and locked securely in their pen. Since the neighbors weren't home, Lyle said he would tell them about it in the morning. He smiled at Heidi and motioned to his horse and buggy. "Hop in, and I'll give you a ride back home."

She did as he suggested, reaching over to touch his arm after he'd untied the horse and they'd both taken a seat. "Danki for your help with the *sei*. Those rambunctious critters can be a handful when they're all stirred up, and our faithful dog didn't help things any with all the barking he did."

"Where's the *hund* now?" Lyle glanced around before clucking to the horse to get him moving down the road.

Heidi pointed in the direction of their house. "As soon as you showed up with the horse and buggy, he made a beeline for home."

Lyle snickered. "Guess he figured I might holler at him for being out of the yard."

"That's quite likely," Heidi agreed. "So how'd things go at the auction?"

"They went well, and there was a good turnout. How was your day?"

"Okay. I got lots done, and I hope your *hungerich*, because I made a pot of stew, and it's keeping warm on the stove."

Lyle thumped his stomach and grinned. "You know me... Always ready to enjoy a good meal."

Heidi placed her hand on his knee and gave it a tender squeeze. Her husband's humor and pleasant attitude were reminders that she'd chosen well when she married him.

"Say, this is a pretty good meal. What's it called?" Lance's brother smacked his lips.

"It's Chicken in a Crumb Basket. The Amish woman I told you about taught me how to make it during the last cooking class." Lance put some coleslaw on his plate and handed the bowl to Dan. "There's something I need to talk to you about."

"Oh? What's up?"

"There's a young woman named Lisa who's also taking the cooking classes, and..." Lance paused and took a quick drink of water. "Anyway, Lisa owns a duplex in Dover. She lives in one side and rents the other one out."

Dan grabbed a pickle and plopped it on his plate. "That's nice, but why are you telling me this?"

"The thing is. . . Well, Lisa's previous tenants moved out unexpectedly, and now she's looking for someone else to rent or lease the place to."

"I'm still not sure why you're mentioning this."

Lance clutched his fork tightly. Did he need to draw his brother a picture? "I thought you might want to take a look at it—maybe rent the duplex."

Dan's brows furrowed. "What for? I own a townhouse, you know."

"Yeah, but it won't be ready for several more months."

"That's okay. Thanks to your generosity, I have a place to stay."

Lance briefly closed his eyes, taking a deep breath. This wasn't going as well as he hoped. Should he come right out and tell his brother that he wanted him to move, or would it be better to let Dan figure it out himself? All Lance knew was he couldn't put up with his brother's irritating habits and inconsiderate actions much longer.

He drew a quick breath and decided to try again, using a more direct approach this time. "I think it might be better for both of us if we weren't sharing the same house."

"I shoulda known this was coming." Dan slumped in his chair. "You're still mad 'cause I painted the kitchen beige without asking you, huh?"

"It's not just the kitchen or the TV you replaced my old one with. We don't see eye-to-eye on many things, and it'd be best if we had our own space."

Dan pressed his lips together. "Wow, I've only been here a short time, and have already worn out my welcome." He pushed his chair back and rose from the table. "Well, don't give it another thought. I'll find someplace else to live till my townhouse is ready. Sorry I've been such a bother to you."

Lance groaned inwardly. He'd offended his brother, and now he felt like a heel. "Listen, Dan, you're not a bother."

"Sure sounds like it to me."

"Okay, look, I'll be the first to admit, I'm set in my ways. Since Flo died I've established somewhat of a routine, and havin' you here has upset my applecart. If you don't want to look at Lisa's duplex, that's fine by me. We'll continue with our arrangement until your place is ready."

Dan gave a firm shake of his head. "No, you're right. It'd be better if we weren't sharing a home. We may be brothers, but we've always been different as nighttime and daylight. If you want to set up a day and time with your friend Lisa, I'll take a look at her place."

Lance wasn't sure if Dan had given in merely to keep the peace, or if he actually felt he'd be better off living on his own. No matter, though. Dan had agreed to look at the duplex, so tomorrow morning they'd head over there and see if anything could be arranged. One thing Lance hadn't mentioned, though, was that he'd promised to help Lisa with anything that needed to be fixed. He'd make sure Dan knew about it before they got to Lisa's place, though, because he figured his brother should help, too.

Lance tapped his chin. *On second thought, it might be better if I wait till we get to Lisa's to mention the work that needs to be done. I'll be harder for Dan to say no in Lisa's company.*

Canton

Todd had finished eating a fried egg sandwich for his evening meal, when his cell phone rang. Seeing it was his mother, he almost didn't answer. But if he ignored her too long, she'd only keep calling and leaving him long messages, which really got on his nerves.

Todd swiped his thumb across the front of his phone. "Hi, Mom. How are you?"

"I'm well, and so is your father. We haven't heard from you in a while and wondered how you're doing."

"Doin' okay. Keeping plenty busy with work and other things."

"I figured as much." There was a brief pause. "Listen, the main reason I'm calling is to see if you plan to be here for Thanksgiving weekend."

Todd glanced at his calendar. Thanksgiving was still a few weeks away. "Probably not, Mom."

"How come?" He could hear the disappointment in her voice.

"I have other plans."

"Oh, I see. So what are your plans for Thanksgiving?"

The truth was, Todd had no holiday plans but hoped he and Lisa might get together that day. He wanted to go out with her a few more times before he asked, though, and didn't want her to think he was moving too fast. The last thing he wanted to do was lay out money for a plane ticket to see his folks and spend Thanksgiving listening to Mom pick apart everything he said and did. Her constant badgering was one of the reasons he'd moved away. The offer to write a food column for the newspaper here had come at just the right time.

"Todd, did you hear what I said?"

"Yeah, sure, Mom. You asked what my plans are for Thanksgiving."

"And?"

"I'm seeing someone I met recently, so. . ."

"You're dating again?"

"Yeah. Sort of."

"I'm happy to hear this, Son. After the breakup with Felicia, I wasn't sure you'd ever want to date again."

Todd put the phone on speaker and moved over to the sink to rinse his dishes. "Can we talk about something else? I'd rather not rehash all that went down with my ex-girlfriend."

"Whatever you wish. Is it all right if I ask a few questions about your new girlfriend?"

"Sure, but right now we're just friends. I'm not sure how she feels about me yet."

"Then why are you spending Thanksgiving with her?"

Todd lifted his gaze to the ceiling. If he didn't hang up soon, this could turn into a session of twenty-plus questions. "I enjoy Lisa's company, and—"

"Lisa who? What's her last name, Todd?"

"Brooks."

"Did you meet her at work, or is she another woman you met on one of those Internet dating sites?"

"I haven't been doing anymore online dating. Once was enough. I met Lisa at a cooking class I've been taking, hosted by an Amish woman who lives in Walnut Creek." Todd moved back to the table and took a seat.

"Cooking classes? An Amish woman?" Mom's voice raised nearly an octave. "Since when did you decide to learn how to cook, and why take lessons from an Amish woman? I'm sure she's not a gourmet chef."

"Of course not, but she's an excellent cook and is teaching us to make some traditional Amish dishes."

"How many others are taking the class?"

"There are six of us. Three men and three women. We meet every other Saturday for a total of six classes."

"Hmm. . . Interesting."

Todd glanced at his watch. In three minutes one of his favorite shows would be coming on TV. "Sorry, Mom but I have to hang up now. Thanks for calling, and tell Dad I said hello."

"All right, Son. I'll talk to you again soon. Oh, and it'd be nice if you called us for a change."

"Okay, Mom. Bye." Todd clicked off the phone. He wished his mother hadn't brought up the topic of his breakup with Felicia. It was a bitter pill, and he wanted to put it behind him. Hopefully, if he and Lisa's relationship developed further, she wouldn't betray him the way Felicia had.

Chapter 29

Dover

Thank you both so much. I appreciate all the help you gave me this morning." Lisa smiled at Lance and his brother as they sat at her kitchen table, eating the lunch she'd prepared. When they'd first gotten here and she'd shown them the duplex, Dan hadn't seemed that interested in the place. Now, however, as he gobbled down some of her homemade chicken noodle soup, he talked about moving in and said he looked forward to being able to spread out.

Dan glanced at Lance with eyes slightly narrowed. "This way I won't be in anybody's way."

Lance ignored the comment and grabbed a roll, slathering it with butter.

Sensing a bit of discord between the men, Lisa handed Lance a jar of apple butter and changed the subject. "Are you looking forward to our next cooking class with Heidi?"

His eyes brightened as he nodded. "The last recipe she taught us to make was good, but I'm hoping for some kind of dessert I can make for Thanksgiving or even Christmas."

"That would be nice. I cater a lot of parties during the holidays, so I'm always looking for new pie, cake, or cookie recipes to try."

"Bet your business is doing well." Dan wiped his mouth on a napkin. "Because this chicken soup you made is sure good."

"Thank you. It's an old family recipe, handed down from my great-grandmother."

"My wife, Flo, used to make good soup. She taught our daughters how to cook well, too." Lance rubbed his hand against his chest, where his heart would be. "Sure do miss her."

Lisa felt like leaving her seat and giving him a hug, but she held back. Except for the times they'd met at Heidi's classes, she didn't know Lance well and thought he might not appreciate a hug from a near stranger. "Loss is hard," she murmured. "It's good you have other family around."

"Yeah." He bumped Dan's arm with his elbow. "I may not always show it or think to express my feelings, but I do appreciate you, Brother."

"Same here. Even though we have our differences, when the chips are down, I know I can count on you."

Lisa's cell phone rang from the living room, so she excused herself to answer it. She took a seat on the couch. "Hello."

"Hi, Lisa, it's Todd. I hope you aren't busy."

"I was having lunch with Lance and his brother, Dan."

"Lance Freemont from our cooking class?"

"Yes. He brought Dan over this morning to look at my rental, and since they helped me with a few repairs, I fixed them lunch."

"Wow, if I'd known having lunch with you would be the reward, I'd have volunteered to come help myself."

She snickered. "And miss work?"

"You're right, I do need to write an article for the paper, but I get a lunchbreak, which I'm taking right now, in fact."

"If you were closer to Dover, I'd invite you to join us."

"That'd be nice, but since I'm not, how about dinner tonight?"

"You want to join me here for dinner?"

"I was thinking of taking you out for another meal." He laughed. "I'm a pretty direct person, but I'd never invite myself to anyone's house, expecting them to cook for me."

"Actually, I'd be happy to fix you a meal, but tonight I'm busy."

"Oh, I see." She heard the disappointment in Todd's voice.

"I'm catering a friend's baby shower this evening, so I won't even have time for a decent dinner myself." Lisa heard laughter coming from the kitchen and smiled. It sounded like the brothers were getting along well, and she was glad. She'd be most happy to have a brother or sister. She hoped Lance and Dan knew how fortunate they were.

"Are you still there, Lisa?"

"Uh, yeah. I need to finish eating, but can we get together for dinner some other night this week—maybe Friday or Saturday?"

"Saturday would work for me."

"Okay, see you at six o'clock that evening. Oh, and plan on eating here this time. I'll fix something special."

"Sounds good, Lisa. See you Saturday."

When Lisa hung up, she sat several seconds, thinking about Todd. Based on some things he'd said during one of the cooking classes, she wasn't sure if he was a Christian or not. She needed to find out soon, before their relationship went any further.

New Philadelphia

After leaving work that afternoon, Allie picked the kids up from school, then went to the bank. As she headed for home, with Nola and Derek talking quietly in the backseat for a change, her thoughts went to Steve. She couldn't believe he'd worked past midnight both Sunday and Monday. Allie had tried talking to him about it this morning, before she took the kids to school, but he'd been evasive. Something had to be going on, and she was determined to get to the bottom of it, once and for all. It wasn't fair of Steve to cause her to worry and wonder like this. Tonight, when he came home—no matter what time it was—she would insist they sit down and have a little talk.

"Mommy, can we take Trouble for a walk when we get home?" Derek's question pushed Allie's thoughts aside.

"We'll see. I need to put a roast in the oven for supper, and you two need to change into your play clothes before we do anything else."

"Can we have cookies and milk?" Nola asked.

"Yes, we'll take time for a snack. Afterward, you can play in the yard with the dog until I'm free to take a walk with you."

"Okay, Mommy," the children said in unison.

Allie smiled. It was good to see them both in pleasant moods, with no teasing or quarrelling. There were times when the kids sat in the back of the van picking on each other until they reached their destination. Nothing got on Allie's nerves more than that.

The grocery store was up ahead, and Allie decided to stop and pick up a few things she needed. "Let's go kids." Allie parked the van and opened the door. "We are going to make a quick trip inside, then we'll go straight home and take care of Trouble."

Once inside, Allie and the kids scooted down each aisle. She was glad her children kept up with her. Rounding the cart to the next aisle, Allie spotted another mother whose daughter was in her son's class. *Oh, fiddle. I was hoping I wouldn't run into anybody. I don't want to take the time for idle chitchat.*

Allie tried to look away, in hopes she wouldn't be seen, but it was too late. Tammy Brubaker approached her cart.

"Nola and Derek, I want you each to pick out a box of cereal you'd like to get while I say hello to Mrs. Brubaker." Allie didn't want to be rude, and hopefully she could make this conversation short.

"Hi, Allie." Tammy smiled. "I haven't seen you in a while."

"Hi, yourself. And yes, it has been a while."

"How are you and your family doing?"

Allie gave a quick rundown and mentioned the puppy she'd recently gotten for the kids. Then Tammy asked how Steve was doing.

"He's good, but his job keeps him from home a good deal of the time."

"I'll bet. Having a job as a police officer, well. . . I'm sure there is never a lull." Tammy pushed her long auburn hair away from her face.

"You're right about that." Allie wished she could find a way to end their conversation, but it would be impolite. The last thing she wanted to talk about with Tammy was Steve or his job.

"Come to think of it," Tammy continued. "I saw Steve recently, when I went to get a cup of coffee at the little café in the mall."

"Oh?"

"Yes. I was parking my car, but didn't get a chance to talk with him, though. He was leaving with a fellow officer. A nice-looking lady with blond hair." Tammy pulled a jar of pickles off the nearest shelf and placed it in her shopping cart. "She looked too young to be a police officer, but then, these days it's hard to tell a person's age."

Allie tensed up, and no words would come. Call it good timing, but she was thankful when the children came running back with their choices of cereal. Did Tammy suspect something was going on between Steve and Lori? If so, Allie hoped she wouldn't mention it to anyone.

"I'm sorry Tammy, but we really have to run." Allie put the cereal boxes in the cart. "The puppy has been home alone all day, and I'm sure we'll have a mess to clean up in his cage." As she pushed the shopping cart toward the front of the aisle, Allie looked over her shoulder and hollered, "It was nice talking to you."

Allie didn't care about the curious expression on Tammy's face. All she wanted to do was get out of that store, take the kids home to care for Trouble, put the groceries away, and start supper. The busier she kept, the more it would help her anger to keep from bubbling over. The last thing Allie had wanted to hear was news of Steve being seen with that blond—especially learning such a thing from someone else.

After making sure the kids were buckled in, Allie got into the minivan. *Now calm down,* she told herself. *It doesn't do any good for you to get so upset—especially when you have no proof of anything.* But the image of Steve and his blond partner having coffee in that cute little café remained in Allie's head.

Millersburg

As Bill headed across the school's parking lot to his truck, he spotted Nicole walking in the direction of the buses waiting to pick kids up. For the first time since he'd met the young woman, he noticed a spring to her step. It was an even bigger surprise to see her walking beside another teenage girl, talking and laughing.

I bet she's in a good mood today 'cause she found out some of her workload will be lifted by having a weekly housekeeper. Bill grinned. It felt good to do something nice for a person in need, even if he didn't know her well. It had been hard to part with the money Bill had been saving for a trip to Alaska he wanted to take, but he had waited this long to go and could wait awhile longer. Besides, he had his upcoming hunting trip to look forward to and the hope of bagging a big buck this year. Bill could almost see a beautiful pair of antlers hanging on the wall in his cabin in Coshocton.

He turned back toward the buses and saw Nicole wave to her friend. Then she started walking down the sidewalk. Bill was tempted to go talk to her, but thought better of it. She might be embarrassed to have anyone see her talking to the school's head janitor. Well, that was okay. He'd talk to Nicole at Heidi's next cooking class. He was curious to hear how things were going for her in school now that she'd been given more time to study.

New Philadelphia

Allie finished putting the roast in the oven and had gone to the kitchen window to check on the kids and the dog, when she saw Steve's SUV pull into the yard. Over and over she told herself, *Keep calm, Allie. Keep calm and don't say anything out of anger or start making accusations.*

When Steve came in, the first thing he did was give Allie a kiss. But before she could ask him any questions, he told her about an unwed woman he'd arrested today for child abuse.

Steve shook his head. "It was sad to see her three kids taken from her, but they'll be better off in foster care."

"What a shame." Allie felt bad for those unfortunate children, as well as for the mother who desperately needed help. Every child deserved to grow up in a stable, happy environment.

Steve ambled across the kitchen and poured himself a cup of coffee. "There are so many kids in the system these days who need good foster parents. Too bad we're not able to take one or two children in."

Allie nodded. "It would be nice, but with both of our jobs, plus caring for our own kids, it's not feasible."

"You're probably right." He drank his coffee and set his mug in the sink. "I talked to the kids before I came inside. They want us to take them and the dog for a walk. Are you free to go with us?"

"I did tell them I would walk the dog, but now that you're here, I'd like us to talk for a bit."

"No problem. We can do that while we're walking."

She shook her head. "What I have to say is not for the kids to hear."

He leaned against the cabinet, folding his arms. "Okay. What's up?"

"I want to know why you're always working late. And I want you to explain—"

Steve held up his hand. "I work late because I have to, Allie. We've had this discussion many times, and unless you want to start an argument and ruin the whole evening, there's nothing more to say— end of story. Now let's get our jackets on and join Nola and Derek."

She heaved a sigh. "Give me a few minutes to change into my sweatpants, and I'll be ready to go."

When Allie walked into the bedroom, she stared at her image in the mirror. Pulling her thick, curly hair away from her face, she secured it with a clip. "I'm not a bad-looking person," she mumbled to her reflection. Running her fingers over her cheekbones, it pleased Allie to have such soft skin. Having an olive-tone complexion, with no wrinkles other than a few laugh lines around the corners of her eyes, gave her a younger-than-thirty appearance. *Steve should be satisfied with me. I'm a good mother, and I do my best to look nice for him.*

She massaged her temples, trying to gain relief from a headache. *Why does Lori Robbins have to be so cute? She can't be much younger than me. Does Steve find her more attractive than I am? Would he rather spend time with Lori than his wife and children?*

Allie turned sideways and ran her hand over her flat stomach. One would never know she had two children. Her arms and legs were toned, too.

She drew a deep, cleansing breath. *Why am I doing this to myself?*

What am I afraid of? Steve and I have a good marriage and two wonderful kids. I need to stop dwelling on all this, or I'll end up causing problems in our marriage. I knew soon after I married Steve, his being a police officer would not be easy. She pinched her cheeks. *Come on, girl—toughen up.*

"Hey, Allie, hurry up! The kids and puppy are raring to go," Steve yelled from downstairs.

"I'm on my way!" With one last look in the mirror, Allie stuck her tongue out at herself and, as if she were a child needing to be scolded, added, "Shame on you. Now go enjoy the evening with your family. Isn't this outing what you've been hoping for?"

Allie felt a little better when she headed outside to go for their walk. If Steve refused to listen to her concerns, there wasn't much she could do. But one thing was certain: Allie planned to keep an eye on things. It truly wasn't Steve she was worried about, though. It was the blond-haired cop. She had too much at stake to let some other woman steal her husband away.

Chapter 30

Walnut Creek

After Heidi got the mail Saturday morning, she decided to stop at the phone shack to check for messages that may have come in since last evening. She was pleased to find one from her mother, inviting her and Lyle to Middlefield for Thanksgiving. It had been a while since Heidi visited her folks, and she looked forward to going. Hopefully, Lyle hadn't already made plans with his parents for that day. She would wait and check with him before responding to Mom's phone message.

She listened to the rest of the messages and wrote down those that were important, then stepped out of the phone shack, pausing briefly to breathe in the fresh morning air.

Heidi was almost up to the house when a car pulled in. She recognized the vehicle, and waved when Kendra got out and took the baby from the car. How wonderful it was to see them again.

"I was hoping you'd be home." Kendra smiled when she joined Heidi near the front porch. "Do you have time to visit?"

"Of course." Heidi gestured to the infant held snuggly in Kendra's arms. "How's my little namesake doing?"

"She's getting along well—gaining the weight she should, too. And as long as she's fed and diapered regularly, my sweet little Heidi is a satisfied baby."

"That's good to hear." Heidi gestured to the house. "Let's go inside where it's warmer."

Kendra followed Heidi into the house, and they found seats in the living room. With a great sense of longing, Heidi gazed at Kendra's precious daughter. *I will not allow myself to feel jealous.* "How are things going now with you and your parents?" she asked. "Any better?"

"Unfortunately, about the same as when I was here before. Dad's still impatient, and Mom—well, she keeps reminding me to keep the baby quiet when Dad's in the house because Heidi's crying gets on his nerves." Kendra's shoulders lifted as she released a deep sigh. "I wish I could get out on my own, but there's no way I can afford to rent a place right now. Maybe when I'm feeling strong enough to look for a job, but then there's the matter of finding someone to watch the baby while I'm at work."

"Won't your mother take care of her granddaughter?" Heidi couldn't imagine Kendra's mother being unwilling to watch the baby. Most grandmothers she knew looked for excuses to be with their grandchildren.

"She probably would take care of the baby, as long it was during the day, when Dad's at work. If I worked during the evening hours, it could be a problem, though."

Heidi was tempted to ask Kendra why her father had agreed to let her move back home if he had no patience with a little one. Instead, she held out her arms. "May I hold the baby?"

"Sure." Kendra handed the infant to Heidi.

She moved from the couch to the rocker and got it moving back and forth as she stroked the infant's silky head. *I shouldn't do this,* Heidi told herself. *Holding Kendra's daughter only increases my desire for a child and makes me wish this little girl was mine.*

Heidi sucked in her bottom lip. It wasn't right to envy, but despite her best efforts, she couldn't seem to help herself. Then the words of Hebrews 13:5 came to mind: *"Let your conversation be without covetousness; and be content with such things as ye have: for [Jesus] hath said, I will never leave thee, nor forsake thee."*

Heidi paused to thank God for the reminders found in His Word, for she certainly had much in her life to bring contentment—a wonderful husband, loving parents, good health, and special friends. Those were the things she needed to focus on and feel thankful for.

———— •⟨ ∘⊙∘ ⟩• ————

Dover

Lisa rushed about the kitchen, getting things ready for dinner with Todd. She felt relaxed and at ease with the world today. Having a renter in the other half of the duplex again would be nice, and since Dan had no pets, she wouldn't have to worry about the place becoming a mess.

Lisa lifted the lid on the crockpot and inhaled the zesty aroma. "Yum. If this smells even half as good as it tastes, I think Todd will be impressed."

Her cell phone rang, and thinking it might be Todd, she hurried across the room to pick it up. Seeing in the caller ID window that it was her mother calling, she quickly answered. "Hi, Mom. How are you?"

"I'm fine, honey. How are things going with you?"

"Doing well." Lisa put the phone in speaker mode and began to set the table.

"Are you busy right now? I hear some clinging and clanging going on."

Lisa laughed. "Todd's coming over for dinner this evening, and I'm setting the table."

"Oh, I see. One of these days you'll have to bring your new fellow by the house so your dad and I can meet him."

"How about Thanksgiving? It would be a good chance for you both to get to know him." Lisa rubbed an itchy spot on the side of her nose. The truth was, she didn't know Todd all that well yet, either.

"You haven't invited him to join us yet, I hope."

"No, Mom, but I thought—"

"In all honesty, I would prefer it just be our family this year. I hope you understand."

No, I don't understand. Her mother's request made no sense to Lisa. In times past, they'd invited many different guests to share their Thanksgiving meal. Why should it be any different this year? "Okay, that's fine," she murmured. "Todd may have other plans for the holiday anyway, and I haven't mentioned Thanksgiving to him."

"I'm glad you're agreeable. We'll see you then, and feel free to come a little early." Mom's tone sounded chipper. Since Lisa kept so busy with her business, she didn't get to see her folks as often as she used to. Maybe that was the reason they wanted her all to themselves this holiday. If her relationship with Todd kept going, Lisa would make sure Mom and Dad got to meet him.

When Todd entered Lisa's kitchen, he lifted his nose and inhaled deeply. "Something sure smells good in here. What have you got cooking?"

She smiled, pointing to the crockpot on the counter. "I made lemon chicken, a tossed green salad, steamed brown rice, and brussels sprouts cooked in coconut oil and fresh garlic."

He jiggled his brows. "Sounds pretty good so far."

Lisa poked his arm. "What do you mean, so far?"

He gave her a kiss on the cheek. "I'm wondering about dessert."

"I made a banana cream pie. How's that sound to you?"

"I like banana cream pie, but I bet it won't taste half as good as your sweet lips." Todd kissed her again, this time a gentle kiss on the mouth. He'd been right. Lisa's kiss was sweet as honey.

Her cheeks colored, and she pushed him gently away. "You're such a big flirt."

"I'm not flirting; I'm serious."

"I'm flattered by the compliment, but now it's time to eat." She gestured to the table. It had been set with fancy dishes and shiny goblets. There was even a scented candle in the middle, surrounded by a small autumn-colored wreath. "Now, if you'll please take a seat, I'll serve the meal."

"Is there anything I can do to help?"

She shook her head. "It won't take me long to set things on, so just sit and relax."

Todd obliged. Being here in Lisa's kitchen was nicer than going out to a restaurant, and much more relaxed. He could get used to spending time with her like this.

After everything was on the table, Lisa took the seat beside him and bowed her head. "Would you like to say the blessing, or should I?"

Todd squirmed uncomfortably in his chair. He hadn't expected she would ask him to pray. Truth was, he wouldn't know what to say. "Uh. . .why don't you do the honors?"

Todd sat with his eyes partially open as Lisa offered a prayer, thanking God for the food and the opportunity to be with Todd this evening. He couldn't help feeling a bit guilty for sticking her with saying grace, but he had not offered any kind of a prayer since he was a boy. And then it was only when he'd spent time with his grandparents, who prayed at every meal. Todd still remembered how Grandma used to make everyone at her table take turns saying a prayer. When it was his turn, he would hurriedly say a little prayer he'd memorized. "God is good. God is great. And I thank Him for this food. Amen." He'd feel pretty foolish if he recited that prayer in front of Lisa, though. It was best that she offered the blessing.

As they ate their meal, Todd's taste buds came alive. The succulent chicken all but melted in his mouth, and the brussels sprouts were done to perfection. "I'm duly impressed with your culinary skills." He gave her a thumbs-up. "Everything tastes superb."

Once more, Lisa's cheeks turned rosy as she nodded her head. "Why, thank you, sir. I am pleased that you like what I cooked for you this evening."

"I'm sorry I misjudged your abilities based on what you fixed for my friends' wedding."

She wrinkled her petite little nose. "Please, let's not go there again."

"Okay." He winked at her and reached for another helping of chicken.

After the meal was over, Todd helped Lisa clear the table and load the dishwasher. Then they went to the living room and spent the next couple of hours visiting.

"Are you ready for some pie?" Lisa rose from the couch. "And how about a cup of coffee to go with it?"

Todd smacked his lips. "Both sound good. Need some help getting it out?"

"Thanks anyway, but I can manage. While I'm in the kitchen why don't you turn on the gas fireplace? It's a little chilly in here, and a cozy fire is always nice during an autumn evening."

"Sure thing. I like the whole 'flick a switch and instant flames' thing. It beats dealing with messy wood and ashes you have to clean out of a wood-burning fireplace, like my grandparents have."

She took a few steps toward the kitchen, but paused and turned to look at him. "Do they live in the area?"

"Nope. Both sets of my grandparents live in Oregon, not far from my folks."

"I bet you miss them."

"Yeah, but I enjoy my independence, so the positive outweighs the negative."

Lisa turned and headed to the kitchen. Todd figured she probably thought it was strange that he'd chosen not to live close to his family. A slight muscle jumped in his cheek as he moved across the room to turn on the fireplace. *Well, if she knew my mom, she might understand. Not everyone has a good relationship with their family.*

Once the fire was going, and he'd set the remote for it to a nice, even temperature, Todd took a seat on the couch again, to wait for Lisa. She returned shortly, carrying a tray with two pieces of pie and coffee mugs, which she placed on the small table in front of the sofa.

"Here we go. Please, help yourself."

Todd didn't have to be asked twice. Just looking at the banana cream pie, he knew he was in for a treat. After taking his first bite, Todd smiled and took hold of Lisa's hand. "This pie is awesome. Not quite as sweet as your lips, but a close second."

She lifted her gaze to the ceiling. "You're incorrigible."

He snickered. "Just trying to be honest."

As they ate their pie and drank the coffee, Lisa told Todd a little about her family. They also visited about the cooking classes and agreed that they'd be sorry to see them come to an end. While the classes might be winding down soon, Todd hoped he'd have the chance to keep seeing Lisa. She was different than any woman he'd ever met, and he wanted the opportunity to see if their relationship could deepen.

When it came time for Todd to leave, Lisa walked him to the door. With no hesitation, he pulled her into his arms for a lingering kiss.

"Before you go, I have a question to ask," Lisa said breathlessly.

"Sure. Ask me anything you like."

"I was wondering if you'd like to attend church with me tomorrow morning. Maybe we can go out for a bite to eat afterward."

He bit down on his bottom lip. *Oh, great. Now why'd you have to go and ruin our nice evening? Do I try to weasel my way out of going or cave in and give church a try?*

"Todd, did you hear what I said?"

"Umm. . .yeah."

Lisa tipped her head and looked up at him. "Yeah, you'll go to church, or yeah, you heard my question?"

"Both."

She smiled and gave him a hug. "I'll see you tomorrow then. Church starts at ten thirty, so if you could pick me up at ten, that'd be perfect. Unless you'd rather I give you the church's address and we can just meet there."

He shook his head. "No, I'd rather pick you up. See you then." He leaned down, gave her another kiss, and rushed out the door. *I must be out of my mind.*

The next morning, when Todd took a seat on a church pew with Lisa, he looked around the sanctuary and cringed. *How did I get talked into this? The only reason I agreed to come here is so I could spend more time with Lisa. Plus, I didn't want her to think I'm not interested in religion, which she obviously is. Why'd I have to choose a woman who's into spiritual things?*

Todd stuck a finger inside his shirt collar to loosen it a bit. Looking at all the people with their holier-than-thou expressions made his stomach tighten. He'd gone to church a few times with his previous girlfriend, and where had that gotten him? A kick in the teeth—that's what. Felicia, with the sweet smile and pearly white teeth, may have pretended to be a Christian, but her actions proved louder than her words. Would Lisa do the same?

Todd glanced over at her, sitting beside him with a pleasant smile, while reading the church bulletin they'd received from an elderly greeter when they first entered the church. Was she a true Christian in every sense of the word?

I need to quit thinking about this, and let Lisa prove herself. Todd didn't know why it bothered him so much, because he was far from being a Christian, but anyone who professed to be one should act like it.

Turning his attention to the front of the room, Todd forced his thoughts aside and tried to concentrate on the announcements being made. According to what was written in the bulletin, they still had singing, scriptures, offering, and a sermon to get through. He gave his shirt collar a tug. *Sure hope I can sit here that long.*

———————⸱❧⸱———————

As they drove toward the restaurant of Lisa's choice after church, Lisa watched him, wondering what was going through his mind. He hadn't joined in when the songs were sung during the service today. Todd seemed distracted, glancing at his cell phone several times throughout much of the pastor's message. Was he bored, preoccupied, or just didn't enjoy the kind of worship service she was used to? Lisa wrapped her fingers around her purse straps, squeezing tightly. *Maybe I shouldn't have invited him to join me today.*

Looking out the window as they drove outside of town, she was finally able to relax as she gazed at the countryside. It was the end of October, and winter would soon be creeping in. Today's weather reminded her of that. It had dipped into the twenties overnight, and so far, she realized, glancing at the thermometer reading on the car's dashboard, it was barely in the thirties.

Todd's vehicle had tight quarters and no backseat, but it was nice and cozy in his little car, since it heated up faster than her minivan.

Continuing to watch out the passenger window, Lisa admired the huge farm they were passing. Cows stood bunched together around a feeding trough, and vapor coming from their nostrils resembled smoke drifting into the air. The good news was, according to the local weather channel, this cold spell would be short lived. Even though she loved the holidays, Lisa wasn't sure she was ready for winter.

She reached across the seat and gently tapped Todd's arm. "Can I ask you a question?"

"Sure."

"Did you enjoy being in church with me today?"

A muscle on the side of Todd's neck quivered. "I enjoyed being with you. Just not in church."

She pulled her hand back. "How come?"

He sucked in his bottom lip. "I should have been straight with you before, Lisa. I'm not a religious man."

"Are. . .are you an atheist?"

"No, but I don't believe in prayer and all that sort of thing. I think religion is for people who can't stand on their own." He lifted his chin. "I'm a self-made man, and I don't need any help from God in order to make it through life."

"I see." A shiver ran up the back of Lisa's neck as the words of 2 Corinthians 6:14 came to mind: *"Be ye not unequally yoked together with unbelievers."* She should have suspected Todd wasn't a Christian because he'd shown no evidence of it. He was good looking, charming, intelligent, and said all the right things to turn a woman's head, but that wasn't enough—not for Lisa, anyway. She needed a man who loved God as much as she did and wanted to serve Him with his whole heart.

Lisa drew in a deep breath. "So if you feel this way, why'd you agree to go to church with me this morning?"

"I wanted to be with you, and I didn't want you to think—"

"Todd, I don't think we should see each other socially anymore."

He looked at her, then turned his head back to the road ahead. "You're shutting me out because I can't buy into religion?"

"I'm not shutting you out. I just don't want to continue in a relationship that can never go anywhere."

"That's stupid. I like you, Lisa—a lot, in fact, and I'm pretty sure you feel the same about me."

She couldn't deny the feelings she'd begun to have for Todd, but a clean break was the best, for both of them. "Sorry, but I won't be going out with you again." Lisa was glad now that her mother had discouraged her from inviting Todd to Thanksgiving dinner. *I wonder if Mom suspects the guy I've been dating is not a Christian.*

Chapter 31

Walnut Creek

With arms folded, Heidi looked at the calendar on the kitchen wall. Today was the first Saturday of November, and she would soon be teaching the fourth cooking class in this series. With her fluctuating emotions during the first three classes, she hoped she'd made herself clear enough and that everyone had understood the directions she'd given them for the recipes they'd made so far. More than that, Heidi hoped the verses she'd written on the back of each person's card had been meaningful to one or more of them. She hadn't done much actual mentoring during the classes—at least not the way her Aunt Emma did during her quilting classes. But if the scriptures Heidi had shared helped anyone at all, she would be satisfied.

Heidi tapped her chin. *Of course, how will I know whether anyone's been helped, unless they say something to me? I certainly can't come right out and ask. That would be like fishing for a compliment, and it would be prideful.*

"I'm ready to head for Millersburg now, Heidi. Is there anything you need me to get while I'm there?"

Lyle's question pulled Heidi out of her musings. "No, I can't think of anything." She snickered. "Something will probably come to mind after you've gone, though. Isn't that the way it usually goes?"

"Jah, it's true." He pulled Heidi into his arms and gave her a firm kiss. "I hope everything goes well with your class today."

"Danki. I hope so, too."

Lyle grabbed his straw hat from the wall peg and slapped it on his head. "See you sometime this afternoon," he called over his shoulder as he headed out the door.

Smiling, Heidi moved over to the cupboard where she kept her baking supplies. Then she took out the ingredients needed to make the apple corn bread she'd be teaching her students to make today. It was an easy recipe and quite tasty—a nice addition to any autumn supper.

After watching out the window as her husband's buggy went down the driveway, Heidi glanced around the section of yard within her vision. So many leaves still needed to be cleaned up, especially where the wind had piled them in corners. "Guess I'll have to get out there soon and get some raking done. Not today, though."

She moved away from the window. The leaves in her flower beds could stay there until the first warm days of spring. It would give the flower bulbs an extra blanket until the coldest weather was done for the season.

She glanced toward the trees in their yard. The only leaves still clinging were on a white oak, which dropped its leaves in the spring. At least the weather had warmed up a bit, and the recent cold snap was over. But with winter coming, things would soon change.

Heidi set everything out on the table, and was about to pour herself a cup of tea, when a knock sounded on the back door. She glanced at the clock. It wasn't quite time for her students to arrive, and normally they wouldn't use the back door.

She hurried to answer it and was surprised to find Loretta Donnelly on her porch in tears. Heidi clutched her friend's hand, leading her inside. "Loretta, what's wrong?"

"It–it's Eli."

"What's wrong with him? Is Eli sick, or has he been hurt?"

Sniffing, Loretta shook her head. "We. . .we had our first disagreement, and I'm afraid my response may have ruined things. Even though I joined the church last Sunday, it might be over between us."

"Come sit down." Heidi hoped none of her students would arrive early and interrupt their conversation, because Loretta obviously needed to talk.

After Heidi fixed a second cup of tea and handed it to her friend, she joined her at the kitchen table. "Now tell me what happened between you and Eli."

Loretta took a sip of tea, then set her cup down. "I had him over to my house for supper last night, and he compared the meat loaf I fixed to one his wife used to make."

Heidi leaned forward, resting her arms on the table. "Is that all there was to it?"

"No. I became upset when he said her meat loaf was similar to mine, but hers was juicier. Eli said his wife was a great cook and he'd never had better meat loaf." Loretta paused long enough to take another sip from her teacup, then she resumed. "This isn't the first time Eli's compared me to her, either. And if he's doing it now, I can only imagine how it would be if we got married." She rolled her shoulders, as if to release some of her tension. "I don't compare Eli to my first husband. Even if I did mentally, I would never say anything to Eli's face. When he makes comparisons between me and his deceased wife, I feel as if I'm not good enough—like I don't measure up."

"Have you explained this to him? Told him the way you feel about things?"

Loretta shook her head. "I was afraid he wouldn't understand my feelings or might not want to talk about it. He's a man of few words, you know."

Heidi placed her hand on Loretta's arm and gave it a loving pat. "Lyle and I have come to know Eli pretty well. I'm almost certain you can share your feelings with him about this."

Hands clasped beneath her chin, Loretta spoke in a trembling voice. "I'll take your advice and try—as soon as I can work up the nerve."

Heidi smiled. "I'll be praying for both of you."

"Thank you. Or should I say, 'Danki?'"

Heidi nodded. "Yes, that's the right word." She was pleased her friend had been making an effort to learn Pennsylvania Dutch. It would certainly help since she was now part of the Amish church.

A knock sounded on the front door, and Heidi jerked her head. "Oh, I bet it's one of my students."

"Sorry, I didn't realize today was one of your cooking classes. I'd better be on my way." Loretta rose from the table and gave Heidi a hug. "Once I've talked to Eli, I'll let you know how things went."

"Jah, please do." Heidi let Loretta out the back door, then she hurried to see who was at her front door.

"Good morning, Heidi. Am I the first one here?" Lance asked when she led the way to her comfortable living room. As usual, the room was tidy—just the way Flo had kept things in their home.

"Yes, you are the first to arrive, but I'm sure the others won't be far behind."

He grinned. "You know, every time I come to your door I feel like I should be delivering a package or something."

"That is how I normally find you on the front porch." Chuckling, Heidi gestured to Lyle's favorite chair. "Why don't you have a seat and relax till the others get here?"

"Thanks. Don't mind if I do." Lance took a seat in the recliner and put the footrest up. "How have you been, Heidi?"

"Fine. How about you?" She seated herself on the couch.

He stretched his arms out wide. "Never better. I feel like I'm on top of the world."

"Did something special happen since you were last here?"

He gave a nod. "You bet! My brother moved out, and I have the whole place to myself again."

"Did he move to the duplex Lisa had for rent?"

"Yep." Lance rubbed his hands together. "Dan and I went over to her place and helped with several repairs while she cleaned the place. He moved in the following day, and even bought a few new pieces of furniture to replace the ones the previous renters had ruined." His smile widened. "Never knew my brother could be so generous. Guess he took a liking to Lisa. She is a pretty sweet gal."

"That's wonderful, but what about your brother's townhouse you'd previously mentioned?" Heidi tipped her head. "Won't it be completed soon?"

"Nope, it doesn't look like it. Things are still going slow with the remodel. I'm guessing my brother will stay in the duplex at least a month—maybe longer."

"I see. Then Lisa will have to look for another renter." Heidi's brows pulled in.

"Yeah, I suppose." Fidgeting in his chair, and feeling a bit guilty for putting Lisa out, Lance looked down at his feet. *Maybe I was too hasty asking Dan to move out. Guess I could have put up with him for another month or so, but our relationship was at stake.* Well, it was too late now. His brother was already moved and temporarily settled. He hoped when Dan moved out of Lisa's duplex, she wouldn't have any trouble finding another renter.

"What are we making today?" Bill asked when everyone gathered around Heidi's kitchen table.

Heidi pointed to the ingredients she'd set out. "Apple corn bread."

"Sounds good." Grinning widely, Bill thumped his belly. "I love apples and most always eat the whole apple—core and all, just not the stem. Some of my buddies tease me about being related to a horse."

Everyone but Lisa and Todd laughed. They'd both been quiet since they'd arrived and had barely glanced at each other. Bill wondered if some sort of issue had developed between them. Well, it was none of his business. He came here to learn how to make something new, not worry about the problems others might be having.

He glanced across the table at Nicole. She seemed more relaxed than usual. With lips slightly parted, and eyes shining brightly, her attention was focused on Heidi's instructions.

"How are things going at school, Nicole?" Bill ventured to ask.

She turned her head in his direction. "Better than before. Think I passed the math test I took yesterday. Course it helped that I had more time to study for it."

"Good for you." Bill was well aware of the reason Nicole had more time to study. He was glad he'd eased things for her by paying for a cleaning lady to come in once a week. He saw it as a blessing to help Nicole and her family out but wondered how she would feel if she knew the gift had come from him.

"Does anyone have a question about this bread before I go on?" Heidi broke into Bill's thoughts.

Allie raised her hand. "Does it matter what kind of apples we use?"

"Not really. The type we are using today is Fuji, but most any apple will do." Heidi handed them each a recipe card. "If you'd like a sweeter-tasting corn bread, then you might want to use a sweeter variety of apple. But if you'd prefer something tarter, I'd suggest Granny Smith apples."

Bill turned over his card. As he expected, Heidi had written another Bible verse on the back. "I am the light of the world: he that followeth me shall not walk in darkness, but shall have the light of life" (John 8:12).

The scriptures their teacher had included on the cards peaked his interest. Especially the one for today. What exactly did it mean to have the "light of life"?

While Todd waited for his corn bread to bake, he alternated between taking notes about Heidi's style of cooking and watching Lisa. His frustration mounted, because Lisa would barely look at him today. He'd said hello when she arrived shortly after he did, but all he'd gotten from her was a brief nod and a mumbled, "Hi." *Why's she so picky about me not being religious, anyway? Can't she just appreciate me for who I am? I'm willing to ignore her religious ways; she should overlook my nonreligious views.*

"What are you writing there?" Lance pointed to Todd's notebook.

"Umm. . ." Todd's face heated. "Just taking some notes."

"You took notes during our last two classes." Lance peered over Todd's shoulder. "What are you up to? Are you writing a book?"

Breathing heavily through his nose and ignoring the man's question, Todd decided to change the subject. "So what's everyone doing for Thanksgiving this year?"

"I've invited my parents, as well as my husband's mom and dad, to our house for the holiday," Allie spoke up. "I just hope Steve doesn't decide to work that day, because most of the work will fall on me if he's not there to help out."

"Won't your parents and in-laws help out?" Lisa questioned.

"I'm sure they would, but Nola and Derek don't get to see their grandparents often enough, so I want our folks to spend as much time with the kids as possible." She tilted her chin down. "Last year we went to my folks' in New York, and because it had snowed the day before, we ended up having a white Thanksgiving. The kids enjoyed being able to play in the snow. My dad even helped them build a snow fort."

"New York usually does get snow early on. Especially if the storms are coming off Lake Erie," Lance chimed in.

Allie got a faraway look in her eyes. "When I was a young girl, I always loved the first snowfall of the year. In fact, I still do."

"Me, too." Bill gave a nod. "Especially when I go up to my cabin to hunt. With snow on the ground, the cabin, the woods—everything looks like a picture postcard."

Todd hadn't expected all this conversation about snow, and he quickly got back on track. "How about you, kid?" He looked at Nicole. "What are your plans for Thanksgiving?"

Her slim shoulders slumped. "We're not having any company, and I'll probably help my dad cook the meal."

"It's good you're taking cooking classes then. Maybe you can fix the bread we're learning to make today to go with your Thanksgiving meal."

Nicole gave no reply to Todd's comment, as she sat staring at the recipe card. The girl had seemed pretty upbeat when she'd first arrived. Todd wondered what had happened between then and now to make her turn sullen.

He looked at Heidi. "The way you cook, I'll bet you're planning a big dinner with all the trimmings. Am I right?"

"Actually, my husband and I will be going to Middlefield to spend

Thanksgiving with my parents. Most of my siblings and their families will be there, too." A wide smile stretched across Heidi's face. "I'll take something to contribute to the meal, of course."

Todd glanced across the table, where Lance sat. "Have you made any big holiday plans?"

"Not yet, but I'm sure to get a dinner invitation from one of my daughters. They take turns each year, alternating whose house the dinner will be at."

"What about you, Lisa?" *If she won't voluntarily talk to me, I'll force her to say something. So far, she'd only been listening to everyone. Surely she won't ignore my question and make herself look bad in front of these people.*

Keeping her focus on her hands, folded in her lap, Lisa murmured, "I'm going to my parents' house, too."

"Good for you." Todd gritted his teeth. *Too bad I wasn't invited. At one time you said you wanted me to meet your folks. How could you change your mind so quickly? Are you gonna let a little thing like religious differences come between us?*

"In case anyone's interested," Todd mumbled, "I'll most likely be spending Thanksgiving alone."

"That's too bad. Don't you have plans to be with your family?" Heidi questioned.

"Nope. They all live in Oregon, and I'm not going there." Todd turned to face Bill. "What are you gonna do for Turkey Day?"

"I'm going deer hunting the Monday after Thanksgiving, so I'll be heading up to my cabin on Thanksgiving Day. I usually start getting the place ready—make sure there's a good fire going in the wood stove and all. Some of my buddies will join me there, but not till the day after Thanksgiving." Bill pointed at Todd's tablet. "You never did say why you're writing stuff down. With Heidi showing us firsthand how to make whatever she's teaching, plus the recipe cards she gives us to take home, I wouldn't think you'd need to take any notes."

Todd's pulse quickened. He set his pen down and crossed his arms. "If you must know, I'm taking notes for an article I'm writing for the newspaper in Canton."

Heidi quirked an eyebrow. "You're writing about my cooking classes?"

He gave a brisk nod. "To be honest, I'm a food critic, and I decided to take this class so I could write about it in my column." There, the truth was out. Now to wait for everyone's reaction—especially Lisa's.

All heads turned in Todd's direction. Some, like Heidi, wore questioning expressions, but the reddening and tightening of Lisa's face let him know she wasn't happy hearing this bit of news.

Heidi's portable timer rang at that moment, and Todd jumped up to get his bread from the oven. *Well, who cares if she's angry or not? I'm glad the truth is finally out, because I don't have to pretend any longer.*

Chapter 32

Lisa could hardly sit in the same room as Todd without letting her annoyance show. Besides his disinterest in religious things, he was a deceiver. *How could I have been so foolish? I should have known by the way he scrutinized everything here and at the restaurants he's taken me to that he had more than a passing interest in the food. I'm glad I won't be seeing him anymore.* She shifted in her chair. *If I'm meant to have a man in my life, there has to be someone out there who's better suited to me.*

She glanced over at Todd as he removed a piece of corn bread from the pan. Not a shred of guilt on his face, or even an apology for misleading Heidi after he'd announced his true profession and admitted the reason he'd signed up for her classes. *I can only imagine what Heidi and the others must be thinking right now as they all sit staring at him.*

Unable to hold her tongue, Lisa left her seat and marched across the room to where Todd stood at the counter after placing his bread on a cooling rack. "How could you be so deceitful?" When he gave no reply, she tapped his shoulder. "The day Heidi first asked each of us what brought us to her cooking classes, why weren't you honest about being a food critic?"

He leaned away from her, creating several inches of space between them. "Don't judge me, Lisa. You're not perfect, you know."

Heat shot up the back of Lisa's neck and quickly spread to her face. "Never said I was." She pointed a finger at him. "But I didn't lie about my reason for taking Heidi's classes. For that matter, I've always tried to be honest and upright."

His nostrils flared. "Wow, I had no idea I'd been going out with a saint. Wasn't I the privileged one, though? I'm surprised you wasted your time with a sinner like me."

Lisa planted her hands against her hips, but before she could offer a retort, Heidi stepped between them. "It would have been nice to know your true reason for being here, Todd, but no harm's been done, and I'm not angry with you."

The hair on the back of Lisa's neck prickled. *Really, Heidi? You're more forgiving than I would be. Guess I'm not living up to my Christianity today.* She pulled in her top lip. *Even if I do forgive Todd, we can never be together. We are unequally yoked.*

After everyone's corn bread had cooled sufficiently, Heidi placed a cube of butter on the table, along with a jar of honey she'd gotten from one of the local beekeepers. "Now it's time for us to sample what we made. Oh, and I have some hot apple cider to go with it."

Bill smacked his lips. "Autumn's the best time to enjoy hot cider. I always take plenty of it when I go to my hunting cabin."

Heidi handed out the prefilled mugs. "I think this cider's the best, because one of our neighbor's makes it with an antique cider press."

Allie lifted her mug and took a sip. "Mmm. . .this is good apple cider."

Lance nodded in agreement.

"The apple corn bread's not bad, either," Nicole added. "Think I might make some for Thanksgiving dinner. I bet Dad would like it, and maybe my sister and brother will, too." Nicole smiled at Heidi. It was nice to see her looking more cheerful again. The other three times Nicole had come to cooking classes, she'd been quiet and sullen. With the exception of Lisa and Todd, everyone seemed to be in good spirits today.

Heidi thought about her previous students, and how some of them had brought their problems to class. She wondered if she should have encouraged Lisa and Todd to air things out. Perhaps she, or one of the other students, would have some good advice to offer these two. But with them being in the middle of cooking, it hadn't seemed appropriate. Now that the lesson was over, if either Lisa or Todd continued with their disagreement, Heidi planned to say something more. If the opportunity didn't arise, she would remember to pray for Todd and Lisa, because as her bishop often said, "Prayer is a powerful tool."

"Is that today's newspaper over there?" Lance pointed to the desk across the room.

Heidi nodded. "Yes, it is."

"I didn't realize you folks subscribed to the paper." He rubbed the back of his neck. "Thought you only read things written by the Amish or specifically for the Amish."

"We read those magazines and papers, as well as the regular newspaper. Lyle likes to keep up with the local and national news."

"There's not much good in the news these days." Bill grunted. "Fact is, I quit subscribing to the paper for that reason. And I really get mad when they put things of importance way back inside the paper instead of on the front page."

"I know what you mean about the news being bad," Lisa chimed in. "Just the other day there was an article about a store that had been robbed and the owner beaten."

"Stuff like that is on the Internet and television news, too," Todd interjected. "Bad stuff happens. Like it or not, it's part of the real world."

Nicole frowned. "Yeah, the real world—that's not always so great. Fact is, most of the things going on in our world stink."

"She's right." Allie's forehead creased. "Last night, when my husband came home, he mentioned three young children who were taken from their mother because of child abuse. It's sad that so many kids in Ohio are waiting for foster homes and in desperate need of someone to care for them. Some of these children are babies, but most are older kids, and many come from abusive situations." Allie slowly shook her head. "It's a shame there aren't more people willing to become foster parents."

Heidi swallowed hard. Maybe she and Lyle should apply to be

foster parents to some needy child. It wouldn't be the same as having a baby of their own, but at least they'd have the satisfaction of helping some poor child in need. When he got home later today, she would talk to him about it.

Canton

After Todd got home from the cooking class, he flopped onto the couch, hoping to relax while he read the newspaper. "Yep," he grumbled, "Bill was right. There's nothing much good in the news these days."

Skimming through the paper, Todd tried to keep his mind off Lisa and how upset she'd gotten with him in cooking class today. His confession about being a food critic had not gone well with her. And now, as he played over some of the things she'd berated him about, Todd wondered if she might be right. "Guess I should have been honest with Heidi, up front." But again, Todd rationalized that he hadn't actually deceived Heidi, or anyone else in the class; he just hadn't told them the truth. His concern was not making a bad impression that first day, or revealing the main reason for attending the class. Taking Heidi's cooking lessons had actually turned into more than Todd expected. He was beginning to get to know everyone, and actually felt more comfortable with some of them than he did his own parents.

It was hard to concentrate on reading the paper. In fact, most of it had become a blur.

Skimming over the local news, though, something familiar caught Todd's attention. A restaurant he had critiqued a while back was going out of business, the article said. He remembered he hadn't given a good review of the place and had criticized several things about the food, as well as the condition of the restaurant.

He continued to read how this family establishment had been in business for a long time, and at the same location since it first opened. The article didn't say why they were closing, but it gave a date when it would last be open. Todd was surprised it would be so soon. The restaurant's final day of business would be this coming Thursday, November 10.

"Maybe I ought to go there." Todd pulled out his cell phone, to check the calendar and make sure he had nothing else going on that day. The tenth was open for him, so he wrote a note to remind himself.

Todd wasn't sure how he would handle the situation, but he was curious to find out the reason they were closing the establishment. Inside, he felt a pang of guilt and hoped his negative critique hadn't brought this restaurant to a close. It had happened one time before, when a new place of business couldn't make a go of things. They'd blamed Todd for the uncomplimentary review he'd written about their hole-in-the-wall restaurant.

"Mind if I come in?" Kendra's sister Shelly poked her head into Kendra's room, where she lay on the bed next to her precious baby girl.

"Sure, come join us." Kendra motioned to the other side of the bed.

"Okay." Shelly lay down, with little Heidi snuggled between them. "My niece sure is growing, huh?"

"Yeah. Babies don't stay little long enough."

"Mind if I ask you a question?"

"Nope. Ask away." Kendra stroked her sleeping infant's velvety cheek.

"Do you have any regrets about not letting the Amish couple adopt your baby?"

"I do have moments of doubt," Kendra admitted. "But when I'm holding the baby, all my reservations melt right away."

"I can understand why." Shelly leaned close to the baby and kissed her other small cheek. "Things are getting better around here between you and Dad, don't you think?"

"I don't know. . .maybe so. He's not barking at me all the time anyhow."

"I'm not defending his previous actions, because I thought it was awful when he kicked you out, but. . ."

"But what?" Kendra lifted her head, eyeballing her sister. "Do you think he was justified in putting his own needs ahead of mine? Do you think it's okay that he sent me away?"

"No, that's not what I was gonna say."

"What then?"

"I can understand a little of how embarrassed he felt when he found out you were pregnant. It was hard for him to acknowledge it to the other church board members."

"Yeah, I know. He was more worried about what they would think of him than me, though." Kendra fluffed up her pillow. "It hasn't been easy, but I've forgiven him for giving me the boot."

They lay silently for a while, until Shelly posed another question. "Would you have married Max if he had asked you?"

"I can't say for sure. Maybe back then I would have, but now, knowing what a louse he is, I'd never agree to marry the guy."

"Do you ever hear from Max?"

"Nope. Why do you ask?"

"Just wondered if you know where he is or what he's been up to since he went into the Marines."

"I haven't a clue."

"Don't you think Max has a right to meet his daughter?"

Kendra's face warmed as she shook her head vigorously. "No way! Max gave up the right to be Heidi's dad when he cheated on me and ran off with another woman." Her toes curled inside her stockings. "I don't want him anywhere near my little girl."

"Suppose I can't really blame you, given the circumstances."

"Thank you for that."

"Think you'll ever find someone you love enough to marry?"

Kendra shrugged. "Who knows? Maybe someday Mr. Right will come along. For now, though, I need to concentrate on being the best mom I can for my sweet little girl." She gazed lovingly at her daughter. *If I'd given you up for adoption, I would have missed out on so much. No, I did the right thing by keeping you, little Heidi. And if I have my way, your biological father will never get the opportunity to lay his snake eyes on you.*

Chapter 33

Walnut Creek

D o we have everything filled out as required?" Lyle leaned over Heidi's shoulder, brushing a gentle kiss across her neck. They'd just finished eating breakfast and putting the dishes away.

She shivered and reached up to touch the side of his bearded face. "Jah, I believe so. I never expected there'd be this many questions, though."

He took a seat opposite her at the dining-room table. "Becoming a foster parent requires several things, including being licensed, which won't happen unless we fill out the paperwork and prove we meet all the necessary requirements."

She drew a deep breath and exhaled quickly. "I hope we get to take in a boppli."

He thumbed his ear. "A baby might not be the best idea, Heidi."

"How come?"

"Eventually, when it's time for the child to return to his or her parents or some other relative, it would be hard to say goodbye to a baby."

She pursed her lips. "It'll be difficult to say goodbye to any child put in our care, but we'll do what needs to be done when the time comes."

Lyle gave no argument. Instead, he rose from his chair, went over to the window, and looked out. "It's only November eleventh, but with the way the gray clouds are looming in the sky, and the chilly temperatures today, it looks like we might get some *schnee*."

Heidi's eyebrows rose. "Ach, I hope not. It's too early for snow."

"I agree, but unfortunately, we have no control over the weather."

She sighed. "Or anything else for that matter."

"Are you thinking of something in particular?"

"Jah. I was thinking about Loretta and Eli."

Lyle slid his chair in closer to the table. "What about them?"

"Well, Loretta stopped by the morning of my last cooking class, before any of the students arrived." Heidi paused to sip some of her mint tea. "She was upset because Eli compared his deceased wife's meat loaf to the one Loretta made when she invited him to join her and the children for supper."

"Did she talk to him about it?"

Heidi shook her head. "I told her she needs to, though. Eli probably doesn't even realize he hurt her feelings." She placed her hand on Lyle's arm. "Has he spoken to you about this?"

"No. The last time I talked to Eli he mentioned that Loretta would be joining the church and said he planned to ask her to marry him once she became a church member. I figured now that she's done that, he'd have already proposed."

"It may not be good to interfere, but would you consider talking to Eli?"

Lyle pinched the bridge of his nose in a slight grimace. "Oh, I don't know, Heidi. Eli might not appreciate me butting in. He could even tell me to mind my own business."

"But he's your friend," Heidi argued. "When a person sees their friend going through a difficult situation, they should say something, don't you agree?"

"I suppose I could drop over to see him soon. Maybe I can get Eli to open up without coming right out and telling him what Loretta said to you."

"Good to hear." Heidi's lips parted slightly. "Now let's get back to filling out the foster-parent paperwork."

———————— ⁂ ————————

Canton

Todd had gotten up early, showered, and fixed himself some toast so he could get to the restaurant that had closed yesterday. He'd had full intentions of going there for supper last evening, but he'd fallen asleep and didn't wake up until two this morning. Surely, the owners would still be there, finalizing everything before the restaurant was vacated.

Todd parked his car and noticed a light glowing from the interior of the building. *Good. Someone's inside.*

After Todd entered the place, he was surprised when the owners, Antonio and Teresa Carboni, greeted him with a smile.

"You probably don't remember me. I'm Todd Collins. I'm a food critic, and I write a column for the local newspaper."

Antonio put his arm around his wife's shoulder and gave it a squeeze. "So what brings you here today, Mr. Collins? You know we are now closed, don't you?"

"Yes, I read about it in the paper. Your last day was yesterday." Todd looked down at his shoes. "I actually wanted to come by last evening, but didn't make it, so I hoped I could catch you here today." He looked up again, barely able to make eye contact with the Carbonis. "I—I need to know something. Was the reason you closed this establishment because of the negative review I wrote about your restaurant a while back? Did it affect your business at all?"

Smiling, Antonio patted him on the shoulder. "Business has slacked off, but it's probably our fault for not putting more money into the place to fix things up and hire a more experienced cook. And actually, son, in some ways your article did us a favor."

Todd scratched his head. "Really? How so?"

"Seeing how business was slacking off, and being too tired to keep pursuing it, Teresa and I decided to do what we've wanted to do for a good while now. In hindsight, we should have done it sooner, because it was getting to be a little much for the two of us to keep the restaurant going. That was most likely the reason you found some negative things about our place."

"I'm sorry about the article I wrote, but as a food critic, I have to be honest and write the truth, which at times, is not easy to do."

"No need to explain." Antonio went on to tell Todd a few things he didn't know. With nothing but the clothes on their backs, and a little bit of money they'd saved, Antonio's parents came to the United States to start up a family-owned restaurant many years ago. "They built this business through perseverance and hard work, and they worked here until they died." Antonio spread his arms out and pointed to the inside of the building. "Growing up, this place was more like home to me than where we actually lived.

"When my parents died, their wish was for me, their only child, to take over the business. They'd prepared me from a young age when I began helping out." Antonio grinned at Teresa, still standing by his side. "I was lucky to marry a woman who stood by me and helped to keep this place going."

"Sounds like it was a lot of hard work."

"Sure was."

Todd listened to more of Mr. Carboni's story, although he wasn't sure why the man was telling him all of this.

"This restaurant my mama and papa started has been a labor of love, but it's getting too much for us now." The wrinkles in Antonio's forehead deepened. "My wife and I are in our late sixties, and we're exhausted working day and night to keep this place going."

She nodded. "My husband is right about that. Truth is, we've never been on a real vacation or taken much time off just to relax. It hasn't been easy to make this decision, but we've both decided we're ready to move on and spend time with our children and grandchildren."

"I'm sure your parents would be proud of you for keeping this restaurant going all these years." Todd was surprised when he noticed tears in Antonio's eyes, and his own eyes started to water. "Thanks for sharing your story with me." Todd felt better after hearing the facts and all the reasons behind the restaurant's closure. "Well, I'm sure you folks have lots to do, so I'll be on my way. I wish you both nothing but the best." Todd shook Antonio's hand, and when he turned to Teresa, she gave him a hug.

On the way home, Todd thought about the Carbonis and began to question his own life. *Do I want to continue in this profession any longer? Do I want to risk possibly hurting more establishments with my* negative critiques and causing hardships on the owners or their families? He didn't know any of these owners personally or the problems they might be facing, but he wouldn't be able to live with himself if more places closed because of his opinion in an article he'd written.

Todd gripped the steering wheel with a sense of conviction. *Maybe it's time for me to make a career change.*

———— ❦ ————

New Philadelphia

Bill grabbed his son, Brent, in a hug. "It's sure good to see you, Son."

"Same here, Dad. We shouldn't wait so long to get together."

"I know. . . I know." Bill led the way to the living room, and they both took seats after Brent returned from putting his suitcase in the spare bedroom. "So tell me how things are going with you these days. Are you still seeing Donna?"

Brent shook his head. "We broke up three months ago."

"Sorry to hear it. What went wrong?"

"Our relationship wasn't going anywhere, even though Donna dropped hints about us getting married." Brent tapped his foot. "I wasn't in love with her, Dad. Also, I want kids, and Donna made it clear that she doesn't."

"All I can say is, she doesn't know what she's missing."

Brent's expression was pensive. "Yeah."

"You know, Son, even though it may have been hard to end the relationship with Donna, love is important in a marriage, as is a shared desire to have a family. So you probably made the right decision."

"Thanks, Dad. I appreciate your support." Brent shifted on his chair. "Now tell me what's new with you."

"Well, I told you about the cooking classes I've been taking."

"Right. I'm glad you're learning new things and getting out so you can meet some new people."

"Same here. It's been a blast." Bill snapped his fingers. "Say, I have an idea. I'd like to take you over to the Troyers' so you can meet my cooking teacher. How about we drive over to Walnut Creek sometime tomorrow for a short visit?"

"Fine by me. In fact, I'm lookin' forward to it."

"Are you hungry for lunch yet?" Bill asked.

"Yes, I'm actually starving." Brent rubbed his stomach, and they both laughed when it gave a loud growl.

"Good. I kinda thought you might be after the drive down here, so I'm going to make something I learned in one of the classes." Bill headed for the kitchen, with Brent on his heels. "It's called Chicken in a Crumb Basket, and I'm positive you're gonna like it."

Chapter 34

Walnut Creek

Heidi hummed as she put a batch of pumpkin cookies in the oven. They were one of her favorites, especially when she added raisins and walnuts to the spicy dough. These cookies were good any time of the year, but even more so this close to Thanksgiving.

Heidi looked forward to spending the holiday with her parents. She could hardly wait to tell them she and Lyle had decided to become foster parents. Heidi felt sure Mom and Dad would support their decision. She'd been tempted to tell them over the phone but decided it would be better to share the good news in person.

Heidi set the timer, then poured herself a cup of green tea. She was about to sit down when a knock sounded on the front door. *I wonder if it's Lance delivering another package.* He'd brought one up to the house yesterday, but it was something Lyle had sent for. Heidi was waiting for the supplements she'd ordered from an Amish-owned health food store in Indiana and hadn't been able to find locally. Perhaps that package had finally arrived.

When Heidi opened the front door, she was surprised to find Kendra on the porch, holding her baby.

Heidi smiled. "Well, this is a pleasant surprise. It's good to see you again, Kendra. Please, come in."

"Are you sure? If you're busy. . ."

"No, not at all. Just baking some pumpkin cookies."

Kendra lifted her head and sniffed. "I can tell. They smell delicious."

"Let's go to the kitchen. You can sample some from the first batch as soon as they're out of the oven." Heidi took Kendra's jacket and hung it on a wall peg; then she led the way to the kitchen. "How is little Heidi doing?"

"Fine. She's a real good baby. Would you like to hold her?"

Before Heidi could respond, the timer went off. "I'd love to hold her, as soon as I take the cookies out and get another batch put in."

"If you'd like to hold her now, I can take care of the cookies." Kendra chuckled. "Thanks to you, I've had a little baking experience."

"True." Heidi grabbed two pot holders. "I'll get the cookies out, then you can take over."

While Kendra dropped the cookie dough onto the baking sheet, she paused to glance at Heidi. She seemed more relaxed than usual, looking content as she held the baby. What a shame she couldn't have children. Motherhood would come naturally to Heidi.

As Kendra continued to take cookies in and out of the oven, they visited about a variety of things.

"Lyle and I have decided to become foster parents." Heidi stroked the baby's head. "We filled out the paperwork yesterday to begin the process. We'll also have to complete a home study, which will be conducted by an assigned licensing specialist."

Kendra smiled. "That's good news. You'll both make good parents."

Heidi lowered her gaze. "The easy part will be caring for a child, but it'll be hard to say goodbye when it's time for the child to go."

Before Kendra could respond, a knock sounded on the front door.

"That could be our mailman," Heidi said. "Would you mind answering it for me?"

"No problem." Kendra left the room. When she opened the front door, and saw two men on the porch, her mouth dropped open. "Brent Coleman?"

"Kendra Perkins?" His brows lifted as he took a step forward. "What are you doing here?" He glanced at the other man, as if looking for answers, then looked back at Kendra.

"I'm here visiting my friend, Heidi. Why are you here?"

The older man spoke before Brent could respond. "I'm Bill Mason, one of Heidi's students, and Brent is my son. I assume you two must know each other?"

"Yes, we do." Brent motioned to Kendra. "We went to high school together. I was a senior when she was a sophomore."

Kendra swallowed hard. Back then she had a crush on Brent, but he never seemed to notice her. She was surprised he remembered her at all. After graduation Brent had gone off to college, and she hadn't seen him again until now. He was tall and muscular, with dark curly hair and vivid blue eyes. Brent was still as handsome as he was in high school, but more mature looking. It was hard not to stare at him.

"Is Heidi expecting you?" she asked.

Bill shook his head. "We just dropped by, hoping to find her at home so my son could meet her."

"Yeah, Dad's told me all about the cooking classes he's taking, and he was excited to introduce me to the woman who's taught him how to make some new recipes he can try out on his hunting buddies. I got to taste one of them for lunch yesterday, and it was exceptional."

Kendra smiled. "Heidi's a wonderful teacher. I took her first set of cooking classes—that's how we met." Remembering her manners, she swung the door open wide. "Come inside. Heidi's in the kitchen with my baby."

As the men stepped into the entryway, Brent paused beside Kendra. "You're married?"

Kendra shook her head. "No. It's a long story." Lifting her chin, in an attempt to look confident, she hurried toward the kitchen.

———— ⟅∽⟆ ————

"Well, this is a surprise," Heidi smiled up at Bill when he and Brent entered the room.

"I would have called first but didn't know how often you check for phone messages." Bill gestured to his son. "This is Brent. He's here for the weekend, and I wanted him to meet you."

Heidi stood, handed the baby to Kendra, and shook Brent's hand. "I'm glad you could drop by. I've enjoyed having your father in my class."

"Not as much as I've enjoyed being here." Bill chuckled. "My cooking was one-dimensional before I signed up for your class, and I'm looking forward to trying even more new recipes in the future. But I want you to know I made the Chicken in a Crumb Basket for Brent yesterday for lunch."

"It was sure good." Brent rubbed his stomach.

"Well, I'm pleased to know that. Would you both like to try out some pumpkin cookies, fresh from the oven?" Heidi gestured to the ones Kendra had previously placed in a canister.

Bill licked his lips. "I won't turn down a cookie or two. How about you, Son?" He turned to look at Brent, who stood staring at Kendra.

When Brent didn't answer, Bill bumped his arm. "Do you want a cookie?"

"Uh, sure. Sounds good." Brent shuffled his feet.

Bill sensed his son's unease. He was fairly sure it had something to do with Kendra—especially since he couldn't seem to take his eyes off her.

"The baby's asleep. Would you mind if I make a bed for her on the couch?" Kendra asked Heidi.

Heidi shook her head. "Of course not. Why don't we all go into the living room so we can visit? I'll bring a tray of cookies and some hot coffee."

Bill didn't have to be asked twice. He headed for the living room, barely glancing over his shoulder to see if Brent followed. At first, Brent held back, but then he ambled in behind Bill and took a seat in the chair nearest the couch.

Kendra came in behind them with the baby and settled the sleeping child on one end of the couch. She smiled at Brent. "I'll sit here to make sure my little girl doesn't roll off; although it's doubtful, since she hasn't rolled over by herself yet."

Bill watched with interest as his son's gaze went from Kendra to the baby. "She's a cute little thing. What's her name?"

"I named her after Heidi." Kendra leaned over and kissed her baby's forehead. "I call her my precious little Heidi."

"So where's the baby's father?"

I'd like to know that myself, Bill thought, as he waited for Kendra's answer to Brent's bold question.

Face turning crimson, she mumbled, "He split as soon as he found out I was pregnant. Said he couldn't be bothered and didn't want any kids."

A vein on the side of Brent's neck bulged. Bill could almost guess what his son was thinking. He wanted to be a father, but his ex-girlfriend didn't want kids. Kendra had a child, but the baby's dad didn't want anything to do with fatherhood. Some things in life made no sense at all.

Heidi came in carrying a tray with a coffeepot, cookies, and four mugs. She placed it on the coffee table and told everyone to help themselves.

Bill waited to see what Kendra and Brent would do, but when neither of them made a move, he poured himself some coffee, grabbed a napkin, and took three cookies. The mere sight of them made his mouth water. He ate one and wiped his lips with the napkin. "Delicious, Heidi. Course, I wouldn't have expected otherwise."

She smiled. "I'm glad you like them."

"Are you gonna teach us in class how to make cookies like these?" he asked, after slurping some coffee.

Kendra and Brent still hadn't taken a cookie or poured themselves any coffee. They sat quietly looking at each other.

"I was thinking for next week's class, I'd teach you all how to make pumpkin whoopie pies," Heidi responded.

"I'm all for that. Anything with pumpkin in it sounds good to me." Bill gave her a thumbs-up.

Heidi pointed to the tray of cookies. "Kendra and Brent, don't you want to try a pumpkin cookie? You especially, Kendra, since you baked most of them."

"Oh, then if that's the case, I'd better try a few." Brent grabbed a cookie and took a bite. "My dad's right. . . . This is real tasty."

Kendra took one, too, nibbling on it as she tucked the baby's blanket under her little feet.

Bill's cell phone rang, so he excused himself and went outside to answer it. He didn't feel right about taking a call inside an Amish home, where phones were not allowed.

The call was from Bill's friend Andy asking if Brent made it to his place okay.

"Sure did. He and I are at Heidi Troyer's right now. I wanted him to meet her."

"Are you having a good visit with your son?"

"Yeah, but the weekend's going too fast. Sure wish I could see Brent more often."

"Maybe you can convince him to move closer." Andy chuckled. "He could join our hunting party. You did teach him the fine art of hunting, right?"

"No," Bill mumbled. He felt bad about it now, but in all the times he'd gone hunting when Brent was growing up, he'd never taken the boy hunting or taught him how to shoot a gun or bow and arrow. The kid seemed more interested in sports and hadn't shown any interest in hunting. Bill wished he could go back and do some things differently, but it was too late.

"Listen, Andy, I should get back inside."

"You're outside talking to me?"

"Yeah."

"How come?"

Bill explained the situation and said he didn't want to be rude by taking the call in Heidi's house. "Did you call for any particular reason or just to shoot the breeze?"

"Just wondered if you're gonna be alone at the cabin on Thanksgiving."

"Most likely. None of the other guys can make it till the following day." Bill rubbed his arm as the wind whistled through the trees. The day seemed to have gotten colder, even more so, since he and Brent had arrived at Heidi's house. "Sure hope it doesn't snow."

"You mean now or on Thanksgiving?"

"I meant now, since my son has to drive home tomorrow. But during hunting season—that's a different story. I'd be eager for some snow."

"Well, I'll let you go so you can get back inside where it's warmer. I'll miss joining you and the guys at camp this year."

"Yeah, we'll miss you, too."

When Bill entered the house, he was surprised to see Brent sitting on the couch next to Kendra, while Heidi sat in the rocking chair holding Kendra's baby. Brent and Kendra were engrossed in conversation, and he hated to interrupt, but figured it was time for them to get going, since he'd planned to take Brent out to lunch at his favorite restaurant in Berlin.

He took a seat, drank the rest of his lukewarm coffee, and stood. "We should get going, Brent. I'd like to get to the restaurant before it becomes too crowded. Saturdays are always busy with tourists and locals who like to go shopping and eat out."

"Oh, okay." Brent stood and handed Kendra one of his business cards. "Give me a call sometime. I'd like to keep in touch."

She smiled. "That'd be nice."

Bill and Brent said their goodbyes and headed out the door. As they climbed into Bill's truck, he turned to his son and said, "Think she'll call?"

Brent's ears turned slightly pink. "I don't know. Guess I'll have to wait and see what happens."

Chapter 35

Millersburg

Nicole was in the kitchen, gathering up her apron and notebook in readiness for Dad to take her to the fifth cooking class, when she glanced out the window and saw her mother's car pull up next to the garage. *Oh, great. What does she want this time? I hope she hasn't been drinking again.*

Holding her breath, Nicole stepped back from the window, out of sight, but positioning herself so she could still see her mother. *If I don't answer the door, maybe she'll go away.* But it was too late. She watched as Dad went out the door and walked up to Tonya. *I hope he holds his ground and tells her to leave. If she doesn't go soon, I'm gonna be late for the cooking class.*

Eager to know what they were saying, Nicole opened the door a crack and listened while peeking through the narrow gap.

"I've been going to Alcoholics Anonymous, and I'm working hard at staying sober." Tonya moved closer to Dad. "Thanks to my drinking and irresponsible attitude, I made a mess of our marriage."

Nicole clenched her fingers. *You've got that right, Tonya. You made a big mess of everything. You don't care about your family, so just go away and leave us alone.*

"I'm sorry for all the hurts I've caused, and I want to do better."

You're lying. You always lie when you want something.

Dad said nothing; just gave a brief nod. Nicole hoped it didn't mean he'd accepted Tonya's apology. Surely he couldn't be that weak where his ex-wife was concerned. Not after all the damage she'd done to this family.

Tonya touched Dad's arm. "I hope once you see that I've changed you'll allow me to spend some quality time with the children—especially around the holidays."

"We'll see how it goes, Tonya." Dad's tone held no malice. He didn't even pull his arm away. "This is not something you can fix overnight, though."

"I realize that, but please give me a chance to prove myself." Her pleading tone was pathetic.

Nicole shook her head. *Don't let her get to you, Dad. She's trying to pry on your sympathies. Do not give in.*

"Do you forgive me, Mike?"

Dad took a deep breath as his shoulders raised, then lowered. Rubbing his forehead, he answered, "Yes, Tonya, I forgive you."

Nicole's spine stiffened. *You've gotta be kidding! How can he forgive so easily? If Dad wants to be foolish where Tonya's concerned, that's up to him, but there's no way I will ever forgive that woman for all she's done.* Nicole shook her head forcibly. *Nope. I don't want anything to do with Tonya—not now, not ever!*

Nicole was relieved when a few minutes later, Dad came into the kitchen. "You all ready to go, Nicole?"

She gave a nod. "I saw you talking to Tonya outside—I mean, Mom. I assume she's gone?"

"Yes, and we'd better get going so you're not late for the cooking class."

"Yeah, okay." Nicole was on the verge of asking Dad if he believed all the things Tonya had said to him, but thought better of it. If he brought it up, she would offer her opinion. Otherwise she wouldn't say anything. No point letting Dad know she'd been eavesdropping.

Walnut Creek

Heidi was pleased when everyone showed up at her house on time. Making the whoopie pies would take a bit of time, so she wanted her students to get started right away. Once everyone was seated at her kitchen table, she explained what they'd be making and handed out the recipe cards, along with all the ingredients they would need.

"I think you will all enjoy these special cookies," she said, standing at the head of the table. "They've always been one of my family's favorites, and the pumpkin whoopies make a wonderful treat during the fall and winter months."

"I'm sure I'll enjoy them." Lance offered Heidi a big grin.

"Same here," Bill chimed in.

Heidi clasped her hands together. "Well, all right then, let's get started."

Allie stared across the table at no one in particular. She had a hard time concentrating on the recipe Heidi had given them for pumpkin whoopie pies. She'd had an argument with Steve last night, and they'd both gone to bed angry. He'd gotten up early and left before she and the kids were out of bed, so there'd been no chance to talk more or offer any apologies.

She clenched her fingers around the mixing spoon, while stirring the cookie batter. *Not that he would have offered any, and I probably wouldn't have apologized either. Seems like all we do is argue lately, but no one ever wins. Steve doesn't want to be with me or the kids anymore. If he did, he wouldn't work unnecessary shifts for others.*

"These cookies would be good for Thanksgiving, don't you think?" Lisa leaned closer to Allie.

"Yes, I suppose so." Allie hadn't even planned what they would have for their Thanksgiving meal yet. She had originally hoped they'd be able to go to her parents for the holiday again this year, but Steve's schedule didn't allow that to happen. Instead, her folks and Steve's parents were coming to their home, but Steve wouldn't be there. He'd told her last night that he was scheduled to work Thanksgiving Day, which had led up to their argument. Allie had even been bold enough to ask if he was in love with someone else, and secretly seeing another woman, but he'd denied it and said Allie was paranoid and worried too much.

"I'll be taking a pumpkin pie to my parents' house for Thanksgiving, but I think I'll take some whoopie pies, too." Lisa interrupted Allie's thoughts again. "There can never be enough desserts for a holiday, right?"

"My sentiments exactly," Bill spoke up. "Think I'll take some whoopies to the cabin with me." He chuckled. "Course I may have them all eaten before my buddies show up the day after Thanksgiving."

"I'll probably take a batch of them to my daughter Sharon's place," Lance put in. "She called last week and invited me to join her family on Thanksgiving." He gave an enthusiastic grin. "My other daughter, Terry, will be there, too, as well as my brother, Dan."

Allie glanced at Todd, to see if he would say anything, but he kept stirring his cookie dough without a word. Same for Nicole. Her glum expression was an indication that she was not in a good mood today.

Well, join the club. Allie poked her tongue to one side of her cheek. *But at least I'm trying not to let it show.*

———————⚬❦⚬———————

After everyone's whoopie pies were baked and cooled, Heidi suggested they go into the dining room to sample what they'd made. "I'll bring in some hot chocolate and coffee to go with the cookies. While you're eating your whoopies, I'll tell you the decision Lyle and I made about becoming foster parents." She gestured to Allie. "I have you to thank for bringing up the topic at our last cooking class."

Allie's lips twitched before breaking into a grin. "That's good news. I'm happy for you, Heidi."

Nicole and the others all nodded.

"My husband and I are looking forward to caring for a child, but I'll tell you more as we're sharing our snacks." Heidi opened a cabinet and took out a large serving tray.

"I'll stay here in the kitchen and help you carry things out," Bill offered.

Heidi smiled. "Thank you, Bill."

Nicole gathered up her whoopie pies and placed them in the plastic container Heidi had given each student. Then she followed the others to the dining room and took a seat at the table between Allie and Lisa. Lance and Todd sat across from them. While everyone chatted about various things, Nicole studied the recipe card Heidi had given them to go with the cookies they'd made. The whoopie pies weren't too hard to make and would probably be something her sister and brother would enjoy. *Maybe I'll make a batch sometime before Thanksgiving. Sure hope Tonya doesn't get any ideas about coming over that day.*

She turned the three-by-five card over and frowned when she read the verse of scripture Heidi had written: *"[Jesus said,] 'If ye forgive men their trespasses, your heavenly Father will also forgive you'"* (Matthew 6:14).

Nicole shifted in her chair, crossing and uncrossing her leg. *Why is it so important to forgive? Tonya doesn't deserve my forgiveness. She hasn't asked for it, either.*

Growing more uneasy by the minute, she pushed her chair back and stood. "Think I'll go see what's taking Heidi and Bill so long."

Nicole headed for the kitchen, and was almost to the door, when she heard Bill mention her name. He was telling Heidi how he'd paid for a weekly housekeeper to help Nicole and her family out. "Not knowing how Nicole would take it, I decided it'd be best to remain anonymous."

Nicole stood at the door, her lips pressed together, as her thoughts scrambled to understand. Why would Bill have done this for her? He hardly even knew Nicole. *Should I go in and say something—tell him I overheard what he said?*

Blinking rapidly, she stood like a statue, barely breathing as she weighed the pros and cons. If she said something, Bill might be embarrassed. If she kept quiet, he would not be thanked for his good deed. Nicole did appreciate it, after all. Still, it upset her that anyone had to even do this for her family. If Mom hadn't bailed on them, there would have been no need. Having the housekeeper had given her more time for schoolwork, as well as the chance to do some other things. No one—especially a near stranger—had ever done anything this nice for her, and Bill deserved a thank-you.

Pushing her sweater sleeves past the elbows, Nicole was about to enter the kitchen, when Bill stepped out, carrying the tray with napkins and paper cups. Heidi came behind him with a coffeepot. Bill's eyes widened as his head jerked back. "Oh, Nicole, I didn't realize you were near the door. How long have you been standing there?"

"Long enough to hear what you said to Heidi about paying for someone to clean my dad's house." She lifted her chin and looked up at him. "I don't know what to say, except thank you."

He winked at her. "You're more than welcome. I was happy to do it."

Tears welled in Nicole's eyes, and she was powerless to keep them from spilling over. Heidi was quickly at her side, slipping one arm around Nicole's waist, guiding her into the kitchen. "Is there something you wish to talk about?"

Nicole gulped on the sob rising in her throat. Desperate to unburden her soul, she blurted out the details of her mother's visit that morning and how Tonya had told Nicole's dad she was going to AA and wanted to spend more time with her children.

A rush of heat flushed through Nicole's body. "She asked for Dad's forgiveness, and I can't believe it, but he actually forgave her. I mean, how could he be so gullible?" She sank into a chair at the table with a groan. "Tonya may have quit drinking for a while, but she'll be at it again, and probably soon. Nothing will change for the better. I can't stand her, and I wish she wasn't my mother."

Heidi took the seat beside her. "Loving people is not always easy, especially if we've been hurt by them. But when we choose to hate and refuse to forgive instead of offering love and forgiveness, it's as though we are roaming around in darkness." She paused and placed her hand on Nicole's trembling arm. "Hatred is disorienting. It takes away our sense of direction."

Nicole sniffed deeply. "I—I don't care. Tonya's done too many bad things. She doesn't deserve my forgiveness—especially when she's just gonna do it again. And people wouldn't have to be helping us out if she'd stayed home and been a real mom."

Heidi handed Nicole a tissue. "I understand—it's not always easy to forgive. Please think about it this week, and remember, I'll be praying for you."

For some reason, Nicole found comfort in knowing Heidi would be praying for her. This young Amish woman was so kind and loving— nothing like Nicole's messed-up mother. It was a shame Heidi didn't have any children of her own. She would certainly be a good mother.

Bill moved close to the table and cleared his throat. She hadn't even realized he'd joined them in the kitchen until now. She'd thought he'd gone into the dining room with the others.

"You know, Heidi, as you've been talking to Nicole, I've been thinking about my own situation. I realize now that I've never forgiven my wife for her part in what turned out to be a painful divorce." Bill shuffled his feet a few times. "I need to do that, and I'll also talk to Michelle and ask her forgiveness for my part in the breakup of our marriage. It's too late for us to get back together, because she's remarried, but at least I'll feel better knowing there's no animosity between us."

Nicole couldn't listen anymore. With head down, she went back to the dining room to join the others and wait for Dad to pick her up. If Bill wanted to forgive his wife, that was his business, but it didn't change the way she felt about Tonya.

Chapter 36

Burton, Ohio

The morning had started out with low, steel-colored clouds. But now, as Heidi and Lyle's driver neared the town of Burton, on their way to Middlefield, the wind came up, pushing the clouds to the west, and revealing a milky sun. The closer they got to their Thanksgiving destination, the more eager Heidi became.

"Look over there." Heidi pointed out the front window of their driver's van. "It looks like smoke up ahead."

"You're right it does," Lyle agreed. "But those huge puffs, resembling smoke, are nothing more than billowing steam coming off the manure being spread by that tractor over there. It's a good time of year to get it done, before the snow falls and blankets the ground."

Squinting, Heidi leaned forward as far as her seatbelt would allow. Sure enough, the man in the tractor drove the outline of the field. Then little by little, he worked his way toward the middle, leaving a steaming trail of manure behind him.

As the van continued on, she noticed all the barren trees on both sides of the road. Everything looked so dismal this time of the year. Dead leaves, brown with no color left, blew across the road in the wind. Several homes they passed, with their once-green yards, now matching the color of wheat, had smoke rising out of the chimneys. Heidi hoped they might have some snow by now, to give more color to the ground and trees. In fact, with the cooler temperatures, she'd expected snowy weather might have already come, or at least that they'd see some before Christmas arrived. It was always special to wake up on Christmas morning and view the beauty of everything blanketed in pristine snow.

I can hardly believe it's Thanksgiving. Heidi shook her head. *Wherever did this year get to?* The holiday had approached so fast, and as they rode by an English man wrapping colored lights around a pine tree in the front yard, it was one more reminder that Christmas would be here soon, too. Two young children stood near the man, jumping up and down. No doubt they were excited about the upcoming holiday, too.

What fun it must be to have children around the holidays. Hopefully by this Christmas, she and Lyle would get to find out. But until then, Heidi had to be patient. *What a blessing it would be for us to bring a child into our home at Christmastime.*

She looked over at Lyle and placed her hand on his knee. "I wonder what Mom and Dad's response will be when we tell them about our plans to become foster parents."

"I imagine it'll be the same as my folks when we told them the other day." He smiled and placed his hand over hers, giving her fingers a tender squeeze. "Your parents will be happy for us, too, and probably offer encouragement, as well as words of wisdom about parenting."

Heidi gave a nod. "We are both so fortunate to have loving parents." She thought about Nicole and the situation with her mother. "Not everyone is blessed with good parents."

───────── ⌘ ─────────

Zoar, Ohio

"Sharon sure lives in a dinky town," Dan commented as he and Lance drove into the historical village south of Canton.

Refusing to let his brother's negative comment rile him, Lance smiled and replied, "Zoar is more than a dinky town. It's an interesting piece of local history."

Dan let go of the steering wheel with one hand and gestured toward Lance. "Oh? How so?"

"For starters, the people who lived here more than a hundred years ago were part of the Separatist Society."

"Is that a fact?"

Lanced nodded. "Due to religious persecution, they left their home country of Germany and fled to America."

"Hmm. . . Sounds similar to why the Amish came here."

"You're right, only the Zoarites were communal and didn't have their own homes. The community association here works hard to keep the spirit and lifestyle of the original village alive."

"Guess that's important."

"Yep. And since the Zoar village used to be an apple orchard, the town is known for its delicious apple dishes. Fact is, Sharon said she was gonna make a dutch apple cake for dessert today. It'll go well with the pumpkin whoopie pies I brought along."

"Both desserts sound good."

They rode in silence for a while, until Lance spoke again. "Say, Dan, before we get to Sharon's place, there's something I need to say."

"What's that?"

"I'm sorry for getting upset with you during the time you were staying at my house. I overreacted on a few things."

Dan waved his hand. "It's okay, Brother. You do things different than I do, and living together was hard for both of us. Things are better now that I'm living in the other half of Lisa's duplex, where I can pretty much do as I please."

"So everything's good?"

"Absolutely."

"Glad to hear it." Lance was tempted to ask if his brother was keeping the place picked up but didn't want to start a discussion that could lead to an argument. Even if the place wasn't being kept super clean, he felt sure Dan would not ruin any of Lisa's furniture or mark anything up. "So, on another note—any idea how long till your own place is ready for you to move back to?" He asked.

"A few more weeks. It probably won't be long after I move out before Lisa finds someone else to rent the side of the duplex I'm in now."

"I hope so. She did us both a favor renting to you—especially knowing it wouldn't be full-time."

"True, but her place is nice, and I'm sure once I move out she'll find another renter."

Lance hoped his brother was right. He would feel bad if Lisa had a hard time finding another person to move in. Most likely she relied on the rent money to supplement her income.

New Philadelphia

Allie put the turkey in the oven and sighed. *I wish Steve could be here to carve the bird when it's done.* The fact that her parents and in-laws would be here for Thanksgiving made Steve's absence seem even worse. Would she be able to keep a lid on her emotions and not let on how upset she felt because her husband couldn't join them? If she said too much, one or both sets of parents might figure out that things were strained between Allie and Steve. *They could even think we're headed for a divorce.*

Should I consider divorcing Steve? Allie wondered. *Would it be better for me? But what about the kids? I have to consider their needs.* She cringed, having gone over this in her mind several times before. Even though Steve wasn't around as much as he should be, Nola and Derek would miss their daddy. When he was home, the kids and their father were practically inseparable.

Tears welled in Allie's eyes. *Truthfully, I'd miss him, too.* Allie had fallen in love with Steve a short time after they'd begun dating. He was everything she'd ever wanted in a man—nice looking, smart, strong, and brave. He had a pleasant personality and got along well with people, too. Allie's father had taken to Steve the first time she'd brought him home to meet her folks. When she and Steve first got married, they were inseparable and communicated well with each other. But as time went on and Steve became more involved in his work, things began to change.

Before this year, Steve had always managed to get off on Thanksgiving, which made his absence today even harder. Allie felt empty as she washed the potatoes and laid them on a paper towel to dry.

Arf! Arf! The kids' puppy darted into the kitchen with Derek at his heels.

"Come back here, Trouble!" Derek shook his finger at the dog. "You need to come when I call you."

Allie glanced at the clock. "Your grandparents will be here soon, so you should put the pup in his cage now."

Derek's nose wrinkled. "Trouble don't like it there, Mommy. It's like bein' in jail." He looked up at her with a pleading expression. "You wouldn't wanna be in jail, would you?"

"Of course not, Son, but Trouble will get into mischief if he's left to run around the house all day." She leaned over and scratched the pup behind his silky ears. "You can keep him out till your grandparents arrive, but then he has to go in the cage. Understood?"

Derek nodded. "When's Daddy gonna be home?"

"Later this evening."

His lower lip protruded. Allie figured she'd better change the subject or her boy would end up whining.

"Where's your sister? Did she clear her toys out of the living room like I asked?"

Derek shrugged. "Don't know. I wasn't watchin'."

Allie lifted her gaze to the ceiling. *What else is new?* She'd go check on Nola, then come back, wash her hands, and peel the potatoes. If she got all the prep work for dinner done ahead of time, the meal would be ready by the time the parents showed up. Besides, keeping busy took her mind off Steve and how much she missed him not being here today.

⊷∘•∘⊶

Cambridge, Ohio

Gravel crackled beneath the tires of Lisa's van as she drove up her parents' driveway. Living in a rural area, they'd never bothered to put pavement down. As Lisa approached the two-story house, she was surprised to see a vehicle she didn't recognize parked outside their garage. *Did Dad buy a new car?*

She parked next to the SUV and stepped out of the van. Since she planned to spend the night, she took out her small suitcase and the plastic container with the whoopie pies in it.

A rustling wind slid through the trees as Lisa made her way to the house. She paused briefly to look at the well-used tire swing hanging from the stately maple. She'd spent many hours in that old swing when she was a girl, daydreaming and wishing she had a sibling. But it was not meant to be. Mom had complications when Lisa was born, and a hysterectomy put an end to her childbearing days. Of course, Lisa had friends to play with, but it wasn't the same as having a brother or sister. She'd determined in her heart some time ago that, if she ever got married, she would have three or four children. Right now, however, marriage seemed to be in the distant future. She'd need to find the right man first, and at present, that seemed unlikely, too.

Halting her thoughts, Lisa stepped onto the front porch and rang the bell to announce her presence. Certain that the door would be unlocked, she opened it and stepped inside. The delicious aroma of roasting turkey greeted her, and she was tempted to head straight for the kitchen. But hearing voices coming from the living room, she set her luggage in the hallway, hung up her coat, and placed the whoopie pies on the entry table.

When Lisa entered the adjoining room, she was surprised to see a young couple with two little, tow-headed boys sitting on the couch. She'd never met them and wondered if Mom had invited a new neighbor or someone from church whom Lisa didn't know.

"Oh, good, I'm glad you're here." Mom rose from her chair, and Dad did the same. They took turns hugging Lisa. Then Mom introduced their guests. "Lisa, this is Tim and Sandy Sawyer." She gestured to the children. "And these two young men are Nicolas and Wesley. Your dad and I invited them to join us for dinner today."

Lisa shook hands with Tim and Sandy, and told the boys hello. Her smile felt forced, however. It didn't seem right that after Mom had specifically told her not to invite Todd, saying today was just for family, that she would invite strangers into their home for Thanksgiving. At least to Lisa these people were strangers. If Mom and Dad knew them, they'd certainly never mentioned it, nor had Mom informed Lisa they'd invited any guests.

I suppose it doesn't matter, though, Lisa told herself, *since I'm not seeing Todd anymore. And maybe these people had nowhere else to go for the holiday. Mom's hospitable and has always reached out to those in need.*

"Lisa, please take a seat. There's something you need to know." Mom pointed to one of the recliners.

A tingle of apprehension slid up Lisa's spine. Mom's tone and expression were so serious. She hoped nothing was wrong. "What is it?" Lisa asked, lowering herself into a chair.

Mom glanced over at Tim, then back at Lisa. "There's no simple way to tell you this, except come right out and say it."

Lisa leaned forward. "Say what, Mom? You're scaring me. Is something wrong with you or Dad? Is that what you're trying to tell me?"

Mom shook her head. "No, we're both fine, and I hope you will be, too, when we share this news."

Lisa sat quietly, waiting for her mother to continue and watching as Mom grabbed Dad's hand. Something big was going on here, and Lisa was eager to find out what it was.

Mom cleared her throat a couple of times. "Tim is my son."

Lisa swallowed hard, touching the base of her neck. *I must have misunderstood. I'm an only child. Mom couldn't have more children, and if she had, I certainly would have known.* "Wh—what are you saying?" Lisa could barely speak. Was Mom playing some kind of a joke on her?

"I know this must come as quite a shock," Tim spoke up. "But as a baby, I was adopted. I've been looking for my biological parents for the last two years, and thanks to the Internet, I've found my birth mother." He paused and moistened his lips. "I'm your half brother, Lisa."

Chapter 37

Lisa sat in stunned silence as her mother explained how twenty-eight years ago she'd had a baby out of wedlock and put him up for adoption. It had pained her to do so, but she was young and immature, with no way to support a child. When Tim contacted her a few weeks ago, Mom invited him and his family here today so they could meet and share a Thanksgiving meal.

"Why am I just now hearing this, Mom?" Clutching the folds in her dress, Lisa tilted her head to one side.

"Your mother wanted to surprise you today." Dad spoke for the first time. "We both thought this would be a good opportunity for Tim to not only meet his biological mother, but his half sister, too."

Oh, I'm surprised, all right. Shocked might be a better word for it. Lisa glanced at Tim. He had blond hair like hers, and it wasn't hard to see that they were related. Even his sons, who sat on the floor across the room, playing a game, resembled Tim, rather than their dark-haired mother. All these years of wanting a brother, and here she'd had one the whole time and didn't even know it. As pleased as Lisa was to hear this news, she felt cheated and hurt by her mother's deception. *Didn't Mom think I deserved to know the truth? Was she afraid I would think less of her because she'd given birth to a child and wasn't married?*

Lisa shifted in her chair. *Would I have been condemning? Would knowing Mom had put my brother up for adoption have made a difference in the way I feel about her?*

She had to admit, it would have been a shock, no matter when she'd learned the truth. But it may have been easier to accept and deal with it if she'd found out sooner.

Tim smiled at Lisa. "I'm anxious to get to know you. I grew up with three brothers and always wondered what it would be like to have a sister."

Lisa's throat constricted. It wasn't Tim's fault they'd been kept apart. *If Mom had told me early on that she'd given birth to another child and put him up for adoption, I could have begun a search for him, and maybe found Tim sooner.*

As the shock of it all began to wear off, Lisa relaxed a bit. Today would be a time to get to know Tim, his wife, and their children. It would be a new beginning for all of them. She truly had something to be thankful for this Thanksgiving.

※

Middlefield

"You outdid yourself on this meal, Rachel." Lyle gave his stomach a pat. "I ate too much, and I'll probably sleep the rest of the afternoon, but it was worth every bite."

"I'm glad you enjoyed it." Heidi's mother laughed. "And you probably won't be the only one taking a nap today." She looked at Heidi's father. "Isn't that right, Irvin?"

"That's correct, because you're a good cook." Heidi's dad grinned as he stifled a yawn.

Heidi looked at all the smiling faces gathered around the extended table, as well as a smaller one for the children. She was glad her brothers, Richard and Sam, along with their wives and children, had been able to join them today. Her sisters, Naomi and Elizabeth, were also present with their families. Now that everyone was together, it was the perfect time to share her and Lyle's good news.

She picked up her spoon and gave her water glass a few taps. "Well, before anyone gets too sleepy—Lyle and I have a special announcement to make."

All heads turned in Heidi's direction, and Lyle clasped her other hand under the table.

A wide smile formed on Mom's lips. "After all these years are you expecting a boppli?"

Heidi shook her head. "It's doubtful that will ever happen, but Lyle and I are going to become foster parents."

Now everyone smiled, and several people asked questions.

"What you plan to do is a real good thing." Dad leaned closer to Lyle and gave his back a few hearty thumps. "I'm sure I speak for everyone here when I say that we support your decision."

Mom bobbed her head. Heidi's siblings did the same.

Heidi inhaled deeply. She was almost certain becoming a foster parent was the right thing to do, and she felt ever so grateful for her family's support.

<hr />

Canton

Sitting alone at a table in a crowded restaurant on Thanksgiving Day was not Todd's idea of having holiday fun. *Maybe I should have booked a plane ticket and gone to Mom and Dad's place after all. It would have been better than sitting here by myself, eating bland food that doesn't even deserve a critique.* He squared his shoulders. *Well, maybe it's not really bland. It's just that nothing tastes good to me today.*

The slices of turkey on Todd's plate held no appeal, and neither did the piece of pumpkin pie the waitress had brought out with Todd's dinner. She'd said they were getting low on pumpkin and wanted to be sure he got a slice.

"Ah, Miss. . ." Todd snapped his fingers to get the waitress's attention. "Could I please have a little whipped cream with this pie?"

"Sure thing."

He nodded in thanks when she returned, shaking a can, then squirted a design of whipped topping on his dessert.

If I hadn't ruined things with Lisa, I would probably be with her right now, Todd fretted. *I bet she's having a great Thanksgiving with her folks. Why'd I have to mess things up by acting like such a jerk? I was on the brink of thinking we were establishing a relationship, but then everything went sour, and it's all my fault.*

Gazing at the pie, Todd thought about the verse Heidi had written on the back of the recipe card for pumpkin whoopie pie cookies. It was about forgiveness. Todd needed to forgive his ex-girlfriend for the things she'd said to hurt him. He also needed to ask God's forgiveness for the things he'd done to hurt others, including Lisa. He'd had a good start when he visited the Carbonis. If their reasons for closing hadn't turned out the way it did, Todd would have done something for them to make up for the negative critique he'd written about their restaurant. What that would have been, Todd wasn't sure, but in his heart, he knew, his intentions would have been sincere. He could feel his heart soften and shift in another direction. He wanted to take a better path from now on. Trouble was, Todd didn't know where to start when it came to God. He had never established a relationship with the Lord, but when the realization hit him, Todd knew what he had to do. The only place he could think to begin this connection was by going to church. Surely the pastor, or someone there, could show him the way.

———— ❧ ————

Coshocton

Bill arrived at his hunting camp early, and after getting a warm fire going in the fireplace and eating a quick breakfast, he was bound for the woods to do a little pre-hunt scouting. When he got back to the cabin, he'd clean things up, set up the foldaway cots, and make sure everything was ready for when Russ and Tom arrived tomorrow. He also wanted to hang his orange blaze hat and hunting vest out on the porch. This way, by Monday morning, the items would have pulled in the natural smells from the woods. Today, though, since Bill wasn't hunting, he'd dressed in camouflage clothes.

Bill couldn't help but think how different it would be this year without Andy joining them. Going to Orlando this time of year certainly didn't interest Bill. It wouldn't feel much like the holidays, being in a warm climate without any anticipation of snow. But since Andy wanted to be with his family, he couldn't blame his friend for that. Bill had to admit he felt a bit envious, too, for it would certainly be nice to have Brent here with him at the cabin.

When he got to the area where his tree stand was located, Bill checked it over thoroughly, and all seemed secure. Climbing the ladder, and putting a camouflage cushion on the seat, Bill sat down to enjoy the scenery and watch for any deer activity. After pulling his thermos from the backpack he had brought along, he opened the lid, poured some out, and sipped the steaming brew.

"Sitting here in my tree stand with a good cup of coffee, now what could be better than this?" Bill grinned and raised his thermos lid in a toast to nature. He loved being up here this time of year. The silence and surroundings were pure delight.

After Bill sat there awhile, his feet grew cold and his legs started to cramp up. He stood and stretched them a bit, but there was not a lot of room on the small wooden platform, so he couldn't move around much.

"I oughta have a bigger tree stand built," he muttered. "There's barely room for me up here, let alone my hunting buddies."

It had rained a bit when Bill first got here this morning, but the downpour stopped after a few hours. The earthy scent from fallen wet leaves lying all over the ground wafted up to greet him. If he had a new stand built, he'd make sure it had a roof and was twice the size of this old one, or maybe even bigger. The tree stand had been here when Bill bought the property, and since he didn't use it all the time, he'd made do. Maybe next year, after he'd built up his savings, he'd see about replacing it. In times past when his buddies were here, they'd traded off—two of them sitting on the platform in tight quarters, while the other two hunted from the ground.

I can't wait till Monday morning. Bill smiled in anticipation. Opening day was always exciting. When would the first shot be heard? Would he get a chance to bag a big buck? Who'd be lucky enough to get the first deer, and would any of them go home empty-handed? It really made no difference to Bill if he got a deer or not; it was the experience of it all that he enjoyed. But once his buddies arrived and they got to talking, Bill knew he'd get excited about getting a deer, too.

As steam from his breathing escaped Bill's mouth, he reminisced about previous years on opening day, climbing up here before it got light. His eyes would adjust, and as dawn began to break, he'd see shadowy images of deer sneaking through before it was legal to shoot. Bill had witnessed some beautiful sunrises from up here, too, and he always looked forward to it, coupled with the thrill of watching wildlife begin to stir. His friends had different ideas about the whole hunting experience and tended to be a bit more competitive.

Bill sat back on his canvas camping chair and tried to relax. At least it was fairly comfortable if he didn't sit there too long. No sign of any deer yet, though. Were they all bedded down, or just avoiding this area because he, the intruder, was near? Bill had forgotten to de-scent his clothes with the special spray he'd brought along, but hopefully any odors from breakfast didn't linger on his hat, shirt, pants, or jacket.

In the distance, Bill heard a few shots. Most likely, someone was sighting in their rifle, which was common to hear this close to opening day. He hoped that's all it was, since shooting a deer wouldn't be legal until Monday.

If nothing came his way in the next hour or so, he'd head back to the cabin to fix supper. Bill had brought potatoes, carrots, and onions from home as the basis for a savory stew. He'd also packed a loaf of apple corn bread he had made yesterday, and that would be his Thanksgiving meal. Bill didn't mind being alone in the woods. He enjoyed the solitude. But with today being a holiday when he normally got together with his buddies, he felt kind of lost.

Wish my boy could have joined me today. Bill shifted on his chair. *It would have been good to have a little more father-son time together. The three days Brent and I shared two weeks ago went too fast. No wonder Andy chose to go with his family, even it meant being in an environment as warm as Florida.*

Bill's attention came to a peak when a rustling noise reached his ears. He turned his head slowly in the direction it was coming from and sat forward in anticipation. *Maybe it's a deer sneaking through after hearing the gunfire a few minutes ago.* He wished he would have put his camera in the backpack, but it was too late to worry about that now. Bill watched and waited and hoped it would be a big buck. It would be nice to know one was in the area and hopefully get a chance to see it on opening day.

The sound grew closer, and when the animal appeared, Bill's eyes widened and his mouth dropped open. Slowly, Bill sat back against the tree as close as he could get and tried not to move a muscle. Down below, a few feet from the tree, stood an enormous black bear. Bill had heard there were bear in the area, but after years of hunting and never seeing any, he'd thought it was only a rumor, or one of those stories people liked to tell while sitting around a campfire. But here was a bear, as big and bold as you please, and he was a beauty.

Bill blinked his eyes rapidly as they began to water. *I cannot believe what I'm seeing. The guys will never believe this. Boy, do I wish I had my camera.*

As the bear stood on all fours, looking around and sniffing the air, Bill was glad he had gone unnoticed. A few times, the bruin looked up in his direction, however with Bill wearing his camo clothes, the material blended in well with the tree's bark. He had read one time, though, that a bear's hearing was exceptional. *I hope he can't hear my heart beating, because it feels like it's about to pop right out of my chest.* Bill released air through his lips as quietly as he could. He tried to swallow, but his mouth felt too dry.

Oh brother, what am I going to do now? I hope the bear leaves soon, or I'll be spending the night up in this tree stand. Bill took short, quiet breaths, so the big creature would not hear him. Barely breathing, he watched the bear stick his nose in the air, as though trying to get a scent of something. *I should have stayed back at the cabin. How long is he going to stand there like that?*

It was cool out, but by now, Bill was drenched in sweat. When the bear started walking around, he could hear the intake of air going through its nostrils as it investigated every stick, sniffing every leaf and what seemed like every blade of brush grass. Then it walked over to the ladder Bill had climbed up on and took a few sniffs of the lower rungs. When the bear stood and looked up at Bill, eyes on each other and unblinking, time seemed to stand still. *Please don't climb this ladder.*

Then as if someone had stuck him with a needle, the bear jumped back and became alert. Just that quick, the animal took off running in the opposite direction. How something that big, could run so fast, Bill could not comprehend.

He stood up to watch, but saw no sign of the bear. All he could hear were sticks breaking and the crunching of leaves, as the lumbering sound grew farther away. After sitting there a few minutes longer, and not hearing anymore noise, Bill hoped it would be safe to leave the tree stand.

By now, it had started spritzing, and as Bill turned to go down the ladder, he heard some cracking noises above his head. He froze, and his scalp prickled when he looked up and saw some dead limbs high above that had begun to rot. The last thing he needed was a tree limb hitting him on the noggin. *This big old oak tree probably needs to be taken down soon.* Bill grabbed his seat cushion, put his thermos in the backpack, and gave the area one last look. *I'm getting back to the cabin where it's safe.*

By the time Bill got to the bottom rung, a steady rain had begun to fall. This time a lot harder than earlier today. He grimaced when the raindrops splattered his face and dripped down the back of his neck.

He'd only made it a few feet from the tree when—*crack!*—the rotting limb broke off and dropped to the ground with a sickening *thud.* Letting out a yelp, he shuffled backward, stumbled on a rock, and landed on the seat of his pants. *Whew, that was too close for me! If I hadn't gotten down from the tree stand when I did, that old limb could have smacked me on the head.*

Bill's heartbeat raced as he clambered to his feet. *If the falling branch had hit me, I could be unconscious or even dead. It's probably not a good idea to be out here by myself. I shoulda waited till the guys could join me tomorrow to do some early scouting. So much for me wanting to brag about seeing a deer when Tom and Russ arrive, but at least I can tell 'em about the bear. Sure wish I had picture to prove it, though.*

Bill's leg muscles spasmed with each step he took as he hobbled toward the cabin. Although not seriously hurt, both knees throbbed. Bill made a mental note to rub some joint cream on them when he got back to the warmth of the fire. On top of that, his teeth chattered from the moisture seeping through his jeans and the opening of his jacket. More importantly, Bill was concerned about putting distance between himself and that enormous bear. This would be a memorable Thanksgiving, although not in a good way. At the moment, Bill didn't care if he bagged a deer Monday morning. All he wanted was to seek refuge and warmth inside the cabin, get out of his wet clothes, and have something to eat. Come morning, he might feel differently—especially once his buddies showed up.

❦

Millersburg

Nicole sat beside her sister at their Thanksgiving table, while Tony sat opposite of them, next to their father.

"The ham turned out good, Dad." Nicole smiled at him. "I like it better than the turkey Tonya used to make."

Dad's forehead wrinkled. "How many times must I tell you to stop calling your mother that? You need to call her Mom."

Nicole lifted both hands in surrender. "Okay, whatever."

"I thought Mom's turkey was fine," Tony spoke up. "She made good mashed potatoes, too." He looked over at Heather. "Don't you think so?"

A cat-like whimper escaped Heather's lips. "I miss Mom so much. Holidays don't seem the same without her."

"You know, kids, your mother is working on getting better," Dad said. "And when she does, you may be able to spend some time with her."

Heather's face brightened. "Really?"

"Yes. Would you like that, honey?"

Heather and Tony both nodded.

Dad looked at Nicole. "How about you? Would you be agreeable to seeing your mother now and then?"

Nicole pursed her lips. "We'll see." Truthfully, she had no intention of spending any time with her mother, but seeing how happy her sister and brother were about the idea, Nicole kept her feelings to herself. There was no point in spoiling the day for her siblings.

Later, while washing the dishes, Nicole glanced out the window from time to time, but her thoughts focused on something Heidi had said during the last cooking class. Was she wrong in refusing to forgive? If Mom meant what she said, and really was trying to get better, shouldn't she be allowed another chance? It wasn't as if Mom would be moving back to their house. She'd only come for visits, or maybe Tony and Heather would go to her place sometime. Nicole didn't want to go, but she wouldn't say or do anything to sway her siblings or turn them against their own mother.

Nicole's chin trembled, and then her shoulders began to quake. For the first time in a long while, she bowed her head and offered an earnest prayer. *Lord, please help me get rid of the anger I have felt since Mom left, and fill my heart with forgiveness toward her.*

Chapter 38

Coshocton

Bill looked up at the clock above the fireplace, wondering when his buddies were going to show up. It was eight thirty Friday morning, and he'd been up since the crack of dawn. Thinking at least one of them would be at the cabin by now, he'd made a fresh pot of coffee, mixed pancake batter, and also fried some maple-flavored bacon. When no one showed up by eight o'clock, Bill ate breakfast alone.

Being used to the quiet, he jumped when his cell phone rang. Bill hoped it wasn't one of the guys saying they weren't coming after all or had been delayed. When he picked up the phone he realized it was his son.

"Hey, Brent, how was your Thanksgiving?"

"I ate too much, but otherwise it was good. How about yours, Dad? Did you see any deer when you went scouting?"

"Nope, but I did see a big black bear."

"Really? So it's not just a rumor about bears being seen in the area?"

"Apparently not, 'cause I saw the creature with my own two eyes."

"It must have taken you by surprise. Glad you're okay, Dad."

"Yeah, me, too." Subconsciously, Bill rubbed the top of his head. "It wasn't just the bear I had to worry about either."

"What do you mean?"

"I may have to take down the old oak where the tree stand is."

"How come?"

"I noticed some dead branches above where I sit, and I came pretty close to getting clunked on my head when one broke off and fell."

"Wow! You're not going to hunt from the tree stand Monday morning, I hope."

Bill heard the concern in his son's voice.

"Definitely not. I'll look for another spot tomorrow, when the guys and I do more scouting. If they ever get here, that is." Pressing the phone tighter against his ear, Bill huffed. "It's not what I want to do, but to be on the safe side, I'll be hunting on the ground this year. I fear the oak tree is too dangerous now."

"Smart move, Dad." Brent sounded relieved.

"It's disappointing, but yeah, it's the wise thing to do."

"Say, Dad, I don't mean to change the subject or anything, but I'd like to ask your opinion on something."

"Sure, go ahead." Bill took a seat in front of the fireplace and put his feet on the coffee table. The heat from the burning logs sent warmth throughout the room.

"You know that day you took me to meet Heidi Troyer, and Kendra Perkins was there?"

"Yeah."

"Well, I've been thinkin' about calling her to see if she'd like to go out with me sometime."

"I see." Bill picked up his coffee mug and took a drink.

"Do you think it's a good idea?"

"Well, that all depends."

"On what?"

"On whether you're looking for a serious relationship or just want to establish a casual friendship."

"I don't know right now. But I'll never find out if Kendra and I don't spend some time together."

"True." Bill set his mug on the coffee table and slouched in his chair. "You don't need my approval to go out with Kendra, but I would like to offer a few words of advice."

"Such as?"

"For starters. . . She has a baby. Are you prepared to raise another man's child if your relationship develops into something serious?"

"I don't know. Maybe. I've never really thought about it." This time Bill heard a hint of doubt in his son's tone. That was good. It meant he was being cautious.

"It's something you ought to think about."

"I suppose."

Bill massaged the back of his neck. "If you decide to pursue a relationship with Kendra, I'd move slow. You don't want to make a mistake you'll be sorry for later."

"Are you thinking of yours and Mom's relationship?" Brent asked.

"Yeah. We had a few things in common when we first got married, but as time went on, our differences pulled us further apart."

The rumble of a vehicle told Bill to look outside, so he rose from his chair. Peering out the front window, he saw Russ getting out of his vehicle.

"Sorry, Son, but I've gotta go. One of my hunting buddies just pulled in."

"Oh, sure, no problem, Dad. I'll talk to you again soon."

"Sounds good. Oh, and be sure to let me know how things go between you and Kendra."

"Will do." Brent chortled. "And if I decide to marry her, you'll be the first person I tell." Before they hung up, Brent added one more thing. "Oh, and Dad—good luck Monday morning. Stay safe and watch out for that bear."

Canton

Kendra had just put little Heidi in the crib when her cell phone rang. When she answered it, she was surprised to hear Brent's voice. She really hadn't expected to hear from him. Kendra had called Brent the other day but got his voicemail, so she'd left a message, giving him her cell number.

"Hey, Kendra, how's it going? Did you have a nice Thanksgiving?"

"Yes, I did. How about you?"

"Good. I ate dinner at my aunt's place, and even though the food was great, there was too much of it."

She laughed. "I know what you mean."

"Say, uh. . . I got your message, and was glad to hear from you. I was wondering if you'd like to go out to dinner with me tomorrow evening."

Blinking rapidly, Kendra tightened her grip on the phone. It had been so long since anyone had asked her on a date, she wasn't sure how to respond. "I'm pleased that you asked, and I'd really like to go, but I'll have to see if my mom or one of my sisters is free to watch Heidi for me."

"Sure, no problem. When do you think you'll have an answer for me?"

"Umm. . . Can I call you back this evening? I should know something by then."

"This evening's good."

"Okay, great. I'll talk to you later, Brent."

Kendra's stomach fluttered as she clicked off the phone. *I hope someone's available to babysit Heidi for me. I'd sure like to spend more time with Brent.*

Cambridge

Lisa sat beside Tim on the couch, engrossed in what he'd been telling her about his childhood. It was amazing how many things they had in common. They both enjoyed cooking, were active in their churches, liked many of the same foods, and spent much of their free time outdoors. Of course, there was also the similarity in their looks. Their hair was about the same shade of blond; however, Tim's eye color was a darker blue than Lisa's. Why she hadn't noticed that when they first met, Lisa wasn't sure, but thank goodness, they did meet.

While she and her half brother got to know each other better, Mom and Dad had taken Tim's wife and the boys shopping. No doubt they wanted to play grandma and grandpa and spoil the children a bit. Lisa couldn't blame them. Finding out Mom had two grandsons, plus a daughter-in-law she'd known nothing about, had been an added bonus to the reunion with Tim. Lisa couldn't remember when she'd seen her mother look so happy. She'd worn a smile throughout the entire Thanksgiving meal yesterday.

Tim tugged on his ear. "You know, I like what I've seen of Ohio so far. If I could find a job and housing, I'd move here in a heartbeat."

Lisa clasped her hands together. "Really?"

He nodded. "I think my wife and boys would like it here, too, and it would sure be nice to live closer to you and your folks."

"What about the parents who raised you?" Lisa asked. "I'm sure they'd be upset if you packed up your family and moved away from them."

Tim shook his head. "You don't understand—my parents are deceased. They were killed in a car accident five years ago."

Lisa brought her hand to her mouth. "I'm so sorry, Tim. That must have been quite a shock."

He dropped his gaze to the floor. "It was a tough time, but with God's help, and the encouragement of our church family, my brothers and I made it through."

Lisa swallowed hard. She could almost feel Tim's pain. "I wonder sometimes how people who don't put their faith in God make it through difficult times." Her thoughts went to Todd. He thought he could do everything in his own strength, but he was so wrong. She hoped one of these days his eyes would be opened to the truth.

Focusing once again on Tim, Lisa turned to him and smiled. "If you should decide to move, I have a two-bedroom duplex I'd be happy to rent at a deep discount. There's someone living in it now, but he'll be moving out soon."

Tim clasped Lisa's hand. "Thanks, Sis. I'll talk to my wife, and we'll give it some thought—sprinkled with lots of prayer, of course."

Moistening her lips with cautious hope, she gave his fingers a tender squeeze. Lisa still couldn't believe she had a brother. How grateful she was that she'd come to her parents' for Thanksgiving. It was one holiday she would always remember. And if things went the way she hoped, she'd have her newly found brother living close by. What a blessing it would be to spend time with Tim, his wife, and their cute little boys. If they moved into her duplex, they'd be living right next door. The only thing that could make Lisa's life any better right now would be if God provided her with a Christian boyfriend.

Chapter 39

Coshocton

Bill, Russ, and Tom started walking toward the cabin after doing some morning scouting. "That's some deer you got a picture of there." Tom thumped Bill's back as they stood looking at the digital camera.

"Yep. I came across this windfall to sit up against, and it seemed like a good spot, since the tree stand is no longer an option." Bill grinned at the photo of the six-point buck he'd taken earlier today, from the new area he'd found to hunt. He'd remembered to take his camera along when he left the cabin this morning. "I watched that deer for a good fifteen minutes as he rubbed his antlers on a tree." Bill leaned slightly forward. "Sure hope I see him again Monday morning. But if not, at least I got a good picture."

"Tom and I haven't seen a thing after traipsin' through the woods all morning," Russ chimed in. "I was hoping to see a deer after we got here yesterday. Now here it is Saturday, and still no luck. I hope that bear you saw on Thanksgiving didn't chase them out of the area. Too bad you didn't get the bear's picture."

"Didn't have my camera with me." Bill gestured to Russ and Tom's orange hunting coats and hats. "Maybe you two should have worn all camouflage today." He pointed to his own clothing. "The buck never saw me this morning, and I was only a few yards away from him. That's why my orange hat and vest are hanging here on the porch. Really don't need them till Monday morning."

"I didn't have a choice, since I forgot my camo jacket." Tom grunted. "Think I shoulda stayed home this weekend." He plunged both hands into his jacket pockets. "The only thing I've gotten so far is a chill seepin' all the way into my bones. Sure hope this isn't an indication of how Monday morning will be."

Russ blew out a breath so strong it rattled his lips. "You should have brought some hand warmers like Bill and I did."

"That's right, and we dressed warm enough." Bill gestured to the cabin as it came into view. "Maybe you should stay inside the rest of the day. You can sit by the fire, drink a cup of coffee, and eat some of the friendship bread I brought to give you fellas. There's also a few pumpkin whoopie pie cookies left."

Tom shook his head vigorously. "And miss the chance of getting a glimpse of a big buck, should one come along? No way! I can drink coffee and try out the bread and cookies when we all go inside, but then I'm heading back out."

Bill chuckled and thumped Tom's shoulder. "Now that's the spirit, my friend."

"It is a bit disappointing about the tree stand, though." Russ looked out toward the woods. "I always liked hunting from up there."

"Don't worry," Bill assured him. "We'll find another, healthier tree, and build an even bigger stand. Maybe one large enough for all of us to be up there together, and we'll put a roof on it, to keep us dry when it rains or snows." Just talking about the plans for a new tree stand gave Bill a sense of anticipation.

"Yeah, I like the idea already." Tom bobbed his head.

"I have a lot of good memories from up there in the old tree stand, but this morning, before I went scouting, I went over to the oak tree and took a good look at things." Bill's forehead wrinkled. "It's a good thing, too, because I discovered some wood dust around the base of the trunk, and that can only mean one thing—carpenter ants."

Grunting, Russ shook his head. "Oh, boy, that's not good."

"Don't know how I missed it yesterday." Bill grimaced. "And if I hadn't gone over to take a look this morning, I may not have noticed it today, either. Guess it must have happened for a reason, though."

He thought about some of the Bible verses Heidi had written on the back of the recipes cards she'd given him and her other cooking students and wondered if God's hand might have been in the situation that spared his life. It was something to ponder all right.

"Building a new tree stand sounds like something we could all work on this coming year." Tom rubbed his hands together, grinning enthusiastically. "I'll bet Andy will be interested in hearing about this, too."

"I agree. It's something we can look forward to." Bill gave a small slap to Tom's back. "Well, let's go inside for a while so we can warm up a bit." He opened the cabin door. "I'll put some fresh coffee on and we can chow down on the rest of the bread and pumpkin whoopies I brought along. You guys are gonna like 'em." While the desserts Bill had brought to share with his friends were not particularly "health foods," they weren't full of artificial ingredients, like some store-bought treats were. Bill had remembered to bring some cut-up veggies for snacks and meals, and he'd made a big tossed green salad to go with their supper tonight.

"Sounds good to me." Tom thumped his belly. "And I can hardly wait to see what you've got planned for lunch. Your cooking's sure improved since you started those classes."

Bill couldn't argue with that. He wished he could continue to learn from Heidi beyond the six classes. But at least he would have the recipes she'd taught them, along with a notebook Heidi gave everyone with helpful tips for the kitchen.

Canton

Kendra stared at her reflection in the bedroom mirror. She wasn't sure what restaurant Brent would be taking her to but hoped she was dressed appropriately. Kendra had chosen a rust-colored skirt and creamy white blouse, which brought out the color of her auburn hair. Dressing up wasn't really her thing, but she wanted to look nice for her date this evening.

Tap. Tap. Tap.

Kendra turned toward the door. "Come in."

Mom poked her head inside. "Well, don't you look nice? Are you going somewhere?"

"Yeah. I have a date with Brent Mason. You said you'd watch Heidi for me, remember?"

"Oh, oh." Mom touched her parted lips. "Sorry, I forgot."

Kendra could hardly believe her mother had forgotten so quickly. It had only been twenty-four hours since she had told her Brent called, and she'd asked if she would watch the baby. "Brent should be here in the next thirty minutes, so are we good?"

Mom shook her head. "Sorry, Kendra, but your dad's boss is having a get-together this evening, and it wouldn't look good if he went without me."

Kendra frowned. "How long have you known about this?"

"Your dad told me this morning." Mom glanced at the baby, sleeping in her crib. "I would suggest that you ask one of your sisters, but they've both gone to the roller-skating party the church youth group is having tonight."

"That's just great." Kendra clenched her teeth. "I wish you had told me about your plans sooner. I would have cancelled my date with Brent." She glanced at the clock on her nightstand. "It's too late now. He's probably on his way here already."

Mom sighed. "Guess I'd better stay home then and watch Heidi." She turned toward the door. "I'll give your dad the news."

"No, that's okay. Your place is with Dad, and you need to keep him happy. When Brent gets here, I'll tell him I'm not able to go out to dinner after all." Kendra figured if Mom gave up her plans this evening to watch the baby, Dad would be upset—probably more with Kendra than Mom, of course. Even though he'd allowed her to move back home, he'd never really accepted the situation and wasn't as attentive to his granddaughter as Kendra would like him to be. The last thing she wanted was to be the cause of more irritation for him. Hopefully, someday her father would wake up and realize what he had right here before him. Until, and unless, that time ever came, Kendra would continue to try and keep the peace.

Mom turned back around. "Say, I have an idea. Why don't you take the baby with you this evening?"

Kendra pinched the bridge of her nose. "That's not a good idea. Heidi might get fussy, and it would be hard for Brent and me to visit if I have to take care of her while I eat and carry on a conversation. Besides, he's expecting this to be a date, not an evening of watching me keep the baby entertained."

"If you feed her now, before he gets here, she'll probably sleep most of the evening."

"I'd rather not chance it." Kendra shook her head. "Go on now, and have a good time with Dad. With any luck, Brent will ask me out again some other time."

"Okay." Adopting a slumped posture, Mom opened Kendra's bedroom door and shuffled out of the room.

Mom obviously felt bad, but that didn't solve Kendra's problem. Raising her hands, she lifted her head toward the ceiling. "How come nothing ever works out for me?"

Chapter 40

The doorbell rang. With regret, Kendra went to answer it, knowing it must be Brent. Sure enough, she found him on the porch, holding a bouquet of red carnations, mixed with pretty feathery-looking greens. He'd obviously gotten them from a florist, since carnations weren't blooming in anyone's yard this time of the year. Grinning, he handed it to her. "These flowers are for you. Hope you like them, and sorry I'm a bit late."

Kendra blinked. Was this guy for real? In all the time she'd been seeing Max, he'd never given her flowers—or much else, for that matter. And her ex-boyfriend had never apologized for being late. "Thanks, Brent. They're beautiful. Carnations are one of my favorite flowers."

"Glad you like 'em." He eyed her with a curious expression—one she couldn't quite read. Did he think she wasn't dressed appropriately for their date? "You about ready to go?"

She drew a quick breath. "I hate to tell you this, but I won't be able to go out with you tonight after all."

Brent's brows furrowed as he tipped his head to one side. "How come?"

She explained about her mother not being able to babysit after all and that both of her sisters had gone out for the evening. "So I have no one to watch little Heidi."

"Not a problem." He leaned closer, his hand on one knee. "You can either bring the baby along, or we can get takeout and eat here."

Now why didn't I think of that? Kendra inhaled quietly. "You wouldn't mind eating here?"

"Nope. Not a bit."

She pressed a palm to her chest. *This guy is really something. Nothing like Max, that's for sure.* She smiled and stepped aside. "Come on in, Brent, and thanks for being flexible."

"No problem. Now that I think about it, eating here would probably be better anyways, because it'll be easier for us to visit in your house than it would be in a crowded, noisy restaurant."

She gave a nod. "Good point." *I'm glad Brent's so agreeable.*

Brent followed her into the living room. After she took his jacket and hung it up, he found a seat on the couch. Glancing over at Heidi, lying in the portable crib, he smiled. "She's a cute little thing. You're lucky to have her."

Kendra leaned over the crib and stroked her daughter's soft cheek. "I know. I feel very blessed."

He got up and stood next to her, staring down at the child. "Someday I'd like to have a house filled with kids."

She turned to face him, lips parted slightly. "You're kidding, right?"

"Well, maybe not a whole houseful, but two or three, that's for sure. Do you want more children, Kendra?"

A warm flush crept across her cheeks. "Yeah, I guess so. Not till I fall in love and get married, though. I made one mistake with Max; I'm not gonna make another."

"I understand." Brent pulled out his cell phone. "What should we order? Are you up for pizza?"

"Sure. I can eat pizza most any time." Kendra glanced at her skirt and blouse. "Even if I am overdressed for it."

"You look really nice." Brent stared at Kendra so hard it made her toes curl.

"Thank you." *Could this be the beginning of a new relationship?* she wondered. *If so, am I ready for it?*

⸻ ❧ ⸻

After they had the pizza, and little Heidi was fed and lay sleeping in her crib again, Kendra and Brent relaxed in front of the TV. Neither one of them watched it, though, as they chatted about their current lives, as well as the days they'd attended the same high school. Kendra felt as comfortable with Brent as she did wearing a cozy flannel nightgown and her fuzzy bedroom slippers. She'd never felt this way with Max. She'd always been on edge, for fear she'd say or do something to rile him. Thinking back on it now, she wondered how she could have given herself to a guy like Max. He was hot-headed and demanding, always making her feel guilty if she didn't do things his way. Some of her desire to be with him could have been rebellion, and part of it was a need to feel as though someone truly cared about her. Of course, she realized that Max had never truly cared, but when he held her in his arms and whispered words of love, Kendra had weakened and let her emotions and physical desires take over.

Kendra took a quick breath to steady her nerves and admitted to Brent the feelings she'd had for him back in high school. "You didn't even know I existed, of course. But I can't blame you. I was only in tenth grade when you were a senior."

"This may surprise you, but I do remember you from our school days." Brent's eyes looked so sincere, it made Kendra's heart do a little flip-flop. "You were that cute little redheaded sophomore I saw standing on the sidelines, cheering our team at the football games. In fact, after one of those games, during half-time, because I was looking at you instead of what the coach was saying, I ended up swallowing my gum."

Kendra giggled. "Really? I had no idea. And by the way, would you care for a piece of gum now?" She reached into the pocket of her skirt, and pulled out a package.

Raising his brows, Brent took it from her. "Spearmint huh? This is my favorite flavor of gum."

Kendra smiled. "I know. It's the kind I like best, too." She didn't tell him that she'd saved one of his old gum wrappers. He might think she was weird or had acted like some silly schoolgirl who'd never gotten over the crush she'd had on him. Her breathing slowed, as the memory took over. *Well, maybe I haven't gotten over that crush. If I had, then why's my heart racing right now?*

Walnut Creek

Heidi sighed contently as she snuggled on the couch beside Lyle, rubbing her bare foot along their dog's silky back. How nice it was to relax for a while before bed and enjoy this quiet time with her husband. Between his busy schedule with auctions and chores, as well as her work around the house, and the time spent preparing for her cooking classes, they didn't get as much time together as she'd like. But then, keeping busy was important for both of them.

"Just think," Heidi commented, "in a few more weeks we'll officially become foster parents. Are you as excited as I am, Lyle?"

"Sure am. I'm also anxious to find out whether we get a *buwe* or *maedel*."

"Either a boy or a girl is fine with me. My only concern is whether he or she will like it here. It's quite likely they have never met an Amish person before and certainly won't have lived in an Amish home. What if the child doesn't like it here? What if. . ."

Lyle placed his fingers gently against Heidi's lips. "Now don't start fretting about things that may never occur. The child may adjust to our way of living with no trouble at all."

"I know. I need to trust the Lord in all things and wait to see what happens." She kissed his fingers. "The best part of all in the joy of waking every day is that it gives us a chance to begin anew. So even if things aren't as we want them to be the day before, we're given another chance to make things right," Heidi quoted from a recent message given by one of their ministers.

"So true," he agreed, "and with tomorrow being Sunday, we'll have the opportunity to worship God with other believers and begin our new week."

Canton

Todd stood in front of his bedroom mirror and straightened his tie. He couldn't believe he was going to church this morning, but it was time for him to turn over a new leaf. At first he had looked in the paper at the different churches he could attend here in town. But in the end, he'd decided to go back to Lisa's church in Dover, where he'd been before. Since Todd had already gone there once and met the minister, he felt semicomfortable about attending there again. Even if Lisa didn't like him showing up at her church today, maybe if he explained his reasons for being there, she would understand.

As Todd put on his overcoat, his cell phone rang. He pulled it out of his pocket and swiped it on with his thumb.

'Hello, Son. It's your mom."

"Hi, Mom." Todd tapped his foot, glancing at his watch. He didn't have much time to get to church, so he'd have to make this brief.

"How was your Thanksgiving? Did you have a nice time with. . . I think you said her name was Lilia?"

"No, her name is Lisa, but I'm not seeing her anymore, and I ended up having Thanksgiving by myself, in a restaurant of all things." Todd braced himself. *Here it comes; Mom's gonna have more questions.*

"Oh, Todd, what happened with you and Lilia—I mean, Lisa?"

"It's complicated, and I don't have time to go into it right now."

"You know, you could have flown home, instead of being there by yourself."

"Mom, I have to go. Church service starts soon, and I'll be late if I don't leave now."

"Church service? Where are you going to church?"

"I'll tell you later. Say hi to Dad for me. Bye for now, Mom." Rushing out the door, Todd quickly hung up and stuffed the cell phone in his coat pocket. *Sure hope I'm not gonna be late. I probably shouldn't have taken Mom's call.*

———— ⌑⌑⌑ ————

New Philadelphia

"Mama, I can't find my church shoes!" Nola shouted from her bedroom upstairs.

Rubbing the back of her neck, Allie lifted her gaze to the kitchen ceiling. She should have left ten minutes ago to take the kids to Sunday school, and if they didn't leave soon, they'd be so late, they may as well stay home.

She stepped into the hallway and cupped her hands around her mouth. "Did you look in your closet?"

"Not there!"

"How about under the bed?"

"Huh-uh."

Allie groaned. "Ask Derek to help you look for them."

While she waited for her daughter's response, Allie took her teacup to the sink and rinsed it out. She'd wash it, as well as the breakfast dishes, when she got back to the house after dropping them off. Steve was working again, of course, and it would be nice to have some quiet time by herself.

The kids' puppy whimpered and brushed against Allie's leg. She bent down and gave him a pat on the head. "Hey, Trouble. . . What do you want, boy?"

The dog barked twice, then raced to the back door.

"Oh, I see. You need to go outside." Allie opened the door and stepped aside as Trouble darted out and made a beeline for the fenced-in yard. *Cute little pup. He's learning fast.*

She closed the door and hollered at Nola again. "Did you find your shoes?"

"No, Mama."

"Then you'll either have to stay home or wear your sneakers today." Allie tapped her foot, her impatience mounting. If Nola had gotten her shoes out last night like she'd been asked to, they could have looked for them then if she'd realized they were missing.

She glanced at the clock and was about to go upstairs to check on things, when the telephone rang. "Now what?" She was going to let the answering machine get it, but decided to pick it up in case the call was important. "Hello. Garrett residence."

"Allie, this is Sergeant Bowers. I'm afraid I have some bad news."

Her heart started to pound, and she leaned against the kitchen table for support. "Wh–what's wrong?"

"Steve's been shot, and is being taken to the hospital in Dover."

A sudden coldness spread through Allie's body as the room began to spin. Every time Steve went out the door to report for work, his life was in danger. Tightening her grip on the phone, she feared the worst. Could her husband's wound be fatal? Would she ever see him again? The fearful thoughts shook her clean to her toes.

Allie covered her ears in an attempt to stop the agony raging in her soul, but it did no good. She needed to get to the hospital right away!

Chapter 41

Canton

Kendra was almost finished getting the baby ready for church when her dad came into the room. Since the door was open, she figured he thought it was okay not to knock.

"Can I talk to you a few minutes before it's time to leave?" he asked.

Kendra, feeling hesitant and not wishing to deal with whatever he wanted to say, shrugged her shoulders. "Well, it might make us late."

He shook his head. "We have ten minutes yet before it's time to leave, and I don't want to go until I've said what's on my mind."

"Okay." Kendra buttoned the baby's pretty pink dress. It was a gift from her friend Dorie.

Dad took a seat on the end of her bed, watching as she finished dressing little Heidi. A few seconds passed. Then he cleared his throat. "I've been doing a lot of thinking lately, and spending some time in prayer."

Oh, great. I suppose he's gonna tell me he made a mistake letting me move back home and now he wants me to find someplace else to live. She bit her trembling lip. "What are you trying to say, Dad?"

He stood and moved over to stand next to her, in front of the changing table. "I owe you an apology, Kendra."

She tipped her head in question but said nothing. *Did I hear him right?* As far back as she remembered, her dad rarely apologized to anyone—at least not to his wife or daughters. She was even more surprised to see tears well up in his eyes. Was it possible that her father truly felt remorse?

He placed his hand on her arm. "My attitude has been wrong

where you are concerned. I shouldn't have demanded you leave the house when you told your mother and me that you were pregnant. I should have been there to offer support and help you make the right decisions concerning the baby. I've been harsh and unfeeling. Will you forgive me, Kendra?"

Her mouth felt dry, and she swallowed hard, barely able to say the words. "I—I—yeah, Dad, I forgive you. Will you forgive me for bringing shame on our family by giving in to my desires and sleeping with Max?"

Dad slipped his arm around Kendra's waist and drew her up close. "Yes, I will, but you need to seek God's forgiveness, too."

A lump formed in her throat, and her voice cracked when she spoke. "I already have."

"That's good." Dad patted her back. "I've done the same." He paused. "I've also apologized to your mother. It hasn't been fair to her being stuck in the middle of all this due to the way I've been acting. I shouldn't have made her feel guilty if she didn't want to take my side."

Kendra felt a sense of relief such as she'd never felt before. For the first time in a long while, she knew without reservation that Dad loved her. All the anger and bitterness she'd felt toward him for so long, melted away.

She looked at him and smiled through her tears. "I love you, Dad."

He lifted his hand and dried the dampness from her cheeks with his thumb. "I love you, too, Kendra, and I'm proud of you. You're a good mother to sweet little Heidi." Tenderness laced his words, like a soft blanket against rough skin. Then, glancing down at the baby, he added with a smile, "And I feel blessed to be the grandfather of such a precious little girl."

Dover

Drawers on medicine carts sliding open and then banging shut grated on Allie's nerves. Even a simple thing like someone's newspaper rattling put her on edge. Her chair creaked as she tried to find a comfortable position. She glanced at her watch. Steve had been in surgery well over two hours. What in the world could be taking so long? Why wouldn't someone come and tell her something?

She left her seat and paced the length of the waiting room. As she passed an elderly woman thumbing through a magazine, Allie stifled a sneeze. What kind of horrible-smelling cologne was the woman wearing? People ought to have better sense than to wear stuff like that.

I am being oversensitive and need to calm down. She walked to the far side of the room, poured herself a cup of hot tea, and returned to her seat. *I wish someone was with me right now. Steve's folks should have been here by now.* A raw ache settled in the pit of her stomach.

When Allie received the news that Steve had been taken to the hospital, she'd called her parents, as well as Steve's folks right away. Then she phoned her neighbor Ella and asked if she could come over to be with the children. There would be no Sunday school for her kids today. Of course, Allie's parents, living in New York, wouldn't be here for several hours. Ella had wanted to go with Allie to the hospital, and suggested her daughter, Tara, could stay with the kids, but Allie insisted on going alone. Big mistake! What she needed the most right now was comfort and someone's support. *Maybe I should have notified the pastor or somebody from the church where the kids attend. At least I could have asked for prayer on Steve's behalf.* In times like this, sometimes prayer was the only thing that could hold a person up. And right now, Allie had been doing a lot more than praying; she'd been begging God to spare her husband's life.

"How's Steve?"

Allie looked up, surprised to see Lori Robbins, the blond-haired patrol officer new to the force, looking down at her. Allie's nostrils flared as she lifted her chin. "What are you doing here?"

"I came to find out how Steve is doing. After he was shot, I had to go back to the office and fill out a report. Otherwise, I would have been here a lot sooner." Lori took a seat beside Allie.

"So you were with him when it happened?"

"Yes." Lori's facial features sagged as she held her hands together.

"Would you please give me the details about the shooting? What I've been told so far has been sketchy, and Steve was already in surgery when I got here." Despite Allie's irritation, since Officer Robbins had been with Steve at the time he'd been shot, she was the best person to talk to about it right now.

Lori leaned slightly forward, staring down at the floor. "We received a call saying there was a robbery at the mini-mart on the other side of town. When we got there, a man wearing a ski mask was running down the sidewalk. He fit the description of the robber, so Steve shouted at the guy to stop, but he kept going." Lori paused and pushed aside a wayward strand of blond hair that had come loose from her ponytail. "While I called for backup, Steve pursued the suspect. Suddenly, a shot rang out, and then Steve slumped to the pavement." Her eyes misted. "I hope he's gonna be all right. Have you had any word?"

Allie's chin quivered as she shook her head. "Nothing since they took him into surgery. I—I don't know what I'll do if Steve doesn't make it. The children and I need him so much."

Lori placed her hand on Allie's arm. "Think positive thoughts and say a prayer for your husband. He's a good man. I've been praying for him, too."

Allie was tempted to quiz Lori about her relationship with Steve, but this wasn't the time or place for an inquisition or accusations. Her focus right now was on her husband, willing him to live and hoping God would answer her prayers.

As Lisa approached the pew where she normally sat, a shiver went up her spine. *Todd. What's he doing here?* She was about to turn around and leave the church sanctuary when he spotted her.

"Lisa, don't go. I need to talk to you."

She put her finger against her lips. "Not here. This isn't the time or place."

"Can we go somewhere after church?" he whispered.

She shook her head.

"Please, Lisa. It's important." He scooted over. "If you don't have time later, then have a seat, and I'll tell you right now."

Lisa glanced around, noticing several people staring at them. The best option would be to take a seat, but with the service about to begin, she certainly wasn't going to carry on a conversation with Todd. She slipped in next to him and whispered, "We can talk in the parking lot after church."

Eyes focused straight ahead, he gave a brief nod.

Lisa shifted nervously on the bench. It was difficult sitting next to Todd, inhaling his spicy cologne and wondering what he wanted to talk to her about. His hand brushed her arm, and the brief contact made her flinch. She didn't trust Todd, and the last thing she needed was to lose her heart to this man. Heat flooded her face, like it always did when she was flustered.

When the worship team gathered on the platform, Lisa forced her attention to the front of the room. The musicians consisted of two guitarists, a young woman playing the keyboard, and a drummer. Four vocalists led the congregation in choruses and hymns. Normally, Lisa would have relaxed and enjoyed singing along, but this morning it was hard to focus, much less unwind and feel one with the music. She'd come to church full of joy after a weekend of learning she had a brother. Now the bliss she'd felt had been replaced with apprehension.

Lisa glanced briefly at Todd, surprised to see he was actually singing along. Or perhaps he was merely mouthing the words. She couldn't be sure with all the voices around her. Todd didn't appear to be bored, like the last time they'd been here together. Was he putting on an act for her benefit, or had something changed in Todd's heart?

Chapter 42

When the church service drew to a close, Todd's hands began to sweat, as negative thought patterns took hold. What if Lisa didn't accept his apology or believe he was trying to change for the better? His thoughts spun faster than a windmill in a gale. She might think he was making it up to try and win her favor. But it was worth a shot, and he couldn't go home until he'd tried.

"Don't forget, I need to talk to you," he murmured in Lisa's ear as they walked out of the sanctuary.

"I remember. Follow me to my car."

Todd paused at the door to shake hands with the pastor and his wife. Lisa did the same and waited while he asked the pastor a question. "Do you think I could meet with you soon? I need someone to talk to." Todd pulled at the tie up close to his throat. It felt like it was choking him.

Lisa stood by and silently watched. He wished she would say something—at least give some indication as to what she was thinking.

The minister handed Todd a piece of paper with his phone number on it. "Give me a call, and we'll set something up."

"Thank you. I appreciate it." Todd shook the preacher's hand again. Then he and Lisa stepped outside.

Todd waited for Lisa to drill him with questions, but instead she remained quiet. The silence between them was deafening, except for Lisa's heels clicking against the pavement.

Out in the parking lot, by Lisa's car, Todd wiped a palm across his sweaty forehead. "I just want to say that I'm sorry for deceiving you about my job. I've made a lot of mistakes in the past, and more since I met you." He stopped talking and studied Lisa's face but couldn't tell what she was thinking. "Lisa, I need to find forgiveness." He crossed his arms in an effort to keep from touching her. What he really wanted to do was take Lisa in his arms and beg her to forgive him. "I—I figured coming to church today would be a good place to start."

Todd saw skepticism in Lisa's pursed lips and squinted eyes, but he continued. "Can you find it your heart to forgive and give me a second chance?"

He waited, but Lisa said nothing, looking deeply into his eyes. Todd's gaze held hers as she seemed to scrutinize his face. He didn't have to wonder what she was doing, for he'd done it many times to others. She was reading him and wondering if what he said had merit.

She looked to the left as someone walked by, then turned to face him again. With her gaze fixed somewhere near the center of his chest, Lisa replied, "I forgive you, Todd, but for now, all I can offer you is friendship."

Todd wasn't sure how to respond. He had to admit, he was disappointed. But at least being friends with Lisa was a good place to start. "Having you be my friend is more than I deserve, Lisa. Thank you for that." He leaned closer and gave her a quick kiss on the cheek.

Lisa pulled back, her mouth forming an O.

His face warmed. "Sorry about that. I did it on impulse."

Her eyes narrowed, and she turned her head away. "Don't worry about it. Some things—or shall I say, some people—never change."

Todd's shoulders slumped. "Yeah, right. Guess I deserved that comment. See you, Lisa."

As Todd walked to his car, he could feel her gaze upon him. Unlocking the door, he hesitated, then looked in her direction.

Lisa looked back at him briefly, then turned, climbed into her van, and drove off.

He watched until she was out of sight. Friends? Was that all Lisa wanted? Well, if it was, then he'd accept it, no matter how much he longed for more. Lisa's friendship was better than nothing.

————— ༝ °༚ ༛ —————

Walnut Creek

Heidi sat on one end of a bench, enjoying pleasant conversation with a group of women after the noon meal that followed their church service. When she noticed Loretta at a table nearby, she excused herself and took a seat on the bench beside her friend. The other night, Lyle had told Heidi that he'd spoken to Eli, but she would not mention it to Loretta. Her friend might see it as meddling.

"Where are your children?" Heidi asked.

Loretta gestured to her daughter, Abby, playing with a couple of young girls a short distance away. "And Conner is somewhere with Eli."

"Would you like to go outside and take a walk with me?" Heidi scooted closer to Loretta.

"That sounds nice. It's gotten kind of stuffy in here, and I could use a breath of fresh air."

"Will Abby be okay by herself?

"Jah. She's busy playing and probably won't even know I've left the building." Loretta chuckled. "My son and daughter haven't had any trouble making friends with the Amish children in this church district."

"I'm glad." Walking beside Loretta, Heidi stepped out of the barn, where church had been held that morning.

As they walked around the building and toward the pasture, Heidi was about to ask how things were going, when Loretta posed a question. "I haven't seen you for a while. How'd Thanksgiving go with your folks?"

"Oh, it was *wunderbaar*. I had such a nice time visiting with my parents and siblings."

Loretta smiled. "It's always good to be with family."

"How was your Thanksgiving?" Heidi asked.

Loretta's eyes gleamed. "Mine was wonderful, too. I had Eli and his parents for dinner, and also my folks. It was the first time they'd had a chance to meet each other."

"How did that go?"

"Quite well, actually. Since my mom and dad were raised Amish, they know the Pennsylvania Dutch language. So they were able to communicate with Eli's parents in both English, as well as their Amish dialect."

"I'm pleased to hear that." The two women paused near the fence. "There's something I've been meaning to ask," Heidi added.

Loretta tipped her head. "Is it about me and Eli?"

"Jah. I've been praying for both of you, and I hope things have gotten better between you two by now."

"They have. In fact, I took your suggestion and spoke to Eli about the way I feel when he compares things I've said or done to his late wife." Loretta touched Heidi's arm. "I forgot I said I'd let you know how things turned out once I'd spoken to Eli about the situation. Sorry about that."

"It's all right. I'm eager to know, though. Did he take it okay?"

"Yes, and Eli even apologized and said he would try not to do it again. He also added that if he slipped and did make another comparison, I should tell him about it right away." Loretta placed both hands against her chest. "I believe everything's going to be all right between me and Eli."

Heidi slipped her arm around Loretta's waist. "Hearing that pleases me very much."

Millersburg

Nicole handed her sister a dishcloth. "Your turn to dry."

Heather wrinkled her nose. "Do I have to?"

"Would you rather wash the dishes?"

"No, washing's even worse. I wish Dad would buy a dishwasher."

"Those cost money, and Dad doesn't have extra cash floating

around, you know." Nicole filled the sink with warm water and added a few squirts of liquid detergent. "So stop complaining and be glad for what we have."

They did the dishes in silence. When they finished, Nicole suggested her sister go outside and ride her bike with Tony. With both kids entertained, it would give her a chance to get some sketching done. She hadn't done any drawings for a few weeks, and it would be nice to have some quiet time to herself.

After Heather put on her hooded jacket and headed outside, Nicole went to the hall closet and took out her art supplies. "Come on, Bowser. You can stay inside for a while and keep me company." She patted the dog's head and laughed when his wagging tail thumped against the wall.

Nicole had just taken a seat at the table when the telephone rang. Since Dad was out in the garage, she went to answer it, with Bowser barking at her feet. "Shh. . . Now go lie down." Bowser crawled under the table and let out a whiney yawn before laying his head on his front paws.

"Smith residence."

"Nicki, is that you?"

"Yeah, it's me." Nicole didn't have to ask who the caller was; she recognized her mother's high-pitched voice.

"Is your dad at home?"

"He's in the garage. Should I go get him?"

"In a minute. Since you answered, I'd like to say a couple of things."

Nicole's gaze darted around the kitchen, wishing she could flee the room. *Oh, great. Here it comes. I'm about to hear the same old song and dance about how much my mother has changed.*

Mom cleared her throat. "I'll be the first to admit, I haven't been the best mother."

You got that right.

"But I'm really trying to clean up my life."

"Uh-huh, I know. The last time you were here, I heard you telling Dad that you're going to AA meetings."

"Yes, that's right. Why didn't you say something, or at least show yourself?"

Nicole clenched the receiver until her fingers ached. Should she tell Mom what she thought? "I didn't want to talk to you. I've been angry about the things you've done to our family, and what all I've had to go through in order to help Dad keep everything together."

"I understand. You have every reason to be upset with me, and so do Heather and Tony." There was a pause as Nicole's mother drew a quick breath. Then she started to cry. "I know it's a lot to ask, but can you find it in your heart to forgive me?"

Nicole flinched, as though Mom had reached out and touched her through the phone. She thought about the scripture written on the back of the last recipe card Heidi had given her. *If I don't forgive others, God won't forgive me.* She stood by the sink several seconds, trying to stop the flow of tears that came unexpectedly. "Yeah, Mom, I forgive you, and I hope things will go better for you from now on."

"Thanks, Nicki—I mean, Nicole. I hope things go well for you, too."

———————— ⌒∘⌒ ————————

Dover

Lisa curled up on the couch with a cup of hot chocolate. She'd been sitting here for a while, reflecting on the joy of learning she had a brother. She felt excited thinking how, in the near future, Tim could possibly be living next door. Lisa was anxious to get to know him better, as well as his wife and boys. Even if only for a short time, she was glad Dan had been able to move into the duplex. It had helped pay the bills, but it would be nice once the place was empty and she could offer it to Tim and his family, should they decide to move to Ohio. Tim was a carpenter, and his wife a nurse, so surely one or both of them could find employment in Dover or one of the nearby towns.

Sighing, Lisa's thoughts turned to Todd. She still couldn't get over him showing up in church today. He'd truly seemed different, and hearing him speaking to the minister caused her to wonder if Todd had been serious about the things he'd said to her. Lisa had forgiven him and offered friendship, but she felt sure he wanted more.

"I'm not ready for that," she murmured, reaching for the Sunday paper. She needed to get her mind off Todd and onto something else.

She read the weather report and some of the local news, then turned to the classified section. Lisa needed a new dishwasher, and hoped she might find a good used one—not someone's hand-me-down on its last legs, but a commercial dishwasher that had been reconditioned.

Seeing nothing at all, she resigned herself to the fact that she may have to let loose of her purse strings and buy a new one.

Lisa set the paper aside long enough to take a sip of her hot chocolate, which wasn't hot anymore. She headed to the kitchen to put the mug in the microwave. While it heated, she glanced out the window. Shortly after Lance's brother moved in, he'd asked permission to hang a feeder in the birch tree out back. Within a few hours, the birds discovered it and had been coming into the yard ever since, seeking food.

Lisa found it relaxing to watch and identify the different species. Some of the birds held fast to their perch, eating one sunflower seed after another, while others would take a single seed and fly off to a nearby branch and peck it open to eat. Since Dan's purchase, Lisa had gone out and bought a suet cake and cage to hang in the tree. The woodpeckers were especially attracted to that.

Along with the suet, Lisa found an interesting book to help determine the different types of birds. In the last few pages near the back of the book was a lot of space to log in the date and kind of birds she'd been able to identify.

As she continued to watch out the window, Lisa spotted a red-bellied woodpecker hanging on the suet cage. The basically pale bird had a brilliant red cap, black-and-white barred wings and back, and a slight tinge of red on its belly, for which it had been given its name.

Lisa grinned. *I should have thought of hanging out a few feeders long ago. Who knew it would be so much fun to watch these beautiful birds?* Birdwatching had become a new hobby for her, and she looked forward to seeing what birds would come into the yard when the weather turned colder and it snowed. It was a good idea to feed the birds during the frigid winter, when nature's food for them was scarce.

Pulling her thoughts aside, Lisa realized that the microwave had beeped several minutes ago, so she hit it for thirty more seconds and continued to watch the woodpecker. When she heard another beep, she turned from the window and took the steaming cup of hot chocolate out, then returned to the living room.

After settling on the couch, she placed her mug on the coffee table and picked up the newspaper. This time, her gaze came to rest on an advertisement placed by a local photographer, Charlene Higgins. The ad stated that Charlene was available to do photo shoots for businesses that wanted to advertise their products in various ways.

"What a great idea." Lisa grabbed a pen and piece of paper to write down the phone number listed in the ad. She would make the call first thing in the morning. Perhaps a bit more advertising was exactly what her catering business needed.

—————— ⁙ ——————

Allie felt relief when Steve's folks arrived and took seats near her in the waiting room. She felt even better when Lori excused herself to make a few phone calls. It was hard to look at her and not feel resentment, coupled with anger. Lori had seemed genuinely concerned, but was it for Allie, or was she frightened for herself? If the new officer was having an affair with Steve, then her concern for his welfare was for selfish reasons.

Desperate to focus on something positive, Allie thought of happy times she and Steve had spent as a family. Would they have an opportunity to spend more time together, or was her husband's life about to end?

She glanced over at Steve's mother, Jeanette, clinging to her husband's hand. Carl, Steve's father, gave his wife's fingers a squeeze, whispering words of hope, while trying to appear strong. They were worried, too. Steve was their only son. If he died, they'd be lost.

Allie recalled how when Steve had decided to become a policeman, Jeanette had tried to talk him out of it. "It's a dangerous profession," she'd said several times. "A dangerous, thankless job." But Steve had made up his mind, and even said he felt that police work was his calling. Wanting her husband's happiness, Allie had neither said nor done anything to stand in his way. Now, with his life possibly hanging in the balance, she wished she could go back in time, regardless of wanting to be supportive, and beg him to seek some other type of employment. Allie had so many regrets, but they got her nowhere.

Her attention was drawn to the door when a tall, dark-haired doctor stepped into the waiting room. "Mrs. Garrett?" He moved slowly across the room.

"Yes, I'm Allie Garrett. Do you have some news about my husband?"

He gave a slow nod, then took the seat beside her.

Her body felt paralyzed with fear. She couldn't speak, couldn't move. It was bad news. She felt it at the core of her being.

Steve's parents must have felt it, too, for they left their seats and came over to stand in front of the doctor, eyes wide and biting down on their bottom lips.

"We got the bullet out, and your husband is in stable condition," the doctor said. "His injuries aren't life-threatening, but he will need plenty of rest. It will be several weeks before he can return to work."

Allie pressed her palms against her eyes, sagging in her chair. Struggling to speak around her swollen throat, she rasped, "I am so relieved."

Steve's mother bowed her head, releasing a ragged breath, while his father made the sign of the cross.

"When can I see him?" Allie asked.

"He's still in Recovery, but as soon as he's settled in a room, a nurse will let you know."

"Thank you, Doctor, for all you've done."

--------------------✦✦✦--------------------

Allie sat in Steve's room, watching his chest rise and fall as he drifted in and out of sleep. His parents had popped in earlier and were now in the hospital cafeteria getting a bite to eat. They'd offered to bring something back for Allie, but she'd declined. Food was the last thing on her mind right now. Lori Robbins had left the hospital, after being told only Steve's immediate family could see him today. She'd asked Allie to give him the message that she'd be praying for his full recovery.

Allie fidgeted in her chair, trying to relax, but her nervousness won out. Negative thoughts regarding the blond officer continued to haunt her. Were Lori and Steve an item? How many times had Allie asked herself that question? *I need to know. I can't go on like this, conjuring up all kinds of scenarios. How would I have felt if Steve had died, knowing Lori was the last person to be with him?*

Steve's eyelids fluttered, then opened. "Allie, I. . ."

She put her fingers to his lips. "Shh. . .don't talk. You need to rest."

He shook his head. "I'm sorry, Allie. So sorry."

Her spine stiffened. This was it. Steve was about to confess. Allie couldn't bear the thought of him admitting his love for another woman. If he asked for a divorce, she would have a meltdown, right here in his hospital room. A nurse would probably come in and ask Allie to either quiet down or leave.

Steve reached for her hand. "I'm sorry for working such long hours and not spending enough time with you and the kids." Tears welled in his eyes. "I only did it so I could buy all of you something really special for Christmas this year. I was hoping to plan a trip to Disney World."

Disney World? Something special for Christmas? "Oh, Steve, I don't care about any of that. All I want is you." She sniffed, swiping at the tears rolling down her cheeks. "As much as Nola and Derek would like to go to Disney World, I'm sure they'd rather have their father, whole, and healthy, and spending quality time with them."

His Adam's apple bounced as he swallowed. "You and the kids are my only reason for living."

"What about Lori?"

Steve's brows furrowed. "Officer Robbins?"

Allie nodded slowly.

"What about her? Was she shot, too?"

"No, she's fine." Allie took a tissue from her purse and blew her nose. "She was here earlier and said I should let you know that she's praying for you."

"Then what did you mean when you asked, 'What about Lori?'" Steve took a breath and let it out slowly.

"You two have been together so much, and I just assumed..."

He stared at her strangely for several seconds before a light seemed to dawn. "Please don't tell me you thought something was going on between me and Lori."

Allie dropped her gaze. "To be honest, the thought had crossed my mind. More than once, in fact."

He coughed, then sputtered. "Oh, for goodness' sakes. Lori is my partner—nothing else. The times we have been together were necessary."

"What about the day I saw you two in the car at the mall?"

"We were talking about her boyfriend and the problem they were having with his folks disapproving of him dating a cop." Steve paused and moistened his lips with his tongue. "I could totally relate, since your folks, and my parents, too, did not approve of my line of work."

Allie released a huge breath, rocking back and forth in her chair as moisture from her eyes continued to dribble down her cheeks.

Steve brushed the tears away with his thumb in a circular motion. "I love you, Allie. You're the woman I will always call sweetheart."

"I love you, too." Allie felt such relief as she watched her husband drift back to sleep. She was glad she'd been wrong about Steve and Lori, but beyond that, Allie was thrilled that Steve wanted to spend more time with her and the children. Perhaps, once Steve felt well enough, they would go to church as a family. It was the least they could do to thank God for sparing Steve's life.

Chapter 43

Walnut Creek

Even though she'd received some good news yesterday, a sense of sadness came over Heidi as she scurried about the kitchen, preparing for her students' arrival on this, their final cooking class. With Christmas fast approaching, she'd decided to teach them how to make a Christmas Crunch Salad. The verse she'd written on the back of their recipe cards this time was taken from Luke 18:27: "The things which are impossible with men are possible with God." Heidi knew this scripture well and had memorized it when she was a girl. She couldn't imagine how anyone could make it through life without knowing God personally. His presence was everywhere: in the sun, moon, and stars; on earth; throughout nature—everything was made by Him.

The good news Heidi had received was twofold—first Eli told Lyle he and Loretta were planning to be married this coming spring. Now that Loretta had been baptized and joined the Amish church, they were free to begin planning their wedding.

The second bit of news was when Kendra called and left Heidi a message early this morning. She wanted Heidi to know that her father had apologized for the way he'd treated her since first finding out she was pregnant. Heidi was thrilled with this news, and planned to call Kendra back later today. Some people might believe certain things were impossible, but God, in His infinite wisdom and mighty power, could turn even the most difficult situation into something good—something that would bring glory to His name.

Heidi paused from her introspections to separate the freshly washed broccoli, cauliflower, onions, and cherry tomatoes into piles, placing them around the table where each of her students would sit. She would wait to set out the ingredients for the dressing until everyone arrived.

While she waited, Heidi continued working on a list she'd started for the things they would need to have on hand as foster parents: extra tissues for sniffling noses; bandages of various sizes; a variety of toys, including coloring books with crayons; and of course, plenty of healthy snack foods. There were so many things to think about. But Heidi and Lyle were eager and more than ready to begin this new adventure.

Heidi tapped her pencil along the edge of the rolltop desk. *Do I need to give up teaching cooking classes now that I'll be parenting full time?* She lifted her shoulders briefly. *Well, it doesn't matter. I have other, more important things to think about now. I will make that decision when the time is right.*

The sound of tires crunching on the gravel brought Heidi to her feet. One of her students had arrived. She set her notebook and pencil aside and went to open the front door, where she saw Nicole getting out of her father's car. The next thing Heidi knew, the girl sprinted toward the house, grinning and waving a blue apron in her hand.

When Nicole stepped onto the porch, she held the item out to Heidi. "I remembered to bring it this time."

Heidi smiled. "That's good, because the old one I've let you use a few times is in the dirty laundry basket right now."

When they entered the house, Heidi paused in the hall. "I have a few things to do yet in the kitchen, Nicole. Would you like to wait in the living room until the others arrive?"

"I'd rather go to the kitchen with you. I have something to tell you, and I'm anxious to share."

"No problem."

They headed to the kitchen, and while Nicole took a seat at the end of the table where there were no vegetables, Heidi took two glasses out of the cupboard. "Would you like something to drink? There's apple cider in the refrigerator, and also some milk."

"I'll just have a glass of water."

"Okay." Heidi filled one of the glasses with water and placed it in front of Nicole. Then she poured herself a glass of apple cider and sat in a chair next to her young student.

"Thanks." Nicole took a drink then cleared her throat. "I did like you said and forgave Tonya—I mean, my mom. I told her that when she called last week. Mom's going to Alcoholics Anonymous, and she's trying to do better, so I need to at least give her a chance." She closed her eyes briefly and released a puff of air. "I felt better after we hung up—like a sense of relief. I've been angry at Mom ever since she left, and it's made me disagreeable. Sometimes the resentment I felt made me feel almost sick."

"I'm glad you were able to forgive her. With forgiveness comes healing." Heidi's eyes filled with joyous tears as she clasped Nicole's hand. "What a wonderful thing to learn on this last day of class."

"I have something for you, Heidi." Nicole opened the manila folder she'd carried into the house. Heidi hadn't even noticed it until now. She pulled out a piece of heavy paper and handed it to Heidi. "It's a picture I drew of your dog. I wanted to surprise you with it."

Heidi gazed at the picture. "It certainly does look like our Rusty." She shook her head slowly. "I had no idea you were an artist, Nicole. This is a wonderful gift."

Nicole tucked her arms in at her sides, looking down at the floor. "It's nothing, really. Drawing is something I do just for fun. I'm not really that talented."

"Oh, but you are." Heidi placed the picture on the table and gave Nicole a hug. "I appreciate your thoughtfulness."

———— ✺◦◦◦◦ ————

Bill stepped onto the Troyers' porch at the same time as Lance. "How was your Thanksgiving?" he asked.

"It was good. I spent it at one of my daughter's." Lance gave a wide smile. "How was yours?"

"I was alone at my cabin on Thanksgiving, but my two hunting buddies showed up the next day." Bill puffed out his chest a bit. "Got me a nice-sized buck on Monday, opening day, with a good set of antlers."

"You gonna hang 'em on the wall in your cabin or display them at your house?"

"Probably at the cabin. I have several others there, too."

"Do you eat the deer meat?" Lance questioned.

"I have in the past, but this year I made a decision to donate the venison to a local food bank. They are always in need of meat."

"That's a nice thing to do." Lance gave him a friendly smack on the shoulder.

Bill knocked on the door. "I can't believe this is our sixth and final cooking class."

Lance nodded. "I know. I'm gonna miss coming here every other Saturday." He chuckled. "Gonna miss the good-tasting food, most of all."

"Yeah, same here. But I'll also miss the time we've spent getting to know each other, as well as our cooking instructor. Heidi's a special young woman. I have the utmost respect for her."

"Me, too." Lance tugged his earlobe. "It's interesting how we all come from different walks of life, yet have found something in common—specifically our interest in Amish cooking."

Heidi opened the door and greeted them both, asking the men to join her and Nicole in the kitchen.

The minute Bill entered the room and took a look at Nicole, he knew something was different about the girl. Gone were her drooping shoulders and downturned mouth. They'd been replaced by a relaxed posture and eyes that sparkled. It had to be something other than better school grades and more time to do homework. He stood with arms folded, staring at Nicole as she fingered her glass of water. Did he dare ask what had brought on such a change?

As if she could read his thoughts, Nicole offered Bill a wide smile. "I wasn't gonna say anything, but it's only fair that you know—I'm not mad at my mom anymore. It feels good to have let it all go."

He stepped behind her and placed both hands on her shoulders.

"That's good news. Life's too short to carry a heavy load of anger in our souls." Bill thumped his chest. "Ask me—I know."

"I wholeheartedly agree," Lance put in. "I've had my own share of things to deal with concerning my brother, but I think it's all good now."

"Life ain't perfect," Bill added, "but it's a lot better when we're at peace with others. I've learned a lot more than cooking from taking these cooking classes." He lifted both hands. "And who knows...I may even start goin' to church sometime in the future."

Heidi smiled. "That's good news."

Bill moved closer to Heidi. "By the way, I know something I think you'll want to know."

She raised her eyebrows. "Really? What's that?"

"My son, Brent, who came with me to meet you before Thanksgiving, had a date last weekend with your previous student, Kendra." Bill scratched the back of his head. "Well, they didn't actually go out on a date. Kendra's babysitter fell through, so they ended up ordering pizza, and Brent spent the evening with Kendra at her folks' house."

Heidi placed a hand on her hip. "Somehow I'm not surprised. I saw the way those two looked at each other when you three were here that day."

"Yep." Bill snapped his fingers. "I wouldn't be surprised if Kendra and Brent don't get hitched someday."

"That would be something all right. Now, did you both remember your aprons today?" Heidi asked, looking at Bill and then Lance.

"Sorry, I forgot," Bill mumbled. This wasn't the first time he'd forgotten his, either.

"I brought mine." Lance held up the paper sack in his hands. Bill hadn't even noticed Lance had been carrying it until now.

"I don't have any clean aprons today, but I can give you a big towel to drape around your neck, if you'd like to keep your clothes clean." Heidi moved across the room and opened a drawer.

Bill waved his hand. "Naw, that's okay. My jeans and sweatshirt are old, so it doesn't matter if something gets spilled." He glanced at the piles of vegetables on the table. "What are we making today, anyway?"

"Since Christmas is only a few weeks away, I decided to show you how to put together what I call Christmas Crunch Salad. It's simple to make and quite tasty. We'll get started on it as soon as the others arrive." Heidi gestured to some empty chairs at the table. "Why don't you men have a seat?"

<hr />

Lisa was getting out of her car when Todd's vehicle pulled in. *I hope he doesn't pressure me to go out with him again. I'm still not ready for that.*

She gave him a polite wave and started for the house. With Todd's long strides, he caught up to her before she reached the porch.

"Too bad this is our last cooking class." Todd stepped close to Lisa and reached out to support her elbow. "I'm gonna miss the friendly banter, and I'll especially miss seeing you." He gave her elbow a little squeeze. "Sorry if I'm being too pushy."

Lisa's purse strap slipped off her shoulder, and Todd quickly repositioned it. Her face grew warm when an electrifying sensation went through her from the touch of his hand. "I'll miss everyone, too. The classes have been fun, and I've been able to try a few of the recipes for myself, as well as some of my clients." Even though her heart had begun to flutter, Lisa couldn't bring herself to say she would miss seeing Todd, too.

Todd moved closer to Lisa—so close she could feel his warm breath on her cheek. "Think you might ever go out with me again?"

"I don't know, Todd. Maybe. We'll have to wait and see how it goes." Lisa stepped onto the porch and knocked on the door. Todd was so charming that it was difficult to say no to him. But she had other, more important things on her mind right now, and they didn't include dating. In addition to meeting her brother and wanting to get to know him better, she'd been asked to cater a large Christmas party next week. It would take lots of planning, not to mention preliminary prep work. And she needed to find someone who could assist her with all that, as well as help set everything up. So, with the exception of being with her folks on Christmas Day, she wouldn't make any social plans until after the New Year.

Lisa felt relieved when Heidi answered the door. No more pressure from Todd—for now, at least. She was anxious to tell Heidi about the meeting she'd had this past week with one of her previous students.

———————◦⊙◦◦⊙◦———————

Heidi greeted Todd and Lisa, leading them to the kitchen, and suggesting they take a chair.

"Oh, yes, I will, but before I do, there's something I want to share with you." Lisa spoke excitedly.

"What is it? I'm eager to hear." Heidi took a few steps closer to Lisa, as Todd pulled out a chair at the table and sat down.

"I met with one of your former students on Thursday evening. Her name is Charlene Higgins."

Heidi gave a nod. "I enjoyed getting to know Charlene. She's a sweet young woman."

"Yes, based on the phone call I had with her, she seems nice. Charlene is going to take some pictures I can use on my new website to help promote my catering business." Lisa's face broke into a wide smile. "You can only imagine how surprised we both were when the topic of food came up and I mentioned that I've been taking cooking classes from you. Then Charlene said she was a student in your first set of classes, and after that, we had a lot to talk about."

"Oh, my, that's wonderful. How is Charlene doing these days?"

Lisa leaned against the counter near Heidi's desk. "She mentioned that she'll soon be getting married to a wonderful guy. And in addition to teaching school, Charlene's started a part-time photography business." She paused to tuck a short strand of hair behind her ear. "Oh, and she also mentioned having to move her wedding date out a bit."

Heidi tipped her head. "Oh? I hadn't heard. I figured by now she and Len were already married. I believe they'd planned for a September wedding. I wonder why the delay."

"I don't know. She didn't say. She did, however, ask me to tell you hello."

"When you speak to Charlene again, please give her my regards." Heidi clasped her hands to her chest. "Charlene won a photo contest for a prestigious magazine during the time she was taking my classes. When she showed us the beautiful picture of a colt and its mother with a glorious sunset behind the animals, I knew she had talent. I'm pleased to learn she'll be using her abilities in a positive way. And I'm doubly happy to hear she and Len are still planning to be married."

"Let us know when your new website is up and running, Lisa," Lance called from across the room. "I'm sure we'd all like to check it out."

A faint blush crept across Lisa's cheeks as she joined the others at the table. "Yes, thank you. I will keep you posted."

Heidi noticed when Todd fixed his gaze on Lisa, and she gave him a brief smile. There had to be something special going on between them, even if neither of them knew it. Perhaps a new romance would come out of this class, after all. Heidi hoped if it happened, Todd and Lisa would keep her informed. It was nice keeping in touch with former students and finding out how they were doing.

No wonder Aunt Emma enjoys teaching her quilting classes so much, Heidi mused. *It's not just about instructing people how to make something; the real joy comes from getting to know the students personally and feeling like you're a part of their lives.*

A knock sounded on the door, and Heidi excused herself to answer it. She was pretty sure it had to be Allie.

A few minutes later, Heidi returned to the kitchen, with Allie at her side. After everyone washed their hands and put on their aprons, Heidi explained how to make the salad. "I also made some Christmas cut-out cookies we can have as a treat afterward," she added.

"The salad sounds good. Think I'll make it to go with our Christmas dinner." Allie smiled. "This is going to be one of our best Christmases, because my husband is alive."

Heidi's brows furrowed as she tipped her head. "What do you mean?"

Allie explained how Steve had been shot by a robber, and ended the story by saying he was going to be all right and wouldn't be working so many long hours anymore. Bill and Todd asked a few questions about the details of the robbery, and then everyone got busy cutting up their vegetables and placing them in a bowl.

"I'd like to tell you all something." Todd looked at everyone individually. "I'm sorry I wasn't honest up front with all of you about my job and the reason I took this class."

Before anyone could respond, he continued. "As soon as I finish writing my last article, which will be about the cooking classes I've taken part in, I'm going to quit my job at the newspaper as a food critic."

Heidi's mouth opened slightly. She wondered what he might say about her classes.

"I've come to realize I can no longer have a job that could rip the rug out from anyone's feet." He looked at Heidi. "Don't worry, because I will have nothing but good to say in my article about your cooking or the classes you've taught. In fact, I'm gonna give it a five star review."

Heidi smiled. "Why, thank you, Todd."

"What did you mean about ripping the rug out from anyone's feet?" Nicole questioned.

"I don't want to chance giving a negative review on a restaurant, and because of it, having the place close down. Who knows what the owner's situation might be?" He lifted his hands as if in defeat. "It's happened before, and I could not live with myself if it happened again because of me."

"What are you going to do now?" Lance questioned.

"I'm not sure. I'd like to work with food in some capacity, though." Todd stroked his chin. "Guess I'll have to start reading the classified ads and see if there's something out there for me."

"Todd, it took a lot for you to admit that to all of us, but I can see a burden has been lifted from you," Heidi commented.

"Yes, and don't fall over, but I've even started going to church." Todd smiled. "The minister there met with me this week, and he's going to help me develop a closer relationship with God." Todd heaved a sigh.

"Hopefully with his guidance, and by studying the Bible, I'll be on the right path for once in my life."

———————✦———————

As Lisa listened to Todd, she could not believe the transformation. It thrilled her to know he was seeking a relationship with God. There was something about his manner that seemed different, too. Todd genuinely seemed sincere.

She also considered what he had said about finding another job and wanting to work with food. *Should I say something, or would he be offended by my suggestion? Oh well, here goes. . .* "Todd, before you look at the classified ads, we need to talk. I may have an opportunity for you."

Todd turned to face her. "Oh?"

Lisa looked around and noticed that everyone seemed to be listening. "I have a huge Christmas party to cater soon, and I'm going to need someone to help me with it. I cannot cater this party alone—it's too big for one person to handle. There will be even more guests than there were at Melanie and Shawn's wedding reception." She paused briefly. "Also, my business is slowly growing, and I'm considering the idea of teaming up with someone who might someday, down the road, want to partner with me in the catering business. We can take things slow, and see how it goes, but Todd, do you think you might be interested?"

"Interested? Are you kidding me? You bet I'm interested!" Todd bumped shoulders with Bill, who sat next to him. "I have a lot to learn about cooking and all the things I'll need to know concerning the catering business, but if you're willing to teach me, Lisa, I'm more than eager to learn."

Smiling, she said, "With your sophisticated palate and understanding of what foods go together well, we should make a great team."

Everyone clapped when Todd and Lisa sealed the deal with a handshake. Afterward, Todd got up from his chair and gave Lisa a kiss on the cheek.

The blush Lisa felt spread from her toes all the way up to the top of her head. "I'd like to also make an announcement."

All heads turned to look at her.

"My family has suddenly increased."

"Oh, how's that?" Heidi questioned.

"Well, I found out on Thanksgiving Day that I have a half brother. I'll tell you all about it when we're eating our snacks."

"Lisa, that's wonderful news. I'm eager to hear the details." Heidi's smile was deep.

"Now it's your turn, Heidi. How have you been since we last saw you?" The question came from Allie, but everyone watched and waited.

"I've been well," Heidi responded. "Lyle and I had a nice Thanksgiving with my family in Middlefield, and yesterday we got word from the caseworker helping us become foster parents that we'll be getting two foster children a few days before Christmas."

"Two kids, huh?" Bill reached for another piece of broccoli to cut up. "Sounds like you'll be kept pretty busy."

Heidi nodded. "But we're looking forward to it. Besides, this will be a good kind of busy."

"How old are the children?" Lisa asked.

"Marsha is three, and her brother, Randy, is five." Heidi clasped her hands, placing them under her chin. "The caseworker explained that the little girl hasn't spoken since her mother and father were killed in a car accident. She also mentioned that the boy has a negative attitude, so it's going to be a challenge."

Todd whistled. "Wow, I hope you're up to it. Sounds like those kids will be hard to deal with."

"If anyone can do, it'll be Heidi and Lyle," Lance interjected. "As their mail carrier, I've gotten to know them fairly well. Why, I bet within a few weeks they'll have those kids wearing smiles, big as you please."

"Thanks for the vote of confidence. My husband and I will do the best we can." Heidi relaxed in her chair. Even though she didn't know how long these children would be with them, she determined in her heart to do the best she could in caring for and offering love to Marsha and Randy. She looked forward to giving them a wonderful Christmas, and thanked God for His special blessings in allowing her and Lyle this unexpected opportunity.

Heidi thought about the scripture she had put on everyone's recipe card for this class: *"The things which are impossible with men are possible with God."* The truth of that verse was definitely being lived out in this small group.

Looking around the table, at each of her students, she appreciated being able to teach them how to make six special recipes. But more than that, Heidi felt thankful she had been given the opportunity to share the love of God and see how He was working in each person's life. She looked forward to the days ahead, and the opportunity of sharing the many blessings she had received.

Heidi's Cooking Class Recipes

Baked Oatmeal

Ingredients:

2 eggs, beaten
1 cup sugar or substitute
   sweetener
½ cup butter, melted

3 cups oatmeal
1 cup milk
2 teaspoons baking powder
Pinch of salt

Preheat oven to 350 degrees. Combine eggs, sugar, and butter in 2-quart baking dish. Add oatmeal, milk, baking powder, and salt. Stir until well blended. Bake for 30 minutes. May be served plain or with milk or whipping cream.

Amish Friendship Bread

Ingredients:

- 1 cup starter (see recipe for starter below)
- 3 eggs
- 1 cup oil
- ½ cup milk
- ½ teaspoon vanilla
- 2 cups flour
- 1 cup sugar
- 1½ teaspoons baking powder
- 2 teaspoons cinnamon
- ½ teaspoon salt
- ½ teaspoon baking soda
- 1 to 2 small boxes instant pudding (any flavor)
- 1 cup nuts, chopped (optional)
- 1 cup raisins (optional)

Preheat oven to 325 degrees. Grease and flour two large loaf pans.

Mix 1 cup starter (recipe below) with eggs, oil, milk, and vanilla. In separate bowl, mix flour, sugar, baking powder, cinnamon, salt, baking soda, instant pudding mix, and nuts and/or raisins, if desired. Add to liquid mixture and stir thoroughly.

Dust greased pans lightly with some cinnamon-sugar mixture. Pour batter evenly into pans and sprinkle remaining cinnamon-sugar mixture on top.

Bake for one hour or until toothpick inserted in center of bread comes out clean.

Options: Use 2 boxes pudding mix. Change flavor of pudding mix. Add up to 2 cups dried fruit or baking chips (note: heavier add-ins may sink to bottom). Decrease fat by substituting ½ cup oil and ½ cup applesauce for 1 cup oil in recipe. Decrease eggs by using 2 eggs and ¼ cup mashed banana. Use large Bundt pan rather than two loaf pans.

Recipe for Starter:
  ¼ cup warm water
  1 (¼ ounce) packet yeast
  1½ cups plus 1 tablespoon
    sugar

3 cups milk
3 cups flour

Day 1: Put warm water in bowl with yeast. Sprinkle 1 tablespoon sugar over it and let stand in warm place to double in size (about 10 minutes). Mix 1 cup milk, ½ cup sugar, 1 cup flour, and yeast mixture. Stir with wooden spoon. Do not use metal spoon as it will retard yeast's growth. Cover loosely and let stand at room temperature overnight.

Days 2–4: Stir starter each day with wooden spoon. Cover loosely again.

Day 5: Stir in 1 cup flour, 1 cup milk, and ½ cup sugar. Mix well. Cover loosely.

Days 6–9: Stir well each day and cover loosely.

Day 10: Stir in 1 cup flour, ½ cup sugar, and 1 cup milk. It's now ready to use to make bread. Remove 1 cup to make your first bread. Give 1 cup each to two friends, along with the recipe for the starter and your favorite Amish bread. Store remaining starter in a container in refrigerator (or freeze) to make future bread.

Chicken in a Crumb Basket

Ingredients for crumb basket:

½ cup butter, melted
6 cups bread crumbs
¼ cup onion, chopped

1 teaspoon celery salt
½ teaspoon poultry seasoning

Mix all ingredients in bowl. Line bottom and sides of greased 2-quart casserole dish with mixture, forming a "basket." Bake at 350 degrees for 15 minutes.

Filling:

¼ cup butter
¼ cup flour
½ cup milk
1½ cups chicken broth
1 cup carrots, finely chopped

1 cup potatoes, finely chopped
3 cups chicken, cooked and
    finely chopped
1 cup fresh or frozen peas

Make white sauce in a kettle by melting butter, browning flour in butter, then slowly adding milk, followed by broth. In separate pot, cook carrots and potatoes in water until soft. Drain. Add chicken and peas. Coat with white sauce. Pour into crumb basket and bake at 350 degrees for 30 to 40 minutes.

Apple Corn Bread

¾ cup cornmeal
¾ cup spelt or whole wheat
   flour
3 teaspoons baking powder
¼ teaspoon cloves
1 teaspoon cinnamon
¾ teaspoon salt

1 egg, beaten
1 teaspoon vanilla
¾ cup buttermilk
2 tablespoons cooking oil or
   melted butter
1 tablespoon honey
2 cups diced apples

Sift dry ingredients together in a bowl. Add egg, vanilla, and buttermilk. Blend well. Add oil, honey, and apples. Mix thoroughly. Pour into greased, 9-inch square pan. Bake at 350 degrees for 25 minutes.

Pumpkin Whoopie Pies

2 cups brown sugar
1 cup vegetable oil
1½ cups pumpkin (cooked or
    canned)
2 eggs
1 teaspoon vanilla
3 cups flour

1 teaspoon salt
1 teaspoon baking powder
1 teaspoon baking soda
1½ tablespoons cinnamon
½ tablespoon ginger
½ tablespoon cloves

Preheat oven to 350 degrees. Cream sugar and oil together in mixing bowl. Add pumpkin, eggs, and vanilla. Mix well. Add dry ingredients and stir until combined. Drop by heaping teaspoon onto greased cooking sheet. Bake for 10 to 12 minutes.

Filling:
2 egg whites
1½ cups shortening
1 teaspoon vanilla

¼ teaspoon salt
4½ cups powdered sugar

In a bowl, beat egg whites and add shortening, vanilla, and salt until combined well. Stir in powdered sugar and mix until creamy. Spread some of filling on cookie. Place another cookie on top of filling. Wrap each "sandwich" in plastic.

Christmas Crunch Salad

4 cups broccoli, cut into small pieces

4 cups cauliflower, cut into small pieces

1 medium onion, chopped

8 cherry tomatoes, halved

Dressing:

1 cup mayonnaise

½ cup sour cream

1 to 2 tablespoons sugar

1 tablespoon apple cider vinegar

Salt and pepper to taste

Put cut-up vegetables in a bowl. In another bowl, combine dressing ingredients. Pour over vegetables and toss well. Cover and chill in refrigerator for 1 to 2 hours.

Discussion Questions

1. For some time after Kendra changed her mind about letting Heidi and Lyle adopt her baby, Heidi grieved. How would you deal with a situation like Heidi's? Would you try adopting another baby or be content in your marriage without children?

2. In addition to teaching her students how to make some traditional Amish meals, Heidi felt compelled to help those in her class who had emotional or spiritual problems. Sometimes, however, she was unable to get through to them. Is there ever a time we should stop trying to help someone?

3. Kendra changed her mind about letting Lyle and Heidi adopt her baby because her parents agreed to let her come home so they could help raise the child. Was it right for Kendra to break her agreement with the Troyers? Would her baby have been better off with them instead of Kendra and her parents?

4. Nicole had a lot of responsibility on her young shoulders: trying to keep an eye on her two siblings, cleaning, and cooking while her father went to work. This ended up affecting her grades because she had less time to concentrate on her studies. Do you think she should have been honest with her father from the beginning and explained that she was falling behind at school due to all her responsibilities at home? Was Nicole trying to prove something by taking on all the responsibilities her mother used to do?

5. Nicole was bitter and angry at her mother for divorcing her dad, and she struggled with her relationships with others. What are some ways we can help a person like Nicole?

6. Lance had an issue with his brother when he came to live with him for a while. Dan kept doing things to get on Lance's nerves, until Lance was fed up and sought some other place for his brother to stay. Rather than taking that approach, would it have helped if Lance had communicated better with Dan when he asked him to stop doing the things he found annoying? Have you ever had someone living in your home temporarily? How did things work out for both of you?

7. Lance was a widower, and his daughters were always trying to play matchmaker, believing their dad needed another wife. Lance was content and didn't want to remarry. How could he have better conveyed that to his daughters?

8. Allie was married to a policeman, and she became upset because he filled in for others on the force, which didn't leave much time for them to be together as a family. Have you ever had a parent or spouse who worked too much and didn't take time to be with his or her family? How did you deal with that situation?

9. Allie suspected that her husband might be having an affair. Do you think she was too hasty in making this assumption? Did Allie's suspicions have more to do with her lack of self-esteem or was it a lack of trust in her husband?

10. Bill liked to hunt and had been saving for a trip to Alaska. But he depleted part of his savings when he did something to help someone in the cooking class, even though he didn't know her very well. Have you ever made a monetary sacrifice for someone you didn't know well? How did it make you feel?

11. Lisa was attracted to Todd, even though he didn't profess to be a Christian. Is it good for someone to date a person who doesn't share their religious beliefs? What does the Bible say about being unequally yoked with unbelievers? Does that also pertain to dating?

12. Although Todd wanted a relationship with Lisa, his dishonesty put a wedge between them. Todd also had a know-it-all attitude. Have you ever known someone like that? How did you respond, and did their attitude drive a wedge between you? Is there a nice way of telling someone who thinks they know everything that it's affecting your relationship?

13. Heidi liked to include a Bible verse on the back of the recipe cards she gave her students. Were there any verses in this book that spoke to your heart? How has God's Word helped you through a difficult time in your life?

14. Did you learn anything new about the Amish who live in Holmes County, Ohio, while reading this book? Why do you think some Amish communities differ in their rules and what the church ministers will allow their people to do?

15. Did you like how some of the characters from Book 1, *The Seekers*, were mingled into this story? Who were your favorite characters from Books 1 and 2, and what did you like about them?

THE CELEBRATION

Prologue

Walnut Creek, Ohio

Heidi Troyer sat on the back porch, watching Marsha and Randy play in the yard. It was hard to believe the children had been living with her and Lyle for the past four months. The time had gone so quickly since their arrival a few days before Christmas.

While not completely adjusted to her surroundings, Marsha had finally begun to speak, but usually only when spoken to. Randy was still moody at times, and occasionally didn't want to cooperate. Heidi continued to look for ways to get through to the children and make them feel loved and a part of this family.

Of course, they aren't really our children, Heidi thought with regret. *They were placed in our foster care and are still grieving the deaths of their parents.*

Breathing deeply, Heidi enjoyed the warmth of an April breeze. Spring was a rejuvenating time of year, especially with the sound of the children's laughter. She chuckled as she watched Randy and Marsha blow cottony seeds from a dandelion. Heidi remembered how she and her siblings had done the same thing when they were children.

She leaned her head against the back of the wicker chair and closed her eyes. *Lord, please give me the grace to accept things if it becomes necessary for Marsha and Randy to leave our home. And give Lyle and me the wisdom to know how to help these precious children adjust to life without their parents.*

"Are you all right?" Lyle asked as he touched her shoulder.

Her eyes snapped open. "*Jah.* I was praying—asking God for wisdom to know how to help the children adjust to their new life."

He took a seat in the chair beside her. "It's only been a few months, and the *kinner* are doing better than when they first came here."

"You're right, but only with us. When other people are around, Marsha doesn't say a word, and Randy sometimes responds negatively." Heidi released a lingering sigh. "After church last Sunday, they both stayed close to me and didn't interact with the other children. I would think by now that they'd be more comfortable around other kinner."

Lyle pulled his fingers through the ends of his thick beard. "Say, I have an idea. You might think it's a crazy notion, but it would be something to think about at least."

Her interest piqued; Heidi placed her hand on his arm. "What is it, Lyle? I'm open to any suggestions that could help Randy's attitude and bring Marsha out of her shell."

"I was thinking you could teach another cooking class."

Heidi's brows furrowed. "How would that help?"

Lyle glanced toward Randy and Marsha, who were kneeling on the grass, petting one of the barn cats. "What if this time, you held the class for children instead of adults? Randy and Marsha would be included, of course. It would give them a chance to interact with other children and, at the same time, do something fun."

Heidi cupped her chin in the palm of her hands. "Hmm. . . That is something to ponder. Of course, Marsha's too young to learn how to cook, but she could watch and maybe take part by stirring things, cracking eggs, or doing some simpler tasks that might be involved in the recipes I choose." She reached over and clasped his hand. "*Danki*, Lyle. It's an interesting idea, and I'll give it some thought."

Chapter 1

Dover, Ohio

Darren Keller poured himself a cup of coffee and headed for the living room to relax for the evening. As a full-time fireman, he had days less demanding. The men would do chores around the fire station and keep up with maintaining the trucks. Then there were days like today: unusually long and full of action. In addition to responding to three house fires, his fire department had been called out to a seven-car pileup on the interstate, involving a propane truck. Several people had been injured, and there'd been a huge fire to put out. Thankfully, no one was killed.

Darren liked his job, but it could be stressful. When his wife, Caroline, died from a brain tumor two years ago, he'd been tempted to find another job. Darren had struggled with whether it was fair to his son, Jeremy, to be raised by a single parent who might not always be there for him. There was always the possibility of being injured. Worse yet, he could be killed during the dangerous situations firemen often face. After having a heated debate with himself and seeking out a friend's counsel, he decided to stick with the job he knew and loved, remembering to take every precaution. He felt thankful for his parents' promise that, if something should happen to him, they would take care of Jeremy.

Brushing his thick, curly hair off his forehead, Darren leaned back in the easy chair and closed his eyes. An image of his beautiful wife came to mind. Darren could almost hear her sweet voice reminding him of the importance of his job. Caroline had always supported his choice to be a fireman, and he felt sure she would approve of him continuing in the profession. He couldn't count the many times his wife had said she was proud of him for the heroic deeds he considered to be normal. Even the smallest of acts, Caroline believed, were valiant, and many times she referred to Darren as a "gallant knight in shining armor." Courageous or not, it was his instinct to help and protect.

I miss you, Caroline. Jeremy misses you, too. I'm doing the best I can to set a good example and teach him all he needs to know. But he needs a mom—someone to show him the softer side of life.

Hearing the *clomp, clomp* of feet racing through the hall, Darren opened his eyes. Stocking footed, Jeremy slid into the room, in hot pursuit of his dog, Bacon. The reddish dachshund zipped behind Darren's chair, and when Jeremy charged after, he slipped and fell.

"You okay?" Darren grabbed the arms of his chair, prepared to get up.

"Yeah." Jeremy blinked, and his cheeks flushed a bright pink. "Guess I shoulda been wearin' my shoes."

"Glad you're okay." Hoping to make light of the situation, Darren pointed to the floor. "Hope the floor's okay, too."

With a groan, and an eye roll, Jeremy clambered to his feet. "That stupid mutt never comes when I call him."

Darren shook his head. "Now don't blame Bacon, and he's not a stupid mutt. The little fella's still a pup, and you shouldn't have been running through the house."

Rubbing his elbow, Jeremy dropped his brown-eyed gaze to the floor. "Sorry, Dad."

Darren clapped his hands. "Come here, Bacon. There's no need for you to hide."

Looking sheepish, as he crawled on his belly, the dog came out from behind the chair.

Darren reached down and rubbed Bacon's silky ears. He'd given the dog to Jeremy for his birthday last month, hoping it would not only offer the boy companionship, but teach him responsibility.

"Hey, Dad, are there any of those cookies left that Mrs. Larsen brought us last week?" Jeremy leaned close to Darren's chair. Corine Larsen was a sweet grandmotherly woman who looked after Jeremy when Darren was at work.

"Nope. I put the last of 'em in your lunch box when you left for school this morning."

Jeremy frowned. "Would ya buy some more cookies?"

"I could, but it might be fun if you learned how to bake them yourself."

Jeremy tipped his head. "Are you gonna teach me?"

Darren reached for the newspaper lying on the side table beside his chair. "No, but I saw an ad earlier about a woman who lives in Walnut Creek. Starting next month, she'll be teaching a cooking class for kids every other Saturday for six weeks. Since you'll be getting out of school for the summer next week, a cooking class might be fun. What do you think?"

"No way! There'd probably be a bunch of girls there." Jeremy folded his arms. "I think it's a bad idea, Dad."

"I don't. In fact, I'm going to call the number listed and get more details."

Berlin, Ohio

Miranda Cooper stared at her reflection in the full-length bedroom mirror. Her straight, shoulder-length auburn hair lacked body. She should probably try a different style, or maybe get a perm to fluff it up. But why bother with that? Miranda wasn't trying to impress anyone—least of all her husband, Trent, who'd moved out of their house a month ago, because she asked him to.

"Well, it doesn't matter." She plumped her tresses. "He's not here to notice anymore. If only he hadn't. . ."

Miranda's six-year-old son bolted into her room through the open door. "Who ya talkin' to, Mommy?"

"No one, Kevin. Well, actually, I was talking to myself."

He stared up at her with a curious expression. "What were you sayin' to yourself?"

"Nothing important." Miranda ruffled the boy's sandy brown hair, then smoothed it down over his ears. She kept the sides long enough to cover her son's ears, which sometimes made him the brunt of other children's teasing. Kids could be cruel. It wasn't Kevin's fault his ears stuck out. His older sister, Debbie, was protective and usually stood up for him. With two years between them, they'd always gotten along well.

Kevin flopped down on her bed, and Miranda tickled his bare toes. "Where's your sister?"

"In her room, fixin' her ponytail." Kevin sat up. "Hey, can we get a trampoline for the backyard? Aaron's parents bought him one last week."

"That might be a question you can ask your dad, but maybe you should wait and see if the fun of it wears off for your friend. I've noticed a lot of trampolines in people's backyards, but rarely see anyone playing on them." Miranda sat beside Kevin. "For now, when you go over to Aaron's house, you can enjoy his."

"Okay, Mommy." Kevin jumped up and ran out of the room.

"Don't forget to pick up your clothes!" Miranda shook her head. Getting Kevin to pick up after himself was like reminding her husband to visit the kids more often.

I wish there was something fun for Debbie and Kevin to do this summer. Miranda twirled her fingers around a strand of her hair. *Maybe I should sign them up for the cooking class I read about in the paper this morning. I think they might enjoy doing it together.*

Canton, Ohio

Denise McGuire sank to the edge of her bed, covering her face with her hands. If ever there was a time she felt like giving up her career as a Realtor, it was now. The events of today had been stressful. Her first appointment had been scheduled for nine o'clock this morning, but thanks to her daughter having a hissy fit during breakfast, Miranda had been forty minutes late. When she finally got to her office, the people had left. Not a good way to start the day—especially with prospective clients.

On top of that, by the time she dropped Kassidy off at her school, Miranda had developed a headache. Who wouldn't get a headache when they'd been listening to their eleven-year-old daughter carry on from the moment she'd taken a seat at the breakfast table until she'd gotten out of Denise's luxury sedan in the school parking lot? Kassidy's tirade had been about something so stupid—wanting to get her hair dyed dark brown like her mother's, because she hated her own red hair. No matter what Denise said to discourage her daughter, Kassidy was relentless—shouting and screaming that she wasn't loved and wished she had different parents. Before he'd left for work, Denise's husband, Greg, had tried to reason with their daughter, but he'd gotten nowhere. Greg had a way of knowing when to bolt, leaving Denise to deal with their daughter. Once Kassidy made her mind up about something, there was no rationalizing with her.

Maybe it's my fault, because I'm so busy with my job and other obligations. I need to find something we can both do together this summer, when Kassidy's out of school. Denise rubbed her forehead. *But when would I have the time? My schedule is erratic, and many people look for houses during the summer.* Normally, sales increased once the weather turned warm, which also meant Denise's income increased.

She rose from the bed and moved over to stand by the window. The sun had already set, and shadows lay across their expansive backyard. Greg was at a meeting with some other lawyers from his firm and would no doubt get home late this evening. "Even if he was here," she murmured, "he probably wouldn't want to discuss the situation with Kassidy."

These days, with Greg's busy law practice, he was rarely at home. When he was, he wanted to relax and be left alone. Denise could relate as she needed some downtime, too. But she always made a little time each day to connect with their daughter, although sometimes she wondered why. Dealing with Kassidy's negative attitude was draining. It seemed there was no pleasing the girl.

Denise leaned her forehead against the window, hoping the cool glass might ease her pounding head. She stood up straight, as a thought popped into her head. After showing another client a home at noon, she had stopped for a bite to eat in Sugarcreek. When Denise left the restaurant, she'd seen a flyer on a bulletin board near the door, advertising cooking classes for children. At the time, she hadn't paid much attention to it, but wished now she'd had the presence of mind to write down the information.

I think I'll go back to that restaurant tomorrow and see what I can find out about the cooking classes. The activity with other children might be good for Kassidy. Denise couldn't count all the times she'd tried teaching her daughter to cook a few simple things. Maybe someone who wasn't related would have better luck.

Chapter 2

Millersburg, Ohio

It's time for bed, Becky," Ellen Blackburn called from the kitchen, where she sat with a cup of herbal tea. She'd put a cherry pie in the oven after talking on the phone with her friend Barb. While Ellen waited for the pie to bake, she jotted a few things down on her grocery list. The store where she frequently shopped had good prices on fresh fruits and vegetables this week, and she wanted to make sure the fridge was restocked with healthy items.

Ellen was careful about food choices, not only for herself, but also for her ten-year-old daughter. She wanted to be a good role model and start Becky out young, teaching her good eating habits. Ellen believed if people ate healthy food, nine times out of ten, they would stay healthy throughout their life. Every so often, though, like this evening, Ellen got in the mood to bake something on the sweeter side.

Hearing voices from the other room, Ellen shouted once more: "Becky, please turn off the TV."

But again, her daughter did not respond.

Setting her cup on the table and pushing her chair aside, Ellen rose to her feet. *Is Becky so engrossed in the program she's watching that she doesn't hear me?*

When Ellen entered the living room, she was surprised to discover that even though the television was still on, Becky was asleep on the couch.

She pointed the remote toward the TV and turned it off, then bent down and gently shook her daughter's shoulder. "Wake up, sweetie. It's time for bed."

Becky's eyelids fluttered, then closed again.

Ellen stroked her daughter's olive-tone face. "Wake up, sleepyhead. You need to brush your teeth and go to bed."

Yawning, Becky sat up and swung her legs over the couch. "I missed the rest of my show, Mom. I wanted to see how it ended."

"I'm sure it'll be back as a rerun soon."

"Yeah, and since school will be out for the summer soon, I can watch all my favorite programs."

Ellen shook her head. "Sorry, honey, but you're not going to spend the whole summer watching TV. There are lots of other things you can do."

"Like what?"

"I'm thinking about signing you up for a children's cooking class." Ellen pointed to the newspaper lying on the coffee table. "I read about one, and I believe you would enjoy it."

Becky squinted her hazel-green eyes, the way she always did when she was thinking. "Would it be just me and the teacher, or would other kids be there, too?"

"I doubt it would only be you. I'm sure other children would take part in the class."

"I don't wanna do it then."

Ellen sighed. Sometimes Becky's shyness got in the way of her making new friends. It was something she needed to work through. Learning how to cook with other children might be exactly what her daughter needed.

"We'll talk about this later. Right now, you need to get your teeth brushed."

"Okay, Mom."

Ellen watched her daughter skip down the hallway toward the bathroom. Then a smoky aroma reached her nostrils.

"Oh no!" Ellen ran toward the kitchen. "Bet I forgot to turn the oven temperature down. Maybe I'm the one who needs cooking lessons."

Walnut Creek

"I'm not tired. I don't wanna go to bed." Randy sat on the living-room floor with his arms folded, staring up at Heidi defiantly. His blue eyes held her steady gaze.

This wasn't the first time the boy had challenged Heidi's authority. Just when she felt they were gaining some ground, Randy exuded stubbornness.

In a firmer tone, Heidi said, "Please do as I say and help your sister pick up the toys."

Randy continued to sit, holding his lips in a straight line. Marsha sat beside her brother, seemingly oblivious to the conflict going on. Her blond ponytail bobbed as she rocked back and forth, holding her baby doll.

With a sigh of exasperation, Heidi turned to look at Lyle. He sat on the sofa reading the latest edition of *The Connection* magazine.

Lyle set the magazine aside and rose to his feet. Then he marched across the room, bent down, and looked directly at Randy. "Okay, little buddy, let's go brush your teeth, and then I'll tuck you into bed."

Without a word of argument, the boy gathered his toys, put them in the wicker basket across the room, and padded down the hall.

Heidi pursed her lips. *Now why couldn't Randy have done that for me?* Although pleased because the child obeyed Lyle, it frustrated Heidi that he hadn't listened to her. *Do I need to take a firmer hand or try to be more patient?*

At times like this, Heidi wondered if she had what it took to be a good parent. *Of course*, she reminded herself, *if I had been given the opportunity to raise a child from infancy, things might be different.*

For a brief moment, her thoughts went to the baby she and her husband had almost adopted—until Kendra Perkins changed her mind and decided to keep her infant daughter. Well, that was in the past, and she needed to move on.

Remembering that Marsha still sat on the floor, holding her doll, Heidi knelt next to the child. "It's time for bed, Marsha." She held out her hand.

The little girl looked up at her and blinked several times. Then, with a quick nod, she took Heidi's hand and stood.

Heidi smiled and hugged the child, relieved that Marsha hadn't put up a fuss. This was progress. Often, when Randy became stubborn, his sister did, too.

Heidi led Marsha down the hall and into the room that would have been their baby's nursery, had they been able to adopt. Since Marsha sometimes woke up crying during the night, Heidi wanted her to sleep in a room close to the bedroom she shared with Lyle. When the children arrived last December, Lyle had set up two small beds in the nursery so Marsha and her brother could be together. But a few months later, Randy decided he wanted to sleep in one of the upstairs bedrooms. The little guy tried to be so independent and brave, but at times Heidi found him crying. She tried to offer comfort, but Randy always pulled away. He seemed more comfortable with Lyle. Heidi assumed the boy had been close to his father and related better to a man.

"Let's put your doll on the bed so we can take off your dress and put your nightgown on." Heidi spoke softly to Marsha, and she felt grateful when the little girl did what she asked.

Once Marsha was in her nightgown, Heidi led her down the hall to the bathroom so she could wash her face and brush her teeth. After the task was done, they returned to the bedroom.

Before Heidi pulled back the covers, she handed Marsha her doll, and then helped the child into bed. Leaning over, she placed a gentle kiss on the little girl's forehead. "Sleep well, little one."

Marsha's eyelids fluttered, then closed. In no time at all, she was asleep.

Seeing a need for the Amish-style dress the child had worn today to be washed, Heidi picked it up and quietly left the room. She'd begun dressing Randy and Marsha in Plain clothes soon after they'd come to live with them. She and Lyle were also teaching the children some Pennsylvania Dutch words. Since Marsha and Randy would be staying with them, perhaps indefinitely, it only made sense to introduce them to Amish customs, as well as their traditional language. Someday, if the children desired it, they might join the Amish faith.

After Heidi put Marsha's dress in the laundry basket, she returned to the living room, where she found Lyle sitting on the sofa reading *The Connection* again.

"Marsha's in bed sleeping. How'd things go with Randy?" she asked, taking a seat beside him.

He placed the magazine in his lap, turning to look at her. "I don't know if he's asleep or not, but at least the little guy is in bed."

"I'm beginning to wonder if he will ever respond as positively to me as he does to you." Heidi sighed. "I think Randy resents me for some reason."

Lyle shook his head. "It's not you he resents, Heidi. Randy is still trying to come to terms with his parents' death, and I suspect he might be angry at them for leaving him and his sister. If there's anything he resents, it's having to live with strangers."

She bit down on her bottom lip. "Do you think he doesn't care for wearing Amish clothes or being asked to learn our language?"

"I don't know. Randy is hard to figure out, but I've never heard him say anything negative about wearing Amish clothes or learning our Pennsylvania Dutch words." Lyle clasped Heidi's hand, squeezing it gently. "We need to be patient and keep showing the children how much we care about them. Eventually they'll come around."

Heidi slowly nodded. "I hope and pray you're right. When Gail Saunders, the social worker, comes around again to see how things are going, I wouldn't want her to think Randy and Marsha don't like it here." Tears welled in her eyes. "I want them to continue living with us, Lyle."

"So do I. We need to remember that if it's the Lord's will for the children to remain in our care, things will work out for everyone."

Chapter 3

"Since I don't have an auction to preside over today, why don't you leave the kinner home with me while you visit your friend Loretta this morning?" Lyle asked as he and Heidi sat at the kitchen table having a second cup of coffee after breakfast.

She blew on the steaming brew. "I appreciate your willingness, but it'll be good for Marsha and Randy to interact with Loretta's children. They need to make some friends; don't you agree?"

"Very true, but you're with the children all day, so I thought you might enjoy some time to yourself."

"If I was going shopping for groceries, I would prefer to go alone. But since Loretta mentioned that her kinner would enjoy spending time with Randy and Marsha, it's best I take them along. Sure wouldn't want to disappoint Conner and Abby."

"All right then, I'll spend the day catching up on a few things around here." Lyle placed his coffee mug in the sink. "Since it's so nice out this first day of June, would you like me to hitch your horse to the open buggy?"

"That'd be nice." Heidi joined him at the sink, running water in both cups to prevent any coffee stains.

"Guess I'll head outside now." Lyle kissed Heidi. "I'll let you know when your horse and buggy are ready to go."

"Danki." She tenderly squeezed her husband's hand before he went out the back door.

Dear Lord, she prayed silently, *I've thanked You many times for this, but again, I'm grateful for Your blessings, including my marriage to such a thoughtful, loving man.*

———⁂———

As Heidi guided her horse down the road toward the Millers' place, she thought about Loretta and how she had joined the Amish church and married Lyle's friend Eli. What a blessing it had been to attend their wedding last spring. Plus, it was nice having Loretta and her two children living closer, since they'd moved into Eli's house. Heidi and Lyle had also attended the wedding of her former student Charlene this spring. Weddings and births were always time for celebration.

Heidi redirected her thoughts when she heard Randy whisper something to Marsha from the back seat of the buggy. She strained to hear what he said but couldn't make out the words.

"Look at the baby *kieh* in the field over there," Heidi called to the children.

"What's a kieh?" Randy questioned.

"It's the Amish word for *cows*." She glanced over her shoulder. "Do you remember the word for baby?"

"*Boppli*."

"That's right. And more than one boppli would be *bopplin*."

"Boppli kieh," Randy said.

Heidi nodded. "You're *schmaert*, Randy."

"You think I'm smart?"

"Yes, I do. You're a bright boy, and you catch on fast to the new words you've been taught."

"My sister's schmaert, too," Randy asserted. "But she don't talk much. Not since Mommy and Daddy died."

Heidi's heart went out to the boy. "You're right, Randy. Marsha is smart." She glanced over her shoulder again and smiled at Marsha. "You're a schmaert little *maedel*."

"What's a maedel?" Randy asked.

"Maedel means girl. Marsha is a schmaert little maedel."

Marsha giggled and repeated what Heidi had said.

Hope welled in Heidi's chest. Marsha was talking a little more and beginning to learn some new Pennsylvania Dutch words.

"I'm glad you and the kinner could come visit us today." Loretta gestured out the kitchen window, where they could see her children and their two dogs playing with Randy and Marsha in the backyard. It was good to see them interacting and having a good time.

"The kinner seem to like both of your *hund*." Heidi nodded toward the happy scene. "Marsha and Randy took a quick liking to our dog, Rusty, too."

Loretta smiled. "It's hard to believe we've had Donnelly over a year already. Eli's dog, Lady, and our Donnelly, get along well. Those two stick together like glue." She chuckled as the sound of laughter rippled through the open window like a pleasant breeze. "I have to admit, though, I wasn't too sure it was a good idea when Eli surprised us with Donnelly last year. He must have known what he was doing, however, because that pup quickly became one of the family."

"Isn't it amazing how our lives have changed in one short year?" Heidi looked toward Randy and Marsha, both squealing with glee as Donnelly lapped kisses on their faces and Lady sat patiently waiting her turn. "And now, because of our foster children, I'm going to teach a children's cooking class."

"Oh yes, that's right. When do you start the first class?" Loretta asked, handing Heidi a glass of lemonade.

"Two days from now." Heidi seated herself at the table. "I am hoping it won't be too big a challenge."

"You're a good teacher. I'm sure you'll do fine." Loretta took a seat across from Heidi. "I would have signed Abby and Conner up for your classes, but they'll be spending a few weeks with my parents this summer, and it will come right in the middle of your cooking classes."

Heidi smiled. "Well, maybe some other time, if I should ever decide to teach cooking to children again."

The sounds of the children's laughter and barking dogs grew silent. Loretta and Heidi jumped up at the same time and went to the window.

"Who's that man talking to the children?" Heidi asked.

"Oh, that's Sam Jones. He was my neighbor before the children and I moved here." Loretta shook her head. "The kids sure miss him, but he visits as often as he can."

Heidi watched as Sam made his way to the back door with the kids following close behind, and the wagging-tailed dogs trying to sniff the bag Sam carried.

"Did you sell your house in Sugarcreek yet?" Heidi asked.

"Jah. It was on the market only a week before a solid offer came in. The last time Sam visited, he told us he got some new neighbors who also have young children." Loretta picked up her glass and took a drink. "I'm sure Sam has them spoiled by now. He was the best neighbor and has the most amazing raspberry patch. I won't be surprised if he brings us some from his first picking. He's been like a grandfather to my kinner. And speaking of children. . . Will Randy and Marsha take part in the cooking classes?" Loretta asked.

Heidi nodded.

"Those two are fortunate to have you and Lyle as foster parents."

"We feel privileged we've been given the opportunity to care for them."

"Have you considered adopting the children?"

Heidi's tongue darted out to lick some sweet lemonade from her lips. "Perhaps if they do well in our care, we will be given the opportunity to become their legal parents."

"From what I can tell, they are already doing well." Loretta leaned forward, placing her hand on Heidi's arm. "I'll be praying for you and Lyle, as well as the kinner."

"Danki. If it's God's will for us to adopt Randy and Marsha, I'm confident things will work out."

Chapter 4

"Are you ready for the big day?" Lyle asked when he entered the kitchen Saturday morning.

Heidi turned from the stove, where she'd been boiling a pan of eggs, and watched her husband wash his hands at the kitchen sink. "I believe so. My only concern is the age difference among those who'll be attending the class. Counting Marsha, the children range from three to eleven years old." She shook her head. "Some of the older ones may catch on quickly, while the younger children will likely have a shorter attention span and may be harder to teach."

After drying his hands, Lyle walked over to Heidi and gave her shoulders a gentle squeeze. "There you go again, worrying about something that may not happen. Remember how you fretted before your other two cooking classes started? And look how well those classes turned out. You made some lasting friendships."

"You're right. I did."

Lyle turned, plucked a grape from the bowl of fruit on the counter, and popped it into his mouth. "You never know. The younger students might surprise you with their ability to follow directions. And maybe some of the older students will help the younger ones if they struggle or fall behind."

"I suppose." Heidi blew out a series of short breaths. "I'm also concerned about how well Randy and Marsha will interact with the other children."

"Isn't that the reason you decided to teach these classes—so they could be with other kinner?"

Wiggling her bare toes, Heidi nodded. "It doesn't mean things will work out the way I'd hoped."

Lyle glanced at the clock on the kitchen wall, then pulled another grape off its stem. "Here, eat one of these. They're sure good." He held the juicy morsel up to Heidi's mouth.

Heidi took the grape and ate it. Her husband was only trying to take her mind off her nerves, but it didn't help much.

She removed the kettle of eggs from the stove and was about to rinse them in cool water, when she heard Marsha's shrill cry from the living room.

"*Ach!* I hope she's not hurt." She hurried from the kitchen behind Lyle. Seeing Marsha on the living-room floor, Heidi rushed forward, stubbing her big toe on the leg of a chair. "Ouch!" *Guess that's what I get for not putting on my shoes this morning.*

Lyle looked at Heidi, his brows pulling in. "Are you okay?"

"I stubbed my toe, but I'll be fine."

They both went down on their knees beside Marsha. "What's wrong?" Heidi asked. "Why are you crying?"

With tears rolling down her cheeks, Marsha pointed at the scratch marks on her arm. Seeing a clump of gray fur on the floor beside the little girl, Heidi realized what had happened. One of the cats must have gotten into the house and scratched Marsha's arm. A crying child—a sore toe—she didn't need to deal with either of these right now, not with her first class starting soon.

Heidi looked at Lyle. "Would you please search for the cat while I put some antiseptic and a bandage on Marsha's arm?"

"Sure thing." Lyle rose to his feet. "Want me to see where Randy is, too?"

"Jah, please do. We all need to be ready before my young students arrive for the cooking class." Heidi helped Marsha up and took her by the hand. Then she limped her way down the hall to the bathroom. Hopefully the rest of this day would go better.

———⌐∘∘⌐———

Canton

"Are you ready to go, Kassidy?" Denise rapped on her daughter's bedroom door.

"Go where, Mom?"

"Remember I told you last night that I'd be taking you somewhere special this morning?"

"Yeah, I remember, but I don't feel like going anywhere today."

Denise grasped the doorknob and stepped into Kassidy's bedroom. She found her pajama-clad daughter sprawled out on the bed, doing something on her cell phone.

Denise's muscles tensed, and her chin jutted out. "I hope you're not texting anyone. And for heaven's sake, Kassidy, you're not even dressed. If you're not ready in the next fifteen minutes, we are going to be late."

Kassidy sat up, swinging her legs over the side of the bed. "Late for what?"

"I told you, it's a surprise."

"Are you and Dad taking me to get a new smartphone?" Kassidy held up her cell phone. "I hope so, 'cause this one's having some issues. Besides, it's outdated, and I'd like a better one. This phone is a piece of junk."

"Your dad's meeting a friend at the golf course this morning, and we'll talk about your phone later." Denise gestured to her daughter's closet. "Now please hurry and get dressed." She left the room before Kassidy could offer a retort.

Denise waited a few seconds, then tiptoed quietly back to the entrance of her daughter's bedroom. Peeking around the doorway, she saw Kassidy throw her cell phone on the bed and stomp her way over to the closet. Then, as she went from hanger to hanger, trying to decide what to wear, Kassidy stiffened her shoulders and repeated her mother's words. "Now hurry and get dressed." She pulled one outfit out, throwing it on the bed, then reached for another. Kassidy didn't realize she had more clothes than some children got in a lifetime.

I hope I didn't make a mistake signing her up for cooking classes. Denise leaned away from Kassidy's door and rubbed her temples. *Did I make the right decision by not telling her about the cooking classes? Should I say something on the way to Walnut Creek, or wait until we get there and hope she's pleasantly surprised?*

————— ⟨∘⟩ —————

Dover

"How come you don't have to work today?" Jeremy asked, looking at his dad from across the kitchen table.

Darren drank some coffee and set his mug on the table. "You're kidding, right?"

Jeremy tipped his head. "What do ya mean?"

"I told you earlier this week that I'd signed you up to take cooking classes. And last night I reminded you. How could you have forgotten so quickly?"

"I didn't forget. Just figured you'd probably get Mrs. Larsen to take me 'cause you'd be working today."

"No, I made sure today would be free for me. I worked Monday through Friday so I could take today off." Darren took another swig of coffee. "Thought I'd drop you off at the home where the classes are being taught, then browse around some of the shops in the area until it's time to pick you up."

Jeremy's brows furrowed. "Sure wish you hadn't signed me up for this. I'm gonna feel stupid taking cooking classes with a bunch of girls."

"You don't know that. There could be other boys there, too." Darren put his empty mug in the sink, reached into his pocket, and put a piece of chewing gum in his mouth. "You'd better go comb your hair so we can get going."

"Aw, Dad," Jeremy whined, "can't you at least stay with me during the class?"

"I'm sure none of the other parents are going to stay with their kids. Wouldn't you feel funny if I was the only one who did?" Darren tried to sound encouraging.

"Maybe. If I don't like the class, can I quit?"

"We'll see how it goes."

————— ⟨∘⟩ —————

Millersburg

Ellen stood on the front porch, waiting for Becky to join her. Ever since she'd been reminded about the cooking class this morning, Becky had dragged her feet. It was out of the girl's comfort zone to interact with strangers. She'd made it clear that she didn't want to go. Ellen would not give in, however. She felt certain something as fun as taking cooking classes was what her daughter needed. Perhaps Becky would make some new friends there, too.

A warm breeze came up, lifting Ellen's hair away from her face. The temperature had been rising the last few days. Summer was definitely on its way. She looked forward to taking days off from the hospital and being able to spend time with Becky. She'd arranged her work schedule so she could have every other Saturday off, which would allow her to attend the cooking classes with her daughter. Maybe after each class was over for the day, they could go out to lunch, do some shopping, or visit one of the parks in the area. Walnut Creek wasn't far from Millersburg and had a nice restaurant, as well as several gift shops to browse in.

Ellen watched the billowy white clouds overhead. Ever since she was a child she'd enjoyed studying the different shapes of the clouds, trying to imagine what her future held and always hoping she could someday be a nurse.

The screen door squeaked open and slammed shut, halting Ellen's musings. She turned and smiled at her daughter. "You ready to go, sweetie?"

Becky shrugged, dropping her gaze.

Ellen clasped her daughter's hand. "It'll be fun. You'll see."

⸻ ⌘ ⸻

Berlin

"Are you two ready? It's almost time to go," Miranda called to Debbie and Kevin as she stood in the hallway beneath the stairs.

"I'm coming, Mom." Debbie's ponytail bounced as she bounded down the stairs. "I can't wait to go to the cooking class."

Miranda smiled. At least one of her children looked forward to attending the class. In fact Debbie hadn't stopped talking about the class since Miranda signed her children up for it.

She wasn't sure about Kevin, though. But at least he hadn't said he didn't want to go. Debbie was always willing and eager to help Miranda in the kitchen, which was no doubt the reason she was excited to learn how to make some kid-friendly dishes.

Kevin plodded down the steps, wearing his favorite baseball hat—a gift from his dad last Christmas. *Too bad Trent doesn't spend more time with the kids instead of getting them gifts*, Miranda fumed. Even before they separated, he hadn't given Debbie and Kevin enough attention. But what was the use in thinking about that now? They needed to get going. It wouldn't be good to be late for the first class.

"Let's go, kids." Miranda grabbed her purse and car keys and herded the children out the door.

After everyone buckled in, Miranda started the car. She'd no more than pulled out of the driveway when Debbie called from the back seat, "What do you think the teacher will show us how to make, Mom?"

"I don't know, honey, but I'm sure it'll be easy for you to make."

"How many other kids will be there?"

"I'm not sure about that either. You'll have to wait and see."

"I can't wait to tell my friend, Linda, about the cooking class." Debbie's tone bubbled with enthusiasm. "She'll probably wish she could take the class, too."

"I hope there'll be some other boys there," Kevin said, sitting beside his sister.

Miranda nodded. She was glad her kids were open to the idea of taking the class, and hoped, for Kevin's sake, that he wasn't the only boy.

Chapter 5

Walnut Creek

As Darren drove his four-wheel drive SUV down the road, following the directions on his GPS, he couldn't help wondering what it would be like to live out here in the country. He spotted several Amish men working their fields and saw children running barefoot through the grass in their yards. Everything seemed peaceful here, at a much slower pace.

He rolled down his window and drew a deep breath. *Too bad Jeremy and I can't live in a place like this, instead of in town. Bet we'd both be a lot happier. I know I would.* With the stress of Darren's demanding job as a fireman, he was always eager to get home and unwind. *Of course,* he reasoned, *having a big yard and acreage to take care of might add more stress than relaxation.*

Darren glanced in the rearview mirror at Jeremy, sitting in the back seat with a scowl. He'd hoped by the time they got to Walnut Creek his son would have mellowed out a bit. So much for wishful thinking.

Darren still didn't plan to stay with his son for the whole time today. Instead of browsing some of the shops, he might stop in at the fire station in Berlin, since it was less than ten minutes from Walnut Creek. Darren had gotten to know a few fellow fire fighters from outside his station, both in Berlin and in Sugarcreek, since a lot of times several stations responded to the same fire. That was one of the things Darren enjoyed about being a fireman—the comradery between fellow fighters. The only time there might be a little competition was when they played a game of baseball. Even then, it was friendly competition, and afterward, they'd all meet at a restaurant to eat. Of course, the losing team had to pay for the winners' meals.

When Darren's vehicle approached a mailbox by the side of the road, showing the address he'd been looking for, he turned his vehicle up the driveway. Another car was parked near the house, and Darren watched as an attractive woman with blond hair got out, along with a young brunette girl who looked to be about Jeremy's age. The woman walked up the porch steps with an air of confidence and knocked on the door, while the girl stood beside her, head down and shoulders slumped. A few seconds later, the door opened, and mother and daughter, both wearing blue jeans and a T-shirt, stepped inside. Darren wondered if the woman planned to stay with her daughter. He hadn't given it much thought until now, but maybe all the parents who brought their kids for the cooking class would stay—at least for today.

Jeremy groaned. "See, I told you, Dad. I'm the only boy signed up for the cooking class. Can't we forget about this and find something else to do today? I'm gonna feel stupid if I'm the only guy here today."

"You won't be the only guy." Darren thought things through a bit and changed his mind about leaving. It might be good to get to know some of the other kids' parents. "I'll be right here with you—at least for today's class, so let's get out of the car and head on in."

Jeremy opened the back door and got out, but he remained unmoving next to the SUV. Darren nudged his son and started walking across the grass toward the house. Dragging his feet, Jeremy trudged along beside him. Well, at least he hadn't gotten back in the car.

———————— ⁓⊙⁓ ————————

"Look Mommy, there's a horse over there in the field," Kevin pointed as they pulled into the driveway.

"Yes, honey, the Amish don't drive cars. They use a horse and buggy as their transportation." Miranda stopped the car midway up the driveway, putting the windows down so her kids could take a better look.

"They have cows, too." Debbie's tone was as enthusiastic as her brother's, and they both looked toward the barn where several cows milled around. "Do you think we can go see the animals after the class is done?"

"We'll see." Miranda took a whiff of the country air. While some people might find it offensive, to her it was calming.

"I didn't know there'd be animals here." Kevin giggled when a cat ran in front of their car. "I wonder what else they have in the barn."

"I don't know, but I hope we find out," Debbie responded. "Wouldn't it be fun if the Amish family took us for a ride with the horse and buggy sometime?"

Miranda smiled as her children laughed, watching one cat chase another into the barn. "Okay, you two. Let me find a place to park, and then we'll head inside." *Maybe this will be a positive experience for my Kevin and Debbie.*

———————— ❧☙ ————————

"What are we doing out here in the middle of nowhere?" From the back seat, Kassidy tapped Denise's shoulder. "I don't see much of anything but farms and a bunch of horses and cows."

"Just relax and enjoy the ride. We're almost there."

"Almost where?"

"Here." Denise turned her car up a graveled driveway and parked it near two other vehicles. Then she turned in her seat to face Kassidy.

Kassidy huffed out a long breath. "What is this place? Looks like an old farmhouse to me."

"It is a farmhouse, and the Amish woman who lives here teaches cooking classes."

"If you're taking some cooking classes I don't see why you brought me along. I'm old enough to stay home for a few hours by myself, you know."

Denise clenched her jaw as she glanced back at Kassidy. Creases had formed across her daughter's forehead, and her eyebrows squished together.

"The classes aren't for me, Kassidy. Heidi Troyer will be teaching children how to cook, every other Saturday for six weeks."

"Huh?"

Denise pursed her lips. "I believe you heard what I said."

"So you signed me up to take cooking classes? Is that your big surprise?"

"Yes. It should be fun. I think you'll enjoy learning how to make some easy dishes."

"I'm not a child. I am almost twelve years old, so I don't need to know how to make easy dishes." Kassidy's lips moved rapidly. "And when will I be old enough to sit up front with you or just use a regular seatbelt? I'm tired of sitting in this safety seat."

Denise drew in some air and blew out a quick breath. "Just get out of the car, please."

Kassidy sat with her arms folded, unmoving.

That's just great. What am I going to do if I can't get her to go inside? Denise opened her door, then looked back at her daughter. "Please get out so we can go inside and meet Mrs. Troyer." She stepped out, went around to the other side of the vehicle, and stood by the back door. When the girl made no move to get out, Denise opened the door. "Kassidy, if you don't get out right now I'll take your cell phone."

Kassidy's eyes narrowed. "That's not fair."

"Neither is your stubborn refusal to get out of the car."

"Okay, okay." The girl's cheeks reddened as she unbuckled and slid out of the safety seat, then shut the car door. "I don't want to take a cooking class, Mom." She glanced around. "Especially not here in the middle of cow country."

"Don't be so melodramatic." Denise motioned to the two-story house. "Let's go knock on the door. I'm sure once you meet the Amish woman and some of the other students, you'll find you like it."

"I don't want to! This is stupid!"

Denise put her finger to her lips. "Keep your voice down. I will not stand for you throwing a temper tantrum out here in the yard."

"Fine, then let's go home." Kassidy's arms flailed in the open air. "You didn't even ask if I wanted to take these stupid classes."

Denise stood her ground. "We are not going home, and you're not going to get your way this time. If you don't go inside with me, I'm taking your phone."

Another vehicle pulled in and parked. Denise watched as a woman with shoulder-length auburn hair got out, along with a young boy and a girl. She turned to face her daughter again. "See, Kassidy, there are other children here today, and they're both smiling. Let's go inside and see who else will be taking the class with you."

Kassidy took a few steps through the grass, then stopped, wrinkling her nose. "Oh, yuck! I stepped in doggie doo-doo, and now my one shoe is ruined!"

Denise glanced at the woman and her two children, all heading in their direction. "Kassidy, please keep your voice down. People are staring."

"I don't care." Kassidy lifted her foot, then hopped over to the porch stairs on the other foot. "How am I gonna get this horrible smell off my shoe?"

By this time, the woman and her children had also reached the porch. The boy pointed at Kassidy's foot and plugged his nose. "Phew! That sure stinks!"

Kassidy's nostrils flared, like a bull ready to charge. "Well, your ears stick out like bat wings." She put her thumbs in her ears and wiggled her fingers.

Horrified, Denise pointed at her daughter. "Apologize to the little boy this instant."

Kassidy shook her head, pulling off her sneaker. "He's the one who should apologize; he said I stink."

"Did not. Said *that* stinks." The boy pointed at Kassidy's shoe.

Denise grimaced. So much for hoping her surprise would be welcome. Not only did her daughter not want to take the cooking classes, but now she had a shoe covered in doggie-doo and she'd made an enemy out of one of the other students. *How much worse can it get?*

Just as the question entered her mind, Denise couldn't believe what her daughter was about to do. Still holding the shoe, Kassidy began scraping the bottom of it on the edge of the porch.

Mortified, Denise's mouth opened. "Kassidy McGuire—stop!"

Chapter 6

Denise held her throbbing temples. She could hardly believe what her daughter had done. Now, in addition to the telltale smelly smudges on Kassidy's shoe, a blob of doo-doo clung to the edge of the Amish woman's front porch.

Standing behind her son, and urging him forward, the boy's mother stepped up to Denise. "I'm sorry about Kevin's rude behavior." She nudged the boy's arm. "Tell the girl you're sorry for what you said."

He pushed his shoulders forward and mumbled, "Sorry."

Denise placed her hands on Kassidy's shoulders. "Now it's your turn to apologize for the hurtful remark you made about his ears."

"I don't want to." Kassidy folded her arms.

Denise's lips pressed together as she whispered, "Guess you're ready to give up your cell phone."

"No, I'm not." Kassidy's hands and arms went limp, as though in defeat. "Sorry for what I said." Her unconvincing tone sounded like a half-hearted apology, but at least it had been said.

Denise glanced at her watch. "It's time for the class to start and we are holding things up." She gestured to her daughter's shoe. "Leave it on the grass beneath the porch, and we'll deal with it, as well as the mess you made on the porch, after class. I'm sure Mrs. Troyer has something you can use to clean it all up."

Kassidy's face reddened as she flapped her hands. "Don't see why I have to do it. It's not my fault some stupid pooch made a mess in the grass. People ought to either keep their mutts locked up or at least, clean up after their dogs when they've done their business." She pointed to her other shoe. "And what should I do with this? I can't go inside with only one shoe on."

"Oh Kassidy, really? Just take it off and leave it here on the porch.

No one is going to say anything. You can just wear your socks." Denise tapped her foot. "This discussion is over. It's time to go inside." She turned and knocked on the door.

A few seconds later, a pretty Amish woman with brilliant blue eyes and dark hair opened the door. "Welcome to my home. I'm Heidi Troyer. Please come inside." She gestured to Denise and Kassidy, and also to the other woman and her two children.

As they entered the house, Denise noticed Heidi wore a pair of flip-flops. When she looked closer, and saw Heidi's black and blue toe, Denise was tempted to ask what happened. However she didn't want to appear nosy or impolite. Especially since Heidi hadn't asked why Kassidy wasn't wearing her shoes. However, that didn't stop another boy, who looked to be close to Kassidy's age, from pointing to her feet and asking what happened to her shoes.

Kassidy wrinkled her nose. "Left 'em both outside 'cause I stepped in doggie doo-doo."

The boy snickered, until the man standing beside him said, "Don't be rude, Jeremy. You need to mind your own business."

"I'm sorry about that," Heidi apologized. "Our Brittany spaniel normally goes out in the field to do her business, but she must not have made it in time. I'll take care of cleaning your shoes after class."

Denise stepped forward. "Actually it's only one of her shoes, and there's a little more than what remains on the shoe to clean off. Thanks to my daughter's impulsiveness, most of it is now stuck to the edge of your porch. I am so sorry about that."

Heidi's brows pulled slightly inward, but then a faint smile formed on her lips. "It's okay. I'm sure we've all done that at least once in our life. We'll deal with it later. Now, if you children will follow me to the kitchen, you can introduce yourselves, and then we'll begin our first class."

———⚬⚬⚬———

Heidi was surprised when the children's parents joined them in the kitchen. She had expected they would drop their kids off and return for them when the class was over. She hadn't set out enough chairs for this many people and wondered how well the children would respond to her with their parents looking on. Surely, the adults didn't plan to accompany their children to every class. Hopefully they would only stay today, in order to help their kids become adjusted.

After they scrounged more chairs to put around the expansive kitchen table, Heidi introduced herself, as well as Randy and Marsha. Randy muttered a quick, "Hi," but Marsha hid behind Heidi, refusing to speak to anyone. This wasn't unusual, since she said very little. Heidi figured the little girl would not join in any of the conversation during today's cooking class.

"Your children are cute." The auburn-haired woman smiled. "Are they going to take part in the cooking class?"

"Yes, they will. My husband, Lyle, and I are foster parents to Randy and Marsha." Quickly changing the subject, Heidi said, "Now, starting on my right, I'd like everyone to introduce themselves. Please tell a little about yourselves and why you decided to take my cooking classes."

The tall man with dark curly hair spoke first. "My name is Darren Keller, and I'm a single father." He gestured to the dark-haired boy beside him. "This is my son, Jeremy, and he's ten years old. I thought taking a cooking class would be something fun for him to do during his summer break." He nudged the boy. "Say hello, Jeremy."

"Uh, hi everyone." A dot of red erupted on Jeremy's cheeks.

Darren smiled at Heidi. "My son was worried he would be the only boy here today."

Heidi felt sorry for Darren's son. Would he have been more eager to speak if his father hadn't been here coaching him? She glanced at the brunette who sat next to Jeremy. "Would you and your daughter like to go next?"

The woman sat up straight, patting her perfect-looking hair in place. "My name is Denise McGuire, and this is my eleven-year-old daughter, Kassidy. I signed her up for the class so she could learn to cook, and also to give her something meaningful to do this summer."

Kassidy rolled her blue-green eyes. "I didn't even know my mom signed me up till I got here today, and I don't want to learn how to cook." The girl looked right at Heidi. "I can think of lots better things to do during summer break than spend time in the kitchen."

Heidi hadn't expected the girl to be so blunt. Maybe cooking classes for kids wasn't a good idea. She hadn't expected she'd be dealing with a problem child like Kassidy. Well, she refused to become discouraged. As time went on, and everyone got to know each other, the sessions were bound to get better.

The next parent introduced herself as Miranda Cooper. "And this is my son, Kevin, and my daughter, Debbie."

Neither child said a word. Heidi hoped her young students might be more talkative once they got busy making today's recipe.

The last parent stood and said her name was Ellen Blackburn, and that she was a single mother. She'd brought her ten-year-old daughter, Becky, to learn how to cook.

Becky's chin dipped toward her chest. No comment from her either.

Poor child, Heidi thought. *Becky must be shy, the way she's keeping her head down and not looking at anyone. It's probably best to keep things moving along.* "Thank you everyone, for your introductions. Now we'll begin making our first recipe."

Heidi went to the refrigerator, took out a tray of fresh fruit, and placed it on the table. "Today I'll be teaching you how to make a fruit salad."

"I hope it doesn't include oranges." Kassidy wrinkled her nose. "I can't stand the smell of oranges, and I'd gag if I tried to eat one."

"I do have oranges available for those of you who would like to include them, but there are other fruits to put in the salad, so you can pick and choose."

After Heidi had all the supplies set out, she asked the children to take turns washing their hands at the sink. Heidi watched in dismay as a couple of parents, obviously determined to be a part of the class, washed their hands, too.

She stood at the end of the long table, holding a stack of index cards. "Here is the recipe I've written out for you to take home today." Heidi moved about the table and gave each child a card. She'd written a verse of scripture on the back, the way she'd done previously for her adult students, but she made no mention of it. Heidi hoped after the children got home, they would discover the verse and it would be meaningful to them.

Heidi had coaxed Marsha to take a seat beside Randy. Even though they couldn't read yet, she'd given them both a recipe card so they wouldn't feel left out. Then she returned to the head of the table to explain what they should do first.

Heidi first demonstrated how to hold and cut up an apple. The children picked up their dull paring knives and apples, and copied what she did on their cutting boards.

Like a mother hen, Miranda moved in close to her boy. "Kevin isn't used to cutting up food. I do all the meal preparations at home." The woman almost reached for the knife, but pulled back.

"I can do this, so don't worry, Mom." Kevin's tongue shot out and rested against the side of his mouth, while he cut up the apple into good-sized chunks.

"He's doing a fine job." Heidi stepped over to watch him and the other children. She wasn't sure how this was going to play out. Heidi could see that some of these children didn't have a lot of experience in the kitchen.

Darren shifted in his seat. He felt ill at ease, being the only man here with his child. In order to hide his embarrassment, Darren concentrated on his son and how he responded to Heidi's instructions.

Next, Heidi showed the children how to peel an orange. Darren wasn't surprised when Kassidy held her throat as though gagging and looked away. Then lowering her voice, she muttered, "That's so easy. Anyone with common sense can peel an orange."

Darren held back a snicker when Kevin took half an orange and squeezed the juice in Kassidy's direction. She responded by sticking out her tongue. "Ha! Ha! You missed me."

"That's enough, Kevin," the boy's mother reprimanded.

Darren was glad it wasn't Jeremy who'd squirted the orange. So far, he'd been minding his manners.

"Children, as long as you are here taking my classes, you will need to be kind to one another," Heidi said. "That includes no intentional squirting or sticking your tongue out at anyone."

Aside from a little more awkwardness with everyone in the room, the kids, for the most part, remained well behaved.

One thing that annoyed Darren a little, though, was the blond woman—Ellen. Instead of allowing her daughter to participate on her own, Ellen did everything for Becky. The girl simply sat, watching her mother take part, when she should have been doing by herself what Heidi instructed. Not only did Becky watch what her mother was doing, but she shyly glanced around at the other kids, who were cutting the fruit on their own.

Darren looked at Heidi. She was also watching Ellen. He assumed from her sober expression that she saw it, too. *Maybe I'll say something to Ellen once the class is over. Would she be offended?*

After all the fruit was prepared, Heidi explained how to mix the two juices and ginger and then pour it over the fruit to lightly toss. The fruit salad looked good, but it would need to chill for half an hour.

Once everyone had put their bowl of fruit salad in the refrigerator, Heidi explained a little about the upcoming classes and what to expect. She told the parents that unless they felt they needed to be there, they weren't expected to stay during the classes. The lessons would last for two hours, so if the parents had something they'd like to do in the meantime, they could return for their children at noon.

Darren figured maybe next time he wouldn't stay, but he'd wait and see first what the other parents did.

———————

After the cooking class ended, Heidi helped clean off Kassidy's shoe, as well as the mess on the porch. Denise apologized once more for the mess her daughter had left, but Kassidy remained silent as she stood and watched, her cheeks crimson.

Heidi didn't mind tending to the job, for she'd learned early in life how important it was to be kind and patient. Maybe this would help the contrite girl to be a little nicer. Heidi could only imagine how it would be to have a daughter as bold as Kassidy. While different from a shy child, Kassidy could also use some help learning how to act around others.

Kassidy seemed a bit more pleasant now that her shoe had been cleaned up. Denise nudged her daughter's arm. "What do you say to Heidi?"

"Thank you," Kassidy mumbled.

"You're welcome." Heidi handed the shoe to the girl.

Kassidy went over to retrieve the other shoe, and slipped it on her foot.

Not long after, Heidi waved as Denise and her daughter got in the car and pulled out of the driveway. Then Heidi grabbed the hose and turned on the water, giving the porch one more good washing.

Soon Randy and Marsha came outside and took a seat on the porch swing.

"How did you like learning to cook with the English kids today?" Heidi asked the children. "Did you both have a good time?"

"I liked eatin' the salad, but it was hard to cut up the fruit." Randy looked at his sister. "It was too hard for Marsha, but I'm glad she gotta taste the salad."

"The next class will be two weeks from today, and then we'll learn to make something else." Heidi put the hose away. "I'm going in the house now to get our lunch started. Do you two want to come inside or stay out here on the porch?"

"Think we'll stay out here awhile." Randy clasped his sister's small hand. "Me and Marsha wanna sit on the swing."

"Okay. I'll call you when lunch is ready." Heidi went inside. As she took a loaf of bread out to make sandwiches, she heard a shrill scream. Dropping the bread to the counter, Heidi rushed out the front door.

Chapter 7

When she stepped out on the porch, a blast of water shot Heidi in the face. Holding her hands like a shield, she gasped.

"Uh-oh." Randy quickly lowered the hose, holding the nozzle so it pointed toward the nearest flowerbed.

Marsha, who stood sobbing across from him, was drenched from the top of her blond head all the way down to her little bare toes.

Heidi wasn't sure what to do—scold Randy or comfort his distraught sister. She shook her finger at the boy, then quickly turned off the nozzle at the end of the hose. "I'm ashamed of you, Randy. What made you squirt your sister with water?"

He gave an undignified grunt. "Marsha said she was hot, so I cooled her off."

"I don't believe being soaked with cold water from the hose was what she had in mind." Heidi placed her hand on Marsha's wet head. "Now, Randy, please put the hose back where it belongs and make sure the spigot where the hose is connected is turned off."

"Okay." Randy paused and looked at his sister. "Sorry for gettin' you wet. Are ya mad at me?"

Still sniffling, Marsha shook her head.

As Randy stepped off the porch, Heidi leaned down and clasped the little girl's hand. "Looks like I got a little bath, too. Come inside with me, and we'll get out of our wet clothes." She was thankful the social worker hadn't shown up for a surprise visit in the middle of all this. If Gail had seen what had just happened, it would not have made a good impression.

Marsha looked up at Heidi with such a sweet expression, it almost melted her heart. Truth was, she had begun to think of these children as her own.

"I don't see why we have to eat here," Kassidy grumbled as the hostess showed them to a table at Der Dutchman restaurant. "I told Hillary I'd be home before one o'clock. She was gonna come over and swim in our pool today." Kassidy reached back to flip her red ponytail.

Denise clicked her freshly manicured fingernails against the table. "In the first place, it's not warm enough to go swimming yet. In the second place, you should not have invited your friend without checking with me first. So settle down, because we are not going home until we've eaten lunch."

Kassidy slumped in her chair. "Are you trying to punish me 'cause of what happened to my shoe?"

"Your shoe is inconsequential. What upset me today was your attitude. You were rude and acted like a spoiled three-year-old child instead of an eleven-year-old girl who should know better." Denise released an exasperated sigh. "I've never been so humiliated in all my life."

"Well, what about me? You shouldn't have signed me up for that stupid cooking class. I already know how to cut up fruit, and everything about the class was boring."

"Is that so? First of all, you need to stop thinking of yourself all the time, and boring or not, you will be taking the next five classes." Denise spoke with clenched jaw and forced restraint. "As far as Hillary is concerned, you can call her right now and say she can't come over because you're on restrictions until you learn to have a better attitude."

Tilting her chin down, Kassidy frowned. "That's not fair, Mom. I was looking forward to spending the afternoon with my friend."

Shaking her head, Denise held firm. She'd given in to her daughter too many times in the past, and it had done nothing to improve the girl's haughty attitude or tame her temper. "Kassidy, I was looking forward to us being at the cooking class together, and look how that turned out. So get on your cell phone and call Hillary right now."

Frowning, Kassidy reached into her pocket. "My phone! It's not here."

"Did you leave it in the car?"

"No, I—I must have left it at that Amish woman's house." Kassidy's face contorted. "I remember setting it down on the table when we were eating the fruit salad. I bet it's still there." She pushed her chair aside and stood. "We've gotta go back, Mom. We need to go there now and get my phone."

"Sit down, Kassidy and quit making a scene." Denise pointed to the menus on the table. "We'll go after we've had lunch."

"But what if something happens to my phone? Those kids Heidi's taking care of are little. If one of 'em fools around with the phone, they might mess up the settings." Eyes narrowed, Kassidy's voice rose as she clutched the neckline of her blouse.

Denise put her fingers to her lips. "Calm down. I'm sure Heidi would have found your phone and put it in a safe place."

"But what if she didn't? What if—"

"All the 'what ifs' in the world won't change a thing. We'll find out about your phone when we get there." Denise pushed the menu closer to Kassidy. "Now make a decision on what you want, or I'll order for you."

Kassidy pouted, but grabbed the menu. After looking it over, she muttered, "Nothing looks good, so I'll just have a burger and fries."

Denise felt relief when a waitress came to take their order. Maybe once her daughter had food in her stomach, she'd be in a better mood. *I know I will be.* She picked up her water and took a drink. *I'm more than ready to eat lunch, and despite whatever Kassidy thinks, everything on the menu here looks good to me.*

Berlin

"What did you think of the cooking class today?" Miranda asked her children.

"I liked it, but I don't care much for Kassidy." Debbie's lips curled. "She wants her way all the time."

"Maybe since we were all strangers to one another, everyone was a little uncomfortable. I'm sure it will get better once we all get to know each other." Miranda had to admit that Kassidy was one spoiled child. *I'm glad my children aren't like that.* "How about you, Kevin? What did you think of the cooking class?"

"Guess it was all right, but I had more fun when that nice man showed us the animals after the class was over."

"It was kind of Mr. Troyer to give you a tour of their barn."

As Miranda drove toward home, she recalled how Heidi's husband had been so patient, answering the children's questions about all the animals they had on the farm. One thing that had really impressed Miranda was when Lyle glanced lovingly back at his wife, and how Heidi smiled at him, watching as he and the children ventured toward the barn.

Miranda blew a breath from her lips. *I remember when Trent used to look at me that way. When did it all go wrong?*

Before returning home, Miranda wanted to make a stop, so she pulled into the local market in Berlin. "Hey kids, how about we go in here and get some things to make toasted cheese sandwiches for our lunch?"

"Sounds good," Debbie and Kevin said in unison.

"We'll need to make it quick, though. We have to get home and let Blondie out."

Blondie was their poodle, and she got the name because of her light-colored, curly fur. Blondie was a friendly, good-tempered dog. The kids loved her, and she'd become an important part of the family.

After picking out some different cheeses, fresh bread, and a bag of potato chips, they returned to the minivan, and Miranda drove the three miles to their home.

When she pulled into the driveway, she spotted Trent's shiny red truck parked by the garage. Her husband stood in the backyard, throwing a stick for Blondie to fetch.

"Dad's here!" Debbie yelled, quickly getting out of the van after it came to a halt.

Kevin was close behind her, and they both ran to greet their father.

Miranda got the bags of groceries out of the back and headed toward the house. Like a faithful friend, the poodle ran up to greet her.

"Hey there, Blondie. Did you miss us?" Miranda smiled as the dog raised up on her hind legs and tried to sniff inside the bags. "Don't worry. I got something for you, too."

As if the dog understood, Blondie gave an approving bark.

After chatting with their dad a few minutes, the kids called to Blondie and continued the game of fetch.

Miranda stopped as Trent approached. He wore a light beige shirt and a pair of darker beige, stylish slacks. While some people might think her husband was average looking, to her, no other man was as handsome as Trent. The first two buttons of his shirt were open, revealing dark curly chest hairs that matched his thick eyebrows. Miranda's face grew warm, as she willed her eyes to rise up and meet his gaze. Even with all the problems between them, she still remembered, and longed for, the way things had been before he'd begun seeing another woman. Of course, Trent denied having had an affair. He insisted the relationship hadn't gone that far before he'd broken things off. But Miranda lost faith in him and wasn't convinced he was telling the truth.

"Nice of you to stop by when we weren't home." Miranda couldn't keep the sarcasm out of her tone. "Why are you here anyway? I thought you were scheduled to work today."

"I did work this morning, but I got off at noon. Oh, by the way, I didn't know you weren't going to be home."

"Don't you remember?" Miranda sighed heavily. "We were at the cooking class I told you about when I called to see if you could take the kids." *Trent never remembers anything I tell him.*

"Oh, yeah, right, I forgot."

Big surprise. "So, why did you stop by?"

"I want to get some of the music CDs I left here when you kicked me out." Trent shifted from one foot to the other. "I have a CD player, but no music to play in it."

"Oh, I see." Miranda's body temperature rose, and it wasn't from the heat. "Then I guess it wasn't because you wanted to see the kids."

"Now don't try to make something out of nothing, Miranda." Trent kept his voice lowered. "Figured when I got here, I'd spend a little time with Debbie and Kevin." He reached out and took one of the grocery sacks.

Miranda didn't want to argue, especially in front of the children, so she invited Trent to stay for lunch. That would allow him some time with the kids.

"Thanks for the offer, but I'll have to take a rain check." Trent looked toward the children, who were still playing with the dog. "I had a busy morning at the dealership. In fact, I sold three cars. So I'm tired and want to get home and relax. If it's okay with you, I'll pick out some CDs and be on my way."

"Sure, take whatever you want." She waved her hand to shoo him on.

"Look, Miranda, I'm trying to be cordial. Quite frankly, when I realized you weren't home, I could have just gone in the house, got the CDs, and left. But I hung around, hoping you and the kids would be home soon. That's why I came out here with Blondie. Figured I'd mess with her a bit while I waited for you."

"Well if you'd paid attention, you would have remembered that I said the cooking class would be over at noon."

"Okay, I admit, I forgot." Trent rubbed the bridge of his nose.

"By the way," she added, "the next cooking class is in two weeks, and I have to work that Saturday. So can you take the kids?"

"I'm scheduled to work, too, but I'll see if I can switch with someone."

"Thanks."

Miranda and Trent entered their ranch-style house. While she put the groceries away, he went to the living room to get what he'd come for.

Debbie and Kevin came running into the kitchen. "Where's Daddy?" Kevin asked.

Miranda nodded toward the living room. The children hurried in to be with their father. *Those poor kids miss their dad so much. I'll never understand that man. If he hadn't messed up, he could still be living here.*

Blondie, who'd been left outside, whined and scratched at the door.

"Did they forget about you?" Miranda held the door open as Blondie pranced in. The cute dog stayed with her in the kitchen, sitting patiently and wagging her pom-tipped tail.

"What do ya say now?" Miranda held her hand out, hiding a surprise.

"*Woof! Woof!*" Blondie rose up in a begging position, reaching her front paws up as high as she could.

"Good girl." Miranda rewarded her with a chewy bone.

She watched the pretty poodle go over to her doggie bed, spin in a circle, and lie down with the bone. Shortly thereafter, Trent, holding a few CDs in his hand, entered the kitchen, with both kids trailing behind.

"Can't you please stay, Daddy?" Debbie held onto her father's arm.

"Sorry, honey. Some other time. I want to go back to my apartment and put up my feet." Trent patted the top of Debbie's head.

Kevin stood silently, not saying a word, but his look of disappointment said it all.

Sugarcreek, Ohio

"Why are we stoppin' here?" Jeremy asked when Darren pulled his rig into the parking lot of a restaurant in Sugarcreek.

"We're going to stop for lunch." Darren glanced in the mirror at his son sitting in the back seat, wearing a scowl. "I'm hungry and figured you would be also."

"Yeah, okay. Guess I could eat something. That dumb fruit salad I had to make during the cooking class didn't fill my stomach. Especially when I had to share it with you."

Darren chuckled. "You wouldn't have eaten it in front of me, would ya?"

"Naw, I was only kidding."

"Are you feeling better about taking the class now that you know you're not the only boy?"

"I guess so, but the other guys are just little kids. I don't have much in common with Randy or Kevin."

"That's okay. You don't have to become best buds. It's just kind of nice to know there are three boys in the class, which evens things out, since there are three girls."

"Four, if you count the little girl who lives with Heidi."

"True." Darren opened the door on his side of the vehicle. "Let's go inside the restaurant and see what's on the menu."

They had no more than stepped into the restaurant when Darren spotted Ellen and her daughter, Becky, sitting at a table near the window. He thought about how the two of them had hurried out the door after class ended today, preventing him from telling Ellen what he thought about her not giving Becky a chance to learn on her own. It was probably for the best, though. No point creating a problem—especially when they'd be seeing each other again at the next cooking class.

Ellen glanced up from perusing her menu and was surprised to see Darren Keller enter the restaurant with his son. When Darren looked her way, she offered a casual wave. He nodded in her direction, before following the hostess to a table. Ellen turned back to Becky. "Did you enjoy the cooking class today?"

Becky lifted her shoulders briefly. "It was okay, but I didn't like two of the boys who were there."

"Which two?"

"Kevin and Jeremy."

"How come?"

"Well, Kevin kept doing things to irritate that girl, Kassidy, and Jeremy kicked me under the table a few times."

"I'm sure he didn't kick you on purpose." Ellen glanced across the room, where Darren and Jeremy sat. They were too far away to hear what Becky had said, especially since she'd spoken so quietly.

"Mom, do they have pizza here?" Becky asked.

"I don't think so." Ellen pointed to the menu. "I'm going to order the baked chicken wrap. You should order something healthy."

"Okay I'll have a wrap."

"We'll have pizza soon," Ellen promised, seeing Becky's defeated expression. "I know pizza's your favorite food. Whenever we decide to have it, maybe instead of ordering a pizza, we can make one together. How's that sound?"

"Okay."

Ellen felt better when Becky nodded in agreement.

"Mom, when I go to the next cooking class, you can just drop me off at Heidi Troyer's and come back when it's done to pick me up."

Ellen shook her head. "I wouldn't feel right about that. I'd prefer to stay during the class." She glanced at Darren again, and was surprised when he left his seat and headed in their direction. Ellen moistened her lips. *I wonder what he wants.*

Chapter 8

"I'm surprised to see you here." Darren smiled as he stood beside Ellen's chair. "Do you come to Sugarcreek often?"

"No. I heard about this restaurant and decided to stop for lunch before heading home." She fiddled with her napkin, nervous all of a sudden. The depth of Darren's blue eyes seemed to bore right through Ellen as he held her steady gaze. "How about you? Have you and your son eaten here before?"

"Nope. It's our first time, too. Got a recommendation from another fireman who lives in Sugarcreek." He grinned. "If anyone knows a good place to eat, it's a guy who puts out fires for a living."

She chuckled. Darren was not only good looking, but he had a sense of humor, something she'd always appreciated in a man— or anyone else for that matter. As a nurse, she'd learned from observing her patients that laughter and a positive attitude were good medicine.

Darren gestured to the empty chairs at Ellen's table. "Say, would it be okay if Jeremy and I joined you? It might be nice to get better acquainted."

Ellen looked at her daughter, wondering how she would feel if Darren and his son sat at their table. When Becky said nothing, Ellen looked back at Darren. "Sure, that'd be fine."

Darren turned and motioned for his son to come over. Jeremy remained in his seat a few seconds, then got up and tromped across the room. "What's up, Dad?"

"We're going to sit here and eat lunch with Ellen and Becky."

Jeremy's brows furrowed. "I thought we had our own table."

"We did, but I decided we should sit over here and visit with Becky and her mother."

"Okay, whatever." Jeremy took a seat next to Becky and slouched in his chair.

She gave him a sidelong glance, but didn't say a word either. Ellen hoped her daughter wasn't holding a grudge against Jeremy because he'd kicked her under the table.

Darren seated himself in the chair beside Ellen, then glanced over at her menu. "I hear the French dip sandwich is pretty good here."

"I'll probably have a salad." Ellen pushed the menu closer to him. "Do you want to take a closer look?"

"Nope. I know what I want." He handed the menu to Jeremy. "You'd better make up your mind soon, 'cause a waitress is headed this way."

"I made up my mind when we were sittin' at the other table." Jeremy nodded in that direction. "I'm gonna have a personal-size pizza."

"I thought they didn't have pizza here." Becky looked at Ellen with furrowed brows. "If he gets to have pizza, why can't I?"

Feeling a headache coming on, Ellen rubbed her forehead. "Okay, Becky, you can have whatever you want. I must have missed seeing pizza listed on the menu."

After the waitress took their orders, it grew uncomfortably quiet at the table.

"Did you enjoy the cooking class?" Darren asked at the same moment Ellen threw out the same question.

He chuckled. "You go first."

"Yes, despite the fact that no one knew each other, I thought things went well for the first class."

"I thought it was a little awkward, though." Darren glanced at Becky, then back at Ellen. "Hopefully the next ones will go better, and the kids will be more comfortable with each other. Don't you think so, Jeremy?" He nudged his son's arm, but all Jeremy did was nod his head.

"Did you like the class, Jeremy?" Ellen asked.

"It was okay." Jeremy glanced at Becky, then looked quickly away.

"How about you, Becky? What did you think?" Darren questioned.

"It was all right," she mumbled without looking at him.

Darren chuckled. "Well, at least our kids think alike where that topic is concerned."

Ellen smiled. "You mentioned another fireman had recommended this place to eat." She took a drink of water the waitress had put on the table. "Are you also a fireman?"

"Yeah. It's what I've always wanted to be." He grabbed his glass of water and took a big swallow. "I tried college after graduating from high school, but only got as far as acquiring my associate's degree in business management."

"I see." Ellen leaned her elbows on the table.

"I knew sitting behind a desk was not for me." Darren didn't want to talk about himself anymore. "How about you? What do you do?"

"I'm a nurse in the pediatric ward at the hospital in Millersburg."

He smiled. "Guess that means you must like kids."

"I do." Her face sobered. "It saddens me, though, to see a severely sick or injured child."

Darren slowly nodded. "It's hard for me to see kids who have been burned or injured because of a fire. So in some ways our jobs are similar."

"Yes, I suppose." Ellen rested her hands beneath her chin.

"Don't mean to change the subject, but are you planning to come to all the cooking classes with your daughter?"

"Yes, I am."

Darren came close to voicing his opinion on that subject, but the waitress arrived with their food. *Maybe once he'd gotten to know Ellen better he would feel free to interject his thoughts.*

<hr />

Walnut Creek

"Are ya still mad at me for playin' with the hose?" Randy asked Heidi as she sat in the kitchen with him and Marsha, eating lunch.

She reached over and gave his shoulder a tender squeeze. "No, Randy. You apologized and I forgave you." Heidi looked at Marsha, her lips covered with peanut butter. "Your sister accepted your apology, too."

"I won't touch the hose again." Randy shook his head vigorously. "Promise."

Heidi smiled. "Sometimes Lyle or I might ask you to turn on the hose, and then it will be okay. I just don't want you spraying anyone with water."

"Okay." He pointed to the cookie jar on the counter. "Can Marsha and I have a *kichli*?"

"Yes, but not until you've finished your lunch. There are only a few oatmeal cookies left, but you and Marsha can help me make more."

Marsha grinned, and Randy bobbed his head. It was good to see him becoming more receptive to her. It also pleased Heidi that Randy had used the Pennsylvania Dutch word for cookie. He was beginning to catch on to more Amish words. When he started school this fall, Randy would have an advantage over the other children, since he already knew the English language. It would be easier for him to make friends and communicate with the other children before and after class if he spoke Pennsylvania Dutch. Marsha wouldn't start school for a few more years, so Heidi would have plenty of time to work with her if she and Lyle were allowed to continue caring for the children.

What a privilege it was to take care of these precious youngsters. *And to think, if one of my previous students hadn't mentioned the need for foster parents, Lyle and I never would have considered such a thing.* It still amazed Heidi how the Lord had worked things out on their behalf, as well as the children's. Despite the disappointment she'd felt over not being able to adopt Kendra's baby, everything had turned out well.

Seeing that the children had finished their sandwiches, Heidi scooted away from the table and went to get the ingredients to make oatmeal cookies. She set a carton of eggs on the counter and was about to get out the oatmeal, when a knock sounded on the front door.

"I'll be right back." She hurried from the room.

When Heidi opened the door, she was surprised to see Denise and Kassidy on the porch.

"Sorry to bother you." Denise's tone was apologetic. "My daughter thinks she may have left her cell phone here."

Kassidy lifted her chin. "I don't think it, Mom. I know I left it here.

I had my phone with me when I was in Heidi's kitchen."

"The children and I just finished eating lunch, and I didn't see any sign of your cell phone in the kitchen. Perhaps you left it somewhere else," Heidi suggested.

The girl's face turned crimson, as she shook her head. "I only took it out when I was sitting at your table, because I wanted to see if I had any text messages."

"Okay, well, let's go to the kitchen and take a look." Heidi led the way.

When they entered the room, where Randy and Marsha still sat, Kassidy scanned the table.

"Your phone's not here," Denise pointed out. "Are you sure you left it on the table?"

Kassidy nodded curtly.

"Maybe one of the others who was here at the class saw the phone and moved it someplace else," Heidi suggested.

"Or maybe someone took it." Kassidy planted both hands on her hips, glaring at Randy and Marsha.

"Now, don't go making accusations, Kassidy." Denise stepped between her daughter and the table.

Kassidy's face tightened. "I need my phone, and I want it back!" She skirted around her mother and leaned close to Randy's chair, looking him right in the face. "I bet you took it, you little thief. You have guilt written all over your dirty face."

"My face ain't dirty." He glared back at her.

"Yeah, it is. There's purple jelly on your chin and a smudge of peanut butter on your cheek."

Heidi was on the verge of intervening, when Denise spoke again. "Kassidy, you can't go around accusing people of taking your things when you have no proof."

"But I do have proof," she insisted. "I left my cell phone here, it's gone now, and the little runt looks guilty."

Feeling the need to end this, Heidi looked at Randy and said, "Did you take Kassidy's phone?"

He started to shake his head, but then slowly nodded. "It was on the table when she left, so I picked it up."

"What'd you do with it?" Kassidy's nostrils flared like an angry bull about to charge.

"I—I put it in my room so I could look at it later."

"You'd better not have played with the buttons or messed up any of my settings." The girl's cheeks turned a deeper shade of red.

"Randy, please go to your room and get Kassidy's phone." Heidi was embarrassed by his behavior and disappointed because he had taken something that wasn't his, without asking. She wondered if his parents had taught him right from wrong.

"Okay, I'll get it." Randy leaped from his chair and bolted out of the room.

"I apologize for his behavior." Heidi looked at Denise. "He's young and doesn't always think about what he's doing."

"Believe me, I understand." Denise gave a sidelong glance toward her daughter.

A few minutes later, Randy returned with Kassidy's cell phone. Before he could utter a word, she snatched it out of his hand and looked it over.

Randy backed away from Kassidy and took a seat next to Marsha.

"Everything seems okay with my phone. Can we go now, Mom?" Kassidy put the phone in her pocket.

"Yes, but before we do, you need to tell Randy you're sorry for talking so sharply to him."

"Okay, whatever." Kassidy went over to where Randy sat, and mumbled. "Sorry for what I said. And you should be sorry, too, for taking my phone." She moved across the room and stood with both hands on her hips.

Denise turned to face Heidi. "Sorry for the interruption and especially for my daughter's rude behavior. We'll look forward to seeing you in two weeks." Denise and Kassidy went out the back door this time.

Heidi looked at Randy. "I'm not going to punish you this time, but if you ever take anything that doesn't belong to you again, there will be consequences. Understand?"

"Jah." Randy scrubbed a hand over his face and turned his head away quickly.

Heidi wished she could do something to reach the boy. One minute things were going along okay, and the next minute Randy misbehaved. Was it the pain he still felt over losing his parents that caused his naughtiness, or did Randy dislike living here? One thing was certain: this had not been a good day for the boy.

That evening before the children went to bed, Heidi would read to them the verse she'd written on the back of the recipe card for fruit salad. Both Randy and his sister needed to understand the importance of obedience.

Chapter 9

Velma Kimball stood at the back door of the run-down double-wide she shared with her husband, Hank, and three of their children. They'd moved from Kentucky to Ohio a month ago but hadn't yet made any real friends.

The sun shone brightly this ninth day of June, but Velma's emotions swirled like a brewing storm. Nothing seemed to go right for her family. Seventeen-year-old Bobbie Sue had dropped out of school six months ago, and worked as a dishwasher at a restaurant in Berlin. It would be time for Velma to pick her up soon.

Velma was glad they'd gotten Bobbie Sue out of Kentucky, for her boyfriend there had been a bad influence, encouraging her to quit school, smoke, and sneak out of the house. Velma hoped things would be better now that Bobbie Sue was away from Kenny.

Clem, their oldest son, had left home two years ago, when he'd turned eighteen. They hadn't heard from him since. Then there was Eddie, their ten-year-old son. The boy had a chip on his shoulder and often got in trouble at school. Maybe now that summer was here, Eddie would settle down and make some new friends. Peggy Ann, age eight, was Velma's clingy child, which sometimes got on Velma's nerves. The girl also needed friends, or at least something to keep her busy during the summer months.

To make matters worse, Velma's husband, Hank, a truck driver, was often gone from home, leaving her to cope with the kids on her own.

As her frustration mounted, Velma kicked the rickety screen door with the toe of her worn-out sneaker. She'd been dealt a bad hand most of her life, and it was getting old. She longed for something better and hoped by moving they'd be getting a new start. Of course, leaving Kentucky wasn't just about getting Bobbie Sue away from

Kenny. Most of it had to do with the rift they'd had with Velma's folks. It was sad to have to cut ties with one's folks, but for Hank's sake, Velma had done just that.

Velma's mouth twisted as she balled her hands into fists. *Maybe I shoulda married someone else—a man my parents approved of, at least. Well, it's too late for regrets. It's time to focus on our new life here in Ohio and hope things go better for me, Hank, and our kids.*

With a gentle breeze blowing in her face, Heidi headed down the road in her open buggy toward Walnut Creek Cheese. She inhaled deeply. It was a warm, dry wind—the comfortable kind of breeze that didn't give you goose bumps and wasn't too humid.

Holding the ends of her covering ties between her teeth so her *kapp* would stay in place, she gripped the reins firmly to keep her horse from sprinting at full speed. Heidi hadn't used Bobbins, their chestnut mare, for a few days, and she seemed eager to run.

It was hard to believe almost a week had gone by since her first children's cooking class. With her second class just a week from tomorrow, she needed to make sure she had everything on hand. Since Heidi would be busy with other things the first several days of next week, today was the best time to get some shopping done. Lyle didn't have an auction, so he'd volunteered to stay home with Marsha and Randy, which allowed Heidi to shop with no interruptions. It wasn't often that she had time to be by herself these days, and she appreciated his willingness to supervise the children. No doubt, they would be good for him.

Their social worker had dropped by yesterday morning, and they'd had a good visit. Gail seemed pleased that Randy and Marsha were getting along well, and when Heidi told her about the cooking classes, Gail said it sounded like an interesting venture and wouldn't mind taking cooking lessons herself sometime.

Driving along, Heidi saw a woman from their church district out mowing her lawn. She waved at Irene, and her neighbor responded with a hearty, "Nice to see you, Heidi!"

The heavy smell of fresh mowed grass filled Heidi's senses, and an image of herself during childhood days came to mind. As a young girl, she loved being cushioned by the sweet-smelling grass and watching big white clouds float slowly across the sky. *I'll have to introduce Marsha and Randy to cloud watching some afternoon.* Heidi smiled. *Another thing I'm sure they would enjoy is a picnic in our backyard.*

The thought of an evening meal of fried chicken, baked beans, potato chips, and sweet tea made her mouth water. Randy and Marsha would no doubt enjoy eating those, too.

Heidi figured the children were due for a reward of some kind. Ever since the incident with the hose last Saturday, plus being caught with Kassidy's phone, Randy had been on his best behavior. Marsha too, but then the quiet little girl always did as she was told. A family picnic seemed like a valid way to show her approval. Plus, her husband was a pushover when it came to her crispy, coated chicken.

She thought about the other night. When she'd tucked the kids into bed and read them the verse from the Bible about obedience, they'd promised to be good. Heidi hoped the other children who'd received a card would also take the verse to heart.

Despite the wind that had increased, the warmth of the sun felt pleasant to Heidi as she continued in the direction of the store. Sunlight always brightened her mood, and today was no exception. Since Randy and Marsha had come to live with them, Heidi had a renewed sense of hope for the future. She hadn't spoken to Lyle yet about the possibility of trying to adopt the children, but hoped to talk to him soon. He'd become a father to their foster children in every way, so Heidi felt sure he would want to make Marsha and Randy legally theirs. She couldn't imagine him saying anything but yes.

After Heidi pulled into the parking area and secured her horse, she headed into the cheese store. Grabbing a basket by the door, she moved along the refrigerator case, eyeing the many types of cheeses they offered.

Heidi noticed an English family picking out some different items. She wondered if they were tourists or lived in the area. The mother and father were soft spoken as they talked to the two children, allowing them each to pick out a treat. The boy seemed content as he chose some cheese and crackers. His sister took longer deciding, until she reached out for a small container of bear-shaped graham crackers.

Heidi turned away and tried a sample of habanero cheddar. It was so hot she couldn't finish eating it, and ended up spitting it in a tissue she pulled from her purse. *I hope no one saw me do that. Lyle might like the hot cheese, since he enjoys putting spicy salsa on some things we eat at home, but it's certainly not for me.* Waving her hand in front of her mouth, in the hope of cooling off, Heidi wished she'd brought her water bottle inside with her.

Not long after, she saw her friend Loretta and visited with her for a bit. They decided to go to another shop in the area and look around, since neither of them had their children along.

As Heidi walked beside Loretta, they shared the latest news, while looking at some of the gift items. Then they stopped for a dish of ice cream before going their separate ways. Of course, Heidi bought a gallon of ice cream that she put in a small cooler she'd brought along so she could take home a treat for Lyle and the children. She would serve it after supper.

Berlin

"Are you ready to head for home?" Velma asked Bobbie Sue as she climbed into the passenger's seat of Velma's older model, mid-sized car. Eddie and Peggy Ann were in the back seat.

Bobbie Sue's face reddened as she crossed her arms. "Oh, I'm ready, all right. The boss just fired me, so I won't be comin' back to this stupid diner anymore." She scrunched her nose. "What a cruddy way to end the week."

Velma blinked rapidly. "Why would Marilyn let you go?"

"Said I was mouthin' off." Bobbie Sue's nostrils flared as she shook her head. "I think she made it up so she can hire her niece who moved here last week from Cincinnati."

"Did she come right out and say that?"

"No, but it don't take no genius to figure it out. All's I did was tell the boss lady that I was sick and tired of gettin' stuck with all the dirty work. I wanna wait on people, not be stuck washing dishes, cleaning tables, and sweeping the floors." Bobbie Sue paused long enough to draw in a quick breath. "Marilyn plays favorites anyways, and when I heard her niece was here and would need a job, I had a feeling I'd probably get fired."

Velma's jaw clenched. Maybe Bobbie Sue was telling the truth, but since she often mouthed off, Marilyn may have let her go for a legitimate reason.

"Would you like me to talk to your boss? With any luck, maybe I can talk her into giving you your job back."

Bobbie Sue shook her head. "Don't bother, Mama. I'm sick of the job anyways."

"Well, like it or not, you need to be working and paying room and board, like I did when I was your age."

Her daughter just stared straight ahead.

"How long till we get to Uncle Patrick's house?"

Keeping her concentration on the road ahead, Ellen responded to her daughter's question. "It will be awhile. Probably about two hours to go yet." Ellen couldn't believe how busy Berlin was today.

"Yeah, but I can wait." Becky folded her hands and rested them in her lap. "I wonder what we will have to eat tonight."

"Your uncle said something about grilling hot dogs and burgers." Ellen smiled. When Becky first learned they were going to her aunt, uncle, and cousins' place for the weekend, she'd been excited. With Ellen's brother and his family living in Wheeling, West Virginia, they didn't get to see them regularly. Since Becky tended to be a bit shy around other children, it was good for her to spend time with her cousins, Alisha and Connie. Ellen was thankful she'd been able to get two days off in a row so they could make the trip. When she'd gotten off work today, she had gone home, put their suitcases in the car, and headed out with Becky. They would return home early Sunday evening, since Ellen's shift on Monday would begin at six o'clock in the morning.

The traffic became heavier, no doubt due to the number of people getting off work, not to mention all of the tourists. And because it was Friday, everyone seemed anxious to get to wherever they were going. Already, one driver had cut in front of Ellen to gain some headway. She found an easy-listening station on the radio and turned the volume down to a soft level, hoping it would help soothe her nerves as she and Becky traveled the rest of the way. She was just as anxious as her daughter to see her brother and his family.

Patrick was two years older than Ellen, and their brother, Dean, was five years older. Because of their close ages, she and Patrick had always had a stronger relationship while growing up. They had a lot in common, too. He was a doctor and she a nurse. They both enjoyed people and shared the same bubbly personality. Patrick had a strong relationship with God, and so did Ellen. Unfortunately, their older brother had strayed from his faith, and it had affected his marriage. Dean and Shelly were now divorced, and their three children lived with her in Texas.

I hope my older brother gets back on track before it's too late, Ellen thought as she approached a stoplight. *Shelly hasn't remarried, so maybe there's a chance that they could get back together.*

Ellen noticed a compact car as it started through the intersection as the light turned green. At the same time, an older-model vehicle on the right sailed through the light without stopping. She gasped at the horrible sound as the vehicles collided, breaking glass and crunching metal.

From the backseat, Becky screamed.

Concerned that one or more of the passengers in either car might be hurt, Ellen pulled onto the shoulder of the road and turned off the ignition. "There, there Becky. It's going to be okay." This was the first time her daughter had witnessed an accident such as this. "Stay right here, though. I need to see if anyone was injured and call for help."

A re you all right?" Velma's heart pounded as she reached across the seat and touched her daughter's arm.

"I—I think so. My neck kinda hurts, though. How about you, Mama? Are you okay?" Bobbie Sue's voice trembled as she sat slumped in her seat.

"I'm not sure." Velma swiped at the wetness on her forehead, certain that it was bleeding. She found a lump there, but no blood, just perspiration.

Quickly, Velma turned in her seat to see if her two younger ones had been injured. "Are either of you hurt?"

Wide eyed, and with her chin trembling, Peggy Ann shook her head.

"I'm okay, too," Eddie said.

Velma heaved a sigh of relief. Then the door on her side of the car opened, and a pretty woman with blond hair looked in. "Are any of you hurt?"

Velma shook her head. "There's a small lump on my forehead from where I hit the steering wheel, and my oldest daughter said her neck hurts a bit, but my kids in the back are okay. Thank goodness those safety seats kept them secure."

"I've called 911, so help should be here soon." The color of the woman's brown eyes deepened. "The man in the vehicle you hit passed out and it wouldn't be wise to try and move him until the paramedics get here and can determine his injuries."

Velma sucked in a deep breath. If the man died it would be her fault, for she had plowed through the intersection without stopping at the light. Thank goodness she'd paid the car insurance premium on time this month.

"It's going to be okay. My name is Ellen Blackburn, and I'm a nurse. I'll stay with you until help arrives." The woman's voice was calm, and she spoke with reassurance. The way the sun shone on her blond hair, it almost appeared as if she were an angel. Not that Velma had ever seen an angel. Truth was, she'd never been a religious person and could only imagine what one looked like.

"Wonder what Papa's gonna say when he finds out what happened." Bobbie Sue's forehead wrinkled as she looked over at Velma.

"He won't be thrilled, that's for sure." Velma moved in the seat, trying to loosen the tight belt that held her in. "This ancient car is our only transportation, other than your dad's semitruck, and I'm sure ole Bessie will need a lot of repair—if she can be fixed at all."

"There's a lot of smoke coming up out there." Her daughter pointed toward the rising fog.

She glanced in the direction of the moving cloud. "Actually, that isn't smoke; it's the radiator steaming. It probably has a crack in it from the accident." Velma groaned and shook her head.

"That's another reason for me to get a new job, and soon." Bobbie Sue popped a stick of gum in her mouth. "We're gonna need more money to afford another car."

"I hope the other driver will be okay. It was stupid of me to have driven through that stoplight." Velma's eyes teared up.

"Mama, it was only an accident. You didn't do it on purpose." Bobbie Sue patted her arm.

"I know what you are saying, but I'm worried about the other driver and wish there was something I could do. I wonder what other folks do in situations like this. All we can do is sit here and wait to hear how they're doing."

"Maybe they pray."

Velma rested her hands against the steering wheel. Although she rarely prayed, Velma sent up a quick plea on the other person's behalf.

"I feel bad for you, having to listen to Papa blow a gasket 'cause you wrecked the car," Eddie spoke up.

Velma groaned. She could only imagine.

———————— ⁕ ————————

Ellen felt relief when the paramedics arrived. She directed them to the passenger in the smaller vehicle first, since he seemed to be hurt the worst. Two of the medics headed in that direction, while a third man went over to see about the passengers in the older-looking car. Two patrol cars arrived a few minutes later, and Ellen waited in her car until they were ready to talk to her.

"What's going on, Mom?" Becky's eyes were wide with fear. "Are the people in those vehicles hurt bad?"

"I don't know, Becky, but now that help is here, they will be looked after and taken to the hospital if necessary."

Becky blinked rapidly, then squeezed her eyes tightly shut. "I'm glad our car wasn't hit."

"Same here." Ellen patted her daughter's arm. "God was watching over us—that's for sure."

When Ellen saw one of the officers approach, she stepped out of her car.

"I'm assuming you must have witnessed the accident?" he asked.

She nodded.

"Would you mind giving me your statement?"

"No, I don't mind at all, but could you tell me how the people involved are doing? Were any of them seriously injured?"

"Other than a couple bumps and bruises the women and children in the one car seem to be okay, but the guy driving the van is still unconscious. He's being taken to the nearest hospital."

Ellen sent up a silent prayer, asking God to be with the injured man, as well as those in the older vehicle.

———————— ⁕ ————————

Canton

"Kassidy, would you please set the table? It's almost time for supper." Denise took the meat loaf out of the oven and placed it on top of the stove. When no response came, Denise turned to see what her daughter was doing. Kassidy sat in the chair at the roll-top desk across the room, doing something on her cell phone.

"Please put that phone away and do as I asked."

Kassidy looked up and wrinkled her nose. "I'm in the middle of something, Mom. Can't you set the table yourself?"

Tapping her foot, Denise took a deep breath. Apparently her daughter had not read the verse Heidi wrote on the back of her recipe card about children obeying their parents. If she had, she'd chosen to ignore it.

Denise marched across the room and snatched the phone out of Kassidy's hands. "I want you to set the table—now!"

Kassidy gripped the sides of her head, as if to cover her ears. "You don't have to yell. I'm sitting right here."

Denise's jaw clenched as she shook her finger. "Don't you talk to me like that, young lady. When I ask you to do something, I expect you to do it with no back talk or rude comments." She set the cell phone on the counter. "If you cooperate, you can have it back tomorrow morning."

Kassidy's mouth fell open. "But, Mom, I—"

"No arguments or you won't get it back tomorrow either." Denise turned toward the hallway door. "I'm going to let your father know supper is ready. By the time I get back, you'd better have the table set."

When Denise entered the living room, she found her husband in his recliner, watching TV.

"Supper's ready, Greg. But before we go in to eat, I want to talk to you about our daughter."

"Can't it wait? I had a long day in court, and I'm too tired to deal with any problems Kassidy may have."

Denise rolled her shoulders in an effort to relieve some of the tension. "You're not the only one who's had a long day. I showed five houses to the pickiest couple I've ever met, and then I came home, made supper, and had to deal with our spoiled daughter."

He picked up the remote and turned off the TV. "Whose fault is it that Kassidy's spoiled? You're the one who's always buying her things."

"This isn't about things. It's about her disrespectful attitude and refusal to obey when I ask her to do even a simple chore."

"Guess it's something you need to work on then." He pulled the lever on his chair and sat up.

Denise moved closer to him. "I've been thinking about this over the past week, and you know what the biggest problem is, Greg?"

"No, but I'm sure you're going to tell me."

Ignoring his sarcasm, she said, "You and I have been putting our careers first. We're both too busy for our daughter, so she acts out to get attention. It's time we call a halt to her temper tantrums and self-centered ways."

"What brought this on all of a sudden? We've never had this discussion before."

"Going to the cooking class last week with Kassidy got me thinking. She acted like a spoiled child, embarrassing me to no end. Truthfully, that's exactly what she is."

He stood, shoving his hands into his pants' pockets. "Our jobs keep us busy, and if it weren't for our jobs, we wouldn't be able to give Kassidy all the nice things she's come to expect and appreciate."

"You're right. She does expect them, but I'm not sure our daughter appreciates anything we do for her." Denise massaged the bridge of her nose. "Maybe we need to work less and spend more quality time with Kassidy. Except for the obsession with her phone, it's apparent all this stuff we give her means nothing."

Greg tipped his head, looking at her through half-closed eyes. "If you want to cut back on your workload and spend more time with our daughter, that's up to you, but I'm not in a position to do that right now." He moved down the hall toward the kitchen, leaving Denise alone, shaking her head.

I can't do this by myself, Greg. If we want Kassidy to grow into a mature young woman who respects her elders and doesn't respond negatively when she can't have her way, it's going to take both of us giving her more of our time and attention. Her chest tightened. *I just hope you realize that before it's too late.*

<hr />

Walnut Creek

Humming one of the songs they frequently sang at family gatherings, Heidi checked on the baked beans in the oven. The fried chicken cooled on a large platter, while Lyle was outside tending the grill. When shopping, Heidi had also purchased some early fresh corn on the cob. Lyle smothered the ears with butter, wrapped them in foil, and heated them on the hot coals.

Heidi's mouth watered as the smell of seasoned chicken reached her nostrils. "Yum. I can't wait to sink my teeth into that meat." Whether hot or cold, fried chicken was a perfect picnic choice for their supper.

With the scent of grilling smoke wafting through the open window, she could hear the children's laughter and Rusty's excited barking. Heidi breathed in a contented sigh. When she'd gotten home a few hours ago, she was pleased to hear what a good time Lyle and the children had together. Randy was eager to share with Heidi how he and Marsha helped Lyle in the barn. Marsha bobbed her head as Randy explained how fun it was to clean the cat's dishes and fill them with fresh water and food. Lyle also piqued their enthusiasm with his plan of purchasing some chickens. The kids seemed excited when they learned their responsibility would be to help collect eggs once the hens started laying. But first Lyle had to ask Eli about building a chicken coop for them, as well as a sturdy fenced enclosure. It would not only keep the chickens in, but help to protect them from predators.

Heidi had to admit, getting some chickens was a good idea, and having farm-fresh eggs to collect every day was a bonus. It would also teach the children responsibility.

Randy and Marsha had been with them six months and were settling in more comfortably. Even Randy's negative attitude had turned more positive, and Marsha was talking more. Here at the Troyer residence, it was starting to feel like they were a real family. Heidi hoped the children might someday open up more about their parents—especially Randy, since he was older and had more memories of his mom and dad. Marsha was still pretty young and probably didn't remember as much. In time, the memory of her folks would fade. But Heidi would not push the children to talk about their past until they were ready.

Heidi thought about the photo albums tucked away in her and Lyle's bedroom closet, which they'd received when Randy and Marsha came to live with them. They belonged to the children's parents, Fred and Judy. All the other belongings from the Olsen household had been auctioned off after they'd passed away. But social services felt these photo memories were important to keep with the children. Heidi and Lyle agreed. Those pictures were part of the children's life, and the only tangible things they had left of their parents. When the time was right, Heidi planned to go through the albums with the children so they could talk about the photos.

When the agency had given Heidi the albums, they had looked pretty worn. Heidi could only assume they'd been looked at many times throughout the years. Along with the family album, inside the box was their parents' wedding album and the children's baby albums. Heidi had scanned through the baby books, consisting of details from the children's birth to one year of age, before putting them in the closet.

As she pulled the casserole dish of baked beans out of the oven and put it on the counter, Heidi heard the crunch of tires on gravel as a vehicle pulled into the driveway. Glancing out the window, she saw a minivan park, and was surprised when one of the students from her second cooking class got out of the passenger's side.

"Oh my, it's Allie Garrett." Heidi wiped her hands on her apron and quickly covered the beans and chicken with foil. She hadn't heard from or seen Allie since early December, when their final class ended.

When Heidi stepped out to the porch, a man in a police uniform was getting out of the driver's side. Heidi assumed it was Allie's husband, Steve, and was glad for the opportunity to finally meet him.

Allie and Steve wore big smiles as they walked up to Lyle standing by the grill. After they introduced themselves and shook his hand, Allie ran over to greet Heidi as she approached.

"Oh, Heidi, it's so good to see you." Allie reached out for a hug. "I picked my husband up from work, and we're heading to Millersburg to eat and do some shopping at Hershbergers' Farm and Bakery." Allie looked over at Steve. "We were going right through Walnut Creek, and I told Steve it would be a shame if we didn't stop. The kids are at church camp for a few days. Otherwise, they'd be with us."

"I'm so glad you came by." Heidi draped her arm around Allie's shoulder as they walked over to join their husbands.

"Heidi, this is my husband, Steve." Allie's eyes shone brightly as she looked at him. "And Steve, this is Heidi—the best cook in Holmes County."

"So nice to meet you, Steve." Heidi shook his hand. Steve's was a gentle, but firm handshake.

"I've heard a lot about you, Heidi. I'm enjoying being Allie's taste tester every time she makes a new dish." Steve patted his stomach. "If I'm not careful, though, it's going to show."

"Tell me about it." Lyle thumped his own belly. "It's a good thing this farm and the auctions I oversee keep me active. Otherwise, I'd have to buy bigger clothes."

Everyone laughed.

Allie scanned the yard. "How are things going with the children?"

"Very well." Heidi smiled, and Lyle nodded. "They're around here somewhere, playing with the dog. When Rusty and those two get together they're inseparable."

At that moment, their dog came bounding from the other side of the house, wagging his tail as he approached the visitors, with Randy and Marsha following.

"Here they are now." Heidi pointed.

When the children got closer and spotted the Garretts, their laughter and giggling halted, and Randy stopped in his tracks. Marsha took one look at Steve, held out her arms, and shouted, "Daddy!"

Chapter 11

As fast as her little feet could go, Marsha ran up to Steve and wrapped her slender arms around his legs.

Steve and Allie looked at each other in bewilderment, while Heidi stood beside Lyle, too stunned to say anything. As Steve squatted down to be eye-level with Marsha, she looked him square in the face.

"Now what do we have here?" Steve touched the end of Marsha's nose. "Aren't you a cute little girl?"

As quick as she had been eager to greet Steve, Marsha was even faster to pull away. Sobbing, she turned and ran over to her brother, hiding her face in his chest.

Even at five years old, Randy was protective of his sister, so it didn't surprise Heidi when he guided Marsha up to the porch, and they went inside the house together.

Heidi looked at Lyle, who appeared to be as bewildered as she was right now. "Allie and Steve, I'm so sorry. I'm not sure what just happened."

"It's okay." Allie turned to Steve. "We'd better go." Then giving Heidi another hug, she said, "I'll catch up with you soon, Heidi, and I hope the children are okay."

After the Garretts' van pulled out, Lyle turned off the grill and joined Heidi on the porch. "I wonder what was going on with Marsha." He reached under his hat and scratched the back of his head.

"I don't know." Heidi rubbed her hand down her cheek and rested it at her throat. "It's not like Marsha to run up to a stranger like that. She's normally pretty bashful. And did you hear her call Steve, 'Daddy'?"

"Jah. It surprised me. Maybe Steve resembles the children's father."

"We better go check on them."

When they went into the house, Heidi heard whimpering coming from the living room. As they walked in, she saw Randy consoling

Marsha, as he gently patted her back. "It's okay Marsha. Don't cry." Even though Randy was trying to be the big brother, they both looked so small, huddled together on the couch.

Heidi went over and sat next to Marsha, then held out her arms. Marsha quickly climbed onto her lap and put her face against Heidi's neck.

Lyle sat next to Randy. "Did something frighten you outside?" he asked.

"Kinda." Randy kept his head down, lips quivering like a leaf in the wind.

"Do you want to talk about it?" Lyle touched the boy's arm.

Randy took a shuddering breath. "When I saw that man in a uniform, it made me think of my daddy. He wore a uniform at his job, too."

"What was your daddy's job?" Heidi questioned.

"He worked at the shoppin' mall." Randy looked at Heidi with such seriousness in his eyes.

"You mean, like a security guard?" Lyle leaned closer to the boy.

"I. . .I think so, but I'm not sure. When we saw him standin' there, my sister thought it was our daddy. Then she got scared when she heard his voice. That's when she knew it wasn't Daddy. Guess it was his clothes that made her think it was Daddy." Randy sniffed. "Wish it had been. And I wish Mama was with him, too."

"I understand." Heidi clasped both children's hands. Tonight, before bed, she would get out the photo albums in their closet and share them with the children. This was definitely the right time.

"You know, sometimes we think we see someone we know, and it turns out being someone else," Heidi continued.

Marsha sat up and looked at Heidi, rubbing her tearful eyes.

"I'll bet there is someone out there who looks just like you." Heidi smoothed the blond hair back that had come loose from Marsha's ponytail. Then she kissed the little girl's forehead.

"How about we go back outside and have that picnic now?" Lyle suggested. "The corn on the cob should be done, and I'll bet Heidi has the chicken and beans ready."

"Yes, and after we've had some ice cream for dessert, I'll share something special with you and your big brother." Heidi smoothed the wrinkles in Marsha's dress. Her heart ached for Randy and Marsha. This was the first time Randy had mentioned anything about where their dad had worked. He, too, had clearly been shaken seeing Steve in uniform. But children were resilient and could usually get over things faster than most adults. Hopefully, Randy and Marsha would find it easier to talk about their parents after looking at the pictures in the album, and their emptiness would slowly wane. Heidi would do everything in her power to make these children feel loved and to give them a sense of belonging.

Dover

It was a slow day at the fire station. "How are things going with you these days?" Darren's friend Bruce asked as they hosed down one of the fire trucks at their station.

"Everything's fine." Darren moved to the front of the truck. "I took Jeremy to a cooking class a week and a half ago, and we'll be going to class number two this coming Saturday."

Bruce's eyebrows lifted. "How come you're taking a cooking class? As I recall, you get around the kitchen pretty well."

Darren shook his head. "It's not for me. Jeremy's taking the class from an Amish woman, along with four other kids, plus the Amish woman's two foster children."

"If it's for kids, then why are you going with Jeremy?"

Darren shrugged. "I wasn't planning to at first, but the other parents stayed instead of dropping off their children, so I figured I would, too. Also, it gives Jeremy and me something fun to do together." He watched a volunteer fireman pull in for his shift. "I thought my son could learn something new with kids his age and have a good time."

"Did you watch or take part in the cooking class?"

"Like many of the other parents, I was mostly a spectator, but there was a young single woman who did just about everything for her daughter." Satisfied that the truck looked clean enough, Darren turned off the hose and put it away. "I ran into Ellen. . ."

"Ellen?" Bruce cocked his head to one side.

"Yeah, her name's Ellen." Darren shrugged his shoulders. "As I was saying, I ran into Ellen and her daughter, Becky, at a restaurant in Sugarcreek when Jeremy and I went for lunch after the first class. We ended up sharing a table with them and got to know each other a bit better. Found out we have a few things in common, which was kinda nice."

Bruce looked at him through half-closed eyelids. "Is something going on between you and this woman? And if so, aren't you moving a little fast?" He picked up a drying towel and began working.

Darren flapped his hand. "Nothing is going on, so get that notion out of your head. My heart belongs to Caroline, and I have no desire to begin a relationship with another woman. Besides, I barely know Ellen. Our kids will be together in this cooking class for a total of six weeks, and it's nice to get to know the other parents." He grabbed a towel and moved along, helping to dry the vehicle. "When we get the truck dried off, we'll need to do some inventory. Oh, and I'm gonna fix a hearty casserole for the guys this evening."

"Sounds good, since we'll be here awhile on our shift." Bruce stood back and studied his work. "Think this rig is ready to go."

"If we get any calls, I'll pop the casserole in the oven on low." Darren finished drying a few streaks of water they'd missed.

Their conversation was interrupted when a call came in about a fire on the other side of town. Darren paused to send up a prayer, just as he did every time he went out on a call. Then, with all other thoughts pushed aside and his focus on the task at hand, Darren and the other men on duty gathered up their gear and headed out, all thoughts of the casserole forgotten.

Berlin

Miranda, dressed for work, tapped her foot in annoyance. Trent was supposed to pick up the kids to take them out for pizza half an hour ago. She hoped he hadn't forgotten.

Miranda clenched her fists. *That man can be so undependable.* She reached for the phone and punched in his cell number. *If only Trent could put others first and try to be less self-absorbed.*

A few seconds later, Trent answered. "Hey, hon, I was just gonna call you."

Her jaw tightened. They'd been separated since the end of April. Why did he still call her "hon"? Did he think she'd be impressed with the endearment and welcome him home with open arms? Well, she'd be a lot more impressed if Trent would show up on time when he promised to take the kids somewhere.

"Where are you, Trent? You were supposed to be here thirty minutes ago. What happened—did you forget about your promise to take Kevin and Debbie out for pizza this evening?"

"I did not forget, and if you'd let me get in a word, I'll explain why I'm not there."

Holding the phone slightly away from her ear, Miranda moved away from the window and took a seat at the kitchen table. "Okay, what's your excuse?"

"It's not an excuse. It's a fact. I'm locked out of my apartment, and the keys to my car are inside."

She lifted her gaze toward the ceiling. "Are you kidding?"

"Wish I was, but I'm not. I would ask the apartment manager to let me in with his key, of course, but he's out of town till tomorrow evening. Can't you explain things to Kevin and Debbie? We'll do pizza some other time."

"It isn't as simple as that. I got called in to work to fill in for someone who's sick, and I need to leave soon. What am I supposed to do about the kids if you can't drive over here to pick them up and spend the evening with them?" Miranda waited, but only heard silence at the other end. "And besides, what were you going to do, now that you're locked out of your place?" she questioned.

"I'm not sure. Haven't figured that out yet." He groaned. "Guess I can call a locksmith, but it would be a while before he arrived, and I have to be here in person to meet him. Why don't you call your sister, and see if she'll watch the kids while you're at work?"

Miranda grimaced. "Do I need to remind you that Kate lives in Akron? For goodness' sake, Trent, it would take her at the very least, forty-five minutes to get here."

"Okay, I get it, but if you need me to watch the kids this evening, you'll have to drive over and get me."

Her chest rose and fell in a heavy sigh. "I'll call my boss and let her know I'll be late, because I have to pick up my kids' sitter."

"Your kids' sitter? Is that all I am, Miranda?" His voice grew louder. "Why not just tell her you're picking up your husband so he can be with the children?"

"Let's not get into an argument about this. The kids and I will be there soon to pick you up. Goodbye, Trent."

Wheeling, West Virginia

"It's sure nice to have you here, sis." Ellen's brother, Patrick, wrapped his arms around her in a hug. "Between your busy life as a nurse and mine as a doctor, we don't get to visit each other often enough."

She thumped his back. "You're right, and I miss all of your teasing."

Patrick grinned and squeezed Ellen's hands before turning to Becky. "And how's my favorite niece?"

Becky snickered. "I'm your only niece, Uncle Patrick. Your brother has two boys, remember?"

Patrick slapped his forehead. "Oh, of course. How could I have forgotten something so important?" He winked, then gestured toward the hall leading to the upstairs. "Glad you're here. We were wondering what was holding you up." He gestured to Becky. "Your cousins are upstairs. Why don't you go on up and say hello? Or would you rather I called them down here?"

"I'll go up." Becky grinned shyly and headed upstairs.

"Where's Gwen?" Ellen asked her brother.

"She's taking a shower. Since we weren't sure what time you'd get in, we decided to take you out for supper, rather than cooking something here. I hope you're okay with that."

Ellen smiled. "Going out to eat is fine with me."

Patrick moved toward the living room. "Let's sit and visit while we wait for Gwen."

Ellen followed and took a seat on the couch, while he seated himself in a leather recliner.

"How was the drive here?" Patrick asked, reaching down for the lever to put the footrest up.

"Well, before getting too far from Berlin, we witnessed an accident." Ellen grabbed a throw pillow and wrapped her arms around it. "We would have been here sooner, but being a nurse, I couldn't leave."

"How bad was it?"

"It could have been a whole lot worse." Ellen explained the details. "So while Becky waited in the car, I called 911, and checked on the people involved. We stayed until the authorities came and took my statement. Fortunately, the rest of the way here was uneventful."

"Glad to hear that. It was good of you to stop and help out." Patrick smiled. "Your daughter's grown a bit since I last saw her. Pretty soon she'll be a teenager, going out on dates and keeping her mom awake at night, trying not worry."

Ellen grunted. "Don't remind me. I'm not looking forward to any of that."

He brushed her comment aside. "You've done a good job raising her. I doubt you'll have anything to worry about."

"I'm doing the best I can." Ellen sat silently for several seconds. "When I first adopted Becky, I never dreamed there would be so many challenges in being a single parent."

"You're right, but then any parent, single or not, faces challenges when they are raising their—"

Ellen heard a gasp, and she and Patrick both turned their heads toward the archway. There stood Becky, her mouth gaping open. Ellen briefly closed her eyes. *Oh no, what have I done? It's too late to take back my words.*

Becky came into the living room and stood right in front of Ellen. "Adopted? I'm adopted?" Her shrill voice reverberated throughout the room. "How come you never told me this? Does everyone know except me?" Tears pooled in Becky's eyes as she scrutinized Ellen.

Ellen swallowed hard. She could hardly look at her daughter. *What am I going to tell her? How do I explain why I kept her adoption a secret all this time? I took a chance speaking to Patrick about it with Becky in the house. This was not how I planned for her to find out.*

Chapter 12

Ellen's throat felt so swollen she could barely swallow as she crossed the room and reached out to touch her daughter's arm. "Let's take a seat, and I'll explain things to you." She moved toward the couch, hoping Becky would follow. The child, however, remained standing like a statue, with her arms held tightly against her sides.

Ellen looked at Patrick, hoping he would say something, and she wasn't disappointed. Speaking softly, he smiled at Becky. "Please take a seat. You and your mother need to talk."

Shuffling her feet across the carpet, Becky took a seat in the rocking chair. Except for the grandfather clock striking the half-past hour, the room was uncomfortably quiet.

Ellen couldn't hide her disappointment. Her desire was for Becky to sit beside her, so she could wrap her arms around the girl and explain her reasons for keeping the adoption a secret.

Becky shot Ellen an icy stare. The daughter who was usually so pleasant, showed no sign of that trait. "Did you ever plan to tell me the truth?"

"Of course, when you were old enough to understand it all, I planned to tell you, but—"

"Who are my real parents?" Becky's voice cracked. "I. . . I can't believe you hid this from me."

Ellen clutched the folds in her skirt. She had put herself in this position by keeping the truth from Becky, and that had obviously been a mistake. Her daughter was clearly upset, with good reason.

"I don't know your biological parents, Becky. I never met them." Ellen paused to clear her throat, hoping to dislodge the lump that had formed. "The adoption took place through an agency, and as far as I'm concerned, I am your real mother."

"But you're a single mom. Didn't you want me to have a dad?"

"It was not my intention for you to be raised without a father, but…" Ellen shifted on her seat. "I've always loved children and wanted some of my own. Since I had no serious boyfriend or any promise of marriage, I decided to adopt a child on my own."

Becky got the rocker moving and gave Ellen her full attention. "So what was the big secret? How come you didn't want me to know?"

Speaking slowly and with conviction, Ellen told how, when she was in high school, her best friend, Lynn, had learned she was adopted. "Lynn was upset and wanted to know about the woman who'd given birth to her," Ellen explained. "My friend's adoptive parents wouldn't tell her much and refused to help her look for her birth mother. Lynn was angry and moved out of their house and found a job after she graduated. It was sad, but she cut all ties with the parents who'd raised her, and as far as I know, she never went back." Tears welled in Ellen's eyes. "I was afraid if you knew you'd been adopted, it might cause problems between us, too. I realize now that I made a huge mistake. I should have been honest with you as soon as you were old enough to understand. Will you forgive me, Becky?"

The ticking of the clock seemed to grow louder in Ellen's ears as she waited for her daughter's response. Finally, Becky nodded. With tears coursing down her flushed cheeks, she rushed across the room and into Ellen's arms. "I still love you, Mom, and I always will."

Ellen breathed a sigh of relief. She never wanted to lose her daughter and would do anything to protect what they had together. She closed her eyes and lifted a silent prayer: *Lord, thank You for a daughter like Becky. Please continue to help me raise her according to Your purpose. Amen.*

"Someday, when you're a bit older, I'll help you search for your biological parents if that's what you want." She opened her eyes and patted her daughter's back. When Ellen looked across the room where her brother sat in another chair, he smiled and gave her a thumbs-up.

Berlin

"How come you're in Mommy's closet?"

Trent whirled around at the sound of his son's voice. "I'm

looking for some of my clothes."

"Why?"

"Because I'm locked out of my apartment and need a place to spend the night."

"Are you gonna stay here?" Debbie questioned, giving Trent's shirttail a tug.

"Yes. I'll be sleeping on the couch downstairs."

Jumping onto the foot of the bed, Kevin frowned. "But you used to sleep in here with Mommy."

"You're right, but we don't live together anymore, remember?" Trent ruffled his son's hair.

"If you and Mommy don't fight this time, maybe you can spend another night at our house." Kevin's expression brightened.

"I rather doubt it," Trent mumbled under his breath.

"Try to get along better with her, Daddy." Debbie stepped closer to him and took hold of his hand. "I wish we all lived together like we did before you and Mommy started fighting so much."

"Yeah, me too," Kevin added.

Trent swallowed hard. He remembered those days well and knew how hard it had been on the kids when Miranda had asked him to move out. He wished he could erase the past and start over again, but he'd done many things that had gotten him in trouble with his wife— one in particular. Trent needed to work on this matter—not just for the kids, but also for him. "I can be nicer to your mom, but I'm not sure she'll want me back." He squeezed his daughter's fingers. "Let's take it one step at a time and see how it goes."

◦⌒◦

When Miranda awoke the next morning, she was greeted with the aroma of coffee. It took a few moments to remember that Trent had spent the night on the living-room sofa. But the smell of coffee was the reminder she needed.

She rose from the bed and stretched both arms over her head. Miranda would never admit it to Trent, but it was kind of nice having him in the house again. She felt protected and knew the kids were happy to have their daddy there, too. It was evident last evening, after he got settled in and they ate popcorn together while watching TV. If only things could be different. If she and Trent could have learned to get along and settle their differences peacefully instead of hollering at each other all the time, maybe he wouldn't have gotten interested in another woman. She still found it hard to believe Trent's protests that his relationship with that person had never developed into an affair. Miranda's heart held no trust where her husband was concerned, and she was still contemplating if divorce was the best option.

I can't think about all this right now. I need to get downstairs and start breakfast. After slipping on her robe, she opened the bedroom door. Miranda heard some contagious laughter rising from the room below. When she entered the kitchen a short time later, she found Debbie and Kevin, all smiles, sitting at the table, each with a glass of milk in front of them. Trent stood at the stove with his back to her.

"What's going on?" she asked.

When Trent turned around, she couldn't believe he was wearing her springtime floral apron. "Our children were laughing at their father's choice of cooking attire," he announced, before turning back to the stove.

Miranda stifled a chuckle. "I can see why there was so much giggling going on."

Kevin grinned and pointed to the bottle of maple syrup sitting in the center of the table. "Daddy's making us pancakes."

"Is that so?" She pressed her lips together to keep from asking Trent why he never fixed breakfast for the kids when he was living here. Was he trying to butter her up via the kids, in the hope of worming his way back in?

Miranda grabbed a mug and poured herself some coffee. *Well, it won't work. Trent hasn't changed. If he had, he'd start by going to church and setting a Christian example for his family. He'd also prove he was responsible and be true to his word.*

Trent looked over his shoulder and smiled at Miranda. "After breakfast, would it be okay if I borrow your car so I can meet up with the locksmith whom I called first thing this morning? I need to get into my apartment again."

"I guess that'll be okay. Today's my day off, so I won't need the car unless I decide to run to the store for something later on."

He flipped one of the pancakes and gave her a wide grin. "Thanks, hon. I appreciate that."

Miranda looked away. *There he goes, calling me "hon" again.* She'd have called him on it, but not here in front of the kids. Miranda would save her accusations for another time when she could speak to Trent alone.

Walnut Creek

After breakfast, Lyle hitched the horse and buggy and set off to Eli's place. He wanted to make arrangements to have a coop built before they purchased some chickens. "I sure hope Eli has time to build one for us." Lyle said to himself, and Bobbins nickered in return. Last evening, after their picnic when things had settled down a bit, Randy talked excitedly about the chickens they would soon be getting. This morning at the kitchen table, even Marsha seemed excited. Brother and sister talked about who would feed the chickens and who would collect the eggs.

Lyle had been relieved that the children recovered so quickly after Steve and Allie stopped by and knew Heidi was happy about it, too.

"Those poor kids." Lyle shook his head, letting Bobbins take the lead. It was hard enough to lose one parent, let alone both at the same time. Lyle felt blessed that his and Heidi's parents were still around. If Lyle could do anything to ease the children's grief and help them understand about losses, he would do it, whatever it took.

It hadn't been that long ago when Lyle thought it was God's will for him and Heidi not to have any children. In fact, he had convinced himself that if it was to be that way, he would be content. But since he and Heidi had become foster parents, he couldn't imagine even a day without Marsha and Randy. Heidi had told him several times that she felt the same way about the children. Last night, before going to bed, they'd even discussed the possibility of adopting Marsha and Randy. Of course that would depend on several things, including how well the kids adjusted to living with them.

Nearing Eli's farm, Lyle breathed in the fresh air as the *clip-clop* of Bobbin's hooves put him in a mellow mood. So clear was the sky, uninterrupted by any clouds for as far as the eye could see.

Pulling into the Millers' lane, Lyle noticed Loretta waving from the yard where she was hanging up clothes.

"*Guder mariye.*" Lyle tipped his hat after he secured the horse to the hitching rail.

"Good morning to you, too." Loretta smiled as she walked to the edge of the yard. "What brings you here on this beautiful morning?"

"I have a project to ask Eli about. Is he around?"

"Jah, he's there in the shop." Loretta pointed. "I'm sure he'll be glad to see you."

"Okay, danki. Have a *gut* day." Lyle turned and walked toward the woodshop. When he entered, he found Eli staining a porch chair.

"Hello, my friend."

"Oh, you startled me." Eli bent to pick up the paint brush he'd dropped.

"Sorry, I thought you may have heard me out there talking to Loretta."

"Nope. I've been concentrating on my work in here." Eli grinned, picking a piece of straw off the brush. "It's good to see you and a fine morning it is, jah?"

"Sure is." Lyle stepped closer to his friend. "Don't want to keep you from your work, but I came to see if you might have time to do a project for me soon."

"Sure thing. I have one other chair to finish for a customer, but no coffins to make right now. So, what did you have in mind?"

Lyle explained about the need for a chicken coop, and was pleased when Eli said he'd be happy to build it. In fact, Eli said he would be able to start by Friday or Saturday of the coming week. Lyle also agreed when Eli suggested the structure be built right there at Lyle and Heidi's place. That way they wouldn't have to worry about transporting the completed coop once it was finished. And Randy and Marsha could watch the progress.

On the way home, feeling like a kid himself, Lyle whistled. He was anxious to tell the children and couldn't get Bobbins to go fast enough.

⸻ ❧❦ ⸻

"You did what?" Velma's husband's face contorted.

"You heard me, Hank. I ran a stoplight and hit another vehicle." Velma stared at her lukewarm coffee sitting on the kitchen table. Ten minutes ago, Hank had returned home with his truck, after being gone three days, and she'd just given him the news that their car was totaled. *Why couldn't that man of mine be a little more sympathetic? Sometimes I feel like I'm married to a grumpy ole grizzly bear.*

Hank pounded his fist, vibrating the table. "What in tarnation were ya thinkin'? You shoulda been payin' attention to your driving."

"I don't know. Guess I was thinking about Bobbie Sue and how she lost her job yesterday afternoon."

He hit the table a second time. "Now isn't that just great?"

Velma drew a sharp breath. "Aren't ya even gonna ask if anyone was hurt? Or do you care more about your precious vehicle than your wife and kids?"

He scrutinized her. "I can see by lookin' at ya that you ain't hurt. I saw Bobbie Sue outside when I pulled my rig into the yard. She looked fine to me."

Velma pulled in a few more breaths, hoping to calm her nerves. Hank had a temper, and while he'd never hit Velma, she often wondered if he might someday. She figured her one saving grace was him being on the road so much. If he wasn't home when something unpleasant occurred, she wouldn't have to hear him blow his stack.

Velma handled most situations with the kids on her own, without him ever knowing about it. However, hitting another vehicle was something she couldn't very well hide, especially since their one and only car had been totaled.

"Eddie and Peggy Ann were in the car also, and luckily, none of us was seriously hurt." She paused for another breath. "But the driver of the other vehicle was taken to the hospital by ambulance. I heard later that he wasn't in serious condition, so that's something to be thankful for."

His eyes glazed over. "That's good news about the other driver, but you're lucky the cops didn't haul you off to jail for runnin' a stoplight."

Oh boy, here we go. . . Mount St. Helens is erupting again. Velma sniffed, struggling to hold back tears. "I did receive a citation—a pretty hefty one at that."

"Great! So now we have that to pay for, too." Hank's face reddened further, and a vein on his neck protruded. "You do realize that we only have liability insurance, so even though our insurance company will pay for the other guy's vehicle and injuries, our car won't be covered. Not to mention our insurance will go up with surcharge points, all because of this accident."

Gulping, she nodded. *Doesn't he know he's making me feel even worse by his continued ranting?*

"So now, on top of daughter number one bein' out of a job and unable to contribute to our finances, I'll have to work twice as hard hauling with my semitruck in order to earn enough money to replace the car."

"I can look for a job."

Hank shook his head vigorously. "Your job is here, takin' care of the kids while I'm on the road." He glanced around. "Where are they, anyhow?"

"Eddie and Peggy Ann are still in bed, and as you already know, Bobbie Sue's outside, hanging up the laundry because we can't afford to buy a dryer."

He raked his fingers through the ends of his thinning brown hair. "That's right, and now, because of your careless driving, a new dryer goes to the bottom of our list."

Velma rested her head on both hands. "I don't know how, but we'll get through this, Hank. We always have."

Chapter 13

New Philadelphia, Ohio

Trent sat at the kitchen table, staring into his empty mug. Thanks to the locksmith he'd called a few days ago, he was back in his dinky apartment. But after spending a night and part of a day with Miranda and the kids in a home he was still paying the mortgage on, he felt depressed. Here in his humble abode, these rooms were too quiet for him.

"Shouldn't be living here alone," he mumbled. "I miss my wife and kids and want to go home."

Trent's apartment was big enough for one person, but it had few furnishings and absolutely no personality. It was drab and dull, and he missed seeing the little touches Miranda had placed around their house. A vase of flowers, little knickknacks, framed photos of the kids—those were the kind of things missing in this dreary place.

"Even my walls are bare." Trent lifted his hands in despair. "But why bother with all that stuff when I'm here all alone?" He first believed his stay here would be only temporary. Now he had serious doubts. "I wonder if Miranda will make good on her threat and file for divorce."

Trent glanced at his cell phone. He had just enough time for another cup of coffee before heading out to pick up the kids for their cooking class in Walnut Creek. It would be good to see them again. *Maybe I can get Kevin and Debbie to work on their mother. If they tell her how much they miss me, maybe Miranda will say I can move back to the house. Sure wish I could do something to prove I wasn't disloyal to her.* He tugged his ear. *Well, maybe I was, but I didn't have an affair. I broke things off with Isabelle before it got that far.*

Trent was about to reach for the coffeepot, when his cell phone rang. The sound made him jump up. Seeing it was his buddy Rod Eckers, he answered.

"Hey, Rod, what's up?"

"I heard you had the day off and wondered if you'd like to meet me for a game of racquetball this morning."

Frowning, Trent tilted his chin down. *Sure wish I could.*

"Trent, are you there?"

"Yeah." He moaned. "But I'm not free this morning."

"How come?"

Resting his elbows on the table, while holding his head in his hand, Trent made it short and sweet. "Gotta take my kids to some cooking class. Miranda has to work today, and she pretty much insisted it was my turn to take them."

"Aw, that's too bad. Let me know when you have your next day off. Hopefully, we can work something out."

"Okay, I'll give you a call. Talk to you later, Rod."

Trent hung up and groaned. When he and Miranda first separated, he'd thought he would have more time to do the things he liked. But moving out of the house didn't make his responsibility to the children disappear. So he would take the kids to Walnut Creek, but he wasn't going to stick around. He planned to drop them off and pick them up when the class was over. Truthfully, Trent had no interest in watching some Amish woman teach a bunch of rowdy kids how to cook or bake something.

He stood up and straightened his button-down shirt. *I need to get going.* Trent poured himself a cup of coffee and took a couple of sips. "I wish a game of racquetball could fit into the time frame of the kids' cooking class." He shut off the coffee maker and carried the mug to his bedroom. Setting his cup on the windowsill, Trent thumbed through the closet, sorting through his insufficient supply of shirts. He really should bring the rest of them over from the house.

"There's my favorite racquetball shirt. Too bad I can't put it to good use today." Trent picked up his cup again and took a drink as he deliberated. *It can't hurt if I sneak away and have some "me" time would it? I deserve a break today from my expected duties.*

Walnut Creek

Lyle stepped outside onto the porch and noticed Eli's horse and buggy at the hitching rail. "I wonder when he showed up." Lyle figured his friend wanted to get an early start.

Lyle had an auction yesterday, but he was free today. It worked out well, since the building where some of his auctions were held was closed today, due to repairs. Since Heidi had a cooking class, Lyle planned to give Eli a hand with the chicken coop.

Lyle unleashed Eli's horse and walked it to the barn. He was surprised Eli hadn't taken care of it himself. After giving Blossom a few scratches behind her ears, Lyle put the horse in an empty stall and headed out to the yard where Eli was working. "Guder mariye, Eli." Lyle approached him. "I didn't hear you arrive."

"Guess I shoulda let you know I was here, but I wanted to get right to work. And if my calculations are correct, the chicken coop should be finished soon."

"You got a lot done on it yesterday." Lyle reached out to hold the board Eli was preparing to hammer to the frame.

"I had a good little helper." Eli chuckled. "That Randy was sure eager to be a part of this project, and I couldn't let him down. So I asked him to hand me nails when I needed them, as well as some other little things he could handle."

Lyle chuckled. "It's all he's been talking about since we told him and Marsha about getting some chickens."

Eli grinned and shook his head. "It'll be good for the kinner to have a part in this. Randy told me yesterday all about the responsibility he and his sister will have: feeding the chickens and collecting eggs."

"Jah. You know how it is when you're young." Lyle reached for another board and handed it to Eli. "Heidi and I hope this will be good for the children and give them an even better sense of belonging. They sure seem eager to help."

"Believe me, I know." Eli finished putting the nails in the board. "Loretta's two are the same way. Whenever there's a project to do at our place, one or both of 'em are eager to help."

"How are Conner and Abby doing these days?"

"Doin' well. They're both like two wound-up pups. Don't know where they get their energy. They'll be at their grandparents visiting soon. And Loretta. . . Well, she's been scurrying around like a busy bee painting each of their bedrooms. She wants it to be a surprise when they get home and see their favorite color on the walls of their rooms."

Lyle pondered things as Eli sawed a few more boards to length. *Maybe it would be a good idea to paint Marsha and Randy's bedroom walls and let them choose the color. That way each of their rooms will feel as though it's really theirs. I'll take care of that soon.*

As Velma walked along the shoulder of the road with Peggy Ann and their dog, Abner, she found herself beginning to relax. The scent of blossoms from a gorgeous rose garden in a nearby yard filled her senses with sweetness. It was nice walking with her daughter, too, and doing some deep thinking. *Boy, I really needed to get away from the house for a while.*

The last few days had been stressful, and the fresh air and sunshine felt good. Walking the dog was a good excuse to be outside on a day such as this.

Facing the sun, she closed her eyes for a second and let the sun's warmth penetrate her skin. The only sounds for the moment were the birds singing and the jingle of Abner's dog tags as he pranced along in front of Velma's daughter.

Peggy Ann insisted on holding Abner's leash, and Velma didn't object, because the black Lab was behaving himself.

"How come you're so quiet, Mama?" Peggy Ann asked, skipping to keep up with the dog.

"Oh, just enjoying the surroundings and thinkin' is all."

"What about?"

Velma shrugged. "Nothing much."

"Wanna know what I'm thinkin' about?"

"What's that, honey child?"

"Papa." Peggy Ann stopped walking so the dog could sniff

something on the ground. "I wish he didn't have to be gone all the time. Bet you miss him, too, huh, Mama?"

Velma slowly nodded. She wouldn't admit it to any of her children, but it was a relief when Hank left early this morning to pick up a load with his semitruck. He'd be gone several days, so she wouldn't have to listen to him harp on the issue of the accident she'd caused and them having no car. Velma was the person inconvenienced. Having to walk or ride one of the kid's bikes was certainly no fun for her. Neither was living with disharmony in their home. Velma wanted a good solid marriage. She needed some answers to fix her dilemma, because right now, nothing seemed right. *Maybe it would help if I had a friend—someone to bounce things off of.*

Velma glanced at a well-kept farm across the road. *Too bad we don't have a horse and buggy like those Amish people do. At least it would get us where we wanna go without worrying about having money to fill the gas tank.* She wrinkled her nose. *Guess keeping a horse wouldn't be cheap, though. It would cost money to feed it.*

As they came parallel to the driveway leading to the Amish house, a Brittany spaniel started barking from the yard. Abner responded with a few *Arf! Arfs!* Then, jerking the leash out of Peggy Ann's hand, the dog broke free and darted across the street.

"Come back here, Abner!" Velma and Peggy Ann shouted at the same time.

Both dogs were now chasing each other around the yard, yipping and yapping so loud Velma felt like covering her ears.

"What should we do, Mama?" Peggy Ann began jumping up and down.

Only one thing to do. Go into the yard after her dog.

———————⚬⚬⚬———————

"I don't wanna learn cookin' today." Randy's lower lip protruded. "Wanna be outside watchin' Eli work on the chicken coop."

"You got to watch and help him yesterday when he started the project," Heidi reminded the boy. "And remember, as soon as Eli finishes building the coop, we'll get some chicks." She pointed to the recipe cards lying on the table. "This morning you'll enjoy making mini corn dogs with the other children, and we'll get to eat them afterward."

"But I was helpin' Eli, and what if he needs me again today?"

"I'm sure Eli will understand. Lyle will be helping him today. Now that he has your rooms painted, he has some free time."

Out of the blue, Marsha spoke up. "I like corn dogs."

Heidi smiled. "I think most kids do—and even some adults like me and Lyle."

The little girl looked up at Heidi with such a sweet smile. "Lyle's my *daadi*, and you're my *mammi*."

"No, they're not." Randy shook his head. "Our mommy and daddy are in heaven."

Marsha squinted, while tipping her head, as if trying to process what her brother said. They'd talked about this before, but apparently Marsha had forgotten.

Before Heidi could offer an explanation, a ruckus coming from outside drew her attention to the window. She was surprised to see Rusty being chased by a black Lab she didn't know. A leash clipped to the Lab's collar trailed behind.

"Oh, dear." Heidi opened the back door and stepped outside. Clapping her hands, she called for her dog, but Rusty kept running and barking, oblivious to her command. This was unusual for her normally obedient dog.

Then a woman with scraggly blond hair dashed into the yard, hollering, "Stop, Abner! Come here right now!" When she picked up a stick and shook it, the Lab quit running and crawled to her on his belly.

"Don't hit him, Mama. Please don't hit Abner." A young girl with reddish-blond hair worn in pigtails ran up to the woman and clutched her hand.

"I ain't gonna hit the mutt. Just wanted to scare him so he'd quit running." The woman picked up the dog's leash, holding it firmly. Then she turned to face Heidi. "Sorry for the intrusion. My daughter and I were takin' Abner for a walk, and when he saw your dog and heard it barking in your yard, he took off like a flash. Peggy Ann couldn't hold him, and the leash slipped out of her hand."

By this time, Rusty had also quit running and was lying on the porch by Heidi's feet, panting. Lyle came out of the barn. "Everything okay up there?"

Heidi waved. "Jah, we're good." She smiled when he nodded, and he went back into the barn.

Heidi came down the porch steps. "It's all right. I understand how dogs can be sometimes." She smiled. "I'm Heidi Troyer. Are you new to the area? I don't recall seeing you or your daughter before."

"Yeah, we moved here from Kentucky about a month ago. My name's Velma Kimball, and this is Peggy Ann. I have two more kids at home: Bobbie Sue—she's seventeen—and Eddie, who's ten. We live down the road apiece in a double-wide."

Heidi wasn't sure she could get a word in, with the woman talking so fast, but she was finally able to say, "It's nice meeting you." Now that she thought about it, she had seen the mobile home set back off the road. It had been for sale a while ago, but she hadn't realized it had sold or that anyone was living there now.

Still holding her dog's leash, Velma reached out her other hand to shake Heidi's. "Nice to meet you, too. Have ya got any kids?"

"None of my own, but my husband and I have two foster children."

"I see. Well, maybe my kids will get to meet them sometime." Velma glanced at her daughter, then looked back at Heidi. "Peggy Ann's kinda shy, and she hasn't fully adjusted to our move. I think it'd be good if she makes some new friends."

Heidi noticed how their dog had begun to pant. The animal's pink tongue hung out the side of its mouth. "Peggy Ann, there is a bucket over by the porch. Why don't you get the hose and fill it with water for your dog? He looks thirsty."

After Peggy Ann filled the bucket, she carried it over and set it down by the Lab. As if the dogs were best friends, Rusty and Abner, heads together, lapped the water at the same time.

"Now would you look at that?" Velma grinned when both dogs laid down in the cool grass together. "Abner's never taken to any dog like that. Seems he's already made a new friend."

Heidi was about to respond, when a car she hadn't seen before pulled in. A few seconds later, Kevin and Debbie got out of the vehicle. Heidi saw a man in the driver's seat, but she'd never met him before.

"I'm sorry to cut our conversation short," she said, looking at Velma, "but I teach a cooking class every other Saturday, and some of my students have arrived."

Velma pursed her lips. "Those kids are your students?"

"Yes, that's Kevin and Debbie. The others aren't here yet but should arrive soon, I expect." Heidi nodded. "It's a cooking class for children, and today will be their second lesson."

Velma rubbed her chin with a thoughtful expression. "Hmm. . . Are the classes expensive?"

Heidi quoted the price and Velma grimaced. "Unfortunately, I don't have any extra money right now. It's a shame, too, 'cause I think learnin' to cook with a bunch of other kids would be real good for my Peggy Ann."

"I may teach more classes for children in the future," Heidi said. "If I do, I'll let you know."

Velma snapped her fingers. "Say, ya know what? I have an idea."

Heidi glanced at Kevin and Debbie. They stood next to the car, talking through the open window to the man who'd brought them. *I need to go introduce myself to him, but I don't want to be rude to our new neighbor.*

"Would ya like to hear my idea?" Velma seemed eager to share her plan.

"Umm. . .certainly."

"I was thinkin', since I can't afford to pay for Peggy Ann to take your classes, I could do some work for you in exchange for you teaching my daughter."

"Well, uh. . ." Heidi moistened her lips with the tip of her tongue. "I'm not sure. . ."

"I'll do any kind of chore you need to have done. I can clean your house, do yard work, and even chop wood. I'm very handy, believe you me, and strong, too." Velma's voice trembled a bit. "Oh, please don't say no. Peggy Ann would surely benefit from takin' your class."

"Well, I suppose it would be all right. Peggy Ann can join the class today, and afterward I'll make a list of some things I need to have done. Then you can choose."

Velma's face broke into a wide smile. "Thanks, Heidi. Thanks so much."

Heidi wasn't sure if agreeing to let Velma work for her in exchange for Peggy Ann joining the classes was a good idea, but she didn't have the heart to say no. Velma seemed almost desperate, and her daughter looked so forlorn. Perhaps she would have the opportunity to minister to them in some way, as she had in the past with many of her previous students.

Heidi looked over at the Cooper children again and was disappointed because it appeared that the man in the car was getting ready to leave.

Excusing herself from Velma, Heidi hurried across the yard.

Chapter 14

When Heidi approached the car, the man sitting in the driver's seat offered her a friendly smile. "Hi there, I'm Trent Cooper—Debbie and Kevin's dad. And you must be their cooking teacher."

She nodded. "I'm Heidi Troyer."

"Daddy brought us today 'cause our mom has to work," Kevin spoke up. "I asked him to come inside and watch us cook, but he said he has to go somewhere."

"That's right," Trent agreed, "but I'll be back around noon to get the kids. That's what time the class ends, right?"

"Yes, but—"

"Good. See you later then."

Debbie and Kevin jumped back from the car as their father hastily pulled out of the yard, giving Heidi no chance to say anything more. Walking beside the Cooper children, she headed for the house, where Velma and her daughter remained by the porch.

Barely giving Velma and her daughter a glance, Kevin poked his sister.

"Hey, stop it!" Debbie moved to his other side.

Velma's dog tried to jump up on Kevin, but Velma yanked Abner's leash. "I'd better take this mutt home now." She looked at Peggy Ann. "You go on in the house with Heidi and get acquainted with the other kids. I'll be back to get you when the class is over."

"Except for Debbie and Kevin, none of the other children are here yet," Heidi explained again.

Velma waved her hand. "Well, never mind about that. Peggy Ann can sit with these two and wait till the others show up."

Peggy Ann gripped her mother's hand. "I thought you was gonna stay with me, Mama."

Velma shook her head. "Not this time. I have some things I need to do at home, but you'll be fine. I want to get Abner home, too." Holding the dog's leash, Velma turned and headed toward the road.

Heidi's jaw clenched. That made two parents who wouldn't be with their children today. She wasn't sure how she felt about the parents participating or not. With the addition of another child to teach, she might need a helping hand. Although with the exception of Ellen, none of the other parents had been very helpful during the first class. Looking back on it, Ellen had actually done too much for her daughter. Becky needed the chance to learn things on her own without her mother taking over. So maybe it was best if the parents didn't stay. That's what Heidi had expected in the first place.

She opened the front door. "You three can go on into the living room. Randy and Marsha are inside. I want to put Rusty in his pen, and then I'll be right in." Heidi waited until the children stepped inside and shut the door behind them.

"Come on, Rusty, let's go to the pen." Heidi clapped her hands.

The dog lifted his head, then flopped back down with a sleepy grunt.

"Sorry, mister, you're going in the pen. My other students will be here soon, and I don't want you creating anymore ruckus."

Rusty got up and ambled down the steps behind Heidi. They were halfway across the yard when he darted to the left and made a beeline for a mud puddle in the driveway. It had rained during the night, leaving several puddles of water in various places throughout their yard.

Heidi cupped her hands around her mouth and whistled, but Rusty ignored her. Now he was chasing a butterfly he'd spooked near the puddle. Jumping up as he gave chase through the damp grass, Rusty's attempts to catch the colorful insect failed. She didn't understand what had come over him today. He was normally so well-behaved.

Well, she couldn't spend any more time watching Rusty's shenanigans. He'd gotten himself into too much mischief already. Heidi didn't want to leave him free to roam in the yard. Plus, she had to get back inside to make sure Randy and Marsha were getting along with the other children.

Heidi clapped her hands and said firmly, "Rusty, come here, boy."

The dog turned in her direction, but when a car pulled into the yard, he plodded down the driveway to greet them.

"Watch out, Mom. There's that stupid mutt coming toward our car." Kassidy tapped Denise on the shoulder from the back seat.

Denise turned to look at her and frowned. "I hope he gets out of the way. Sure wouldn't want to hit Heidi's dog." She slowed the car and crept forward just a bit, waiting to see what the Brittany spaniel would do. It was a pretty dog but not very bright. She was surprised the Troyers hadn't trained it to stay away from cars. *Of course*, she reasoned, *the dog's probably not used to many cars coming onto their property, since their main mode of transportation is by horse and buggy.*

Denise couldn't imagine having to hitch a horse to a buggy, not to mention traveling so slow compared to riding in a car. Whenever she went anywhere, she wanted to get there as quickly as possible.

"What's wrong with that dog, anyways?" Kassidy complained. "Why won't it get out of our way?"

"Just be patient. The dog will eventually move."

"Look, Mom. Heidi's coming now to get the dog." Kassidy pointed again.

Denise stopped the car, waiting for Heidi to approach. Once Heidi had a hold of the dog's collar and had guided him off the driveway, Denise moved her vehicle forward and parked it near the barn. She and Kassidy opened their doors and got out at the same time. But just as Kassidy started walking toward the house, Heidi's dog got away from her. The animal raced across the yard and jumped up, putting his dirty feet on Kassidy's chest. Kassidy screamed so loud, it must have frightened the dog, for it raced off and darted into the barn.

A few minutes later, Heidi's husband came out, carrying the spaniel. He said a few words to Heidi, then put the dog in its pen. In the meantime, Kassidy sat on the front porch steps, crying hysterically. Denise went immediately to her side.

"Calm down, Kassidy. The dog didn't bite you, did he?"

"No, but he did this!" She motioned to the muddy paw prints and wet grass stains on the front of her cream-colored blouse. "We've gotta go home, Mom. I can't go in there looking like this."

Heidi joined them on the porch with a pained expression. "I am so sorry, Kassidy. I tried to hold Rusty, but he got away. Don't know what's come over him today. He's normally better behaved."

Lowering her gaze, Kassidy folded her arms. "My blouse is ruined, and I'm not in the mood to learn how to cook anything today. Every time I come here, there are problems with your dog. First, my shoe. Now this." Kassidy pointed to her blouse. "I bet the stains will never come out!"

"Your blouse isn't ruined," Denise spoke up. "I'm sure the mud and green stains will wash out. I'll take care of it as soon as we get home."

Looking up, Kassidy blew out a noisy breath. "What am I supposed to do in the meantime? I look a mess!"

"I'd offer to loan you one of my dresses, but they'd be too big for you." Heidi tucked a stray piece of hair back under her white head covering. "I do have an apron you can wear today. It will cover the front of your blouse."

Kassidy looked at Heidi as if she had two heads. "I wouldn't wear one of your—"

"Thank you, Heidi," Denise interrupted before Kassidy could say more. She gave her daughter a look, daring her to say another word. "We seem to be the only ones here so far, so let's go inside. You can put Heidi's apron on before anyone else arrives. Then you won't have to be embarrassed about anyone seeing the mud on your blouse."

"Actually, a few of the other students are inside," Heidi said.

"Oh, great." Kassidy looked down, mumbling something else under her breath.

"What was that?" Denise nudged her daughter's arm.

"Nothing, Mom."

Denise smiled. For the moment at least, it appeared that she'd won this battle of the wills. She hoped Kassidy would be cooperative during the cooking class today.

"Sure hope we make something good this time." Jeremy leaned over the seat and bumped Darren's arm as they turned up Heidi's driveway.

"I'm sure it will be good. The salad you made during the first class was pretty tasty."

"I guess—if you like a lot of fruit chopped up in one bowl. I'd rather eat a banana or an apple by itself instead of with other fruit."

Darren didn't comment. He was too busy watching Ellen and her daughter get out of their vehicle. Ellen was not only pretty, but from the few times they'd visited, she seemed intelligent and well grounded. He wanted to get to know her better.

"Say, Dad, I've been wondering about something."

"Umm. . .what's that, Son?"

"Do you know why the Amish wear such plain clothes?"

"No, I don't. Why don't you ask Heidi?"

"I don't know. She might think it's a dumb question."

Darren parked next to Ellen's vehicle, turned off the engine, and hopped out. "Hey, it's good to see you again." He offered Ellen what he hoped was a pleasant smile. "How have you been?"

She smiled in return. "We've been fine, and we're looking forward to another cooking lesson." Ellen looked at her daughter. "Isn't that right, Becky?"

The girl shrugged. She wasn't a very talkative child. Not like Jeremy, who had been known to talk nonstop when it came to something he was interested in, such as playing soccer, going fishing, or teaching his dog new tricks.

"How are things going with you?" Ellen asked.

"Good. Jeremy and I are going hiking next week. We're looking forward to that."

Ellen's eyes brightened. "Sounds like fun. I've enjoyed hiking since I was a young girl. Used to go on hikes with my dad, and sometimes we went fishing."

"Now isn't that something? Jeremy and I both like to fish." Darren looked at Becky. "Do you enjoy fishing?"

Without meeting his gaze, she mumbled, "It's okay, I guess."

Darren couldn't help noticing the face Becky made as she turned and looked toward the house. Ignoring Ellen's daughter, he continued. "Maybe the four of us could go fishing sometime. We could make a trip to one of the lakes or ponds in the area and take a picnic lunch along. We'd park the car some distance away, and hike in, of course." He grinned. "It'll make it more fun that way."

Jeremy tapped Darren's arm, and said in a low voice, "Can we go inside for the class now?"

"Just a second, Son." He rested his hand on the boy's shoulder.

Ellen repositioned her purse's shoulder strap and nodded. "That does sound like an enjoyable outing. After we get inside, I'll give you my phone number. When you have a date in mind to go fishing, you can let me know, and then I'll see if Becky and I are free to go."

"Dad, we need to get to the class. I'm sure Heidi's waiting." Jeremy kicked at a pebble.

Darren looked at his watch. "We're fine. We've got a few minutes yet."

Becky looked up at her mother through half-closed eyes but said nothing. Darren had a feeling the girl wasn't thrilled about the idea of going fishing with them. For that matter, based on the frown his son wore right now, he guessed neither one of the children wanted to go. Well, it didn't matter. If he and Ellen could work out a day when they were both free, the kids would have to go along whether they liked it or not. Maybe some time fishing and enjoying the great outdoors would be good for all of them.

Chapter 15

Once everyone gathered around the kitchen table, Heidi introduced her newest student. "I'd like you all to meet Peggy Ann. She and her family live down the road a ways, and Peggy Ann will be joining us today, as well as the next four classes we have." She placed her hands on the young girl's slender shoulders. "Please make her feel welcome by introducing yourselves."

Denise, Ellen, and Darren went first, then their children.

"You met Kevin and Debbie when they first arrived," Heidi said.

After the introductions were made, Heidi explained that they would be making mini corn dogs. She was about to hand out the recipe cards, when Randy leaped off his chair and raced to the back door. "I hear Eli pounding with his hammer!"

"Eli's been out there a good while, and I'm sure Lyle is helping him. You can check on their progress after class is over." Heidi gestured to the table. "Please come back, Randy, and take your seat."

With slumped shoulders, the boy shuffled across the room and flopped into his chair with a grunt. "Eli's gonna wonder why I'm not helpin' like I did yesterday."

Heidi shook her head. "He knows we're having a cooking class today."

"Who's Eli?" Kevin asked, leaning closer to Randy.

"He's a nice Amish man, and he's buildin' a coop so me and Marsha can have some chickens."

Kevin grinned. "Oh, boy, that sounds like fun. Can I see your chickens when you get them?"

Randy bobbed his head. "Course ya can. I'll show 'em to everyone here if they want."

"I'd like to see them," Debbie put in.

"Me too." Peggy Ann nodded affirmatively.

"How 'bout you?" Randy asked, looking at Darren's son.

Jeremy shrugged. "Maybe."

Randy looked at Becky next. "Would you like to see the chickens?"

"I guess so," she said quietly.

"I don't want to see any stupid old chickens." Kassidy wrinkled her nose. "And I don't see what the big deal is either."

"Bet you don't have any chickens." Randy looked Kassidy square in the eyes. "Me and my sister will get to gather eggs and feed the chickens."

"Oh, that sounds like so much fun." Kassidy rolled her eyes. "Chickens are smelly, and even if you paid me, I'd never want any."

"Well, ours won't be smelly." Randy crossed his arms. "I'll keep their coop nice and clean."

Kassidy answered by holding her nose, and her mother looked fit to be tied.

Heidi figured it was time to get back to the topic of making the corn dogs, before an argument started. "As you can see on your recipe cards, in addition to a package of hot dogs, we'll be using white flour, cornmeal, baking powder, salt, shortening, butter, and milk."

"How come so many things just to make hot dogs?" Peggy Ann blinked rapidly, and when she tipped her head, one of her braids fell across her face.

Marsha giggled and pointed at her. "You look funny."

Heidi shook her head. "Marsha, it's not nice to make fun of others."

"But she's right." Kevin snickered. "Peggy Ann looks like she's wearin' a giant mustache."

All the kids laughed—even Becky, who up until this time had seemed quite sullen. Peggy Ann, on the other hand, pressed a fist to her lips, as though holding back tears. Or maybe she was trying to refrain from saying something mean back to Kevin.

Heidi was certain if the boy's mother had been here, she would have scolded him for teasing. Perhaps his father would have as well. But neither parent was here today, so Heidi felt it was her place to say something.

"Now, Kevin, I'm sure you wouldn't want someone to poke fun of you, so you shouldn't do it to anyone else. Don't you think you should tell Peggy Ann you're sorry?"

He leaned his elbows on the table. "Don't see what for. I didn't say anything bad. Just told the truth."

Debbie poked her brother's arm. "Quit arguing and just say you're sorry. If you don't, I'm gonna tell Daddy when he picks us up."

Frowning, Kevin glanced at Peggy Ann, then looked away. "Sorry," he mumbled.

It wasn't much of an apology, but it was better than nothing.

"So now," Heidi said, after clearing her throat, "Let's begin our lesson."

Berlin

As Trent wandered around Heini's Cheese Chalet, tasting samples of various cheeses, he thought about the kids and wondered how they were doing. If he'd had more time, he would have driven to New Philly and joined his buddy for a game of racquetball. But if he went there, he'd be late picking up the kids and felt sure one or both of them would tell their mother about it.

Trent checked his watch, wondering if there would be time to go anywhere else, but he thought better of it. Two hours could go by quickly, especially if a person wasn't paying attention, so he would just browse around here a little more.

Trent grabbed a clean toothpick, and took another sample of cheese. *This stuff's good. Maybe I'll buy a few packages and give one to Miranda. I've got to do something to get back in her good graces again.*

He put two packages of baby Swiss in his shopping basket, along with some mild cheddar and a package of Gouda. As he neared the cash register, he spotted some milk-chocolate bars and put those in the basket for the kids. *If I give 'em candy to eat on the way home, they might be less apt to tell their mother I bailed on them this morning.*

While the clerk rang up the customer ahead of him, Trent thought he might make another stop. *Maybe I'll go to a store nearby for a homemade pretzel. That'd be good, because I'm still hungry. All those cheese samples did was whet my appetite. I may even indulge in a double scoop of ice cream.* That was one thing nice about living where the tourism was hot—plenty of businesses selling his favorite treats.

⸺⸺◦~◦⸺⸺

Walnut Creek

Ellen stood quietly, watching as Becky mixed the butter, shortening, and milk in with the dry ingredients Heidi had given each of the children. *I wouldn't mind taking a cooking class myself. It's fun to watch the children, although it is hard to resist doing my daughter's work.* Ellen was making an effort not to take over for Becky as she'd done during the first cooking class. With Becky being her only child, sometimes it was difficult not to smother her.

Even though Becky had said she loved Ellen and forgave her for keeping the adoption a secret, things weren't quite the same between them as they had been before the visit to Patrick's. Becky seemed withdrawn and disinterested in most things. *I know I've betrayed my sweet daughter's trust, but I must believe that in time the Lord will help me with this.*

Ellen bit down gently on her bottom lip as she stole a quick glance at Darren. *Hiking and fishing with him and Jeremy would be something fun for us to do. I hope we can work things out with our schedules so we can make it happen. I, for one, am looking forward to it—not only for the fresh air and exercise, but I'd like the chance to get to know Darren better.*

Ellen noticed a bee come into the room and fly to the kitchen window. "Um, Heidi, do you have a fly swatter around?"

"Yes, I do. I'll get it." Heidi retrieved the swatter hanging in the corner of the kitchen.

"Hey, everybody, look there. Heidi is gonna swat that ole bee." Peggy Ann piped up.

"Wish I could kill it." Kevin hopped down from his seat.

Heidi took a swing and missed the insect the first time. The bee flew around the room and came back to the window. All eyes seemed to be on the fly swatter, as well as its target. Heidi's arm drew back like a loaded spring, then she released it with a *smack!* The bee hit the sink and didn't budge. Kevin cheered and everyone else clapped. Heidi scooped the insect onto the weapon of its undoing and carried it outside. When she returned, she washed her hands and came back to the table.

"Now that everyone has their ingredients mixed well, it's time to roll out the dough." Heidi owned three rolling pins, which she'd previously placed on the table. "We'll take turns rolling the dough before we cut it in rounds. She handed one rolling pin to Debbie and one to Kassidy. The other one she used to demonstrate the correct way to flatten and roll out the dough.

"Can I go check on Eli while I'm waitin' my turn?" Randy asked.

She shook her head. "It won't take long to get your dough ready for the hot dog, so I want you to remain at the table and watch the others."

Randy bent his head forward, sitting in a hunched position, but at least he stayed seated.

After Heidi demonstrated with the rolling pin, she watched as Kassidy and Debbie rolled theirs. They both did it easily, and then it was Randy and Kevin's turn. The boys, being younger, needed a bit of assistance, but once their dough was rolled out adequately, the rolling pins were given to Becky and Jeremy.

"This looks easy." Jeremy glanced at Becky, through half-closed lids. "Bet I can get mine rolled out before you do."

With a determined expression, Becky began rolling hard and fast.

"Slow down, sweetie. There's no need to hurry." Ellen touched her daughter's shoulder.

Becky shrugged and kept rolling.

Lips pressed tightly together, Jeremy rolled his dough so hard that it split down the middle.

"Now look what happened." Darren shook his head slowly. "You're too competitive, Son."

Heidi was at a loss for words. She couldn't understand what the problem was between the two children or why there would be competition. But then Heidi didn't understand a lot of things these days—such as why, whenever Marsha called her mammi, or Lyle, daadi, Randy seemed upset. She doubted that he would ever call them anything except their first names. But it was okay. At least his overall attitude had changed for the better, and as with the chicken coop, he'd taken an interest in more things.

Heidi smiled when she saw Marsha, kneeling on a chair, while reaching over to touch the dough Debbie had rolled.

"Are we makin' a pie?" the little girl asked.

"No, dear one," Heidi explained. "The dough we mixed up is sort of like what we'd make for a pie, but it'll be wrapped around our mini corn dogs."

Eyes wide, Peggy Ann spoke up. "Ain't the dough too big for a little bitty frankfurter?"

Heidi smiled, biting back a chuckle. "Our next step, Peggy Ann, is to cut out the dough in a circle, and then we'll place the small frankfurter in the center of it."

"How we gonna cut it—with a pair of scissors?"

"No. We'll use the lid from a canning jar," Heidi responded. "It's simple enough, and everyone, even Marsha, should be able to do it."

Heidi moved across the room to get a few of her wide-mouth canning lids, but was interrupted by pounding on the back door. She went to answer it, thinking either Lyle or Eli wanted something. *Of course,* she reasoned, *if it were Lyle, he would not have knocked.*

Heidi opened the door, and Velma, dressed in what looked like a pair of men's overalls, stepped inside. Strands of blond hair stuck out from under the red paisley hankie scarf tied at the back of her neck, and she seemed out of breath. "I know it's not time for the class to be over, but I'm here to do whatever work ya need done. After I got Abner taken care of, I changed and came right back."

"Well, I'm right in the middle of class." Heidi tilted her head. "Didn't you say you had things to get done at your place?"

"Oh, that." Velma waved off Heidi's question. "Those chores can wait. This is more important to me."

Oh, dear. Heidi massaged her forehead. She hadn't expected Velma would want to get started so soon, and truthfully, she hadn't had a chance to even think of what she might want to have done.

With the door still open, Randy must have seen this as his chance to escape, for he leaped off his chair, and raced outside before Heidi could call out to him.

The class was only half over, and already things seemed topsy-turvy. Heidi wasn't quick enough to stop Marsha from taking a chunk of dough from Debbie's rolled-out piece, and popping it in her mouth, like it was candy. Once more, Heidi wondered if teaching a children's cooking class had been a good idea. If she continued teaching classes, she might stick to adults only. At least they weren't so impulsive—although some of her previous students had other problems.

Chapter 16

"Now that's some chicken house you're makin' there."

Heidi turned at the sound of Velma's voice. She hadn't realized the woman had followed her into the yard where Lyle and Eli had moved the structure and were now working on its roof.

Heidi hated to be rude, but she hoped Velma wouldn't take up too much of her time talking. She was halfway through today's class and needed to get back inside.

"Yes, indeed." Velma slapped her knee. "I've built a few chicken coops in my time. We had a really nice one when we lived in Kentucky. Housed enough chickens to give us plenty of eggs for our use, plus enough to sell." She paused long enough to draw a quick breath, then kept talking. "I need to get one built at our place. Just haven't made the time to do it yet. But I'd be glad to help you finish this one if ya like."

When Velma quit talking, Eli jumped in. "I appreciate the offer, miss, but Lyle and I are almost done here, and everything's under control."

Before Velma could comment, Randy stepped forward, giving the leg of Eli's trousers a tug. "You said I could help ya finish up with the coop." He pointed to the house. "But I'm stuck in there makin' some dumb old corn dog."

Eli tapped the boy's shoulder. "As soon as you're done, you can come out and help us put the finishing touches on."

"And don't forget," Lyle added, "you'll get to go with me to pick up the chickens next week."

Randy's face brightened. "Can Marsha go, too?"

"Of course she can." Lyle gestured to Heidi. "I think my *fraa* might want to accompany us as well."

Heidi nodded. "I wouldn't miss it."

"Okay!" Randy grinned.

Heidi felt relief when the boy started back to the house, swinging his arms. She smiled at the men. "There'll be enough corn dogs to eat when they are done, so if you two would like to join us, you're more than welcome."

"Sounds good." Lyle thumped his stomach. "I've been working up an appetite. How about you, Eli?"

Eli grinned. "Same here, but I think I might pass on the offer. I'll be taking Loretta out for an early supper this evening, and I want to save plenty of room for the Farmstead Restaurant's buffet."

"Okay, well, I'd best get back to my class." Heidi looked at Velma. "You're welcome to come watch if you like."

"I would, but I came here to get started on some chores for you, like I promised." Velma shifted from one foot to the other. "What about your garden? Does it need to be weeded?" She looked toward the yard where the garden was planted, then tucked a strand of wayward hair back underneath her scarf.

Heidi glanced toward her garden. "I do appreciate the offer, and I would say yes, but the weeds aren't too bad yet." She could see by the downward curve of Velma's mouth, that she was disappointed.

Since Heidi wasn't sure what she wanted to have done, nor did she want to take the time to show Velma right now, she said, "Why don't you plan on coming over one day next week to do a chore? By then I'll have a better idea what I'd like to have done."

Velma's forehead wrinkled as she hesitantly nodded. "Guess that'd be okay. All right then, I'll go inside with you and watch the proceedings."

"Where's Heidi? When is she coming back?" Kassidy's chin jutted out as she pointed to the clock on the far wall. "It'll be time for us to go pretty soon, and we won't have made a thing."

"Don't be so impatient," Denise reprimanded. "I'm sure Heidi will return soon. Besides, we don't have any plans for the rest of the day, so there's no hurry."

Kassidy frowned. "I don't wanna be here all day, Mom. I might want to get together with one of my friends."

Jeremy glanced her way. "Ya know what, Kassidy? You whine too much."

"Do not."

"Yeah, you do."

"No, I don't, and you should mind your own business."

Before a full-blown argument could brew, Denise quickly changed the subject. "Who likes mustard on their corn dogs?"

"I do." Peggy Ann's hand shot up. Little Marsha followed suit.

"I don't like mustard," Debbie said, "but I do like plenty of relish."

"I like ketchup," Kevin announced.

"Same here." Jeremy nodded.

"How about you, Becky?" Denise asked. "What's your favorite thing to put on a corn dog?"

"Ketchup, I guess." The girl spoke quietly. "Sometimes I like mustard."

"I'll bet Heidi has ketchup and mustard." Darren looked at Ellen and smiled. "What's your favorite condiment?"

"I'm okay with ketchup and mustard, but what I really like on my regular hot dogs, or even a corn dog, is sauerkraut."

"Same here." Darren's smile widened. "Looks like we have one more thing in common."

Denise suppressed a smile. It didn't take a genius to see the fireman was infatuated with the nurse. She remembered back to when Greg used to look at her like that. With both of them absorbed in their busy careers, they'd drifted apart. He rarely took the time to really look at her anymore, much less with such a happy expression.

Denise's contemplations came to a halt when Heidi entered the kitchen with a frumpy looking woman with faded blond hair sticking out of a red paisley hankie scarf. The woman reminded her of a funny card she'd seen at the store recently. Except for not wearing a straw hat or having missing front teeth, Denise could swear it was the same lady pictured on the hilarious birthday card.

"Everyone, I'd like you to meet Velma Kimball. She's Peggy Ann's mother."

"Sorry for the interruption," Velma said, "but Heidi said it was okay if I came in and watched." She gestured to Denise, as well as the other two parents. "Looks like I'm not the only adult here, though."

"That's right," Heidi agreed. "This is Denise McGuire, Darren Keller, and Ellen Blackburn. Ellen's daughter, Becky; Darren's son, Jeremy; and Denise's daughter, Kassidy, are my students." She motioned to the boy and girl sitting across from Kassidy. "And you've met Debbie and Kevin Cooper. Neither of their parents is here today."

Velma nodded. "Yeah, I was outside with you when their dad dropped them off." She placed her hand on top of Marsha's blond head. "And this cute little girl I've already met, along with her brother." Velma reached out, as if to touch Randy, but he slunk down in his chair. Denise figured the boy was either shy around strangers or didn't care much for Velma. *Maybe she reminds him of someone he knows and doesn't like.*

"Okay, now, let's start where we left off." Heidi washed her hands at the sink and handed each of the children a wide-mouthed canning jar lid. "Just press it into your dough and when you lift it off, you'll see that you've made a circle. Keep doing that until you have several circles."

"What about the dough Marsha pulled off of mine and ate?" Debbie glanced at Heidi with a look of concern.

"It's okay," Heidi reassured her student. "You still have plenty of dough." Heidi shook her head at Marsha. "Please don't eat any more dough, okay? It's not good for you."

Slowly, Marsha nodded.

"Now what do we do?" Jeremy asked after he'd made his circles.

"You will place half a hot dog on each of the circles. Then bring the sides of the dough up and pinch it in the center." Heidi took one and demonstrated.

"This is easy-peasy," Kassidy said. "If you want my opinion, it's baby stuff."

Jeremy squinted. "Nobody asked for your opinion."

"Oh, yeah, well, for your information—"

Heidi broke in quickly, as though hoping to divert a confrontation. "The next step will be to place the frankfurters wrapped with dough on a greased cooking sheet. We'll set the oven temperature to 350 degrees and bake them for twelve to fifteen minutes. Once they have cooled sufficiently, we can take the mini corn dogs outside and eat them at the picnic table."

"Got any potato chips to go with 'em?" Peggy Ann wanted to know.

Heidi smiled. "Yes, I certainly do. We can also have some cold lemonade to drink."

Peggy Ann clapped her hands. "Oh, good! It'll be like a picnic. It's been a long time since we had a picnic, huh, Mama?"

Velma nodded.

"We used to do picnics all the time before our daddy moved out of the house." Kevin looked over at his sister. "Ain't that right, Debbie?"

She scowled at him. "*Ain't* isn't good English, and you shouldn't be blabbing stuff about us. It's nobody's business but ours."

Kevin sneered at his sister. "Well, it's not like I'm makin' stuff up or anything. It's the truth. We did a lot more fun things when Daddy lived with us."

Denise felt sorry for these children whose parents were obviously separated, or maybe even divorced. She wondered if Kassidy knew how good she had it.

————— ೦⋄⊙ —————

After everyone's corn dogs were adequately browned, Heidi provided paper plates and suggested they take the food outside. "I'll bring out the condiments, and if some of you parents don't mind helping, you can bring the lemonade, chips, and some napkins."

"I'll bring the chips," Darren offered.

"And I'll get the lemonade."

Denise smiled. "Guess that leaves me to carry the napkins."

"What about paper cups? Do you have any of those?" Velma asked.

"Yes, of course." Heidi didn't know why she felt so mixed up today. She'd had everything planned out ahead of time, but things hadn't turned out the way she'd expected—starting with Velma and her daughter showing up before class.

"Always be prepared for the unexpected," Heidi remembered her father saying.

It's hard to be prepared for things you weren't planning to happen, she mused.

After the children went outside with their plates filled, Heidi and the parents followed them out the door with the rest of the items. When Heidi saw Lyle look her way, she motioned for him to join them at the picnic table.

She was about to suggest that everyone bow their heads for silent prayer, when Jeremy picked up the plastic bottle of ketchup and held it over one of his corn dogs. Nothing came out, so he gave it a good squeeze. This time, though, he angled the container, while at the same time, looking at something across the way. The next thing Heidi knew, ketchup squirted out of the bottle and all over the front of Becky's shirt.

Becky gasped, and so did all the adults. But, with the exception of Becky, the children must have thought it was funny, because they all laughed.

Becky started crying and raced for the house. Ellen followed.

Heidi cringed. *So much for a nice picnic lunch.* She debated on whether to go inside to check on Becky or stay put and let the girl's mother handle it. She didn't have to think about it long, for Darren got up and grasped his son's arm. "Come with me, Jeremy. You owe Becky an apology."

The boy shook his head. "Don't see why I have to say I'm sorry. It was an accident, Dad. I didn't mean to squirt her with ketchup."

"That may be so, but you're the one who caused it, so you need to apologize." Darren held his ground and led his son up to the house.

"Eww. . . Mom." Kassidy pointed. "Look what a bird just did on your shoulder."

"Goodness, gracious." Denise turned her head and grimaced when she saw a white blob on the navy-blue blouse she'd worn today. Taking a napkin, and trying to rub it off, Denise only managed to smear it.

"Guess when we get home you'll have to soak your blouse and mine." Kassidy snickered. "Maybe Heidi should have given you an apron to wear."

Heidi closed her eyes briefly. She would be glad when this day was over.

Chapter 17

New Philadelphia

The next Wednesday morning, Trent sat at his kitchen table, mulling things over. Although Kevin and Debbie hadn't made a big deal out of him not staying for their cooking class last week, he felt guilty for bailing on them. At the time, he didn't feel like sitting through the class, but in hindsight Trent wished he had hung around. He also knew if the kids had told Miranda, it would give her one more reason to be upset with him.

Trent rapped his knuckles on the table. There had to be something he could do to redeem himself with her. He'd had enough of living alone and cooking his own meals. Of course, that was only part of the reason he wanted to come back home. Truthfully, he missed his wife and kids. So it was time to take stronger measures in getting Miranda to let him come home.

Let's see. . . . What does she like? He snapped his fingers. *Flowers. Miranda loves flowers. Probably not a good idea to get her a bouquet of cut flowers, though. Those don't last long.* Maybe he could find some nice potted flowers to plant. He'd be on the lookout for roses the same color as the ones Miranda had carried in her wedding bouquet.

Trent glanced at his watch. He didn't have to be at work until noon today, so he had all morning to put his plan into action. And he knew exactly what it would be. He just hoped Miranda would like it.

Walnut Creek

"Them little chickens are sure cute." Randy leaned close to the pen and peered in. Marsha had gone inside with Heidi soon after returning from Baltic, where they had gone to purchase the poultry.

"They're fun to watch, aren't they? Lyle leaned in, observing their cute behavior. "We have a good variety of breeds here. I especially like the Plymouth Rocks, but the Araucana chickens and Rhode Island Reds are nice, too."

"Those brown striped ones are sure neat lookin'." Randy pointed at one and smiled. "I could watch 'em all day. Can I hold one again?"

"Sure, go ahead. The one you are after is a Rhode Island Red chick. We'll get nice brown eggs from it when it's fully grown." Lyle knelt next to Randy.

The boy scooped up one with care and stroked the soft brown, down feathers on its back. "I like having these babies around to take care of." Randy looked closer at the fluffy chick. "Are these its feathers growing out on its back?"

"Yep. They're called pin feathers, and in no time, these little guys will grow them all over their bodies." *Randy and I have something fun we can do together now.* Lyle smiled, observing the boy's delight.

"It sure wants to move around in my hands." Randy petted the chick.

"Taking care of these peepers will be a big responsibility," Lyle said. "Are you sure you're up to it, Son?"

"Umm. . . I guess so." Randy's forehead wrinkled a bit as he looked up at Lyle, while holding on to the peeping fledgling. "What all am I supposed to do?"

"Well, you'll need to feed and water the chicks and keep their pen clean." When Lyle saw the boy's perplexed expression, he quickly added, "Would you be willing to let me help you? We can do the chores together until you have the routine down. Then, when you feel more comfortable with it, you can do the chores on your own. How's that sound?"

"Sure, I'd be glad for the help till I know what I'm doin'." Randy's expression changed to one of obvious relief. At the moment, the little fellow looked much older than his six years.

Lyle smiled. No way he'd let Randy take care of the chickens all by himself—at least not until he felt confident enough to take on the responsibility alone.

At times like this, Lyle felt as if Randy was actually his son. He didn't think the feeling was mutual, however, because the boy kept a safe emotional distance most of the time. Lyle noticed Randy's guard lowering, even though it may have been for brief moments. He hoped in the near future, he and Heidi would gain this young man's trust.

Lyle hadn't brought up the topic of adoption to Heidi for some time, and he certainly didn't want to rush into anything where Randy and Marsha were concerned. But here lately, he'd begun to think adopting these special children might be the best thing—for Randy and Marsha, as well as for him and Heidi.

"Hi there. Is Heidi at home?"

Lyle rose to his feet and turned around. He'd been so preoccupied with Randy and the chickens that he hadn't realized anyone had come into the yard. He recognized Velma right away, though. She wore the same pair of baggy overalls she'd had on last Saturday, but this time she had a dark blue hankie scarf on her head.

"Yes, my wife is here," he responded. "She's in the house."

Velma joined them by the chicken coop. "I see ya got your chicks. They're not as little as I thought they'd be."

"That's right." Lyle nodded. "These chickens are four weeks old, so they should be fine out here in the coop."

"I can tell by their color that those ones there are Rhode Island Reds." Velma whistled, pointing to the brown striped ones. "You picked some good breeds. They're not only good egg layers, but they are good eatin', too."

"No one's gonna eat my chickens." Randy looked up at Lyle and blinked. "Are they?"

"Definitely not." Lyle raised his eyebrows at Velma. "These chickens are strictly for egg laying."

"That's good." Randy crossed his arms and lifted his chin.

"Don't blame ya none." Velma pointed to the chicks. "I'd rather have the eggs, too." She ran her fingers across the chicken-wire enclosure. "It's good you made a place so they can be outside for some sunshine and bug pecking." She tucked her unruly hair back under her scarf. "Chickens need that, ya know."

Randy looked up at her and tipped his head. "You seem to know a lot about chickens."

"Yep. I've raised my share of poultry over the years. Even when I was growing up, we had chickens. We raised Leghorns mostly. They lay lots of eggs." She swatted at a fly buzzing around her head. "Whelp, guess I'll go on up to the house and talk to Heidi now. Came here to do some work for her today."

She sprinted toward the house so quickly Lyle didn't have a chance to say anything more. Although a bit unconventional and seemingly impetuous when she spoke, Velma seemed like a decent sort of person. He had a hunch she would work hard at whatever chores Heidi gave her to do.

Velma stepped up to the door, and seeing it was open a crack, she knocked once and stepped inside. Tipping her head to one side, she heard voices coming from the kitchen.

Velma moved in that direction. "Hello!"

Eyes wide, Heidi stepped out of the kitchen. "Oh, you startled me, Velma."

"Sorry about that. The door was open so I came right in. That's how it is at our place." Velma's lips twitched. "If a door's open it means folks are welcome to come in."

"I see. Well, come into the kitchen. Marsha and I are baking cookies. Perhaps you'd like one."

Velma smacked her lips. "You bet I would."

Heidi led the way. When they entered the kitchen, Velma saw little Marsha sitting on a stool at the table, forming cookie dough into balls with her delicate hands. "Well, aren't you the big helper?" Velma placed her hands on Marsha's shoulders, but the little girl shrugged them away.

"Sorry about that," Heidi said. "She's still a little shy around strangers."

"I can understand that." Velma moved away from the table, putting a safe distance between her and Marsha. "My Peggy Ann is a shy one until she gets to know ya."

Heidi held a plate of ginger cookies out to Velma. "Here you go."

Velma didn't have to be asked twice. She grabbed a cookie and took a bite. "Yummy. Yummy. This is one good cookie. And your kitchen sure smells good from all the baking that's been going on."

Heidi smiled, brushing off some flour clinging to her apron. "Would you like another?"

"It's real tempting, but I'd better not. I can't stand around all day, shootin' the breeze and eatin' all your cookies. Came to work, so what have ya got for me to do?"

Heidi went over to her desk and picked up a piece of paper, which she handed to Velma. "I've written a few things down and thought you could decide which of the jobs you'd prefer to do."

Velma studied the list. "Let's see now. . . Gather the cut-up wood out behind the house and stack it by the barn. Dust the living-room furniture and shake out the throw rugs. Wash all the lower windows, inside and out. Paint the porch railing. Put new stain on the picnic table." She paused, clamping both hands against her hips. "I don't have to choose. I'll do at least one of those chores each week to pay for my daughter's cooking classes."

"Oh, no," Heidi was quick to say. "I don't expect you to do all the chores. I only made the list so you could decide what you would rather do."

Velma shook her head vigorously. "Nope. I insist on doin' everything you mentioned. It's the least I can do to repay your kindness."

───── ❧ ─────

Millersburg

Gathering up her keys, Ellen hollered up the stairs for her daughter to hurry. If she didn't drop Becky off at the sitter's soon, she might be late for work.

"Okay, Mom, you don't have to shout. I'm coming." A few minutes later, Becky plodded down the stairs. She carried along a tote with a drawing tablet and colored pencils inside. "I have a book on animals, and I wanted to try drawing horses like the ones out by Heidi's place."

"That sounds like a good idea. I can't wait to see your picture when we get back home this evening."

Ellen was almost out the door when her cell phone rang. She pulled it out of her purse, and when she looked at the caller ID, she didn't recognize the number. Figuring she ought to answer anyway, she said, "Hello."

"Hi, Ellen. It's Darren Keller. I hope this isn't a bad time to call."

"Well, I was about to head out the door, Darren, but I have a few minutes to talk." She glanced over at her daughter.

Becky looked upward, rolling her eyes.

"I found out I don't have to work this Friday, and wondered if you and Becky would be free to join me and Jeremy for a day of hiking and fishing."

Ellen's face grew warm as she glanced at her work schedule, pinned to the bulletin board in the kitchen. "As a matter of fact, I have Friday off, too. So yes, we'd be glad to join you."

"That's great. If you'll give me your address, we'll be by around nine Friday morning to pick you up. Or is that too early for you?"

Ellen tried to swallow, but her throat had gotten dry. She grabbed the water bottle close to her purse and took a drink. "No, nine will be fine. I'll pack a picnic lunch for the four of us."

Darren laughed. "I was just going to say that I'd be happy to furnish our lunch, but if you really don't mind, I'll leave it up to you."

"I don't mind at all. Is there anything special you or Jeremy would like?"

"Naw. Just throw some sandwiches together and we'll be content."

"Any particular kind?"

"I'm not picky, and neither is Jeremy—except for tuna fish. He doesn't like tuna sandwiches at all."

"No worries. I won't fix tuna fish."

"Okay. See you Friday." Darren paused. "I'm looking forward to it, Ellen."

"Me too. Bye, Darren."

When Ellen hung up, Becky clasped her arm. "Why'd ya tell him we would go, Mom? I don't want to go fishing with Darren—and especially not Jeremy."

"How come? You enjoy fishing. I'm sure you'll have a good time."

"No, I won't. Jeremy is a know-it-all, and he doesn't like me." Becky held her stomach as though she was in pain. "The truth is, I don't like him either."

"Don't be that way, Becky. Do you remember the Bible verse Heidi wrote on the back of the corn dog recipe card? It's 1 John 4:7."

"No, not really. What'd it say?"

"Beloved, let us love one another."

"It's hard to like some people, and I could never love Jeremy." Frowning, Becky shook her head. "He gets on my nerves."

"It's not always easy to love or even like some people, but as Christians we are commanded to love one another. And who knows, once you and Jeremy get better acquainted, you might see him in a different light."

"Can't I stay with one of my friends on Friday? You can still go fishing with Darren and Jeremy, if that's what you really want."

Ellen shook her head. "Darren invited both of us, and I already said yes, so we're going."

Becky rushed out the door and trumped down the porch steps. She was obviously not happy about this. But she would get over it once they got to the lake and started fishing. At least, Ellen hoped that'd be the case.

Chapter 18

Berlin

The minute Miranda stepped out of her car, she knew something in the front yard was different. The space where she'd thought about planting some dahlias was now full of pink-and-white roses.

"What in the world?" She scratched her head. "Where did those come from?" Miranda couldn't imagine how this happened. What a treat to find such gorgeous colors at home in the once empty spaces bordering her walkway.

Not only did she favor the color of the flowers, but for a special reason, roses were her favorite. Their beauty drew her toward them, and the intoxicating scent coming off the velvety petals made her bend closer to inhale the fragrance. Miranda stared at the beautiful roses a few more seconds, then hurried into the house. There, she found Debbie and Kevin watching TV with Carla, their middle-aged babysitter. "Hey, kids. Do either of you know where those roses came from in the front yard?" Miranda questioned.

Carla pulled out her earbuds and gave Miranda a blank stare. "What's up?"

Miranda repeated her question.

"Daddy did it." Kevin bobbed his head. "He said it was a surprise for you."

Carla gave a twisted smile. "It was supposed to be a nice gift for your mother."

"Yeah," Kevin agreed, "but I think he did it 'cause he felt bad that he didn't stay at Heidi's last Saturday to watch us cook."

Debbie's elbow connected with her brother's arm.

"Ouch," Kevin rubbed the spot. "Hey, what'd ya do that for?"

"You weren't supposed to say anything about that. You have a big mouth."

Kevin squeezed his eyes shut and covered his mouth. "Oops! I forgot."

Miranda's skin prickled as agitation took over. "If your dad didn't stay with you during the cooking class, where did he go?"

Kevin shrugged. "Don't know. He never said."

Debbie shot him an icy stare. "You've already ratted on Dad, so you shouldn't be lying to Mom now." She looked up at Miranda. "Dad went to the cheese store in Berlin. He said he bought some cheese for you, but then he decided to keep it for himself. Guess that's because he didn't want you to know he dropped me and Kevin at Heidi's and then went off to do whatever he wanted."

Miranda glanced at Carla. She was a pleasant woman, and Debbie and Kevin both liked her, but she tended to be a bit of a gossip. The last thing Miranda needed was for the kids' babysitter to blab around the neighborhood, or even at church, anything about the Cooper family. It was bad enough that most of their friends and family knew Miranda and Trent were separated. Too many well-meaning people had already offered their unsolicited thoughts and opinions about the situation.

"Umm, we can talk about this later, kids." Miranda gestured to the TV. "I'd like you to turn that off and go into the kitchen so you can help me get supper going."

After Debbie hit the remote and she and Kevin had left the room, Carla rose from her chair. "Now that you're home from work, you won't be needing me anymore this evening, so I'll head for home."

"Thanks, Carla." Miranda smiled. "I'll see you next Monday, when I'm scheduled to work again, and I'll pay you then if that's okay."

"Sure, no problem." Carla gathered up her purse and started out the door with a farewell wave.

Miranda paused to think and offer a quick prayer before heading for the kitchen. She did not want to say anything negative to the children about their father. She would, however, have a talk with Trent when Debbie and Kevin weren't around. He needed to know that he couldn't buy her love or work his way back into her good graces through the act of planting flowers—especially ones that reminded her of their wedding day.

Walnut Creek

Heidi was getting ready to start supper when she heard a familiar *thunk* and knew wood was being chopped. Assuming Lyle had returned home, she went outside to tell him what time their evening meal would be ready. Instead of Lyle, however, she found Velma by a stack of uncut wood, holding Lyle's axe in her hands.

"Velma, what are you doing?" Heidi walked across the yard, swatting at a cluster of gnats that seemed to form out of thin air. "When I asked you to stack the wood that had already been chopped, I didn't expect you to do this." She gestured to the pile Velma had already cut.

Velma lifted her hand, encased in a pair of dilapidated-looking work gloves, and slapped the dust off her overalls. "Well, I got the other wood stacked, so figured I may as well add some more to the pile."

Heidi shielded her eyes from the evening sun—and the annoying bugs. "I appreciate you wanting to do some work as payment for Peggy Ann's cooking classes, but you've worked several hours already and should really go home. I imagine your children are getting hungry and expecting their mother to fix supper."

Velma's head moved quickly from side to side. "Naw, I won't be cookin' supper tonight. It's Bobbie Sue's turn in the kitchen."

"I see." Although Heidi hadn't met Bobbie Sue, she knew from talking to Velma that her oldest daughter was seventeen, certainly old enough to cook a meal. If Velma's children had been with her right now, Heidi would have invited them all to stay for supper. Perhaps some other time she would extend an invitation. It would be nice to meet Mr. Kimball, too.

"I appreciate the work you did here today." Heidi smiled. "It more than covered Peggy Ann's first cooking class. In fact, it probably covered two."

"Naw." Velma touched the side of her face, leaving a smudge of dirt behind. "I plan to do several chores and work at least one day each week that my young'un comes here for a class. It's the least I can do for your kindness." She leaned the axe against the side of the woodshed, and rubbed her eyes when more bugs aimed for her face. "Boy, these gnats are relentless. It must be gonna rain." Velma swatted at them, but it seemed to aggravate the insects even more. "Well, I've had enough of this. Guess I'm a little sweaty, and I am gettin' kinda hungry, so think I'll call it a day and get on home."

"Okay. Thank you, Velma. I'll see you sometime next week."

As Velma headed down the driveway, swinging her arms, Heidi paused and said a prayer for the woman. Moving into a new neighborhood in an unfamiliar state would be difficult for anyone—especially when they were having financial difficulties. Heidi planned to speak to Lyle about the Kimballs' situation. Perhaps they could think of other ways to help. Allowing Velma to do some work in exchange for her daughter's lessons was simply not enough.

———•❧❧•———

Walking briskly toward home, Velma whistled, glad that the bugs had finally dispersed when she got to the road. She hadn't minded working for Heidi today. Despite the pesky gnats, and the sore muscles she expected to end up with, it felt good knowing she was able to pay for Peggy Ann's classes by helping the Troyers with things needing done. She'd meant to ask how Peggy Ann did during Heidi's second cooking class, but she'd forgotten to say anything about it. Hopefully her daughter hadn't missed too much by not attending the first class.

Velma reflected on how nice it would be to have a beautiful flower bed growing out front of her place, like the one Heidi had. It would take a lot of time and work, but it'd be worth it. However, she couldn't afford to spend extra money right now—unless it was a necessity.

As Velma continued her journey, she thought about Hank. He'd be home, either late tonight or early tomorrow, and would probably stick around a few days. In some ways, she looked forward to him being there, but in other ways she dreaded it. He'd no doubt start harping at her again about the accident that had totaled their car.

"Well, I won't let him get under my skin," she murmured. "Everyone makes mistakes, and he's sure not perfect."

Velma remembered how one Fourth of July, Hank had thrown a firecracker into her birdbath and blew it to smithereens. Of course, that didn't compare to wrecking a car. But the birdbath had been a birthday gift from Velma's sister, Maggie. Velma was quite upset when Hank ruined it, although she'd decided not to make a big deal out of it. What was the point, anyway? Fussing and fuming wouldn't bring back her birthday present, and it would have only made Hank mad. What really riled her, however, was Hank never even apologized for what he'd done. At least she'd had the decency to say she was sorry about wrecking their car.

Life sure has its ups and downs, she thought. *Wish I'd been lucky and was born with a silver spoon in my mouth. But no, my folks were poor as church mice.*

Soon Velma's driveway came into view, and as she turned to start heading toward their mobile home, she spotted a motorcycle parked near the small storage shed to the left of the trailer-house. She recognized the skull and crossbones insignia on the back of the cycle. It belonged to Bobbie Sue's boyfriend, Kenny Carmichael. Her muscles tensed, and she bit the inside of her cheek so hard she tasted blood. *What's he doin' here? That fellow never was anything but trouble.*

Velma hurried her footsteps. She planned to march right in there and send the old boyfriend packing.

Velma was almost to the door when Kenny stepped out, with Bobbie Sue clutching his arm. "Look who came to see me, Mama." Bobbie Sue gave Velma a wide grin, then looked adoringly back at Kenny.

"Nice to see ya again," Kenny mumbled.

With a curt nod, Velma waited.

Kenny put his arm around Bobbie Sue and pulled her close to his side. "I sure have missed my girl. Wish you all hadn't up and moved."

"I'm goin' for a ride with Kenny." Without waiting for Velma's response, Bobbie Sue followed him over to his motorcycle and climbed on the back.

Velma was almost too dumbfounded to say anything, but she found her voice before Kenny had a chance to start up the cycle. "You can't go anywhere right now, Bobbie Sue. It's time to eat supper, which you should have ready for us by now."

Bobbie Sue shook her head. "I was thinkin' about starting something when Kenny showed up. We're going to the burger joint in Berlin."

Anger bubbled in Velma's soul, and she slapped both hands against her hips. "Oh, yeah? Who says you're goin' anywhere?"

"Well, I. . ."

"Aw, come on Mrs. Kimball," Kenny interrupted. "It's been way too long since I saw my girl. Ya can't be mean enough to try and keep us apart."

"I am not trying to be mean." Velma spoke slowly, curbing her anger. "I've been workin' hard most of the day for one of our neighbors, and my daughter was supposed to fix supper for all of us tonight. Then I show up here, dog-tired, and she wants to run off and spend the evening with you, which would mean I'd have to do all the cooking." Heat flooding her face, Velma tapped her foot a couple of times.

Kenny pulled his fingers through the ends of his black, shoulder-length hair. "Now don't go gettin' yourself all worked up over nothin'. If ya don't want Bobbie Sue to go out with me to grab a bite, I'll eat supper here with your family."

Velma blinked. *The nerve of that boy! Just who does he think he is?* She drew a deep breath and silently counted to ten. *I suppose having Kenny here for the evening would be better than my daughter going out with him on that motorcycle and leaving me stuck with the cooking. At least if he's here, I can keep an eye on things.*

She forced a smile and said, "Sure, Kenny, you're welcome to join us for supper. You'll get to see what kind of a cook my daughter is." *You just won't be staying long after we're done eating*, she added silently as Bobbie Sue gave her an icy stare.

Chapter 19

Canton

Denise stood at the living-room window, watching as Greg pulled out of their yard. Her husband had been in such a hurry to get to the office today he hadn't even taken the time to eat breakfast.

She glanced at the stately grandfather clock across the room, gonging on the half hour. In a few minutes it would be time to take Kassidy to her friend's house for the day. After she dropped her off, Denise would be hosting a Realtors' open house for a new listing. If this home sold at the price it was listed for, she could make upwards of thirty thousand dollars.

Better not get my hopes up too high, at least not yet, she reasoned. Still, given that it was Friday, Denise hoped they'd have something to celebrate soon.

After pulling her sleeve back to check the time on her diamond-studded wristwatch, Denise turned and was about to call her daughter down from upstairs, when Kassidy burst into the room.

"Just look at my blouse, Mom. Those stains you said would come out are set in for good. I even tried scrubbing the blouse when I found it on the floor of my closet this morning, but it didn't do any good." Frowning, Kassidy held out the item in question. "It's ruined, and now I'll have to throw it away."

Denise's gaze flicked upwards. "If you had put it in the laundry when we got home from the cooking class last week, like I told you to, I most likely could have gotten the stain out." She swept her hands impatiently. "I don't have time to debate this with you. We have to go right now or I'm going to be late for my open house."

Kassidy stomped her foot. "Mom, you're not listening to me—my blouse is ruined."

"Yes, I heard you—loud and clear. But there is nothing I can do about it, so get your things and let's go."

"I need a new blouse, and I want one today." With an angry-looking scowl, Kassidy tossed the blouse on the floor, then grabbed her backpack and stomped out the door.

I think Greg and I created a monster by allowing our daughter to get away with her temper tantrums since she was a little girl. Denise picked up her purse and followed. There would have been a day she'd have given in to her daughter's demands, but not anymore. Until Kassidy learned how to ask for things nicely, she would not be getting anything new other than necessities.

Millersburg

"I sure like this weather we're having," Darren commented as he walked beside Ellen on the trail leading to the lake he'd chosen for fishing today. Tall trees—a mix of evergreens and hardwoods—shaded the pathway, while a warm breeze tickled Darren's bare arms. He wasn't sure if it was the weather or strolling down the footpath this close to Ellen that seemed to make his senses tingle.

She looked over at him and smiled. "You're right. We couldn't ask for a better day." Ellen turned and called over her shoulder, "Hurry up, Becky. You're falling behind."

Darren paused. "Maybe we're walking too fast."

Ellen shook her head. "She's been dawdling since we got out of the car."

"Not Jeremy." Darren pointed ahead. "He acts like he's rushing to a fire or something." He chuckled and started walking again. "My boy's always enjoyed going fishing with me. I'm sure that's why he's running ahead. Probably thinks if he gets to the lake first he'll catch the most, or biggest, fish."

"Maybe he will." Ellen stopped walking and looked at her daughter again. Becky had almost caught up to them, but the grim twist to her mouth let Darren know she was anything but happy to be here today. Ellen had said previously that Becky enjoyed fishing and hiking, so he figured her lack of enthusiasm might be because of him or Jeremy. *Does Becky feel threatened by my interest in her mother? Or is it simply that she doesn't like my son very much?* Either way, Darren was determined to win the girl over, because he definitely liked Becky's mother. Maybe things would go better once they reached the lake.

———————⌒⟲∾⟲⌒———————

When they arrived at the spot where Darren suggested they set up, Ellen couldn't believe how beautiful it was. The area felt like some secret place, undiscovered by anyone but them. Wild grass grew up to the water's edge, with trees surrounding the sides and far end of the lake. All the way around, the body of water looked promising to fish from its bank.

"It's so pretty here." Ellen glanced over at Darren as she set the picnic basket down, along with the duffle bag that held the blanket. "Do you and Jeremy come here often?"

"As much as we can. We've been to other places, but we like it here best." Darren pointed to a trash can several feet away. "Other people fish here, too, because there's usually evidence in the can. But we always seem to time it right and usually have this spot all to ourselves."

Darren walked over to a level area under the shade of a tree. "How about we spread your blanket out here for later, when we have lunch?"

"Sure, this looks like a good place." Ellen looked toward the water again, taking in the alluring reflection from the sun and clouds overhead.

"I can tell you this. Jeremy and I have pulled some good-sized fish out of this lake."

"Regardless if I catch a fish or not, it's just nice being here." Humming, Ellen rolled her shoulders forward. Up above, a robin sang its cheery melody, and a frog began croaking.

"I know exactly what you mean." Darren took the fishing rods over to a log near the water, then came back to get his tackle box.

Unfolding the large blanket she'd purchased a few years ago at a yard sale, Ellen glanced over at her daughter. Tight-lipped, Becky stood with her arms folded. Ellen was about to suggest that her daughter grab the other end of the blanket, to help her spread it out over the grass, when Jeremy ran up to Becky. "Do you know how to skip stones over the water?" Jeremy held a few flat stones in his hand.

"Course I do." Becky put her hands on her hips, giving him quite the stare.

"Well then, come on. Let's see who can make one go the farthest." Jeremy handed Becky a few stones, and off to the water's edge they both ran.

"Here, let me help you, Ellen." Darren reached down and took the other end of the blanket. After they had it spread on the ground, they got a few things out of the basket.

"Kids. Always trying to outdo each other." Darren chuckled, looking over his shoulder at Becky and Jeremy. Their stones skimmed over the water's surface before disappearing.

"I hope they don't scare the fish." Ellen knelt on the blanket to get a few snack bags out.

"Nah, Jeremy skips rocks every time we come here, and it never seems to bother them."

Once Ellen made some snacks available, Darren reached his hand out to help her up. "Come on, let's do some fishing."

It was a peaceful morning, and while Darren and Ellen sat on the log, talking and keeping an eye on the red-and-white bobbers floating in the middle of the lake, her body relaxed. Jeremy and Becky were fishing, yards apart, over on the bank toward the right. Neither of them wanted to use a bobber, but preferred to throw their line out, then slowly reel it back in. It was easy to see they were competing again, only this time with casting their fishing lines.

"I hope if anyone catches some fish, it's the kids." Ellen smiled. "Right now, at least, they seem to be tolerating each other."

"Yeah, kids can be funny—one trying to upstage the other." Darren looked out where his line went into the water. "So far, I haven't gotten any bites."

"Don't feel bad. I haven't either." Ellen chuckled. "But who cares?"

Just when all seemed content, Jeremy yelled, "I got one!"

"So did I!" Becky squealed a few seconds later.

"Bet mine's bigger than yours." Jeremy struggled, reeling his line in until it revealed a nice trout flopping on the end.

Ellen watched as Becky pulled her fish in next. "Oh, she got a nice one, too."

Darren and Ellen got up to check out the fish. Jeremy walked over to Becky, proudly holding up his catch. Becky did the same, placing hers right next to his.

"Looks like a tie to me." After eyeing the trout, Darren picked up a stick and held it next to his son's fish, then did the same to Becky's. "Now, how about that? They are exactly the same length."

Ellen smiled as Darren took the fish off their hooks, put them on a stringer, and set them back into the water along the shoreline.

"I'm glad they each got a trout, but now I'll bet they'll both try for a bigger one." She pointed as Becky and Jeremy ran back to their fishing spots.

Darren strolled back to the log, while Ellen continued to watch their children. Jeremy cast his line out. Becky put more bait on the end of the hook and extended her arm back to cast. What looked to be a good fling of her line, ended up getting snagged on a shrub behind where she stood.

"Oh great! My line is tangled." Becky groaned.

"Here, let me help you." Jeremy offered, setting his fishing pole down.

Ellen walked over to Darren, raising her eyebrows. "Will you look at those two?"

"Jeremy's a good kid. Sometimes it just takes him awhile to warm up to someone." Darren looked fondly at his son as he helped Becky free up her line.

Ellen recognized the proud feeling Darren had for Jeremy, for she felt the same about Becky. "Looks to me like we are both fortunate parents."

"You've got that right." Darren's lips parted slightly as he moistened them with his tongue. "Mind if ask you a personal question?"

"No, not at all."

"How long have you been a single mom?"

"Well. . ."

He pulled his fingers down the side of his face. "Guess what I really wanted to ask is, are you a widow or a divorcee?"

"I'm neither." Ellen briefly explained how she'd adopted Becky, leaving out the part about not telling her daughter until recently. "How about you?" she asked. "I assume you were once married."

"Yes, my wife died from a brain tumor two years ago." Darren pressed a fist against his chest. "Losing Caroline was difficult for me, as well as Jeremy." He paused, staring vacantly across the lake. "I do my best with Jeremy, but my son needs his mother."

Ellen reached out and touched his arm. "I'm sorry for your loss."

"Thanks. I'm doing better, but there are still times when I think about Caroline and all we had."

"While I've never lost a mate, I struggled with depression after my grandma died. We were very close, and I still miss her."

"Loss of any sort is hard, but life goes on, and all anyone can do is keep pressing forward and try to focus on the good things—like those two." Darren pointed to Becky, who had made a successful cast now that her line had been untangled. Jeremy stood a little closer to Becky than before, and a few giggles erupted as they talked.

Ellen couldn't help hearing part of the kids' conversation, and was surprised when her daughter said, "Thank you, Jeremy, for untangling my line."

"You're welcome." Jeremy grinned, although he kept his focus on the water.

This day was turning out better than she imagined. Ellen felt comfortable around Darren as they opened up to each other and also discovered some more things they had in common. Ellen couldn't remember the last time she'd felt so lighthearted. She wondered if Darren might ask to see her again, and hoped if he did that Becky and Jeremy would continue to get along.

Walnut Creek

Velma's fingers clenched around her coffee mug so tightly that her veins protruded. Soon after she and the children had eaten breakfast this morning, she'd found a note on her desk in the kitchen. Reading it for the second time, before starting lunch, her nose burned with unshed tears.

> *Dear Mama,*
>
> *I'm sure you won't like this, but I'm running away with Kenny. In two weeks I'll be eighteen, and we're gonna get married.*
>
> *Don't worry about me. Kenny and I will both get jobs, so we'll be fine. Once we're settled, I'll send you our address and phone number. I love you, Mama, and I hope you and Papa will forgive me for doin' this. I love Kenny and wanna be with him.*
>
> *Love,*
Bobbie Sue

Velma let go of her mug and slammed her fist on the table. "I knew that snake was up to no good when he showed up here two days ago. Shoulda sent him packin' like I wanted to do."

"What's going on, Mama?" Peggy Ann asked when she and Eddie entered the room. "Who were you talkin' to?"

"Myself. I was talking to myself."

Eddie glanced around, as if looking for answers. "How come?"

"Because I'm upset." Velma picked up the note and waved it about. "Found this awhile ago, and I just finished reading it again."

Peggy Ann tipped her head. "What is it?"

"It's from your big sister. She ran off with Kenny Carmichael sometime during the night." Velma swallowed hard. "And ya may as well know, there's a good chance we'll never see her again."

"What?" Peggy Ann lowered her head and started to wail.

Eddie scrunched up his nose. "Just wait till Papa gets home. Bet he'll go after Kenny and punch him in the nose."

The words were no more than out of his mouth when Velma heard the roar of an engine. Rising from the table, she went to the kitchen window and peered out. Sure enough, Hank's rig had pulled into the yard.

"Oh, great." Velma blew out a quick breath and turned to face her children. "Not a word to your dad about Bobbie Sue. Understood?"

Peggy Ann's forehead wrinkled. "How come, Mama? Papa's gonna know somethin' ain't right when he asks where she is."

"I realize that. I just need to be the one to tell him. So when he comes inside, you can both say hello, and then I want you to go to your rooms till I call ya for lunch."

"Okay, we'll zip our lips." Eddie bumped his sister's arm. "Right, Peggy Ann?"

She pushed him away. "You're not my boss, so don't be tellin' me what to do."

"I wasn't."

"Uh-huh."

Velma stepped between them. "That's enough, you two. Ya don't want to be bickering when your dad comes in, now, do you?"

Both children shook their heads.

A few minutes later, Hank entered the house and came into the kitchen. "Hey, how's my little brood?" He leaned over and patted Eddie's head, then scooped Peggy Ann into his arms. "Have you two been good for your mama while I was gone?"

"Yes, Papa." Peggy Ann wrapped her arms around his neck and gave it a squeeze.

"How about you, Son?" Hank looked down at their boy.

"I've been good, too." Eddie looked up at Velma. "Right, Mama?"

She nodded. "Now, why don't you and your sister skedaddle to your rooms? I'll call ya when it's time to eat."

Hank set Peggy Ann down, and she scurried out of the kitchen behind her brother.

"Would ya like a cup of coffee?" Velma asked, moving across the room to the stove.

"Sure." He followed Velma and placed a sloppy kiss on her cheek. She took it to mean he wasn't angry with her anymore.

After she'd poured coffee into his mug and handed it to him, Velma suggested they take a seat at the table.

"Aren't you gonna fix me some lunch?" Hank asked.

"I will shortly. But first, we need to talk."

Turning his head, he cleared his throat. "If it's about the car. . ."

"No, it's not the car. It's Bobbie Sue."

"Where is that girl anyway? Is she at work? Did Bobbie Sue find another job while I was gone?"

"No." Velma pulled out a chair and sat.

Hank took the seat across from her. "What's this about? Do those creases in your forehead mean somethin' is wrong?"

"Afraid so." Velma took in a gulp of air and quickly relayed how their daughter had run off with Kenny and left a note.

Hank's nostrils flared, and sweat beaded on his forehead. "Why that no good so and so." He stood and pushed back his chair with such force it toppled over. "I'm gonna get back in my rig and go lookin' for Bobbie Sue. And when I find that girl, I'll drag her right back home."

Velma lifted her hands. "What good would that do? Bobbie Sue will be eighteen in two weeks, and then she can do whatever she pleases."

Hank shuffled back a few steps. "Oh, that's right. I'd forgotten her birthday was comin' up soon."

"I don't like this any better than you do, Hank, but I think it's best we leave well enough alone. Hopefully, our daughter will smarten up and come home on her own. She'll soon find out how rough it is out there in the real world with no support from her family."

Squinting, Hank rubbed the back of his neck. "If she takes after her older brother, we won't see any sign of her again."

Moaning, Velma held both hands tightly against her body to keep from shaking. Hank's final words had pierced her soul. If she was honest with herself, Velma would have to admit that she may never see Bobbie Sue or Clem again. The mere thought of it took away any appetite she may have had this morning. But life didn't stop because they'd been thrown another curve ball. For the sake of her two younger children, she'd fix lunch and somehow muddle through the rest of the day.

Chapter 20

Berlin

As Heidi sat in the waiting room at the dentist's office Monday morning, she took a notepad from her purse and made a list of the ingredients she would need for Saturday's cooking class. Marsha sat quietly next to her, looking at a children's picture book, while Randy had his teeth cleaned and saw the dentist for an evaluation. It would be Marsha's turn next, but since she was so young and insecure, Heidi intended to go in with her.

She chuckled to herself, thinking about Randy's independence when she asked if he wanted her to go with him when it was his turn. Putting on a brave face, he'd shaken his head and said, "Nope. I'm a big boy and don't need no one to sit beside me."

When the children's appointments were over, Heidi planned to take them to lunch at one of her favorite restaurants. Afterward, they would stop for ice cream at Walnut Creek Cheese.

A smile reached Heidi's lips, remembering how many years she'd dreamed of doing these things with her own children. Having Randy and Marsha in her life had turned out to be the most precious blessing, and she prayed it would keep getting better.

Heidi glanced out the window in the waiting room. There wasn't a cloud in the sky. After a weekend of off-and-on rain, it was nice to see blue skies again. The buggy ride here had been pleasant, with warm breezes pushing away the damp air. The only evidence of the soggy weather was puddles of water that hadn't dried up yet. *Guess Velma was right last week when she mentioned rain might be coming.*

Pulling her attention back to her notebook, Heidi wrapped her fingers around the pen as she thought about this Saturday and how she would teach her young students to make strawberry shortcake. Since there were plenty of ripe strawberries in her garden right now, this would be the perfect dessert to make. She was sure everyone would like it—especially since she planned to make some homemade whipped cream to put over the top of the berries after they were spooned onto the shortcake.

The verse she planned to write on the back of their recipe cards this time was Proverbs 20:11: "Even a child is known by his doings, whether his work be pure, and whether it be right." No one had said anything about the scriptures she'd included so far, but Heidi hoped one or more of the children in class, or perhaps a parent, might memorize the verses and find help through them.

"Mama, what are they doin' to Randy?" Marsha placed her small hand on Heidi's arm.

"The hygienist is cleaning his teeth, and then the dentist will look in your brother's mouth and let me know if there are any problems. You will go in after Randy comes out."

Marsha shook her head. "Don't want no one lookin' in my mouth. Only you can brush my teeth."

"I'll be right there with you when they clean your teeth. I've had mine cleaned many times." Heidi patted the little girl's hand. "It'll be fine. I promise. They will most likely give you a new toothbrush, too, and even let you pick out the color you want."

Marsha looked up at her with a dimpled grin. "Okay, Mammi."

Heidi's heart nearly melted. Even though Marsha was not her biological daughter, every day spent together seemed to draw them closer.

<hr />

Walnut Creek

In order to keep her mind off her runaway daughter, Velma decided the best remedy was to stay busy. She had more work to do at the Troyers', of course, but didn't want to leave Peggy Ann and Eddie by themselves. Her plan was to work for Heidi this Saturday, while Peggy Ann took part in the cooking class. Since Bobbie Sue was no longer around and

Hank was on the road again, no one would be home to keep an eye on Eddie. So Velma would enlist his help on whatever chore Heidi gave her to do. It was either that, or let the boy attend the class with Peggy Ann, which wasn't a good idea. Quite often, Eddie could be quite mischievous. No telling what kind of trouble he might cause that could interrupt Heidi's teaching. No, it was safer to keep him close by Velma's side.

Velma thought about Heidi and the way she and other Amish women in the area dressed. *Sure can't picture myself wearing a long dress while building a chicken coop. I like Heidi. She's a good person, and her ways, even though they're different, aren't bad.*

Velma's contemplations came to a halt when she looked out the window at the clean sheets flapping in the breeze. *Guess it's time to get some work done around here. It would go a lot quicker if my wayward daughter was still with us.* Her eyes misted.

She went outside, took the bedding off the line, and hauled it inside. Velma paused to inhale the fresh fragerence. "Now those are some nice smellin' sheets for Eddie's bed." She carried them to his room.

Coming in through the door, the not-so-nice smelling bedroom needed a good airing. Velma dumped the sheets on the bed and opened the window as wide as it would go. The curtains swayed back and forth with the fresh breeze entering the room.

Turning her attention to Eddie's twin-size bed, Velma began searching through the bedding for the pillowcase to put on, but it was not there.

She hurried from the room and found it lying in the hallway on the worn carpet. "Even the laundry isn't cooperating today." Velma picked up the pillowcase and headed back to Eddie's room, trying to focus on something positive.

Yesterday, in between rain showers, Velma had begun building a chicken coop in their backyard, so that was positive. She hoped to finish it today. Velma had seen some laying hens advertised in the local paper for a reasonable price and planned to pick them up on Wednesday. Having fresh eggs to eat, and maybe sell, would be nice.

Any little extra income in their pockets would surely be beneficial.

When Abner barked excitedly, Velma opened the front door and glanced toward the road. Hope welled in her chest as she heard a noisy vehicle approach. It sounded like a motorcycle. Maybe Bobbie Sue had changed her mind and come home.

But as the cycle sped by, Velma realized it didn't belong to Kenny. The elderly man driving it waved, and so did the woman in the sidecar. They were a happy-looking couple—probably reliving their youth and enjoying every moment they had together.

Velma envied them. It had been a long time since she and Hank had done anything purely for fun. With his long days on the road, plus their lack of money, she couldn't envision them doing anything fun in the near future either. Fact was, with her two oldest children leaving home, Velma had been left with a huge void in her life, so nothing seemed enjoyable anymore. She felt like an unfit mother who had driven her children away.

Dropping to her knees, just inside the door, Velma gave in to her tears. Had she done something in her past to deserve such misery? Had she failed her children somehow? Maybe their negative behavior was because of how she'd raised them.

Berlin

Miranda said goodbye to Carla and the children, then headed out the door. She didn't have to be at work for another hour and a half but needed to run a few errands on the way.

She'd no more than stepped out the front door when she saw a silver-gray SUV pull in. At first, she wasn't sure who it was, until Trent got out of the vehicle. It made sense after she noticed the license plate with the dealership's name on it. Since her husband sold cars, he sometimes drove a demo instead of his own. While this might not be the best time to confront Trent about the flowers he'd planted, she wouldn't pass up the opportunity.

Miranda brought her hand up to the strands of hair grazing her forehead, waiting until Trent finished dabbing a spot off the car. Then she stepped up to him as he approached.

"Hi, how are ya doing?" He gave her a dimpled grin—the kind of sweet smile that used to cause a stirring in her heart.

"Okay, I guess. Nice car you're driving."

"Wish it were mine, but it's only a demo." Trent continued to smile, never taking his eyes off of her. "You look great, Miranda."

A shiver went through her as Trent's gaze slowly roamed from her head, down to her toes, and back to her face again.

"Is that a new shade of lipstick you're wearing?"

She lifted her chin and gave him a probing gaze. In all the time they'd been married, he'd never once mentioned her lipstick. Or much of anything else about her appearance, for that matter. Why the sudden interest now? *I bet he's trying to butter me up.*

"It's not new." Miranda spoke slowly, deliberately. "I've worn this same lipstick many times in the past."

"Okay then, but you do look nice this morning. Are you on your way to work?"

"Yes, I am. And what might you be here for? Did you come to plant more flowers?" Miranda couldn't keep from speaking in a tone of sarcasm.

Trent lifted both hands. "All right, you've found me out. I did plant the roses. Do you like them?"

She slowly nodded. "They're beautiful, but I'm not happy about the reason you put them there."

He tipped his head slightly. "What do you mean?"

"Don't act innocent, Trent. You felt guilty for not staying with the kids during the cooking class, so you—"

"Okay, okay, I admit it. I did feel bad about not sticking around. But the real reason I planted the roses was to remind you of our wedding day. Remember the beautiful bouquet you carried as you walked down the aisle toward me—your eager groom?"

Miranda shifted her weight, clutching her purse close to her side. "Of course I remember."

"I still love you, honey, and I want to come home."

She swallowed hard, hoping he wouldn't know how close she

was to letting her tears fall. Thinking back to their wedding day, Miranda recalled how she'd thought she and Trent would always be happy together, making beautiful memories throughout the years. But those hopes and dreams had gone out the window when her husband admitted he had feelings for another woman and wanted to pursue a relationship with her. It wasn't long after Miranda insisted he move out of their home that Trent said he was sorry and pleaded with her to forgive him. Of course, Miranda said no. She couldn't trust him anymore. And with good reason. He couldn't even keep a simple promise to take the kids to cooking class.

She bit her bottom lip. *Trent did take them. He just didn't stay there like I expected him to. And he asked the kids not to tell. That's deceitful behavior from a man who claims to love me.*

"Well, aren't you going to say anything, Miranda? Can I come home or not?"

Trent's question pulled her back to the present. "No. I can't believe you think that just because you planted some roses in my flower bed, our marriage should be back on track and everything would be peachy—or should I say rosy?"

Trent huffed impatiently. "What's it gonna take to convince you to give me another chance? What do I have to do to get back in your good graces?"

"For one thing, you'd need to take an interest in spiritual things." Her chin jutted out. "And I don't mean just going to church."

"What exactly do you mean?"

"You need to make a serious commitment to God and become the spiritual leader in our home."

He spoke as though his words were chosen deliberately. "I am not a bad person, Miranda. And I'm getting sick and tired of you making me feel like one. Just because I almost got caught up in an extramarital affair doesn't mean I'm headed down the road toward—"

She held up her hand. "I don't want to discuss this with you anymore, Trent. And I won't be late for work on account of you."

He glared at her. "Why do you always have to blame me for everything? Did it ever occur to you that your holier-than-thou attitude might be part of our problem?"

Trent's words stung like a slap across the face. If she didn't leave now, Miranda knew she would either say something mean or break down in tears. "Sorry, Trent, but I have to go. Debbie and Kevin are inside with their babysitter if you want to say hello." Miranda hurried to her car and opened the door. Short of a miracle, she doubted that she and Trent would ever live together again.

Miranda closed her eyes and took in a breath. *I just wish the children weren't affected by all of this. They deserve two parents who love the Lord, as well as each other.* She sniffed deeply. *Perhaps that's too much to hope and pray for, but I have to trust God to help me get through this without losing faith and becoming a bitter person.*

Chapter 21

Kevin leaned his elbows on the table and stared at Miranda as she fingered the handle of her teacup. "Mommy, are you mad at Daddy?"

She blinked. "Why would you think that?"

"'Cause he said so when he came by the other day."

Debbie poked her brother's arm and put one finger against her lip.

"What's going on?" Miranda asked. "Has your father been talking about me behind my back?"

Debbie dropped her gaze to the table, while Kevin slumped in his chair.

"Okay, kids—out with it. What did he say?"

"Just said you was mad at him for plantin' the flowers."

Miranda felt a flush of heat on the back of her neck. She took a moment to gather her thoughts before responding to her son's statement. *What I wouldn't do for a God-fearing husband in this house. If only Trent would get his act together and be that kind of man for his family.* "I am not mad at him for that." She spoke in a soft tone, glancing at her watch. "And you know what? You two need to go brush your teeth so we can leave for Heidi's on time. You don't want to miss her third cooking class."

After finishing his glass of orange juice, Kevin pushed away from the table. "Wonder what she'll teach us to make today."

"I hope it's something good." Debbie left her seat, too.

Kevin wrinkled his nose. "The corn dogs we made last time were okay, but they were so little."

"Course they were, silly. That's why Heidi called them 'mini corn dogs.'"

"I ain't silly."

"Are so."

"Huh-uh."

Miranda put her cup in the sink and turned the water on full blast, hoping to drown out Debbie and Kevin's bantering. She'd been tempted to tell them the reason she was mad at their father, but stopped herself in time. It wasn't right to involve the children in her and Trent's problems, and she certainly didn't want them to take sides. Their separation was hard enough on the kids, and she disliked even asking them what their father had said. They were already in the middle of this mess, and the last thing either child needed was to become an informer.

Miranda turned off the water. She heard the faucet running in the bathroom and knew one of them was in brushing their teeth. She combed her fingers through her shoulder-length hair, and watched a pair of turtle doves in the yard. She thought about Trent's comment that she was partly to blame for their relationship falling apart.

"It might be true," she murmured. "I may have done things to drive him away." Miranda lifted her hands with intertwined fingers, bowing her head in prayer. *Lord, if it's meant for Trent and me to be together again, please show us both what we need to do in order to work things out. And help me learn to be more forgiving.*

———————— ❧◦❦◦❧ ————————

Millersburg

"Are you ready to go, sweetie?" Ellen called to her daughter. "We don't want to be late for class number three."

"Okay, I'm ready, Mom." Becky met Ellen at the door with a smile. "How do I look in my new blue-and-white-striped shirt?"

"You look nice, and a little nautical with your red sneakers." Ellen winked, pointing to Becky's feet.

She was happy to see her daughter in a good mood this morning. It seemed she was looking forward to the cooking class, which was a pleasant change. Ellen had a hunch it had something to do with the way things had gone when they'd been fishing with Darren and Jeremy. It had turned out to be a fun day for all, and for the first time since Becky met Jeremy, they'd actually gotten along.

Ellen smiled as she grabbed her cell phone and put it in her purse. She looked forward to seeing Darren today and appreciated the things they had in common. In addition to being single parents, they both enjoyed the outdoors, shared Christian beliefs, and had careers of a helpful nature. It might be too soon to think this way, but Ellen could almost see a future with Darren. It was the first time since she'd adopted Becky that she'd been seriously interested in a man.

"Are we going, or what?" Becky tugged on her mother's arm.

"Of course." Ellen followed her daughter out the door, locking it behind them. *I wonder if Darren's been thinking of me.*

Dover

Darren eyed his son, sitting across the table from him, staring at his bowl of cold cereal. "Aren't you hungry this morning?"

Jeremy shrugged. "I guess."

"You guess you're not hungry, or did you mean you are?"

"I'm not hungry. My stomach doesn't feel right, Dad. Think I might be comin' down with the flu."

Darren wasn't sure whether to take his son seriously, since Jeremy sometimes feigned sickness to get out of doing something. "You wouldn't be trying to get out of going to the cooking class, would you?"

Jeremy lowered his head, rubbing his hand through his messy hair.

"I thought now that you and Becky are getting along better, you wouldn't mind going."

"She's not my best friend, Dad." Jeremy dropped a piece of his toast on the floor for his dog.

Darren didn't approve of feeding the dachshund table scraps but decided not to make an issue of it this time. Bacon looked like he needed some more meat on his bones. "I wasn't insinuating that you and Ellen's daughter are best friends, Jeremy. I just thought—"

"Can we talk about somethin' else?"

"Sure. What do you want to talk about?"

"I don't know. Anything other than Becky or her mother."

"Okay." Darren drummed his fingers on the table. *Does my son have something against Ellen. Do I dare ask?*

Clearing his throat, Darren blurted the question. "How do you feel about Becky's mom? Do you like her, Jeremy?"

"She's okay, I guess." Jeremy rubbed his forearms. "She did catch a nice trout the day we went fishin'."

"That she did." Darren chuckled, remembering Ellen's surprised expression when she reeled in the fish. "So you wouldn't mind if I ask Ellen to go out to dinner with me—just the two of us this time?"

Jeremy blinked rapidly. "How come?"

"Because I enjoy being with Ellen, and I'd like the chance to get to know her better."

"Okay, sure, whatever."

"Maybe we can plan it so you can spend the night with one of your friends."

Jeremy frowned. "I'm not a baby, Dad. I can stay here by myself."

Darren shook his head. "You're not even close to being an adult yet. And until you're a few years older, I will not leave you alone for a long period of time."

Jeremy tossed the dog another piece of toast. "Guess if you think you have to see Ellen alone, I'll talk to my friend, Todd. See if I can spend the night with him."

"Good. I'm glad we got that settled. Now finish your breakfast so we can get on the road. I don't want you to be late for Heidi's class."

"Sounds like you're the one who's excited about going," Jeremy mumbled, picking up his spoon. "Bet the only reason is so you can see Becky's mother again."

Ignoring his son's comment, Darren changed the subject. "I still need to shave, pick out a shirt, and comb my hair."

"Okay." Jeremy spooned some cereal in his mouth.

Darren couldn't deny it. Ever since their time spent at the lake the previous week, Ellen had been on his mind. So much so, that he'd decided to sit in on the cooking class again today. And if he had the opportunity to speak to her privately, before or after the class, he planned to bring up the idea of a dinner date.

Canton

"I don't want to go to Heidi's today. Something bad will happen to me like it did before." The muscles along Kassidy's jawline tensed.

"Life is full of ups and downs, Kassidy." Denise handed her husband a cup of coffee when he took a seat at the kitchen table. "Isn't that right, Greg?"

"Absolutely." He brushed his fingers across his mustache and looked over at Kassidy. "So you'd better get used to it, because you'll be faced with many obstacles over the course of your life."

Kassidy's face slackened as she hunched over. "Well, if that's how it is, then life really stinks."

Denise placed her hand on Kassidy's shoulder. "It does stink sometimes, but if we keep a positive attitude and try to do what's right, it will be easier to deal with problems when they come along. Besides, you'll learn over time the challenges we experience give us a chance to do things better the next time around." Denise thought about her own situation, where the owners of the expensive house she'd hoped to sell had changed their mind and taken it off the market.

Kassidy picked up her glass of milk and took a drink. "It's kinda hard to have a positive attitude when people make fun of my red hair or think it's funny when something bad happens to me. Some of the kids at Heidi's cooking class thought it was hilarious when my blouse got grass and mud stains on it." Her forehead wrinkled deeply. "I don't like any of those kids, and I wish I didn't have to take any more of Heidi's classes."

"Just remember this." Denise touched her daughter's arm. "No matter what age we are, we're never too old to gain knowledge and learn from our mistakes. Same goes for the other kids in the class."

Kassidy grunted. "Well it doesn't seem like they've discovered how to be nice yet."

"Perhaps you could start by setting a good example. Did you read the Bible verse Heidi wrote on the back of the recipe card she gave you during the last class?"

Kassidy shook her head.

Denise rose from her seat and returned to the table with the card. "This is what it says: 'Beloved, let us love one another.'"

Greg looked at her through squinted eyelids. "Is that Amish woman teaching cooking classes or doing a Bible study?"

"We are not studying the Bible, Greg. The Amish are God-fearing people, and I think Heidi just wants to share a little of her faith with the class."

"Yeah, well, that's fine and dandy. Just don't let it go to your head so you end up coming home in a preaching mood." Greg pushed his chair away from the table. "I've got to head out. I'm supposed to meet my friend Arnie at the golf course today." He bent and kissed Denise on the cheek, then landed a quick peck on Kassidy's forehead. "You two have fun at the cooking class."

Kassidy's eyes brightened a bit as she looked up at him. "Okay, Dad, I'll try."

Chapter 22

Walnut Creek

Heidi popped a fresh strawberry in her mouth. Its sweet, juicy flavor made it tempting to eat more, but the others in the bowl were for the strawberry shortcake they'd be making today. She looked forward to another class. Her doubts about teaching children had been erased, for she'd soon learned what a pleasure it was to spend time with them, watching as they learned to make a new recipe. The mouthwatering smell of sweet shortcake she'd made for dessert tonight rose from the oven and brought back memories of Heidi's childhood when her mother made the tasty dessert for their family during the warm summer months.

Looking out toward the garden, an image of Marsha came to mind, with the red stain of strawberries all over her face and hands. Heidi chuckled, thinking how much fun Randy and Marsha had helping her yesterday as they picked the plump berries. The children had eaten more than they picked, but that was the fun of it all.

Heidi had started washing the breakfast dishes when Randy dashed into the kitchen. Sliding to a halt in his stocking feet, he announced, "Someone's car is pulling into the yard out front."

"Okay, thanks for letting me know. Now, please head upstairs and put your shoes on. My students will be here soon for the cooking class."

Randy nodded. "I'll make sure Marsha is wearin' her shoes, too."

"Good idea, Randy. I appreciate you being so helpful."

He scampered out of the kitchen, and Heidi dried her hands on a paper towel, then hurried to the front door to see whose vehicle had pulled in. Since her class wouldn't start for another half hour or so, she figured it wasn't one of her students. But it could be their mailman,

Lance, bringing a package to the house, as he often did.

When Heidi went out to the front porch, she was delighted to see Kendra getting out of her car. She waited in anticipation as the young woman opened the rear door and took her ten-month-old baby girl out of the safety seat. Kendra looked like she'd lost all her baby weight, and she was wearing a pretty, floral dress with pink sandals.

As she watched them approach, Heidi realized this was the first time she'd seen her little namesake without her heart being filled with regrets. Kendra had a right to raise her own child, and Heidi's life had become filled with the joy of taking care of the Olsen children. She and Lyle had talked earlier this week and decided to move forward in taking the necessary steps to adopt Randy and Marsha. It had been over six months since the children's parents died and they'd become wards of the state. In all that time, no relatives had come forth to seek custody, so Heidi felt safe in seeking to adopt Marsha and Randy.

"It's good to see you." When Kendra stepped onto the porch, Heidi greeted her with a hug. "How are you and your little one doing these days?" She reached out and touched the sweet child's silky hair.

Kendra grinned, hoisting her daughter a bit higher on her hip. "Real well. As you can see, little Heidi is growing by leaps and bounds."

"Yes, I can certainly tell."

"If you're not busy, I'd like to come in. I have some exciting news to share with you."

"I'll be teaching another cooking class today, but my young students aren't due to arrive until shortly before ten, so please come in." Heidi opened the front door. "Let's take a seat in the living room and we can visit awhile."

"Okay." Kendra glanced at her watch. "But I'll only stay a few minutes. I apologize for not calling ahead."

"It's not a problem. I'm always pleased to see you and the baby." Heidi reached out her hands. "May I hold her?"

"Of course." Kendra handed her daughter to Heidi, and they both took a seat on the couch.

Heidi stroked the little girl's soft cheeks. "I'm eager to know. What is the exciting news you want to share with me, Kendra?"

Kendra extended her left hand and pointed to the sparkling diamond ring on her finger. "Brent and I got engaged last night. We're planning to be married this December."

Heidi clasped Kendra's hand. "That's wonderful news. I only met Brent the one time when Bill stopped to introduce his son, but he seemed like a nice young man."

"You're right about that, and he's so good with the baby. I think he'll make a great father for little Heidi, not to mention a wonderful husband for me. I'd like it if you and Lyle could come to our wedding in December. I'll send you an invitation as the time gets closer."

"It would be so nice to be a part of your special day."

"I can't stop looking at my ring." Kendra wiggled her hand back and forth as the light caught the diamond and made it sparkle. Then she pointed at the box of toys across the room. "I'm guessing you and Lyle are still foster parents to the children who came to live with you toward the end of last year."

"Yes, we are. Marsha and Randy are upstairs, putting on their shoes. Lyle and I have become quite attached to those two." Heidi leaned closer and lowered her voice. "We are seeking to adopt them, but they don't know yet. No living relatives came forward after their parents died, so we assume that either there are none, or no one wanted the responsibility of raising them. Now, we're just waiting to see if our application gets accepted."

"Now that is good news." Kendra reached into her purse and pulled out a tissue, then wiped a wet spot off the baby's chin. "Sorry about that. She's on the verge of cutting another tooth, so she drools a lot."

Heidi nodded. "They do grow quickly, don't they?"

"You can say that again. It won't be long before my daughter will be toddling all over the place. Ever since she learned how to crawl, the little stinker's been getting into things." Kendra looked at little Heidi with such adoration. "Course, I am not complaining. I'm enjoying every phase of my daughter's babyhood, and so are my folks, as well as my sisters."

"And that's how it should be." Heidi chuckled when the baby stuck her thumb in her mouth and made loud sucking noises.

Kendra rolled her eyes. "She doesn't know about good manners yet."

A forceful knock on the front door interrupted their conversation. Heidi glanced at the clock. It was a quarter to ten. She hadn't heard any vehicles pull into the yard, and figured it might be Velma, since she'd previously come on foot.

"Excuse me, Kendra. I'd better answer that." Heidi handed the baby to her mother and hurried across the room. When she opened the door, she found Velma on the porch with Peggy Ann, as well as a young boy with dark brown hair and eyes that matched.

"I'm here to do more work for you, while Peggy Ann takes her cooking class." Velma motioned to the boy. "This here's my son, Eddie. I didn't want to leave him home alone, so he's gonna be helping me today."

"Oh, I see. Well, perhaps he'd like to come in and take part in the cooking class with his sister."

With a pinched expression, Velma shook her head. "I can't afford to pay for Eddie's lesson, and believe me, it's best that he helps me outside. I'll chop some more wood, and he can stack it for me. Unless there's something else you'd rather have done today."

"No, that's fine. You can start with that. I'll be out later to tell you what else I'd like to have done. That is, if you have time to do anything more than chop wood today."

"I'm sure I'll have the time." Velma dropped her gaze to the wooden planks on the porch. "Workin' helps take my mind off the troubles that seem to keep coming my way."

Heidi was about to comment, when Velma gave her daughter a little push. "You go on inside now, Peggy Ann. And you'd best do whatever Heidi tells you during the cooking class, ya hear?"

Looking up at her mother, Peggy Ann nodded.

Velma turned, took hold of her son's arm, and stepped off the porch. "Come on, Eddie. Let's you and me get to work."

Shoving his hands into the pockets of his bib overalls, the boy mumbled something Heidi didn't understand, but he went along with his mother, kicking a few pebbles in the dirt. It was obvious Velma's son did not want to be here today. He'd probably rather spend the day doing anything other than work.

Back inside, Heidi introduced Peggy Ann to Kendra, then suggested the young girl choose a toy to play with until Randy and Marsha came downstairs or some of the other children arrived.

Kendra gathered up her purse and stood, holding her baby daughter. "Looks like things are gonna get busy around here, so I'd better go. I'll let you know when Brent and I have set an exact date for our wedding. And again, we'd be honored if you and Lyle could be there."

Heidi smiled. "It would be an honor for us to attend." She wrapped Kendra in a warm hug and watched as the young woman went out the door.

A few seconds later, Randy and Marsha appeared, both fully dressed, including their shoes. Without saying a word, they took a seat on the floor next to Peggy Ann. It pleased Heidi to see them interact with the girl. Since Peggy Ann was new to the area, she needed a friend or two.

"I hope that stupid mutt of Heidi's isn't running around the yard today," Kassidy muttered as they approached the Troyers' driveway. "I'm glad I don't have any pets."

Denise glanced in the rearview mirror at her daughter. "What do you mean? Have you forgotten about Tokai?"

"She's not my cat, Mom. She's yours." Kassidy's nose crinkled. "Besides, Tokai doesn't jump on me with dirty paws."

Seeing no other vehicles parked in Heidi's yard, Denise pulled up close to the house. She figured if the dog was running around outside somewhere, the front door wouldn't be too far for them to go.

Seeing no sign of the dog, Denise signaled Kassidy to get out of the car, and she did the same. They were almost to the house when a young dark-haired boy, wearing a pair of faded overalls and a T-shirt with several holes in it, stepped in front of them. "Hey, I'm Eddie. Who are you?"

"My name is Denise McGuire, and this is my daughter, Kassidy. Are you here to take Heidi's cooking class?"

He shook his head briskly. "No way! Cookin' is for girls, not boys."

"How so?" Kassidy crossed her arms.

"My papa says a man's place isn't in the kitchen."

Narrowing her eyes, Kassidy's face tightened. "Oh, yeah? Well, for your information, there are three boys taking Heidi's class. And besides, sometimes, when he has the time, my dad likes to cook, too."

He sneered at her. "So what? Don't mean I wanna cook, so just leave me be."

"Hey, you're the one who approached us. And you know what?"

"What?" Eddie asked, squinting at her.

"You look dorky in those bibs you're wearing." Kassidy's hands went quickly to her hips. "I wouldn't be caught out of the house in those faded old things."

Just then Rusty came bounding around the house. The dog ran up to Eddie and sat by his feet. Eddie knelt on one knee and talked to the dog. "You're a good boy, aren't ya?"

"I see you made a furry friend." Kassidy snickered. "You two mutts deserve each other."

Eyes narrowing into tiny slits, Eddie stood up, but before things could escalate, Denise grabbed her daughter's hand. "You're being rude. Let's go inside."

Kassidy gave Eddie a dismissive nod and quickly stepped onto the porch. Denise followed, giving the boy a backwards glance as he and the Troyers' dog disappeared around the side of the house.

Denise pointed her finger at Kassidy. "What you said to that boy was uncalled for. And let me remind you, young lady, you own a pair of bib overalls yourself."

"But mine are the latest style. They aren't faded and tattered, like his are."

"You haven't learned a thing, have you?" Denise grew more disappointed as she looked at her daughter, wanting to say more. Instead, she turned and gestured to the door. "Let's drop it for now, but don't think this discussion is over."

It was a good thing Eddie wasn't taking part in today's class. Those two would probably go at it the whole time. Kassidy had certainly met her match.

When Darren pulled his SUV into Heidi's yard, he was pleased to see Ellen getting out of her car. This would be the perfect opportunity to talk to her alone.

As soon as Darren got out of his rig, he called out to Ellen. She turned and smiled.

"Can I talk to you a minute, before you go inside?" he asked.

"Certainly." Ellen looked at Becky. "Why don't you go ahead in?"

The girl shook her head. "That's okay. I'll wait till you're ready to go in the house."

Oh, great. Darren struggled not to give an impatient huff. *Should I ask Ellen for a date, with her daughter standing here?* Of course, Jeremy had gotten out of the car now, too, and stood near Darren, shifting from one foot to the other. *Well, it's better to have it out in the open with Becky and Jeremy here,* Darren decided, since he'd already discussed it with his son.

He moved closer to Ellen. "I was wondering if you'd like to go out to dinner with me one night next week. Just the two of us this time."

Ellen glanced at Becky, then looked back at Darren. "That sounds nice. Would Friday night work for you?"

Nodding, he grinned. "That'd be great. I'll pick you up at six, if that's okay."

"Six will be fine."

Whew, that's a relief. Darren closed his eyes briefly. When he opened them again and saw the obvious displeasure on Becky's face, the joy he felt seconds ago was replaced with concern. Apparently Ellen's daughter wasn't thrilled about him dating her mother. *Well, our kids will have to deal with it, because Ellen and I have the right to date whomever we choose.*

Chapter 23

"I wish you and Daddy could both take us to the cooking class," Kevin announced from the back seat of Miranda's minivan. "Then we could all learn to cook together."

"Mommy already knows how to cook," Debbie put in. "Besides, Daddy has to work today."

Kevin spoke again. "I miss him and wish he'd come home to live with us, like he did before."

Miranda cringed. Sometimes she felt guilty for asking Trent to move out, especially knowing how much the kids missed him. Even so, she couldn't let him come waltzing back until she saw a true change in his behavior. Sending gifts and making promises he might not keep in order to lure her in simply wouldn't do.

Shifting mental gears, Miranda turned into the Troyers' driveway. Seeing that three other vehicles were already there, she hoped she and the children weren't late.

New Philadelphia

Trent had only been at work an hour, when a stabbing pain started on his right side, radiating to his back, and making him feel nauseous. As he rubbed the area, and took a deep breath, Trent tried to recall what he might have done to make it hurt this much. But he hadn't done anything strenuous lately, except being on his feet several hours at work yesterday.

Oh no! Trent rubbed the bridge of his nose as he leaned against a shiny new car in the showroom. *I hope this isn't another kidney stone.* Trent remembered all too well the stone he'd passed a few years ago. It was the worst pain he'd ever experienced, and he'd hoped he would never have to go through anything like that again.

As Trent headed toward his boss's office, he felt relief that for a Saturday, no customers had shown up yet. He found Herb sitting at his desk going over some papers. "Trent, come on in and sit down. It's been a slow morning so far, hasn't it?" Herb got up to pour himself a cup of coffee. "Would you like a cup?"

"No thanks." Trent inhaled sharply as the pain grew worse. "Think I need to head home. I'm not feeling well all of a sudden."

"Sure, sure, Trent." Herb's thick eyebrows furrowed. "I can handle things here. Do you think you're coming down with something?"

"I can't say for sure, but I believe I'm having a kidney stone attack."

"Oh my, you'd better get on home then. My brother gets kidney stones, and I know from what he's told me, how bad they can be—especially if they're difficult to pass." Herb's brows came together in a frown. "Do you want me to drive you home?"

"Thanks, but my apartment isn't far from here." Trent started to leave, then turned back. "Hopefully, if I pass this stone quickly, I'll be back to work on Monday."

"Just let me know." Herb waved him off. "Get going now, and be careful driving home."

Walnut Creek

"Now that the Coopers have arrived, let's all go into the kitchen." Heidi led the way, and everyone followed.

Ellen noticed her daughter's solemn expression as she took a seat at the table. *Becky doesn't want me to go out with Darren. She's had me all to herself since she was a baby and obviously feels threatened by me dating for the first time in ten years.*

Ellen took a step away from the table, contemplating things further. *Should I tell Darren I've changed my mind about going out with him and end this relationship now, before it goes any further?*

Ellen felt trapped between wanting to please Becky and fulfilling her own needs. She could see herself perhaps having a future with Darren, but not if Becky wouldn't accept him. *I'm thinking ahead too far,* she berated herself. *It's too soon to know if there's even a possibility of a future with Darren.* She tipped her head. *I wonder how Jeremy feels about his dad going out with me. If I give this relationship a try, maybe Becky will come around and be okay with it. I certainly hope so, because the more I get to know Darren, the more I like him.*

"As you can see, everything you will need to make the shortcake is on the table." Heidi gestured to the dry ingredients, as well as the milk, vanilla, softened butter, and one egg for each child. "Now, the first thing you'll need to do is cream the sugar and butter in your mixing bowl."

Peggy Ann's pale eyebrows squished together. "How are we supposed to make the sugar and butter turn into cream?"

Heidi smiled at the child's innocent question. "It won't turn into cream, Peggy Ann. When I said 'cream the sugar and butter,' I meant, stir the ingredients in the bowl until they are creamy."

Peggy Ann's cheeks puffed out as she huffed. "Why didn't ya just say that then?"

Heidi lifted her hands and let them fall to her sides. "You're right. I should have explained it better. So now, let's all get our butter and sugar mixed." Heidi stood next to Marsha and helped her put the ingredients in the bowl and stir them around.

Marsha looked up at Heidi and grinned. "This is fun, Mammi."

Heidi smiled in return. "I'm glad you're enjoying it, and I hope everyone else is also."

"Not me. I think this is boring, and if you ask me—"

Denise poked her daughter's arm. "Kassidy, I'm warning you."

Kassidy's mouth clamped shut, and she picked up her wooden spoon.

While Heidi couldn't say she noticed much improvement in the young girl's belligerent attitude, she did see a change in Kassidy's mother's behavior. Denise seemed more determined to make her daughter behave. Kassidy was one of the oldest children taking this class, but so far, she wasn't setting a good example for the others. Heidi could only hope that in time things would improve, but she wished there was something specific she could say or do to make it happen quickly.

Once the children had finished the first step, Heidi asked them to add the milk, egg, and vanilla, and then mix well. She was impressed with Randy and the younger children in their determination to do a good job and keep up with the older students.

"This smells good. I can't wait to eat the cake when it's done." Kevin smacked his lips. "Bet my daddy would like it, and I think he'd be proud of me for learnin' how to cook."

Heidi smiled. "I'm sure he would, and I'm pleased that you followed directions."

"What do we do next?" Debbie wanted to know.

"You'll add the dry ingredients." Heidi was pleased that none of the parents here today stepped in and took over for the children—although it was nice to have their assistance when needed.

Once everyone had mixed their dry ingredients, Heidi showed them how to pour the batter into their baking dish. "We can bake four at a time, and when those are done, the other three can go in. Who would like to be first?"

Peggy Ann's hand shot up, and so did Randy's. "Okay, why don't we let the younger children bake their cake first? That would be Peggy Ann, Randy, Marsha, and Kevin."

"How come they get to go first?" Kassidy's eyes narrowed. "I shouldn't have to bake mine last just because I'm older than them."

"Kassidy. . ." Denise spoke firmly, and her daughter backed down.

"Okay, whatever."

"While the first pans are in the oven, you children can chop and sweeten the berries. As you're doing that, I'll whip the whipping cream with my egg beater."

Peggy Ann's face scrunched up. "What's an egg beater?"

"This is what I'm talking about." Heidi held up the device. "When you turn the handle really fast, it will stir things up quickly."

"My mom uses an electric mixer to make whipping cream and stuff like that." Becky snickered. "One time she beat the cream too long and ended up with butter."

Ellen's cheeks grew pink. "Guilty as charged, I admit. That's what can happen when a person starts thinking about one thing while doing something else."

"What were ya thinkin' about?" Peggy Ann asked.

"Well, that happened some time ago, and I don't remember what it was. All I know is we couldn't use the whipping cream on our pudding that night."

Heidi glanced at Jeremy. While he'd done everything she asked and had his cake batter ready to go into the oven, the boy hadn't said one word since he'd come into the kitchen. And he hadn't so much as cracked a smile—not even when someone said something funny.

I wonder if he's upset about something. Or maybe Jeremy isn't feeling well today. Heidi was on the verge of saying something to the boy, when he grabbed his stomach, leaped out of his chair, and raced for the bathroom. The other children sat with their mouths partially open, while Darren ran down the hall after his son. Heidi wasn't sure what to do.

Finally, after gathering her wits, she helped the younger ones put their cake pans into the oven. Hopefully, Jeremy wasn't seriously ill, and things would go better for the rest of this class.

New Philadelphia

The drive from the dealership was short, but with the pain Trent was in, the road seemed to stretch for miles before he got home to the comfort of his apartment. All he wanted to do was take an ibuprofen, lie down on his bed, and wait for the pain to subside. *I wish Miranda was with me right now. I need some TLC.*

Sometime later, after the stone had passed, Trent collapsed on his bed, exhausted.

Like the last time after the kidney stone passed, Trent had a few bouts of pain, but it didn't compare to what he'd just been through. "Guess I won't go back to work today," he mumbled. "I better take it easy till Monday."

Trent fluffed up his pillow and stared at the ceiling. *Wonder how the kids are doing at the cooking class this morning? Maybe I should surprise them and drive to Heidi's. It would probably surprise Miranda, and she might even think it was nice if I showed up.*

But after thinking it through, Trent realized he wasn't up to going anywhere right now.

After resting for an hour in a comfy pair of sweatpants, he got up, made his way to the kitchen, and fixed himself a cup of coffee.

"What am I gonna do now?" Rubbing his hand through his thick hair, Trent looked around his too-quiet apartment. *Maybe I'll clean my golf clubs and wash the towels that are in the bag.* "I'm sure they need it."

Trent still used the clubs and bag Miranda had bought him on their first anniversary. He smiled, remembering the day she'd surprised him with this special gift.

Sipping at his coffee, he took each of the clubs out and laid them on the table. Then he went through the different compartments and pulled out the terry-cloth towels. He held them up to his nose. "Oh yeah, these definitely need to be washed."

Trent went to another pocket of the golf bag and unzipped the closure. Reaching in, he pulled out an envelope. Inside was the anniversary card Miranda had given him many years ago with the golf clubs and bag.

Trent smiled as he fondly remembered that day. They were so much in love and enjoyed every minute of being together. His smile faded. *What went wrong anyway?*

He looked at the front of the card with two doves holding a heart. Then he opened it and read the hand-written message Miranda had included inside the card:

> *Trent,*
>
> *Happy Anniversary to my wonderful husband. This first year of our marriage has been like a fairy tale for me, because you are in my life.*
>
> *I know, as the years go by, we may have problems or challenges to face, but as long as we can work through them together, our relationship will only grow stronger.*
>
> *Thank you for giving me a wonderful first year.*

I am so blessed knowing I'll be spending the rest of my life with you.

> *I'll love you forever,*
> *Miranda*

Closing the card and holding it against his chest, Trent blinked tears from his eyes. His heart felt empty without Miranda. He missed his wife, he missed his kids, and he missed doing things together as a family. It was scary being sick all alone this morning, remembering how his wife had fussed when he'd dealt with his first kidney stone.

How could I have been so stupid as to jeopardize our marriage like I did? Somehow, I have to prove to Miranda that it will never happen again. I have to gain her trust, and maybe now, I know how.

Chapter 24

Walnut Creek

Darren waited outside the bathroom until Jeremy finished emptying his stomach. He felt like a heel, forcing the boy to come to class when he'd complained earlier that his stomach bothered him. But Darren figured his son might have been using it as an excuse to stay home. If he'd had any idea Jeremy was really sick, he would have called Heidi and left a message, explaining their absence.

When Jeremy stepped out of the bathroom, his pale face and sagging features said it all. "Dad, I'm sick. My head hurts, and my belly's still churning."

Darren placed his hand on Jeremy's shoulder. "Sorry, Son. I should have listened to you this morning when you said you weren't feeling well." He handed Jeremy his keys. "Why don't you go out to the car and wait for me? I'll explain the situation to Heidi, and let her know that I'm taking you home."

"Okay." Holding his stomach, Jeremy made his way down the hall and out the front door.

As Darren headed back to the kitchen, he berated himself for not paying closer attention to Jeremy. What made it worse was he knew the reason.

Unwrapping a piece of peppermint gum, he popped it into his mouth. *I didn't want to miss seeing Ellen today. That's the real reason I ignored my son's complaint.*

When Darren entered the kitchen, he crossed over to Heidi and said, "Jeremy is sick, so I'm taking him home. Someone else can enjoy his shortcake when it's done."

"I'll finish Jeremy's dessert and then bring it by your house after class," Ellen offered.

Darren smiled. "That's nice of you, but I don't think Jeremy will be up to eating much of anything the rest of the day."

"It will keep in the refrigerator for a few days," Heidi spoke up. "Since I've made extra, I'll give one to Ellen for you, too."

"Okay, thanks." Darren hesitated, wishing he could speak to Ellen privately. But then if she was coming by later, he'd have a chance to talk to her then. Right now, he had to get his son home. Darren said a quick goodbye to everyone and headed out the door.

———————— ❧◦⁀◦❧ ————————

"I bet that kid has the flu." Kassidy blew out a breath that rattled her lips. "And now everyone here will probably get it, because he was spreading his germs all over the place."

Denise tapped her daughter's shoulder. "You can't be sure. It might be something else that upset Jeremy's stomach. Besides, if he does have the flu, it doesn't mean the rest of us will come down with it."

"That's right," Ellen agreed. "In my years of nursing, I have seen many patients get sick with the flu, while none of their family came down with it."

Kassidy made an unladylike grunt and looked the other way.

"Mom, you're not going inside when you drop off Jeremy's dessert, I hope." Becky clasped her hands together, positioning them under her chin.

Ellen shook her head. "I'll take the shortcake up to the door, and you can wait in the car."

"Okay, but don't get too close to Jeremy. Like Kassidy said, he could be contagious."

"I'm sure it won't be him who comes to the door," Ellen assured her daughter. "Besides, didn't you hear what I said about the flu? If it even is the flu Jeremy has come down with."

Becky bobbed her head. "I heard, but I think Kassidy's right. We could all end up sick because of him. He shoulda stayed home today."

"Bet he didn't feel sick this mornin'," Peggy Ann spoke. "I threw up at school once, but I felt fine when I first woke up."

Feeling the need for a topic change, Heidi broke in. "Let's finish baking our shortcakes and cutting up the berries. Then, when the cake is cooled enough, we can go outside and sit at the picnic table to enjoy the dessert."

———————————•ↄ∞ↄ•———————————

Velma paused from chopping to see how Eddie was doing. He'd taken a wheelbarrow full of wood around the corner of the barn fifteen minutes ago and still wasn't back. She reached under her scarf and scratched her head. *I'm sure it couldn't have taken him that long to unload that kindling.*

She set the axe aside, pulled a hanky from the back pocket of her overalls, and wiped her sweaty forehead. Then Velma grabbed her bottle of water and took a swig. Still no sign of Eddie.

"Ouch." Velma winced, almost choking on the water. Throwing the bottle aside, she leaned down and picked up the axe that had fallen against her knee. Pulling up her pant leg, she rubbed the spot where the handle hit. *I'll probably have a black-and-blue spot by nightfall. At least it was the handle, and not the blade, that walloped into me.* She rubbed her knee a few more times, then pulled her pant leg down. *Don't even wanna think about what coulda happened if the blade of the axe had hit my knee.*

Making sure she propped the axe in a safer position, Velma looked around. *I wonder what that boy is up to. Wouldn't be surprised if he's not off somewhere, playin' with the Troyers' dog.*

Velma limped toward the woodshed, and was halfway there, when she spotted Eddie squatted beside the chicken coop with his nose pressed against the screened enclosure. "What are you doin' out here?" Velma came alongside of him. "You're supposed to be stacking wood."

"I did stack what I put in the wheelbarrow. But when I was done I decided to come look at the chickens." Eddie pointed. "They're sure scrawny-lookin', ain't they, Mama?"

"That's 'cause they're not fully grown." Velma knelt next to him. "Why, by the end of summer, these chicks will be fully grown—just like the chickens we'll be gettin' soon."

"Havin' chickens means a lot of work, don't it, Mama?"

"Yeah, but we'll all take turns feeding them and cleaning their coop. It'll pay off, too, when they start layin' eggs."

Eddie tipped his head to one side as he looked at her. "Who's 'we all,' Mama? Papa ain't home that much 'cause of his job, so there's just you, me, and Peggy Ann to do everything. It ain't fair."

"I know, Son, but we'll manage."

"Sure wish Bobbie Sue wouldn't have run off." With tears gathering in his eyes, Eddie's shoulders drooped. "Guess she don't care about us no more."

"No, I don't think it's that."

"Maybe she left 'cause you yelled at her so much. It ain't fun to be hollered at all the time, ya know."

Velma's chest ached, and tears blurred her vision. Eddie was right. She did yell a lot. Once more, she felt like an unfit mother, who probably should have never had any children. She sure wouldn't be getting any mother-of-the-year awards. That she knew was a fact.

—————◦◦◦◦————

After everyone's shortcake had cooled sufficiently, Heidi asked if Ellen, Miranda, and Denise would oversee the children while they each cut up their berries. Then, everyone would go outside.

Denise smiled. "Of course, I'd be glad to do that."

Ellen nodded. "Same here."

"I'm fine with it, too." Miranda got up from her chair. "You do whatever you need to do, Heidi. We're more than happy to help out."

"Thanks, ladies. While you're doing that, I'll go outside and see if Velma and Eddie would like to join us at the picnic table. I'm sure they could use a break from the work they've been doing for me this morning."

"That makes sense," Miranda said. "You go right ahead."

When Heidi entered the backyard a few minutes later, she was surprised to see Velma and Eddie kneeling beside the chicken coop. As she drew closer, she realized they were both crying. Heidi hesitated, wondering how best to approach them.

She didn't have to ponder things long, for Velma must have heard her coming. Sniffing, she reached up and dried her eyes, using an old hanky, then quickly stuffed it back in her pocket. "Sorry about that. You caught me bawlin' like a baby, when I shoulda been workin'." She rose to her feet, pulling Eddie up as well. "We'll get right back to work."

Heidi shook her head, watching Eddie swipe a finger under his nose. "There's no need for that. It's time for you both to take a break. In today's cooking class we made strawberry shortcake, and we're going to eat it out on the picnic table soon. I came out to invite you and Eddie to join us."

"That's real nice of you, but I think we'd better pass." Velma gestured to the smudges of dirt on her face. "I must look a mess."

"I'm not worried about that, and I'm sure it won't bother the others either. What I am concerned with is why you've been crying. Is there something you wish to talk about?"

A crimson flush crept across Velma's cheeks. "I don't wanna take up your time with my problems. You've got better things to do than listen to me bellyaching."

Speaking softly, Heidi touched Velma's arm. "I don't mind listening at all. Talking about your problem might help you feel better."

Velma turned her head toward the house when three ladies and the children filtered out the door toward the yard. "O–okay." She looked at Eddie. "You go on over to the picnic table and join the others. I'll be there shortly."

"Ya mean I get to have some cake?" Eddie looked at his mother first, then over at Heidi.

Heidi smiled. "Yes, you sure do."

The boy didn't have to be told twice. He whirled around and took off toward the picnic table like a bee was in hot pursuit of him.

Velma grunted. "My boy has more energy than he knows what to do with. Maybe that's why he gets into so much trouble at times."

Heidi motioned to a wooden bench Lyle had built and placed under the shade of a maple tree. "Let's take a seat over there, and you can tell me what has caused you to feel so troubled."

Velma followed Heidi silently to the bench, and once they were seated, she proceeded to pour her heart out. She began by sharing details of how her oldest son had left home a few years ago, and they'd lost contact with him.

"Oh my, this is so hard to talk about." Tears slipped from Velma's eyes and rolled down her blotchy, red cheeks. The dirt on her face ran down as well, and smeared like wet paint that had been thinned too much. Reaching into her pocket she took out the hanky and wiped it across her cheek. "Then to make things worse, my oldest daughter, Bobbie Sue, ran off with her boyfriend one night last week. She didn't bother to tell her dad or me, face-to-face, of course—just left a note that I found the next day."

Velma paused long enough to wipe her nose with the hanky. "I feel like a terrible mother, who must have let her kids down. I mean, why else would Bobbie Sue and our son Clem have run off without tellin' us why? They both must have hated their life at home. We'll probably never see either of them again."

Heidi tugged her ear, thinking about the best way to respond. She certainly didn't want to say anything that would make Velma feel worse. *Help me, Lord. Please give me the right words.*

"I'm scared outa my wits, Heidi. If things don't change for our family soon, I fear my two youngest kids might run off during their teen years, too."

Heidi reached for Velma's hand and gave it a tender squeeze. "Do you attend church anywhere, and is there a minister you can talk to about all this?"

Velma shook her head. "Never been one to go to church. Hank don't go, neither. He thinks it's a waste of time and says there are too many hypocrites in church." She chuckled. "My thoughts are, if the church is full of hypocrites, then I guess there's room for two more, because me and my husband sure ain't perfect. If we were, our kids wouldn't have turned out so bad."

"I think you're being too hard on yourself. None of us is perfect, and life can be difficult, even when we are trying to do what is right." Heidi paused to collect her thoughts. "Even for those of us who attend church regularly and try to set a Christian example, we have no guarantee that our children or other family members will not go astray.

We do the best we can, and ask God daily for wisdom and strength to endure the trials we sometimes must face. And when things go wrong, and we feel like we can't cope, we reach out to others and ask for help." Heidi slipped her arm around Velma's shoulder. "I'll be praying for you, and whenever you need to talk, please feel free to share your burdens with me. It always seems to help when I'm upset about something if I talk it out."

Velma pressed both palms to her chest. "Whew, I feel like I've just been to church and heard a great message—one I needed to hear, mind you. Thanks, Heidi."

"You're welcome." Heidi rose from the bench. "Now, should we join the others for a refreshing dessert?"

"Yeah, that'd be nice."

As they made their way across the grass to the picnic table, Heidi sent up a silent prayer. *Heavenly Father, please show me something specific I can do to let Velma and her family know how much You love and care about them.*

Chapter 25

Dover

"How do you even know where Darren and Jeremy live?" Becky asked when Ellen turned off the main highway and into Dover.

"He gave me their address the day we went fishing with them."

"Oh."

Ellen glanced back at Becky, slouched in her safety seat. "We had a good time that day, huh?"

"Yeah, I guess."

"It was good to see you getting along better with Jeremy. I think he's a nice boy, especially when he untangled your fishing line."

Becky hunched her shoulders. "He's okay."

"Darren's nice, too. I enjoy being with him."

"Yeah, I can tell."

Ellen turned left at the next street, drove a few blocks, and stopped. "This must be their place. I see Darren's SUV parked out front." She turned off the engine, picked up the plastic containers on the seat beside her, and opened the car door. "I'll be back in a few minutes."

As Ellen walked across the yard, she couldn't help admiring Darren's tan-colored, split-level home with a brick facade. It had a welcoming feel, and so did the well-manicured yard. She wondered how he found the time to keep it looking so nice.

When Ellen stepped onto Darren's front porch, she was surprised to see a pot filled with petunias hanging next to a hummingbird feeder. She smiled. Feeding the birds and appreciating flowers added to the list of things she and Darren had in common.

As Ellen stood quietly, she heard a buzzing sound she thought was a bee. But when she turned slightly, she saw a hummingbird hovering near her head. It flicked back and forth mere inches from her face. Then just as quickly, it swooped down and landed on the feeder. Ellen had to suppress a giggle, watching the tiny bird's beak dart in and out between sips. Then another hummingbird appeared out of nowhere and dive-bombed the one at the feeder, giving chase to it up toward the trees.

Turning back, Ellen was about to ring the doorbell when the front door opened, and Darren, with a little dog following him, stepped out to greet her. "I was watching a hummingbird at your feeder." Ellen pointed to the trees. "Then another one chased it off."

"They're at each other constantly." Darren shook his head. "I even put another feeder out back, hoping they could feed without being so territorial, but they chase after each other there, too."

"Aw, what a cute little dog." Ellen looked down at the dachshund, which was sniffing her shoes.

"This little fella is Jeremy's dog, Bacon." Darren's cheeks colored. "Well, he's kinda my dog, too. I can't help but love the pooch." He reached down to pick the dog up.

Ellen giggled when Bacon licked doggie kisses all over his face. Then she asked, "How is Jeremy doing?"

"About the same. He's running a fever, so I'm almost sure it's the flu."

"Sounds like it. Be sure to give him plenty of fluids."

Darren grinned. "Yes, Nurse Ellen."

Her cheeks warmed. "Sorry about that. Whenever anyone is sick, my nursing instincts kick in."

"It's okay. I don't mind." His brows furrowed. "If Caroline were still alive she'd be playing nursemaid, and I wouldn't have to do anything more than worry."

Ellen saw the pain in Darren's eyes. No doubt, he still missed his wife. Hoping to lighten the mood, she handed him two plastic containers filled with strawberry shortcake. "Heidi sent one for you, and one for Jeremy, when he feels up to eating."

"Thanks. I'll enjoy mine tonight, but it may be a day or so before Jeremy eats his."

Ellen shifted her weight. "Well, I'd better go and let you and your dog get back inside."

"Okay, and thanks for coming by." Darren touched her arm. "I'm still planning to take you out for dinner next Friday, but if Jeremy isn't better by then I'll let you know."

She moved her head slowly up and down. "I'll be praying for him, and if there's anything I can do, please let me know."

"I will." Darren pulled his hand aside. "Have a good weekend, Ellen."

"You too." She turned and hurried to her car. *Oh, Darren, you're such a nice man. Where have you been all my life?*

Berlin

When Miranda pulled her minivan into her driveway, she spotted Trent sitting in a silver-gray mid-sized car. *No doubt another vehicle from the dealership where he works. I wonder what Trent wants this time.*

"Daddy's here! Daddy's here!" Kevin shouted from the back seat. "I hope he brought us something."

Miranda grimaced. Trent's gifts, even for the kids, meant nothing to her. She wished he would realize that.

She'd barely turned off the ignition, when Debbie and Kevin hopped out of the van and ran up to greet Trent as he stepped out of his vehicle.

By the time Miranda joined them, he was squatted down with his arms surrounding both kids. "What are you doing here, Trent?" she questioned. "This is not your weekend with the children."

"I am well aware." He stared at her intently. "I came by to give you something."

Miranda stiffened. "No thanks. The last time you brought me something there were strings attached. You can talk to Debbie and Kevin for a while if you want to, but I've got work to do inside." Without waiting for a response, she whirled around and hurried into the house.

As Miranda marched off, Trent stood, clenching his jaw. *Why couldn't she have at least given me a chance to show her the card I found? Maybe I should give it to one of the kids and ask them to show it to their mom.* His forehead wrinkled. *Or would it be better to wait for another time, when Miranda's in a more receptive mood? Of course, that may never happen. What does she want from me, anyway? Am I supposed to sit up and beg like a dog?*

Kevin tugged on Trent's hand. "How come you're frowning, Daddy? Don't ya like what I said?"

Trent swept a hand across his furrowed brow. "Sorry, Son, I must've missed it. What did you say?"

"I was tellin' you what we made at the cooking class today."

"Oh? What was it?"

"Shortcake, and we put strawberries from Heidi's garden over the top."

"And don't forget the whipping cream," Debbie interjected. Her eyes looked as bright as shiny new pennies. "It was sure good."

"I'll bet it was." Trent's thoughts went to Miranda again, and the delicious strawberry shortcakes she'd made over the years. In addition to wishing for his wife's companionship, he missed her great cooking.

"Did ya bring us anything, Daddy?" Kevin asked, pulling Trent's thoughts aside once more.

"Uh, no. Not today, Son. I did bring your mother something, though."

Debbie frowned. "Mommy doesn't like it when you bring her gifts. I heard her say so when she was talking to Grandma on the phone the other day."

Trent resisted the urge to say something negative about his mother-in-law. The kids loved their grandparents, and he wasn't about to spoil their relationship. He could only imagine, though, what Alta's response was when Miranda told her that. Whenever Trent had been around Miranda's folks, he'd always felt that he never quite measured up. It was like they—especially, Alta—felt as though their daughter could have done better in choosing a husband. He wasn't sure if it was his job they didn't approve of, or maybe his personality rubbed them the wrong way.

"I don't think your mom will mind what I brought for her today." Trent opened the car door and reached inside, where he'd placed the card on the passenger's seat. He'd kept it in its original envelope so it wouldn't get wrinkled. "Would you please see that your mom gets this?" He held the envelope out to Debbie.

She hesitated at first, but finally reached for the card.

"Thanks, sweetie." Trent bent down and hugged both kids again. "I should get going now, but I'll see you guys next Saturday."

"Why can't you stay, Daddy?" Debbie's soulful eyes looked directly at him.

"I would, honey, but this morning I wasn't feeling well. I passed a kidney stone, so I'd like to go home and rest a little more."

Kevin looked up at Trent with a hopeful expression. "Are we gonna do anything fun when you pick us up next Saturday?"

"Yeah. I'm not sure what yet, but I'll come up with something you and your sister will enjoy." He opened his car door, but then turned back around to face Debbie. "Don't forget to give your mom the card."

"Okay, Dad."

Trent got in the car and sat watching as the kids went into the house. Clenching his fingers around the steering wheel, he murmured, "I hope that card jogs Miranda's memory and she comes to her senses. If this doesn't do the trick, I'll have to come up with something else."

Walnut Creek

After setting lunch on the table, Heidi stepped outside to call Marsha and Randy. It was no surprise when she discovered them standing by the chicken's enclosure.

"Lunch is ready." Heidi put a hand on top of both of their heads.

"Can we come back and watch the *hinkel* after we eat?" Randy asked.

Heidi smiled. It was a pleasure to hear him using the Pennsylvania Dutch word for chickens. "Of course you can. And a little bit later, you can give them fresh water and more food."

Randy grinned up at her. "I like takin' care of the hinkel."

"You've been doing a good job." She pointed to the house. "But right now, lunch is waiting."

"Okay." Randy grabbed his sister's hand. "Let's go, Marsha!"

Heidi followed, but she'd only made it halfway to the house when Lyle's driver pulled into the yard. She waited until Lyle got out of the van.

"How'd your class go today?" he asked, joining her on the lawn and slipping his arm around her waist.

"For the most part it was good, but one of my young students got sick and had to go home. I think Jeremy may have come down with the flu."

"That's too bad. I hope no one else gets it." Lyle handed Heidi his lunch pail. "Would you mind taking this into the house while I go out to the barn to check on our horse? She was favoring one of her back legs before I left for the auction this morning, and I want to make sure she's okay."

"No problem. I hope Bobbins is all right. But before you go, I'd like to ask you a question."

He paused. "Sure, what's up?"

"Well, today, when I went out to invite Velma and her son to join us for strawberry shortcake, I found her in tears. Him too."

He tipped his head. "Oh? Did she tell you what was wrong?"

"Jah. Apparently, Velma's teenage daughter ran off with her boyfriend recently, and Velma is quite depressed. Her oldest son also left home a few years ago, and they've had no contact with him since."

Lyle shook his head. "What a shame. It has to be difficult for Velma and her husband."

"It is, and also for the younger kids, too. As I've mentioned before, they've had some financial problems since they moved here, which I'm sure has contributed to Velma's emotional state. I'm wondering if there isn't something we can do to help that family."

"I'll have to give it some thought, but in the meantime, why don't we invite them over for an indoor supper or an outdoor barbecue some evening? It will give us a chance to get to know them better," Lyle suggested. "I've seen her husband a few times, but all we did was wave at each other. If we spend some time with them, it might give us a better idea of their needs and how we might help out."

Heidi nodded. "Good idea. I'll contact Velma sometime next week and extend an invitation to supper."

"Oh, and speaking of next week. . . Don't forget about the auction coming up on Saturday. There will be lots of good food available and some interesting things to see. I think it will be a fun outing for Marsha and Randy."

Heidi smiled. "I believe you're right. And now, I'd better get inside and make sure the kids washed their hands before sitting down at the table."

Lyle slipped his arm around Heidi's waist again, hugging her tenderly. "I'll be in soon to join you for lunch."

Before heading inside, Heidi glanced toward the birdhouse at the far end of their property. The other day, while watering her flowers, she'd watched a pair of bluebirds catching bugs and taking them into the birdhouse—a sure sign they had a family to feed.

As Heidi walked slowly across the yard, she squinted her eyes to get a better look. "Hmm. . . Now why does it look so odd?"

When she drew closer to the little house Lyle had attached to a fence post, Heidi realized one of their barn cats sat upon the roof of the birds' dwelling. Little tweets and chirps came from inside, as the parent birds frantically swooped toward the cat, then landed in the nearby tree. Their loud and frantic *chit, chit, chit* let Heidi know the bluebirds were not happy with this intruder so close to their home with babies inside.

Scurrying to get there quickly, Heidi picked up her pace. Just as the cat reached a paw inside the small entrance, Heidi clapped her hands. "Oh no you don't! Shame on you. Now scat!"

The orange-colored feline had been so intent on trying to get the baby birds, the sound of Heidi's clapping startled him. It was hard to suppress her giggles when the tabby jumped off the roof, with his paw still inside the opening, and dangled there in midair a few seconds before dropping to the ground. It looked like a streak of orange as the cat made a beeline toward the barn.

"That will teach you." Heidi watched a few more minutes, as one of the bluebirds flew into the little house. A few seconds later, it zipped out again, while the other parent bird sailed in with a bug in its mouth.

Satisfied, after hearing little chirps coming from the hungry babies inside, Heidi hummed as she made her way back to the house. Next week would be busy, but she didn't mind. Between doing something neighborly for Velma and her family, and spending time with the children, she felt sure it would be a satisfying week.

Chapter 26

"How come you're limpin' 'round the kitchen, Mama?" Peggy Ann asked as Velma moved slowly about the room, getting supper ready.

"I told you before—my knee hurts from where the handle of the axe fell against it today." Velma grunted. "Don't ya listen to anything I say?"

Peggy Ann's hair hung in her face as she lowered her head. "S–sorry. Guess I forgot."

Shuffling over to her daughter, Velma pulled the child into her arms. She wished she could take back her harsh words. "No, I'm the one who should be sorry. Didn't mean to be so cross. I'm just tired, hurtin', and hungry, to boot."

Eddie burst into the room. "I'm hungry, too. What's for supper, Mama?"

She pointed to the stove. "I'm heating some leftover vegetable soup, and we'll have cheese and crackers to go with it. Nothing exciting, but at least it'll fill our bellies."

"Will we be havin' any dessert?" Peggy Ann wanted to know.

Velma shook her head. "Nope. You two had your dessert at Heidi's, remember?"

Eddie smacked his lips. "It was sure good."

"That it was. And since your sister came home with the recipe, we can make strawberry shortcake sometime. I'm sure it'll be as good as what we had today." Velma took three bowls down from the cupboard. "You two go wash up now, while I dish out the soup."

The children scampered out of the kitchen, and Velma hobbled over to get the soup ladle.

Pulling and tugging, Velma blew out an exasperated breath. "Now why won't this stubborn drawer open?" She rattled it and jiggled it in every direction, but it wouldn't budge. "Come on you stupid thing. Don't I have enough troubles already?"

Velma stopped for a minute to catch her breath. She hoped Hank would be home soon with some money. Their food supplies were running low, and some things needed to be fixed around the house— including now, this kitchen drawer.

Once more, Velma wished she could look for a job. But what would she do with Eddie and Peggy Ann while she was at work? She couldn't leave them home by themselves. That would be asking for trouble. And then there was her need for transportation. If she took a job at one of the stores or restaurants anywhere—even one of the small towns here in Holmes County— it would require a car.

Staring at the drawer, Velma knew it wouldn't open itself. She grabbed the handle one more time, and with one final tug, the drawer flew open, almost sending Velma backward to the floor. Apparently the soup ladle had been stuck, keeping the drawer from opening. It was bent, but, at least, still usable. "Why can't anything ever be simple?" she mumbled.

"Cause it ain't."

Velma jumped at the sound of her husband's booming voice. "Hank, I—I didn't hear your rig pull in. How long have ya been here?"

"Long enough to say hi to the kids." He moved toward Velma. "What's the matter with you, woman? Are ya goin' deaf? That truck of mine's loud enough to wake the dead."

Velma's chin quivered. "You don't have to holler, Hank. I'm standing right here."

His eyes narrowed. "What's going on? You look like you're gonna start bawling."

"I'm tired, and I've had a rough day." She motioned to the pot of soup on the stove. "The kids and I are about ready to have supper. Have you eaten yet?"

"Nope."

"Okay, I'll set you a place." Velma took out another bowl and put it on the table where Hank normally sat when he was at home. "Can I talk to you about something?"

"Sure, what's up?" He pulled out a chair and sat down.

Velma moved to stand beside him. "I was talkin' to Heidi today—told her about our two oldest running off."

His face tightened. "Ya got no call to be tellin' other people our business. What happens in the Kimball home stays right here." Hank slapped his hand on the table. "A nosy neighbor starts gossiping, and pretty soon the whole county will know what's goin' on at our place."

"But Heidi isn't like that. She's not a nosy neighbor, and I doubt she will tell anyone what I told her."

"*Puh!* I wouldn't be so sure about that. The Amish don't have TVs or run around in motorized vehicles. What else do they have to do all day but spread gossip?"

Velma's fingernails bit into her palms as she fought for control. "You are not being fair. Are you prejudiced against the Amish?"

He shook his head vigorously. "Course not. I just know how people like to talk—not just the Amish, but anyone with a waggin' tongue."

"Well, like I said, I don't think Heidi would gossip about us. When I talked to her today, she seemed to truly care." Velma drew in a quick breath. "Heidi mentioned church also."

"What about it?"

"She asked if we attended church or had a minister we could talk to about our problems."

"Humph! Church is the last thing we need. Now, if you wanna start goin', I won't stop ya, but there's no way I'll step inside a church building." Hank pushed his chair aside and strode across the room. After opening the refrigerator door, he took out a carton of milk and poured himself a glass. "Is this all the milk we have?" He shook the carton.

"Yes, it is, and I could use some money to go grocery shopping."

"Figured you'd be askin' for money." He lifted the glass to his lips and took a big drink. "You really oughta find a job."

"We've been over this before." She sighed. "If I went to work, I'd need to pay someone to watch the kids—not to mention some form of transportation."

"Eddie and Peggy Ann are big enough to stay by themselves."

"No they're not, Hank. They're just children."

He took another drink. "Yeah, well, when I was Eddie's age, I was helpin' my pa at the lumber mill."

She plopped her hands against her hips. "Just because your dad trusted a boy to do a man's job doesn't mean we should leave our kids alone while we're both off working." Velma could see by her husband's placid expression that she wasn't getting anywhere with him. She was stubborn, but Hank was even more hard-headed. He rarely agreed with her on anything.

Hank flopped back in his chair. "So, are we gonna eat now, or what?"

"Yeah, I'll go get the kids." Velma clenched her fists as she limped out of the kitchen. No kiss on the cheek today when Hank got home. It seemed they were getting further and further apart. "Guess absence doesn't make the heart grow fonder, like some people say," she muttered. Nothing would probably ever change for the better in her life, so she may as well accept it. *I bet he didn't even notice me limping.*

Berlin

Miranda was getting ready to climb into bed when someone tapped on her door. "Who is it?"

"It's me, Mommy. Can I come in?"

"Of course, sweetie," Miranda called.

The door opened, and Debbie stepped into the room. "I have something for you. It's from Daddy, and I promised to give it to you, but I forgot until now."

Miranda's lips pressed together. *Oh, boy, here it comes.* "What did your father ask you to give me?"

"This." Debbie held out a cream-colored envelope. "I was supposed to give it to you when me and Kevin came in the house after Dad left. But then you told us we should change clothes before lunch, so I put the envelope on my dresser and forgot about it till now."

"Okay, thanks." Miranda took the envelope and hugged her

daughter. It wasn't Debbie's fault Trent was using her to deliver his gift. "Did your dad visit with you and your brother a little before he left?"

"No. Daddy said he had to go home and rest. Something about a kidney stone."

"Your father had a kidney stone?"

"Yep, I think he said he passed it, whatever that means."

Miranda didn't ask her daughter any more. "Now off to bed you go."

"Night, Mommy. Sweet dreams."

Miranda smiled. "Sweet dreams to you, too."

After Debbie left the room, Miranda took a seat on the bed and opened the envelope. She recognized the card right away. It was one she'd given Trent on their first anniversary, when they were so very much in love. She'd written such lovely things to him—promising, no matter how many struggles they might encounter, or how difficult or challenging situations may get, they'd always work things out together.

I wonder if I should call him to see if he's okay. The last time he had a kidney stone attack, it lasted for two days. No, I better not. Trent would have called if it had been too bad.

Tears welled in her eyes and dripped onto the card. Miranda couldn't deny that she still loved Trent. She just wasn't sure they could be together again.

Chapter 27

Charm, Ohio

I'm glad your son is feeling better." Ellen smiled at Darren from the passenger seat of his SUV.

"Me too. He was only sick about twenty-four hours, so I'm pretty sure he had a stomach virus and not the flu." Darren slowed as they drove through the small village of Charm. "I'm glad neither you nor Becky got sick, and I hope none of the others who were at Heidi's that day came down with it."

"I hope they didn't, either. So where is Jeremy this evening?" she asked.

"He's spending the night with one of his friends. I'll pick him up in the morning sometime after breakfast. The boys will probably go to bed late and sleep in Saturday morning. I may just catch some extra z's myself—that is, if Bacon lets me." Darren glanced over at Ellen. "What's Becky doing tonight?"

"A friend of mine from church came over to be with her. Of course, Becky thinks she's too old for a babysitter, but as far as I'm concerned, she is not old enough to be left alone for any length of time—especially after dark."

Darren bobbed his head. "We're on the same page regarding that. Say, I hope you like the Bavarian-style food they serve here," he said as he pulled his vehicle into the parking lot of the Chalet in the Valley restaurant. "I should have asked."

"Yes, I do, and I've actually been here a few times with Becky." Ellen smiled. "Believe it or not, she likes bratwurst with sauerkraut, which is also one of my favorites."

"That's a dish I enjoy eating, too." Darren chuckled. "Your daughter has good taste. Guess she must take after her mother."

"Yes, she does in many ways." Ellen's face sobered. "Just not in appearance. But then, that's because she's not my biological child."

He tipped his head. "Most people would never guess it, though."

"Probably not." Ellen shifted in her seat. "Becky didn't know she'd been adopted until recently. It came out when she overheard a conversation I had with my brother."

"How'd she take it?"

"Not well. It was quite a shock."

"Why did you wait so long to tell her?"

"I was afraid for her to know the truth." Ellen explained, "You see, when I was a girl, I had a friend who found out she was adopted, and it ruined the relationship that had been established with her adoptive parents."

Ellen's eyebrows gathered in. "I regret not telling Becky sooner. I'm afraid it's put some distance between us."

"Really? If so, it's not obvious—at least not to me."

Ellen sighed. "Well, things are better, but not quite how it was before Becky found out the truth."

"How are things different?"

"For one thing, Becky's not as talkative as she was with me before. And she spends more time alone in her room than she used to."

Feeling her frustration, Darren reached over and clasped Ellen's hand. It felt warm to the touch, making him wish he could hold it all night. "I'll bet things will go back to the way they were once she's had enough time to work through it."

"I hope so. Thanks for listening. It helped to be able to share this with you."

"That's what friends are for, Ellen." Darren's lips parted slightly as he struggled with the temptation to pull her into his arms and offer a kiss. But it may be too soon for that. Before their first kiss, Darren wanted to be sure about Ellen's feelings for him.

The feelings stirring within Darren surprised him. Ellen was so beautiful, and at the same time, looked so vulnerable after revealing her concern over Becky. All he wanted to do was hold her and make everything right.

Ellen's stomach rumbled softly, and she quickly placed her hand on it. "My tummy seems to be talking to me. Guess we need to go into the restaurant so I can feed it."

Darren gave Ellen a thumbs-up. "I'm all for that."

Walnut Creek

Velma stepped into the bedroom she shared with Hank and stopped. Wearing the most faded, threadbare jeans in their closet, he lounged, shirtless, on the bed.

"What are you doing? You need to get dressed or we'll be late for our supper at the Troyers'." She stood at the foot of the bed, squinting at him.

He yawned, stretching both arms over his head. "Wish you hadn't told 'em we'd go there tonight. I don't get much time at home these days, and I'd planned to kick back and relax all evening."

Her pulse quickened. "Then ya shoulda told me that before you agreed to go."

"Wasn't thinkin' much about it at the time. I was probably half asleep when you asked."

Velma stared straight at Hank as she pushed her shoulders back. "Well, the invitation was extended, and we accepted, so ya may as well get up and get dressed, 'cause we're goin'." Velma wasn't normally this assertive with her husband, but with the way things were going between them lately, her nerves were on edge. Truth be told, she was looking forward to spending the evening with Heidi and her family—and Eddie and Peggy Ann were excited about going there, too.

"Okay, okay. . . Don't get so pushy." Hank pulled himself off the bed, ambled across the room, and opened a dresser drawer. The T-shirt he pulled out caused Velma to gasp.

"You're not gonna wear that old thing, I hope."

He shrugged his broad shoulders. "Don't see why not."

She shook her head. "It's not appropriate."

"It is to me." He slipped the dingy white shirt with a couple of small holes in it over his head.

She recoiled, wrinkling her nose. "You have better T-shirts to choose from. Please wear one of those colorful ones in your drawer. Or better yet, how about a long-sleeve cotton shirt that will cover up your tattoos?" Velma glanced at the cotton dress she wore, hoping it looked presentable.

Hank gazed at the tattooed panther on his left arm, then gestured to the eagle on his right arm. "You think your Amish friends will have somethin' against my tats?"

"I'm not sure what they'll think, but whether they do or not, I'd appreciate if you would wear somethin' decent."

He planted his feet in a wide stance. "Either I wear what I've got on, or I ain't goin'."

Velma's posture sagged. "Okay, Hank, wear whatever you want." She could only imagine what the Troyers would think of her sloppy, boisterous husband.

———————⟡⟡⟡———————

"This is some mighty good tater salad." Hank emitted a loud burp, then reached under his T-shirt and scratched his belly. "Mind if I have some more?"

"No, not at all." Heidi handed the bowl to Lyle, who passed it on to Hank. "I'm glad you like my salad. It's a recipe that's been in our family for a long while, and it has been handed down to each generation."

"Everything is good." Velma pointed to the barbecued chicken. "You and Lyle outdid yourselves on our account, and we thank you for it." She glanced over at her husband as if expecting him to agree, but he was silent. Heidi figured Hank's appreciation was being shown through the manner in which he was eating the food, as he sat there licking barbeque sauce off his fingers.

"I understand you're a truck driver." Lyle looked over at Hank.

"Yep." The man bobbed his head and shoveled another spoonful of potato salad into his mouth.

"That's why Hank's away from home so much," Velma put in. "Sometimes he's gone for just a few days. Other times it could be a week or longer."

"Me and Peggy Ann don't like it when Papa's gone," Eddie spoke up. "It means more work for us to do." He glanced at his mother, then looked quickly away.

"Yep, I got word before we came here that I have to leave tonight on a run," Hank added. "And I probably won't be back till Monday sometime."

Both Eddie and Peggy Ann groaned, while Velma grew silent.

Heidi wanted so badly to come right out and ask Velma if they could do anything for her family, but she didn't want to embarrass her in front of everyone. She knew from some of the things Velma had told her that money was tight and they were in need of a car. A vehicle was something she and Lyle couldn't help with, but maybe they could loan the Kimballs some money. Of course, that might be a touchy subject. Some folks didn't want to be beholden to anyone, and she had a feeling Hank might be one of those people.

Heidi touched the base of her neck, where a mosquito had landed moments ago and left its mark. *Guess this is one more thing I need to pray about. Hopefully, something will come to me soon about the best way to help the Kimballs.*

Chapter 28

Between Berlin and Charm

By the time Heidi and the children arrived at the Doughty Run School Auction on Saturday, things were in full swing. Lyle had gone early, since he was the head auctioneer, but Randy and Marsha didn't get up in time for them all to go with him. So right after breakfast Heidi hitched her horse to their open buggy, and she headed to the auction with the children.

They arrived at eight thirty, in time for the auction to begin, but missed the breakfast that had been served at seven. School auctions were important to the Amish community, and Heidi was glad she could bring Randy and Marsha here today. Randy would attend the Amish schoolhouse near their home toward the end of August, and she and Lyle would be involved in many functions centered on the school. Parental involvement was important to the children, teachers, and Amish school board.

After guiding her horse and buggy into the area reserved for parking, Heidi climbed down and secured Bobbins to the hitching rail provided. She felt thankful the mare's leg was now better. Then she clasped the children's hands and headed to where the action was. In addition to all the activity in the auction tent, vendors were selling barbecued chicken, root beer floats, ice cream, and lots of baked goods.

"I smell somethin' good." Randy pointed to a booth selling kettle popcorn. "Can we go get some?"

"We will a little later." Heidi smiled. "I thought we would go into the auction tent for a bit and see how things are going. You'll get to see Lyle there, too."

"Can we talk to him?" Marsha asked.

"Probably not. He will be busy auctioning items and making sure everything is running smoothly." Heidi led the way to some benches, where they all took a seat. She enjoyed watching as several handmade quilts were auctioned, as well as some nice pieces of furniture made by one of the local Amish men. She caught a glimpse of Loretta and Eli across the way and waved.

Randy and Marsha both giggled.

"What are you two laughing about?" Heidi smiled as they pointed at Lyle.

"He's talkin' funny." Randy smirked. "And really fast."

Heidi explained about how auctioneers talked when they were bid calling.

Hearing her name called, Heidi glanced to the right. She was surprised to see Allie Garrett in the row directly across from them.

Heidi smiled and waved. Allie waved back, and then she left her seat and came over to where Heidi sat. "It's good to see you," Allie whispered. "Can we find a place to talk for a few minutes? It'd be nice to get caught up."

Heidi glanced at Randy and Marsha. They both seemed intent on watching as Lyle got the crowd bidding on a beautiful oak desk. She leaned close to Randy. "Will you two be okay if I go outside the tent for a few minutes to talk to my friend?"

Randy moved his head up and down.

"Okay. Just stay right there on the bench. I'll be back soon." Heidi stood and followed Allie out of the tent.

"I have some good news." Allie spoke excitedly. "Steve's taken a desk job, so he won't be patrolling or out on the streets where his life has been in constant danger." She leaned closer to Heidi. "He's spending more time with me and the kids now, and it was his idea to bring me and the kids here today."

Heidi tenderly squeezed Allie's shoulder. "I'm glad things are working out."

"So how are things going? I saw your foster children sitting on the bench with you."

Heidi nodded. "Marsha and Randy are adjusting pretty well."

"That's wonderful, Heidi. Did the officials ever find out if the children have any living relatives who might want to raise them?"

"No, and because we love Randy and Marsha so much, Lyle and I have decided to adopt the children. It's a process, and we're waiting until things are closer to being finalized before we tell the kids."

"I'm sure everything will move forward without a problem. After all this time, any relatives would have come forward." Allie hugged Heidi. "You and your husband will be good parents for those children."

"We will do our best, and we're looking forward to the days ahead—watching Randy and Marsha grow up, and hopefully both of them someday joining the Amish church."

"That time we stopped by your place, we felt bad after we left, seeing how upset the children were—especially little Marsha."

"Apparently your husband reminded the children of their father until he spoke," Heidi explained. "It was his uniform. Apparently their dad was a security guard at the mall."

"Oh, my. How traumatic for them to see someone who resembled their dad."

"It's okay. We had a picnic that evening, and afterward I was able to sit down with Randy and Marsha and look through a photo album that had belonged to their parents." Heidi paused. "I believe it helped for the children to be able to talk about their mom and dad as they looked at all the pictures."

They chatted a bit longer, until Heidi said she should go back and check on the children.

"Yes, I should check in with my family, too." Allie hugged Heidi once more, and they walked back inside together. "Please let me know how everything goes with the adoption."

Heidi nodded. "I certainly will."

———————————— ⁓ ————————————

Loudonville, Ohio

"You kids are gonna have a great time here today," Trent said as he pulled his newer-model truck into a large parking lot. He was glad the parking was free, because there was an admission fee for the event. The cost was minimal, however, and they'd probably be here most of the day, so he would get his money's worth.

"I like when you let us sit up front with you, Daddy." Debbie grinned.

"If I had some safety seats, you'd be sitting in the seat behind me. But the seat belts have you good and secure."

Kevin, who sat beside Trent, tapped his arm. "I forgot. What'd ya say is goin' on here today?"

"It's the Great Mohican Powwow. We're going to see all kinds of Native American events and activities."

"Like what?" Debbie peered around her brother, looking curiously at Trent.

"There will be things like singing, dance and drum competitions, tomahawk throwing, fire starting, storytelling, flute making, and most likely lots more." Trent wiggled his brows. "I found out about this event on the internet, and it said there would be over forty traders, artisans, and craftsmen."

"Will there be food to eat?" Kevin wanted to know.

"Yep. There'll be plenty of that."

"How come the Native Americans get together like this?" Debbie asked.

"It's a chance for them to sing, dance, renew old friendships, and make new friends, too," Trent explained. "It's also a time to reflect on their ancestors' old ways and preserve their people's heritage."

Kevin's eyes gleamed. "Can we get outa the truck now?"

"In a minute, Son. I need to ask your sister a question first." Trent leaned around Kevin so he could see his daughter's face. "Did you take the envelope I gave you last Saturday to your mother?"

She nodded.

"What'd she say when she opened it?"

"I don't know, Daddy. I just handed it to her and said it was from you. Then I headed back to my room 'cause it was time for bed."

"Did your mom say anything about it the next day?"

"Huh-uh."

Trent sagged against his seat. If the words Miranda had written on the card still meant something to her, surely she would have contacted him this past week. He would have to come up with some other idea now to win Miranda back.

Walnut Creek

Slicing a pineapple she'd purchased at the market yesterday, Velma sighed. She'd already been up a few hours after a fitful night of little sleep. She'd tossed and turned, done a lot of crying, and punched her pillow numerous times as well. So early this morning she'd risen from bed before the sun had come up.

After sprucing up the living room and kitchen, while Peggy Ann and Eddie were still sleeping, Velma had gone to the living room, opened the drawer of an end table, and pulled out a dull white album that held her and Hank's wedding pictures. Since they could not afford a professional photographer back then, Hank's brother, who lived in South Carolina, had offered to take the pictures for them. A few weeks later, after the film was developed, her brother-in-law mailed them the pictures, which were inserted in a standard off-white album. Enclosed was also an envelope with the negatives, along with a card telling them the album and wedding pictures were his wedding gift to them. Velma remembered feeling grateful because his gift saved them a lot of money.

Her mouth puckered as she bit into a slice of pineapple. *So long ago.* Velma heaved another sigh, flipping through the worn-out pages of the album. They were decent enough photos, and a few were exceptional. Years ago, Velma had intentions of purchasing an actual wedding album, picking out a few of the better prints, and having the pictures enlarged to put in a special keepsake album. After looking at many beautiful scrap books in the local card store, she gave up. There always seemed to be something more important to spend the money on, since the keepsake albums were not cheap.

"Humph!" Velma mumbled out loud as she glanced around the small kitchen. "Like a lot of things I'd always hoped for, that wedding album never happened."

Looking at the pictures took her back in time. Except for the birth of her children, Velma couldn't remember a happier moment than the day she married Hank. She sniffed and grabbed a napkin from the holder to wipe at a tear rolling down her cheek. Today was their twentieth wedding anniversary, and she'd be spending another one without her husband, since he was out on the road.

The first couple of years of their marriage, Hank made sure to take the day off. He'd do something simple on their special day. Sometimes it was giving her a bouquet of cut flowers or some other sweet memento, along with a nice card. Velma still had every card Hank had given her. Sometimes they would start celebrating early and attend Fourth of July events around their hometown, with the evening ending in a stunning fireworks display. But as time went on, his romantic gestures waned, until their anniversary became like any other ordinary day.

Things sure do change, Velma brooded. At times it really tore at her heart. *Guess I should be used to it by now, though.*

Eddie chose that moment to come bounding into the kitchen, his brown hair uncombed and unruly. "Mornin', Mama." He grinned at her before getting the carton of milk out of the refrigerator, and then slid in his stocking feet all the way to the small pantry for his favorite box of cereal.

Velma got up and put the album back, then went to the kitchen to get a bowl for her son.

"Is cereal all ya want for breakfast? I can make an egg and toast if ya like, or even some pancakes."

"Nope, cereal's fine." Eddie winked one of his chocolate-colored eyes.

"I'll have cereal, too." Peggy Ann skipped into the kitchen.

"Goodness." Velma lifted her eyebrows. "You two are mighty chipper this morning."

After pouring milk on his cereal, Eddie handed the carton to his sister. "It's Saturday, Mama, and our favorite cartoons are on." He scooped up a spoonful of colorful crunchy puffs and put them in his mouth.

Peggy Ann nodded while stirring the milk through her bowl of honey-flavored oats.

"Okay, but you can only watch TV for an hour. Then I have some chores for you both to do."

Without argument, her children looked at her and nodded. *That's odd.* Velma looked at her daughter, then her son. *Normally they would fight me on doing chores.*

"You can take your bowls to the living room and set up TV trays, if you'd like to eat there. Also, here are some slices of pineapple to have with your cereal." Any other time, Velma didn't allow them to eat in the living room, but this morning, she made an exception.

"Oh yummy." Eddie took a slice of the fruit and had it eaten before he bounded out of the kitchen.

"Thank you, Mama." Peggy Ann put her pineapple slice on a napkin, then followed her brother.

Velma got a bowl of cereal for herself and sat back down at the table. She could see the kids through the open doorway, sitting quietly, eating, and watching TV. *I wonder if those two heard me crying during the night. It wouldn't surprise me as loud as I got. Maybe that's why they were bein' so nice.*

———————•⸎◦⸎◦⸎•———————

Canton

"I don't see why I have to go with you today," Kassidy complained as they headed to the home where Denise would be conducting an open house in the afternoon. "I'm old enough to stay by myself, you know."

Denise clicked her newly manicured fingernails against the steering wheel. "How many times must we have this discussion?"

Kassidy said nothing.

Some parents might be comfortable leaving their eleven-year-old at home alone for a good chunk of the day, but Denise wasn't one of them. Besides, bringing Kassidy along would give her daughter something to do besides fooling with her cell phone. Denise still didn't understand why Greg thought it necessary to give their daughter her own phone at such a young age. It would make more sense if Kassidy was older, and had a car or a job. As far as Denise could tell, the only thing Kassidy used her phone for was texting friends, taking selfies, and

and sharing them with friends. Occasionally, she found her playing a game, but were those things reason enough to pay for the extra phone?

"You know, someday when you grow up, you might decide to become a Realtor, so helping me at the open house today can be beneficial."

"I don't see how, Mom. All I'm gonna do is just stand around. Good thing I brought my cell phone along so I'll have something to do."

Denise shook her head. "You are not going to play on that phone today. In fact, when we get there, I want you to give it to me."

"What?" Kassidy groaned. "How come?"

"Because it's a distraction you don't need. Today I'll need you to keep an eye on the brochures I will have set out, and if the pile goes down, you can replace them with more from my briefcase."

"That's gonna be boring." Kassidy kicked the back of Denise's seat.

"You can also make sure the plate of cookies I brought gets refilled as needed." Denise glanced in the rearview mirror. "And please stop kicking my seat. It's distracting."

"Okay, whatever. What I wanna know is what are you gonna do the whole time during the open house?"

"I will be answering the door and showing prospective home buyers through the house."

"That sounds like more fun than what I'll be doing."

Denise released a puff of air as she turned up the driveway leading to the house with the For Sale sign. This home would also bring a good commission if she found a buyer willing to pay the full asking price.

At least Kassidy wasn't putting up too much of a fuss at this point. Denise parked the car. *Maybe the scripture verse Heidi put on the back of a previous recipe card about children obeying their parents is getting through to my daughter. I wonder what verse Heidi will share with the class next week when we go to her house.*

Walnut Creek

After lunch, Velma pulled weeds, while the kids gathered up their toys that were strewn all over the yard. Something strange was going on, but she wasn't about to question anything. It was rare when the kids did what she asked without moping about it or suddenly making themselves scarce.

Earlier, after watching their favorite cartoon, Peggy Ann and Eddie had actually cleaned their rooms and even removed the sheets from their beds so Velma could put fresh linens on.

To the best of her knowledge, Hank wasn't due home until sometime Monday. *I'll bet he doesn't even call to give me an anniversary wish.* As she pulled some stubborn dandelion stems out of the dry dirt, her thoughts went back to their wedding day.

Velma had been nineteen when she walked down the aisle to the man she had fallen in love with. The man she wanted to make dreams, have children, and grow old with.

Back then they'd started with nothing, and twenty years later, they still had very little. Except for having children, not many of their dreams had come true.

"You'd think after this many years, we'd be further ahead in our life." Velma stood up, wiping a dirty hand across her sweaty forehead. Her knee still hurt, but not as bad. Still, she was careful not to put a lot of pressure on it and cause more problems. They certainly couldn't afford any unnecessary medical bills.

Hearing a horn honk, as an unfamiliar car pulled into the driveway, Velma shielded her eyes from the sun and watched the vehicle come to a stop. She could barely see someone waving through the tinted glass.

Wiping her hands on the back of her coveralls, Velma started walking toward the car, when a woman wearing sunglasses, and dressed in a stylish blouse with neatly pressed twill slacks, got out.

"Velma!" The woman hurried in her direction.

"Nellie!" Velma recognized her voice. "Is it really you?" Meeting her halfway, she smothered her childhood friend with a huge hug.

"Oh, Velma, it's been way too long." Nellie's voice caught. "But life gets in the way sometimes. I'm just glad you sent me your change of address when you and your family moved here from Kentucky."

"It's wonderful to see you. I had no idea you were coming."

"Sorry, I should have called, but I wanted it to be a surprise."

"I'm surprised, all right. So glad I'm home today." Velma took Nellie's arm and steered her to the plastic resin picnic table under their one and only tree. "My, my. . . Just look at you. Except for your hair being styled a bit shorter, you haven't changed one bit."

"Oh, I don't know about that." A blush crept across Nellie's cheeks.

"Look at me. I'm a mess." Velma quickly crossed her arms to hide her dirty hands. "Can I get you something to drink, or have you had lunch yet?"

"Maybe something cold to drink. I stopped at a restaurant for lunch about an hour ago."

"Come inside with me while I wash these grungy hands, and afterwards I'll make us some lemonade. We can come back out here and catch up with each other at the picnic table."

Nellie grinned. "Sounds wonderful."

After Velma mixed the lemonade and poured them each a glass, she and Nellie headed back out to the yard.

"Come here, Eddie and Peggy Ann," Velma called to her kids once she and Nellie got seated. "I want you to meet someone special."

When the children ran up to them, Velma introduced Nellie. "Peggy Ann and Eddie, this is my friend Nellie Burns." Velma touched Nellie's arm. "We grew up together when we lived in Kentucky, and were very close, almost like sisters. Nellie moved away before you two were born."

"Hello." Peggy Ann grinned shyly.

"Nice to meet ya," Eddie said with a nod.

"Well it certainly is nice to meet you both, as well." Nellie reached out and shook the children's hands.

"Okay, you two, go on in and pour yourself some lemonade, and then continue with what you were doin'. Afterwards, you can relax; you both did a good job today." Velma smiled as they ran toward the door, each trying to get inside first.

After the kids went inside, Velma looked at Nellie. "I've thought about you often over the years. Wondered how you were doing. Did you ever get married again after Ted died?"

Nellie shook her head. "I never remarried. I've been single so long now I'm sort of used to being on my own." Nellie took a sip of her drink. "What about you? What's happened with you since we last saw each other?"

Velma lowered her head. "Not much to talk about. I'd hoped when Hank suggested we move here, things would get better for us."

"And they haven't?" Velma saw pity in her friend's eyes.

"Nope." Velma went on to tell Nellie about her two oldest children leaving home. "Most recently, our teenage daughter, Bobbie Sue, left a note and ran off with her boyfriend, Kenny, saying she plans to marry him as soon as she turns eighteen. Who knows—they're probably hitched by now."

Nellie didn't say anything but continued to listen.

"Bobbie Sue's boyfriend would not have been my choice for our daughter, but then it's sorta fitting I guess. My parents didn't approve of Hank either, but I still married him. You know the ole saying: what goes around comes around." Velma stopped talking and sniffed. "Hank owns a semitruck and is gone a lot, so it's been kinda lonely since we moved here. Other than an Amish woman who lives down the road, I haven't made any friends."

Nellie placed her hand on Velma's arm. "I'm sorry. I wish I'd kept in better touch."

"Yeah, me too." Velma released a lingering sigh. "To make matters worse, today is Hank's and my wedding anniversary."

"I really should have called ahead. I hope I'm not in the way of any plans you and your husband have for today."

Velma shook her head. "Plans? What plans? Hank's not here to help me celebrate, and he didn't even leave me a card before he headed out on the road." A lump formed in Velma's throat, and she swallowed a couple of times, hoping to push it down.

"That's too bad." Nellie gave Velma's arm a motherly pat.

"So, what brings you to Ohio? I'm sure you didn't come here just to see me." Velma asked, not wanting to talk about her husband anymore.

"Well, I'm actually heading to Pittsburgh, where my son, Dale, lives. He and his wife, Kay, had a baby boy recently, and I'm anxious to meet the little guy." Nellie smiled. "They want me to move there, and

I'm seriously considering it. Being close to family will be better than living alone."

Velma nodded. "I hope it all works out."

"Same here." Nellie turned her head in the direction Eddie and Peggy Ann were pointing at something in the yard. "Peggy Ann reminds me of you at that age."

"You think so?"

"Definitely."

When a cloud floated over the sun, a moment of cool air passed through the leaves above them. Velma lifted her head toward the limbs overhead. The air felt so refreshing. Then she looked back at Nellie. "Ya know, even though me and Hank have had some struggles along the way, things could always be worse."

"Velma, I'm really sorry for all you've had to go through." Nellie patted Velma's arm again. "I wonder if there is such a thing as a perfect marriage. It seems everyone I know who's married, even those who seem to have a good relationship, has something they're dealing with— either in their marriage, with their children, or even the in-laws."

"Well, it's hard, but I'm tryin' to do my best with the situation we're in." Velma waved her hand, as she motioned around the yard. "We don't have much, but I keep hopin' for some sort of miracle, and that our situation will look brighter someday."

"I know there are people who seem to have it all: a big expensive house, nice cars, and all the other bells and whistles one would think makes a person happy. But you know what? Those folks are some of the saddest people I know." Nellie's head moved slowly up and down. "So don't go thinking those objects bring happiness into a person's life, 'cause they don't."

"Guess you're right," Velma agreed. "We have our health, and I pray our two youngest children don't leave us, too."

"You know Velma, there seem to be many opinions floating around these days on how to raise children, but I doubt there is one book ever published that explains how to do it right all the time." Nellie spoke in a calming voice.

"Well, I'm tryin' to improve and do some things differently."

"Such as?"

"For one thing, starting tomorrow, I'll be takin' the kids to church." Velma went on to explain about Heidi and what an influence she'd made on her. "Yep. She's opened my eyes to a lot of things, and the realization that I've been missing something important without God in my life. I'm hopin' if these kids of mine can learn something by going to church, maybe they'll end up with a better attitude about life than our two older children did."

"What about you, Velma?" Nellie's expression was one of concern. "Do you have any expectations for yourself?"

"I'd like to finish high school someday. Maybe take a few night courses and get a decent job." Velma looked toward her children again. "It'll have to be when they're older though."

"Don't you miss the good ole days when we were growing up together?"

"Sure do. Things were so simple back then. We didn't have much when we were kids, but as I look back on it, I can see that we had what was important."

Velma and her friend visited awhile longer. Then Nellie looked at her watch. "I hate to rush off, but if I'm going to make it to Pittsburgh before suppertime, I'd better hit the road."

"Okay, Nellie. Thanks for stopping by. It's been so nice to catch up." Velma wrapped her arm around her friend, and they walked to the car. Eddie and Peggy Ann ran up to them.

"Are ya leavin' now?" Eddie asked.

"Yes, I'm heading to Pittsburgh." Nellie ruffled his hair. "Maybe you all can come to visit me and my family sometime."

"Can we?" Peggy Ann asked, standing close to Velma.

Velma put her arms around both of the kids. "God willing, we'll sure try—especially if Nellie moves to Pittsburgh."

Nellie and Velma shared a parting hug.

"I think you are heading in the right direction by going to church tomorrow." Nellie smiled. "My life would have no meaning if God wasn't a part of it."

"I'm hopin' my life will have more purpose. I just hope the roof doesn't cave in when I walk through those doors tomorrow morning." Velma giggled and grabbed Nellie's hand. "Your visit meant more to me than you will ever know. Let's stay in touch now, okay?"

"For sure." Nellie gave Velma's hand a final squeeze before getting into her car.

As Velma watched her friend's vehicle pull onto the main road, she felt as hopeful as she had after Heidi talked with her.

Dear God, I have no right to ask this, since I've ignored You all these years, but please bear with me, and help me to be strong for my kids, my marriage, and even myself. Show me the way to keep hope alive, and please forgive me for all the mistakes I've made.

Velma looked up toward the sky, and a sense of peace came over her. As she headed inside, she knew what she was going to do first. It had been many years, but she said a little prayer that her grandma's old Bible would give her some answers.

Chapter 29

S eated in the back row of the community church she and the kids had walked to this morning, Velma felt conspicuous and as out of place as an elephant in a candy shop. Hank hadn't made it home yet, but he would have refused to join them anyway. Of course, Velma didn't let that stop her. She was determined to follow Heidi's suggestion and give church a try. After all, what did she have to lose?

Velma glanced to her left, where Peggy Ann sat, clinging to her hand. The girl's reddish-blond ponytail bounced as she bobbed her head in time to the music. *Maybe coming here will be good for my little girl. She seems to be enjoying herself.*

Velma didn't recognize any of the songs being sung. But then she hadn't set foot in church since she was a young girl. Velma's parents were not the religious type, but her maternal grandmother was. She'd taken Velma to Sunday school a few times when she came to visit on some weekends. She remembered singing songs like "Jesus Loves Me," "Down in My Heart," and "The Lord's Army." But none of those were being sung here today. One of her favorite songs had been "Onward Christian Soldiers."

She pursed her lips, staring at the songbook in her lap. *Guess that's what I get for stayin' away from church so long. I'm out of touch with everything that goes on.*

Eddie, sitting on the other side of Velma, nudged her arm. "I'm bored. When are we goin' home?"

"Shh. . . Be quiet." Velma glanced around, hoping no one heard what her son said.

Eddie crossed his arms and slumped farther down on the benched pew seat.

Velma had hoped she and the kids would make a good impression, in case they decided to come back again, but they weren't off to a very good start.

When the music stopped, and the people on the platform who'd led the singing sat down, a man dressed in a dark blue suit stood in front of the congregation and offered a prayer. Velma closed her eyes, hoping her children would do the same. But no, Eddie decided to start chomping real loud on his gum. She opened her eyes, and was about to whisper for him to take the gum out of his mouth, when he blew a rather large bubble. The next thing Velma knew, the bubble popped, leaving gum all over her boy's face.

Velma quietly opened her purse and fished around for the small pack of tissues. Nudging her son's elbow, she frowned. With a sheepish look on his face, Velma watched Eddie pull the sticky gum off his mouth and put the wad in the tissue she held out to him.

The prayer was still going on, but Velma noticed several people around them had opened their eyes and were looking in their direction with disapproving expressions. *They probably think we're hicks from the sticks.*

Velma groaned inwardly. *So much for making a good impression. This may be the first and last time we ever visit this church. Why can't Eddie be as well behaved as the other children sitting around us?*

Berlin

"It's good to see you. How are things going these days?" Miranda's friend, Shelly Cunningham, greeted her as soon as she and the children entered the church they regularly attended.

"About the same as usual. I'm still cashiering part-time at our local grocery store." Miranda gestured to Debbie and Kevin. "And these two completed their third cooking class a week ago, Saturday."

Shelly squeezed both children's shoulders. "That's great. Are you two enjoying the class?"

Debbie nodded, but Kevin merely shrugged. Then, seeing his friend Scott enter the building, Kevin ran over to greet him. A few seconds later, Debbie wandered off in the direction of four young girls about her age.

Shelly rolled her eyes. "Kids—you gotta love 'em."

"You're right," Miranda agreed, as she and Shelly stepped away from the front entrance. "I'm just glad my two like coming to church—even if the main attraction is to see their friends. Some parents have a difficult time getting their kids to go to church—especially when their father refuses to go and doesn't set a Christian example."

"Are you thinking about Trent?"

"Uh-huh. If he could only see how important it is for him to be the spiritual leader in our home." Miranda sighed. "He's been trying his best to get me to take him back, through gifts and preying on my sympathy."

Shelly tipped her head. "Are you considering it?"

"No. I won't go back to the way things were. There would need to be a heartfelt change in my husband before I'd consider trying again."

"What about a marriage seminar? Do you think Trent would consider going to one?"

Miranda turned her hands palms up. "I'm not sure. Do you know of one in our area?"

"Sure do. In fact, it will be taking place here at this church in August." Shelly reached into her purse and pulled out a brochure. "All the information is right here. Look it over, and if you think it's something the two of you should attend, you might talk to Trent about it. If he's serious about wanting to get your marriage back on track, then maybe he will consider going."

"Okay, thanks." Miranda put the pamphlet in her purse.

Shelly hugged Miranda. "I've been praying for you, my friend, and I'll keep on until God gives you clear direction."

Miranda appreciated her friend's concern. Maybe this marriage seminar was the miracle she'd been hoping for.

———— ✦ ————

Walnut Creek

"The kinner are sure quiet back there," Lyle commented as he guided their horse and buggy toward home after leaving Eli Miller's, where church was held that morning. "I wonder if they fell asleep."

Heidi turned and glanced over her shoulder. Sure enough, Marsha's head drooped against Randy's shoulder, and the children's eyes were closed.

She turned back around. "Jah, they're both snoozing."

"Guess they must need it." Lyle grinned. "It was nice seeing Randy and Marsha mingling with some of the kinner after our noon meal. I'm glad they're adjusting so well."

"Me too." Heidi released the tight grip she held on her purse straps and tried to relax. "I just wish we'd hear something from our lawyer soon about the adoption proceedings. It's difficult waiting for news."

"I agree, but the wait will be worth it. You'll see."

As they approached their home, Heidi noticed a car parked across the road. A gray-haired man stood beside it. But as Lyle began to turn the horse and buggy up their driveway, Heidi looked back and saw the man hurriedly get into his car.

"I wonder who that is." She looked over at Lyle. "Did you recognize him?"

Lyle shook his head. "Probably some tourist looking to get a few photos of Amish people. You know how it is. Sometimes curiosity gets the better of folks, and they stop along the road to stare at us or snap a few pictures." His face sobered. "Guess they don't realize we're just human beings like they are. We may dress differently and use a different mode of transportation, but in here, we're the same as everyone else." Lyle touched his chest.

Heidi's skin prickled. She wanted to believe the man was only a tourist, but she had an odd feeling that something wasn't right. She'd always been intuitive, and the way the man had hurriedly gotten into his car made her suspicious. She wondered if he'd planned to break into their house and rob them while they were gone. Perhaps his quick getaway was because they'd seen his face.

It wasn't unusual for robberies to take place. Plenty of accounts of break-ins and thievery appeared in the newspaper every month. Heidi thought about one of her previous students, Ron, and how he'd stolen some things from them while they were gone. Hopefully, Lyle was right about the man they'd seen by the road. Heidi certainly didn't need one more thing to worry about.

Chapter 30

"No, please. . . . You can't take them! They belong here with us."
Rolling onto his side, Lyle gently shook Heidi's shoulder. "Wake up, Heidi. You were talking in your sleep."

Her eyes opened, and when she sat up in bed, Lyle noticed his wife's nightgown was drenched in sweat.

"W–what time is it?" Heidi looked toward the window.

"It's morning, around the time we normally get up."

"I was dreaming." She blinked several times. "Oh, Lyle, it was a horrible nightmare, and it seemed so real."

He sat up next to Heidi and clasped her hand. "What was it about?"

"I dreamed some unknown relative showed up here and wanted to take Marsha and Randy from us." Heidi paused and drew a shuddering breath. "It was dark outside, and the man or woman—I'm not sure which—pulled the kinner into their vehicle. I hollered at them to stop and to leave the children with us, but they drove away into the night."

"It was only a dream." Lyle spoke soothingly, hoping to alleviate her fears.

Heidi swept a hand across her forehead. "Oh, Lyle, I'm so frightened. What if someone should show up and try to take Randy and Marsha from us?" Her voice trembled. "I don't think I could suffer another disappointment."

Lyle slipped his arm around Heidi and pulled her close. "It was only a bad dream. Your fears are unfounded."

"I suppose, but after Kendra decided to keep her baby and the adoption was called off, I can't help but worry that something will happen to prevent us from adopting Randy and Marsha."

Lightly stroking his wife's arm, and fumbling for the right words, Lyle whispered, "We need to trust God. If it's meant for us to raise those children, nothing will stand in our way."

She leaned her head against his shoulder. "Danki for listening, and especially for the reminder to trust the Lord. Sometimes, I find it easier to tell others how to strengthen their faith, but it's much harder when I'm dealing with my own problems."

"That's how it is with most people." Lyle kissed her damp cheek. "Now I think we'd better both say a prayer before we get out of bed."

Heidi bowed her head. Lyle did the same. *Heavenly Father*, he silently prayed, *please chase away my fraa's doubts and concerns. Help us be strong and accepting if something should go wrong and we're not able to adopt the children.*

————————

Heidi stood in front of the kitchen sink, washing the breakfast dishes. It was hard to believe it was the middle of July and today was her fourth cooking class. She hoped the egg-salad sandwiches she would teach her young students to make would be appreciated. While some children might not care for egg salad, it had been a favorite of Heidi's since she was a young girl. Heidi's maternal grandma had given her the recipe she would share with the kids today. She was eager to teach the class, too, hoping it would get her mind off the horrible dream she'd had early this morning. Although she wanted to believe everything would work out, it was difficult to get rid of the niggling doubts.

"I need to trust God, like my husband said," she murmured. "Perhaps my faith is being put to the test."

Heidi glanced out the window and smiled when she saw Randy and Marsha feeding the chickens with Lyle. In addition to bringing both of the children much joy, their little poultry venture was giving Randy, in particular, a meaningful chore and something he looked forward to doing each day.

She hoped helping take care of the chickens was also causing Randy to draw closer to Lyle as they worked together. The boy still hadn't called Lyle "Daadi" or her "Mammi," but Heidi hadn't given up hope of that happening someday. She felt certain Lyle had begun to think of Randy as his son in every way.

She smiled, watching Marsha dart away from the chicken enclosure to chase a pretty butterfly. Heidi would have been tempted to join the little girl if she didn't need to get the dishes done before her young students arrived.

Randy and Marsha had brought them much joy. At times like this, Heidi's heart felt like it would burst with enthusiasm and hope for the future.

<hr />

Millersburg

"Your breakfast is sitting out, Becky," Ellen called when she left the kitchen and stepped into the hall. "And if you don't hurry, we'll end up being late for the cooking class."

"I'll be right there!" A few minutes later, Becky entered the room. She stopped in front of the table and frowned.

"What's wrong?"

"I thought we were having pancakes today. You mentioned it last night when you got home from the hospital, remember?"

Ellen nodded. "I had planned to make them, until I came into the kitchen and looked at the time." She gestured to the clock above the refrigerator. "So we wouldn't be late, I decided it would be better to have cold cereal this morning."

Becky sat down with an undignified grunt.

"Aren't we the grouchy one today? Didn't you sleep well last night?" Ellen pulled out a chair beside Becky.

"I slept fine. Just woke up grumpy."

"How come?"

"I don't know."

"Well, let's pray. Maybe you'll feel better once you've had something to eat."

They bowed their heads, and Ellen offered the prayer. "Dear Lord, please bless this food to the needs of our bodies, and give us a safe trip to Heidi's today. Be with the others who'll be traveling there too. Amen."

Becky remained quiet as they ate, even when Ellen tried to make conversation. "Is something wrong? Aren't you looking forward to the cooking class today?"

"Yeah, I guess. But I'm not lookin' forward to going to the Firemen's

Festival with Darren and Jeremy later today."

"Why not, for goodness' sakes? From what Darren told me, it'll be a fun event, and after it gets dark, there will even be fireworks." Ellen smiled. "That should be fun, right?"

"Maybe. I just don't understand why we have to see Jeremy and his dad twice in one day."

Ellen picked up her coffee cup and took a drink. "The Firemen's Festival simply happens to be on the same day as the cooking class, Becky. It's not like Darren planned it that way."

With only a shrug, Becky grabbed her spoon and started eating. Once more, Ellen wondered if Becky resented Darren and wanted to keep things the way they were between mother and daughter. Was there room in Becky's heart for a stepfather and stepbrother?

Ellen shook herself mentally. *Now where did that thought come from? I'm just beginning to know Darren, and there's certainly been no mention of marriage. I need to stop thinking about something that may never happen, especially if my daughter doesn't approve of me seeing Darren.* She added a bit of cream to her cup and stirred it around. *Hopefully, Darren will win Becky's heart, the way he's beginning to win mine.*

<hr>

Berlin

Miranda had started clearing the breakfast table when she heard a vehicle pull into the yard.

"Bet that's Daddy!" Kevin leaped out of his chair and raced for the back door. Debbie was right behind him.

Miranda was scheduled to work this morning, so Trent had agreed to take the kids to their cooking class again. She hoped this time he would stay with them and not go off on his own. When she got home from work this afternoon, she would quiz the kids about what went on.

Miranda placed the dishes in the dishwasher, and as she closed the door, Trent entered the kitchen, both kids clinging to his hands.

"Morning, Miranda. How's it going?" Trent's cheerful attitude made her wonder if he was up to something. She still hadn't asked him about attending the marriage seminar, but she'd wait to do it until he brought the kids home this afternoon.

"It's going," she responded. "How are you?"

"Doin' okay, but I'd be better if. . ." Trent stopped talking, let go of the kids' hands, and moved across the room. "If you're not doing anything this evening, I'd like to take you somewhere so we can talk."

I bet you would. Miranda bit her lip to keep from verbalizing her thoughts. "What do you want to talk about?"

He nodded with his head in the direction of Kevin and Debbie, who had moved over to stand by the back door. No doubt, they were eager to go.

"Is there a problem?" She spoke quietly.

He shook his head. "Not really, but there are some things we need to discuss."

I bet he wants to talk about a divorce and doesn't want our son and daughter to hear. Miranda's muscles tensed. "I'd need to get a sitter. Sure can't leave the kids here alone."

"No, of course not." Trent fingered the top button of his pale green shirt. "If you can line someone up to stay with the kids, I'd be happy to pay the sitter."

Miranda tilted her head from side to side, weighing her choices. If she and Trent were alone, regardless of his agenda, it would give her a chance to bring up the marriage seminar. *Maybe Trent wants a divorce. If so, he'll never agree to go to the seminar with me.*

"Okay, I'll go, but not till after the kids are in bed. I don't want them asking a bunch of questions."

"That's fine. I'll come by around nine. Will that be okay?"

She nodded. "I'll see you then."

When Trent went out the door with Debbie and Kevin, Miranda released a lingering sigh. *I hope I made the right choice agreeing to go somewhere with Trent this evening. Maybe I should have suggested he talk to me here, after the kids have gone to bed. But then if he should bring up the topic of divorce, it's not something I want the children to hear.* They would have to be told, of course, but Miranda wanted to be the one to tell them. Hopefully, she could do it in a gentle way so they wouldn't be too stunned and could accept it.

Chapter 31

Walnut Creek

When Darren pulled his SUV into Heidi's yard, he glanced around, hoping Ellen would be there by now. But there was no sign of her car. He needed an opportunity to talk to her before the class but figured it could wait till later. He just wanted to make sure Ellen and Becky were still planning to go with him and Jeremy to the Firemen's Festival later today.

Darren set the brake, turned off the engine, and got out of his vehicle. When he turned to shut the door, he was surprised to see Jeremy still sitting in the back seat. "Hey, are you getting out or what?"

"In a minute." Jeremy fiddled with something in his hand.

"What have you got there?" Darren leaned over and stuck his head inside the rig.

"It's nothing, Dad. I'm gettin' out now." Jeremy hopped out and shut his door. Then, with his hands in his jeans' pockets, he strolled up to Heidi's front porch.

Darren closed the door on the driver's side and followed. He wondered if Jeremy had brought his pocket knife along, even after he'd been asked to leave it at home.

Woof! Woof! The Troyers' dog bounded over from the other side of the house.

"Hey there, Rusty ole boy." Darren stopped to pet the dog's silky head, watching his stubby tail wiggle back and forth. "Are you the official greeter today?"

After a few more barks, Rusty ran up to greet Jeremy, apparently in need of more attention.

As Darren followed his son to the house, he realized the boy was in need of a haircut. Jeremy's thick hair curled around his ears and had even worked its way under his shirt collar. *When Caroline was still alive, she would have noticed our son's hair way before me and taken him to the barber. I might be an okay dad, but I fall short in the area of mothering.*

Allowing his mind to wander a bit, Darren imagined what it would be like to be married to Ellen. How would Jeremy take to the idea of having a stepmom? Would he appreciate all the motherly things she would bring to their home, or would he resent her?

Shaking his thoughts aside, Darren stepped onto the porch, joining his son by the door.

"Did you knock?" Darren asked.

Jeremy nodded.

A few seconds later the door opened. Randy stood looking up at them. "Guess ya must be here for the cookin' class, huh?"

Darren smiled. "That's right. Are we the first ones?"

"Yep." Randy opened the door a bit wider. "Heidi's in the kitchen. Said I should tell ya to come in."

"Okay, thanks, we will."

When they entered the house, Randy darted away, and Jeremy excused himself to use the bathroom. Darren took a seat in the rocking chair. Glancing around the tidy room, his thoughts returned to his wife again. Caroline was an immaculate housekeeper, although she never nagged him about picking up after himself. If things got a little disorganized, she quietly put them away herself.

I should have been more considerate, he thought. *Too bad there are no second chances for me. If there were, I'd do a lot of things differently.*

Darren got the chair moving and sat quietly, until Jeremy came back to the room and took a seat on the couch.

Tap. Tap. Tap. Someone was obviously at the door. Darren hoped it was Ellen, but before he had a chance to see who it was, Heidi came into the room. "Hello, Darren. Hello, Jeremy. You're the first ones here, so just make yourself at home. I'm sure the others will be along shortly." She gave them a brief smile. "A few minutes ago Randy came into the kitchen to let me know you were here, but just now, I thought I heard someone knock on the front door."

He nodded. "You did."

Heidi's cheeks looked flushed, and she fanned her face with both hands. "Guess I'd better see who it is."

———————— ❦ ————————

"Guess what?" Velma asked when Heidi greeted her at the door.

"I don't know. But from the looks of your cheery smile, I'd say it must be something good."

"Sure is." Velma looked down at Peggy Ann, standing beside her on the porch. "Me and the kids went to church last Sunday, and I think I'm gonna take 'em another time, too."

Heidi smiled. "That's good. If you're planning to go again, you must have enjoyed the service."

Velma's head moved up and down. "Can't speak for the kids, but I sure did." She lowered her head a bit. "I didn't know any of the songs, though. They were nothin' like the ones I sang when I was girl and attended my grandma's church a few times. Guess after I go awhile, I'll catch on. Of course, I may try a different church next time."

"It may be a good idea to try a few until you find a church you are comfortable with." Heidi opened the door wider. "Why don't you two come inside and join Darren and his son? I assume Eddie didn't come with you today?"

"Nope. Hank's home for the weekend, so Eddie's there with him." Velma nudged Peggy Ann. "My daughter's here for the class, but I won't be comin' in. Came here to work, not sit around." She turned toward the yard, then looked back at Heidi again. "Got anything outside ya want me to do? It's a beautiful day for yard work."

Heidi tapped her chin. "Well, I suppose you could do some weeding in my vegetable patch. Those sneaky little weeds have a way of coming up a few days after you pull them."

"Did you and the kids get to do any weeding together? You'd mentioned it when I first started doing some tasks for you."

"Actually, we did work in the garden one afternoon, but the weeds keep growing, so it needs to be done again." Heidi stepped out onto the porch and gestured toward the garden plot.

"Well, just point me to your gardening tools and I'll get started on it."

"Everything is in the barn. If you'll follow me there, I'll show you where I keep everything."

"Sounds good." Velma tapped her daughter's shoulder. "You go on inside now and have a good time. You can show me what ya made after your class is over."

"Okay, Mama, but can't I stay outside till everyone gets here?" Peggy Ann tipped her head back to look at Velma. "I wanna see how Randy's chickens are doing."

Velma looked at Heidi. "Is that okay with you?"

"Certainly. But if you step inside and speak to Randy and Marsha, I'm sure they'd like to go out to the coop with you." Heidi chuckled. "Those two never miss a chance to hang out by the chickens."

Peggy Ann grinned. "I'll get 'em!" She hurried into the house.

Velma slapped her knee. "That girl. She sure is eager to see them chickens."

Woof! Rusty plopped down in front of Heidi as they turned to head for the barn.

Heidi leaned down and patted the dog's head. "Okay, Rusty, you can come with us."

The dog must have understood, for he jumped up and ran ahead of them all the way to the barn.

"Poor pup." Heidi looked at Velma. "Since those chickens arrived and are getting all the attention, Rusty's been feeling kind of left out."

"He's a nice dog. How 'bout he keeps me company while I'm weeding your garden?" Velma asked. "If it's okay with you, that is."

"Sure. I'm positive Rusty would love it."

———————— ❧ ————————

"I wonder what you'll be making today," Ellen said as she turned her car up Heidi's driveway.

In the back seat, Becky didn't answer. In fact, she'd said only a few words since they left home this morning. Ellen figured her daughter's gloomy mood might have something to do with her not wanting to go to the Fireman's Festival later. Once they got there, and she saw all the festivities, maybe she'd be more interested and have a better disposition. Ellen certainly hoped so, because she looked forward to spending the evening with Darren and wanted it to be pleasant.

She noticed Darren's SUV parked near Heidi's house and figured he and Jeremy must be inside. Eager to see him, she hopped out of the car, but Becky remained seated with her arms folded.

Oh, great. Now she's going into her stubborn mode. "Come on, Becky. Let's go inside."

"You go ahead. I'll be in soon. Randy, Marsha, and that girl with the pigtails are out by the chicken coop. I'm gonna go say hello."

"Okay." Ellen closed her door. It was nice to see her daughter wanting to socialize with the other children.

"The last time you were here, did your cooking teacher say what you might be making today?" Denise asked her daughter when they arrived at Heidi's and had gotten out of the car. "I don't recall."

Kassidy lifted her gaze toward the sky. "Are you hard of hearing?"

Denise pointed a finger at Kassidy. "Don't use that tone with me, missy. I asked you a question, so please answer me respectfully."

"No, Heidi never said what we'd be making today." Kassidy's upper lip curled. "It better be something good, though."

"I'm sure whatever she teaches you to make will be tasty."

When they got out of the car, Denise noticed Peggy Ann, Randy, Marsha, and Becky standing outside the coop. "Before we go inside, why don't we go over and see how much Randy and Marsha's chickens have grown?" she suggested.

"Why?" Kassidy wrinkled her nose. "It stinks over there, and chickens are dumb."

"Oh, really? Well, you don't complain when you're eating their eggs."

"That's different. Eating store-bought eggs is not the same as standing beside a smelly coop and staring at a bunch of dumb little clucking birds."

"Well, nevertheless, let's take a walk over there and say hello to the children who apparently do enjoy looking at chickens." Denise guided her daughter in that direction.

"Oh, no!" Kassidy pointed, then whirled around. "Here comes that mutt."

Denise looked where her daughter was pointing and saw Rusty running ahead of Heidi and Velma, who had just stepped out of the barn area.

Denise put her hand on Kassidy's shoulder. "Don't worry. Heidi's dog is friendly. Just be nice to him, and you'll see how fast he warms up to you."

"We'll see." Kassidy trudged toward the chicken coop as Rusty ran past, with a wagging tail.

"It's nice to see you both again." Heidi called, before gesturing to the coop. "Those chickens are going to get spoiled with all the attention they're getting."

"You're probably right." Denise cupped her hands around her mouth. "We'll be in shortly."

"Take your time. We have a few minutes before class starts."

As Denise walked toward the children, she glanced across the way and noticed Velma, pulling weeds in the Troyers' garden. She could barely hear the woman's soothing voice as she held a one-way conversation with the dog, who had made himself comfortable a few feet away. Rusty must have enjoyed the attention, as he tilted his head as though listening.

Denise had no more than stepped up to the chicken enclosure, when Kassidy looked over at Randy and blurted, "I don't know what you think is so special about your chickens. They're just dumb birds who eat bugs and scratch around in the dirt."

Randy's chin quivered. "I like my hinkel."

"Hinkel? What's a hinkel? Is that anything like a wrinkle?" Kassidy got right in his face.

Before Denise could say or do anything to correct her daughter, Becky stepped up to Kassidy and bumped her arm. "That was mean. Tell Randy you're sorry."

Kassidy stood rigid and sneered at her. "I am not sorry, and I don't have to say I am, either. Besides, I wasn't talking to you."

"Well, I'm talking to you, and you had better apologize." Becky clenched her fists.

Denise held her breath, certain that her daughter would back down.

But instead of telling Randy she was sorry, Kassidy grabbed a handful of Becky's hair and yanked. The next thing Denise knew, Becky retaliated. After a few whoops and hollers, both girls were on the ground, rolling around. The other children stood with their mouths gaping open, except for Marsha, who clung to her brother's arm and sobbed.

"Stop! Stop that, you two!" Denise yelled.

Chapter 32

Hearing a ruckus outside, along with Rusty's barking, Ellen and Heidi rushed out the front door. Ellen could hardly believe her eyes. Her normally timid daughter was on the ground in a scuffle with Kassidy, while Randy and Peggy Ann looked on as though in disbelief. From where she stood, it appeared that Marsha was crying.

Ellen's fingers touched her parted lips. *What in the world could have brought this on? I've never known my girl to provoke a fight, much less do battle with someone like this. Did Kassidy do something to hurt Becky?*

Ellen dashed across the yard, with Heidi running along beside her. She saw Rusty down on his front paws barking at both of the girls. Denise shouted at Kassidy to stop, and as they drew closer to the area outside the chicken pen, Ellen did the same. But the hair pulling, slapping, and rolling about continued. Ellen was beside herself. Never had she been so stunned or humiliated by her daughter's actions.

With a determined set of her jaw, Heidi clapped her hands and spoke in short, strong sentences. "Girls, you need to stop fighting right now. This is wrong, and it's not the way to settle a disagreement."

To Ellen's amazement, Becky let go of Kassidy's hair and Kassidy let go of hers. Then both red-faced girls stood up and moved to stand by their mothers.

"What is the meaning of this, Becky Blackburn?" Ellen struggled to keep from shouting. "I have never known you to do something like this." She gestured to the other children, huddled nearby. "And what kind of an example are you setting?"

"I didn't provoke it, Mom. She did." Becky pointed to Kassidy.

"You're the one who started it." Kassidy, breathing hard, sneered at Becky.

"Did not. You were making fun of Randy's chickens, and when I defended them, you grabbed hold of my hair." Becky blinked rapidly, placing both hands against her flaming red cheeks, and Rusty started barking again.

"She ain't lyin'." Peggy Ann pointed at Kassidy. "What she said about Randy's chickens made me so mad, I felt like punchin' her in the nose."

"Nobody should be punching or making fun of anyone." Heidi leaned down and took hold of Rusty's collar, which helped him settle down. "It was wrong for you two young ladies to become physical."

"I tried to stop them," Denise interjected. "But they wouldn't listen." She wiped her brow where perspiration had gathered, and looked at Ellen. "I apologize for my daughter's behavior."

Ellen had never seen the usual put-together woman look so distraught. She felt sorry for Denise. "It's not your fault." Ellen placed her hand on Denise's arm. "It's our girls who are at fault for not controlling their tempers."

By this time, Kassidy and Becky were both sniffling. But neither would apologize. Ellen was ashamed of her daughter. Becky knew better than this.

"Debbie and Kevin aren't here yet," Heidi stated. "We all need to go inside so Becky and Kassidy can wash up before the other children arrive." She picked Marsha up and gently patted her back. Fortunately, the little girl's crying had subsided.

No one argued the point as they walked to the house. Ellen could only imagine how the rest of the day might go. If not for her wanting to spend time with Darren, she would have canceled her plans and taken Becky home as soon as the cooking class was over.

I wonder if Becky did this on purpose so I would decide not to go. One thing's for certain—when Becky and I do go home, a lecture and some form of punishment will be forthcoming.

⁘

From where she knelt in Heidi's garden, Velma had heard and seen what transpired between Kassidy and Becky. She was surprised her daughter hadn't been in the middle of the scuffle, knowing the temper she had. Velma had been about to set her weed pulling aside and break up the fight, but seeing Heidi and Ellen come out of the house, she'd decided to let them handle it. Since the fuss didn't involve her daughter, it really wasn't her business anyway. Seeing the way Rusty had carried on, Velma wasn't surprised when Heidi put the dog away in his kennel.

She remembered back to when she was a girl and had gotten into disagreements with some of her schoolmates. She was a scrapper and often ended up in a kicking or hair-pulling match. Seeing how Becky and Kassidy looked as they'd rolled about on the ground, caused Velma to feel shame for her childish and mean-tempered conduct all those years ago. It was her duty as Peggy Ann and Eddie's mother to teach proper behavior, and by attending church, it would give them a stronger foundation in knowing right from wrong.

Gripping the shovel and digging it into the dirt, Velma made a decision. In addition to going to church on Sundays, she would look for the old Bible she'd inherited from her grandma and read a few passages every day.

Another car pulled in, and Velma watched as Debbie and Kevin got out of the vehicle. The same man who'd brought them here a few weeks ago followed them up to the house. She assumed he was their father. He paused once, and looked in Velma's direction, then gave her a friendly wave. *Goodness, he just missed seeing a bit of excitement.*

———————— ⁓⁓ ————————

"Step away from the window, Jeremy. They'll think you've been watching them." Darren gestured for his son to take a seat.

Jeremy's mouth slackened as he moved back to the couch. "Can you believe Becky picked a fight with that Kassidy girl? I can't wait to find out what she said to her. Never figured Ellen's daughter could be so tough."

Darren shook his head. "When they come into the house, you are not to say anything about what you saw."

"How come?"

"Because it would be rude. I'm sure their mothers are embarrassed by what their daughters did. I would be if you'd ended up in a scuffle with one of the other kids here today."

"So I can't ask Becky what happened?"

"Not here, Son. If you feel you must ask her, then wait till we take Ellen and Becky to the Firemen's Festival."

Jeremy huffed and flopped onto the couch.

A few seconds later, Heidi stepped into the house, along with Ellen, Denise, and the children. Kevin and Debbie came in right behind them, along with a man Darren assumed was their father. The two older girls looked a mess—rumpled clothes smudged with dirt, hair sticking out at odd angles, and bright red faces. Darren had to admit he, too, was tempted to ask what had happened to cause the skirmish. But he bit his tongue. If Ellen or Becky wanted him to know, the topic would come up later. He hoped this little incident with Becky wouldn't affect their plans for the afternoon.

Heidi clasped the edge of the table, praying for a sense of peace here in her kitchen. Ever since they'd come inside there had been a chill in the air, and it had nothing to do with the weather. Becky and Kassidy had both gotten cleaned up and sat silently at the table. Heidi was disappointed that neither of them would apologize for their part in the scuffle. She'd never seen two girls carry on like that—and over such a small matter. While it wasn't right for Kassidy to make fun of Randy's chickens, it was not a reason for Becky to lose her temper. *There must be something more behind the girl's aggression,* Heidi thought. *If I knew what it was, maybe I could help.* Heidi could see that Ellen was embarrassed by her daughter's outburst, as she kept her gaze downward. Denise appeared more subdued than usual. No doubt, she regretted Kassidy's unpleasant behavior.

Since she couldn't do anything about this problem, Heidi began her class. "Today we'll be learning to make egg-salad sandwiches."

"Egg salad?" Kassidy lips puckered. "I don't like eggs all mashed up and spread on bread. I only eat fried or scrambled eggs at breakfast time. That's when they're supposed to be eaten." Her lips pressed into a white slash.

"This egg salad is different than most," Heidi explained. She refused to let Kassidy influence the other children. "It's from an old family recipe, and—"

"I don't want to make it." Kassidy shook her head determinedly. "And no one's gonna make me eat it!"

Heidi glanced at Denise, who stood behind her daughter, rubbing her forehead. Kassidy's mother didn't say anything for several seconds, then she stepped forward, placed both hands on Kassidy's shoulders and said, "I will eat the sandwich, but you're going to make it."

Peggy Ann's hand shot up. "I like egg salad. Mama said when the chickens we're gonna get start layin', we can make all sorts of things with them eggs. We're even gonna sell some 'cause we need the money. Someday, Mama's gonna buy another car." The girl shook her head. "Course it won't be a new one 'cause they cost too much."

"I'll never be poor, because my folks are rich." Kassidy looked at Peggy Ann with a smirk. "We have three cars, and when I turn sixteen and learn how to drive, my dad's gonna give me one."

Heidi wasn't sure how to respond, but Denise relieved her of that problem.

"Kassidy McGuire! If you don't stop bragging—"

"What?" Kassidy's tone grew louder. "Were you gonna say that you'd take me home? If so, then I'm glad, 'cause I wanna go home!"

"Oh, Kassidy, give me a break." Denise left the room, apparently out of patience.

"Kassidy," Heidi said in a firm voice. "I have a chair over there in the corner. Do you want to spend the entire class sitting in it, or are you going to be a good student?"

The girl squirmed and heaved a sigh. "Okay, whatever."

Heidi held her hands behind her back, wondering how she could get through to Kassidy or Becky. And then there was the Kimball family. They needed help, too. *All I can do is pray for my students, but I don't feel it's enough.*

———— ❧ ————

Trent sat back and listened. He'd felt the tension as soon as he walked into the house. Except for Darren, the parents seemed on edge.

I should have stayed the last time I brought the kids. It's strange, though, they never mentioned any problems going on within their class.

As Trent half-listened to what Heidi was instructing, he was glad everything seemed to have settled down. Denise had rejoined her daughter in the kitchen, and Ellen seemed more relaxed.

Once more, Trent's thoughts turned to his wife. He missed the life he used to have with her and the children. Even their occasional squabbles seemed minor now. Trent would overlook them if given the chance to begin again with Miranda. It was like watching the wheel of time turn round and round as he remembered their first kiss, then their wedding day, and later the birth of their children.

My wife is a wonderful mother, and she's the perfect wife. How could I have been so stupid as to get caught up in another woman's charms? No wonder Miranda is afraid to trust me. But how can I prove myself to her and show that I've learned my lesson and will never do anything like that again? Would I trust her if she'd done it to me?

Chapter 33

Heidi handed out recipe cards to each of her students, and then gave them the ingredients to make her special egg salad. She could see from a few of the children's expressions that they weren't too enthused. Well, it was too late to fix something else, but at least she noticed a few of her students turning the card over to read the Bible verse. This week she'd used Isaiah 54:13: "And all thy children shall be taught of the Lord; and great shall be the peace of thy children."

Maybe the verses are getting through to some of these children, or even their parents. Heidi hoped that was the case.

"Now the first thing we will do is boil some eggs." Heidi pointed to the egg carton, as well as the kettle she'd set on the table. "If you'll each take one and gently place it in the pan, I'll put it on the stove to boil. Be very careful, though. We don't want to break any eggs."

Heidi had no sooner spoken the words when Peggy Ann picked up an egg and dropped it into the kettle. The shell cracked on impact, and the yolk, mixed with white, seeped out.

Peggy Ann burst into tears.

Trent stared at the child in disbelief as she ran out of the room. He glanced at Debbie, staring at the broken egg with a sober expression. *Wonder how my daughter would have reacted if it happened to her.*

"What's that girl's problem?" Trent directed his question to Heidi. "It's only a broken egg. Seems overly emotional to me."

"Peggy Ann has many reasons to be emotional." Heidi spoke in a quiet tone. "She and her family are fairly new to the area and they've had a rough go of it since their arrival."

"What kind of problems have they faced?" he questioned.

"For one thing, Velma—Peggy Ann's mother—was in an accident and totaled her car. Her insurance won't cover the damages, and Velma and her husband don't have the money to buy a new vehicle." Heidi moved away from the table. "I need to check on Peggy Ann. Would one of you please take over until I get back?"

"I'll do whatever you ask," Ellen spoke up. "Should I see that the eggs get boiled?"

"Yes, thank you." Heidi hurried from the kitchen and found Peggy Ann crouched in one corner of the living room, tears streaming down her face.

Heidi knelt beside the little girl and patted her trembling shoulder. "It's okay. No harm's been done. You can start over with another egg."

"I can't never do nothin' right. My brother says I'm a klutz, and I guess it's true." Peggy Ann sniffed, swiping at her tears. "Mama always says we shouldn't waste food, but I wrecked a good egg."

"Don't worry about it, Peggy Ann. I've broken plenty of eggs, too." Heidi shook her head. "And you're not a klutz. It was an accident and could have happened to anyone."

Peggy Ann blinked rapidly. "You think so?"

"Most certainly." Heidi gave the child a sympathetic squeeze. "Now let's go back to the kitchen." She rose to her feet and reached for the child's hand.

Peggy Ann blew her nose on the tissue Heidi handed her. "Okay."

Heidi smiled. At least one problem was solved. Now, if she could just get Kassidy and Becky to apologize to each other and act civilized, it would be a successful day.

As Trent sat between his children, waiting for the kettle of eggs to boil, he thought about the things Heidi had said concerning Peggy Ann's mother needing another car. While he couldn't provide her with a new one, he might be able to buy a reliable used car. It may not prove he was trustworthy yet, but it would be a good deed and could help gain points with Miranda, which, in turn, might pave the way further to a reconciliation.

Trent's tongue darted out to lick his lips. *Yep. Come Monday morning I'll get on it. I'm sure the right car that would fit my budget and work for the struggling family's need is sitting on my boss's lot, waiting for a new owner.*

Trent bumped his son's shoulder and grinned. *Hang in there, buddy. It won't be long and your dad will be coming home where he belongs. Then our family will be complete again.*

———————⌐✦⌐———————

Denise looked over at her daughter, sitting with elbows on the table and wearing a smug expression. *Does my daughter think she's won the fight with Becky, or does she have something else up her sleeve?* Kassidy seemed to be making an attempt to get along with all the other children except Becky—and especially Jeremy.

"Do you have any pets?" Kassidy smiled sweetly at Darren's son, although her question sounded far from sincere.

"I have a dog named Bacon," Jeremy answered with little enthusiasm. "Thought I told you before."

"No, you never mentioned him to me," Kassidy said in an all-too-friendly tone. "You should bring him to class next time."

"Naw. That wouldn't be a good idea." Jeremy turned his back on Kassidy and made conversation with Randy. Denise couldn't blame him for that. He probably didn't care much for her daughter, with the way she acted.

When Heidi returned with Peggy Ann, Kassidy spoke up. "Are you okay now, Peggy Ann?"

The young girl nodded.

Denise watched with suspicion when Kassidy smiled, then turned her conversation to Debbie. "Maybe sometime you can come to our place, and we can spend an afternoon together."

"Maybe." Debbie glanced at her father, but he said nothing.

Denise felt pity for Becky, frowning and fidgeting in her chair as she eyed Kassidy. *I wonder what that poor girl is thinking.*

"Kassidy, quit disrupting the class and pay attention to Heidi," Denise whispered so that others wouldn't hear. She felt sure Kassidy was up to something, but couldn't figure out what.

———————⌐✦⌐———————

Velma paused from weeding long enough to watch a mother robin pull a worm from the grass and feed her baby. Even birds and animals cared about their young and provided for their needs.

Her heart clenched. *I wonder where Bobbie Sue is living now. Is she doing okay? If we would only hear something from her I'd feel a bit better.* She squeezed her eyes shut, reflecting on her son, Clem. He obviously didn't care about his family anymore either. *Maybe I'm getting what I deserve.*

Velma thought about her parents and the falling-out she'd had with them before she and Hank packed up their family and moved to Ohio. It was a heated argument that never got resolved. Velma had been so upset when they moved, she'd decided to sever the relationship with her folks. They'd never approved of Hank, and her obligation was to him, so Velma felt she had to choose. Some days she thought about trying to make amends, but she wasn't sure they would want anything to do with her—especially after the horrible things that had been said on both sides. Hank was even angrier than Velma, and he'd made it clear when they moved that he never wanted to see her parents again. So if she chose to contact them, she'd have to do it secretly. It might be worth taking the chance, however. At least then, she wouldn't have to live with guilt.

When she heard her name being called, her eyes snapped open. She looked toward the house and saw Heidi heading her way. Velma stood, and wiped her face with her hanky, hoping there were no tears.

"I came out to tell you that the children have finished making their egg-salad sandwiches," Heidi said. "We made a few extras, so would you like to join us as we eat our sandwiches?"

"Oh, I don't know." Velma self-consciously brushed a splotch of dirt off her T-shirt. "I'm not really presentable for socializin'."

"It's okay. Nobody is dressed fancy, and since Kassidy and Becky have dirt and grass stains on their clothes, no one will even notice the soil on yours. Besides, a little dirt from the garden shows how hard you've been working."

"A sandwich does sound good." Velma stuffed her hanky into one of her overalls' pockets. "Before we go into the house, can I ask you a question?"

"Certainly."

"If you had a disagreement with your folks, and your husband didn't want you to have any contact with them, what would ya do?"

"That would be a difficult situation." Heidi rubbed the base of her neck. "Does Hank have a good reason for not wanting you to speak with them?"

Nodding, Velma groaned. "We had a fallin'-out with them before we left Kentucky, and some ugly words were said on both parts. Truth is, my parents have never cared much for Hank, so that makes it even harder."

Heidi placed a comforting hand on Velma's arm. "If I were in your situation, the first thing I'd do is pray about it."

"Yeah, I kinda thought I should be doin' that." Velma puckered her lips. "Prayin' don't come easy to me, though, and it may take some practice."

"You know, Velma, praying isn't anything more than talking to God. He wants us to talk to Him—not just about our requests—but to praise and thank Him for our many blessings."

"Guess you're right about that. I just don't feel worthy to even be talkin' to God. All these years I've pretty much ignored Him, thinkin' I could do things by myself. So why would He listen to me now?"

Heidi shook her head. "If we based our relationship with God on our worthiness, none of us would measure up. But He wants us to humbly come to Him in prayer and supplication, so we should never be afraid to approach the throne with our requests. No prayer is too small or unimportant in God's eyes."

Velma's lips parted as she leaned closer to Heidi. "Know what I think?"

"What?"

"I think you'd make a good preacher."

Heidi's cheeks flushed. "Oh, my, no. I'm not qualified for that. Besides, in our Amish faith, only men are chosen to be ministers."

Velma tipped her head. "Is that a fact?"

Heidi slowly nodded.

"And why is that?"

"We believe the Bible tells us that women are not to teach men. Our ministers, deacons, and bishops are chosen by lot, and women are never included."

"Looks like I've got a lot to learn. Especially about my Amish neighbors." *If Hank heard what Heidi just explained, I'm sure he'd agree with this Amish rule, but not for the same reasons.*

Chapter 34

As Heidi reached into the laundry basket to hang a towel on the line, she noticed a car at the end of her driveway. It just sat there with the engine running, but she couldn't make out the driver. Could it be the same vehicle she'd seen out by the road a few weeks ago? Was it the same color? She didn't remember.

Her heartbeat quickened. Today had been stressful and her nerves were on edge. She didn't need one more thing to worry about.

Should I walk out there and see who it is? Perhaps it's only someone who is lost and needs directions. Her fingers clenched as she dropped the towel back into the basket. *I wish Lyle were here right now. He'd know what to do.*

Heidi started walking toward the driveway, but the car backed out and headed down the road. She sighed and resumed her task. Then hearing the squeal of laughter, she glanced in the direction of the children, playing on the front porch. After her students departed today, Heidi had expected Randy or Marsha to mention the quarrel they'd witnessed between Becky and Kassidy. But surprisingly, neither child had brought it up. Heidi couldn't imagine it not bothering them, for it still disturbed her.

Apparently Marsha, who had been quite upset at the time, now had other thoughts on her young mind. Kassidy and Becky had not set a good example for the younger, impressionable children. This was all the more reason Heidi was determined to give Randy and Marsha a good upbringing. Oh, how she looked forward to the day those sweet children would truly belong to her and Lyle.

A flash of blue, along with frantic chirping, caught Heidi's attention. She stood motionless, holding the towel she'd dropped back in the basket moments ago, and watched two male bluebirds seemingly in battle. She assumed the one bird was guarding his territory. Heidi expected the baby birds would soon leave the safety of their box. Last evening at dinner, Lyle had told her he'd noticed the young birds sticking their little heads out the entrance. They seemed anxious to discover the world awaiting them.

She looked toward the nesting area and saw the female bird watching the ruckus from the roof of the bird box. The fighting males flew at each other, wings flapping and feet extended. They dropped to the ground and continued to challenge each other. Heidi feared one of them might break a wing as they flew at each other. Finally, the battle ended. The female's mate, with a few feathers ruffled, joined her on top of their little home.

Heidi could relate to those birds and how they took care of their family. Without a doubt, she and Lyle would do whatever it took to provide for and protect Randy and Marsha.

She finished hanging the laundry, hoisted the empty basket, and stepped onto the porch. "Would you two like a snack?" Heidi asked, smiling down at the children.

Marsha grinned as she bobbed her blond head. "Jah, Mammi. Do you have any kichlin?"

"As a matter of fact, I do. Would you like peanut butter cookies or chocolate chip?"

"I want the chocolate ones," Randy spoke up.

Marsha licked her lips. "Peanut butter."

"All right then, I'll set some cookies and milk on the table, while you two go in and wash your hands."

The children clambered to their feet and raced into the house. Chuckling, Heidi followed.

———— ⌒∾⌒ ————

Millersburg

"I can't understand why you didn't want the kids to come along this evening." Miranda looked over at Trent as they neared the town of Millersburg. "And just where are you taking me?"

He glanced over at her and smiled. "It's a surprise. You'll see soon enough."

She fiddled with her purse straps. *Why do I have the feeling he's up to something again? First it was the flowers. Now, who knows what?*

Trent turned on the radio to an easy-listening station, and Miranda tried to relax. She moistened her lips with the tip of her tongue, wondering if she should bring up the marriage seminar or wait until they got to their destination. *Maybe I'll let him tell me whatever he wants to say about the kids before I mention the seminar.*

Twenty minutes later, they pulled up to Fox's Pizza Den, and Trent turned off the ignition. "We're here." He grinned over at Miranda.

Her brows furrowed. "We're having pizza? What's that have to do with our children?"

Trent's ears turned pink. "No, I—" He placed his hand on her shoulder. "Remember when we came here on our first date, and then we went bowling at Spare Things Lanes?"

She shook her head. "No we didn't, Trent. On our first date we went to LaPalma Mexican Grill. Bowling and the pizza place was our second date."

"Oh, boy. Guess I blew that one, didn't I?" Trent's blush covered his ears and down his neck. "So much for trying to impress you."

Miranda tugged her ear. "I didn't think we came here so you could impress me or take a walk down memory lane. I thought you wanted to talk about Debbie and Kevin."

"I do. Just thought. . ." He paused and cleared his throat. "The kids miss me, Miranda. They want me to come home, and I was hoping you might want that, too."

Miranda felt trapped. Trent was using Kevin and Debbie to pry on her sympathies again. He should know by now it was not the way to win her back.

Miranda's muscles twitched as she clasped her hands tightly in her lap. "Our marriage needs an overhaul, Trent. There are so many weak areas, and nothing will be resolved by sweeping things under the rug."

"What exactly are you saying?"

"We need help."

Trent slapped his forehead. "Here we go. You want us to see a marriage counselor, right?"

"Maybe, but to begin with, I'd like you to attend a marriage seminar with me that my church is having next weekend. It starts on a Friday evening, and then continues on Saturday for most of the day." She held her breath, waiting for his response.

Trent clutched the steering wheel as if he were holding a shield. "I—uh—will have to think about it."

"Okay, but I'll need an answer by the first of next week so I can sign us up for the event."

"I'll give you a call Monday evening." Trent rubbed his chin. "Now, I'd like your opinion on something."

"What is it?"

"There's a young girl taking Heidi's cooking class. Her name's Peggy Ann."

Miranda nodded. "She lives near the Troyers, and her mother, Velma, does some work for Heidi to pay for her daughter's class."

"That's right, and from what I overheard, the family is struggling financially and they need a car." Trent made strong eye contact with Miranda. "So I was thinking I ought to look into getting a reasonably priced used car for Velma."

"It's a nice thought, but I doubt they could even afford a secondhand car."

He shook his head. "I'm planning to buy the car myself and give it to them."

"Really? Can you afford to do that?"

"Probably not, but I feel sorry for the family, and I want to do something to help."

Miranda touched the base of her throat. She'd never known her husband to be so generous, especially to a perfect stranger. Was he doing it as a genuine good deed, or could it be that Trent was only trying to impress her? For now, she would give him the benefit of the doubt. The real test would be whether he would agree to attend the seminar with her.

Canton

"Do you want to tell him, or should I?" Denise's forehead wrinkled as she handed Greg a platter full of baked chicken. Greg had been playing golf all afternoon with his lawyer buddies, so he had no idea what had transpired at the cooking class earlier that day.

"Tell me what?" Greg looked from Denise to Kassidy.

Kassidy picked up the ear of corn on her plate and chewed off the kernels, leaving several pieces stuck to her face.

"Your daughter got in a fight today before class started." Denise forked a piece of steaming broccoli and blew on it.

"A fight?" Greg looked at Kassidy. "Was it a verbal argument or an actual fist fight?"

"It wasn't a fist fight, Dad." Kassidy grabbed a napkin and wiped the butter dripping down her chin. "Just a bunch of shoving."

That girl makes me so mad. Denise inhaled slowly feeling her frustration mounting. "That fight involved more than shoving, and you know it. You were pulling each other's hair and punching. Furthermore, it doesn't matter what kind of fight or argument it was. You should never have let it happen."

"It was Becky's fault, too," Kassidy retorted.

"Maybe you need to spend the rest of the night in your room." Greg reached for an ear of corn off the platter.

"But Dad, I was good in class afterwards, and even tried to be nice to the other kids. But Mom keeps harping at me."

With furrowed brows, Greg looked at Denise. "At some point, all kids get into fights. Doesn't make it right, but that's part of growing up. I'm sure you had a fight at least once during your childhood."

"No, I did not. Besides, it's not the point. Our daughter didn't even apologize to Becky. I think she should be grounded for a couple of days, or maybe—"

Kassidy lifted her chin. "Becky didn't apologize either."

"You see." Greg wagged a finger. "The other girl's at fault, too. Just let 'em work it out, Denise."

Denise wiped her mouth and took her plate to the sink. *Why bother to argue? As usual, Greg's mind is made up, and once again, Kassidy has gotten her way.* She reflected on the verse Heidi had written on the back of the recipe card she'd given Kassidy at the last cooking class. "And all thy children shall be taught of the LORD; and great shall be the peace of thy children."

Denise rubbed the bridge of her nose and sighed. *Perhaps Greg and I have made a mistake by not seeing that our daughter gets religious training. We have taught her nothing about God, and I have to wonder if we should all start attending church, in search of God's peace.*

⁓

Berlin

Darren slipped his arm around Ellen's waist as they meandered around the Fireman's Festival, looking for the best place to sit during the fireworks display. Their kids walked ahead of them, neither saying a word. Jeremy had been quiet all evening, and Becky seemed to be pouting. *She's probably still fretting about the encounter she had with Kassidy this morning.* Darren wished he felt free to talk to her about it, but he didn't know how Becky would take it. And Ellen might not appreciate him reprimanding her daughter.

Darren spread out the blanket he'd brought along and suggested they all take a seat. With hands in his pockets, Jeremy shook his head. "I'd rather stand."

"Okay, but make sure you're not blocking anyone's view." Darren was pleased when Ellen sat on the blanket, and he quickly took a seat beside her, watching to see what her daughter would do.

"I'm gonna find a restroom," Becky mumbled, looking down at her mother.

"Okay, but hurry back, or you might miss the fireworks."

"Have you enjoyed the festival?" Darren asked, leaning closer to Ellen.

She smiled. "Very much. I admire and appreciate what you and all the firemen in our area do. It's a difficult and sometimes dangerous occupation."

"Yeah, but I like my job, and I bet you like yours as a nurse, too."

"I do, although there are stressful times. But I suppose that's true with most professions."

"Uh-huh." Darren looked up and pointed as the fireworks started, then he turned to look into Ellen's eyes. The glow from the exploding lights illuminated her beautiful face.

Almost of its own accord, Darren's hand reached out and caressed her cheek. When he tilted her chin upwards, everything around them seemed to disappear, except for Ellen's warm breath feathering his face. Darren slipped his other arm around Ellen's waist, lowered his head, and kissed her tenderly. He was pleased when she didn't pull away and returned his kiss. Ellen's lips were soft as rose petals.

The spell was broken when Jeremy returned to the blanket and plopped down in front of them. So much for the evening ending on a romantic note. Darren had to wonder if his son had seen them kiss, and intentionally interrupted.

Becky returned a few minutes later and sat in front of Ellen as the fireworks continued to burst overhead.

"Say, I have an idea." Darren reached for Ellen's hand. "How would you and Becky like to go with me and Jeremy to the Farm at Walnut Creek next Saturday? It'll be fun to ride in one of their horse-pulled wagons and see all the animals roaming about."

"That sounds good, and my schedule just changed so that I don't have to work next Saturday," she replied. "And I'm sure my daughter would like to go, too." Ellen nudged Becky. "Right?"

The girl shrugged.

Darren gently squeezed Ellen's fingers. He looked forward to spending more time with Ellen. Hopefully, their kids would be in better moods.

Chapter 35

"Who wants a glass of cold lemonade?" Miranda asked when she and the children entered the house after running errands Monday afternoon.

"I do! I do!" Kevin shouted.

"I'd like one, too," Debbie added. "And also some cookies."

"I think that can be arranged." Miranda chuckled. "Let me change out of my work clothes, and I'll meet you both in the kitchen." She hung her purse on the coat tree and hurried down the hall to her bedroom. It had been a busy day at the grocery store, and all she wanted to do was prop up her feet. Standing at the register all morning and afternoon, Miranda felt weariness set in.

When Miranda returned to the kitchen, she found Kevin sitting with his elbows on the table. Debbie had gotten out the cookie jar and set napkins out.

Miranda smiled. "Thank you, sweetie. You're such a big help."

"You're welcome." Debbie stared off into space.

Miranda wondered what her daughter was thinking about. She opened the refrigerator and took out the lemonade.

"Can I ask you something, Mom?" Debbie asked after Miranda gave her a glass of lemonade.

"Sure, honey, what is it?"

"Do I have to go over to Kassidy's house if she invites me?"

Miranda took a moment to think how best to answer, but Kevin spoke first.

"I'd never go over there." He held out his glass, while Miranda poured the cold drink. "I don't like Kassidy. She's mean."

"Never mind." Miranda tapped her son's arm, then turned to Debbie. "If she does extend an invitation, and you don't go, that's fine.

I certainly won't force you to go someplace where you wouldn't be comfortable."

"Thanks, Mommy. I can't figure her out. She's been so nasty, and then all of a sudden Kassidy acts like she wants to be my friend. Makes me wonder if she's only being nice 'cause she wants something."

"It's hard to know what another person is thinking. Perhaps Kassidy has a hard time making friends. Or maybe she wants to change her ways, but doesn't know how." Miranda noticed that her children were looking at her intently. "Maybe if you're kind to Kassidy, she will be kind back."

Debbie tipped her head. "I can be nice during the cooking classes, but I don't wanna go to her house. She'd probably brag about everything she has."

"Yeah," Kevin chimed in before reaching for a cookie. "That girl's a bragger, all right."

Miranda handed her son a napkin. "Let's wait and see what happens. Kassidy may forget about asking either of you to visit her home."

Miranda's cell phone rang, and she went to retrieve it from her purse. A quick look, and she knew the call was from Trent. "You kids finish up your snack while I take this call."

So they wouldn't hear her conversation, Miranda stepped into the utility room and closed the door. "Hello, Trent."

"Hi. What took you so long to answer? Figured I'd end up leaving a message."

"I was in the kitchen with Debbie and Kevin, and my phone was in my purse."

"Do you have a few minutes to talk?" he asked.

"Sure."

"I've been thinking about our conversation Saturday night, and your suggestion that we attend a marriage seminar."

Miranda stood silently waiting for him to continue.

"If you still want to go, I'm willing to attend it with you." His tone was upbeat, which gave her hope that he wasn't doing it out of some sort of obligation.

"Yes, I do want for us to go. Hopefully, we'll both get something good from it." She leaned against the washing machine, waiting for his response.

"I have no idea what to expect, 'cause I've never been to that kind of thing."

"And I never thought we'd need to attend something like this, but I've heard good things from others who went to previous seminars."

"What time should I pick you up Friday evening?"

"The event starts at seven, so if you could be here by six thirty, that would be great. I'll get a sitter for the children."

"Okay, sounds good. See you soon."

"Bye, Trent." Miranda clicked off the phone and closed her eyes. *Heavenly Father, please let this seminar be the beginning of a healing in my marriage.*

Canton

When Kassidy entered the living room, wearing a pair of navy-blue shorts and a white blouse, Denise set the real estate listings she'd been looking at aside. "Is Hillary still coming over to play tennis?"

"Yeah, Mom. She should be here soon." Kassidy flopped onto the couch. "I wish it wasn't so hot out, though. We shoulda played earlier in the day."

"That would have been fine if either your father or I had been home. But since we both had to work this morning, and you spent that time with my folks, it didn't work out for you to have your friend over until this afternoon."

Kassidy focused on her white tennis shoes. "When are you gonna realize I'm old enough to be left alone? Hillary, and some of my other friends, have stayed home by themselves lots of times." Her bottom lip protruded. "You and Dad think I'm still a baby."

Denise shook her head. "We don't think you're a baby, but you aren't an adult either."

"Yeah, I know." Kassidy pushed a strand of curly red hair behind her ear.

"You should be happy your dad said you could have Hillary over to play tennis. If it were up to me, you'd have been grounded this week because of the fight you had with Becky last Saturday." Denise leaned forward in her chair. "Where did you get that barrette in your hair? I've never seen it before."

Kassidy's cheeks colored as she reached up and touched the golden hair clip. "Um. . . I borrowed it from one of my friends."

"Which friend? Does it belong to Hillary?"

"No, it's uh. . ." Kassidy jumped up and raced to the window. "Think I heard a car pull in. Yep, I was right. . . It's Hillary's mother, dropping her off." She hurried to open the front door and stepped outside.

That girl. Denise pursed her lips. *I wish she wouldn't borrow things from her friends. If she loses the barrette, she'll have to buy a new one, but the money to pay for it won't come from me. I will take it out of Kassidy's allowance. She needs to learn a lesson.*

<hr />

Walnut Creek

Walking barefoot through the grass, Velma shielded her eyes from the late afternoon sun. Abner lay panting in the shade of a willow tree on the side of their mobile home. It had warmed up considerably yesterday, and today the weather was even hotter. They had no air-conditioning, and she dreaded going to sleep tonight. "Maybe you, me, and the kids oughta sleep outside," she said, bending down to pet the black Lab. "It'll be a lot cooler than in that stuffy old double-wide." Velma had given the kids vanilla ice cream after lunch, and it melted before they could finish what was in their bowls.

Abner barely lifted his head, looking up at Velma with sleepy brown eyes. The poor dog looked as miserable as she felt.

She knelt on the grass next to him, then fanned her face with her hand. The hot muggy air made her feel weighed down. If this warm weather kept up, with no rain in sight, their yard would turn brown.

Velma glanced toward the porch, where the kids were spread out on a couple of old cots Hank had picked up somewhere. No doubt the heat wave had gotten to them, too.

Hearing a *cluck. . .cluck. . .cluck*, she turned her attention to the chicken coop she'd finished building this morning. Soon afterward, she had walked down the road about half a mile and purchased three hens. Then she'd walked back, carrying them in a metal carrier. When Hank got home with some money later this week, Velma hoped to buy a few more hens, as well as a rooster. She'd spent the last bit of cash Hank had given her before he left on the three chickens. Once again, she wished she could go out and get a job. Velma was tired of pinching pennies and barely having enough money to put food on the table and pay the bills. On top of that, she was lonely and wished her husband had a job that would allow him to spend more time at home. His being gone so much was hard on Peggy Ann and Eddie, too.

Velma sat back, with both arms spread out behind her, drawing in a deep breath. Yesterday, being Sunday, she'd planned for her and the kids to try out a different church, but they'd all slept in, and by the time everyone had breakfast and gotten dressed, it was too late to make it to church on time.

She leaned her head back and looked up at the cloudless sky. *Maybe next week we'll go.*

The smell of chocolate permeated the kitchen, making Heidi's stomach growl. It brought back memories of her mother baking, when the warm sweet aroma of cookies seeped into every room of the house. Even though Heidi had baked chocolate chip cookies earlier today, the aroma lingered—probably from the warmth of the kitchen. In fact, the heat was almost stifling.

Moving over to the back door, Heidi glanced through the screen to check on Marsha and Randy. They'd gone out to play in the yard half an hour ago, but the sounds of laughter were no longer drifting through the kitchen window.

Seeing no sign of the children, Heidi opened the screen door and stepped onto the porch. She cupped her hands around her mouth and hollered: "Randy! Marsha! Where are you two?"

No response.

She caught sight of Rusty, lapping water from his dish near the back porch. It seemed strange the kids weren't with him, especially when they'd said they were going outside to play with the dog. *Now where did those children get to?*

Heidi called: "Come out, come out, wherever you are!"

Still no answer.

She ran around the side of the house, and then to the front. "Randy! Marsha!"

Maybe they're playing in the barn.

Heidi dashed across the yard and flung the barn doors open. "Marsha! Randy! Are you in here?"

The only sounds were the soft nicker of their buggy horse and the cooing of pigeons from the loft overhead. *I've warned them about it so many times—surely they wouldn't leave the yard.*

The hair on the back of Heidi's neck prickled as a dreadful feeling formed in the pit of her stomach and an image of the vehicle she'd seen twice by the entrance to their driveway came to mind. *What if my precious children have been kidnapped?*

Chapter 36

With sweat pouring down her face, and her chest so tight she could barely breathe, Heidi ran down the driveway toward the road. Over and over, she called the children's names. No reply. *Where are they? Dear Lord, please help me find them.*

When Heidi reached the end of the driveway, she looked up and down both sides of the road. An English man sped by in his noisy pickup, blowing her dress all about. She clenched her teeth and held onto her skirt. Some of the locals drove too fast on the back roads.

What should I do? Who should I call? Oh, I wish Lyle was here. He was auctioneering again today, and probably wouldn't be home until close to suppertime. This problem had fallen on Heidi's shoulders, and she needed to find Randy and Marsha. Her first course of action was to walk down the road and search for the children. If she couldn't find them, she would go back to the phone shack and call the sheriff.

As Heidi looked up and down the road, she bit down on her bottom lip. *Which way should I go—left or right?*

As Velma pulled weeds on the back side of the mobile home, she thought more about her idea of sleeping outside tonight. Peggy Ann and Eddie would probably enjoy it, and they could pretend they were camping. It would be fun to look up at the twinkling stars in the coal black sky and watch fireflies coming up from the grass.

A sigh escaped Velma's lips. "Haven't had a good time with my kids in a while. We should sleep pretty good out here, too."

Some giggling nearby broke the silence. Thinking it must be Eddie or Peggy Ann, Velma went to see what they thought was funny. She was surprised to see two young children dressed in Amish clothes in the front yard. It didn't take Velma long to realize it was Marsha and

Randy. Heidi had stopped by with the kids last week to drop off some produce from her garden, so Randy and Marsha knew where she lived. However, Velma thought it strange that Heidi wasn't with them today.

She hurried over to the children. "What are you two doing here?"

Randy smiled up at her. "We came to look at the hinkel."

Marsha remained quiet as she bounced on her toes.

"What's a hinkel?"

"It's a chicken," the little girl spoke up.

After a bark of laughter, Velma asked, "Now, how'd ya all know I had any chickens?"

"Cause Peggy Ann said you was gonna get some."

Velma tapped Randy's shoulder. "Well, I guess she did. But where's Heidi?"

"Mammi's at home." Marsha looked up at Velma with all the innocence of a child.

"Does she know you're here?"

Randy shook his head.

"Oh, boy! You two need to skedaddle on back then." Velma reached for Marsha's hand. "I'll walk you both home."

"But I wanna see the chickens." Randy inched closer to Velma.

"Okay, you can take a quick look, but then I'm escortin' you back where ya belong. If Heidi knows you're gone, she's probably worried sick."

Marsha's forehead wrinkled. "Mammi's sick?"

"No, that's not what I meant. But she might feel sick if she worries too much." Velma led the way to the coop, surrounded by wire fencing. "Now hurry and take a peek."

Randy and Marsha stood giggling as the two hens chased each other around the enclosure. "They're funny." Marsha clapped her hands.

Several minutes later, Heidi rushed into the yard. "Oh, Velma, the children are missing. Have you seen any sign of. . ." She stopped talking, and her mouth formed an *O*, as she focused on Marsha and Randy. "Oh, my!" She ran to the children, bent down, and grabbed them both in a hug. "What are you two doing over here? Don't you know how worried I was?"

"Came to see Velma's hinkel." Randy pointed to one of the hens. "They're bigger than our chickens, though."

Tears gathered in Heidi's eyes. "I'm glad you're okay, but you should not have left the yard without my permission." She shook her finger. "And never go anywhere outside of our yard without me or Lyle along. Do you both understand?"

Randy nodded, and Marsha's chin quivered. "S–sorry, Mammi. We didn't mean to make ya sick."

"What?" Heidi glanced at Velma.

"I told 'em if you discovered they were gone, you'd be worried sick," Velma explained. "And just so ya know—I was about to take 'em home when you showed up."

"I see." Heidi hugged the children again. "You're not in trouble, but please don't ever leave the yard again by yourselves. Something bad might have happened to you." She rose to her feet. "Let's go home now."

As Heidi left the yard with the children, she called over her shoulder, "Thank you, Velma. I'll see you and Peggy Ann a week from Saturday."

Velma watched as they walked down the driveway and turned in the direction of Heidi's house. She glanced toward the double-wide, surprised that Eddie and Peggy Ann were not on the porch. "Bet they're inside watchin' TV," she muttered, heading in that direction.

Dover

Darren entered Jeremy's bedroom to call him for supper and was surprised to see him standing in front of his dresser, rummaging through one of the drawers.

"What are you doing, Son?" Darren questioned.

"I—I'm just lookin' for something."

"What is it? Maybe I can help you find it." Darren stepped forward.

Jeremy's ears reddened as he quickly shut the drawer. "It's nothin', Dad."

"Really? Then why the guilty expression?"

Jeremy's gaze dropped to the floor, and he shuffled his feet on the carpet.

"Come on, Son, fess up. What were you looking for?"

Jeremy lifted his head. "I've been lookin' for that fancy doodad Mom used to wear in her hair."

"Do you mean the barrette I bought for her a few months before she died?"

"Yeah."

Darren rubbed a spot on his forehead, just above his brows. "Why would you be looking for it in your dresser?"

"Cause it's missing."

"I know that, Son. It went missing a few days before your mom passed away, and we never found it."

Jeremy lowered his head again. "I found it down the side of the couch last Saturday, before we left for the cooking class."

"Was that what you were fooling with in the car?"

"Yeah."

"Why didn't you tell me you'd found it?"

"I don't know. Guess I thought you'd be upset 'cause I wanted to keep it." Jeremy looked up at Darren with tears in his eyes. "I miss her, Dad, and I wanted to have something of Mom's to remember her by."

Filled with compassion, Darren pulled Jeremy into his arms. "We have lots of things in our house to remind us of your mother. I was planning to give you some of her personal things when you got married someday, but if there is something you'd like now, just let me know."

"I wanted the hair clip because I knew it was special to her." Jeremy's voice broke. "But now I've stupidly lost it."

"You had it last Saturday, though, right?"

Jeremy nodded. "It was in my jeans' pocket, except for the time I took it out and was looking at it."

"So maybe you lost it someplace at Heidi's. And if that's the case, we can ask her about it when we go to your cooking class a week from this Saturday."

"Do we have to wait that long? Can't we go back there now?"

Darren shook his head. "I'm on call this evening and may have to fill in for one of the men who is sick. I work tomorrow, too, so we'll have to wait till Wednesday to go to Walnut Creek to see Heidi."

Jeremy flopped onto his bed. "If Heidi did find it, I bet she threw it away. I'll probably never see Mom's hair clip again."

"Don't give up, Son. If you lost it at Heidi's, I'm sure you will see it again." Darren gave Jeremy's arm a squeeze. "I'm going back to the kitchen to make myself a cup of coffee. Let me know if you need anything."

Jeremy nodded. "Okay, Dad. I'll probably go to the living room and watch TV."

When Darren entered the kitchen, he poured himself a cup of coffee and stood by the window. As he looked out, he thought about Jeremy and the special keepsake symbolic of his mother. It had been only a little over two years since Caroline's death, but certain things, like the mention of her barrette, brought back memories and kept the pain alive.

In Darren's eyes, his marriage to her had been no less than perfect. *Well, maybe not perfect,* he admitted. *But we were happy and filled with hope for the future until Caroline began having severe headaches.* The pain had been manageable at first, but then the headaches got so bad she found it hard to do anything except lie down. When Caroline went to the doctor after about a month of misery, he ordered an MRI and several other tests. The results were devastating. It was discovered that she had an inoperable brain tumor. The prognosis was that his wife had less than six months to live. Caroline declined having any treatments. She wanted to live life as normally as possible and didn't want the side effects of chemo.

Darren remembered how they'd explained things to Jeremy and the way his son had taken it like a little man. But Darren also remembered walking by his son's room one night, a few weeks later, and hearing him sobbing into his pillow.

Darren cried too, but privately. He wanted to be strong for Caroline. But no one was stronger than his precious wife. Her insistence on living life as normally as possible kept her going, even though she dealt with pain, dizziness, and disorientation. The doctor gave her a prescription for medicine that helped her function for a while.

About three weeks before she died, Caroline could no longer manage even the simplest of chores. She became couch-ridden, preferring to recline there rather than in the bed she had previously shared with Darren. She was so brave and beautiful from the inside out, even though the tumor wracked her body with pain. She lost weight but still had her beautiful hair, and that is why Darren bought her the barrette. She wore it every day, but no one seemed to notice when it fell out of her hair and apparently got lodged between the couch cushions. Her condition by then had grown hopeless. Jeremy and Darren cherished every last hour, minute, and second with Caroline.

Darren's thoughts took him back to the night when Jeremy had snuggled up to his mom on the couch and they had fallen asleep together. . . .

Darren sat in the dark, with only the light of the moon filtering in through the living room, watching his son and wife, with tears streaming down his face. Then sometime around two o'clock, Darren could no longer keep his eyes open, and he nodded off.

Sometime later, Darren was awakened when he heard Jeremy cough. He looked over at his wife and saw that she was looking at him.

Darren picked up his son and carried him to his room, being careful not to wake the boy. Then tiptoeing down the hall, he went back to the living room to be with his wife.

Caroline reached out and clasped his hand. "I need you to promise me something," she whispered.

"Of course, honey, anything."

"I want you to be brave and not mourn for me after I'm gone."

"I will try to be brave, but I can't promise not to mourn." Darren could barely speak around the lump clogging his throat.

She lifted a shaky hand and stroked his cheek. "Thank you for being such a wonderful husband and father."

"It's easy to do, since I love you and our son so much."

"And I love you, but I want you to move on with your life when you're ready to let go. Do not feel guilty if you find love again." Caroline paused

and drew a shuddering breath. "I will always have your love with me right here." She touched her chest where her heart would soon stop beating.

Darren couldn't talk. He simply gathered his precious wife into his arms. She clung to him, and then took one last breath. He felt her body relax, and just like that, his beloved wife was gone.

———————————⚬⚬⚬⚬⚬———————————

Darren shuddered, and he wiped the corners of his eyes as his mind returned to the present. He never thought he would find love again, but now with Ellen, he knew that wasn't true. Given the chance, he was almost certain they could build a strong relationship.

As Darren finished his cup of coffee, now lukewarm, he stared out the window. It was something, how when a person left the earth, life still went on. Darren, like others who had lost loved ones, had been numb with grief. Each day he'd had to get used to waking up without Caroline. At times he could almost feel her right beside him. But on other days, he was afraid he would forget her beautiful face. As the weeks drifted into months, and the months into more than two years, the horrors of what he and Jeremy had gone through were replaced by all the memories they shared. Not a day went by when something didn't remind him of Caroline and her sweet ways or reflect on things they used to do as a family.

Now that he and Ellen were getting close, he had to put some thought into their relationship and decide how serious he wanted it to get—especially with how his son felt. If only Jeremy could learn to appreciate Ellen as much as Darren did.

Chapter 37

Walnut Creek

"Sure hope if Heidi found Mom's barrette, she didn't throw it away." Jeremy sounded desperate.

"Try not to worry," Darren called over his shoulder, keeping his eyes on the road.

"But Dad, today's already Wednesday, and if she did find it someplace in her house, she wouldn't have known who left it." Jeremy grunted. "Most likely she'd have thought it belonged to one of the girls in our class. Someone could've already come and claimed it by now."

"Not likely, Son. Since it doesn't belong to one of the girls, there'd be no reason for them to claim it. Now stop fretting. We're almost there."

When Darren pulled into Heidi's yard, he spotted her on the grass, tossing a ball back and forth to the children. They looked like they were having a good time.

Darren parked the car, but before he could open his door, Jeremy hopped out and raced over to Heidi. Darren sprinted across the lawn to catch up with his son.

"Did you find my mom's barrette?" Jeremy stepped in front of Heidi after she threw the ball to Randy.

She quirked an eyebrow. "I'm not sure what you're talking about."

"Jeremy had his mother's hair clip with him last Saturday, and he thinks he may have dropped it someplace in your house or yard," Darren explained. "Did you happen to see it anywhere? The barrette was gold, with little red stones along the top."

"I haven't seen anything like that around the house or in the yard." Heidi gestured to Randy. "Have you seen a fancy hair clip?"

"Nope." Randy bounced the ball a few times.

Heidi looked at Marsha, and the little girl shook her head.

Jeremy groaned. "I had it with me Saturday; I know I did. Dad, remember when you asked me what I was holding in my hand, before I got out of the car?"

"Yes, I do remember." Darren felt his boy's frustration.

"You're welcome to look around out here if you like." Heidi made a sweeping gesture of the yard.

"Thanks." Darren pointed to the driveway. "Let's start where we parked the car that day." He headed in that direction, and Jeremy followed. Heidi joined them in the search. They looked everywhere Jeremy remembered walking, but found nothing.

"What about the house? Can I look in there?" Jeremy bit down on his bottom lip. "I've gotta find it. The barrette was special to my mom, and now it is to me."

Heidi suggested they all go inside and search for the hair clip. Marsha and Randy looked none-too-happy when she asked them to put the ball away and go into the house, but they did as they were told.

Darren and Jeremy followed her and the children in, and Jeremy retraced his steps. "I was here in the living room, and when everyone got here, we all went to the kitchen."

"All right, let's look in those two rooms," Heidi said.

"You also went to the bathroom," Darren reminded. "Why don't you look there, while I check out the living room?"

"While you two are doing that, I'll search in the kitchen." Heidi offered Jeremy a sympathetic smile. "If it's here in the house, I'm sure one of us will find it."

———————— ◦ ⌣ ◦ ————————

Another hour went by, but the barrette was not found. "I'm sorry." Darren clasped his son's shoulder. "We may as well give up and go home."

With shoulders slumped, Jeremy lowered his head. "Guess it's my fault for bringin' it to class with me. I shoulda put it somewhere safe in our house." He shuffled toward the front door.

"I'll keep looking, Jeremy," Heidi called. "If I find it, I'll let your father know right away."

Jeremy went silently out the door.

Darren turned to face Heidi. "Thank you for taking the time to help us look. Jeremy took his mother's death pretty hard, and on top of that, he's having a difficult time accepting the fact that I'm interested in another woman."

Curious, Heidi tipped her head to one side. "Ellen?"

"Yeah. To tell you the truth, I don't think her daughter's too thrilled about it either."

"Children, like adults, can find it difficult to move forward after losing a loved one. We can try to be patient and find ways to encourage them along." Heidi rested her hands against the front of her apron.

"I've been trying to be patient, and I'll keep at it."

"Dad, are you coming?" Jeremy called from outside.

Darren looked over his shoulder, then back at Heidi. "We'll see you soon."

Heidi stood by the front door, watching them get into their vehicle. *I need to keep Darren and Jeremy in my prayers. I can't imagine what it's like to be a single parent, and I pray that never happens to me.*

———————— ·ᴄ·ᵒᵒᴑ·ᵕ· ————————

Millersburg

"I don't see why we have to see a bunch of animals with Jeremy and his dad this Saturday," Becky complained as she and Ellen filled the bird feeders in their yard. "I've been to the farm before with my class at school, and it wasn't that exciting."

"Really?" Ellen stopped what she was doing and placed both hands on her hips. "As I recall, when you came home that day, all you could talk about was the llama that spit, and how much fun it was to see the baby giraffe. I would think you'd want to go back and see how all the animals are doing. You'll get to feed them again, you know."

Becky folded her arms. "Well, it might be more fun if it was just the two of us. Jeremy will probably say a bunch of stupid things, and his dad..." She stopped talking. "Oh, never mind. I can tell you wanna go, so I'll get through it."

Get through it? Ellen could hardly believe her daughter's attitude.

Is she jealous of Darren? Does she think he will come between us?

"Sounds like those birds are mighty hungry." Ellen looked toward the trees. "We have one more feeder to do, and then we're done." Ellen reached for the feeder, and slid open the top, while Becky held the funnel to fill it with seeds. If Becky's attitude toward Darren didn't improve, Ellen realized she may have to stop seeing him.

New Philadelphia

Trent sat at his desk in the dealership, staring at the paperwork for the sale of a mid-size car he was considering buying at a reasonable price. If he went through with the deal, he'd take the vehicle to the cooking class a week from Saturday and give it to the woman who needed a car. *I bet Miranda will be surprised that I went through with my plan. I hope Velma will be willing to accept my gift.*

From where his desk was positioned, Trent could watch the lot where all the new and used vehicles sat. It had been a slow day so far, and only an elderly couple browsed up and down the rows of cars.

Trent paused at what he was doing and held his breath. *Oh no, not that one.* The man and woman stopped at the car he was thinking of purchasing. He watched as they walked all around the vehicle and peered inside at the interior.

Should I go out and see if they have any questions? Truth was, he hoped they'd move on to another car. When he saw them reading the information sheet attached to the passenger window, Trent walked out and joined them.

"May I help you?" he asked, approaching the couple.

"We're looking for a used car, and this one caught our attention." The man smiled.

"I'm not sure I like it, though." The woman walked around the car again. "I was hoping for something a little smaller."

"My name is Trent Cooper." He extended his hand to the man. "I'll let you look around some more, and if you decide on anything, please come inside so we can talk."

"Thank you, Mr. Cooper." The man had a good grip. "My name is

Howard Witmer, and this is my wife, Marie. We'll keep looking and let you know if we decide on a car."

"Okay, I'll be at my desk. It's to the left of the door."

Trent walked back inside. He hoped they would find another car better suited for their needs.

As he sat back down at his desk and watched the couple go down another row of vehicles, his thoughts turned to the seminar he'd agreed to attend with Miranda in two days. He didn't see how it could repair their marriage, but he was desperate to get Miranda back, and hoped by going it might be his ticket home. *And who knows. Maybe I'll learn something.*

Walking over to the water cooler, Trent filled a cup and took a drink. Glancing back outside, he saw the couple get into their car and drive off the lot. "Guess that takes care of that." Trent smacked his hands together and smiled as he walked back to his desk. "Looks like my plan for Velma is going to work out after all."

Chapter 38

Walnut Creek

L ook over there—here comes some animals eager to be fed." Darren pointed to the deer running toward the wagon where he, Jeremy, Ellen, and Becky were seated on a long wooden bench. An elderly Amish man drove the wagon, pulled by two sturdy horses.

Across from them sat five other people, all here for the same fun-filled tour. Everyone had been given a small bucket full of food to feed the animals.

"You must stay in the wagon at all times, and you'll need to remain seated whenever we're moving," the Amish man instructed. "Most of the critters will need to be fed by pouring some of the feed out of the containers and onto the floor of the wagon so they can reach it. However, the two-legged feathered animals with beaks can be fed directly from the bucket," he added. "Just be sure to hold on tight, because if the bucket drops we won't be able to stop and pick it up."

"Oh, look, there's a zebra coming," Ellen shouted, as several deer ate the food on the floor of the wagon. She was obviously enjoying herself, but Darren wasn't sure about Ellen's daughter. Even though Becky had poured food on the wagon floor, she sat with a placid expression. Darren watched Jeremy. He sat quietly, too.

When the zebra came up to the wagon, Ellen reached out and stroked behind the animal's ear. "It feels so soft and silky." She gestured to Becky. "Why don't you try it?"

"No, that's okay." The girl shook her head. "I'll just watch."

Ellen turned to Jeremy then. "Why don't you pet the zebra? It's really. . ."

Jeremy's brows furrowed. "If I wanted to pet the critter, I would." He looked away.

Darren was stunned by his son's sharp tone. "Jeremy, you need to apologize to Ellen."

"Sorry," his son mumbled without looking her way.

Darren rubbed his forehead. This day was not going like he'd planned.

Next, they saw an ostrich with a long neck and pointed beak. Darren couldn't help but chuckle as he held his bucket out, allowing the ostrich to stick its beak in and get some food. In and out. In and out—the big bird's head bobbed back and forth.

Ellen laughed, too. "I think this enormous bird is trying to eat all the food."

Jeremy and Becky remained quiet. It was obvious to Darren that neither of them wanted to be here. *I don't think Becky likes me, and Jeremy doesn't care for Ellen either.*

Darren looked at Ellen and swallowed hard. *Without our kids' blessing, this isn't going to work. As soon as I have a chance to speak to Ellen alone, I'm going to tell her that I think it's best if we don't see each other socially again.*

———— ✦ ————

As the wagon tour concluded, Ellen's shoulders sagged. This outing could have been such a fun day, but Becky and Jeremy's disinterest put a damper on things.

Ellen bit the inside of her cheek. *If only my daughter could see Darren for the nice man he is and realize there's room in my heart for both of them. Becky hasn't given him a fair chance.*

She glanced over at Jeremy, staring at the wagon floor. *He's not happy about his father seeing me either. I bet it's just a matter of time before Darren says he doesn't want to see me anymore.* Ellen pulled in a quick breath and released it slowly. *Maybe it would be best if I break things off. The first opportunity I get to speak to Darren alone, I'm going to tell him I don't think we should see each other outside of the cooking class.*

———— ✦ ————

Berlin

Trent squirmed in his chair, trying to find a comfortable position. Already it felt like he'd been here all day. Last night he and Miranda had attended the first two-hour session of the marriage seminar. Today's gathering, which had begun early this morning, would go on until late afternoon. Trent was glad there was more than one speaker. Listening to the same voice for hours on end would have probably put him to sleep.

He looked around at the other couples who had come here today and wondered if they were all having marital problems. Or perhaps, as one of the earlier speakers had pointed out, some had come to merely strengthen an already healthy marriage. Trent recognized a few of the people from Friday night's meeting. Some were young couples, and a few others looked to be around the same age as he and Miranda. What surprised him, though, was the elderly couples who'd come to the seminar. *I would think those old timers would have all the answers by now. But then, I guess a person is never too old to learn new ways to improve their marriage.*

So far, Trent hadn't gotten a lot out of the class, other than being reminded that a husband and wife should do nice things for each other and work on their communication skills.

Rubbing a hand across his forehead, he felt worry lines creasing his skin. *I've tried to be nice to Miranda, and where has that gotten me? And how am I supposed to communicate with someone who doesn't want to talk to me most of the time and thinks nothing I say is important?*

He glanced in his wife's direction, noting her serious expression as the speaker brought up a new topic.

"A husband's role as head of the house is to be the spiritual leader." The gray-haired man spoke with a tone of authority as he quoted a verse from Ephesians 5:25: "Husbands, love your wives, even as Christ also loved the church, and gave himself for it."

Trent leaned forward, listening intently as the minister read the thirty-third verse of the same chapter: "Nevertheless let every one of you in particular so love his wife even as himself; and the wife see that she reverence her husband."

Trent swallowed hard. *Oh, boy. How can I expect Miranda to respect me when I haven't earned her trust?* Trent leaned back in his seat, and when he glanced in his wife's direction, he saw tears dribbling down her cheeks.

"I love you with all my heart," Trent whispered, clasping her hand. "And with God's help, I want to be the spiritual leader in our home."

"Does that mean you'll start going to church with us as a family?" Miranda spoke quietly against his ear.

He nodded and gently squeezed her warm fingers. It was too soon to ask if he could move back home, but when he'd proved himself and earned her trust, he would ask.

Miranda could hardly believe the words her husband had whispered to her. For the first time since she and Trent had separated, Miranda felt a ray of hope that there might be a reconciliation. It would take some time for him to prove he was serious about attending church and becoming the spiritual leader of their home, but at least he was willing to try. She also felt confident that once it was proven, learning to trust him would be easier.

She closed her eyes and offered a prayer: *Heavenly Father, please lead my husband down the path You want him to follow, and help me to be an encouragement to him. Help me say the right words whenever I speak to Trent, and grant me the wisdom to know when it is right to invite him to come home. If Trent and I resume our marriage, I want it to be for good this time.*

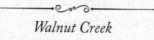

Walnut Creek

After they'd left the farm, Darren had stopped at an ice-cream stand, hoping it would ease some of the tension. All kids loved ice cream, and he'd anticipated Jeremy and Becky would be in a better mood after they had a sweet treat.

Unfortunately the kids' moods had grown worse, and now as they headed to Millersburg to take Ellen and Becky home, his vehicle was filled with nothing but silence. Darren rehearsed in his mind what he would say to Ellen when he dropped them off. He planned to walk them to the door and then, before they went into the house, ask Ellen if he could speak to her alone.

His insides twisted as he thought about saying goodbye and never having the chance to see where their relationship might take them. But he saw no way they could keep seeing each other without their children's approval.

"Hey, Dad, did ya hear those sirens?" Jeremy asked as they approached the road where they always turned off to go to Heidi's.

"Yes, I did." Darren looked in his rearview mirror and saw a fire truck approaching. Then another one, coming from the opposite direction, appeared.

Darren pulled his SUV onto the shoulder of the road to let them pass and was surprised when both vehicles turned up the same road where the Troyers lived. He turned to look at Ellen, sitting beside him with an anxious expression. "I hope you don't mind, but I'd like to follow the trucks and see what's going on. It might be someone we know or maybe they could use some extra help."

Ellen was quick to nod. "I hope nothing has happened at Heidi's place."

Chapter 39

The heat and flames that had started in the kitchen when she left a frying pan on the hot stove sent Velma screaming through her double-wide. She'd tried to put out the fire, but to no avail. "Peggy Ann! Eddie! Where are you? We've gotta get out of the house!" When neither child responded, Velma's fear escalated to panic.

Smoke filled Velma's lungs as she raced down the hall, coughing, disoriented, and calling her children's names. Thick smoke filled the air, and she groped her way along, until she reached her daughter's bedroom. The door was open, and she stepped inside. "Peggy Ann, are you here?"

Velma tipped her head when she heard a faint whimper.

"Peggy Ann!" Velma moved forward, trying to focus through the smoky haze.

Suddenly, her daughter was there, gripping Velma's hand. "Are we gonna burn up in the fire?"

"No, honey, we'll be okay." Velma swept a hand across her forehead. She needed to call 911, but was unable to get to the phone. "Where's your brother?"

"I—I don't know, Mama. Eddie said he was gonna take the dog for a walk, but I don't know if he went outside or not." Peggy Ann coughed. "Oh, Mama, I can't breathe."

Velma pulled her daughter to the floor and instructed Peggy Ann to hold tight to her arm. "Don't worry, baby. I'll keep my arm around you, and we'll crawl out together." She remembered hearing once that, when trapped in a fire, the safest place to be was on the floor, and that a person should try to follow the wall. Velma had to get Peggy Ann to safety and then find Eddie.

Hearing sirens in the distance, she felt a glimmer of hope. One of her neighbors must have seen the blaze and called the fire department.

"Look over there! Do you see the smoke?" Lyle pointed as he guided their horse and open buggy up the road in the direction of their house. They'd taken the children out for an early supper and were on their way home, never expecting to encounter such a tragedy.

Heidi tipped her head back. Lyle was right—there must be a huge fire up ahead. Dusk was approaching, and when they continued on, she saw a red glow in the sky. "Ach, I hope it's nobody we know, and I pray no one's been injured."

As they drew closer, two fire trucks came up behind them, sirens wailing, and horns blaring. Lyle pulled the horse and buggy onto the shoulder of the road and waited for them to pass.

Their horse threw her head back and whinnied. "Whoa, Bobbins, steady, girl," Lyle said in a calming voice. The horse pawed the ground and snorted, but finally settled down.

Lyle pulled back onto the road, but they'd only gone a short distance, when Heidi recognized the location of the fire. "Oh, no! The Kimballs' double-wide is on fire! We need to see if they're all okay."

Lyle turned up the Kimballs' driveway and halted the horse near a tree that stood a safe distance from the burning mobile home. He turned to a wide-eyed Marsha and Randy and said, "You two stay in the buggy with Heidi, while I check on things." Lyle stepped down and raced across the yard.

Trembling, Heidi remained in the front seat, while the children stayed seated behind her, both whimpering.

Randy tapped Heidi's shoulder. "Are Velma and her kinner gonna die in the fire?"

"I hope not, Randy. I pray everyone has safely gotten out of the house."

"What about the hinkel?" Marsha asked. "Are they gonna be all right?"

"Jah, the coop is away from the house, so the chickens should be fine." Heidi felt bad that the children had to witness such a horrible sight, but no way could she and Lyle take them home until they knew if Velma and her family were out of danger.

Desperate to know what was happening, Heidi reminded the children to stay in the buggy, and then she got out. She needed to see for herself if the Kimballs were okay.

———— ✦ ————

As soon as Darren pulled his vehicle into the yard of the burning mobile home, Ellen hopped out of the car. He could almost tell by the determined set of her jaw what she had in mind.

"Where are you going?" Becky leaned out the back window and shouted at her mother.

"Someone may be hurt, and since I'm a nurse, I need to see if I can assist in any way." Ellen turned to look at Becky. "I want you to stay right here in Darren's SUV where it's safe. Do you understand?"

"Okay."

"You stay put too, Jeremy," Darren instructed, before climbing out of the car. "I'm going to see if my help is needed." He waited until his son nodded, then sprinted across the yard.

"Is anyone in the house?" Darren hollered to one of the firemen he recognized.

"Don't know yet. Two of our men went inside when they heard someone screaming, but I haven't seen anyone come out."

Acting on instinct, Darren made a dash for the door, but the fireman stopped him. "Sorry, friend, but you can't go in there. You're not suited up, and this fire is not in your district."

"I know, but—"

"There are no buts about it. You know the rules."

With a reluctant nod, Darren backed off. It wasn't in him to stand around and do nothing, especially when lives could be at stake. He glanced to his right and saw Ellen talking to Heidi Troyer and her husband. A few other Amish folk were milling about. He wasted no time in joining the Troyers. "Do you know who lives here?"

Lyle nodded. "It belongs to Hank and Velma Kimball."

Darren's brows shot up. "The same Velma whose daughter's been taking Heidi's cooking classes?"

"Yes, and this is their double-wide engulfed in flames." Heidi tugged the narrow ties of her head covering. "I wish we knew if Velma or any of her family is inside." She closed her eyes briefly. "I pray no one's been hurt."

Darren stood helpless with the others, as he watched the mobile home continue to burn, despite the firemen's attempts to put out the flames. As the water from the hose hit the scorching inferno, it made a sizzling sound mixed with the popping of things exploding inside. From where he stood, the mobile home was nearly consumed by the fire. And a harsh wind had picked up, making the firemen's efforts that much more difficult.

A few minutes later, one of the firemen exited the home with Velma and her young daughter. Darren looked at Ellen and mouthed the words, *Thank goodness*.

"Where are Velma's son and her husband?" Ellen clasped her hands in a gesture of prayer.

"I don't know. Let's go find out." Darren led Ellen over to where Velma and Peggy Ann stood trembling, despite the blankets draped across their shoulders. Neither appeared to be burned, but their hair and clothes were black with smoke.

"What happened, Velma? Where's your son?" Ellen shouted.

"I don't know," Velma rasped. "Peggy Ann said Eddie was gonna take Abner for a walk, and I pray he and the dog aren't still in the house."

Woof! Woof! At the sound of a dog barking, Darren rushed forward. He couldn't stand out here idly watching when the life of Velma's son could be at stake.

───────── ⚭ ─────────

Velma shook her head vigorously, pushing aside the oxygen mask the paramedic tried to place over her nose and mouth. "I need to find my boy!"

"You need to calm down," the man insisted, holding firm to Velma's arm. "We can't let you go back in the house. If your son is in there, one of the firemen will make every effort to find him."

Ellen and Heidi stepped up to Velma. "It's going to be okay," they said in unison.

Velma rocked back and forth as a wave of dizziness washed over her. "I don't know about that. Bad things always seem to happen to me." She gulped in some air. "Hank will never speak to me again when he finds out my carelessness with hot oil started the fire. And if anything happens to Eddie, it won't matter if he doesn't forgive me, because I'll never forgive myself."

Heidi put her arm around Velma's waist, and Ellen took hold of her hand. They tried to offer her hope, but Velma found no comfort at all. No matter how angry he might get with her, Hank was needed right now and she wished he was here instead of out on the road. He never seemed to be around when she needed him, though.

After what seemed like hours, Darren emerged from the front door of the double-wide, his face blackened with soot. He carried Eddie in his arms and Abner was at his side.

Velma rushed forward. "Is my boy all right?"

"He's inhaled a lot of smoke, but I think he's going to be okay."

The paramedics took over then, offering first aid to Velma and both of her children, while Ellen and Heidi looked on. A fireman took their dog and checked him for injuries. Other than needing some oxygen, Abner was okay.

"You'll need to go to the hospital to be treated for smoke inhalation and observation," one from the medical team told Velma.

"But what about my dog?" Velma felt so disoriented she could barely think. Her home, along with everything in it, was gone, and Hank didn't even know what happened.

"That's my best friend and fellow firefighter, Bruce Ferguson, taking care of your pet," Darren informed Velma.

Abner was now wagging his tail as Bruce removed the oxygen mask. "Don't worry about Abner, Velma. He's in good hands, and I'll see that he's taken care of for you tonight."

Tears welled in Velma's eyes as she murmured a quiet, "Thank you." She had no home and didn't know what the future held for her family, but at least she and the kids were all alive. That was something to thank God for.

———————— ❦ ————————

When Ellen and Darren returned to his vehicle, Becky and Jeremy got out and hugged their parents.

"We were so scared, Mom. Did anyone die in the fire?" Becky sniffed, clinging to Ellen's hand.

"No, Becky. Velma and her children are going to be fine. Their dog is okay, too."

Running a jerky hand through his hair, Jeremy looked up at his dad. "I was worried you might be killed tryin' to save someone's life."

"I'm fine, Son. Just a little smoke ridden is all." Darren gestured to the black Lab at his side. "Velma's dog needs a home for the night. Think you might want to help me take care of him?"

"Bacon might not like having another dog in the house, especially one that's bigger than him. But I guess the poor mutt needs somewhere to go, so I'll help you take care of him."

Darren smiled. "Thanks, Son. I knew I could count on you."

Jeremy looked over at Ellen. "I'm glad you're okay, too. Becky and I were worried about you and my dad."

"He's right, we were," Becky agreed.

Ellen felt a sense of relief. Not only were their children getting along better, but they seemed more cordial toward each other's parents. Maybe there was hope for a relationship with Darren after all. There might be no need for her to break things off—at least not tonight. Ellen would give it more thought before making a decision that could affect the rest of her life. Right now, she needed to concentrate on looking for a way to help Velma and her family.

Chapter 40

It had been a week since the fire, and Velma couldn't believe how much had happened since then. Heidi and Lyle had generously invited Velma, Hank, and the kids to stay with them until they could secure a new place to live. On top of that, when Hank came home and discovered their double-wide had burned, instead of being angry with Velma, his attitude toward her and the children actually improved. He was especially grateful for the Troyers' generosity, and even more so when Lyle told him their Amish community would help them build a new house on their property. Neither Velma nor the children had any serious ill effects from the fire, and that was something to be thankful for, too.

Hank took some time off work to be with his family. Every day he and the kids walked down the road to their property. Randy and Marsha often went along to help feed the Kimballs' chickens, while Hank checked on the progress of things after the fire. Abner remained his playful self and was getting along well with Rusty.

Velma was amazed at how the Amish community pulled together to help after the flames destroyed everything. She and Hank, with the assistance of Ellen, Darren, and the Troyers, had gone through the ashes to see if anything could be salvaged. Unfortunately, the double-wide was like a matchstick, and the intense heat of the fire destroyed everything. A week later, most of the rubble had been cleared, making way for construction to begin.

Velma smiled as she dried the dishes Heidi had just washed. They would soon have a real house, and not just an out-of-date, rundown mobile home with creaky floorboards and peeling wallpaper. *Good things come to those who wait*, she told herself. *Maybe my life isn't such a train wreck after all.*

She placed the clean plates in the cupboard and shut the door. *Now if amends could be made with my folks and if our two older children would come home, or at least make contact with us, I'd feel complete.*

Velma glanced across the room at Heidi, who was busy setting out the things she would need for today's cooking class. *Such a sweet woman, with a generous spirit. I'm glad I've gotten to know her. Heidi deserves only the best.*

⸻ ⚬~~⚬ ⸻

Heidi glanced at the clock on the far wall, then looked over at Velma. "My cooking class will start in half an hour, so I think I will go outside and check for phone messages before the students arrive."

Velma looked out the window. "I see Hank coming back with the kids. Wonder how everything's going at our place?" A contented smile spread across her face. "My husband sure enjoys your kids. As a matter of fact, I do too."

"Randy and Marsha have taken a liking to both of you as well." Heidi moved across the room. "Guess I'd better head out to the phone shack now."

"Okay. I'll finish drying the dishes and then get to work on the laundry while you teach your class."

"You're doing more than your share of work around here." Heidi paused near the back door. "Why don't you take it easy today and join the class? You might enjoy seeing what Peggy Ann and the others will be making."

Velma planted her feet in a wide stance, while shaking her head. "With all you and Lyle are doing for us, the least I can do is help out at your place. Besides, I still owe you some work to pay for my daughter's cooking classes."

"I'm not concerned with that, Velma. You've done enough work around here this past week to more than pay for Peggy Ann's lessons."

"I don't mind a'tall. I'd like to repay all your kindness to me and my family." Velma placed the dish towel on the counter, stepped over to Heidi, and wrapped her in a hug. "Some folks I know wouldn't lift a finger to help their neighbor, but you and Lyle have gone the extra mile."

"We just try to do what the Bible says: 'Be ye kind one to another.'" Heidi tapped Velma's arm. "I'm sure you would do the same if someone you knew needed assistance."

"You got that right." Velma opened her palms. "Course, in our current situation, we couldn't do much for anyone in need."

Heidi gestured to the clean dishes in the drying rack. "You've been doing helpful things for me."

A circle of red erupted on Velma's cheeks. "That's different."

"No, it's not. Your help is much appreciated."

"Thank you, Heidi. You've become a good friend."

Heidi smiled. "I think of you as my friend, too."

Denise glanced in the rearview mirror at her daughter, sitting quietly in the back seat. Kassidy hadn't said more than a few words since they'd left home this morning.

"I wonder what you'll learn to make today. When your last class ended, did Heidi say what she would be teaching you today?"

"Nope, she never said."

Not much of a response, but at least Kassidy had answered. Denise decided to try again. "When we get home after class today, why don't you invite Hillary over?" Denise looked in the mirror again.

"She's not home. Hillary and her family are visiting relatives in Nebraska."

"You know, you should invite the kids from the cooking class sometime, like you mentioned two weeks ago."

"I changed my mind about that. I don't have anything in common with those kids. Besides, most of 'em don't like me, so I'm sure no one would come."

"You won't know unless you ask. If you spent a little more time with them, you might find you do have a few things in common."

Switching her gaze from the rearview mirror and concentrating on the road ahead, Denise clasped the steering wheel a little harder when Kassidy didn't respond. *Is there any hope for that daughter of mine? Why must she be so difficult and moody?*

—————————•❧∞❧•—————————

"Here we are." Darren set the brake and turned off the engine. He glanced in the back and was surprised to see Jeremy slumped in his seat. "Come on, Son. A few other cars are here, so we need to get inside. I'm sure class is about to start."

"Sure wish I knew where Mom's barrette got to," Jeremy mumbled. "The last time I saw it, we were sitting right here, and I remember putting it in my pocket. I must've dropped it somewhere."

Darren's gaze flicked upward. *How many times is Jeremy going to bring this up? I know he feels sad about losing his mom's hair clip, but rehashing it won't change the fact that it's lost and he may never find it.*

Thinking a change of subject would be good, Darren turned in his seat to make eye contact with his son. "Before we go in, I'd like to clarify something with you."

"What?"

"On the way home last Saturday, after the fire at Velma's, you said you'd be okay with me continuing to see Ellen."

Jeremy slowly nodded.

"So when I see Ellen today, if I ask her for another date, you won't have a problem with it?"

"Said I wouldn't, so why do ya keep askin'?"

"Probably for the same reason you keep bringing up your mother's barrette."

"What do ya mean?"

"Seeing Ellen is important to me, and I want to be sure it's okay with you, because someday, if things work out the way I hope, I might ask Ellen to marry me."

"Seriously?" Jeremy's eyes widened.

Darren nodded. "Would you be okay with that?"

"If that's what you really want, Dad, I won't mess things up for you."

"I appreciate that, but I'm not sure yet if Ellen's the woman God wants me to have." Darren paused. "Before your mother died, she said she wanted me to find love again. I think I may have found it with Ellen."

Jeremy sat quietly for several seconds, then slowly nodded. "I'm goin' inside now, okay?"

"Yes, we need to do that. Sure don't want to hold up Heidi's class today." As they walked up to the house, Darren draped his arm over Jeremy's shoulder. *In just a few short years, my son will no longer be a boy. Oh, how I wish Caroline could have seen him grow up to become a man.*

Another car pulled in, and Darren stopped walking to see who it was. He recognized Denise's vehicle and watched as she and her daughter got out of the car. *I hope Kassidy doesn't cause any trouble today,* he thought. *That girl has a way of getting under people's skin.*

When Darren and Jeremy stepped onto the porch, Denise and her daughter joined them.

"Good morning." Denise smiled at Darren. "It's hard to believe, after this one, our children only have one more cooking lesson to go."

He was about to comment, when Jeremy pointed at Kassidy and shouted, "Hey, where'd ya get the barrette you're wearin'?"

"I found it in Heidi's driveway the last time we were here. It's beautiful, isn't it?"

Jeremy lowered his brows, and his cheeks sucked inward. "That's my mom's barrette. I had it with me at the last cooking class and must have dropped it. You have no right to keep something that's not yours, and I want it back!"

Her lips pressed together as she shook her head. "My dad's a lawyer, and I heard him say once that possession is nine-tenths of the law."

"What's that supposed to mean?" Jeremy's eyes narrowed.

"It means I found it, so now the barrette is mine." As if to taunt him, Kassidy pushed her hair away from her face, letting her fingers travel over the hair clip. "If it meant so much to you, why didn't you come back and look for the hair clip?"

"We did come back. In fact, Heidi helped us look for the barrette. It's no wonder we couldn't find it, 'cause you had it all along."

Darren was on the verge of saying something, but Denise spoke first. "Kassidy, I want you to give this boy his mother's barrette right now. Do you hear me?"

Kassidy's lower lip jutted out. "What's he gonna do with a hair clip, Mom? It looks better in my hair than it would his."

"That's not funny." Denise reached out and pulled the barrette from Kassidy's hair. "I'm sorry, Jeremy. My daughter is rude and selfish." She handed him the hair clip. Then taking Kassidy by the arm she led her into Heidi's house.

Darren glanced at Heidi, standing in the open doorway, and wondered if she'd heard what just happened. He felt bad for Jeremy. Caroline's barrette meant a lot to him, and Darren was glad he'd gotten it back. He gave Jeremy's back a pat. "You okay?"

"Yeah." He handed Darren the barrette. "Here, Dad. You'd better hang on to this. Sure don't wanna lose it again."

Darren put the hair clip in his pocket and hugged his son. "I love you, Jeremy."

"Love you too, Dad."

With his arm draped over Jeremy's shoulder, Darren led the way into the house. "Now let's see what you'll be cooking today."

Chapter 41

Heidi couldn't help overhearing the conversation that had transpired between Jeremy and Kassidy. It was hard to understand why some children were so sweet and kind, while others, like Kassidy, wore a frown most of the time and tried to provoke others. Was it her parental upbringing, unhappiness at home, or did the girl merely enjoy making trouble?

Heidi didn't want to keep everyone waiting, so she asked her students to move into the kitchen.

"If it's all right with you, I think I'll wait in the dining room today while Becky takes the class," Ellen spoke up. "It would be good for her not to have me watching over her shoulder."

"Thanks, Mom." Becky headed straight for the kitchen.

"I'll go along with that and sit in the dining room, too" Darren was quick to say.

Heidi looked at the other parents. "What would the rest of you prefer to do? I'm fine with whatever you decide."

"I'll sit with Ellen and Darren. It'll give me a chance to get better acquainted." Miranda smiled. "And my kids won't have to worry about their mom asking unnecessary questions or trying to help them too much."

"I'll stay with the other adults, too," Denise said.

"What about you, Velma?" Heidi questioned. "Would you prefer to join us in the kitchen or stay in the dining room with the other parents?"

Velma tugged on the collar of the blouse Heidi had bought her Monday. In fact, she and Lyle had purchased a few sets of clothes for Velma and the children, since all their clothes other than the ones they'd been wearing the night of the fire had been burned. "I think it'd be best if I do the laundry while you're teaching Peggy Ann, like I said before. Eddie can occupy himself outside in the barn with Hank and Lyle."

It was clear to Heidi that Velma felt uncomfortable sitting among the other parents, so she went along. When the meatballs were done, she would invite Velma to join them for a taste test.

As the adults sat in Heidi's dining room, drinking iced tea and visiting, Denise only half listened to their conversation. She was more interested in what was going on in the other room. She heard Heidi say she was going to check on Velma, so when she left the room, Denise turned an ear in the direction of the children waiting in the kitchen for Heidi's return.

Through the partially opened door, Denise saw Miranda's son, Kevin, sitting at the table beside Jeremy.

"How come only your dad and not your mom have come here with you?" Kevin bumped Jeremy's arm.

"My mom died of a brain tumor." Jeremy lowered his head.

"That's sad. Bet ya miss her a lot."

"Yeah. Everything changed after she died." Jeremy heaved a sigh. "Now, whenever my dad goes to work, he calls a lady from church to stay at our house with me."

Denise glanced sideways at Darren to see if he'd heard his boy's comment, but Jeremy's father seemed to be absorbed in something Ellen was saying to him.

"You're not the only one who gets stuck with a sitter, but the lady who stays with me when Mom's at work is nice." From where she sat, Denise couldn't see Becky, but she recognized her voice.

"When our mom has to work, Debbie and I have a babysitter, too." Kevin bobbed his head.

"My mother leaves me alone sometimes," Kassidy said in her usual bragging tone. "But not for very long, of course."

Now where did she come up with that? I've never once left Kassidy alone at the house. Denise was tempted to intervene, but remained in the dining room, watching and listening to the children. *I'll bet my daughter wants to appear grown-up in the other kids' eyes.*

Kevin thumped the table with his knuckles. "If my daddy moved in with us again, he could be with me and Debbie sometimes when our mom has to work at the grocery store." He paused and sniffed a couple of times. "I miss him a lot and wish he and Mommy would get back together so we could be a family again."

Denise heard Miranda's intake of breath, and when she looked her way, tears glistened on her cheeks.

Denise realized that each family represented here today had their own issues to deal with, and so did she. Even families that appeared to be perfect often dealt with serious issues. She wished there was a simple answer that could fix everyone's problems. But life held no guarantees, and for some, the problems they faced might never be resolved. *Even mine*, she concluded with regret.

Denise caught a glimpse of Kassidy when she got up to get a drink of water. Except for her comment a few minutes ago, she was surprised her daughter hadn't said something hurtful to one of the children or bragged about how perfect her life was. In fact, she'd suddenly become abnormally quiet.

Denise thought back to earlier that morning, when she and Greg had a disagreement. She'd asked him to get some things done outside that morning, because a storm had been predicted for later in the day. The gutters needed to be cleaned, but Greg declined, saying he'd made arrangements to go golfing with one of his lawyer friends, and then out to lunch to discuss an upcoming case. Greg had also added that the gutters could wait.

Denise pursed her lips. *Greg was trying to justify going golfing. I'll bet whatever they had to talk about could have waited until Monday.*

She looked at Darren and Ellen again. They seemed oblivious to everyone else in the room. She couldn't remember the last time Greg had looked at her in the tender way Darren was fixated on Ellen.

Turning away, she gazed out the window. The sky had darkened, and storm clouds brewed in the distance. *I hope we get home before the rain comes. It looks as if it could get nasty.*

"All right, class, I'm ready to begin now," Heidi announced when she returned to the kitchen. "Today I'm going to teach you how to make some yummy meatballs."

———⌾∾◌⌾———

When Heidi's class ended, and they were ready to eat what the children had made, it began to rain, and the muffled sound of thunder could be heard in the distance. "Since a storm is coming, we'll eat in the dining room today," Heidi said. She asked Ellen to get out the cut-up vegetables she'd prepared earlier and put in the refrigerator so they would stay cool and crispy.

"I'd be happy to do that." Ellen rose from her chair.

"I'll help get things on, too. Just tell me what to do," Miranda offered.

"Would you mind setting the table?"

"Not at all." Miranda went to the kitchen.

Denise pushed her chair aside and stood. "I'll help her."

"Thanks. I'll see if Velma, Eddie, and the men would like to join us." Heidi grabbed an umbrella and hurried out the back door.

———⌾∾◌⌾———

A short time later, Velma sat with the other parents and their children around Heidi's dining-room table, enjoying the delicious meatballs and cut veggies. With the exception of Kassidy, the other children seemed pleased when they received compliments on the meatballs from their parents.

While listening to the conversation going on at the table, Velma's mind wandered. *Once we get settled in our new house, I'm going to get involved in some community and church activities. I also need to get better acquainted with the Amish and English folks in the area. Who knows, maybe someday I'll have an opportunity to help someone out.*

A knock sounded on the front door, and Heidi went to answer it. When she returned, a tall man with brown hair was with her.

"Trent—what are you doing here?" Miranda sputtered, nearly spilling her glass of iced tea. "I thought you had to work today."

"I worked this morning, and now I'm here on a mission." He looked at Velma and smiled. "I heard you and your family need transportation, so I brought you a secondhand car that is in good shape."

Velma blinked rapidly as her mouth slackened. "Oh, you shouldn't have done that. My husband and I don't have enough money to buy a car right now. You probably haven't heard, but a week ago, we lost our mobile home and everything in it." She dropped her gaze to the table. "Right now, we're in the worst financial shape we've ever been."

"You don't understand." Trent moved closer to the table. "The car is a gift. I don't expect anything for it."

Velma stared at him with her mouth slightly open. The words would hardly come. "I—I can't believe you would do that for a stranger."

Trent glanced at Miranda and grinned. "My wife told me about your situation, and then I learned more the day I came to the class with Debbie and Kevin." He looked back at Velma. "So, you're not really a stranger. I feel like I know you, and it's my pleasure to help out."

Velma placed both hands against her hot cheeks, barely able to swallow due to her swollen throat. "Thank you, Mr. Cooper. I humbly accept your wonderful gift." Overcome with emotion and gratitude, tears coursed down Velma's cheeks. *Thank You, God, for bringing so many good people into my life when I needed it the most.*

Chapter 42

Canton

Ever since they'd left Heidi's house around one, Denise had tried unsuccessfully to engage her daughter in conversation. It was probably for the best, since she needed to keep her focus on the road now that the rain had increased and the storm was overhead.

Denise had never liked driving in bad weather, and today was no exception. Since the wind had picked up, at times the rain came down sideways. Up ahead, she caught sight of a flapping plastic grocery bag caught on a tree branch. Dark clouds raced across the sky, and a jolt of lightning split the skies. Pools of dirty water quickly formed in low spots in people's yards and along the shoulder of the road.

Denise turned on the radio in time to hear a flash-flood warning. *Oh great.* She gripped the steering wheel, mentally calculating where all the creeks and streams were on the way home.

Denise glanced in the rearview mirror and saw her daughter flinch when a boom of thunder sounded so hard the car windows rattled. The windshield wipers slid back and forth in a futile effort to keep up with the pelting rain. Turning them on the highest speed didn't seem to help.

A vehicle coming toward them sent up a spray of water as it passed through a low spot quickly filling from the intense downpour. Denise pushed hard against the seat, as water hit the windshield with such force it sounded like a million pebbles.

"Did it break the window?" Kassidy screamed above the noise.

"Everything's okay. It just sounded bad. Stay calm." Inside, Denise was nothing but calm, but she didn't want to upset her daughter. "Just a little ways to go, and we'll be home."

Denise felt relief when she drove her car through the open gate at the entrance of their expansive driveway. They were almost there. She couldn't wait to put the car in the garage and get into the house, where she could relax with a cup of her favorite tea.

As she pulled her vehicle into their three-car garage, she was surprised to see Greg's parking spot empty. He certainly couldn't be out on the golf course in this horrible weather, with lightning and thunder all around. Then she remembered he'd mentioned having lunch with his lawyer friend after they finished golfing. Most likely Greg was still at the clubhouse, waiting out the storm.

After she'd parked the car in her bay, Denise followed Kassidy into the house. "Thank goodness the garage is attached to our home. Even with an umbrella, we'd both be soaked to the bone if we had to come in from outside."

Kassidy was silent.

"Did you get enough to eat at Heidi's, or would you like me to fix you a snack?" Denise tapped her daughter's shoulder.

"No, thanks. I'm goin' to my bedroom to watch TV," Kassidy mumbled without turning around.

"I'm not sure I'd put the TV on with the lightning this close."

"If I hear it thunder real loud again, I'll turn it off." Kassidy disappeared down the hall.

Denise made her way to the kitchen. Along with her beverage, she might indulge in a chocolate brownie.

After fixing a cup of chamomile tea, and placing a succulent-looking brownie on a plate, she took a seat at the bar where she often sat to eat breakfast. *Should I or shouldn't I?* She pondered the thought. *Oh, why not?*

Denise went to the refrigerator and got out a can of whipped cream. *What's a brownie without a little sweet cream?* Denise shook the can and squirted a layer over top of her treat. *Now I'm ready to indulge.*

Even though the rain was still coming down hard, she felt relaxed inside her cozy, well-equipped kitchen. Denise watched as water poured over the edge of the clogged gutters outside the window.

She took a bite of the whipped-cream-covered brownie and closed her eyes. "Yum... This is so good."

Taking a sip of tea, Denise read the recipe card for meatballs Heidi had given Kassidy today. She turned it over. Sure enough, a Bible verse had been written on the back. "'Pray without ceasing.' 1 Thessalonians 5:17." She read the scripture out loud and pondered it a few seconds. *Would God listen to me, even though I'm not a regular churchgoer? Does He care about my marriage, our daughter, the struggles we face? Maybe so. Maybe not. I don't know. We probably should attend church more often.*

Denise finished her brownie and was deliberating about whether to eat another one, when Kassidy rushed into the kitchen, wide-eyed and trembling.

"Kassidy, what's wrong?"

"I just heard on the news that a man got struck by lightning on the golf course—the one near our home. I think it's the place Dad belongs to." She sucked in a breath as beads of perspiration formed on her upper lip. "Oh, Mom, what if it's him who got hurt? People who get hit by lightning can die, you know." She clung to Denise's arm. "I don't want to lose you or Dad, like Jeremy lost his mom."

Denise pulled her daughter close and patted her back. "Calm down, Kassidy. Did the news reporter give the name of the man who was hit?"

"No, but Dad's not home yet, and that's why I think it could have been him."

"If it was, I'm sure we would have received a call." Denise patted the stool next to her. "Take a seat, and I'll get you a brownie with whipped cream and a glass of milk."

Kassidy flopped down and Denise went to get the milk and a brownie, which she set on the bar in front of her daughter.

Kassidy took a few nibbles, and then put the brownie back on the plate. "Are you and Dad gonna separate, like Debbie and Kevin's parents did?"

"Of course not. Why would you ask that?"

"Because I heard you two arguing this morning before we left for class."

"Parents sometimes have disagreements, but it doesn't mean we're going to leave each other." Denise reached for the phone and punched in Greg's cell number. A few seconds later, he answered.

"Hey, I was getting ready to call you. Things got pretty bad on the golf course today when the storm blew in."

"Are you okay?"

"I'm fine, but one of the guys I don't know well was slightly injured while playing golf."

"Oh, my! What happened?"

"Lightning struck a tree close to where he was playing. From what we were told, the man started back to get the clubs he'd left under the tree, and that's when the lightning hit." Greg went on to say that the power of the strike knocked the man to the ground, but other than ringing ears and tingly arms, he wasn't seriously hurt.

"That's good to hear. Kassidy and I were worried about you."

"Well, you can set your concerns aside now, because I'll be home soon."

When Denise hung up, she turned to Kassidy and smiled. "It wasn't your dad who got hurt, and the man who did is going to be okay."

"I'm so glad." Tears pooled in Kassidy's eyes, and she hugged Denise. Maybe today had been a turning point for her daughter. For all of them, really.

⸱⸱⸱⸱⸱⸱⸱⸱⸱⸱⸱⸱⸱⸱⸱⸱⸱

Berlin

Miranda couldn't get over Trent's generosity toward Velma and her family. She'd invited him over for supper to spend time with her and the children and as a way of saying thank you for his selfless deed. Although she still wasn't ready to invite Trent to live with them again, Miranda felt as if they might be headed in that direction.

She glanced out the kitchen window. The storm they'd had earlier had died down, but a steady rain continued. Tomorrow, if the sun came out, it would no doubt be humid.

"Well, that's what summer often brings," she murmured, turning on the water to fill the teakettle. At least the yards in the area were nice and green, unlike some years when they didn't get much rain at all.

"Who are ya talkin' to, Mom?" Kevin skipped into the kitchen and tugged on her arm.

Miranda tickled him under his chin. "I was talking to myself."

He giggled. "Do ya answer yourself, too?"

"No, but sometimes I'm tempted to."

"Is Daddy still comin' for supper?" Kevin asked.

"Yes, and I'm trying to figure out what to fix. What do you think he would like?"

"Hot dogs and potato chips!" Kevin gave a thumbs-up.

Miranda lifted her gaze to the ceiling. "Tell the truth now, Kevin. Hot dogs and chips is what you'd like to have, not what you think your dad wants, right?"

He moved his head quickly up and down.

"Daddy likes hot dogs, too."

"You're right, so maybe if the rain lets up we can sit outside around our portable fire pit and roast hot dogs. We can also have potato chips, and I'll make a yummy macaroni salad to go with it. How's that sound?"

Kevin's smile stretched wide. "Okay!" He turned and started out of the kitchen, but turned back around. "Is Daddy movin' back with us?"

Miranda bit the inside of her cheek. "I don't know, Son—maybe. But not tonight. Your dad and I still have some things we need to work through."

Kevin grabbed her hand and squeezed it. "I'm goin' to tell Debbie the good news."

Miranda shook her head. "Please, Kevin, don't say anything about the possibility of your dad moving back home. I'll tell you both if and when anything is decided."

He looked up at her and grinned. "No worries, Mommy. I was only gonna tell Debbie we're havin' hot dogs tonight." Kevin darted out of the room.

Miranda set the teakettle on the stove and turned on the burner. She hoped things would work out between her and Trent, for it would be difficult to disappoint the children.

Chapter 43

Millersburg

Ellen and Becky had left the grocery store, and were heading to the car, when Becky stopped walking and clasped her mother's arm. "I can't quit thinkin' about something, Mom."

"What is it, honey?"

"During the last cooking class, Jeremy was talking about how his mom died, and it was really sad. It got me to thinking about the woman who'd given birth to me. I keep wondering if she's alive, and if so, where does she live?"

Ellen moistened her lips. "Let's talk about this in the car."

"Okay."

Once the groceries were put in the trunk, and Becky was seated in the back seat, Ellen slid in next to her. This was the first time Becky had brought up the topic of her birth mother since learning she'd been adopted.

Ellen reached for Becky's hand. "There are usually ways for a person to locate their birth parents, and as I've mentioned before, when you are older and ready to do that, I'll help you with it."

"Thanks, Mom." Becky squeezed Ellen's fingers. "Even if I do find my birth mother, you'll always be my mom."

Ellen swallowed hard. "And you, sweet Becky, will always be my daughter."

Walnut Creek

"I still can't believe this beauty is ours. Sure never figured someone we don't know would up and give us a car." Hank tapped the steering wheel of their secondhand vehicle, then ran his hand over the dash.

They'd had the car a week already and driven it someplace almost every day since. This morning Velma and Hank went to the grocery store to pick up a few things for Heidi and had just now returned.

Velma looked over at her husband and touched his tattooed arm. "There's something I need to ask you."

"Ask away."

Velma wadded up the tissue she'd pulled from her overalls' pocket—the only pair she had left from before the fire.

Hank's forehead wrinkled. "What's wrong? You look so serious all of a sudden."

"I'm kinda nervous."

"Whatcha got to be nervous about?"

"The question I'm about to ask."

He swatted her arm playfully. "Never had any problems askin' me questions before."

"This is different. You might not like what I'm about to say."

He grabbed hold of her hand. "For heaven's sakes, woman, just tell me what's on your mind."

She drew a quick breath, hoping to calm the fluttering in her chest. "It's about my folks."

"What about them?"

"I'd like to call them, Hank. They need to know about the fire that destroyed our home, and I'd like to ask if they've heard anything from Clem or Bobbie Sue." There, it was out. Velma released a breath of air that lifted the hair off her damp forehead.

Hank rubbed his jaw then moved his hand to the back of his neck. "Guess it would be all right. It's been a long time since you talked to your ma and pa. It's not been fair of me to come between you and your folks."

Releasing her hand from his grasp, Velma sagged against the seat, pressing both palms against her cheeks. "Thank you, Hank. Think I'll go out to the Troyers' phone shed and make a call to my mama right now."

"Okay, and while you're doin' that, I'll haul the groceries in, and see if Randy and Marsha wanna go with me, Eddie, and Peggy Ann to our place to feed and water the chickens."

"Sounds good. I'm betting the kids will be eager to help." She grinned. "Randy never has to be reminded to care for his chickens. Heidi and Lyle are doin' a good job raising him and his sister."

"Yeah. They're sure cute kids, and polite, too. They've had a lot to deal with in their young lives. Let's hope when Marsha and Randy get older they don't decide to up and run off the way our two oldest did."

Velma shook her head. "I'm sure they won't. Heidi and Lyle love those kids, and they're raising them well. Teachin' them all about God, too." She opened the car door. "Well, I'd best get on out to the phone shed. I'll let ya know later what my mama has to say." Velma hopped out. Truth was, she could have stayed here all day talking with Hank. But things needed to be done—beginning with a long-overdue phone call to Kentucky.

——————⌇~⌇——————

Velma entered the small wooden building and took a seat on the folding chair. Her fingers tingled as she picked up the receiver. *What if Mama doesn't want to talk to me? What if she hangs up the phone as soon as she hears my voice?* They'd had a pretty nasty argument with Velma's parents before moving to Ohio, so a reconciliation might not be possible.

"Well, ya won't know till ya try," Velma muttered. She punched in her folk's number and held her breath.

"Hello."

"Mama, it's me, Velma."

Silence.

"Did ya hear what I said?"

"Yeah. Never thought I'd hear a peep outa you again."

Velma's left knee bounced uncontrollably. She placed her free hand on it and pressed hard. "I wanted to let you know that our place here in Walnut Creek caught fire, and it burned to the ground."

"Oh, my! Is everyone all right? Are you okay, Velma?"

"Yeah, I'm fine. Hank wasn't home when it happened, but thanks to the firemen, me and the kids got out okay. Except for breathin' in a lot of smoke, all three of us, and even our dog, were fine."

"That's a relief." Her mother paused. "By the way, how are those youngsters doing these days?"

"Eddie and Peggy Ann are good."

Velma explained about the cooking class and how she'd been doing some chores for Heidi to pay for Peggy Ann's lessons.

"If you need any help financially, all ya have to do is ask," her mom offered.

"I appreciate that, Mama, but thanks to the help of some people in the area, we're managing. Losing everything in the fire was horrible, but some positive things happened because of it."

"Good to hear. So, where are ya staying?"

"Heidi, the Amish lady who teaches the cooking class, and her husband, Lyle, took us in. Some other Amish folks from the community are gonna help build us a new house. The community support's been amazing."

Velma went on to tell about the car they'd been given, and then brought up the subject of Bobbie Sue and Clem. "Have ya seen or heard anything from either of them?"

"As a matter of fact, Clem called a few months ago. He joined the army and is stationed at Fort Polk, Louisiana."

"Is he doin all right?" Velma's voice trembled a bit.

"Seems to be."

"What about Bobbie Sue? Do you know where she is?"

"Sure do. That girl's sittin' right here at my kitchen table." Another pause. "She and that creepy boyfriend broke up, so she came here, askin' if she could live with us."

"So they didn't get married?"

"Nope. Bobbie Sue got a job as a waitress at a place not far from here. Seems to like it there."

"Can I talk to her?"

"Sure, but first, there's somethin' I wanna say."

"What is it, Mama?"

"Just wanted to say I'm sorry for all the hurtful things me and your pa said about Hank before you all moved. It was wrong of us to drive a wedge between you and your man. Hank was your choice for a husband, and we should have accepted it and welcomed him into the family instead of pointing out his faults. Had we done right from the start, you'd still be livin' here and not in Ohio among strangers."

"Heidi and Lyle have become our friends, Mama. But you're correct. Had it not been for the things said about Hank, and even to his face, we'd most likely have stayed put." Velma opened the door of the phone shed a crack and drew a deep breath. "I'm sorry for my part in the blowup we had with you and Papa before we moved."

"All's forgiven. It's in the past. So, do ya think ya might ever come back? You'd be welcome."

"Maybe for a visit, but we like the area here, and we're settling in."

"That's important, Velma. I'm glad everything's workin' out for you." Velma heard her mother blow her nose. "We'll look forward to you comin' to see us, and hopefully that won't be too long."

"Maybe once we get the house built we can make the trip." Velma doodled on the writing tablet next to the phone as she thought about a verse her grandma had taught her when she was a girl. She couldn't remember where it was found in the Bible, but knew what it said: "Honour thy father and mother; which is the first commandment with promise." By making this phone call, and apologizing, Velma felt that she had honored her mother, even in some small way.

"I'm ready to talk to Bobbie Sue now," she said.

"Okay, sure. Take care now, ya hear?"

"You too, Mama."

Velma's knee started twitching again. She hoped she wouldn't mess up and say something to aggravate her daughter.

"Hi, Mama." Bobbie Sue's voice sounded far away—like she might be holding the receiver away from her ear.

"It's good to hear your voice, Daughter. I'm glad you're okay and are livin' with my folks. I've been worried about you."

"What about Dad? Has he been worried, too?"

Velma shifted on the chair. "I'm sure he has. You know how things are. Your dad don't talk about things the way I do."

"Yeah, well I've been worried about you, too, but scared to reach out. Figured you'd be plenty miffed with me for leavin' like I did."

Velma was tempted to ask Bobbie Sue to come back to Ohio,

but thought better of it. She was obviously content to live with her grandparents, and if she came back to Ohio, there might be conflict again. "Bobbie Sue, we all make mistakes. I sure know that. But the good part about mistakes is you can learn from 'em."

"I've had my eyes opened," Bobbie Sue admitted. Then she changed the subject. "How are things going there, Mama? Is everyone okay?"

"We are now, but. . . Well, your grandma can fill you in. I told her all the details of what's been happening with us."

"Okay."

They talked until Bobbie Sue said she had to hang up and get ready for work.

"All right then, I'll let ya go for now, but let's not be strangers. We need to talk now and then."

"I'm fine with that. Oh, before I go, would ya give my love to Papa, and also to my little brother and sister. I kinda miss them sassing me."

Velma chuckled. "I'll be sure and give 'em the message. They'll both be glad I talked to you. They miss their big sister, too."

"I miss them, too."

When she hung up the phone, Velma noticed the light blinking on the answering machine. No doubt, the Troyers had several messages. Since it wasn't her place to check them, she left the phone shed and headed for the house to tell Heidi about her call home, and also mention the blinking light.

Chapter 44

Heidi hummed as she dusted the living-room end tables. It was amazing how quickly a film of dirt could develop when the windows were open during the hot summer months. August would be over soon, though, and then fall would be on its way, with cooler days and chilly nights, which she found most welcome. It would certainly be a pleasant change from the sticky humidity that came after the summer rains.

Heidi thought about Randy, and how he would be starting first grade the week after next. For sure, it would be an adjustment for him. But he was a smart little boy, and Heidi felt confident he would do well in school.

She stopped humming and turned toward the door when Velma stepped in. "Did Hank bring all the groceries in?" Velma asked.

"Yes, and they're all put away."

Velma snapped her fingers. "Sorry, I shoulda been here to help with that. I went to the phone shed to call my mom."

Heidi nodded. "Hank mentioned it. How did things go? If you don't mind me asking, that is."

"Don't mind a bit."

Velma took a seat in the rocker, and Heidi seated herself on the couch across from her. She sat quietly, waiting for Velma to speak.

"It went better than I expected. Mama and I had a good talk. And guess what?" Velma grinned. "Bobbie Sue was there, and I got to talk to her, too."

"I'm glad. Is she staying with your folks?"

"Yeah." Velma let her head fall against the back of the chair. "Bobbie Sue broke up with her good-for-nothing boyfriend, and she's got a job at a restaurant near my folks' house. I'm sure glad she's all right. Oh, and Mama said they've heard from our oldest boy. Guess Clem joined the army."

Heidi smiled. "It must be a relief to know your children are safe and doing okay."

"You got that right. After everything we went through with those two, it sounds like they are going down a better path in life—one they've chosen on their own. Guess it's good to let kids learn from their own mistakes rather than tryin' to make 'em do something you think they should do. That causes resentment and rebellion—at least in our case it did."

Velma closed her eyes and rocked silently for a few minutes, but then her eyes snapped open, and she sat up straight. "Whoa! I better not get too comfy here or I'll be out like a light."

"Maybe you should go up to the guest room and take a nap," Heidi suggested.

"No way." Velma stood. "I need to get busy doin' something. So what have ya got for me?"

Heidi straightened her headscarf, which she wore whenever she worked around the house and didn't want her white covering to get soiled. "Let's see now. . . You could go out to the garden and see if any of the produce needs to be picked. I'm fairly sure more string beans are ready. We got a lot the last time we picked them, and it looked like more were on the way."

"No, problem. I'll get to it right now." Velma started for the door, but turned back around. "Oh, I almost forgot. . . When I was makin' the call to my mom, I noticed the light on your answering machine was blinking. Figured you'd probably like to know, so you can check the messages."

"Actually, Lyle checked early this morning, before he left for the auction he's in charge of today. There's probably no reason for me to check it again until sometime this evening."

"Okay." Velma turned and grasped the door handle. "I'm heading outside now. Give a holler if you need me for anything."

———⟨•◦⟩———

Dover

When Darren entered the house, carrying a black-and-white puppy, Jeremy jumped off the couch. "Wow, Dad, where'd ya get the mutt?"

"It's not a mutt." Darren stroked the dog's silky ears. "As near as I can tell, this is a cockapoo."

Jeremy tipped his head. "What's a cockapoo?"

"Part cocker spaniel, and part poodle."

"Oh." Jeremy didn't show much enthusiasm.

Darren lifted the whimpering pup and held it out to his son. "She's a cute little thing, isn't she?"

"I guess so, but why'd you bring the dog here?"

"I rescued her earlier this morning from an abandoned building close to one that had caught fire. Poor little thing was so scared she was shaking all over when I found her."

"Wonder what happened to its mommy." Jeremy stroked the dog's head.

"I'm not sure, but she was nowhere around, and this was the only puppy in the building. Now you understand why I couldn't leave it there." Darren rubbed the puppy's nose and it started chewing on his finger. "Looks like this little gal is hungry. How about we go warm up some milk?"

"Okay, but what are you gonna do with her?"

"Thought maybe we could give her a home here."

Jeremy held up his hand. "No way, Dad! Bacon would have a fit if we brought another dog into our home. He hid under my bed the night we brought Velma's dog home, and he didn't come out till we took the black Lab to Heidi's place the next day."

"True. Guess I'll take the pup with us to Heidi's next Saturday and see if any of the kids would like her."

"But that's a whole week away. What are we supposed to do with her till then?"

"Good question." Darren snickered when the puppy licked his ear. "Do you think Bacon could deal with the pup for a week? We could keep her in the utility room at night, and outside in our fenced yard during the day."

Jeremy shrugged. "It might be okay, but what happens if none of the kids from the cooking class want a puppy?"

"I'll deal with it then." Darren shifted the pup in his arms. "Where's Mrs. Larsen?"

Jeremy nodded with his head in the direction of the kitchen. "She's baking cookies again."

"I should have guessed." Darren sniffed the air. "I'll go show her the pup. Maybe she'd like a dog to take home."

Canton

Denise and Greg sat on chairs inside their screened-in patio, sipping lemonade. The overhead fan rotated on medium, keeping it comfortable, despite the outside heat.

"It was nice going for ice cream after lunch, Greg." Denise looked at her husband, feeling a tenderness she hadn't felt in a while. "I can't remember when we last did something fun as a family, or when an ice-cream cone tasted so good."

"It's my fault for not taking the time to be with you and Kassidy more." Greg rubbed his thumb over a brow. "We're going to do more of that from now on." He looked toward the door leading into the dining room. "By the way, where is our daughter?"

"She's on the phone, telling Hillary about our outing today." Denise shook her head. "I have to tell you, Greg, our daughter was more excited about spending time with us today, than about all those niceties we've given her over the years."

"Objects don't give or show your love, that's for sure." Greg took a deep breath. "I'll tell you something else. Last week, when the lightning struck close to that guy at the golf course, I had an epiphany."

"What do you mean?"

"I realized how quickly someone's life can change." Greg snapped his fingers. "Lightning could have struck me, and it may have turned out far worse than it did for that man. Imagining you and Kassidy having to fend for yourselves really put a scare into me."

"Last Saturday was an eye-opener." Denise inhaled sharply. "Even for Kassidy."

"Really?" Greg cocked his head. "But you're right. I have noticed a difference this week in our daughter's attitude. What has changed?"

"During the cooking class last Saturday, I overheard the kids talking in the kitchen while we parents waited in the dining room. And then later, Kassidy told me she heard one of the boys tell how his mother had died from cancer. Kassidy was quiet the whole time Jeremy told how he has to have a babysitter whenever his dad has to work. Jeremy also said he missed his mom, and it's hard for his dad to do everything."

"Wow, imagine our daughter learning a lesson from another kid."

"Yes, it certainly wasn't planned. And coming from someone who has had a huge loss in his life made her think what it would be like if something happened to one of us. In fact, when she heard about the lightning strike on the news, she was highly upset and feared it was you. You can only imagine how relieved we both were when I called and you answered the phone."

"I was a bit nervous myself," he said. "Just thinking about you driving home from class in that terrible weather had me on edge."

"Thank the Lord, we are all okay." Denise placed her hand on her husband's arm and gently squeezed it.

"You know, this is nice sitting out here, just the two of us, talking. I need to stay home more instead of playing golf so often. I still have my work, of course, and so do you, but when we have free time, we're going to spend it as a family. Besides, I have a lot of catching up to do around our property—especially taking care of those gutters."

Denise clinked her glass against Greg's before they took another sip of lemonade. She almost felt like a young woman again who'd been kissed for the first time.

———— ❧ ————

Walnut Creek

Heidi put a kettle of freshly snapped beans on the stove. They would go well with the ham and potatoes baking in the oven for supper. Having the oven on had heated up the kitchen, so they would eat their meal outside this evening.

Heidi was about to light the gas burner but decided to hold off a bit, since Lyle wasn't home yet. After working in the garden several hours, Velma had gone to take a shower, and Hank was in the living room, keeping all four kids entertained. That was evidenced by the giggles coming from the other room.

Think I'll go out and check for phone messages. There might be something from our lawyer or the social worker about the adoption proceedings.

Heidi dried her damp hands on a paper towel and scooted out the back door. As she approached the phone shed, Rusty ran across the driveway in front of her. She jerked to one side, nearly losing her balance.

"Rusty, you scared me." She shook her finger at him.

Arf! Arf! The dog ran around her in circles, and then dropped at her feet, looking up at Heidi with his big brown eyes.

She paused and bent down to pet him. "So you need some attention, do you? Where's your new friend, Abner?"

Woof!

Heidi laughed and looked toward the shade tree in the backyard where Velma's dog was stretched out. "That's what I thought. You played him out, huh?" She gave Rusty a few more pats, then continued on her trek to the phone shed.

Once inside, she closed the door so her dog wouldn't follow. It was hot and stuffy inside, so she would hurry and jot down any messages she found.

Heidi took a seat and punched the button to retrieve the first message.

"Hello, Mr. and Mrs. Troyer. This is Gail Saunders, and I have some unexpected news to share with you."

Heidi leaned forward, eager to hear what the social worker had to say. *Please let it be about the adoption. It would be wonderful to have some good news to share with Lyle when he gets home.*

"I know this may come as a surprise, because it did to me, but Randy and Marsha's grandfather has contacted the agency. Mr. Olsen wants to see the children as soon as possible, so. . ." Gail's voice was cut off. Apparently Lyle hadn't deleted enough messages this morning, and now their voice mail was full.

Heidi brought a shaky hand up to her head, where she felt the beat of her heart in her temples. *How could this be? We were told the children had no living relatives. Who is this man who says he's their grandfather, and why has he come forth now after all these months?*

Heidi released an uncontrollable whimper. *Oh, no. . . He's come to take the children away from us.* Tearfully, she bent into the excruciating pain. *Dear Lord, what are we going to do?*

Chapter 45

Heidi spent the next hour fixing supper and keeping her ear tuned for a car that might pull into their yard. She could only imagine what it would be like when the children's grandfather showed up and demanded that Randy and Marsha go with him. She hadn't returned the social worker's call, fearful of what she would say. But if he was coming to see the children, Heidi needed to know when it would be so she could prepare them.

Heidi looked up at the clock on the far wall. It was too late to call Gail now. She would have already left her office for the day.

She rubbed the bridge of her nose, trying to clear her thoughts. Since this was Saturday, Gail might not have been in her office at all when she made the call. Did she call yesterday, and somehow Lyle missed the message when he'd gone to the phone shed this morning? So many jumbled and conflicting thoughts raced through Heidi's mind. It was hard to concentrate on anything else.

She glanced out the kitchen window. *I hope Lyle gets here soon. I need to talk to him about this before we say anything to the children.* Heidi held her arms tightly against her sides. She feared that she and Lyle were about to suffer yet another shattering disappointment. *Why would God allow something like this? Doesn't He care how much we love Marsha and Randy?*

"Are you okay, Heidi?" Velma asked when she entered the kitchen. "Your face is the color of fresh-fallen snow."

"I. . .I. . ." Heidi stuttered. *Should I tell her, or wait until I know something more?*

Velma rushed forward and slipped her arm around Heidi's waist. "You look like you're about to pass out. Why don't ya sit down?" She pulled out a chair at the table and guided Heidi to the seat.

"Where are the children?" Heidi asked.

Velma took a peek into the living room, then quietly returned to the kitchen. "Hank must have played them out. All four kids are sound asleep, and Hank's snorin' away in the rocking chair." Velma rubbed Heidi's arm. "Now what has you so upset?"

A moan escaped Heidi's lips as she answered quietly. "We may lose Randy and Marsha."

Eyebrows raised, Velma took the chair beside Heidi. "What do you mean?"

With a desperate need to tell someone, Heidi told Velma about the social worker's message. She sniffed back tears threatening to spill over. "I can't believe this is happening to us. We were told the children had no living relatives." Heidi paused to pick up a napkin and blow her nose. "If this man Gail Saunders spoke of is truly the children's grandfather, then where has he been all this time, and why did he wait till now to come forward?"

"I—I don't know. It makes no sense to me."

"I'm not sure what I'll do if we lose Randy and Marsha. I love them so much, and Lyle and I have been looking forward to adopting them." Heidi nearly choked on the sob rising in her throat.

Velma stroked Heidi's forearm with a gentle touch. "Maybe the man isn't really their grandpa. He could be an imposter tryin' to steal their inheritance."

"There is no inheritance." Heidi shook her head. "From what we were told, the children's parents barely had enough insurance for burial expenses. And the money they had in the bank was meager. Basically, they were living from paycheck to paycheck."

"Did they own a house and a car?"

"No house. They were renting. They did have a car, but it was totaled when they were hit by another vehicle." Heidi sat quietly for a few seconds, staring at the table. "If the man is really the children's grandfather, his interest in them would not be for any money he might receive."

She stood and moved over to the stove to check on the ham. "Please don't say anything about this to Randy and Marsha, or even Lyle. I'll discuss this with him, of course, but not until after the children have gone to bed. Lyle and I need time to talk this through and decide the best way to tell them."

Velma's head moved back and forth. "Don't worry, Heidi. I won't say a word."

* * * * * ❧❧ * * * * *

Millersburg

The doorbell rang, and Ellen took one last look in the hall mirror to make sure she looked okay. Opening the front door, she put on her best smile. Darren looked so handsome there on the porch, holding a bottle of sparkling cider. Jeremy stood beside his father, wearing a cheerful smile.

"It's nice to see you both. I'm glad you could come for supper this evening."

Darren grinned and handed her the bottle. "We're glad you invited us." He looked at Jeremy. "My son gets tired of his dad's bland cooking."

She laughed. "Come on in."

They followed Ellen into the living room. She smiled when Jeremy flopped down on the couch beside Becky. There had been a day when those two would never have sat beside each other.

"What's new with you?" Jeremy asked, looking at Becky.

"Nothing much. How 'bout you?"

"My dad brought home an abandoned pup, but we're not gonna keep the mutt, since we already have a dog." Jeremy bumped Becky's arm. "Say, how'd ya like to have a dog? You don't have any pets, right?"

"Actually, we do," Ellen spoke up. "We got a cat last week, and most cats and dogs don't get along very well, so we'll have to pass on the pup."

"We went to the pound and got a cat that needed a good home," Becky explained.

Just then the pretty calico entered the room and meowed.

"There she is now." Ellen pointed. "Guess she heard us talking about her."

"What did you name the cat?" Jeremy asked.

"We call her Callie." Becky giggled when the cat walked over and rubbed against her leg.

Jeremy looked up at his dad. "Guess there's not much point in takin' the cockapoo to the cooking class next week. Peggy Ann and Eddie already have a dog, and so do Randy and Marsha." Jeremy tapped his chin. "Come to think of it, Debbie and Kevin told me one time after class that they have a dog named Blondie."

"Theoretically, Rusty is the Troyers' dog, but since Marsha and Randy live with them, I guess they figure the dog is theirs, too," Darren interjected. "Anyway, there's still Kassidy to ask. She might be happy to take the puppy."

Becky's nose scrunched up as she shook her head. "I wouldn't even bother asking her. She's too snooty and prissy to take care of a pet."

"Be nice, Becky," Ellen warned. "You don't know Kassidy well enough to make a judgment about what she would or would not do."

"Your mom's right," Darren put in. "So it won't hurt for me to ask." He leaned close to Ellen and stroked her arm, sending shivers up her neck. "Now lead the way to the kitchen, and I'll help you get supper on the table."

"Thank you." Ellen smiled. *What a thoughtful man. I'm glad you came into my life when you did.*

———— ⌘ ————

Berlin

"Sure am glad you and the kids were free this evening. I've wanted to take you all out for a picnic supper, and this is the perfect night." Trent looked over at Miranda and smiled.

"Yes, it's a beautiful evening." Miranda waited until the kids were in the back, along with their dog, and then she slid into the passenger's seat. Unconsciously, she reached over and took his hand. "I know I've said this before, but I'm so pleased that you gave the Kimballs a car they so desperately needed." She gently squeezed his fingers. "I'm proud to be your wife."

He leaned closer and whispered in Miranda's ear. "Does that mean what I hope it does?"

She nodded slowly. "I'd like you to move back in with us whenever you're ready."

"Is tonight too soon?" His eyes glistened.

"Tonight would be fine. When the picnic is over, we can stop by your apartment for a few of your things. The rest you can bring home at your convenience."

Trent turned and looked in the back seat. "Did ya hear that, kids? Your dad's coming home."

Debbie and Kevin clapped their hands and shouted, "Hooray!"

As though not wanting to be left out, Blondie joined in with a few excited barks.

Trent pulled Miranda into his arms and kissed her tenderly. When the kiss ended, he looked into her eyes and said, "I can't promise to be the perfect husband, but I will always try to do my best. And I'll go to church with you, and study the Bible on my own, because I want to be the kind of husband and father you and the kids deserve."

Walnut Creek

As Heidi sat at the picnic table during supper, she could barely eat anything. She stared at the slice of ham next to the few green beans she'd put on her plate, and as her thoughts took her to the message she'd listened to earlier today, her fear and insecurity increased.

Lyle must have sensed something, for he looked over at Heidi and pointed to her plate. "You've barely touched a thing. Aren't you *hungrich* this evening? Or is the oppressive heat we've had lately getting to you?"

"A little of both, I guess." She wanted to blurt out the real reason for her loss of appetite but was committed to waiting until the children were in bed before she told Lyle about Gail's message.

"Well, the heat hasn't hurt my appetite any. I'm hungry as a mule!" Hank reached for a second baked potato and slathered it with butter and plenty of sour cream. "You're married to one fine cook." He grinned at Lyle.

Lyle smiled back at him. "You're right. That's why Heidi's the perfect woman to teach others how to cook."

Normally, Heidi would have blushed at the compliment, but this evening she felt so flustered, all she could manage was a quick, "Danki."

She continued to pick at her food, only half listening to the conversation going on around her.

Everyone had finished eating, and Heidi was getting ready to clear the dishes, when a car pulled into the yard. Her mouth went dry. It was the same vehicle she'd seen parked across the road and again at the end of their driveway. When a short man with silver-gray hair got out and started walking toward them, her adrenaline spiked. Could it be him? Was this man Marsha and Randy's grandfather?

With fists clenched so hard her nails bit into her palms, Heidi sat rigidly waiting for him to approach.

"Good evening, folks. I'm sorry to barge in like this unannounced, but I'd like to talk to you." He walked up to Lyle and extended his hand. "I'm Gerald Olsen, and I understand that my grandchildren live with you."

Heidi's stomach clenched, and her mouth felt so dry she had trouble swallowing. This was like reliving the nightmare she'd had several weeks ago. Her precious foster children were about to be snatched away, and she was powerless to stop it from happening. *I should have told Lyle about the phone message when he first got home. We could have prepared Randy and Marsha for this.*

Gerald looked at each of the children who sat at the picnic table. Then his gaze came to rest on Marsha. "You have to be Judy's daughter. Same color hair. . .same blue eyes." He gestured toward Randy. "And you must be my son's boy. You look so much like Fred when he was about your age."

Randy and Marsha looked up at the stranger with fear in their eyes. If they'd ever met the man, they obviously didn't recognize him.

Lyle's eyes narrowed. "Is this some kind of a joke? We were told that the children had no living relatives."

Gerald shook his head. "It's not a joke. My son was their father. When he ran off and married his high school sweetheart, my wife, Maggie, and I lost all contact with them." He paused and drew in a breath. "After Maggie died, I moved to Europe to pursue my desire to write."

Heidi glanced at Velma, needing some support. Velma reached over and touched Heidi's arm.

"I came back to the States a few months ago and decided to see if I could locate my son. When I hit a brick wall, I hired a detective, and he found out about the accident that killed Fred and Judy. He also found out they had a couple of kids and that they'd become wards of the state until an Amish couple took them in." Gerald looked at Heidi, then turned his gaze on Lyle again. "I'm guessing that'd be you and your wife."

With a pained expression, Lyle nodded. He, too, must be realizing what was about to happen. Heidi rose from the bench she sat upon and moved toward Gerald. "I listened to a phone message from our social worker this afternoon, saying that you wanted to see the children. But I had no idea it would be this soon or that you would come here without calling first."

He nodded. "Yes, I've spoken to her. I had to go through quite an ordeal to prove who I was."

"I can't believe any social worker worth her salt would give out someone's address and let you come here unannounced." Hank eyed Gerald suspiciously. "Are you on the level?"

"I most certainly am." He focused on Lyle. "And the social worker did not give me this address. I got it from the detective I hired." Gerald stood with his arms folded, staring at the children with a look of longing.

Heidi's hands fluttered as she spoke in an emotion-choked voice. "Please don't take them from us, Mr. Olsen. My husband and I love Randy and Marsha so much, and we're on the verge of adopting them."

"You're gonna adopt us?" Randy leaped off his bench and ran up to Heidi.

She gently patted his head. "Yes, we have been trying to do that but didn't want to tell you until we got the word that it was about to become official."

Marsha left her seat, too, and darted up to Lyle. Looking up at him, her chin trembled. "We don't know this man. Please, don't let him take us."

Before either Heidi or Lyle could say anything, Gerald spoke again. "You little ones have nothing to worry about. I'm not here to steal you away from people you obviously love." Gerald tweaked Marsha's nose. "And I can see they love you very much, too. I just wanted to connect with my grandchildren, and if possible, have some sort of relationship with them." He stopped talking and swallowed so hard, Heidi saw his Adam's apple bob. "I won't stand in the way of the adoption. I'm just happy my son's children have found a good home and will be raised by nice people who will love them the way they deserve."

Struggling to find the right words, Heidi took hold of the man's hand and shook it. "Thank you, Mr. Olsen. Thank you, ever so much."

Bobbing his head, Lyle moved over to stand beside them. "Why don't you join us for dessert, Gerald? We'd like the opportunity to get acquainted, and I'm sure the children would, too."

Tears welled in the older man's eyes. "I'd enjoy that very much."

Heidi looked upward and prayed silently, *Thank You, Lord, for answering my prayer.*

Chapter 46

As Heidi set out the ingredients for her final cooking class, she felt like she was walking on air. The past week had been so exciting. She was anxious to share it with her young students and their parents this morning. Heidi would be teaching them to make surprise muffins, and what she had to share was most certainly a surprise. "The Lord works in mysterious ways," Heidi murmured.

"Is that from the Bible?" Velma asked, joining Heidi at the table, where she'd placed the children's recipe cards.

"No, it's not; although folks often quote it as though it's a verse of scripture. Those words are actually from a hymn written in the nineteenth century by a man named William Cowper." Heidi smiled. "We often pray for things and then are surprised when God answers in ways we never expected."

"I know exactly what ya mean." Velma nodded enthusiastically. "Never in a million years did I expect someone would give us a new car or that so many people, including you and Lyle, would be so generous toward us. The fire was terrible, but so many positive deeds have come about because of it. And did I tell you? When Hank came back from our place the other day, he handed me my grandma's Bible. Said he found it lying on top of the chicken coop. How it got there I don't know. Maybe one of the construction workers found it in the rubble."

Heidi's smile widened. "You are so right. See what I mean about the Lord working in mysterious ways? I was beside myself with worry after I got the phone message from Gail. My mind went in a totally different direction than how it turned out. I certainly didn't expect Randy and Marsha's grandpa to show up and say he was happy the children were with us. And I'm sure you were equally surprised when your grandma's Bible was found."

"Yes, most definitely." Velma moved toward the window. "I hear a vehicle pulling in. Yep, it's Darren's rig. He just got out and he's holdin' a puppy, of all things."

Heidi joined Velma at the window. Sure enough, Darren held a black-and-white ball of fluff.

"I wonder why he brought a dog with him today." Velma grunted. "Thanks to Abner being here, you already have two mutts runnin' around your place."

"I'll go out and talk to him. There must be a good reason he brought the dog." Heidi opened the back door and stepped outside, then popped her head back in. "Velma, I hope you are going to join us today for class, since it's the last one."

"Yep, I'd love to."

❦

When Darren saw Heidi coming toward him with eyebrows squished together, he began to have second thoughts. *Maybe I shouldn't have brought the pup here today. She might not appreciate having another dog running around the place. If it weren't so hot I'd leave the pup in my vehicle.*

Darren glanced over at Jeremy, who was kneeling on the ground, petting Heidi's dog, Rusty. Then Velma's black Lab showed up and pawed at Darren's leg. The pup got all excited and tried to wiggle out of his arms. *Oh, great. This probably was a mistake.*

"Good morning, Darren." Heidi tipped her head up to look at him. "Oh, how cute. Where did you get the puppy?"

As Heidi reached out to pet the dog's head, Darren explained how he'd found the pup, and then added, "I brought her with me today, hoping Kassidy or one of the other kids might want to adopt her." He looked at the other two dogs and shook his head. "But it wouldn't be good to let her run loose in your yard during the class."

"It could get a bit chaotic." Heidi pointed to the barn. "Why don't you put her in there for now? After class, you can bring the puppy out and see if anyone would like to take her home."

"Good idea. If you'd like to lead the way, you can show me where in the barn I should put her."

"Okay, but would you mind if I hold the puppy?"

"Course not." Darren could see Heidi had a soft spot for the cockapoo. He laughed along with her when the puppy licked her face.

"You're such a cute little thing. I wish I could keep you, but hopefully you will find a good home soon." Heidi repositioned the puppy in her arms and looked toward Jeremy, who now had the Lab and the Brittany spaniel vying for his attention. "When you've had enough of their friendly greetings, you can go on up to the house," she told him. "Randy, Marsha, and Peggy Ann are waiting inside."

"Where's Eddie? Will he be joining us today?" Jeremy asked.

"He went fishing with his dad early this morning."

Jeremy looked up at Darren. "When are we goin' fishing again, Dad? You can invite Becky and her mom if you want to."

Darren grinned. It was good to see his son had accepted them. If things should work out and Ellen was to become his wife, he felt sure Jeremy would be okay with it now. Becky, too, for that matter. It was too soon to bring up the subject of marriage to Ellen, but he'd sure be thinking about it.

———— ❧ ————

Once all her students had arrived and everyone sat around the kitchen table, Heidi explained that they would be making surprise muffins. The children were all ears as they listened to her directions. There seemed to be excitement in the air this morning. What surprised her most was Kassidy. Instead of the defiant look she usually had, the girl looked happy. *I wonder what happened in the last two weeks to bring about this change.*

"What about the muffins are a surprise?" Debbie wanted to know.

"We will be putting a small amount of jelly in the center of them before they're baked," Heidi explained. "And when someone, like your parents—who are sitting in the dining room again—eat a muffin, they'll discover the little surprise."

Marsha grinned and bounced on her chair. "I like surprises!"

"Who doesn't?" Jeremy put in.

The other children nodded in agreement.

"I can't wait to make these for my dad," Kassidy said. "He loves most kinds of jelly, and will be surprised when he bites into a muffin."

Heidi smiled. "Well, that's good. After these muffins are baked, and we're all eating our treat, I'll share a surprise with you and your parents."

"Bet I know what it is," Randy spoke up.

Heidi put a finger to her lips. "Shh..."

"Don't worry. I won't say nothin'."

"Anything," she corrected, then patted his head. "Now, please get busy mixing your muffin batter."

<hr>

When the muffins were done and had cooled sufficiently, everyone went outside to the picnic table to enjoy the treat.

"This is sure tasty," Denise commented after she'd taken her first bite. "Kassidy, you did a good job making your muffins."

The girl fairly beamed. "Thanks, but keep eating. There's a surprise inside."

Denise took another bite and smiled. "Oh, yum. There's strawberry jam inside."

The other parents enjoyed their treats, too, and everyone agreed that the surprise muffins were a hit.

"Can I say something?" Darren spoke up.

Heidi nodded. "Of course."

"I want you to know that both my son and I have enjoyed your classes. And even though I've neglected to say anything, the verses you included on the back of the recipe cards were an inspiration."

"I agree with Darren," Denise spoke up. "Those scriptures were most helpful."

The other parents nodded their heads as well.

Heidi's cheeks warmed. "Thank you. The idea came to me when I was preparing to teach my very first class, and I've been doing it ever since." She tapped her spoon against her glass of iced tea. "And now, I would like to share my own surprise with all of you."

All heads turned in her direction as she gathered Randy and Marsha to her side. Lyle was there, too, sitting next to Heidi. "My husband and I applied to adopt Marsha and Randy, and yesterday..." She paused and looked at Lyle. "Maybe you'd like to share our news."

He shook his head. "That's okay. You go ahead."

Heidi placed her hands on the children's shoulders. "Yesterday we signed the final papers, and the adoption became final. These two special children, whom we love dearly, are now officially Randy and Marsha Troyer."

A round of applause went up, and Miranda shouted, "Congratulations! Such wonderful news."

Randy and Marsha clapped the hardest and hugged their new parents.

Heidi noticed a few women wiping their eyes. The others congratulated them, as well, and when things settled down, Velma spoke up. "I think we should all get together sometime and have a real celebration."

"I'm all for a little celebrating, too," a strange voice announced from behind.

Just as Heidi turned around to see who it was, she heard Velma's sharp intake of air.

"Clem! Oh, Clem, what a surprise! I can't believe you're really here."

Heidi's mouth opened as she watched Velma and Peggy Ann rush over to the young man in uniform with outstretched arms.

Heidi glanced around at the others who sat at the picnic table. Ellen held her hand in front of her mouth, and Denise swiped at a tear running down her cheek. Miranda reached in her purse and offered the women a tissue, then she dabbed at her own eyes.

After the emotional greeting, Velma and Peggy Ann returned to the table, clinging to the soldier as if he might disappear.

"This is my oldest son, Clem," Velma announced. "He's in the army, and he told me he came here to be with us while he's on leave."

More clapping transpired and even some stomping of feet. Then Lyle stood up. "Please join us, Clem. Oh, and we have room if you'd like to stay here while you're visiting your folks."

"Thank you, sir. I would be most appreciative of that. I have a lot of catching up to do with my family." Clem pulled his mother close and kissed her cheek.

Velma looked at Heidi and sniffed. "I can't remember when I've been this happy."

"I'm sure I speak for all of us when I say we're happy for you, too."

Everyone nodded in unison. Then Darren stood up. "I have a little surprise also. I'll be right back." He sprinted off toward the barn.

When Darren returned with a squirmy pup, he explained how he'd found her and asked if anyone wanted the dog.

"If it's okay with my mom, I'd like to take the puppy." Kassidy looked at her mother. "I promise to take good care of her."

Denise smiled and nodded. "I think it would be good for you to have a pet."

Kassidy reached for the pup. "Think I'm gonna call her Patches."

"I like that name." Becky moved closer to Kassidy. "Sorry about the fight we had. I lost my temper when you said mean things to Randy, but that was wrong."

"I'm sorry, too." Kassidy lifted the pup. "Wanna hold her?"

"Sure." Becky took the puppy and stroked behind its ears. "She's so soft."

Heidi was surprised when Kassidy went over to Randy and apologized for making fun of his chickens.

"Kevin and I have something special to share that happened since we were last here, too." Debbie looked over at her mother. "Is it okay if I tell 'em?"

Miranda nodded.

"Our dad's living with us again, and we all went on a picnic supper."

"Yeah, even our dog Blondie came along," Kevin added.

"That's wonderful." Heidi clasped her hands to her chest. It seemed that everyone had cause for celebration today. How thankful she was for the opportunity to teach cooking classes, where she'd met so many wonderful people. She didn't know what the future held, but one thing was for certain: she would thank and praise God on a daily basis, for He had brought her and Lyle so many good things.

Tenderly, she hugged Marsha and Randy. It didn't matter that she wasn't their biological mother. Heidi loved these two children as if they'd always been hers. Someday she might teach another cooking class, but for now, she would simply enjoy being a mother—something she'd been wanting for a long time.

Epilogue

One year later

Heidi laid down the announcement they'd received in today's mail on the table. Kendra and her husband, Brent, who'd gotten married last December, were expecting a baby this coming November. *My namesake, little Heidi, will have a new brother or sister by Christmas.*

Heidi smiled at her own sweet baby, nestled in her arms. One-month-old Laura had come to live with them a few weeks ago, and there was no chance of her being taken away. The adoption had been prearranged so that Heidi and Lyle would take the baby soon after she was born. Now they had three precious children to raise.

Randy had done well during his first year in school and looked forward to starting the second grade. Marsha seemed to enjoy Laura as much as Heidi did, for she hovered around the baby and sang her some silly songs.

Both Randy and Marsha had become fluent in the Pennsylvania Dutch language. *But then*, Heidi reasoned, *children learn more quickly than most adults.*

Laura's eyes fluttered open, then closed again. She was such a good baby—truly a blessing.

More good news had come a few days ago, when Darren, Ellen, Jeremy, and Becky stopped in for a surprise visit. Heidi was pleased when they asked if she and Lyle would attend their wedding in September. This news in itself was cause for a celebration.

Heidi felt certain the Lord had been with her through every cooking class she'd taught. Many people's lives had changed for the better, and she, as well as her students, had made some new friends.

Her gaze came to rest on the Bible, lying on the table beside the rocking chair where she sat. Heidi reflected on Psalm 6:9, the verse that she'd written on the recipe for surprise muffins: "The LORD hath heard my supplication; the LORD will receive my prayer."

Heidi's thumb caressed the baby's soft cheek. Even though she couldn't bear children of her own, God had given Heidi the desire of her heart by allowing her and Lyle to raise three precious children. *Thank You, Lord, for receiving my prayer. May every day with my friends and family feel like a celebration.*

Heidi's Cooking Class Recipes

Fresh Fruit Salad

Ingredients:

6 peaches, peeled, pitted, and chopped
1 pound fresh strawberries, rinsed, hulled, and sliced
½ pound seedless green grapes

½ pound seedless red grapes
3 bananas, peeled and sliced
Juice from one lime
½ cup pineapple juice
1 teaspoon ground ginger

In large serving bowl, combine cut-up fruit. Toss gently. In smaller bowl, whisk together lime and pineapple juices with ginger to make light dressing. Pour dressing over fruit. Toss gently to combine. Cover and chill fruit for half an hour or so before serving.

Mini Corn Dogs

Ingredients:
- 1⅓ cup flour
- ⅓ cup cornmeal
- 1 tablespoon baking powder
- 1 teaspoon salt
- 1 tablespoon shortening
- 3 tablespoons softened butter
- ¾ cup milk
- 1 package hot dogs, each hot dog cut in half

In medium bowl, mix dry ingredients with shortening, butter, and milk. Using rolling pin, roll out dough on greased cutting board or mat. Cut circles from the dough. A wide-mouth canning jar lid works fine for this. Place ½ of hot dog on each circle. Bring the sides of the dough up and pinch in the center. Place on greased cookie sheet. Bake at 350 degrees for 12 to 15 minutes.

Strawberry Shortcake

Ingredients:
- ½ cup sugar
- 4 tablespoons softened butter
- 1 egg, beaten
- ½ cup milk
- ½ teaspoon vanilla
- 1½ cups flour
- 2 teaspoons baking powder
- Pinch of salt

In medium bowl, mix cream, sugar, and butter. Add egg, milk, and vanilla. Mix well. Add flour, baking powder, and salt. Mix well. Pour into greased 9-inch pie pan. Bake at 350 degrees for 25 to 30 minutes. Top with fresh strawberries and whipped cream.

Egg-Salad Sandwiches

Ingredients:

3 hard-boiled eggs, chopped
⅛ cup mayonnaise, or more if mixture is too dry
¼ teaspoon vinegar
⅛ teaspoon salt

⅛ teaspoon celery salt
1½ teaspoons yellow mustard
1½ teaspoons sugar
⅛ teaspoon onion salt

In medium bowl, mix chopped eggs with all other ingredients, stirring well. Serve on bed of lettuce or make sandwich using fresh bread. A leaf of lettuce, pickles, or sliced olives may be added.

Meatballs

Ingredients:
- 1 pound ground beef
- 1 large egg
- ¼ cup finely chopped onion
- ⅓ cup old-fashioned oats
- ¼ cup milk
- 1 teaspoon Worcestershire sauce
- ⅛ teaspoon salt
- ⅛ teaspoon pepper
- 1 cup tomato sauce or ketchup

Using shortening or coconut oil, grease 13x9x2-inch baking dish. Set aside. Mix ground beef, egg, onion, oats, milk, Worcestershire sauce, salt, and pepper in bowl. Use tablespoon to scoop mixture and shape into 1½-inch balls. Place meatballs in prepared baking dish. Pour tomato sauce or ketchup over meatballs. Bake at 400 degrees for 20 to 25 minutes. Makes about 25 meatballs, depending on size.

Surprise Muffins

Ingredients:

1 egg	¼ cup sugar
1 cup milk	3 teaspoons baking powder
¼ cup cooking oil	1 teaspoon salt
2 cups flour	Strawberry or blueberry jam

Grease bottom of 12 muffin cups or use paper baking cups. In medium bowl, beat egg with fork. Stir in milk and oil. Blend flour and other dry ingredients until mixture is moistened. Batter may be a bit lumpy. Do not overmix. Fill muffin cups half full of batter. Drop scant teaspoonful of jam in center of batter on each muffin cup. Add more batter to fill cup so it's two-thirds full. Bake at 400 degrees for 20 to 25 minutes or until golden brown. Muffins will have gently rounded and pebbled tops. Loosen from pan immediately and remove with spatula. Serve warm or cold. Makes 12 medium muffins. Discovering the jelly inside the baked muffin is the surprise.

Discussion Questions

1. As in the case of the Troyers helping the Kimballs, would you be able to open your home to a family in need without hesitation?

2. Do you think Hank was too harsh on Velma about the accident she'd caused that left them without a car? Why do some people react to bad news in a negative way?

3. Has a tragedy ever brought positive results into your life and made a bad situation better, like the fire did for Velma?

4. Do you think Velma should have neglected her parents because of the disagreement she and her husband had with them?

5. Do you agree with Velma that it's best to let our children learn life's lessons from their own mistakes?

6. Miranda gave Trent a second chance. Would you be willing to do the same when a person you don't trust is trying to prove they can be trusted?

7. Do you think it is wrong for a couple who is going through an unsettled marriage to use their children as go-betweens or to ask questions about the other spouse the way Trent did?

8. Did Ellen wait too long to tell Becky she was adopted? When is the right time to tell a child about their adoption?

9. Should a parent let their children's influence get in the way of happiness as Darren and Ellen almost did? Would you find it difficult to love again after you've lost your soul mate?

10. How would you handle a child such as Kassidy? Do you think children today are being pacified with too many material objects? Does giving a child a lot of gifts cause them to take important things for granted?

11. Do you think Denise's husband put too much responsibility on her for raising Kassidy? Was it right for Greg to spend so little time with his wife and daughter while he worked long hours at his law firm?

12. How did you feel about Becky standing up for Randy when Kassidy made fun of his chickens? Is there ever a time when it's all right for a child to become physical? What kind of damage can bullying cause a child?

13. In a blazing fire or any situation where it means risking your own life, would you be able to save another person, or even their pet, the way Darren did?

14. After losing a loved one, have you kept a memento that reminds you of them, as Jeremy did with his mother's barrette? How would you feel if you lost that special item?

15. Do you think any of the children or their parents received help from the scriptures Heidi wrote on the back of the recipe cards? Were any of the Bible verses your favorite, and if so, which ones?

16. Which of the characters in this book do you feel changed the most by the end of the story? How did Heidi's influence affect any of these changes?

17. Was it good for the children's parents to attend the cooking class with them, or should they have dropped their kids off and come back to pick them up after the class?

18. If you had the opportunity to take a cooking class hosted by an Amish woman, what questions might you ask her?

New York Times bestselling and award-winning author Wanda E. Brunstetter is one of the founders of the Amish fiction genre. She has written more than 100 books translated in four languages. With over 11 million copies sold, Wanda's stories consistently earn spots on the nation's most prestigious bestseller lists and have received numerous awards.

Wanda's ancestors were part of the Anabaptist faith, and her novels are based on personal research intended to accurately portray the Amish way of life. Her books are well-read and trusted by many Amish, who credit her for giving readers a deeper understanding of the people and their customs.

When Wanda visits her Amish friends, she finds herself drawn to their peaceful lifestyle, sincerity, and close family ties. Wanda enjoys photography, ventriloquism, gardening, bird-watching, beachcombing, and spending time with her family. She and her husband, Richard, have been blessed with two grown children, six grandchildren, and two great-grandchildren.

To learn more about Wanda, check out her website at www.wandabrunstetter.com.